# THE DUBLIN STAGE,
## 1720–1745

## Lehigh University Press Award Winners

The Trans-Alaska Pipeline Controversy
PETER A. COATES

The Dublin Stage, 1720–1745
JOHN C. GREENE AND GLADYS L. H. CLARK

# THE DUBLIN STAGE, 1720–1745

## A Calendar of Plays, Entertainments, and Afterpieces

John C. Greene and Gladys L. H. Clark

Lehigh
University
Press

Bethlehem: Lehigh University Press
London and Toronto: Associated University Presses

Associated University Presses
440 Forsgate Drive
Cranbury, NJ 08512

Associated University Presses
25 Sicilian Avenue
London WC1A 2QH, England

Associated University Presses
P.O. Box 338, Port Credit
Mississauga, Ontario
Canada L5G 4L8

The paper used in this publication meets the requirements of the American National Standard for Permanence of Paper for Printed Library Materials Z39.48-1984.

**Library of Congress Cataloging-in-Publication Data**

Greene, John C., 1946–
    The Dublin stage, 1720–1745 : a calendar of plays, entertainments, and afterpieces / John C. Greene and Gladys L. H. Clark.
        p.  cm.
    Includes bibliographical references and indexes.
    ISBN 0-934223-22-X (alk. paper)
    1. Theater—Ireland—Dublin—Calendars.  2. Theater—Ireland—Dublin—History—18th century—Sources.  I. Clark, Gladys L. H., 1900–  .  II. Title.
PN2602.D8G7   1993
792'.09418'3509033—dc20                                        91-58886
                                                                CIP

PRINTED IN THE UNITED STATES OF AMERICA

This book is dedicated
to the memory of the late
Professor William S. Clark II.

# Contents

# Key to Abbreviations

| | |
|---|---|
| AS | Aungier Street Theatre |
| *BD* | *The Biographical Dictionary of Actors, Actresses, Musicians, Dancers, Managers, . . .* Highfill, et. al. |
| BL | The British Library |
| CAP | Capel Street Theatre |
| CG | Covent Garden Theatre |
| *DI* | *Carson's Dublin Intelligence* |
| DL | Drury Lane Theatre |
| *DC* | *Reilly's Dublin Courant* |
| *DDIN* | *Dalton's Dublin Impartial Newsletter* |
| *DDA* | *Dublin Daily Advertiser* |
| *DDP* | *Dublin Daily Post* |
| *DEP* | *Dublin Evening Post* |
| *DG* | *Dublin Gazette* |
| *DM* | *Dublin Mercury* |
| *DWJ* | *Dublin Weekly Journal* |
| *ENL* | *Esdall's Newsletter* |
| *FDJ* | *Faulkner's Dublin Journal* |
| GBDS | Great Booth, Dame Street |
| GF | Goodman's Fields Theatre |
| *HIN* | *Harding's Impartial News-Letter* |
| *HDJ* | *Hoey's Dublin Journal* |
| *HDC* | *Hume's Dublin Courant* |
| *LDG* | *Daily Gazeteer* London |
| LIF | Lincoln's Inn Fields Theatre |
| *LS* | *The London Stage, 1660–1800: A Calendar of Performances.* Van Lennap, et al. |
| NBDS | New Booth, Dame Street |
| *NHI* | *New History of Ireland.* Moody, et. al. |
| NLI | National Library of Ireland |
| ORD | Office of Records of Deeds, Dublin |

| | |
|---|---|
| *PO* | *Pue's Occurrences* |
| *RNL* | *Reilly's Dublin News-Letter* |
| RS | Rainsford Street Theatre |
| SA | Smock Alley Theatre |
| *SJEP* | *St. James's Evening Post* |
| STRETCH | Stretch's or Ward's Great Booth, Dame Street |
| TCD | Trinity College, Dublin |
| TR | Theatre Royal |
| V | Performance verified |
| *WO* | *Weekly Oracle* |

# Preface

This book is a documentary history and calendar of the Dublin theatres from 1720, the year of Joseph Ashbury's death (and the terminal year of W. S. Clark's *The Early Irish Stage*) to 1745, when Thomas Sheridan assumed the management of the united Dublin theatres. It is the first history of the Dublin theatres during this period written since 1938, when La Tourette Stockwell's *Dublin Theatres and Theatre Customs 1637–1820* appeared.

The reader will note that this book is modelled without apology upon *The London Stage, 1660–1800,* the exhaustive work of Van Lennep, Avery, Scouten, Stone, and Hogan. We have adopted their general organizational structure, placing the daily calendar of performances at the center, prefacing to it a short analytical introduction, and concluding with appendixes, bibliography, and indexes. Within the introduction and calendar we have again followed their format insofar as it is useful in writing about the Dublin theatres. We have given special attention to areas that have been neglected in previous histories; for example, we have treated dance and dancers of the period in much more detail than music and musicians, since the latter subject has been the concern of several books in recent years.

In preparing this book we have consulted all documentary sources thought to be relevent to the subject and have attempted to synthesize the useful work of our predecessors. Whenever possible, we have limited our generalizations to those derived from evidence gleaned from sources within the period 1720–1745.

The Dublin stage histories written in the eighteenth century are all ultimately based on the two eyewitness accounts, the earliest by William Rufus Chetwood who worked in the Dublin theatres at the beginning of the century and then returned at the end of our period. His recollections were published in *A General History of the Stage* (1749). The next person to write about the Dublin stage in this period was Robert Hitchcock (*An Historical View of the Irish Stage* [1788–94]) who, as prompter and actor in the Dublin theatres in the last half of the century, was able to consult some of the surviving actors as well as contemporary playbills and newspapers.

The work of these men is very valuable, but in many instances it (and particularly Hitchcock's) is factually inaccurate and incomplete. Most importantly, the books provide little information about individual performances. The theatre histories of the late eighteenth-century and early nineteenth-century writers Benjamin Victor (*The History of the Theatres of*

*London and Dublin* [1761]) and John Genest (*Some Account of the English Stage* [1832], insofar as they relate to the period 1720 to 1745, are derived in large part from Chetwood and Hitchcock and contain only a few score citations of Dublin performances in total, gleaned mainly, it would seem, from newspapers and playbills. Later historians, J. F. Molloy (*The Romance of the Irish Stage* [1897]), Peter Kavanagh (*The Irish Theatre* [1946]), Christopher Fitz-Simon (*The Irish Theatre* [1983]) are syntheses and make few, if any, original contributions to our knowledge of the subject or the period, remaining content, for the most part, to add anecdotes derived primarily from a few autobiographies and biographies of performers and playwrights active during our period.

In the late nineteenth and early twentieth centuries the painstaking Irish scholar William J. Lawrence made extensive notes relating to the Dublin theatres. Some of these notes are particularly important because they are transcriptions of materials that were destroyed in the burning of the Dublin Public Record Office in 1922. We have incorporated in this book Lawrence's research notes as well as those of the late Professor William S. Clark, who was engaged in research for a history of the Dublin theatre during this period at the time of his death.

La Tourette Stockwell (who also acknowledges a great debt to Lawrence's research), in the portions of her ground-breaking work concerned with this period to which we have already referred, concentrates on the architecture, management, and audiences of the theatres, introducing performance data only in a few instances. Stockwell was, therefore, unable to discuss such topics as the repertory and personnel in much detail or with much cogency. This did not prevent her from making generalizations (some unwarranted) about, for example, the audience and repertory. Furthermore, Stockwell, in her turn, relied upon Chetwood and Hitchcock rather more than she ought to have and was led into perpetuating a number of factual errors.

Professor Esther K. Sheldon's excellent *Thomas Sheridan of Smock Alley* (1967) contains a daily calendar for Smock Alley and Aungier Street theatres during the years of Sheridan's management there (1745 to 1754; 1756 to 1758), but makes only slight reference to the Dublin theatre world prior to 1745. T. J. Walsh (*Opera in Dublin 1705–1797* [1973]) surveys the operatic singing of the period and provides a short list of first performances of the more important operas, masques, and stage oratorios produced in Dublin theatres and music-halls in the eighteenth century. Most recently Brian Boydell, in *A Dublin Musical Calendar, 1700–1760* (1988), has supplemented our knowledge of musical performances (including theatre music) in Dublin for the years between 1700 and 1760.

The present work presents a great deal that is new about the subject. In particular, it greatly expands our knowledge about the plays and entertainments enjoyed in Dublin audiences and about the actors, actresses, and other stage personnel active in Dublin. We hope we have clarified the chronologies of the theatre managements, the locations and chronologies of the various theatres, and the makeup of the Dublin repertory. In light of this information and that published by scholars of the London stage during this era, we have speculated about the indebtedness of the Dublin theatres and actors to their contemporaries in London and the interrelationships between these theatres. As a service to future scholars in this field, we have also included the locations of rare copies of plays and prologues. Finally, we have attempted to rectify factual and conceptual misapprehensions inherited and perpetuated by our predecessors whenever we have recognized them as such.

But this work is by no means complete or perfect, and a word of caution must be inserted; the natural desire to generalize about the Dublin theatres during this period must be tempered with the knowledge that we are not in possession of all of the information we might like to have to support such generalizations. The calendar upon which the analysis is based consists, in the main, of theatre performances gleaned from advertisements found in the Dublin newspapers of the time. As we have observed, little other performance information has survived. For eight of the first ten seasons of the period such advertisements are scarce, due in part to the fact that relatively few newspapers survive from those years, and in part to the fact that until 1735 the Theatre Royal in Smock Alley held a virtual monopoly of stage entertainment in Dublin. Seemingly, its managers considered it unnecessary to advertise in the newspapers, relying instead on handbills, posters, and word-of-mouth for publicity.

There is abundant evidence that suggests that many more performances took place than we have record of, particularly during the first eight seasons of the period. For example, documentary proof survives of only five performances for the 1720–21 season, six for 1721–22, and one for the entire 1726–27 season. The fact that at Smock Alley as many as forty nights of acting are recorded during the 1722–23 season, when there is no discernible reason for a sudden or unusual burst of theatrical activity, strongly suggests more performances during the two preceding seasons. Then too, during the 1727–28 season there were certainly many more plays staged than the twelve performances of *The Beggar's Opera* that comprise our only record for that season. Indeed, the fortieth night of that popular ballad opera following its Dublin premiere in March 1728 was advertised as early as December of that year although only eighteen of these performances can now be verified. During the 1728–29 season, furthermore, we can confirm only thirteen nights of acting during the usually busy months between February and June when there exists a potential of at least forty additional performances even if plays were acted only two nights each week.

Thus, it is probable that at least twice as many nights of acting occurred in the course of the twenty-five seasons under consideration than we can verify. There exists the potential for no fewer than eighty-five performances per season at each principal theatre, if we postulate an average theatrical season beginning in the second week of October and ending in the second week of June during which plays were staged only on Monday and Thursday evenings with one additional performance every three weeks (and allowing for periods during which the theatres were traditionally dark). Such a number is confirmed by the calendars of the 1740–41 through 1744–45 seasons: during the 1743–44 season, for example, ninety performances are recorded at Aungier St. theatre alone. Therefore, a conservative estimate of the total number of performances in the Dublin playhouses (including minor theatres) between 1720 and 1745 would be nearer 3000 than the 1400 of which we have record.

The authors have drawn on the work of many scholars in the preparation of this book and have acknowledged their debts whenever possible. We would particularly like to thank Professors Philip H. Highfill, Kalman A. Burnim, and Edward A. Langhans for permission to use unpublished information about theatre personnel that they have prepared for the *Biographical Dictionary*. Professor Thomas Kinsalla came to our assistance at a crucial time, for which we thank him. Virginia Mueller gave invaluable editorial and clerical assistance in the various stages of manuscript preparation. Paul Rieder of Associated University Presses has our sincere thanks for his meticulous copy-editing.

We also owe a debt of gratitude to the librarians and staffs of many libarries, particularly those of the British Library; the Folger Shakespeare Library; the Library of Congress; the National Library of Ireland; Marsh's Library, Dublin; the Trinity College, Dublin, and University College, Dublin, libraries; the library of the Queen's University of Belfast; Mrs. Anne Cornell of the Blegen Library, the University of Cincinnati; and the library of the University of Southwestern Louisiana.

We thank the editors of *Eighteenth-Century Ireland* for permission to reproduce the article "The Dublin Repertory 1720–1745," 2 (1987): 133–48, which appears here in an edited form.

Dr. Greene wishes to thank the committee of management of the Institute of Irish Studies, the Queen's University of Belfast, for a one-year senior research fellowship spent, in part, in doing research for his book. He also wishes to thank the British Academy and National Endowment for the Humanities for travel grants to collections. Thanks can never compensate his wife and daughter for seven years of Saturdays.

Finally, the authors especially wish to acknowledge the assistance of Professor Harry W. Pedicord and to thank him for years of assistance, encouragement, advice, and friendship without which this book would, truly, not have been written.

# THE DUBLIN STAGE,
## 1720–1745

# Introduction

## The Playhouses: Location and Description

### *First Smock Alley Theatre (October 1662–March 1734)*

The structure of the Theatre Royal Smock Alley described in detail by William S. Clark in *The Early Irish Stage* (52–55) is not known to have undergone any significant modifications prior to its demolition in 1734. The "small but neat and well-lighted" building covered an area about 55 feet wide by 110 feet and fronted on "a dirty street, called Smock Alley" (Dunton 1699, 340). The auditorium contained a pit, a lower level of boxes, middle and upper galleries (Adair 1866, 303) as well as small rooms called lattices on the level of the middle galleries located over the two sets of twin procenium doors which flanked the stage. The small orchestra occupied a music loft placed above the center of the proscenium (Dunton 1699, 339).

As early as 1721 the resident company had observed in "An Epilogue Spoke by Mr. Griffith" that the nearly sixty-year-old theatre might be "not of long duration" and had voiced the hope that a worthy replacement might soon be provided by the "gallant Nation" (*HDC* 4 Oct. 1721). This elicited no response from the playgoing public, and for another fifteen years the Smock Alley players had to make the best of a steadily deteriorating house.[1]

A replacement theatre in Aungier St. was nearing completion when, on 4 March 1734, "Part of the House" at Smock Alley collapsed, putting an abrupt end to any further theatrical activity at Dublin's first Theatre Royal.

### *Aungier Street Theatre (9 March 1734–ca. 1746?)*

When Thomas Elrington died in 1732 his successors to the management of Smock Alley Theatre decided to proceed with his plan for the construction of "a good and sufficient Playhouse in some Convenient Place within half a Mile of the Tholsel" (MS. 83/299/58966 ORD) as a replacement for the delapidated structure in Smock Alley.

Before Christmas 1733 they had chosen a site near the fashionable St. Stephen's Green area on the northwest corner of Aungier and Longford Streets, and had begun to clear the ground at that location. On 28 February 1733 the Theatre Royal managers signed leases for two adjoining parcels of land near the corner of Aungier and Longford Streets: (1) from David Digges Latouche, at a yearly rental of £24, a walled lot, 78' wide and 170' deep, on the north side of Longford Street between Stable Lane and Mr. Parry's house, which faced Aungier Street; (2) from Samuel Taylor, brewer, at a yearly rental of £20, a vacant lot, 46' wide and 135' deep, on the west side of Aungier Street, extending westwards to the rear of the Latouche ground (*DEP* 19–23 Dec. 1732; MSS. 72/165/50246 and 72/197/50373 ORD). On 15 March 1733 these two leased properties were assigned to John Waite, presumably as security for a loan (MS. 74/140/50394 ORD).

They had also by this time secured the assent of Sir Edward Lovett Pearce, the Surveyor General and the architect of the magnificent Parliament House, to design and construct the theatre (MS. 75/140/50394 ORD). Before February he had drawn up plans for the building and had interested "many gentleman of fortune" in sharing the cost of the construction.[2]

Work on the foundations began on 19 March 1733 (*DEP* 17–20 Mar. 1733), and by the end of the 1732–33 season the construction of the new Theatre Royal was well under way. The directors had signed a final contract with Sir Edward Pearce on 21 February whereby in return for the playhouse they would pay him and his heirs for each play, concert, or other entertainment given there a fee at the rate of 2s. 6d. on every £100 expended in construction (MS. 83/299/58966 ORD). The fee was to be collected each night out of the first box money received. Furthermore, Sir Edward, in order to underwrite his building costs, could secure any number of subscribing sharers, none to pay less than £100, and each to receive a silver ticket for admission to any part of the playhouse on any performance night. Two weeks after signing this contract, the foundations of the new structure were begun (*DEP* 10 Mar. 1733) "on the very spot where once stood a stately Monastery of the Order of Grey Friars. . . . In King Charles the 2d's Time, the Earl of Longford made it his Residence, after whose Decease it fell into Ruin" (*HDJ* 12 May 1733).

Because of the corner location Dublin citizens and newspapers during the construction of the playhouse referred to it variously as the theatre in Longford Lane, or in Longford Street, or in Aungier Street (*HDJ* 12 May 1733). After its completion, however, the more fashionable name of Aungier Street was almost universally used.

The formal laying of the four cornerstones took place on 8 May 1733, with "Plenty of the choicest Wines for the Gentry and a Barrel of Ale given to the Populace" (*FDJ* 12 May 1733). The Rt. Hon. Richard Tighe placed the first stone; Major General Robert Napper, the second; Mr. William Tighe, the third; and Sir Edward Pearce, the fourth. Under each stone Thomas Griffith, the eldest of the Theatre Royal directors, put several medals struck for the occasion (*FDJ* 12 May 1733). Trumpets, drums, band music, and applause added a festive touch. An elegant dinner concluded the day's proceedings; the invited "persons of quality" drank fourteen toasts, the last three wishing for "Prosperity to All the Sons of the Muses," "Prosperity for Ireland," and "Success to the New Theatre" (*SJEP* 22 May 1733). Instead of a dinner, the men working on the playhouse received presents of money so that they too could "complete the day in drinking" (*HDJ* 12 May 1733).

The frequent winter storms, "the like of which had not been known in the Memory of any Man at this season of the Year" (*PO* 15 Dec. 1733), had delayed construction but little. Within a week of the Smock Alley collapse the actors, of necessity, moved to Aungier Street Theatre.

The new Theatre Royal was considerably more spacious and elegant than their former residence. Perhaps the new proprietors respected Elrington's wish that the new playhouse be fashioned "after the Form of that in *Drury-Lane, London*" (Chetwood 1749, 137). Indeed, an early French visitor thought that "the new playhouse in Aungier Street . . . yields to none in Europe and surpasses those in London" (*Four Letters,* 26). Constructed of brick, the main entrance faced south and the door to the middle and upper galleries opened off the passage on the playhouse's west side directly opposite Longford Lane (Rocque map 1756). The theatre had a breadth of forty-six feet and a length of ninety-four feet, with a pit twenty-six feet in depth; its stage, twenty-nine feet wide from box to box, and fifty-four feet deep (*FDJ* 4 Feb. 1758) was equipped with the customary traps and "Side Runners for Two Setts of Scenes" (MS. 83/299/58966 ORD).

The building's most striking feature was the "commodious Box-Room . . . finely ornamented and large enough to hold all the Company that [could] sit in the Boxes; from whence they all immediately retir[ed] at the end of the Play, as to a Drawing Room. There they convers[ed] with each other till they [were] called to their Carriages" (Victor 1761–71, 2:261). The box room seems to have been built as an annex behind the northeast corner of the theatre with a corridor leading to an entrance on Aungier Street where coaches could deposit or pick up their passengers (Rocque map 1756). This room may have been the "Great Room in Aungier-Street playhouse" to which over fifty blind patients of the noted oculist Dr. Taylor resorted for treatment in April 1745 (*FDJ* 2–6 Apr. 1745).

The new Theatre Royal in Aungier Street opened on 9 March 1734. Though impressive inside and out, the playhouse soon revealed grave defects as a place for stage entertainments. "Experience proved that . . . it required uncommon powers of voice to fill every part of the house, and on full nights a great part of the people in both galleries could neither hear nor see" (Hitchcock 1788–94, 1:89). W. R. Chetwood, the Drury Lane prompter who rejoined the Dublin theatre community in 1741, expressed the professional consensus:

The architect had more View to the Magnificent than the Theatrical: the Audience Part is ornamented with rich Embellishment, that gives it a superb Countenance, but . . . this might have been [made] more convenient with less Cost. The

Contriver had an Eye more to ridottos than to the Drama. . . . (Chetwood 1749, 71)

That "the Contriver" may have considered the needs of ridottos is confirmed by an announcement in the *DEP* of November 1735 which proclaims that the interior of the new Aungier Street playhouse has been finished "magnificently for the accommodation of the nobility and gentry in a far more elegant manner than ever was in this Kingdom" and is particularly suitable for the presentation of serenatas, oratorios, and ridottos.

In the summer of 1740 an attempt was made to remedy the acoustical problem when workmen "lower'd the Sounding Board near seven feet" (*RNL* 25 Oct. 1740), although the effect of this modification is unclear.

By the end of 1741–42 season the financial strain of six years of uninterrupted rivalry with Smock Alley was beginning to tell not only on the finances of the proprietors but also on the fabric of the building itself. The theatre seems to have decayed into a state of some disrepair for in June of that year the managers were requested to "cause the Nails to be carefully pulled out of their Benches in the pit, otherwise nine Gentlemen out of ten will be a Pair of Stockens out of pocket every Time they go there" (*DM* 5 June 1742).

In July 1742 Thomas Elrington's widow, Frances Elrington, decided to rid herself of the theatre and sold it to Lord Mountjoy, his heirs, and the rest of the subscribers and proprietors, "together with All the Cloaths, Scenes, Machines, Decorations, Property and other Implements and Utensils . . . belonging in anywise to the said Theatres [*sic*]." In return she was to receive during her lifetime an annuity or yearly rent charge of £56 17s. 6d. in four equal quarterly installments, along with a further annuity of £50 payable "out of the money yearly granted by the Lord Lieutenant or the Lords Justice for the use of the Aungier Street Theatre." This arrangement was to continue to her or her heirs until the £810 she had advanced for the use of the Theatre Royal (plus £310 interest) was paid her. Each year Lord Mountjoy, his heirs, and the proprietors were to remunerate Mrs. Elrington or her heirs with all the net profits after salaries and expenses, in order to repay as speedily as possible the debt of £810, over and above the yearly rental of £50 (MS. 106/420/74508 ORD).

The following autumn George Cornelius Swan, the new manager, made some minor alterations to the interior of the theatre. He explained:

> Whereas there have been great complaints made by the Ladies that the Boxes in the Aungier Street Playhouse were excessive cold, the Manager of said Theatre thinks proper to advertize, that apprehending the same proceeded from Holes cut in the Door by Servants waiting in the Passage, and want of Curtains over the Door, he has made all the Boxes quite close, and gotten Curtains to every Door, and given orders that no Servants shall wait in said Passage, which he hopes will answer, and if not [he] will execute any Method [he] shall be Advized [of] for warming the House, or otherwise for the Convenience and Satisfaction of the

Audience, [and] he has likewise got a new Set of Lamps to burn Tallow at the Front of the Stage, the Oyle being offensive, and has mended all the Seats round the House. (*FDJ* 23 Nov. 1742)

When the long-contemplated union of the Smock Alley and Aungier Street companies took place at the beginning of the 1743–44 season the United Company made its home at Aungier Street under the management of Thomas Griffith. Despite the short-lived opposition from Thomas Sheridan and other disaffected actors at Smock Alley, the Theatre Royal in Aungier Street emerged victorious in February 1744 when Sheridan accepted an offer to play at Drury Lane and the Smock Alley company disbanded.

After Sheridan's departure the United Company played occasionally at each theatre, preferring the larger Aungier Street playhouse for plays for which they expected large audiences, and Smock Alley for plays less likely to attract large houses.

### Managers: Old Smock Alley and Aungier Street Theatres

Upon Joseph Ashbury's death the management of Smock Alley theatre devolved to Thomas Elrington (Hitchcock 1788–94, 1:37). It would appear, however, that within a very short time Thomas Griffith and perhaps Louis Layfield were also sharing his responsibilities. This is suggested in the preface to the 1725 edition of Charles Shadwell's *Works,* in which the author implies that Elrington and Griffith were the principal managers by that date when he writes:

> As to the present State of the Stage in Dublin, I must own I think Mr. Elrington and Mr. Griffith have spared no Pains nor Charge in Order to Divert; They both are Excellent in their way, and with a little more Encouragement from the Town, the whole Company might soon be made to Excell both in Comedy and Tragedy.

Elrington may well have confined his efforts to acting and directing. Thomas Griffith's principal managerial tasks were choosing the repertory and writing the occasional prologues and epilogues. In "A Preface to the Reader," which appears only in the 1729 Dublin edition of Coffey's *The Beggar's Wedding,* the playwright states that he submitted his manuscript "to Griffith" on 30 October 1728, but Griffith elected not to undertake production while *The Beggar's Opera* was still drawing large houses.[3]

An advertisement in the *DNL* of 17–20 December 1743 stating: "Whoever have any lawful Demands on the Theatre Royal Aungier Street, are desired to bring them to Mr. Layfield, at his House in Marlbro Bowling-Green" suggests that Lewis Layfield may have coordinated the financial side of the management, and, as former overseer of the Dublin city music (he was dismissed for neglect of duty in 1733) may also have had a hand in supervising the theatre musicians.

After Thomas Elrington's death in 1732 the management passed to "Mr. Francis Elrington, brother to the late manager, in conjunction with Mr. Griffith, Mr. Layfield, and some others whose names have not reached us" (Hitchcock 1788–94, 1:71). Leases from this period indicate that Anthony Moreau and James Vanderbank also became "associate" sharers in the theatre and these five men may have set up a joint directorate (MSS. 71/165/50246, 72/197/50373, and 83/299/58966 ORD) but it is not now possible to say whether Moreau and Vanderbank had a hand in the actual management of the playhouse.

Thomas Elrington's demise "was a severe blow to the interests of the drama in Ireland, and the stage began to decline rapidly" (Hitchcock 1788–94, 1:71). Hitchcock relates that "whether from want of judgment or conduct, or other causes unknown to us, the affairs of the theatre soon began to wear an unpromising aspect" (74).

At this juncture the succession to the managership of Aungier Street theatre has become confused. Hitchcock tells us that, in order to forestall the decline in standards, an unique system of management was put into operation when the Smock Alley company moved to the new theatre in Aungier Street in 1734. "There certainly never was a more noble or disinterested design than that first formed of building and conducting this theatre," Hitchcock continues. The new proprietors, a group "of noblemen and gentlemen of the first rank and consequence in the nation" assumed the overall direction of theatrical affairs, and all of the profits derived from the performances were to be "solely dedicated to the public service." From their number they chose a committee and chairman who met every Saturday "to appoint the plays, distribute the parts, and settle the great variety of business, which unavoidably arises from so great an undertaking." (87–88). The "chairman" was probably the same George Cornelius Swan who was appointed by the proprietors "to superintend the management" (87–88). Stockwell (1938, 73) believes that Elrington, Griffith, and Layfield continued to carry out the actual theatre business under Swan.

The experiment failed. Those "Gentlemen the Proprietors soon found their Error, and resigned the Conduct of the Business to the Actors. . . . But as the Gentlemen still remain'd their Paymasters, and as the Principles of those Actors were equal to their Policy, they continued to make it a losing Game, and by that means, in a short Time after, got the whole into their own Hands. . . ." (Victor 1761–71, 1:17). Hitchcock says that the reason generally given for the failure was "that the former managers of Smock Alley [i.e. Elrington, Griffith, and Layfield] *who were continued by the proprietors*, conducted business so injudiciously that they could not lay any claim to encouragement or success" (1:89, emphasis mine). He adds that Swan's inexperience in theatrical management and the poor acoustics of the Aungier Street playhouse also contributed to the failure (89).

Despite the evidence of Hitchcock and Victor, the noble experiment in committee management of Aungier Street probably took place several years later than Hitchcock suggests. The *DNL* for 17–20 January 1741 contains an advertisement that announces triumphantly that Aungier Street is under new management and that the new managers "are Persons who are qualified to discern the Method to please . . . and [will] furnish the Auditors with the best Plays by the best Authors, as well as procure the best Performers in all Characters. . . . The Gentlemen, the Proprietors of the Theatre Royal Aungier Street, have disposed matters under so happy a Regulation and Oeconomy, that the many Enormities, which hitherto disgusted the Audience, will, for the Future, be avoided, and no Care, Labour, or Expense, will be spared to render the Theatre the Seat of Rational Pleasure. . . ."[4]

Such objectives are strikingly similar to those described by Hitchcock above in reference to the committee of noblemen and gentry. Furthermore, the earliest record we have of Swan's association with the Dublin stage is as an actor in a notice for the benefit performance of *Othello* of 15 May 1742 when the title role was played by "a Gentleman, whose friendship for Mr. Worsdale [the benefit recipient] has engaged him in the undertaking." Later that season "Mr. Swan" played Oroonoko opposite Susannah Cibber's Imoinda. (The famous London actor James Quin also appeared at Aungier Street during the 1741–42 season). Early the following season (4 November 1742) Swan, "the gentleman who played Othello for Mr. Worsdale's Benefit," acted the title role in *Tamerlane*.

Twelve days later the advertisement announcing Swan's reappearance as Othello tells us that "the Manager of Aungier St. proposes a subscription series of Shakespeare plays, one a week for eight weeks." (The importation of excellent actors and the staging of plays of the first quality are desiderata referred to in both Hitchcock's account of the aims of the committee of management and in the advertisement of 17–20 January 1741).At the beginning of the 1742–43 season the Aungier Street manager, presumably Swan, made several improvements to the interiors of the theatre's boxes and "got a new Set of Lamps to burn Tallow at the Front of the Stage, the Oyle being offensive" (*FDJ* 20–23 November 1742).

Later yet, at the end of another performance of *Othello* on 1 January 1743, Swan spoke a prologue attacking the management at the rival Smock Alley for encouraging acrobatics and tumbling at their theatre. Swan was clearly the spokesman for the company, and this, as well as the evidence from the notices for the performances of *Comus* on 17 and 24 January 1743, point almost certainly to Swan as the company's actor/manager. However, with the formation of the United Company at the beginning of the 1743–44 season, Swan's name disappears from the record.

Consequently, if Hitchcock is correct in linking George Cornelius Swan's management of Aungier Street to the "noble experiment," it is virtually certain that his chronology is incorrect. The committee of proprietors seems not to have been directly active in the affairs of the new theatre at the time of its construction in 1734 or for a number of years thereafter; rather, Griffith, Elrington, and the others who formerly managed Aungier Street "were continued by the proprietors" and managed the company during the seven seasons 1734-35 to 1740-41. They relinquished control only as late as January 1741 when Swan assumed the management of the theatre for a part of the 1740-41 and all of the 1741-42 and 1742-43 seasons.

That Swan was acting as deputy of the noble proprietors in 1743 is clear from Theophilus Cibber's "Proper Reply" of July 1743 in which he tells how he came to Ireland to perform at Aungier Street: "Mr. Desbrisay, and other Gentlemen (Men of Worth and Honour) had, by Message, and Letter of Attorney granted to Mr. Swan (who came to *England* on purpose) invited me to the other [Aungier Street theatre]."[5]

At the beginning of the 1743-44 season the proprietors of both theatres at long last formed a united company comprised of the best actors of both houses. The battle had been long, acrimonious and expensive. It certainly brought Lewis Duval, the Smock Alley manager, to the verge of bankruptcy, and, if Thomas Sheridan is to be believed, the union of the theatres was only effected after the proprietors engaged in "an expensive Law-suit" which "from first to last" cost "more than twelve thousand pounds" (Sheridan 1758, 69).

Who precisely managed the united company is not clear, although Francis Elrington and Thomas Griffith remained in the new troupe.[6] Lewis Layfield moved to Smock Alley briefly during the short season of Sheridan's management. Spranger Barry made his very successful debut with the united company in February 1744, and Sheridan states that Barry appeared soon thereafter "at the Head" of the Aungier Street company (Sheridan 1758, 17).

Yet, this attempt, too, ended in failure and "Towards the close of this winter [1744-45], the proprietors of Aungier Street and Smock Alley theatres finding their affairs beyond their power to retrieve, and the stage reduced to the lowest ebb, as their dernier resort, and at the request of the public, solicited Mr. Sheridan to return, and take on himself the sole direction and management of the stage, offering to vest him with unlimited authority to act in every respect as he should think proper" (Hitchcock 1:148-49).

### Signora Violante's Booth, Dame Street (1730-1731)

"Signora" or "Madame" Violante Lorini seems to have come to Ireland first to perform at Smock Alley Theatre at the invitation of Thomas Elrington. In December 1729 Sga. Violante and the small company that she brought with her from the Haymarket Theatre, which included her daughter, Miss (or Madamoiselle) Rosina Violante; Monsieur Charles Lalauze, a French dancing master; and William Phillips, a "Posture Master" later more commonly known as "Harlequin" Phillips; joined the Smock Alley company.

Upon arrival Sga. Violante was advertised as "the most famous Rope-Dancer now living" (DI 23 Dec. 1729). Some twenty years after the fact W. R. Chetwood described her as "an Italian lady celebrated for Strength and Agility; . . . the Strength of the Limbs which these Sorts of Undertakers expose . . . is shockingly indecent, but hers were masculinely indelicate and were of a Piece with the Features of her Face" (59). This description suggests how "an ill-natured report that she was a Man" arose at Shrewsbury where she performed enroute to Dublin (DI 22 Nov. 1729). Nevertheless, the Shrewsbury "Ladies of Distinction caress'd her extremely, and entertained her at their Assemblies and their own Houses, and soon found [the report] to be groundless" (DI 22 Nov. 1729).

By mid-December Sga. Violante and M. Lalauze were entertaining the Theatre Royal audiences with their particular specialties: the former "walk[ing] on a rope from the stage to the upper gallery and then flap[ping] down the same on her breast without being fastened thereto," the latter doing a solo French peasant dance in wooden shoes (DI 30 Dec. 1729). Their performances must have been very popular for by early March 1731 a prologue printed by an anti-Violante faction complained that for her troupe "the House is crowded thrice a week."[7] At the invitation of "several of our First Quality" the Violante troupe set out for Cork at the end of the 1729–30 season (DI 28 Mar. 1730).

When Sga. Violante returned to Dublin in mid-November 1730 she had apparently determined to establish her own place of entertainment in that city, for, instead of appearing again at Smock Alley, she contracted for the building of a wooden theatrical "Booth," containing a middle and upper gallery as well as a pit (DI 14 July 1731). It was located on Dame Street near College Green and opposite the Bull's Head Tavern, in the garden behind the "Great House" where a Mr. Maguire had lately resided and managed a bank (DWJ 16 Mar. 1728; 19 Dec. 1730; FDJ 13, 16, and 20 Feb. 1730; 8 July 1732).

There is no evidence to indicate on which side of Dame Street near College Green either Maguire's Bank or the Bull's Head Tavern stood. J. Rocque's map of 1756 suggests that the Maguire property, with Violante's booth to the rear, was probably situated on the street's south side between Trinity Lane and George's Lane (later South Great George's Street), perhaps in Spring Garden Lane, in which a surveyor's map, ca. 1760–80, shows a "Tennis Court" that could well be Violante's booth converted (Flintscroft).

The booth was completed by early January 1731, for a deed of George Ford, carpenter, dated 8 January 1731 and conveying to William Montgomery, merchant, and Casper White, Alderman, for £107 13s. 2d. "a Booth lately erected on a piece of Garden or Ground behind the House where Mr. Maguire the banker lately lived in Dame Street" (MS. 66/35/44998 ORD). Richard Maguire, banker, died 12 July 1727, and his son William continued his father's banking business at the same house for a time (DG 15 July 1727).

Presumably the owners Montgomery and White leased the booth to Sga. Violante.

Hitchcock (1:47) is the only authority for the statement that Violante's first booth was built in a house in Fowne's Court, formerly occupied by Lord Chief Justice Whitchel, and standing on ground on which Fowne's Street was afterwards built. He fixes her removal to George's Lane in about 1730 (75), an equally erroneous date. Chetwood, it is to be noted, says nothing whatever about her Dame Street booth, although all subsequent historians of the Dublin stage have cited this evidently spurious theatre.

Sga. Violante enlarged her company by engaging five dancers from Smock Alley and performances began at the "New Booth" in February or early March. Apparently the Violante company enjoyed a popularity similar to that which it had experienced at Smock Alley the previous year for "one of the greatest Companys seen at Public Divertions this Season" was present at Sga. Violante's benefit in April, and when the booth closed for the summer in August "a vast Concourse of People of all Ranks" attended (*DI* 4 Aug. 1731).

The 1731–32 season was even more successful, Sga. Violante having varied the usual fare of pantomime, rope dancing, and dancing with performances by the juvenile "Lilliputian" company, which included the young Peg Woffington.

The Dame Street booth was also used occasionally for private stage entertainments. On 15 December 1732, for example, *Julius Caesar* was performed "by some of the young Gentlemen in Dr. [Thomas] Sheridan's School."[8] Thomas Sheridan, later the famous Dublin actor-manager, played Mark Anthony in the performance (Sheldon 1967, 8).

At the end of that season Sga. Violante visited England, appearing in September at the Richmond Wells and Haymarket Theatres (*LS* Pt. 3:1:231–32). When she and her business associate, M. Lalauze, returned to Dublin during the early spring of 1733, however, they did not reopen the booth in Dame Street.

The vacant booth soon tempted a group of adventurous young apprentice actors, led by Luke Sparks, John Barrington, and Miss Mackay, to form a company and rent the booth for £3 per week (Chetwood 1749, 63). Sparks, who had acquired his stage experience with a strolling company, assumed the post of manager. Costumes were borrowed, "some from Friends, and some to be paid for" (63), and they commenced acting with Farquhar's *The Inconstant* in October or November 1733.

The first production aroused so warm a response that the company was enlarged and in due course held benefit performances, the first night going to Miss Mackay as leading actress. When the Theatre Royal players were alerted to the fact that "Several Ladies of the first Rank expous'd her Cause and brought upwards of forty Pounds to the Occasion" (Chetwood 63) they immediately petitioned the Lord Mayor to forbid further competition by the unlicensed company, claiming exclusive stage rights within the city by virtue of their Royal patent. The Lord Mayor acquiesced and issued the prohibition, but allowed a farewell benefit, Bullock's comedy *Woman is a Riddle*, which attracted "a good house" to Dame Street (63). This interference, however, only served to arouse the determination of the fledgling actors and supporters alike to open a theatre in competition to the Theatre Royal outside the Lord Mayor's jurisdiction.

### Stretch's or Ward's "Great Booth," Dame Street 1721?–1736?

A second, and perhaps even a third, theatrical booth was operating in Dame Street at the same time as Sga. Violante's. Faulkner's *Dublin Journal* of 27 April–1 May 1731 announces that a number of young comedians, "separated themselves from those of the Theatre-Royal, but upon what Account we cannot yet tell." This group, which included Mr. and Mrs. [John?] Ward, advertised a performance of Congreve's *The Double Dealer* for 5 May 1731 "At the Great Booth in Dame Street"—the only theatrical performance known to have taken place in that structure.

Hitchcock's assertion to the contrary (1:55), this booth could hardly have been Sga. Violante's theatre since her own company was playing there regularly at this time and was always distinctively called the "New Booth." Possibly, the "Great Booth" was the one in Dame Street owned by Randal Stretch, the puppeteer.[9] Although Stretch had transferred his activities to a booth in Capel Street by 1736 at the latest (*DEP* 27–30 Mar. 1736), in 1729 Stretch apparently still gave his puppet shows in a Dame Street venue.[10] By the time Sga. Violante opened her booth Stretch may have already moved to Capel Street and vacated the Dame Street site, or perhaps he rented it out during periods when he himself was not performing there. Stretch died before 13 March 1744 although puppet shows continued to be performed at his theatre for some time (*FDJ* 10–13 Mar. 1744).

Hitchcock, whose dates are seldom to be trusted, says that in 1735 there were three theatres in Dublin [i.e. Smock Alley, Aungier Street, and Rainsford Street] "not to mention Madam Violante's, and the theatre opened by Ward in Dame-Street" (1:96). If Hitchcock has not contradicted himself (we have already seen that he stated that the Wards' performance took place at Sga. Violante's booth) Ward must have opened a booth, whether his own or Stretch's we cannot now say, sometime after this performance. John J. Mac Gregor, an early nineteenth-century writer on the architecture of the city of Dublin, states (without citing his authority) that in 1734 "Ward's theatre" existed in Dame Street (Mac Gregor 1821, 314).

### Sga. Violante's Booth, George's Lane (1733–34)

Instead of opening the "New Booth" in Dame Street when she returned from England in the spring of 1733, Sga. Violante built another booth in a location only a short distance north of the projected Aungier Street playhouse. This second building occupied a site similar to that of the first: it stood "in the garden behind the house wherein John Martin, plasterer, live[d] on the West side of George's Lane" (MS. 73/336/513 ORD). Lying exactly opposite Fade Street, the passage that led from George's Lane to the booth exists today between nos. 59 and 60 South St. George's Street.[11] The new structure, apparently somewhat larger and better finished inside than its predecessor in Dame Street, contained boxes in addition to pit, middle, and upper gallery, and was "well wainscotted and lined with Woolen Cloath." The interior was "finely illuminated after a new Manner" (*FDJ* 4 June 1734).

The booth in George's Lane was opened by May 1733 although the record of performances there is slight, and it may well have been in operation much earlier in the season. The new "little theatre" evidently did not yield sufficient profit in its early operation: the two proprietors needed financial assistance, for on 19 July 1733 in order to procure a loan of £70 they assigned their rights in the booth "lately built behind John Martin's house" to William Montgomery and Casper White, the two men who also held a mortgage on the Dame Street booth (MS. 73/336/513 ORD).

Although the "New Booth in George's Lane" was used occasionally during the 1733–34 season, Sga. Violante's association with the theatre probably ended sometime during that winter. In November 1733 when Cummins announced that he was taking his benefit on the thirtieth, he again, as in the preceding June, specified that it would be staged at "Madame Violante's Booth in George's Lane" (*DEP* and *FDJ* 24 and 27 Nov. 1733). When, however, Walsh advertised his benefit for 13 February 1734, he described the location as "the New Booth in George's Lane" (*FDJ* 12 Feb. 1735). Perhaps, therefore, Sga. Violante had given up managing the booth and had left Dublin. She had certainly returned to London by April 1734 for her young daughter, Mlle. Violante, was dancing at Goodman's Fields Theatre on 27 April (*LS* Pt. 3:1:391).

There is no record of any use of the booth for theatricals after March 1735.

### *Rainsford Street Theatre (5 Feb. 1733–ca. June 1736)*

The dispossessed company who had occupied Sga. Violante's Dame Street Booth and who were prohibited from acting there by the Lord Mayor lost no time in carrying forward their project for erecting a playhouse outside the city limits and thus outside the jurisdiction of the Lord Mayor of Dublin and the Theatre Royal's patent. Gaining the patronage of the Earl of Meath and reorganizing themselves as "the Earl of Meath's Comedians" with Benjamin Husband and Lewis Duval as managers, they resolved to build their theatre within the Earl's "Liberty," a large private tract which stretched across southwest Dublin almost to the City Basin. A suitable property was found on Ransford (now Rainsford) Street to the south of the present Guinness's Brewery buildings at James's Gate.

In the eighteenth century Rainsford Street, a rather narrow thoroughfare running parallel to Thomas Street, connected Thomas Court with the fashionable Rope Walk, now Portland Street (Rocque map 1756). Charles Brooking's map of 1728 mistakenly designates as Ransford Street the thoroughfare (now Crane Street) which runs south from Thomas Street near James's Gate. Early eighteenth-century deeds, however, describe Ransford Street as a "new" street running east and west, with the "King's pavement" on it by 1715 (MSS. 7/391/2739 and 22/191/11761 ORD). The troupe hastened to prepare "a very neat, compact" playhouse (Chetwood 1749, 66), possessing boxes, pit, and middle as well as upper gallery near the intersection of Rainsford Street and Sugar House Lane (now Belview Gardens) (*DEP* 9, 13, 16 Mar. 1736). This general location is strongly suggested by later newspaper advertisements offering the playhouse property for sale or let and describing it as "The Theatre in Randford-Street, with a good Brick House adjoining, well wainscotted, and great Conveniency of Water: Which may easily be fitted for a Merchant, Brewer, or Sugar-Boyler . . . Enquire of Mr. Lewis Duval at his House in Grafton-Street, or of Mr. William Dryden in Dame-Street" (*HDJ* 26 June 1736; *FDJ* 28 Sept. 1736). Indeed, the site is now occupied by the stores of Guinness's brewery.

These accommodations were reported to be "capable of containing a hundred Pounds at Common Prices," approximately the capacity of the new Goodman's Fields Theatre in London according to Chetwood (60). If he is to be believed and if Arthur H. Scouten is correct in his estimation of the capacity of Goodman's Fields Theatre, Rainsford Street seated about seven hundred patrons (*LS* 3:1:xxvi).

The "New Theatre in Ransford Street" opened on Monday, 5 February 1733, and by 1 March was having such success that the Smock Alley players complained bitterly of the shift in popular favor. However, the fortunes of the Rainsford Street company went into a decline after the opening of the spectacular new Aungier Street Theatre in March 1734. Despite the brief popularity of the burlesques of the Theatre Royal's repertoire, which restored the reputation of Duval's company for the 1734–35 season, its remote location and the physical limitations of the Rainsford Street playhouse had long since been recognized as insuperable obstacles to any continued prosperity there.[12] Consequently, by the end of the 1734–35 season its managers decided to move the company back into the city and selected the site of the old Smock Alley theatre as the location for their new playhouse.

The construction of the new Smock Alley Theatre required that the Company remain in the Rainford Street location for the first few months of the 1735–36 season where they again performed their satire of the *Henry VIII* coronation scene. The last of these performances was on 1 December 1735 when a "numerous audience" gathered to observe the farewell night of the

Rainsford Street Theatre (*WO* 15 Nov. 1735). Though less than two years old, it had become little more than an outpost of the Dublin stage (*HDJ* 26 June 1736 and *FDJ* 28 Sept. 1736). The building was used at least once more on the occasion of a benefit for a "Gentleman in Distress" on 16 March 1736, but thereafter the playhouse seems to have been closed permanently.

Chetwood (66) states that he never saw the Rainsford Street playhouse, suggesting that the building had been demolished by the time he returned to Dublin in 1741.

### New Smock Alley Theatre 1735–1787

The remoteness and the physical limitations of the Rainsford Street playhouse inevitably forced Louis Duval, its ambitious manager, to seek a larger playhouse at a better location. Consequently, Duval took steps to construct a new building on the site of the old Smock Alley theatre almost as soon as the venerable structure was abandoned in the spring of 1734. It was, by common consent, "the most convenient situation in the Entertainment of the Town" (*WO* 20 May 1735).

Duval secured as business partners two interested merchants, Charles Birch of Essex Street and Charles Meares of Castle Street. These three men, for a yearly rental of £65, became lessees of "all that piece of Ground whereon the Old Theatre and other Tenements joyning thereto stood situate on the north side of Smock Alley . . . containing in front to Smock Alley 63¼' and in depth backwards to the Blind Quay 139' and in breadth to the said Quay 67' . . . with appartments on which said premises the said Lewis Duvall hath lately built or caused to be erected a new theatre" (MS. 82/149/57330 ORD). At the same time Duval raised sufficient funds from fourteen subscribers to ensure the erection of a satisfactory playhouse.[13]

Duval also sought the same official recognition of his theatrical enterprise as the Aungier Street management enjoyed, and to this end he persuaded influential friends to make representations on his behalf to Edward Hopkins, Master of the Revels, so that in early January Hopkins granted Duval a license as Deputy Master of the Revels.[14] This license accorded Duval the powers of a royal patentee (the same authority as Thomas Griffith of Aungier Street had held for years) and enabled him at once in playbills and newspapers to designate the Rainsford Street company "His Majesty's Company of Comedians" (*FDJ* 8 Feb. 1735; *DEP* 8 and 25 Feb. 1735).

Demolition of the first Smock Alley theatre commenced before the end of January 1735. The new theatre would possess "convenient Passages from the Front to the Blind Key, and commodious Passages at both Ends for the benefit of the Coaches, and more speedy Conveyance of the Company" (*FDJ* and *PO* 7–11 Jan. 1735). Four months later, on Monday, 19 May, subscribers and "other Gentlemen of Distinction" attended the laying of the foundation stone to the new building that was being "erected pursuant to His Majesty's royal patent" (*FDJ* and *WO* 20 May 1735). Although "several Pieces of Gold were given to the Workmen to drink Their Majesties Healths and Success to the Undertaking" (*WO* 29 May 1735), the occasion was celebrated with much less formal festivity than marked the similar Aungier Street ceremony exactly two years before.

Construction at Smock Alley had reached the point by mid-September where "the Walls [were] almost finished, and only the Timber [had] to be put up, and the Slates nailed, and the Inside plastered, and the Box Pit and Gallery begun and ended" (Swift 1963–65, 4:396–97). Dr. Helsham, one of the subscribers, assured Swift that the curtain would be raised in the new structure on 30 October, and that "the Town reckon[ed] upon it" (4:396–97). Dr. Helsham was, however, too optimistic in his prediction.

In the event, the new Theatre Royal in Smock Alley was used for the first time on the evening of Thursday, 11 December 1735 (*WO* 13 Dec. 1735). "So eager were they to open (or to get money) they began to play before the Back-part of the House was til'd in" (Chetwood 1749, 71). Perhaps because the theatre was unfinished the Town did not anticipate the premiere and "not Half an Audience" was on hand to view the first performance (71).

Notwithstanding the "uncommon expedition" which the now unknown Smock Alley architect exercised, he "studiously avoided the errors and mistakes of former builders" (Hitchcock 1:93). He constructed an auditorium that far surpassed Aungier Street in acoustics, stage visibility, and convenience of seating. The new theatre also held an audience "a Fifth Part more in number" (Hitchcock, 1:93; Chetwood, 72). Smock Alley's greater capacity resulted partly from the inclusion of "slips": slit-like compartments with benches, inserted directly above the upper side boxes (more often called "lattices") and on a level with the upper gallery (O'Keeffe 1826, 1:287; *FDJ* 25 Sept. 1753; *PO* 29 Sept. 1753). The Aungier Street theatre apparently had no such accommodation, but it did possess a somewhat larger stage both before and behind the proscenium (Chetwood, 72).

*Exshaw's Gentleman's and London Magazine* (59:500) contains an engraved likeness of the theatre as it appeared in 1789. The second theatre in Smock Alley, finished in brick with cut stone framing of the front doorway and windows followed its predecessor in facing away from the River Liffey and towards the heart of old Dublin (Rocque map 1756). Since the theatre stood back several yards from the eighteen-foot-wide street (Rocque map 1756; "Survey of Dublin Streets"), a spacious thoroughfare existed for coaches to pass the entrance to the boxes, which was located in the center of the ground floor and protected by a shallow, canopied portal (*Exshaw*). An ample passage on the east or right side of the playhouse connected Smock Alley and the Blind Quay, and led to the door for the pit and middle gallery. A door on the west or left side, approached by a flight of steps, led to the upper gallery, which was divided by a wooden partition into a pay gallery and a free gallery for footmen (*Exshaw*). In February 1743 "several unruly Persons, disguised like Servants, endeavoured to break down" this partition.[15]

The exterior of the new building looked quite plain and must have contrasted strongly with the decoration within, described by early visitors as "elegant" (Hitchcock, 1:93; Luckombe 1783, 15).

*Managers: New Booth, Dame St./Rainsford St./ New Smock Alley Companies*

The reason assigned by Chetwood for the establishment of a theatre to rival Smock Alley is that Siga. Violante, "finding her business decline, let her theatre to Mr. Luke Sparks, Mr. John Barrington, and Miss Mackay, afterwards Mrs. Mitchell, (three of her young performers) for three pounds per week. . . . These young adventurers were joined by several others whom love of fame, more than hopes of profit, incited. Mr. Sparks as being the oldest, and having played before in a country company, was appointed manager" (Hitchcock 1:76).

While waiting for the Rainsford Street theatre to be built, however, the company reorganized itself as the "Earl of Meath's Comedians" (*DEP* 3 Feb. 1733) and selected two experienced managers (*PO* 17 Feb. 1733) with quite different qualifications: Benjamin Husband, "a Gentleman of exact Conduct" (Chetwood 173) who had shown himself an able but not superlative actor at Smock Alley for thirty-five years; and Lewis Duval, a choreographer and former dancer of French descent and training, who had come from London a year or two previously.

Since Duval is not known to have performed on the stage in any capacity during his career in Dublin, we must assume that his involvement in the Irish theatre was mainly entrepreneurial and managerial. That several dances "composed" by Duval were performed at his benefit on 16 April 1733 suggests that he (and perhaps his wife Arabella) had been a dancer in earlier days, probably on the Continent, since he is not known to have danced in London. The John Duval who was advertised as "lately from London" (but having no London record) when he first appeared at Smock Alley in 1730 and who received two other Dublin notices before disappearing from playbills in 1739, may have been a relative. If, however, Lewis Duval was nearly ninety when he died in 1766, as Hitchcock asserts, he would have been well into middle age by the time he assumed the Rainsford Street management and past his prime as a dancer.

Despite initial success at Rainsford Street Duval apparently realized that if he was to give the Aungier Street company serious competition he would be obliged to move closer to the center of the city. Duval approached the proprietors of the derelict old Smock Alley theatre and purchased the site from them. In January 1735, at about the time that construction of the new Smock Alley playhouse began, Duval was appointed to the Deputy

Mastership of the Revels. How Duval acquired the title is not known. He simply may have purchased the office, but the Dublin newspapers of 7–11 January 1735 carried the following notice: "Last week arrived here a special Messenger from the Rt. Hon. Edward Hopkins, Esq.; Master of His Majesty's Revels, in the Kingdom of Ireland, with the Deputation of his Patent, in behalf of Mr. Lewis Duval and Company of Comedians now acting in Ransford-Street, according to the full Power and extent of the same. . . ." Duval could now legally build a patent house within the Dublin city limits and call his troupe "His Majesty's Company of Comedians."

Hopkins died a year later, on 17 January 1736, and the new Master of the Revels in Ireland, Luke Gardiner, did not reappoint Duval Deputy Master. The new Smock Alley company evidently secured a license to play in Dublin from the Lord Mayor and acted thereafter "by Permission of the Lord Mayor."

As manager, Duval took two benefits at Smock Alley in 1735–36 and 1736–37 seasons (both commanded by the Lord Mayor, Aldermen, Sheriffs, and Common Council of Dublin), and in the latter summer took the new Company on its first tour of northern venues, including Belfast and Derry.

In the *DDP* of 26 January 1739 Duval is praised for "having introduced a certain Regularity of Management" at Smock Alley. At the beginning of the 1737–38 season Duval announced the first of his reforms of the theatre. In future, the curtain would rise promptly and the audience was assured that performances would not be cancelled at the last minute because of poor houses (*DDP* 22 Sept. 1737). In the 1740–41 season Duval departed from accepted custom and required that the gentlemen take tickets for the boxes and pit before they were seated (*DDP* 27 Nov. 1740).

Duval may well have been in financial difficulties as early as March 1736 because he mortgaged the theatre property for £100 and was forced to take out another mortgage in March 1738. He lost, or relinquished, his post as deputy master of the revels, for *FDJ* of 21 February 1741 indicates that Worsdale from Aungier Street has been appointed to that position.

Duval gave up sole proprietorship of Smock Alley on 21 April 1741. That he had been under considerable pressure to do so for some time is suggested by an exchange of letters which appeared in the Dublin newspapers in early May 1741. Duval had initiated the paper war with a pamphlet (now lost) in which he aired his grievances in public. Duval claimed that William Bradford, one of the Smock Alley subscribers, had tried to force him to quit the theatre, first, by inciting Duval's creditors to set a bailiff onto him, and, second by compelling the Smock Alley actors to abandon Duval in mid-season and go over to Aungier Street. Bradford and the other Smock Alley subscribers vehemently denied having engaged in any deceitful practices, but Duval published the sworn affidavits of two of his principal actors, Robert Wetherilt and Elizabeth Furnival, in which they swore that Bradford, had, indeed, attempted to force them to desert Smock Alley.[16]

Whatever the truth of the matter, it is interesting to note in the subscribers' part of the correspondence that they clearly had been dissatisfied with Duval's management for some time: "he having often trifled with us, and endeavoured to defraud us of our just rights . . ." and were trying to orchestrate a union of the two theatres even as the bum-bailiffs pursued the unfortunate Duval (see *FDJ* 4–9 May; 9–12 May and 12–16 May 1741; *DNL* 12–16 May 1741).

Despite relinquishing (financial?) management of the Smock Alley company, Duval stayed on in some managerial capacity for at least one further season. Hitchcock tells us that in the summer of 1741 Duval took the company to Belfast and Newry "as usual," and an advertisement for the performance of 12 October 1741 specifies that "Mr. Duval" will open the theatre for the season and has engaged W. R. Chetwood as "Director" of the company, though by 15 September Thomas Philips had taken over that duty. As in the preceding season, Duval was given two benefits, suggesting that he remained in a strong position in the company. When, in July 1742, the theatre apologized to the Lord Mayor of Dublin and his party for not having the Royal box reserved for their use at the previous night's performance, Duval's name appears above those of Thomas Philips, Thomas Furnival, James Morris, Robert Wetherilt, and William Este in the advertisement, which certainly suggests that he was still preeminent in the company.

In the 1742–43 season Duval is not mentioned in the record until 9 May when, because of internecine wrangling, he took his benefit at Aungier Street instead of at Smock Alley. Suffering from gout and unable to wait upon his patrons in person, Duval again complains in a letter to the newspapers that Philips and the Smock Alley company have refused to allow him a benefit at Smock Alley "unless I would take it upon their own ill-natured and oppressive terms; neither would they suffer Mr. Sheridan . . . to play for me" (*DNL* 23–26 Apr. 1743). He explains that he would be indigent if it were not for the kindness of the "Smock Alley subscribers." Things became worse, and in 1743 "one of the Company" had stood bail for Duval, probably for unpaid debts, and Duval had forfeited that bail. That the affair was still not settled by the following autumn is clear from another letter, probably written by Duval, in which the author complains that the present lessees, Sheridan and Elrington, had no right to either the theatre or its wardrobe (*FDJ* 1 Nov. 1743). Duval's active involvement in the Dublin theatre ended after the 1742–43 season. He and his partners transferred all rights in the Smock Alley property on 14 April 1744 for a sum of money and, if T. Sheridan is correct, "annuities to the amount of upwards of £400" per annum (Stockwell 1938, 86).[17]

When, in April 1741, Duval signed over the lease of the Smock Alley playhouse as well as his interest in its scenes, machines and costumes it was to Thomas Philips, Ralph Elrington, Robert Wetherilt, John Morris, Thomas Furnival, William Este, William Phillips, and William Dryden. As we have seen, Duval remained at least nominally in charge of the company for over a year, but Thomas Philips was also principal manager during this period. Although Philips made a brief visit to London in the spring of 1742, he was again listed among the "Lessees or Manag[e]rs of the Theatre in Smock Ally" when the group were granted concessionnaire's privileges in 1742 (cited in entry for Thomas Philips in *BD*).

Thomas Philips acted in Dublin from as early as the 1722–23 season and made frequent appearances there throughout our period before assuming control of Smock Alley. He either managed the company very badly or affairs at Smock Alley had come to such a pass that there was little he would do to save it. Certainly Louis Duval ascribes the blame for his own financial ruin directly to Philips, whom he implies is managing the theatre. Thomas Sheridan confirms Philips's mismanagement when he relates that when he arrived to prepare for the performance of *Cato* on 14 July 1743 he found that Philips had absconded with a part of the company's wardrobe. When the Smock Alley theatre was advertised for auction in January 1744 Philips was working in London, where he remained.

### Capel Street Theatre (1745–July 1746)

The ubiquitous William "Harlequin" Phillips and his wife reappeared in Dublin at the beginning of the 1744–45 season. First, Phillips danced in Ralph Elrington's company at Smock Alley before joining the United Company where he put on his version of the popular pantomime *The Hussar*.[18]

In the late winter of 1744 Phillips gathered together some of the disgruntled players of the United Company and went with them to a new theatre he had built in Capel Street. Phillips leased a strip of land fifty by one hundred feet on the west side of Capel Street between Little Strand Street and Mary's Abbey and erected a small playhouse of approximately the same dimensions (MS 116/323/80604 ORD). This building should not be confused with Stretch's Theatre, the little theatre near Mary's Lane with only a pit and gallery, which Stretch used for his puppet shows. Advertisements in Faulkner's *Dublin Journal* indicate that Stretch was performing at his "house" at the same time as the new theatre opened. Called either the "New Theatre in Capel Street" of "City Theatre in Capel Street," Phillips's playhouse stood some fifty feet back from the street, behind nos. 136 and 137 Capel Street, with a passage out to Capel Street itself.

The theatre auditorium contained boxes, lattices, pit, and first and second galleries. However, the hastily-built little theatre apparently caused some concern for its durability, for the new manager issued a statement:

Mr. Phillips, to remove any Reflections or Injurious Aspersions calculated to prejudice him in this affair, will take care to obtain the judgment and Certificates of the best Master Builders, as to its Warmth, Strength, and Security [of the new theatre]. . . . (*FDJ* 15 Jan. 1745)

On opening night, 17 January 1745, the *DC* reported that "there appeared a numerous and polite Audience, who seemed entirely pleased with the Performance [of *The Merchant of Venice*] and confirmed the strength and security of the House." Acting on Mondays and Tuesdays in January, they extended their productions to three or four times a week in February and March.

As early as 28 January 1745 Mr. Phillips would appear to have reached some sort of associative agreement with Samuel Foote, the comedian and dramatist who was later to become the greatest mimic of his age, but who made his Dublin debut with the united company in October playing major roles in comedy and tragedy. Foote may have found the circumstances at Capel Street Theatre more congenial, for at Smock Alley he was sharing the applause with Spranger Barry who also made his Dublin debut this season. An anonymous letter now in the British Library dated 20 February 1745[19] suggests that Foote was very successful at Capel Street Theatre, if only for a short while:

> The attention of the Publick has been lately taken up by the two rival theatres, the old one in Smock Alley and a new one, *under the direction of Mr. Foot* in Capel-Street; but the last is in the greatest esteem at present Mr. Foote having played Wildair, Bayes, and Pierre five time each, to as crowded Audiences as ever were known. (emphasis mine)

The letter suggests that an arrangement had been reached whereby Mr. and Mrs. Phillips confined their activities to pantomime, while Foote directed the company in comedy and tragedy. By April, however, patronage had fallen off greatly, and Capel Street Theatre's stage was used infrequently until July when its doors were closed for good.

Samuel Foote was acting at Drury Lane at the beginning of the next season. When, that summer, the Phillip's left Dublin is not known, but their departure was hasty, for, as W. R. Chetwood observed, in order "to shew his Dexterity," Phillips "played a Harlequin Trick, and . . . made his Escape . . . back to England, but did not forget to take more Money than his own along with him" (21).

## The Theatrical Season

### *Opening Night*

Performance evidence suggests that the Dublin theatre season usually began shortly after Michaelmas (29 September) and coincided with the opening of the Irish Parliament (every second year in Dublin) or with the commencement of the judicial and university terms in the years when Parliament did not meet.

Prior to the 1736–37 season none began earlier than 25 September (1731–32 season) or later than 30 November (1724–25), although more often than not the first recorded performance took place in the third week of October or later. Such information may be misleading, however, because it is derived entirely from notices announcing plays in honor of one or another of the Royal anniversaries and, therefore, does not preclude earlier unrecorded performances. The managers certainly delayed opening until the town was sufficiently "full" again with returning nobility, gentry, members of Parliament, lawyers (and their wives and children), and students who presumably had spent the summer in the country or abroad and who constituted the bulk of the audience.

After the 1733–34 season, when at least two theatres were operating in Dublin simultaneously, the date of opening is more certain. The Aungier Street company regularized its opening night, commencing on the anniversary of the coronation of George II (11 October) in all but two of the ten ensuing seasons (35–36, 1 September; 37–38, 15 September). Smock Alley, on the other hand, normally opened its doors to audiences sometime between 1 and 22 November (except in 1737–38, on 22 September; and 1741–42, 14 October), three or more weeks later than Aungier Street in all but one season (1741–42). The company seems not to have returned to Dublin from its summer tour of the north until around 1 November.

## Nights of Performance

Throughout the period by far the most popular nights for performing were Monday (35 per cent of performances) and Thursday (33 percent) which together account for nearly 70 per cent of all performances. There were occasional performances on Wednesday (10 per cent), Saturday (10 per cent), Tuesday (7 per cent) and Friday (6 per cent) nights as well. The theatres were always dark on Sundays.

The Dublin theatres also closed for the whole of Passion Week. There is no record of whether or not the Dublin managers ever shared the pre-1730 London custom of not performing on Wednesday or Friday during Lent, but it is certain that they did schedule plays for those days after 1732 and continued to do so even after the Licensing Act of 1737 made such Lenten opening illegal in London. They seem to have preceded their London counterparts by one year in staging a performance on Ash Wednesday (Smock Alley on 9 April 1732).

The theatres closed for the Christmas holiday on 22 December—the only exception being the 1739–40 season when a performance was advertised at Smock Alley for Christmas Eve—and generally reopened on 27 December or shortly thereafter. They were always dark on Christmas Day, Boxing Day, and New Year's Day.

Other circumstances also caused the theatres to close. Mourning for the death of Queen Caroline darkened them from 30 November 1737 to 7 January 1738. Severely cold and inclement weather forced the cancellation of several performances between December 1739 and late February 1740, while civil unrest and an influenza epidemic adversely affected performance schedules for short periods in other years.

### End of Season—Summer Season

The regular season usually ended by the third week in June. Thereafter, visiting actors from London (whose season there ended the last week in May (*LS* 3:1:xliii) played the Dublin theatres until mid-August or, occasionally, until early September, supported by actors from the Dublin companies. Summer seasons are recorded in 1732–33, 1734–35, and, perhaps as a result of the restrictions placed on acting in London by the Licencing Act of 1737, in every season from 1736–37 to the end of the period.

### Seasonal Tours

The Dublin companies made regular tours of the provincial towns at the end of the regular or summer season and, occasionally, at other times of the year as well. The Smock Alley troupe acted in Cork as early as 1713, but there is no further record of any seasonal tour until June 1728 when they went to Drogheda to assist in the celebrations associated with the riding of the franchises. The same company is known to have visited Cork in July 1733, but they may have relinquished the south to the Aungier Street company and established a regular summer tour of the northern towns by 1736. Hitchcock reports that they visited Belfast and Derry in that year, and, although they were in the southern town of Waterford in July of 1737, (accompanied by the visiting London players) they are nevertheless recorded in Drogheda in late-October 1738 and 1740. By 1741, Hitchcock tells us (1:114), the company was "as usual" making a tour of the northern towns of Belfast and Newry.

In June 1742 the Smock Alley company made a brief visit to Carlow to perform before the visitors to the annual race-meeting. Later that summer they embarked for England to perform at the Preston Jubilee, but they were delayed by unfavorable winds, missed the Jubilee, and played for several nights in Liverpool instead. The visit was so successful that they returned to Liverpool to perform the following summer.

The Aungier Street players toured the towns of the south of Ireland, in their first season together, setting out for Carlow races in July 1735. In July and August 1736 they visited Clonmell, Cork, and Carlow, and they are known to have made a brief visit to Cork for the April Assizes in 1739. The company was probably in Cork again in September 1741 accompanied by James Quin from London.

## Benefit Performances

Benefit performances were a regular part of the Dublin theatre calendar by 1720. During the period under study there is record of over 750, constituting nearly 60 percent of all recorded performances.

Benefits were of four types: those for actors and actor/managers (nearly 80 per cent of the total); those for charities (10 per cent of the total); those for house servants (9 per cent of the total); those for playwrights (3 per cent of the total). There is also some evidence that suggests that benefits were occasionally granted either in addition to or in lieu of payment to merchants for services rendered or goods provided to the theatre. The printer to Smock Alley theatre, for example, received an annual benefit, no doubt to recompense him for his services in the printing of play- and handbills. On other occasions benefits are recorded for a jeweller, a wine merchant, and a general merchant.

All Dublin theatre employees appear to have been entitled to some form of benefit performance from which the recipient kept the profits, minus the running expences of the theatre. We have no record of the amount of money required to meet these house charges in Dublin, although in London during this period they came to as much as £50 or £60 (*LS* 3:1:cxiii). The charges would have included the salaries of the performers and ancillary personnel, a set fee for general wear-and-tear to the theatre fabric, costumes, and scenery, as well as a charge for candles and oil to light the building. In addition to the fixed house charge, the benefit recipient also paid to advertise the play in the newspapers and playbills as well as for the printing of the tickets. He also probably paid for the distribution of the playbills and handbills.

The benefit recipient did not rely entirely on printed notices to gain patronage. Bringing his tickets with him, he was expected to make personal calls on well-to-do patrons and to solicit the attendance of themselves and their friends. Recipients who, because of disability or ill-health, were unable to make personal visits to patrons often felt obliged to apologize in the newspapers. Tickets to benefits were also sold at the recipient's residence as well as at the theatre.

Wealthy patrons had considerable influence, too, on the choice of programs presented at benefits, for it is by no means unusual for actors to advertise that a particular play is being performed "at the particular desire of several persons of quality and distinction" or to announce a change of program at the insistence of such people. The general audience also had some influence in this regard as is evidenced by the April 1728 Smock Alley benefit for Mrs. Sterling whose very popular rendering of Polly in *The Beg-*

*gar's Opera* resulted in the audience "demanding" that she be given a benefit.

A sometimes embarrassing requirement of the benefit performance was that the recipient pay to the theatre a portion of the "common expenses" or house charges in advance of the actual performance by way of a deposit. W. R. Chetwood tells us that the unfortunate playwright Thomas Walker was unable to produce the required one-half of house charges before his advertised Aungier Street benefit of 1 June 1744 with the result that "the doors were ordered to be kept shut" and the audience turned away (Chetwood 1749, 247). Similarly, the tearful Louis Duval was forced to appeal to his assembled company for assistance when in April 1741 he "had not credit for the incidental charge of a Night's playing (see entry of 9 May 1743 Aungier Street).

The Dublin theatres seem to have made a standard practice of raising the normal admission charges for benefits from early in the period. In the first year of its opening in 1735 Aungier Street advertised benefit prices of 5s. 5d. for the boxes, stage, and lattices, 3s. 3d. for the pit, and 2s. 2d. for the first gallery, representing an increase of about 1s. 1d. in each seating category. In 1743 these charges remained the same and were being advertised as "the usual benefit Prices." Benefit tickets at Smock Alley and the minor theatres were increased similarly from as early as 1729.

The profit that a benefit realized depended upon a number of factors, the most important being the recipient's position in the hierarchy of theatre personnel. Preeminent were the actor-managers and the principal performers. Actor-managers took at least two and as many as five benefits each season; principal performers usually contracted for two. Secondary performers, principal musicians, and senior house servants, such as the treasurer and the prompter, were allowed one unshared benefit and occasionally a second which they shared. Occasionally, also, they opted for two shared benefits. Tertiary performers, musicians and lesser house servants such as pit- and box-keepers, wardrobe keepers, and dressers usually shared a benefit with one or as many as three others. The advantage of the shared benefit was, of course, that the house charges were also shared, for it is unlikely that many minor employees could afford to meet even the one-half deposit on house charges unaided. Tertiary personnel occasionally shared benefits with performers of higher rank, but as a rule they shared with persons on the same rung of the hierarchical ladder.

Another factor affecting the profits at a benefit performance was its position in the theatrical calendar. The process of benefit allocation seems to have been as follows: upon being engaged (or upon renewal of his contract) the performer agreed to take his benefit or benefits (assuming that his contract included a benefit) during a certain term, be it Michaelmas, Hilary, or Whitsun. At a later time, and perhaps as often as once a term, the management "fixed out" the precise date of the performance in consultation with the company. Presumably the play to be performed and the cast were also assigned and agreed to at this time.

Once the date was fixed all parties were bound to honor it, and changes were made only with considerable difficulty. In February 1743, for example, the managers "begged" the Widow Este to defer her benefit so they could avoid a dispute with the actor/manager Louis Duval who wished to take his on the same night (see entry for 9 May 1743 Aungier Street). Benefits were, furthermore, seldom deferred. Of the 750 benefits recorded, only 60 (8 per cent) were put off to another night once they had been advertised. When a benefit had to be deferred some explanation was usually given in the newspapers, the most common excuses being illness on the part of the recipient or a principal performer, a desire to avoid scheduling the benefit on the same night as another (more popular) performer at a rival theatre, or the request of persons of quality who wished either to attend a conflicting benefit or entertainment, such as a concert or ridotto. Other reasons given for deferring benefits were bad weather, riots, inadequate preparation of scenery or machinery, and compositors' errors on the part of the newspapers or playbill printer.

The theatre management usually reserved the first four months of the season for its own profit. Only actor-managers and first rank performers were allowed the first of their benefits during this time, the weeks immediately preceding Christmas being the most desirable. The other categories of personnel had to wait until February or later to take theirs. Because of the need to make personal calls on patrons to sell tickets, it was preferrable to obtain one's benefit as early in the general benefit period as possible. Since there were sometimes as many as three benefit performances each week at each theatre, the potential patrons would have become less amenable to purchasing tickets after several months of what must have been almost daily solicitation.

Over 70 per cent of all benefits occurred during the months of February, March, April, and May, and of these nearly 25 per cent took place in February. Again, actor-managers and first-rank performers had first choice of dates, and they frequently took benefits in late January or early February. They were followed by the secondary performers from mid-February to mid-March and then by the shared benefits of the tertiary personnel which often ran into June. The spring and early summer months saw a sprinkling of final benefits of the principal performers as well.

The competing theatres appear to have made serious efforts to avoid scheduling benefits on the same night. Even during the decade of the most intense rivalry between Smock Alley and Aungier Street theatres, it was unusual to have more than five such conflicts during a season, the exception being the 1741–42 season when there were conflicts on sixteen occasions. On the nights when simultaneous benefits were advertised, the clash was almost always between employees of similar standing in the hierarchy—

usually tertiary performers or house-servants. Conflicts between the benefits of first-rank performers and employees of lower standing were very rare and when they did occur were usually the result of accident and elicited some comment in the next editions of the newspapers (see 18 Feb. 1740 and 20 Apr. 1743). Benefit conflicts between theatre employees and charity performances were also very rare (only two), and two charity performances were given for different recipients on the same night at different theatres were very unusual (see 22 Jan. 1739 and 4 Dec. 1740).

A final factor affecting the success of a benefit performance was the choice of program. All classes of benefit recipient chose standard plays in the repertory for presentation. Although practically every mainpiece presented during the period was performed at least once for someone's benefit (of the eighty-three plays performed more than three times only two were not), benefit recipients showed a distinct preference for Shakespeare and comedy. Of the mainpieces chosen nearly 65 per cent were non-Shakespearean comedies, 20 per cent were Shakespearean dramas, and 15 per cent non-Shakespearean tragedies.

The comedies of Congreve, Colley Cibber, Farquhar, and Gay were the most popular choices, fifteen mainpieces by these playwrights accounting for nearly 60 per cent of all comedy performed for benefits (*The Beggar's Opera* [27], *The Twin Rivals* [15], *The Recruiting Officer* [11], *Love and a Bottle* [6], *The Constant Couple* [17], *The Beaux' Stratagem* [13], *The Provoked Husband* [17], *The Careless Husband* [9], *The Double Gallant* [10], *Love Makes a Man* [17], *Love's Last Shift* [13], *The Double Dealer* [10], *Love for Love* [18], *The Old Batchelor* [17], *The Way of the World* [21]).

Five tragedies—*Hamlet* (23), *Othello* (17), *King Richard III* (17), *Julius Caesar* (13), and *Macbeth* (11)—account for nearly 70 per cent of the performances of Shakespeare plays presented as benefits. Of Shakespeare's comedies only *I Henry IV* (17) can be said to have been a frequent choice of benefit recipients, although *The Merry Wives of Windsor* (7) and *The Merchant of Venice* (7) were in modest demand.

Of the non-Shakespearean tragedies performed for benefits, over 70 per cent of the performances were of six plays by Phillips, Rowe, Congreve, and Otway (*The Distrest Mother* [17], *The Fair Penitent* [12], *Jane Shore* [8], *The Mourning Bride* [12], *Venice Preserved* [14], and *The Orphan* [7]).

Some plays were seldom performed except as benefit mainpieces. *The Fatal Marriage,* for example, was never staged except for benefits and some eighteen mainpieces were chosen as benefits at least three of every four times they were performed.

Two-thirds (five hundred) of all benefit performances were advertised as double-bills, and recipients displayed distinct preferences in their choice of afterpiece as well as mainpiece. Of the ninety-nine named afterpieces performed in Dublin during this period the eight which were staged more than twenty times account for nearly 50 per cent of all benefits. The twenty-five afterpieces performed between three and nine times account for 25 per cent of the total; the forty-six pieces performed fewer than three times comprise less than 9 per cent of the total.

Benefit recipients also demonstrated a preference for plays which had not hitherto been performed during the current season. No doubt because of their novelty value, actor-managers and principal performers frequently chose plays or afterpieces that had either never been performed in Ireland or which had not been performed for many years (ten years being the most common period, but twenty years was not uncommon and one play was revived after fifty years).

Occasionally first-rank personnel advertised premieres of both main and afterpieces for their benefits. It is interesting to note that despite the time and expense involved in staging new plays for benefits, they were not often repeated later in the same season. In fact, of twenty-four benefit pieces advertised as Irish premieres, fifteen never saw a second night. Revivals were repeated more frequently, usually for the benefits of lesser employees. Afterpieces were much more likely to be repeated for benefits than were mainpieces. While over 60 per cent of benefit mainpieces were performed only one time each season and less than 7 per cent were staged more than three times, less than 40 per cent of afterpieces were performed once in a season and nearly 20 per cent more than three times.

In addition to the drawing-power inherent in the date of performance, the cast, and the choice of program, theatre personnel used a number of devices to make their benefit programs more attractive to the public. Actors and actresses usually chose plays in which they performed a role for which they had achieved some notoriety in the past; principal musicians and dancers usually included extended or new programs of entr'acte entertainments in which they featured prominently. Attempts were frequently made to stimulate interest in a benefit by advertising that either or both of the pieces would not be performed again that season. On a few occasions triple bills were advertised composed to either one mainpiece and two afterpieces or of three afterpieces (e.g. 12 June 34; 6 June 33; 26 Mar. 39, 21 Feb. 40, 7 May 41).

Other special features advertised for benefit nights included special lighting (wax instead of the smokey, tallow candles), special seating arrangements (part of the pit enclosed to form box seats for the comfort of the ladies), new and popular dances, musical pieces, songs and ballads, as well as new prologues and epilogues written especially for the occasion.

Tertiary performers and house servants could not, of course, expect to attract audiences by their own talents and relied entirely on the drawing-power of the program and performers to fill the theatre for them. Indeed, the contracts of the principal performers occasionally seem to have included the requirement to appear in the benefits of an agreed number of their colleagues. This is suggested, negatively, in a sharp exchange of letters between Mlle. Chateauneuf and Thomas Wright in January 1744. The very popular

Mlle. Chateauneuf's name had been included in the playbill for Wright's benefit without her permission, and the offended dancer warned the public that she would neither perform in Wright's benefit nor in the benefit "of any other Player" while in Ireland, not being obliged by her articles, she asserted, "in any Manner to perform" (see entry for 23 Jan. 1744 Aungier Street). That the managers could exercise considerable authority in controlling the participation of actors in the benefits of others is suggested further by an incident which occurred at Smock Alley in May 1743 when Thomas Sheridan, having agreed to perform in a benefit for Louis Duval, was prohibited from doing so by the managers to the detriment of Duval's pocketbook.

## Charity Benefits

In addition to the benefits for theatre employees, the managers allocated a few nights each season for charity performances. Nearly eighty charity benefits are recorded, and these are divided fairly evenly between distressed families or individuals; the various Dublin hospitals and institutions for poor relief, such as almshouses and orphanages; and groups such as prisoners and distressed Freemasons.

Benefits for needy individuals were usually one-off occurrences, although occasionally such people were granted two or even three benefits. In 1738 and 1739, for example, Thomas Kirby, a linen printer who had been in prison for seven years for a debt of £150, was granted a third benefit night when the proceeds from the first two were insufficient to secure his release.

But the managers may not have been as generous to the recipients of charity benefits as appears at first glance, for it is clear that they, too, were usually required to pay not only the house charges but also a portion of these in advance. The £110 received by Thomas Kirby was "the clear Produce" of his three benefit nights, and when, in March 1742, the Smock Alley band was engaged to play at Handel's concert at the Music Hall, M. De Rheiner, "a distressed foreign Gentleman," was forced to defer his benefit and "obliged to give a considerable Praemium to obtain another Day, besides other extraordinary Expenses." More telling yet is the 14 December 1742 Smock Alley benefit advertised "For a Child who has the Money of the House owing."

It is not clear if the various hospitals which were granted annual benefits were also required to pay house charges, but in one instance at least a "clear" night was given. This occurred on 12 February 1737 at Aungier Street when Mercer's Hospital was awarded "the whole Receipts of the House free of Expenses," and suggests that the occurrence may have been unusual. If advances on house charges were required for such benefits, they were apparently paid or at least guaranteed by the relevant Board of Governors or Trustees. Benefits in aid of the distressed Freemasons or the prisoners in the Dublin marshalseas were presumably guaranteed by the Grand

Master or by a sponsoring philanthropic group, such as the Charitable Musical Society, at whose instance the benefits were requested in the first place.

Profits from charity benefits could be considerable. As early as April 1721 a Smock Alley benefit for the distressed weavers of Dublin, with an original epilogue by Swift, raised £73. By 1740 charity benefits were frequently realizing over £190. With the help of the proceeds derived from its charitable benefits the Charitable Musical Society announced that it had released 142 prisoners from the marshalseas in 1737 and 141 in 1738 (*PO* 1–4 Dec. 1739).

*Authors' Benefits*

The few premieres of new plays by authors who were physically present in Dublin to demand a benefit makes it difficult to determine whether the Dublin theatres followed the London custom of awarding benefits to authors on the third, sixth, and ninth performances of their plays. No play of this sort reached its ninth night during this period, although several authors were awarded benefits on the third performances of their works and at least one was given a benefit on the sixth night.

It seems to have been a frequent occurrence for a benefit to be awarded to an author at the premiere of his play. In every case, however, the first performance was also the play's last, and we are led to suspect that the benefit was given more as a charity benefit than as recompense to a successful author. That Dublin playwrights depended heavily upon the benefit—and not the sale of their plays—for remuneration is suggested by the advertisement for Charles Coffey's *The Beggar' Wedding* in March 1729 in which it was stated that the benefit would be "the Author's sole Emolument."

## Command Performances

Although not all Irish vice-regents evinced the same interest in the theatre, the commands of the Lord Lieutenant (during his biannual periods of residence) and of the Lords Justice (in the Lord Lieutenant's absence) had a significant effect on the choice of program. During his years in Ireland the Duke of Dorset commanded some thirty performances. The Duke of Devonshire called for some fifty-four nights of acting during his years in office. About half of these performances can be ascribed to the Dublin custom of government nights at which the ladies were granted free admission to the boxes. The total number of performances of tragedies would, for example, be considerably smaller without the nineteen performances of Rowe's *Tamerlane,* which was commanded each year on 4 November, the anniversary of the birth of William III.

The noblemen who served as Grand Masters of the Freemasons of Ireland also frequently ordered plays, usually for the benefit of their distressed brothers. Important too was the influence of those "Ladies and Gentlemen of Quality" who request plays "by particular desire." Over 180 such requests appear in the newspapers during the period, and they often indicated a request for an alteration of program (sometimes at very short notice).

Indeed, commands or requests from the nobility and gentry comprise nearly 25 per cent of the total number of performances.

## Actors and Other Theatre Personnel

Over three hundred people looked to the Dublin theatres for employment and some form of livelihood in the quarter-century between 1720 and 1745. Most were performers: actors, actresses, dancers, singers, musicians, tumblers, and rope-dancers. But to run smoothly and efficiently, each theatre also depended on a staff of ancillary personnel (houseservants): dressers, wardrobe-keepers, pit- and box-keepers, treasurers, guards, doorkeepers, stage-officekeepers, and, of course, charwomen.

Because little information has survived about the day-to-day backstage workings of the Dublin theatres, we must depend heavily on inference and surmise to form a picture of this aspect of the Dublin stage, although, clearly, the Dublin playhouses were run in much the same way as those in London, about which we know a great deal more.

We have already observed that theatre personnel worked within a fairly rigid hierarchical structure. At the top was the management. Each theatre had one or more managers in overall control of the running of the theatre. The managers were responsible to the subscribers, frequently called "proprietors"—a group of (usually wealthy) men, which sometimes included the managers, who each ventured an initial sum of money in the construction of the playhouse in exchange for a portion of the weekly receipts commensurate with the size of their investment and a silver token permitting the subscriber or a member of his family to attend a specified number of performances each week free of charge.

Subscribers sometimes had an important voice in the management of the theatre, and exerted pressure on managers for various reasons. Such was the case at Smock Alley theatre in 1741 when, because the theatre was on the verge of financial ruin, the subscribers sought to rid themselves of their manager, Louis Duval, in order to form a united company of actors from both Smock Alley and Aungier Street. The "noble experiment" in which the proprietors at Smock Alley attempted to manage the theatre by committee on a charitable basis is discussed above.

The manager was ultimately responsible for every aspect of the successful running of his theatre although his principal concerns were with repertory and personnel. He employed several people to help him with the administration of the company: a boxkeeper was available each day at the theatre to sell tickets to the boxes (admission to the other areas would seem to have been collected by the various doorkeepers either at the door to the various seating areas, after the audience was seated or upon entry in the case of late-arrivals). The treasurer kept the theatre's accounts and prepared the actors' weekly wages for disbursal.

To assist him on the performance side of the business the manager employed a prompter (sometimes called the "director") who undertook all of the duties of the present-day prompter as well as those of stage manager. In conjunction with the manager he prepared the acting version of the play, cutting (and sometimes adding) lines and characters; blocked the movements of the actors; assigned the speeches and characters; ensured that the actors were in the proper positions to make their entrances (probably with the help of a call-boy); blew a whistle to alert the scene-shifters of a scene change and rang a bell to cue the orchestra for entr'acte music. He was also responsible for cueing off-stage sound effects. All this in addition to supervising daily rehearsals of scenes from impending plays.[20]

That the treasurer and prompter held senior positions is suggested by the fact that both were given their own benefit each season, a perquisite otherwise reserved for principal actors and managers. On the other hand, the wardrobe-keeper and dresser, who assisted the actors with their costumes and properties, shared a benefit with other house servants such as doorkeepers or with minor actors. Stagehands would seem to have worked for wages only.

## The Acting Profession in Dublin

About 280 performers practiced their art on the Dublin stages between 1720 and 1745. Most were actors or actresses who were supported in the programs by small groups of dancers, singers, musicians, and other specialty artists.

The average size of the principal Dublin theatre company (excluding house-servants and musicians) was twenty-five performers, consisting of about seventeen men and eight women, (a ratio of about two to one). The average figure of twenty-five is probably somewhat low due to the fact that supernumerary roles were seldom listed in the newspaper advertisements upon which the bulk of our record is based. Scouten indicates that in the London theatres between 1729 and 1747 the average number of actors (excluding dancers) employed at Drury Lane was about fifty and at Covent Garden fifty-five, the ratio of men to women being about thirty-five to twenty.[21]

Of course, the numbers of performers and the ratio of men to women varied somewhat each season according to the needs of the repertory and the personnel available. During the 1728–29 Smock Alley season, for example, the names of some thirty-five performers are recorded, the increase resulting from a requirement for a group of boy-actors recruited solely to perform in *Chuck; or, The School-Boys Opera*. Occasionally, too, additional personnel were drafted in for short periods when plays requiring large numbers of supernumeries were produced. In addition to actors and actresses, each company employed at least two and occasionally as many as eleven dancers or singers each season.

An examination of the careers of the members of the companies who performed at old Smock Alley/Aungier Street and at the Rainsford Street/ new Smock Alley theatres during the period reveals a great deal about the profession in Dublin at the time, and particularly about the stability of the Dublin acting company and the movements of actors between Dublin theatres and between Dublin and London.

Assuming that the calendar is a reasonably accurate record of the length of stay of the performers in Dublin (and excluding the thirty theatre musicians known to have performed in Dublin during the period as well as the twenty-one London performers who visited Dublin only for the summer seasons) we see that nearly 230 actors, actresses, singers, and dancers worked on the Dublin stages for some part of our period.

About one-half of these (111) are known to have stayed for only one year; many of this number were either child-actors or amateurs trying the stage for a lark. Another fifty-five professional performers stayed in Dublin for from two to four years, and represent about twenty-five per cent of the total. Thus, about two-thirds of the Dublin performers remained in the theatres for less than five years. Of the remaining one-third, nearly forty performed from five to nine seasons and about twenty-five from ten to twenty-five seasons.

### Actors: Old Smock Alley/Aungier St. Company

In the typical season at old Smock Alley/Aungier Street about one-third of the actors and actresses had been members of the company for most of their careers: Thomas Elrington (from 1712 until his death in 1732), Francis Elrington (ca. 1714 until his death in 1746), Ralph Elrington (ca. 1717 until he retired in 1758), Lewis Layfield (from 1719 until 1747), Thomas Griffith (from ca. 1698 until he died in 1744), Mr. and Mrs. James Vanderbank (he from 1720 until 1748, she from 1721 until 1739), John Watson, Jr. (1719 until 1760), Alcorn (1721 until his death in 1733), and Mrs. and Mrs. Anthony Moreau (from 1718 until 1752 and 1745, respectively).

Other actors joined the company and stayed with it more or less exclusively for many seasons: Dash (1721–1729), Daugherty (ca. 1707–1734), Joseph Elrington (1736 until his death in 1755), Mr. and Mrs. Henry Giffard (1716 until 1729 when they moved to London), Thomas Hallam (1707 until 1727), Benjamin Husband (1696 until 1733, when he went to Rainsford

Street), Robert Layfield (1728 until 1757), Mrs. Martin (1698 until 1727), Mrs. Sterling (1716 until 1732), Mrs. Knapp (from 1721 until 1727), Rosco (1722 through 1729), George Sheridan (1728 until 1737), Mr. and Mrs. John Ward (moved from new Smock Alley in 1736 and stayed at Aungier Street until 1741), and Mrs. Wrightson (1732 until 1741).

A few performers joined the company on several occasions for short periods: Mrs. Reynolds (1729 until 1743, she also acted at new Smock Alley at various times), Thomas Philips (visited frequently from 1722 until he absconded to England for good in 1743), and Mrs. Lyddal (at old Smock Alley from 1717, moved to new Smock Alley 1733 until ca. 1740, when she returned to Aungier Street to retire).

Around this core of experienced professionals was assembled the majority of the performers who joined the company for one to four seasons and then left.

### Actors: Rainsford Street/new Smock Alley

The Rainsford Street/new Smock Alley company was much less stable than that of Aungier Street. It too had at its core a small number of personnel who remained with the company through most or all of its existence: Lewis Duval, the manager, John Barrington, John Beamsley, Benjamin Husband (from old Smock Alley), Luke Sparks, Mr. and Mrs. Robert Wetherilt (from 1735), Ralph Elrington (from 1736), Thomas Philips (from 1736) and perhaps Bourne (or Berne). Duval's company was also much more dependant than Aungier Street on short-term principal and secondary actors to make up its numbers, many coming for short visits from the London theatres. With the exception of the actors just mentioned, the record shows that no performer stayed at Smock Alley for more than three seasons in succession.

The chief reason for the stability of these core companies seems to be that most of the members had important financial or familial ties with the company, often as managers or sharers. Although Aungier Street actors did, occasionally, defect to the rival house in Smock Alley, they seldom remained there for long. Actors were far more likely to spend a season or two with Duval and then move to Aungier Street at the first opportunity.

### Actors: Mobility

If we eliminate those performers who worked in Dublin for a night or two and then disappeared from the record entirely, available biographical information indicates that only about twenty professional performers confined their careers solely to Dublin. Thus, the Dublin theatres were staffed by people most of whom spent significant periods of their working lives in Great Britain, either in the London professional theatres and theatrical booths or in provincial playhouses and strolling companies. Many Dublin singers, dancers, and specialty artists were Continentals (usually French or Italian) who came to Ireland via London.

The question of the importance of Dublin as a nursery for London performers is a complex one, but the evidence suggests that during this period the London theatres furnished Dublin with at least as many trained performers as ventured east across the Irish Sea. Many, probably the majority, of the principal and secondary actors who worked regularly in Dublin during this period were of British birth and made their stage debuts in London. They came to Dublin for a few seasons, and then returned to Great Britain. There were, of course, notable exceptions: such Irish-born performers as Peg Woffington, Spranger Barry, Thomas Sheridan, and Denis Delane received most or all of their initial training (and success) on the Dublin stage and went on to enjoy long-careers in London, although most of the above-mentioned actors returned to Dublin for extended periods after establishing themselves in London.

How many British-born actors journeyed to Ireland with the specific aim of broadening their repertoires and gaining practical stage experience (presumably because they were not yet considered skillful enough to work in London) is unclear. Dublin managers made regular visits to London in order to recruit important actors, but there is little evidence to suggest that novices were encouraged to come to Ireland in any capacity. It is evident, however, that many experienced London performers saw the Irish stage as a convenient employment alternative to London, usually during the summer when the major London theatres were closed (see section on summer seasons, p. 38). Other London-based actors sought Dublin employment as a temporary haven in times when their talents were out of favor or during disputes with London managers over contracts or status (e.g. Theophilus Cibber's visit to Dublin in 1743 and David Garrick in the winter of 1745).

On at least one occasion, during the 1742–43 season when Aungier Street theatre was under Swan's management, an unsuccessful "cartel" was drawn up and signed with the object of excluding all "English" actors from the Dublin theatres.[22] Since, as has been demonstrated, most of the Dublin actors were "English" by nationality, the aim here seems to have been the exclusion of short-term London actors from making their seasonal depredations in Ireland.

Few visiting London actors saw their stay in Dublin as an opportunity to appear in new characters; visiting actors of whatever caliber usually performed parts in stock plays in which they had been successful before arriving in Dublin. An important exception to this generalization is the case of Susannah Cibber who, during her visit to Dublin in 1742, assayed for the first time the role of Polly in *The Beggar's Opera,* a part which she had always coveted but which at Drury Lane was reserved exclusively for her colleague and rival Kitty Clive.

## Actors: Contracts and Conditions

Little evidence has survived relating to the contractual agreements under which Dublin actors worked. It seems likely, however, that such arrangements were very similar to those which pertained at the time in London.[23] No acting contracts for Dublin actors have survived, and it is probable that Irish actors, and their London counterparts, were not given written contracts but rather entered into the theatre treasurer's pay book the terms agreed between themselves and the managers and this served as the official record.

The terms upon which actors engaged themselves varied according to their standing in the company. Sharers, who were usually also subscribers, managers, or principal performers of long standing, normally received a fixed percentage of the nightly profits of the theatre. James Quin acted as a sharer during the 1743 season and refused to allow the curtain to be raised until he had received his money (Sheridan 1758, 17).

The "articles" of most performers included an undertaking to act in a specific number of performances each week at a fixed nightly or weekly rate. (In his "Humble Appeal" (Sheridan 1758, 53), Sheridan states that he paid his actors at the Treasurer's Office each Saturday). Such agreements also specified the number and form (shared or individual) of benefit to which the actor was entitled and also the approximate date (term) in which the benefit would be scheduled.

Although they date from slightly beyond our period, the documented contractual arrangements made between the Dublin theatre management and the up-and-coming London actor David Garrick are illuminating and illustrative. In the autumn of 1745 Garrick was asked to perform in Dublin and was offered a provisional contract (called a "Memorandum") which specified that he would receive the sum of six hundred guineas for acting from Christmas until the end of the season, a "clear benefit before any other actor or actress; and also *six hundred guineas,* and a clear benefit before any other actor or actress for the next season" (Garrick 1963, 1:68). In the event, Garrick declined these terms, settling instead on the following: he would share the management of the theatre with Sheridan, act twice a week until March, "the profits arising from it are to be divided into three shares, one of the Proprietors, another to Sheridan, and the third to myself. I am to have *two benefits* ; the first will be the fourth night of my playing, clear of all expences; the second any time in January, paying 15 1. for it" (69).

## Salaries

Specific references to the salaries of Dublin actors are uncommon; however, at most levels resident Smock Alley or Aungier Street actors would seem to have been paid about the same as their colleagues in London on a per diem basis. From newspaper items published in the early months of the 1743–44 season we learn that the managers of the united company offered Thomas Sheridan £150 certain for the season, regardless of how often he performed, and a benefit which the managers guaranteed would bring in another £100. Sheridan declined this offer, insisting instead on half profits. Mrs. Furnival was paid £3.00 per week, or about 30s. per acting night, and Mlle. Chateauneuf, the dancer, was offered a certain £100 for the season and a benefit. Good secondary actors, such as Isaac Sparks, earned 12s. a week (Sheridan 1758, 51), while imported first line performers such as Mrs. Cibber had £300 from proprietors of Aungier Street (52). As a child Peg Woffington may have been paid as much as thirty shillings a week during the 1731–32 season for her "lilliputian" performances with Sga. Violante's company (*Memoirs of . . . Mrs. Woffington*, 15).

It seems that the managers rather than the actors were more likely to risk infringing upon the terms of their agreements. Sheridan tells us that Dublin actors were sometimes not paid "a Shilling Subsistence" for several months at a time (Sheridan 1758, 51). In August 1742 the Smock Alley managers stopped paying the actors and musicians entirely for a period of four months and the musicians refused to play thereafter. At other times the performers received only one-half of their salaries, the treasurer keeping back the balance as security for the expence of their benefits (17).

## Costume

Costume was an important financial and artistic consideration for the Dublin theatre managers. Throughout the eighteenth century clothing of any kind was very expensive by modern standards, principally because both the cloth and the garment had to be hand-made. In Ireland, where much of the finer quality cloth was imported, clothing was particularly dear. We know that in the London theatres during this period costume costs involved a large part, sometimes as much as one-tenth, of the entire management budget[24], and it is likely that Dublin managers spent proportionately as much on costumes, although their budgets were much smaller.

The absence of inventories or accounts for the Dublin theatres prevents us from knowing the extent of their wardrobes, but each theatre certainly kept a stock assortment of costumes which was owned by the proprietors and from which actors and actresses took clothing as their roles required. The theatre management undoubtedly purchased the majority of the costumes which the wardrobe contained. The *Dublin Intelligencer* of 5 April 1729, for example, announced that the Smock Alley manager Thomas Elrington had taken leave of his London friends and was returning to Dublin with a "great Parcell of Velvet, Brocade and Embroidered suits, for the embellishment of our Stage. . . ."

Costumes were obviously thought to make an important contribution to the splendor of the spectacle of the theatrical production, and the managers seldom missed the opportunity to advertise the fact that the actors in important or novel plays, and particularly pantomimes, were "new dressed" or had been furnished with "new cloathes" and "habits." Adding and replacing season by season, the managers must have accumulated sizeable collections of costumes.

Each principal theatre employed a wardrobe-keeper whose duties included the maintenance and safeguarding of the costumes. But wardrobe-keepers can nod, as is illustrated by the *Dublin Intelligencer* of 8 July 1729 that announces the theft on 1 July of "an Irish Lustring gown, white ground with red, blew, and green flowers, lined with a cherry Lustring and petticoat of the same, without a lining; a cherry coloured whole sattin petticoat, trim'd with false tabby, and spangles, with other things."

A second important source of costumes was from donations, especially from the nobility. The *Dublin Evening Post* of 26–30 December 1732 observes that "The fine Cloaths lately given by the Right Honourable the Lord Viscount Mountcashell, were for the use of the whole company belonging to the Theatre Royal; so it is hoped, that our nobility and gentry will follow that noble and generous Example." In 1734 the Rt. Hon. William Conolly "in order to encourage our Diversions" gave 50 guineas to decorate the Aungier Street theatre for the premiere of *King Henry VIII*, "which hath met with so much Success in London for its fine Appearance," and over £300 was "already laid out for Dresses to the said Play" (*FDJ* 10–14 Dec. 1734).

It seems likely that costumes were assigned to each actor by the manager in order that petty squabbles about the use of costumes or accoutrements such as wigs and capes could be kept to a minimum. The hostilities between Thomas Sheridan and Theophilus Cibber at Smock Alley in 1743 originated from Sheridan's refusal to perform on 14 July because, as he thought, the long robe he was to have worn that night specifically to cover "Defects" and to add "Gravity and Dignity" to his person as Cato had been stolen by the manager, Thomas Philips, who had absconded to England. In fact, Philips had merely returned the robe to its owner from whom it had been borrowed (*Cibber and Sheridan*, 11–13). It seems likely that the Dublin managers frequently availed of the simple expedient of borrowing clothing to supplement their wardrobe.

The importance of the historical verisimilitude of costumes in the Dublin theatre was stressed from an early date. In 1662 Mrs. Katherine Philips (1705, 96) complained of the unhistorical costuming at a Smock Alley performance of *Othello* with the consequence that the following year, when her own tragedy *Pompey* was acted there, her friend the Earl of Orrery "advanc'd a hundred Pounds towards the Expense of buying Roman and Egyptian Habits" so that the spectacle might be more impressive and plausible (119).

In 1725 the costumes, manners and physical appearance of some of the actors in a Smock Alley revival of Nathaniel Lee's *The Rival Queens* were so inappropriate that one theatregoer was inspired to submit an amusing list of regulations for the improvement of the Dublin stage:

(1) That No Hero, especially Alexander, should have a big Belly.
(2) That the Play House Taylor should apply for Information of the Fashions of the Several Ages to the Antiquarians.
(3) That the Stage Barber whom the Present Age calls Wigmaker, shall supply those who have no Hair of their own with something instead of it, which shall look like Hair.
(4) And lastly, that if the Mock Queens and Heroines are unwilling to part with their Circle Petticoats, at least they shall take due care, out of regard to the memory of those whom they represent, to fall with their Heads towards the Pit. (*DWJ*, 27 Nov. 1725)

The Dublin managers thereafter seem to have paid reasonably close attention to the historical accuracy of the costuming. Announcements such as the one advertising the premiere performance in April 1737 of William Havard's *King Charles I* in which the "Characters will be entirely new dressed, suitable to them times" or like the one for the performance of *The Indian Emperor* at Aungier Street on 12 December 1738 which proclaims "The characters to be entirely new dressed in rich Feather Dresses after the Manner of the Indians and the Spaniards dressed in new Spanish dresses" are not uncommon.

## Scenery and Machinery

Lists of scenery in the late seventeenth-century Smock Alley promptbooks give detailed descriptions of the scenic repertoire of that theatre. W. J. Clark (1955, 73 ff), in his analysis of this scenery, concludes that the "Dublin company exercised the same economy in staging which its London contemporaries pursued. Stock sets appeared over and over again . . . [but] while stock sets formed the backbone of its scenic representation, the array of these on hand by the late 1670's afforded a considerable diversity of stage pictures."

In the first half of the eighteenth century the stocks of sets at the Dublin theatres must have expanded even further in order to keep pace with the ever-growing emphasis on spectacle dictated by the audience demand for new pantomime and musical entertainments. The calendar is replete with notices such as that for the revival of *The Necromancer* at Smock Alley on 6 December 1729 which proclaims that the production will include "New scenes, shapes and machines" and for the 2 May 1737 premiere of *The Hussar; or, Harlequin Restored* for which "no Expense has been spared in the Scenes, Machines, Dresses, Sinkings, Flyings, and other Decorations. . . ." During the periods in which two or more theatres engaged in competition, new scenery was often touted as a reason for attending one theatre's production rather than that of another.

Unfortunately, Dublin lacks the many lengthy descriptive accounts of stage scenery that exist for the London theatres of this time; consequently, we can only speculate about its quality.[25]

Smock Alley would seem to have employed a scene-painter and designer on a regular basis by the autumn of 1722 when the management advertised that for the forthcoming production of *The Rival Queens* the stage would be enlarged "and Ornamented after the Manner of the Theatres in London, with large lofty Scenes entirely new and Painted by Mr. Vanderhegan, lately arrived from London." The fact that the Smock Alley managers for the first time made a point of naming the scene painter in advertisements further suggests the importance that scenery was assuming.

Some previously unnoticed details of the career of William Vander Hagen (died about 1745) are given in an article (printed as a letter from "G. N. S." of Limerick and dated April 1814) entitled "Anecdotes of Vander Hagen," in *The Monthly Museum; or, Dublin Literary Repertory for May 1814,* 473: "Vander Hagen was a landscape and marine painter; but I have seen his own portrait painted by himself, in a fine tone of colouring, with the handling and shadows executed after the purest practice of the French school." The writer goes on to say that, having failed to find any account of Vander Hagen in contemporary printed sources, he had "recourse to the most likely oral resources, but found that the lapse of seventy or eighty years has left but a scanty portion of tradition concerning him. It is said that he was a native of the Low Countries, and when on a voyage was driven into one of the southeast ports of Ireland through stress of weather." "G. N. S." thinks that Vander Hagen had undertaken a voyage for the sake of studying effects at sea, and having visited Ireland and obtaining some encouragement in his profession, had taken up a temporary residence among his new friends. "To support this opinion I have to observe that many old houses have pannels painted by him; generally with marine subjects, and that these houses, though now fallen in estimation, were once the mansions of the opulent. Pieces of later date than these are in a better style, and such as are dated from 1730 to 1736 have all the excellencies I have mentioned above."

Today Vander Hagen is remembered primarily as a landscape and decorative painter; some of the portraits and decorations in fine houses referred to by "G. N. S." survive, as do several of the commissioned studies relating to the Williamite wars intended to be depicted on tapestries to be hung in the Irish House of Lords in Dublin (Crookshank 1978, 55–60).

Vander Hagen certainly painted in the English provinces, but we have no record of his activities on the London stage. It seems likely that he worked there for a time, perhaps with the great John Devoto and Francis Haymen at Drury Lane. These men painted "slanted scenes" or *scena per anglo,* the technique introduced from Italy at the end of the 17th century which stressed "angular asymmetrical perspective. . . . resulting in the impression of diagonal placement of scenic architecture, and opening the stage to previously undreamed of loftiness and vastness" (*LS* 3:1:cxxi). When Vander Hagen painted his "large lofty Scenes entirely new" for Smock Alley he very likely employed this technique in Dublin for the first time.

Vander Hagen's association with the Dublin stage probably continued for more than a decade: *FDJ,* 24–27 March 1733 announces the premiere of *Cephalus and Procris* at Smock Alley: "the Scenes are finer Painted than any ever seen in his Kingdom, done by the famous Mr. Vanderhagen."

By the 1739–40 season the duties of scene painter had been assumed by Joseph Tutor (?1695–1759), who painted the scenery for Theophilus Cibber's *The Harlot's Progress; or, The Ridotto Al'Fresco,* which had a very successful run at Smock Alley. Tutor, newspaper advertisements tell us, painted the scenes "from the celebrated drawings of Hogarth." Although little is known about Tutor's career, he may have been a pupil of Vander Hagen (Crookshank 1978, 61), and it is possible that he, too, was in some way associated with John Devoto who had painted the scenery for *The Harlot's Progress* when it premiered in London in 1733 (Rosenfeld and Croft-Murray 1965–66, 52).

Tutor would certainly seem to have been influenced by the school of more naturalistic scene painters such as Devoto and Hayman which was coming to the fore at this time. He probably designed both "the Prospect of Vauxhall Gardens as they were fitted up for the Entertainment of the Nobility and Gentry of England," which was included in the Ridotto al Fresco portion of Cibber's *Harlot's Progress* at Smock Alley on 26 February 1739 and the "Grand Additional Scene, which exactly represents the Manner of Drawing the State Lotteries at Guild-Hall in London" which was employed in the December 1739 Aungier Street production of Fielding's *The Lottery.*

If it was Joseph Tutor who painted the Vauxhall Gardens set, we might suspect the influence of the Drury Lane designer and painter Francis Hayman who, on 22 May 1736, brought out "A new Entertainment after the Manner of Spring Garden, Vauxhall, with a new Scene representing the Place."[26]

During the 1740s Tudor won the Dublin Society premium for landscape painting no fewer than four times (Rosenfeld and Croft-Murray 1965–66, 52) and worked intermittantly at both of the principal theatres. He is credited in the bills as having painted the scenery for the 11 December 1740 Aungier Street premiere of *The Judgment of Paris; or The Nuptials of Harlequin,* with new music, dances, sinkings, flyings, machines, and entirely new decorations including a "magnificent Temple of Hymen" and for the 27 January 1741 Smock Alley staging of *Harlequin Metamorphosed,* the scenery "done to imitate the Original, as performed with great Applause in London."

Clearly, Tudor kept abreast of the scenic novelty in London and sought to imitate it in Dublin whenever possible.

## Technical design: Scenery and Machinery

The conventions of the repertory would have made it necessary for the Dublin theatres to employ the standard wings, borders, and shutters of the London playhouses. The bottom edges of two or three sets of wings and shutters were probably placed in grooves pegged to the stage, and the top edges held in a similar fashion. A scene could be either "flat," that is, parallel to the front edge of the stage, or aligned obliquely in the Continental fashion. In the early years of our period when a scene change was required the wings and shutters would have been pushed on and off simultaneously, along the grooves, by sceneshifters at a signal from the prompter.

Although the London theatres may have used machines to move scenery as early as 1673 (Hume 1980, 77), the Dublin theatres seem to have persisted in changing scenes manually for another seventy years. As much is suggested by the *Dublin News-Letter* of 21 July 1739 which reports that a "clever Device" has been introduced at Smock Alley by the famous Harlequin Henry Woodward from Drury Lane who was appearing in Ireland for the first time. Woodward's machine altered the stage "so that the side Scenes [wings] from the Upper Part to the Lower, may move together, which will be of infinite use to the Plays, particularly to the Historical Ones of Shakespeare." The precise system of scene changing described here cannot be determined, but in all likelihood it involved some arrangement of ropes and pulleys located under the stage that allowed one or two staff to control the movement of the wings automatically.

Woodward may have taken his "Device" back to London with him when he left Dublin or perhaps his was a relatively primitive mechanism, because at the beginning of the 1741–42 season the newspapers announced that Lewis Duval had "engaged a Machinist from the Theatre-Royal in Drury-lane, and is fitting up his House in Smock-alley, in an entire new manner, after the Model of those in London. . . ." (*FDJ*, 29 Sept.–3 Oct. 1741). Hitchcock, writing much later in the century (1:116), tells us that at W. R. Chetwood's direction "a machinist from one of the London theatres was engaged, who first worked the wings by means of a barrel underneath, which moved them together at the same time with the scenes. This was publicly boasted of as a master-piece of mechanism; at present is well understood and constantly practised."

The machinist referred to was Thomas Ludlow, about whom the London record is silent.[27] It seems likely that the machine he installed at Smock Alley and that is described by Hitchcock was similar to the system in place at Covent Garden by 1744 in which the wings were set into carriages and the shutters in grooves in such a way that an entire set could be changed simultaneously and automatically (Hume 1980, 78).

In addition to machinery for shifting scenery, the Dublin theatres also had the facilities for trapwork and descents. Although descriptions of machinery are few, from as early as 1729 the Smock Alley management was including mentions of new machines in its advertising, and both theatres frequently boasted of the expence they had gone to in providing "new scenes, machines, sinkings, and flyings."

The mention of sinkings implies that the stages in Dublin were equipped with traps, although their number and location are unknown. By means of traps actors, machines, and other equipment could be raised onto the stage from below or lowered down out of sight of the audience. "Flyings" could vary considerably in complexity and lavishness and could involve an actor or property being either lifted from the stage into the flies above or vice versa. As Colin Visser has observed, flyings and sinkings are both "associated with supernatural manifestations of various kinds" and are usually employed in masques, pantomimes, operas, and afterpieces (Hume 1980, 101–2). In Dublin, for example, machines, sinkings and flyings are advertised in such plays as *The Necromancer, The Hussar, Macbeth, The Judgment of Paris, The Rehearsal, The Rival Sorcerors, The Tempest,* and *Comus.*

The "grand Machine representing the zodiack and moon world," which was advertised for the 1 February 1739 performance of *The Emperor of the Moon* at Smock Alley, was probably a fairly elaborate set piece that was lowered from the flies. Some form of carriage suspended from the flies was no doubt used at Smock Alley on 13 February 1742 to enable Harlequin to descend from the sun in *Thomas Koulikan, the Persian Hero.*

That flying had its dangers is attested to by the 26 November 1741 Smock Alley production of *The Lancashire Witches* for which had been prepared "two new Flyings for the witches to fly with; and also the Wings and Scenes on the stage made to move in a moment, by an engine obtained at a great Expense" [presumably Ludlow's machine]. The actor Charles Morgan, who was to fly on the back of a witch, "Thro' the ignorance of the workers in the machinery, the fly broke, and they fell together, but thro' Providence neither of them were hurt" (Chetwood 1749, 139). In the advertisements for the second performance the wary audience was assured that "Particular care is taken, that the Flyings and machinery may be performed without the least Danger."

The revival of the original version of *The Tempest* at Smock Alley on 15 February 1742 "with the original Music, Flyings, Sinkings, Risings, Thunder, Lightening, Rain, Showers of Fire, all executed in the same Manner as at the Theatre-Royal Drury Lane" implies that Smock Alley also possessed machines to produce the illusions of wind, thunder, and lightning.

# Lighting

The principal source of lighting in the Dublin theatres at this time was almost certainly tallow candles. Large rings or hoops of these would have hung above the stage; and may have been raised or lowered, depending on the demands of the scene. Other candles were fitted into wall-brackets spaced throughout the auditorium. The scenic area was probably lit by other hoops of candles which were suspended from the flies and more candles or oil-lamps could have been attached to the back of each wing. On special occasions, such as command performances or important charity benefits, the house was "illuminated with Wax" that is, brighter, cleaner beeswax candles were substituted for the usual tallow.

The main acting area on the fore-stage was certainly illuminated by foot-lights. Initially, the light was provided by candles, but these were later replaced by oil lamps. That oil lamps were unsatisfactory is illustrated by the fact that in November 1742 the manager at Smock Alley advertised that he had "got a new Set of Lamps to burn Tallow at the Front of the Stage, the Oyle being offensive. . . ." (*FDJ*, 23 Nov. 1742). It may have been possible to lower the footlights under the stage and to raise them again when certain lighting effects were required.

# Dancing

Songs and dances were included in Smock Alley programs from the first season of its opening. Mrs. Philips's translation of Corneille's *Pompey,* first performed on 19 February 1663, included five original songs and three dances (Clark 1955, 63). By 1720 singing and dancing, both as a part of the play and as entr'acte entertainment, had become an established part of the programs at Smock Alley. Entr'acte entertainments of singing and dancing were probably a regular part of the Smock Alley program no later than 1709 (127–28).

The first documentary evidence of dancing during our period appears in the advertisements for the 16 October 1721 command performance of Aphra Behn's comedy *The Rover,* wherein "several new entertainments of dance never performed before" were announced. Although mentions of dancing and citations of specific dances are unusual before 1730, the presence in the company of the dancers Mr. and Mrs. Anthony Moreau from about 1719 onwards strongly suggests that dancing was a part of practically every evening's program.

The great popularity in Dublin of *The Beggar's Opera* during the 1727–28 and 1728–29 seasons apparently forced the Moreaus to seek their bread elsewhere, at least temporarily. They spent the 1728–29 season at Lincoln's Inn Fields, returning to Dublin in June 1729. Their stay in Ireland must have been brief, for *DI* of 2 December 1729 announces that Moreau, "The famous French Dancing Master; who has been for some time past on his travels thru' England and France, is again come over to make his residence here. . . ."

The 1729–30 season saw unusual activity in the field of dance at Smock Alley. In addition to the Moreaus, who presumably presented entr'acte entertainments, Sga. Violante's company arrived at the beginning of the season and presented rope dancing, pantomimes, and a variety of unspecified "Entertainments." Her troupe included Charles Lalauze, William Phillips, and Miss Violante, all dancers. The entertainments boasted an ensemble piece entitled "The French Peasants" and "comic" dances by Lalauze. Later in the season a dancer named Pitt "and one of his scholars" danced "The Black Joke" a piece that was "performed in the dress of a man and a woman from the Fingal district of County Dublin" (see performance of 9 April 1730). On 14 May 1730 a benefit performance was given to a new dancer, John Duval ("lately from London"). Besides Duval the dancers included the Moreaus, Leigh, and "others" (possibly James Cummins).

When Sga. Violante opened her new booth in Dame Street in January 1731 it was obviously with the idea of specializing in equilibres, pantomimes, and dance. During the winter and spring her company, which now consisted of Cummins, John Duval, Lalauze, Pitt, Miss Violante, with the addition of a Master Lefavre, and the Moreaus, whom she lured away from Smock Alley for a time, performed regularly. Although only one dance title has survived from this season—Cummins's "'The White Joke Dance' by the Old Woman with Pierrot in a Basket"—evidently every performance included some dancing. Sga. Violante repeated the same sorts of programs of "entertainments" in the early months of the following season at her booth, but she devoted herself entirely to the "lilliputian" players once their success had been established. Thereafter, dancing was again advertised at Smock Alley, although, with the exception of a Mr. William Delamain, neither the titles of the dances nor the names of the dancers are given.

The only dancers known to have performed at Smock Alley during the 1732–33 and 1733–34 seasons were the Moreaus; at the recently opened Rainsford Street theatre in 1733 the manager, Louis Duval, advertised new dances composed by himself. We have already observed (see section on Rainsford Street/new Smock Alley management above) that Duval was probably too old by this time to have actually performed the dances. The Rainsford Street company programs regularly included dances during the two seasons of its existence. Similarly, at the booth in George's Lane, Walsh and Cummins ("dancing masters") performed "a variety of dancing" for their own benefit in the 1732–33 and 1733–34 seasons. Leigh, also advertised at this time as a "dancing master," shared a benefit there with Walsh in June 1734.

The company that moved from Smock Alley to Aungier Street included, in addition to the Moreaus, a group of dancers who had formerly worked elsewhere: William Delamain, probably Pitt (referred to in an advertisement as "the Highland Piper who dances at the Booth" with a child of four years old), Master Pitt ("Mr. Pitt's son, a child of four year old, who performed once before at the Theatre in Rainsford St.") and Peg Woffington. Before season's end this group presented new "pastoral dances" and many other unspecified pieces. Moreau performed "The Dancing Devil," and the child prodigy, Master Pitt, danced "The Dusty Miller."

The 1735-36 season saw the amalgamation of many of the dancers from George's Lane with those from Aungier Street: Cummins, William Delamain, Moreau, Walsh, and Miss Woffington, with the additions of Samuel Hinde, Naylor, and Miss Vanderbank. In addition to the usual unspecified dances, their repertory this season included "A Grand Fury Dance," "A Sailor's Dance," "A Pastoral Dance," and "The Dusty Miller."

Dancers who were members of the Rainsford Street company, which moved to the new Smock Alley theatre this season, were the Pitts, senior and junior, Cummins (who abandoned Aungier Street), and a number of new names: Miss Barnes, Charles Bourne (or Byrne), Robert Delamain, and John Morris. The earliest surviving detailed listing of Dublin entr'acte dancing is given in the advertisement for the evening of 3 April 1736: "End Act I a Pierrot by Morris; Act II Scotch Hornpipe by Pitts [sic]; Act III Wooden Shoe by Morris; Act IV Dance to the Key of the Cel[1?] by Master Pitts; Act V dance by Robert Delamain; End of Afterpiece a new Country Dance." Late in the season Pitt and Byrne added "Two Pierrots," "Two Punches," and "Jack Lattin" to the repertory; Miss Barnes and Pitt danced "Pierrot in the Basket."

The calendar of dances for the 1736-37 season at Aungier Street mentions only Miss Woffington, William Delamain, and Moreau (Mrs. Moreau was dancing in London this and the following season). The named dances credited to them are "Two Harlequins and a Columbine," a dance to the tune of "Lillibalero," a dance "in the character of a Freemason and his wife." Also performed was "the last new Dance composed by M. Moreau." Later that season the three danced new entr'acte entertainments entitled: "A Comic Dance," "A Serious Dance," "A New Dance to 'The Berwick Jockey'," "A Scotch Jig to the [Tune of the] Drought," and "A Minuet and Louver."

The Smock Allen company remained stable for the 1736-37 season except that Samuel Hinde came over to them from Aungier Street during the season. Advertisements for dancing are frequent but seldom specific. The dancers did introduce "The Dutch Skipper and His Frow" to the repertory. In May, John Barrington from Smock Alley, who is not previously mentioned as a dancer, and a new performer, John Dumont ("lately of Paris"), joined the company and attempted "The Squeeking Punch and Monkey" and "The Dancing Punch."

At the beginning of the 1737-38 season the dancers at Aungier Street changed again. Moreau and William Delamain remained. Miss Woffington left Dublin for London early in the season, and the Pitts joined the company. Although dancing was presented regularly, no named dances were advertised.

At Smock Alley the personnel identified as having danced are Cummins, Dumont, Mrs. John Dumont, Mrs. Martin, J. Morris, and Miss Bullock. However, other dancers listed in the Smock Alley company who also may have performed in this respect without being mentioned in the bills are Barrington, Byrne, and Samuel Hinde. Smock Alley introduced the following new dances in the course of the season: "'A Grand Rural Dance' (Performed at the Theatre Royal London)," and "a new pantomime dance called 'Pigmalion and the Ivory Statue'."

The 1738–39 season at Aungier Street saw Moreau and his wife and the Pitts remaining, with the addition of Miss Moreau (her debut), Master Cormick (or Cormack), and Robert Layfield (Lewis's son). The Smock Alley dancers recorded are Cummins, W. Delamain, Dumont, and J. Morris. No new dances were advertised at Aungier Street; those advertised for Smock Alley include "A Grand Masquerade Dance," [A Dance to the Tune of] "Camargo," "The Huntsman and Hounds," "The Highlander and His Mistress," and "Four Pierrots."

Only Master Pitt and Walsh are mentioned as having danced at Aungier Street during the 1739–40 season. Anthony Moreau, who had been with the company since the beginning of the period, left to join the Smock Alley company at the beginning of the season. Only a handful of programs including dancing appear, and no new dances are recorded.

The Smock Alley dancers for the 1739–40 season are the same as those of two years earlier, except that Moreau deserted Aungier Street, and a Miss Elizabeth Thomson joined the troupe. Moreau quickly introduced a number of "Entirely new Dances." Dumont composed a new "Grand Rural Dance." Also new is "The Grecian Sailor's Dance," "A Shepherdess," "A new Dance between a Boatswain and his Mistress," and "A Dance between a Pierrot and a Pierrottess."

The Aungier Street management apparently sought to revitalize its dance program at the beginning of the 1740–41 season, which sparked off several seasons of rather spirited competition in dance at least. In addition to Cormack, the Dumonts (from Smock Alley), the Pitts, and Miss Thomson, the managers imported by December two dancers from London: Fromont (from Drury Lane) and Baudouin, in addition to Cantarino (a rope dancer who came from Paris in early May). The only record we have of Fromont is his introduction of "a pantomime dance called 'Pigmalion'." No other new dances are recorded for Aungier Street during the regular season.

For the summer season at Aungier Street the very popular Mlle. Chateauneuf, who was to spend several seasons there, arrived from Drury Lane and danced two new pieces: "La Provincalle" and "La Tambourin." Later in the summer she was accompanied by Lalauze (now at Drury Lane), who also performed dances "proper to the Mask" of *Comus*. Lalauze and Oates (from Covent Garden) danced "Two Pierrots," and Lalouze, Mlle. Chateauneuf, and Master Louis Layfield danced "The Drunkard's Dance."

At Smock Alley Cummins (who died in April), W. Delamain, J. Morris, and the three Moreaus formed the backbone of a troupe that was supplemented by the addition of William "Harlequin" Phillips and his wife, and a dancer named Giles. Phillips, in addition to his vaulting on the slack rope "as performed at Theatre Royal Drury Lane," danced his "The English Maggot" in which he introduced a "Horn Pipe and the pantomime miller's dance, 'Double Jealousy'". Phillips also contributed "The Drunken Peasant," a "new Dance in which Mr. Phillips introduces a Quaker's Sermon on the Violin," and a new dance in the character of a Clown (perhaps a dance staged later in the season called "Country Revels"). Other dances new to Dublin but not attributed to Phillips include "a grand dance called 'A Country Wedding', and "The Running Footman."

The competition between Smock Alley and Aungier Street theatres, consisting, in the main, in the presentation of novelty acts, pantomimes (which usually included dancing), and additional entr'acte dancing, continued through the 1741–42 season. Mlle. Chateauneuf was convinced to remain in Dublin for the season with the support of the Moreaus, Oates, Jr. (who also performed at Smock Alley) and the younger Pitt. Mlle. Chateauneuf performed almost every night, although references to the specific dances she presented are few. These include "A Serious Dance," "La Paisant Dequise [The Peasant Disguised]," "A Grand Peasant Dance," and "A Comic Dance."

At Smock Alley a less glittering troupe consisting of Miss Bullock, Cormack, W. Delamain, P. Morris, Oates, Senior and Junior, and Master Pitt performed regularly. Although entertainments of dancing were advertised frequently, the only named dances performed at Smock Alley were "A Hornpipe Solo," "A Scotch Dance," and "A Peasant Dance."

In the summer of 1742 Aungier Street managers imported two dancers from London: Sga. Barbarini (from Covent Garden) and Henry Delamain (from Drury Lane). The three Moreaus supported them. Advertising themselves as "from the Opera in Paris," Sga. Barbarini and Delamain danced "The Italian Peasants," "The Rural Assembly," "A Louvre and Minuet," "A new Scots Dance," "A new Mussett," and "A Grand Ballet."

The competition between the theatre dancers would appear to have abated somewhat by the beginning of the 1742–43 season. The only dancer whose name appears in the Aungier Street bills is Moreau, and he is credited with no new pieces, although Mlle. Chateauneuf returned to Dublin in mid-June 1743 and brought with her two French male dancers: Muilment (from Covent Garden) and Picq (from Covent Garden). With Moreau's assistance they performed a number of "new" comic "Peasant" dances (notably, "The Jealous Peasant" and "Badinage Provencal"), "Pastoral" dances, a "Tambourine," and a "Grand Ballet," entitled "La Rendezvous Gallant." Mlle. Chateauneuf also danced "The Italian Sailor."

At Smock Alley the dancers' names that appear in the bills this season are those of W. Delamain, Master Pitt, P. Morris (performing "A Basket Dance," the only new piece performed by the regular company this season), and Cormick. Miss Bullock and Mr. and Mrs. J. Morris remained with the company and may have danced. During October, November, and December the sole performers at Smock Alley were a company of tumblers and equilibrists of mixed nationality which included Dominique, Madame Dominique, Madame German, Guitar, Jonno, and the "Russian Boy." Later in the season Jonno also danced entr'acte entertainments in addition to Harlequinades, and Guitar performed "A Peasant Dance." Dominique and Madame German danced "Harlequin and Harlequinetta" as a part of the pantomime *Harlequin Triumphant in His Amours* and doubtless performed a number of similar (but not advertised) pieces during their stay in Dublin.

The 1743–44 season saw the union of the Aungier Street and Smock Alley companies, although after a few weeks a group of disaffected actors and dancers reopened the Smock Alley theatre in competition with Aungier Street. Their effort petered out in early February 1744. The dancers whose services were retained by the United Company were Mlle. Chateauneuf, W. Delamain, and Moreau. John Dumont (advertised as "lately arrived from Paris" at the beginning of the season) rejoined the company. The playbill advertising the performance of 28 February 1744 includes a dancer named "Morris" (presumably P. Morris from Smock Alley). There is little novelty in the offerings; new dances this season include "An Italian Dance after the Manner of Faussana" and "La Marie."

The dancers in the short-lived rebel company at Smock Alley included P. Morris, W. Phillips, and an import, Mlle. Roland (from Lincoln's Inn Fields). In December Phillips performed a "'Scaramouche Dance' never performed by him but at the Opera in Paris" as well as his standard "The Drunken Peasant." Later in the season his offerings included "A Clown" dance. Mlle. Roland danced frequently during her stay but no dances are named.

In the final season of our period, advertisements for dancing at the United Company are relatively few. The bulk of the dancing was done by Moreau, occasionally assisted by Master Pitt. The only dancer on the roster of the new Capel Street company is Cormick although the William Phillips's doubtless danced as a part of their pantomime entertainments. None of the dances at either theatre is assigned a title.

## Music in Dublin

Music was very important to the eighteenth-century Dublin theatre. We will observe (in the section on the repertory below) that musical entertainments of various types, particularly ballad operas and operettas, began to dominate the afterpiece repertory following the premiere of Gay's *The Beggar's Opera* in 1728. If we consider, too, that each evening's program began and ended with orchestral music; that most full-length plays (even tragedies) contained or were adapted to contain songs and dances; and that each interval between acts or between plays was filled with entr'acte singing or dancing; we can easily conclude that little that occurred on the stage was not in some way affected by music.

Gathering to listen to concerts of vocal and instrumental music was an important part of Dublin social life.[28] Prior to the opening of Mr. Johnston's Great Room in Crow Street in 1731, the first custom-built venue large enough to accommodate large concert audiences, public musical presentations took place in the great hall at Dublin Castle, at the Tholsel (or City Hall), at St. Patrick's and Christ Church Cathedrals, at the larger Dublin churches, such as St. Andrews's Round Church, and at Smock Alley theatre. The cathedrals and churches continued the long tradition of church music, employing semi-professional choirs, and members of these choirs supplemented the choral sections needed to perform oratorios.

Dublin Castle employed professional composers, such as William Viner, Johann Cousser, and Matthew Dubourg, each of whom served as Master of State Music and whose duties were to compose the annual occasional odes for the King's birthday and to compose and conduct for the state musicians who performed at Castle balls and other public assemblies. Some of the state musicians, of whom there were customarily eleven, supplemented their incomes by playing in the orchestras of the Dublin theatres (see below).

Musical performances were also promoted by a dozen musical societies, usually philanthropic associations of non-musicians. The best known of these was the Charitable Musical Society for the Relief of Imprisoned Debtors, which for years met at the Bull's Head Tavern in Fishamble Street and which in 1741 built the "New Musick Hall," also in Fishamble Street, where Handel's *Messiah* was first performed.

Other of the more important musical societies active during our period were the Musical Academy for the practice of Italian music which built Crow Street Music Hall in 1731; the Charitable Musical Society of Vicar's Street, who supported benefits for Dr. Steevens' Hospital; the Charitable Musical Society for the relief of distressed families; and the Charitable Musical Society for the support of the hospital for the incurables on Lazer's Hill, which gave concerts at Crow Street Music Hall and at the Philharmonic Room in Fishamble Street. Small concerts were performed in taverns, such as the Bull's Head, in various "Great Rooms" such as that managed by Mr. Geminiani in Spring Gardens off Dame Street, or at the Taylors' and Stationers' Halls. In the fair weather of spring and summer open-air concerts were held at the City Basin (or reservoir) in James Street and at the Marlborough Bowling Green.

## Music in the Theatres

### Orchestra

The backbone of theatre music was, of course, the orchestra. Although precise information is lacking for Dublin, it is probable that the theatres followed the London practice of beginning each evening's program with three instrumental pieces, known as the First, Second, and Third Music, by way of overture. Later, introductory music was played before the afterpiece began (*LS* 2:1:cxxxvi). The orchestra then accompanied songs and dances contained in the plays as well as for the entr'acte entertainments.

The size of the theatre orchestras is not known precisely, but it seems unlikely that the number of instrumentalists exceeded a dozen, except on extraordinary occasions. The smaller theatres would have been unable to accommodate (or afford) orchestras of even that size. We know that Smock Alley theatre employed at least eight musicians in 1742, as correspondence associated with the the Smock Alley musicians "strike" of 12 August suggests (see performance of that date).

Theatre musicians apparently reached non-exclusive agreements to perform at one or more theatres, and also played at other non-theatrical Dublin venues. In February 1744 Thomas Arne complained, for example, about the difficulty in appointing a night to perform one of his musical works because the Dublin musicians were so busy:

> Mondays and Thursdays are taken up [at the theatres] with Benefits for 6 weeks.
> Tuesdays, Vicar's-st Concerts and the Bear on College Green, which take up all the best Hands.
> Wednesdays, the Philharmonick Society and Crow-st, where they [the best hands] are likewise engaged.
> Friday, Fishamble-st Concert, where they are obliged to perform. (*FDJ*, 11–14 Feb. 1744. Quoted in Boydell 1988, 97)

### Musicians

Below are listed the musicians who are known to have performed in Dublin theatre orchestras during this period. The list does not include virtuosi who performed exclusively as soloists even if they spent more than one season in Dublin. There follow lists of State Musicians known to have been present in Dublin during this period.

### Theatre Orchestra Musicians

[Asterisk* indicates those musicians who refused to return to work at Smock Alley because of non-payment of wages in August 1742 (see performance of 12 Aug. 1742)].

Alcock: performed in concert Aungier St. 26 Apr. 1743; shared benefit play Smock Alley 5 Mar. 1745. Bassoonist.

*Blackwood, John: benefit play at Aungier St. 4 May 1737.

Connor, William: shared benefit play Aungier St. 27 Apr. 1738 and Smock Alley 15 Mar. 1739

Delahoyde, (Oliver or Thomas): shared benefit play Aungier St. 3 June 1741.

*Dowdall, Francis: perhaps same as or related to Sprackling Dowdall, state musician 1717, 1725 and 1740.

*Fitzgerald, George: 10th state musician 1740; shared benefit play Capel St. 7 May 1745.

Gunan, Dominick: shared benefit play Smock Alley 28 Apr. 1740; benefit play Smock Alley 29 Apr. 1742

Heron, William: shared benefit play Aungier St. 13 Dec. 1739. State Trumpeter 1717 (Boydell 1988, 281).

Johnson (or Johnston), John: benefit play at Smock Alley 3 Apr. 1736. According to W. J. Lawrence's transcriptions of Treasury Ledgers destroyed in 1922 (see below), John Johnson was 4th state musician in 1725 at a salary of £30 and 1st musician in 1740 at £40. Perhaps the same man who was listed as state musician in 1717 (Boydell 1988, 282) and/or the man who built and managed the Crow St. Music Hall.

*Johnson, Thomas: 2nd state musician 1740.

Kountze (or Kounty): performed Smock Alley 19 May 1742. Kettle-drum. May have only visited Dublin.

Layfield, Lewis: known principally as an actor and singer, Layfield was "Major Hautboy" in the City Music in 1723 and a member from 1720–33. It is probable that he had some hand in the Smock Alley orchestra if he was not the leader.

Lee: benefit play as Aungier St. 6 June 1737; Smock Alley 21 Apr. 1738.

MacCarty (M'Carty or McCarthy), Callaghan: benefit play at Aungier St. 18 May 1736; shared benefit play Aungier St. 6 Feb. 1739; shared benefit play Aungier St. 12 Mar. 1741. MacCarty not included in the 1725 list but was 9th state musician in 1740 at a salary of £20.

*Mainwaring (or Manwaring), Bartholomew (or Bartel. or Barty): brother of William. Shared benefit play 21 Apr. 1740; shared benefit play Smock Alley 30 Apr. 1741; shared benefit Smock Alley 19 May 1742 with William. Violinist.

*Mainwaring (or Manwaring), William: shared benefit play 15 Mar. 1739; shared benefit play with brother Smock Alley 19 May 1742. Violinist.

Walsh: shared benefit play Aungier St. 3 June 1741; shared benefit play Capel St. 7 May 1745.

Whitnall: shared benefit play Smock Alley 21 Apr. 1740.

Wilks: shared benefit play Smock Alley 21 Apr. 1740.

Winch: benefit play Smock Alley 27 Feb. 1742. French horn soloist.

*Woder, Francis: benefit concert at Aungier St. 3 Mar. 1736; shared benefit play Smock Alley 15 Feb. 1739; shared benefit play Aungier St. 13 Dec. 1739; shared benefit play Smock Alley 15 Mar. 1742. Woder was listed as a State Musician in 1717 (Boydell 1988, 293), was 8th state musician in 1725 at the salary of £25, and 4th state musician in 1740 at £30.

Woder, Master (John?): shared benefit play Smock Alley 30 Apr. 1741. Presumably the son of Francis Woder.

## State Musicians

W. J. Lawrence transcribed the following lists of state musicians (and their stipends) from a Dublin Public Record Office Treasury Ledger destroyed in 1922 (Notebook 4: 33, Notebook 8: 28).

### State Musicians 1725

| | | |
|---|---|---|
| 1st  musician | John Coussar | £80 per annum |
| 2nd musician | Matt. Dubourg | 50 |
| 3rd  musician | Chas. Kemenis | 30 |
| 4th  musician | John Johnson | 30 |
| 5th  musician | Thos. Johnson | 30 |
| 6th  musician | Simon Button | 20 |
| 7th  musician | Chas. Ashbury | 20† |
| 8th  musician | Fras. Woder | 25 |
| 9th  musician | Sprackling Dowdall | 20 |
| 10th  musician | Lewis Layfield | 20 |
| 11th  musician | John Steppenson | 10 |

†A note appended to this page indicates that this Charles Ashbury, who succeeded to a vacancy of one of the state musicianships on 5 April 1720, was not the son of the Dublin manager Joseph Ashbury because Charles died in 1719.

### State Musicians 1740–41

| | | |
|---|---|---|
| Master and Composer | Mat. Dubourg | £100 |
| 1st musician | Jn. Johnson | 40 |
| 2nd musician | Thos. Johnson | 30 |
| 3rd musician | Wm. Davis | 30 |
| 4th musician | Fr. Woder | 30 |
| 5th musician | S. Dowdall | 30 |
| 6th musician | Geo. Angell | 30 |
| 7th musician | Geo. Wade | 20 |
| 8th musician | Ben. Johnson | 20 |
| 9th musician | Call. McCarthy | 20 |
| 10th musician | Geo. Fitzgerald | 10 |

*Concerts*

While the bulk of the concerts of vocal and instrumental music were performed in the various Dublin concert halls, Dublin's theatres frequently offered a convenient venue.

The first full-fledged concert recorded at a Dublin theatre during our period was given by Sga. Stradiotti at Smock Alley on 26 September 1725. The concert, at which the Lord Lieutenant, Lord Carteret, his Lady, and the Lord Chancellor were present, as well as "a numerous concourse of the Nobility and Gentry," may have been the first at which an Italian prima donna appeared in Dublin.[29] A later Stradiotti concert, advertised as "A Cantata composed by Philip Percival Esq.," consisted of a program of some ten of Handel's arias, perhaps the first such programs of excerpts performed in Dublin.[30]

Subsequently, full-length concerts were occasionally given in Dublin theatres although these usually were presented at the various Dublin music halls. A concert of vocal and instrumental music held at Aungier Street for the benefit of Mrs. Davis in December 1734 is perhaps significant in that the venue of the concert had been changed from the Music Hall in Crow Street to Aungier Street, presumably because the new Aungier Street theatre had greater seating capacity.

*Serenatas and Oratorios*

During the 1735–36 season, in an apparent attempt to lend more variety to their programs, and, perhaps, to raise the tone of the musical entertainment being presented at Aungier Street, the managers announced their intention to present a series of "Serenatas, Oratorios and Pastorellas" on Saturdays evenings during the season. The music would be "conducted and managed by the Direction of Gentlemen, Lovers of Musick, which truly raises the Soul to a more than ordinary pitch. . . ." (*DEP* 4–8 Nov. 1735). The first of these of which we have record was presented on 25 October 1735 although the title of the piece has not survived. Indeed, the only title we have is that for the performance of the anonymous "Pastoral Opera" ["Pastorella"?] *Aminta* on 13 December 1735 for the benefit of Signora Mari Negri.

Oratorios, particularly those written by Handel and Arne, were as popular in Dublin as they were in London. This aspect of the Dublin musical scene has been ably discussed by Walsh and Boydell and need not detain us here.

*Ridottos*

The fashion for ridottos—entertainments consisting of a program of singing and instrumental music followed by a supper and communal dancing—

was of longer duration than that for serenatas. As early as March 1731 a series of monthly ridottos, under the direction of Thomas Griffith, had been proposed, but the public was disappointed when the aldermen of Dublin refused to allow the use of the Tholsel, the only venue fit for the purpose (*FDJ,* 20–23 Mar. 1731). In late November 1731 Griffith and a Mr. White "from England" reached an agreement with Mr. Johnston for use of his new music hall in Crow Street, and the first Dublin ridotto was held there at 9:00 p.m. on the evening of 29 November. A "very great Assembly" of people was present, and the ridotto did not break up until 4:00 a.m. (*FDJ,* 23–26 Oct. and 30 Nov.–4 Dec. 1731).

A subscription series for two such assemblies was first instituted by the Aungier Street management in the autumn of 1735 (*DEP* 18–22 Nov. 1735). By the following February the Aungier Street ridotto had become so popular that "the streets were so thronged with coaches and chairs, that several Ladies were forced to wait above two hours before they could get up to the Play-House door" (*DEP* 21–24 Feb. 1736). Subscription series of ridottos were offered at Aungier Street the following four seasons, often in competition with the ridottos offered by Mr. Johnston at his Music Hall in Crow Street. After the 1739–40 season ridottos at Aungier Street were no longer advertised.

### Instrumentalists

Virtuoso performers (domestic and foreign) playing on various musical instruments were frequently heard in the Dublin theatres. During the 1738–39 season, for example, Burk Thumoth gave entr'acte solo performances on the trumpet and German flute. Mr. Charles, "an Hungarian, the famous French Horn," (but also proficient on the "Clarinet, the Hautbois d'amoir, and the Shalamo [which] were never heard in this Kingdom before") performed Handel's "Water Music" at Smock Alley on 17 May 1742 at a time when Handel himself was visiting Dublin. Later that season Richard Pockrich gave the first Dublin performance on the musical glasses. The program included Vivaldi's "Spring" and additional variations "some of which cannot be executed on any instrument but the Glass" (see performance Smock Alley 3 May 1743).

### Vocalists

The Dublin managers could rarely afford the luxury of engaging personnel whose sole function was to sing; the boy soprano Master Mott (1731–32 season) seems to have been one of the few. Instead, they employed actors and actresses who were multitalented and who could attract audiences by their singing and dancing, as well as by their acting. Among these were

Lewis Layfield (also a musician), Vanderbank, Mrs. Lyddal, and Mrs. Sterling.

Even the first-line singers who visited Dublin from London and elsewhere, such as Mrs. Clive, Mrs. Arne, Mrs. Storer, and Thomas Lowe, acted in musical entertainments in addition to singing in concerts and in entr'acte entertainments.

The material which the singers performed was of three types. First, songs which were integral to the plays, as was the case with the bulk of the songs in the various plays loosely classed as "musical entertainments." These occasionally had nationalistic significance as was the case with the six songs with Irish tunes, among them "Eileen a Roon" and "The Highway to Dublin," included in Charles Coffey's ballad opera *The Beggar's Wedding*.

Second, songs which were interpolated into plays to enhance their audience appeal. As early in our period as 7 November 1720, for example, we find such singing when Lewis Layfield sang a "ballad" in the character of the innkeeper in Matthew Concanen's new comedy *Wexford Wells*. Such, too, would appear to be the song "Mad Tom of Bedlam" sung "by a Gentleman for his Diversion" and inserted into *King Lear and His Three Daughters* in March 1729.

Finally, vocalists sang entr'acte entertainments. The titles of few entr'acte songs survive, but they seem usually to have been solos which seldom bore any relation to the theme of the accompanying play. Most were "favourite songs" (songs extracted from currently or perennially popular pieces such as "Britons, Strike Home" from *Bonduca*), love songs or ballads ("Sum up all the Delights," "Peggy Grieves Me" and "Dear Pretty Youth") or songs for which a particular entertainer had achieved some renown.[31] For example, John Barrington, a popular stage Irishman, sang "Teague's Travels" and "Arrah, my Judy" "by particular desire of several Persons of Quality" at a Smock Alley performance of *The Stage Coach* on 5 April 1736. Samuel Hinde, whom Hitchcock tells us was the original in the song of "Mad Tom" in Ireland, was asked to perform that very popular song season after season (1:90).

From as early as 24 June 1725 we have record of special Masonic benefits at the Dublin theatres. The evening's program inevitably included the singing of masonic songs, such as "The Free Mason's Apprentice's Song," between each act.

## The Repertory

### *Number of Performances*

The Dublin stage calendar upon which the following analysis is based consists, in the main, of theatre performances gleaned from advertisements found in the Dublin newspapers of the time; little other performance information has survived. The principal Dublin newspapers which carried theatrical notices during the period are *The Dublin Gazette,* Harding's *Impartial Newsletter, The Dublin Weekly Journal,* Dickinson's *Dublin Intelligencer, The Dublin Evening Post,* Reilly's *Dublin Newsletter,* Pue's *Occurrences,* and, particularly, Faulkner's *Dublin Journal.*

As we observed in the preface, there is abundant evidence to indicate that during this twenty-five year period the Dublin theatres almost certainly presented over three thousand performances rather than the fourteen hundred of which we have record.

## The Program

In Dublin the eighteenth-century playhouses operated on a repertory system, staging thirty to forty different plays in the course of about ninety nights of acting for very short runs. A typical evening at the principal Dublin theatres could extend over five or six hours and consisted of a mainpiece, frequently with a prologue and epilogue, followed by one, and occasionally two, afterpieces. Entr'acte entertainments of singing, dancing, music, and, occasionally, tumbling and rope-dancing were also standard.

Mainpieces were full-length plays that headed the bill, afterpieces shorter one-, two-, or three-act farces, pantomimes, or musical entertainments performed, as the name indicates, after the mainpiece. However, this familiar pattern is complicated somewhat by a small number of programs that either consisted solely of short pieces (sometimes as many as three) normally performed as afterpieces, or programs in which the shorter piece was performed prior to the mainpiece, which happened occasionally, usually when an afterpiece received its Dublin premiere.

## Mainpieces

Dublin theatre managers were distinctly conservative in their choice of mainpieces, displaying little inclination to produce new plays and depending instead on a relatively small number of established standard plays or stock pieces to draw audiences. Analysis of the approximately 175 mainpieces performed in Dublin during the period indicates that only about fifty plays (approximately 30 percent of total) were performed ten or more times, yet these accounted for nearly 75 percent of the total of performances. About thirty-five plays (21 percent of total) were performed fifteen or more times but represented 60 percent of all mainpiece performances.

The standard Dublin mainpiece repertory consisted largely of the plays of Shakespeare; the Restoration comedies of Congreve, Wycherley, Vanbrugh, and Farquhar; the more recent comedies of Cibber and Steele; Gay's *The Beggar's Opera;* and a handful of Restoration and eighteenth-century tragedies, particularly Southerne's *Oroonoko,* Phillips's *The Distrest Mother,* and Otway's *The Orphan* and *Venice Preserved.* During the period, twenty-one different Shakespearean plays were performed (in adaptations and in the original) for approximately 280 performances, representing over 20 percent of all mainpiece performances and making Shakespeare the most frequently performed dramatist by far. Shakespeare's major tragedies and a few of his comedies, such as *The Merchant of Venice,* account for the bulk of these.

It is perhaps significant that while the popularity of most of the fifty or so stock plays spanned the entire period, few were performed in Dublin more than once or twice each season: over sixty percent of all mainpieces were performed only once in a season, less than 7 percent were performed more than three times, 12 percent three times only, 20 percent twice only. This certainly suggests that the managers sought to instill some variety in their programs by deft manipulation of a core of reliable standards. It, of course, assumes a reasonably stable company of actors who were able to fill roles in such pieces year after year.

Only twenty-six original mainpieces premiered in Dublin in the course of the twenty-five years under study (fig. 1), and in only five seasons were the managers adventurous enough to present more than one new play.[32] Very few of these saw a second night: four were performed three times, and only two achieved four performances. Of this group only Charles Coffey's *The Beggar's Wedding,* T. A. Arne's *Death of Abel,* Thomas Sheridan's *Brave Irishman,* and Swift's satire *Polite Conversation* were performed in London (with modest success) subsequent to their Dublin debuts.

Figure 1. Dublin Premieres

(C = Comedy, T = Tragedy, P = Pantomime, BO = Ballad Opera, F = Farce, Burl. = Burlesque, * = later performed in London. Dates are those of the first performances)

*Mainpieces*

| Title | Performances |
|---|---|
| *All Vows Kept* (C, 1733) | 1 |
| *\*Beggar's Wedding* (BO, 1729) | 3 |
| *Cobler of Preston's Opera* (BO, 1728) | 1 |
| *\*Death of Abel* (Oratorio, 1744) | 2 |
| *Deceit* (C, 1723) | 1 |
| *Earl of Westmoreland* (T, 1742) | 5 |
| *The Faithful Shepherd* (F, 1740) | 1 |
| *Fate of Ambition; or, The Treacherous Favourite* (T, 1733) | 1 |
| *Johnny Bow-Wow; or, The Wicked Gravedigger* (BO, 1732) | 1 |
| *Leonora; or, The Faithful Lover* (T, 1736) | 3 |
| *Love and Ambition* (T, 1731) | 6 |
| *Love and Loyalty; or, Publick Justice* (T, 1744) | 2 |

| | |
|---|---|
| *The Miser Matched; or, A Trip to Brussels* (C, 1740) | 1 |
| *Nature* (C, 1742) | 1 |
| *Parthian Hero* (T, 1741) | 1 |
| *The Patriot* (T, 1744) rev. of *Gustavus Vasa* | 4 |
| *Prude; or, Win Her and Wear Her* (C, 1744) | 1 |
| *Punch's Opera* (Burlesque, 1744) | 2 |
| *The Rival Generals* (T, 1722) | 2 |
| *The Sharper* (C, 1738) | 4 |
| *Tamar, Prince of Nubia* (T, 1739) | 1 |
| *Three Humps* (C?, 1738) | 1 |
| *The Treacherous Husband* (T, 1737) | 3 |
| *Turnus* (T, 1739) | 1 |
| *Wexford Wells; or, The Summer Assizes* (C, 1721) | 1 |
| *Wife and No Wife* (C, 1724) | 1 |

### Afterpieces

| | |
|---|---|
| *The Birth of Harlequin; or, The Triumph of Love* (P, 1731) | 1 |
| *The Honest [later, Brave] Irishman* (F, 1743) | 12 |
| *Chuck; or, The Schoolboy's Opera* (BO, 1736) | 1 |
| *The Comic Rivals; or, Columbine Coquette* (P, 1737) | 1 |
| *The Cooper Deceived* (P, 1736) | 1 |
| *A Cure for Jealousy* (F, 1735) | 1 |
| *The Female Officer* (F, 1740) | 7 |
| *Harlequin Triumphant in His Amours* (P, 1743) | 2 |
| *Harlequin Triumphant; or, The Father Deceived* (P, 1733) | 1 |
| *Harlequin Turned Physician* (P, 1737) | 1 |
| *The Intriguers* (F, 1741) | 1 |
| *The Jealous Farmer Deceived* (P, 1738) | 8 |
| *The Jealous Husband Deceived* (P, 1731) | 1 |
| *The Judgment of Paris; or, Harlequin Metamorphosed* (P, 1731) | 9 |
| *The Maid's Last Prayer* (F?, 1736) | 1 |
| *Matrimony Displayed; or, A Cure for Love* (F, 1736) | 1 |
| *Medley* (Entertainment?, 1736) | 1 |
| *No Death Like Marriage* (F?, 1738) | 1 |
| *The Oculist; or, Harlequin Fumigated* (P, 1745) | 1 |
| *Polite Conversation* (Satire, 1738) | 2 |
| *The Prize; or, Harlequin's Artifice* (P, 1745) | 1 |
| *The Ridiculous Bridegroom* (BO?, 1741) | 1 |
| *The Rival Beaux; or, Vanity Reclaimed* (F?, 1743) | 1 |
| *Scaramouche Turned Old Woman* (P, 1738) | 1 |
| *Vernon Triumphant; or, The British Sailors* (F?, 1741) | 1 |
| *Whittington and His Cat* (Operetta, 1738) | 1 |

The most common type of play performed in Dublin was eighteenth-century comedy (including full-length ballad opera, 30 percent), followed by

Shakespearian drama (20 percent), Restoration comedy (15 percent), Restoration tragedy (12 percent), and 18th-century tragedy (10 percent). Comedy was the most commonly performed genre (50 percent), with tragedy accounting for some 25 percent of the recorded performances. Genre aside, eighteenth-century plays made up 37 percent and Restoration drama some 26 percent of the repertory. Similarly, we find that about 27 percent of all performances were of eighteenth-century comedies, 20 percent Shakespeare, 16 percent Restoration comedy, 10 percent Restoration tragedy, and 8 percent eighteenth-century tragedy.

### Afterpieces

By 1720 the typical Dublin playbill probably included at least one afterpiece. Although, as we have already observed, the record of performances is sparse for the first eight seasons of our period, it is certain that afterpieces formed an important part of the Dublin theatre program as early as the 1722–23 season, for on 1 April 1723 John Gay's farce *The What D'Ye Call It* was advertised with *The Mourning Bride* at Smock Alley and the event elicited no comment that has been recorded. No subsequent advertisement for an afterpiece survives until the 1728–29 season, but thereafter they became an ever-increasing part of the bills at the principal Dublin theatres. In 1728–29 only 10 percent of the notices advertised an afterpiece; by 1734–35 this had risen to 50 percent; in 1737–38 the figure stood at 70 percent; and by the 1741–42 season 85 percent of all performances consisted of double and occasionally triple bills. Indeed, over 50 percent of all Dublin theatre programs included both a mainpiece and at least one afterpiece.

As fig. 2 indicates, three of the five most frequently-performed plays in the active repertory were afterpieces, the most popular being *The Devil to Pay,* followed by *The Hussar,* and *Damon and Phillida.* Of the seventy-three plays performed ten or more times, nineteen (nearly 30 percent) were afterpieces. Only one, *The Rival Sorcerors; or, Harlequin Victorious,* was a one-season phenomenon (1741–42); the rest retained their audience appeal and were called for year after year.

By the 1728–29 season, short "ballad operas" were vying with farce as the most popular type of afterpiece.[33] Although the arrival in Dublin of visiting companies of pantomime artists tipped the balance of favor of that genre during several seasons, musical entertainments (described also as interludes or operettas) and especially ballad operas (more than 270 performances) were the most frequently advertised form of afterpiece, followed closely by farce (220) and pantomime (180). Masques, satires, drolls, burlesques, and dramatic tales were performed occasionally.

The "failure" rate for afterpieces was very high in relation to the total number of different plays presented. A successful play was one that was performed at least three times and thereby earned for its author the net profit of at least one benefit performance, a very successful play was one

Figure 2. Most Popular Main- and Afterpieces, 1720–1745

Listed by number of performances. @ = afterpiece.

| Title | Performances |
|---|---|
| *The Beggar's Opera* (BO, 1728) | 69 |
| @ *The Devil To Pay; or, The Wives Metamorphosed* (BO, 1731) | 48 |
| @ *The Hussar* (P, 1737) | 46 |
| *Hamlet* (T) | 43 |
| @ *Damon and Phillida; or, Hymen's Triumph* (BO, 1729) | 34 |
| *Love for Love* (C, 1695) | 34 |
| *Othello* (T) | 34 |
| @ *Harlequin's Vagaries; or, Pierrot in Distress* (P, 1739) | 33 |
| *The Constant Couple* (C, 1699) | 32 |
| *The Provoked Husband* (C, 1728) | 32 |
| *King Richard III* (T) | 28 |
| @ *The Stage Coach* (F, 1704) | 28 |
| @ *The Virgin Unmasked* (BO, 1735) | 28 |
| *Love Makes a Man* (C, 1700) | 27 |
| *I King Henry IV* (History) | 26 |
| *The Recruiting Officer* (C, 1706) | 25 |
| @ *Comus* (Masque, 1712) | 24 |
| @ *The Mock Doctor* (BO, 1732) | 24 |
| @ *The Necromancer; or, Harlequin Doctor Faustus* (P, 1723) | 24 |
| *Venice Preserved; or, A Plot Discovered* (T, 1682) | 24 |
| *The Way of the World* (C, 1700) | 24 |
| *The Conscious Lovers* (C, 1722) | 23 |
| *The Distrest Mother* (T, 1712) | 22 |
| *Julius Caesar* (T) | 22 |
| *The Rehearsal* (Burl., 1671) | 22 |
| *The Twin Rivals* (C, 1703) | 22 |
| *The Beaux' Stratagem* (C, 1707) | 21 |
| *Macbeth* (T) | 21 |
| *The Committee; or, The Faithful Irishman* (C, 1662) | 20 |
| *Flora* (BO, 1720) | 20 |
| *The Miser* (C, 1733) | 20 |

performed ten or more times during the season. Nearly 50 percent of the dramatic pieces not revived after their first performance were afterpieces, as were 45 percent of those which failed to achieve a third night. Of these, pantomime, farce, and musical entertainments are about equally represented, suggesting that no genre was especially unpopular or prone to failure. However, we would do well to recall G. W. Stone's caveat regarding "unsuccessful" plays, for many of the afterpieces that received fewer than three performances were not, strictly speaking, failures at all ("The Making of the Repertory," in Hume 1980, 200). The small number of performances that they received may have been the result of one or more causes. In seasons for which the performance record is slight it is possible, if not probable, that unrecorded multiple performances of some of these afterpieces actually took place. This is particularly likely in the case of those afterpieces for which the management had gone to extraordinary expense in preparing new scenes, machines, and decorations (e.g. *Cephalis and Procris; or, Harlequin Grand Volgi,* for two performances at Smock Alley in 1732–33). Several pantomimes were performed exclusively by touring companies during their short visits to Ireland and included specialist dancing, tumbling, or rope dancing, such as those advertised for *The Cheats of Harlequin* by Sga. Violante's Company at Smock Alley in 1730 and *Harlequin Triumphant in His Amours* as performed by M. Dominique's troupe at Smock Alley in January 1743. Other afterpieces were apparently staged solely as special attractions for the benefit of specific performers, as was the case with *Harlequin Triumphant; or, The Father Deceived* presented at the Great Booth in June 1733 for the dancers Walsh and Cummins.

## Competition

Rivalry between two or more Dublin theatres appears to have exerted a relatively minor effect on the Dublin repertory. Despite occasional, brief challenges from Sga. Violante in 1733 and, later, the Rainsford Street company, Smock Alley had a virtual monopoly of Dublin theatricals until 1735, when the building of the new Smock Alley theatre and the removal of the Rainsford Street company there brought an end to the predominance of one company and one stage. For the next eight years two companies, Smock Alley and Aungier Street, more or less equally matched in facilities and personnel and showing little appetite for spirited competition, necessarily divided the limited Dublin audience and box-office receipts, drawing playgoers first to one house and then to the other according to the lure of their respective programs.

Most of the time the tenor of competition between Aungier Street and Smock Alley was amicable. The managers avoided performing on the same night, preferring instead to play on alternate evenings, particularly during the benefit months of February and March. Occasionally, however, one theatre premiered its own main- or afterpiece on the same night that its rival presented a new offering, and, less often, both theatres presented the same play on the same night.[34]

Another competitive tactic was employed by Aungier Street toward the end of the 1736–37 season: Smock Alley, sparing "no Expence in the Scenes, Machines, Dresses, Sinkings, Flyings, and other Decorations," staged a wholly new pantomime, *The Hussar; or, Harlequin Restored,* which was immediately successful. As soon as Smock Alley concluded the season and its manager, Duval, left for London on a recruiting trip, the Aungier Street management boldly offered its own version of *The Hussar* in order to profit by the current favor it enjoyed.

But despite these few instances of head-to-head competition the theatres generally avoided duplicating plays that had already been performed at the rival theatre in the same season. An average of less than 14 percent of the mainpieces performed were thus affected. However, nearly 30 percent of the performances during the period included these plays, which phenomenon may be explained by the fact that those plays performed in the same season by both companies were, without exception, either stock plays or very popular new pieces which regularly attracted large audiences. The same afterpieces were much less likely to be performed at both theatres: only 7 percent were the objects of competition, and they comprised only about 16 percent of the total number of performances.

A list of the "new" plays presented at the two principal Dublin theatres is provided in figure 3. Here reference to "new" pieces denotes not only those few plays that received their world premieres in Dublin, but also the first Dublin performances of plays which premiered earlier in London as well as plays revived in Dublin after long (more than three years) intervals. Some useful generalizations about this aspect of the repertory may be made in regard to the competition between Smock Alley and Aungier Street. With the exception of the first season of competition (1735–36), when Aungier Street presented fifteen new pieces compared to Smock Alley's seven, in most succeeding seasons Smock Alley produced a few more new plays or afterpieces than Aungier Street, although there was never any great disparity between the two theatres in terms of numbers until the crucial 1741–42 season when, in what would appear to have been an unsuccessful attempt to avoid ruin, the Smock Alley company brought out twice as many new pieces as Aungier Street.[35]

Figure 3. New Plays and Long-term Revivals in Dublin, 1735–36 to 1742–43

(* = premiere; a = afterpiece)

| Smock Alley | Aungier St. |
|---|---|
| **1735–36** | |
| Gamester | Aminta |
| Leonora* | Albion Queens |
| Pasquin (after AS) | Don John |
| Man of Taste | Fair Quaker of Deal |
| Cooper Deceived (a) | Pasquin |
| Penelope (a) | Prophetess |
| Spaniard Deceived (a) | Rehearsal |
| | Sir Courtly Nice |
| | Squire of Alsatia |
| | Tempest |
| | Honest Yorkshireman (a) |
| | Maid's Last Prayer (a) |
| | Medley (a) |
| | Wrangling Lovers (a) |

## 1736–37

City Wives
King Charles I
2 Henry IV
Volpone
Columbine Courtezan (a)
Comic Rivals (a)
Hussar (a)
King and the Miller (a)
Rival Queans (a)

Drummer
History and Fall of Caius Marius
Honest Irishman (a)*
Freemason's Opera (a)
Harlequin Turned Physician (a)*
Lover's Opera (a)
Rival Theatres (a)
Virgin Unmasked (a)

## 1737–38

Amphitryon
Bonduca
King John
Love and a Bottle
Timon of Athens
Man's Bewitched
Sharper
Three Humps*
Country Lasses (after AS)
Anatomist (a)
Cure for a Scold (a)
Jealous Farmer Deceived (a)*
No Death Like Marriage (a)*
Polite Conversation (a) (after AS)

Country Lasses
Indian Emperor
Measure for Measure
Wit Without Money
Oedipus
Lucius Junius Brutus
Dragon of Wantley (a)
Sir John Cockle (a)
Polite Conversation (a)*

## 1738–39

Mustapha
Treacherous Husband*
Harlequin's Vagaries (a)
Harlot's Progress (a)
Whittington (a)*

Emperor of the Moon
Ignoramus
Turnus*
Female Officer (a)*
Margery (a)
Scaramouche (a)*

## 1739–40

Faithful Shepherd*
Miser Matched
Plain Dealer
Sir Walter Raleigh
Assembly (a)
Britons Strike Home (a)
Matrimony Displayed (a)*
Preceptor (a)
Raree Show (a)

Tamar*
Aesop
Walter Raleigh (same night as AS)
Cure for Jealousy (a)*
Robin Hood and Little John (a)
Sharpers (a)

## 1740–41

Comus
Greenwich Park

Successful Straingers
Wife's Relief

Rehearsal (after AS)
Mad Captain (a)
Author's Farce (a)
Nancy (a)
Judgment of Paris (a)
Intriguing Chambermaid (a)

Rehearsal
Author's Farce (same night as SA)
Harlequin Metamorphosed (a)
Intriguers (a)
Queen of Spain (a)
Ridiculous Bridegroom (a)*
Sequel to the Rehearsal (a)
Vernon Triumphant (a)*
L'Arlequin Mariner (a)*

### 1741–42

As You Like It
Humourous Lieutenant
Lancashire Witches
Mithradates (Lee)
Pamela
Merchant of Venice
Parthian Hero*
Lying Valet (a)
Blind Beggar (a)
Grand Sultan (a)
Rival Sorcerers (a)
Strollers (a)
Thomas Koulikan (a)

As You Like It (after SA)
Betrayer of His Country
Man of Mode
Nature*

### 1742–43

Mithradates (Racine)
Non-Juror
Wonder
Harlequin Triumphant (a)
Hymen (a)
Rival Beaux (a)*
Opera of Operas (a)

Love and Glory
Rosamond
Scornful Lady
Twelfth Night
Vintner Tricked (a)
Miss Lucy in Town (a)

Thus, we see that in an average season the two principal theatres produced approximately the same number of new entertainments, neither relying on novel mainpieces to attract audiences. On the other hand, both theatres produced relatively large numbers of new afterpieces: at Smock Alley they account for some 25 percent and at Aungier Street over 35 percent of all afterpieces during the eight seasons in question, and at both theatres they represent over 35 percent of all afterpiece performances during that period.

Infrequently, the managers sought to counter the popularity of a competitor's new piece by getting up one of their own, but such reaction was seldom immediate. Indeed, the theatre directors as often as not permitted the competition to wring the maximum financial advantage from any new piece. For example, Smock Alley produced *A Cure for a Scold* for a long run of twelve performances during the 1737–38 season, *The Harlot's Progress* for seven during 1738–39, *Harlequin's Vagaries* for twenty-three performances during the 1738–39 and 1739–40 seasons, and *The Lying Valet* for ten during the

1741–42 season, but none of these was performed at Aungier Street. Aungier Street, on the other hand, presented *Comus* for multiple performances each season from 1740–41 to the end of the period, *Twelfth Night* for five during the 1742–43 season, and *The Vintner Tricked* for six performances the same season, but none was performed at Smock Alley. This courtesy was due in part, no doubt, to the fact that many new plays were staged expressly for the benefit performances of important members of the company.

Such live-and-let-live cooperation degenerated markedly, however, after the 1740–41 season, when all-out war commenced between the theatres. It became the rule that both theatres performed on the same nights, identical or similar programs became more common, and both companies offered extended summer seasons. The result of this deliberate splitting of the limited theatre-going audience (and box-office receipts) was the eventual financial ruin and disbandment of the Smock Alley company at the end of the 1742–43 season and the formation of a united company which used both theatres.

### London Influence

The repertories of the London and Dublin theatres were clearly inextricably linked; clearly, too, Dublin was almost totally dependent on London for its theatrical material. We have already observed that only twenty-six entirely original mainpieces premiered in Dublin in the course of the twenty-five years under study, and only four of those are known to have been performed in London subsequent to their Dublin debuts. The remainder of the plays came to the Dublin theatres by way of London. Nevertheless, a comparison of the London and Dublin performance calendars reveals some interesting, if not startling, facts.

If we examine the repertories of the Dublin and London theatres for the ten seasons between 1735–36 and 1744–45—it is likely that the Dublin stage calendar for these ten years is nearly complete for several seasons and about 75 percent complete overall—we see, first, that during the 1735–36 season about twenty-five new pieces premiered in London (see fig. 4).[36] Of these eighteen were successful; seven were very successful.

How did Dublin managers react to the twenty-five new and successful London plays? They chose to stage two. Fielding's satire *Pasquin* opened at the Haymarket Theatre in London with some fifty consecutive performances. In Dublin this very popular piece was ready for the stage only six weeks after its London debut and enjoyed a successful run of five performances at Smock Alley and two at Aungier Street. James Miller's play *The Man of Taste* saw many scores of performances at Drury Lane after its premiere this season, and, again, a successful Dublin production followed ten months later.

The next season London audiences witnessed the premieres of about nine-

Figure 4. Number of London Plays performed soon after in Dublin

| Season | "New" | | Revivals | |
|---|---|---|---|---|
| | London | Dublin | London | Dublin |
| 1735-36 | 25 | 2 | 16 | 1 |
| 1736-37 | 19 | 3 | 9 | 1 |
| 1737-38 | 8 | 1 | 3 | 1 |
| 1738-39 | 4 | 2 | 2 | 0 |
| 1739-40 | 9 | 3 | 4 | 0 |
| 1740-41 | 9 | 1 | 8 | 2 |
| 1741-42 | 5 | 2 | 0 | 0 |
| 1742-43 | 3 | 0 | 1 | 0 |
| 1743-44 | 7 | 1 | 6 | 0 |
| 1744-45 | 5 | 0 | 6 | 0 |
| TOTAL: | 94 | 15 | 55 | 5 |

[Note: This table has been amended slightly since its initial publication ("The Dublin Stage Repertory," *Eighteenth-Century Ireland*, (2) 1987, 133-48) in light of Robert D. Hume's estimates for "new" London plays for the 1735-36 through 1737-38 seasons (Hume 1983, 299)].

teen main- and afterpieces. Of these, three were performed soon after in Dublin: William Harvard's tragedy *King Charles I* eight weeks subsequent to the London debut, Dodsley's *The King and the Miller of Mansfield* (approximately sixty Drury Lane performances) and Carey's *The Dragon of Wantley* (approximately one hundred Haymarket performances) eight weeks and eight months later, respectively.

From 1737-38 season to the end of the period the number of new plays performed in London fell precipitously, due in large part to the ramifications of the 1737 Licensing Act. Of the eight new pieces performed in London during the 1737-38 season (the first under the Act) only one, Dodsley's *Sir John Cockle in Court*, was performed in Dublin. It was staged a mere three weeks after its London debut—a prodigious feat considering the grim hardships of land and sea travel from London to Dublin at the time and the obvious necessity to rehearse any new piece.

To avoid a tedious season-by-season account of the Dublin reaction to London plays suffice it to say, as figure 4 indicates, that during the seven seasons after 1737-38 London staged some forty-two new plays, nine of which were performed in Dublin soon thereafter. Among these was Henry Carey's two very successful afterpieces *Margery* and *Nancy,* Fielding's *Miss Lucy in Town,* and David Mallet's tragedy *Mustapha.*

Obviously, Dublin was aware of London taste in plays and, to a degree, reacted to it. But how are we to explain the following? In 1735-36 Aaron Hill's very successful tragedy *Zara* premiered at Drury Lane and received a staggering (for a tragedy) fifteen consecutive performances, yet was never performed in Dublin during the period. Indeed, in the course of that London season four extremely successful pantomimes were performed for the first time, and each was repeated scores of times, but none of these or, indeed, any of the eight other successful and very successful London pieces was performed in Dublin until several years later, if at all.[37]

While the effects of the inhibitions placed on both London theatre managers and playwrights by the Licensing Act of 1737 is incalculable, the Act appears to have been paid little heed in Dublin. In brief, the Licensing Act was instituted by the government of Sir Robert Walpole to put an end to the theatrical activities of opposition playwrights whose works held him and his administration up to public ridicule. It required that a manuscript of each new play be submitted to the Lord Chamberlain's office for approval before being performed in either of the two London patent theatres, the only theatres in which (according to the act) legitimate drama was permitted to be performed.

Debate ensued about whether or not the act applied outside of London, but clearly the Dublin theatre managers did not consider themselves to be affected by it. In the months prior to the Act coming into effect they produced two pieces—*Pasquin* and *King Charles I*—both of which were clearly antigovernment and which enjoyed success in London. However, during the 1736–37 season Fielding's two biting anti-Walpole satires *Eurydice Hissed* and *Historical Register,* which had very successful London runs of over twenty and thirty-five performances respectively, were ignored by the Dublin managers, although they did produce Havard's controversial political allegory *King Charles I.* Later, after passage of the Act, the Dublin theatres presented two plays—Mallet's *Mustapha* (May 1739) and Henry Brooke's *The Patriot* (a revision of *Gustavus Vasa* December 1744)—both of which had been banned from the stage in London because of their political content, yet neither production seems to have caused the least stir in Dublin.

Dublin theatre managers, then, would seem neither to have deliberately sought out nor avoided plays that were embarrassing to the British administration. Furthermore, there is little evidence from the repertory to suggest that during this period the Dublin stage was used as a deliberate instrument for political comment critical of the Dublin municipal government, the Irish parliament or Viceregal administration.

While it is true that some of the plays staged in Dublin had followed close on the heels of successful London premieres, it is, nevertheless, significant to our purpose here to note that the Dublin managers sometimes put on plays which had been distinctly unsuccessful in London. In the 1739–40 season, for example, Smock Alley staged E. Phillips's *Briton's Strike Home,* a piece which had received only one London performance. The following season Smock Alley produced Dodsley's *The Blind Beggar of Bethnal Green,* some eight months after its only London performance. In 1743–44 Smock Alley produced *The Queen of Spain; or, Farinelli in Madrid* a mere three months after a rather mediocre London debut of four performances. Finally, in 1744–45 Miller's *The Picture; or, Cockhold in Conceit* was performed in Dublin less than two months after its one Drury Lane performance.

Furthermore, an examination of the Dublin reaction to London revivals (plays staged after an interval of three or more years) indicates that in this respect London influence on the Dublin repertory was even less significant than was the case with new plays. During the 1735–36 season about sixteen plays were revived in London, but only one of these can also be said to have been revived in Dublin that season. It is worth noting, too, that during that season Dryden's *King Arthur* was revived in London after some forty years for a run of about forty consecutive performances but was not revived in Dublin. The following season about nine plays were revived in London, three of which were very successful, including Shakespeare's *Much Ado About Nothing* and *King John*. Of these only *King John* was revived in Dublin, a year later, as was the much less successful revival of Farquhar's *Sir Harry Wildair*. The 1737–38 season saw three London revivals, only one of which was repeated in Dublin. This was *The Cobler of Preston,* which received one performance in London after some seven years. Despite this lackluster showing, the piece was revived in Dublin four weeks later. Interestingly, *The Cobler of Preston* had been performed in Dublin the previous two seasons— are we therefore to discern some Dublin influence on the London repertory? Two very successful revivals appeared in London during the 1738–39 season, including Colly Cibber's *The Lady's Last Stake* which subsequently became a London standard, yet again neither was performed in Dublin. During the remaining six seasons of the period only two—Shakespeare's *As You Like It* and *Twelfth Night*—of the twenty-five successful London revivals also appeared in Dublin.

A close examination of the actual London and Dublin performance records, then, reveals that while it is certainly true that no play in the Dublin stock repertory had not originated in London and was not also a popular standard there, it is nevertheless a fact that of the nearly one hundred main- and afterpieces which premiered in London during the ten seasons 1735–36 through 1744–45 only about fifteen were seen in Dublin within one year; and of the fifty-five that were revived in London during the period, five were also revived in Dublin.

Dublin theatre managers undeniably shared the taste of their London counterparts as far as the standard repertory was concerned, but they clearly were very selective about which "new" plays from the London theatres they produced.

## Conclusion

If the profound revision that eighteenth-century Irish history is presently undergoing holds any immediate lesson for us, it is to be dubious of rigid visions of the past. All too many of the generalizations that have been made about this era have been based on the shaky foundations of inadequate and occasionally even distorted evidence. In our preface we have provided a cautionary note about the nature and scope of the evidence we have here analyzed; if we have tended to be conservative in our generalizations it is to avoid misleading the unwary. By way of concluding this introduction we offer the following general remarks about the Dublin theatres during this period.

It is now commonplace to observe that during the Restoration and eighteenth century, Dublin was the "second" city of the burgeoning British Empire and supported a rich and varied cultural life. Although population figures are still disputed, Dublin, which may have numbered as many as sixty-five thousand inhabitants, displayed more vitality than any other city of the Empire except its capital. Architectually, Dublin was entering upon an era of vast improvement. The city was expanding rapidly, new streets and bridges were being laid, elegant townhouses for the wealthy and several important buildings, such as the Parliament House and the library at Trinity College, were constructed. The first half of the eighteenth century also saw the rise of both portrait and landscape painting in Ireland. The founding of the Dublin Society in 1731 led to the establishment within ten years of the Society's school of art: "one of the finest art schools in Europe, finer by far than anything established in England till 1768" (Crookshank, NHI, 499).

Dublin was beginning to attract, if only for brief visits, some of the best musicians and singers from London and beyond. Frequent "concerts of vocal and instrumental music" were given in several newly-built music halls and in Dublin's churches. Outdoor concerts and other musical entertainments became increasingly popular during the spring and summer, and fashionable Dubliners resorted in large numbers to the diversions offered in Marlborough and St. Stephen's Greens and at the City Basin. Other popular nighttime social events available to Dublin patrons were ridottos and assemblies.

During the entire twenty-five years under study in this volume, Dubliners had available to them, in addition to the above, a wide variety of public entertainments ranging from bear-baitings to masquerade balls and puppet shows. But the professional theatre was the most popular form of public diversion, although the quality and quantity of the theatrical fare varied considerably in the course of the period.

An assessment of the quality of Dublin performances must be based largely on surmise. Little contemporary comment has survived, and that which has is usually biased. Nevertheless, the evidence suggests that under the management first of Thomas Elrington at Smock Alley and later of Thomas Griffith at Aungier Street, the stage was "supported with a considerable degree of credit," in the words of Charles Macklin's biographer, William Cooke. Lewis Duval, too, was praised for making several reforms when he took over the management at Smock Alley in 1735, but his success was brief.

Thereafter, and until about 1743 when Thomas Sheridan became associated with the theatres, the quality of productions declined until they "were sunk into the lowest contempt" (154).

At their best, the Dublin theatres presented daily programs that virtually rivalled those of London, although the Dublin theatres lagged behind their counterparts in London in making technological improvements, such as scene-shifting machinery and stage lighting, and it is probable as well that Dublin productions were less lavish in terms of the sumptuousness of their scenes and costumes. When new, both the Smock Alley and Aungier Street playhouses were praised by visitors from England and the Continent alike, and were considered as beautiful (internally) and as functional as any in Europe.

A slump in quality undoubtedly occurred; however, it must be viewed from the perspective of the very high standards of production that preceded and succeeded it. Every aspect of theatrical production was criticized at one time or another. (This, incidentally, can also be said of the London theatres of the time). The theatres were "ill-directed," few good performers were available nor were they even sought after by the managers; new costumes and sets were seldom provided. Some elements in the audience, particularly the bucks who watched the performances from seats on the stage and the servants and footmen in the second gallery, were sometimes unruly, and the managers seemed unable to control them. Performances were frequently late in getting under way, gentlemen were not required to pay for their places in the pit and boxes until after they were seated, which led to inconvenience on the part of other members of the audience when the ticket takers came to collect. The tallow candles were too smoky, the auditoriums too cold or too hot. Advertised plays were changed at short notice and performances cancelled at the last minute if the audience was too small. Plays were underrehearsed, and actors sometimes read their parts rather than enacting them, and so on.

Yet, it is doubtful that the theatres in Dublin between 1734 and 1740 were as consistently bad as they are said to have been. Throughout this period two or more theatres competed for the same, limited audience. Could any theatre have been guilty of every infraction for any length of time and remained in business? It is more likely that at various times each theatre was guilty of one or more faults, which the competition, in turn, claimed to have remedied at its house.

Considering this period of "decline" as a whole, it would appear that the quality of the performances at Aungier Street, in general, were superior to those at Smock Alley. Aungier Street had more talented performers who seem to have had a more permanent commitment to that playhouse. Actors certainly appear to have preferred to work there and remained there longer. Aungier Street's repertory was also somewhat more imaginative and novel, and they may have spent more money for new costumes and scenery more frequently than their competitors at Smock Alley, whose finances were in a chronically perilous state.

As for the quantity of Dublin performances, at no time was there less than one theatre in operation, and for nearly fifteen years at least two (at times three and, perhaps, as many as five) were open simultaneously. Although the minor Dublin theatres were short-lived and staged plays only sporadically, the major theatres span the period and had seasons which averaged about 90 nights. This is a very respectable figure if we consider that the major theatres of London, which had ten times the population of Dublin, averaged about 180 nights of acting during seasons of the same length. Clearly, Dublin audiences consisted of regular theatregoers.

But who were these people? La Tourette Stockwell, in her history of the Dublin stage (1938), presented the current view of the Dublin theatre audience in the eighteenth century. It was

> West British, rather than Gaelic, both in its spirit and in its expression, because its audience, consistently, for three centuries, was representative only of a minority group of the total population. This group constituted a psychological unit, composed of the landlord classes and urban tradespeople. Its country was England, its civilization was English, and it looked toward London as Mohammedans look to Mecca. How little the theatre was affected by or influenced the greater part of the population, the native Irish, can be quickly perceived by even a cursory reading of Daniel Corkery's *Hidden Ireland*. (174)

In the last sixty years, most of the assumptions upon which Stockwell bases her view of the eighteenth-century audience have been reexamined and refuted or revised. Putting aside the question of whether theatregoers have ever represented anything more than a "minority group of the total population" of any nation, recent research indicates that the Protestant minority, which formed at least one-quarter of the population of the island, was particularly strong around Dublin. Far from being a group made up entirely of "the landlord classes and urban tradespeople," the Protestant minority included "significant numbers at every level" of society, including workmen, shopkeepers, and tenant farmers. They also possessed a much underestimated Gaelic element (Beckett, NHI, xliv).

Nor were they quite the homogeneous, Anglocentric clique that Stockwell describes; rather, it is becoming increasingly evident that the Protestant minority was far more diverse in religious and social outlook than has previously been realized. While the Anglo-Irish culture clearly "was essentially an English culture, modified by local circumstances" (426) and shared the important protections and privileges afforded by the mantle of an ascendent Protestantism, they "certainly regarded themselves as Irish" and "had no doubt at all that they themselves formed an integral part of the Irish nation; and some spoke and acted as if they formed the whole of it" (xlv).

Yet, in regard to the theatre history of Dublin, Stockwell's central implication—that the Dublin theatre audience was comprised almost exclusively of "English" people or at least Anglo-Irish ("West Britons")—has not been refuted entirely. Unfortunately, today we know little more about the actual composition of the Dublin theatre audiences between the years 1720 and 1745 than was known in 1938. Looking beyond the confines of this period, considerably more can be said, but here we have, with few exceptions, deliberately limited ourselves to the consideration of evidence from within the period.

Although our research into the Dublin repertory and the interrelationships between the Dublin and London theatres and actors has revealed an independence of mind and spirit on the part of the Dublin theatres to which previous students of the Dublin stage were blind, we are unable to determine with any more certainty than Stockwell was, the identities of those who actually sat on the benches in the Dublin theatres. Well-to-do Protestants of the nobility, gentry, merchant, and military classes probably represented the bulk of the audience, or at least they filled the more costly seats. This is implicit in the fact that the theatrical season coincided with the sitting of Parliament and the beginning of the terms of the courts and university. To fill their playhouses, theatre managers necessarily waited until the town was "full" to commence acting, and they seldom continued performing much past the early summer, when the wealthy left Dublin for their country residences or for Great Britain and the Continent.

But at least one of the Dublin theatres played to full houses in the summer, as the "predatory" visits of important actors from London confirm. Year after year actors like James Quin, David Garrick, and Dennis Delane risked the hazards of the Irish Sea voyage and returned to London in the autumn after long and lucrative visits. Clearly, the audiences they entertained must have been composed of more than just the wealthy, and they almost certainly included members of a variety of social classes.

The extent to which the Dublin theatres affected the Gaelic, Catholic Irish is also unclear. It is certainly a gross overstatement to assert that there was none. Daniel Corkery, whose historical objectivity must be called into question in any event, made no explicit statement about the drama. As far as we are able to discover the only bar to theatre attendance was the ability to pay the price of admission. The ability to understand and speak English would not seem to have imposed any obstacle to the Gaelic Irish of Leinster and Dublin by our period (O Cuiv, NHI, 383). At the very least, some of the Gaelic Irish had access to the theatre by sitting in the servants' gallery, which was admission-free. The fact that actors and actresses bearing Anglicized Gaelic names were performing in Dublin coupled with the fact that by midcentury several of the foremost playwrights and actors were of Gaelic Irish extraction, makes it probable, if not self-evident, that in their formative years they were able to attend the theatre, although such evidence is, admittedly, very flimsy.

The theatre is the most mercenary of art forms; Dublin audiences, in general, wanted to see the old standards and fashionable new London plays. As our discussion of the Dublin repertory indicates, Dublin theatre managers were conservative as a result, but nevertheless generally eager to please in this respect, although they did not imitate London taste nearly as slavishly as has been claimed. It must also be remembered that in London during the early years of this period (1720 to 1737) the theatre managers were not very receptive of new plays of any kind (Hume 1988, 14) and after the imposition of the stage Licensing Act of 1737 they became even less so.

However regrettable, the "cross channel" nature of Anglo-Irish society made it inevitable that, given the fact that Irish playwrights and actors must make a living, most emigrated to London, where opportunities were more plentiful and the rewards for talent greater. The per diem salaries in London were roughly the same as those in Dublin, but the fact that London actors could act in twice as many performances made their annual salaries much greater. Why the Dublin theatre artists' preference for London should have been looked on so disdainfully by later (Irish) commentators is puzzling since London has undeviatingly been a principal "Mecca" for Irish men and women, of whatever religion, class, or calling. Their fault, it would seem, was not remaining in Dublin to help to found a "national" theatre.

What the nature of an early eighteenth-century Irish "national" theatre would have been is hard to say. Presumably, it would have presented plays with Irish themes and settings which were written by Irish playwrights and acted by Irish actors. But, had such plays and personnel been available, would Dublin audiences have attended? Few distinctly Irish plays were staged in our period, and of these only Thomas Sheridan's afterpiece farce *The Brave Irishman* enjoyed any success in Dublin. Coffey's *The Beggar's Wedding* (1729) barely managed to scrape together an audience for the Irish author's benefit night and was considered by him to have been a failure in Dublin, though it was subsequently very successful in London. The handful of plays on Irish subjects that had been staged in Dublin a few years earlier— Charles Shadwell's *Irish Hospitality* (1718) and *Roderick O'Connor, King of Connaught* (1719); and William Philips's *St. Stephen's Green* (1699) also had little success and were not revived. An Irish "national" theatre would have to wait for an audience sympathetic to a strong nationalistic movement and is an aspect of Irish theatre history to be treated in a later volume of this work.

## Notes

1. Elrington made extensive repairs to the building in September 1722 and again in February 1730 when Capt. Thomas Burgh, Engineer and Surveyor-General of Ireland, certified in the newspapers that the theatre was structurally sound (*HIN* 29 Sept. 1722; *FDJ* 3 Feb. 1730; Stockwell 1938, 64–65).

2. Letter of Sir Edward Pearce, dated 2 February 1733, as printed in Lenihan 1866, 331.

3. Further evidence that Griffith exerted strong influence in the management may be found in Jonathan Swift's satirical prologue "Billet to the Company of Players" in which a strolling player bribes Griffith: "To speak to Elrington, and all the tribe, / To let our company supply their places."

4. That a major shake-up in the management at Aungier Street occurred this season is further suggested by the fact that Francis Elrington, a manager of long standing, and several other performers deserted Aungier Street for Smock Alley in February 1741, although Elrington returned the following season. Several members of the Smock Alley company also defected to Aungier Street.

5. In later years Swan returned to York and lived to 1782 or thereabouts. A letter from him to Garrick from York is preserved in Garrick's correspondence. In it Garrick states that Swan "is formerly a manager & actor & since retir'd upon a fortune left him at York" (1963, 1:913). See also Boaden's *Life of Mrs. Jordan* (1831), 1:37–39 for anecdotes of him and also Tate Wilkinson's *Memoirs* (1790) 2:44.

6. Benjamin Victor (1776, 1:121), letter of 23 December 1746 tells us that at that time the united company had thirty-six proprietors.

7. "A Prologue upon the Beaux, for Mrs. Davis's Benefit at Smock-Alley" (3–10, 13–24), a Dublin broadside in the Trinity College, Dublin, Library, reprinted in Gilbert 1854–59, 3:190. There is no record of this performance. The broadside was evidently printed when no Smock Alley player dared to deliver it.

8. From a Dublin Broadside entitled "A Prologue to Julius Caesar, As it was Acted at Madam Violante's Booth, December the 15th, 1732, by some of the young Gentlemen in Dr. Sheridan's School" (Folger Shakespeare Library).

9. Rev. S. C. Hughes, *The Pre-Victorian Drama in Dublin* (1904, 19), identifies Stretch's first name as Randal.

10. A poem, "The Puppet Shew," which appeared in *SJEP* 21 April 1721, contains the earliest reference to "great Stretch" and his "artful hand." Eight years later, a satirical broadside aimed at Charles Coffey entitled "Dr. Anthony's Advice to the Hibernian Aesop; or an Epistle to the Author of the B[egger's]. W-[edding] (BL 1890 e. 5) advises Coffey to "Adapt your Muse to *Dames Street* Stage. / But ah! from thence you have been chas'd, / By Punch, of most distinguish'd Taste." This and other internal evidence indicates that the broadside was written shortly after March 1729.

11. In 1745 Dr. Bartholomew Mosse (1712–59) renovated the booth and on 15 March his Lying-In Hospital "in George's-Lane facing Fade-Street opened" (*FDJ* 26 Mar. 1745; Chetwood 1749, 61n.; Hughes 1904, 5, identifies the site as No. 53 South George's St.; Gilbert 1854–59, 3:189, says No. 59).

12. In March 1734 and several times during the previous winter Duval had moved their successful burlesque to the George's Lane Booth, close to the home of their rivals (*FDJ* 18 Mar. 1735).

13. Ten of these subscribers were: William Bradford, Hon. Major Thomas Butler, Robert Curtis, Hugh Eccles, Sir Robert Echlin, James Grattan, Dr. and Mrs. Richard Helsham, Marcus Anthony Morgan, John Rochford, John Rutland, Theobald Taafe, William Usher, Robert Whitehall (MS. 92/122/64093 ORD); Hitchcock 1788–94, 1:93, and Stockwell 1938, 329, give an incomplete list, but Stockwell (79) records all these names with one misreading.

14. *PO* 17 Jan. 1735. Sheridan 1772, 7; Hitchcock 1788–94, 1:97; and Stockwell 1938, 74, set down incorrect accounts of these proceedings and mistakenly describe the Duval-Smock Alley enterprise as a city theatre authorized by the Lord Mayor of Dublin.

15. *DNL* 22–26 Feb. 1743. William Dunkin (1769–70) contains a piece entitled "The Murphiead" apparently referring to this period at Smock Alley. Several Trinity College students disguised themselves as footmen in order to gain admission to the gallery and see the plays *gratis*.

16. Whether as a result of pressure from the subscribers or not, Duval lost at least three of his principal actors and several dancers to Aungier St. in March and April of the 1740–41 season: Barrington left after 4 April, Mrs. Pasquilino 7 March, Mrs. Reynolds after 15 April; Mr. and Mrs. Dumont and Mrs. Martin were the dancers.

17. The terms of the 1741 lease change indicate that the new proprietors had agreed to give Duval forty shillings a week until the debts due the theatre were paid. They also granted Duval a free benefit play each year in November, which privilege he seems to have enjoyed until his death (Stockwell 1938, 80–81).

18. The assertions of Stockwell (1938, 87) and Sheldon (1967, 54 n.) to the contrary, Chetwood (1749, 21) was correct in stating that William "Harlequin" Phillips and not Thomas Philips was the manager of the first Capel Street theatre. The authors of the *BD* in their entry for William Phillips stress that Stockwell's contention (followed by Sheldon) is "certainly incorrect." Thomas Philips confined himself to acting and was with the Covent Garden company constantly during the 1744–45 season. The confusion of identities is no doubt compounded by the apparent fact that both Dublin managers were light-fingered and left Ireland precipitiously.

19. Quoted in *BD* entry on Foote.

20. A great deal of research has recently been done in the area of promptbook evidence, and some of the most informative of the surviving promptbooks were used at Smock Alley in the 1670s and 1680s. The only Smock Alley promptbook for our period is that of 1720 London edition of *Richard II* now in the Folger Shakespeare Library. The prompter's markings are relatively few and do not suggest that practices described by Clark (1955, 72–83) had changed at Smock Alley since the Restoration. See Leo Hughes, "The Evidence from Promptbooks," in Hume 1980, 119–42 and Langhans 1981, passim.

21. (*LS* Pt 3:1:cxxv. Recent research strongly suggests that London companies may have been much larger than Scouten has estimated. Covent Garden may have employed as many as 133 performers and servants, excluding the band. See Milhous and Hume (1990), "John Rich's Covent Garden Account Books for 1735–1736".

22. Cibber, "Proper Reply," in *Cibber and Sheridan*, 43. Sheridan suggests that the cartel was aimed at excluding Cibber only and that he quashed it.

23. For a detailed examination of company management in the London theatres during the 18th century see Judith Milhous, "Company Management," in Hume 1980, 1–34.

24. *LS*, Pt. 2:1:civ, estimates that during the 1724–25 season at Lincoln's Inn Fields John Rich spent as much as £900 of a £10,000 budget on wardrobe. See also Arthur H. Scouten's critical introduction to *LS*, cxvii–cxx, for a discussion of costumes in the London theatres during this period.

25. For discussions of scenery and machinery in the London theatres during our period see the critical introductions to the *LS* volumes of both Scouten and Avery as well as Colin Visser, "Scenery and Technical Design," in Hume 1980, 66–118.

26. *London Daily Post and General Advertiser,* 28 Feb. 1736 quoted in *LS* 3:1:cxxii.

27. *DG*, 21–24 December 1742 indicates that "Tom Ludlow, Machinist to the Theatre in Smock Alley, lately arriv'd from England, has found out an Infallible Method of Curing Smoaky Chimnies. . . ." For Chetwood's own account see his *History* (1749), 73].

28. T. J. Walsh and Brian Boydell have amply demonstrated that the Dublin audi-

ence shared with its London counterpart an enormous appetite for musical entertainment. For extended discussions of music in Dublin during the eighteenth century see T. J. Walsh, *Opera in Dublin 1705–1797* (Dublin: Allen Figgis, 1973); Brian Boydell, "Music, 1700–1850," in *A New History of Ireland*, volume 4 (Oxford: Clarendon Press, 1986) and *A Dublin Musical Calendar 1700–1760* (Dublin: Irish Academic Press, 1988). We are indebted to these works for the summary that follows.

29. *SJEP*, 2–4 Nov. 1725; T. J. Walsh 1973, 23, makes this observation of the Stradiotti concert of 8 Dec. 1725.

30. The arias are listed in Walsh 1973, 23. A previously unnoticed item in *The Dublin Weekly Journal* of 21 May 1726 announces the marriage, evidently in Dublin on 25 April, of "Madam Giovanna Stadiotti, singer, to Carlo Gambarina" after consultations with "Devines [*sic*] of Protestant and Roman Churches" only her father still objects to the marriage.

31. See index for a list of song titles.

32. More than one new piece premiered in Dublin in the following seasons: 1737–38 (2); 1738–39 (2); 1739–40 (2); 1741–42 (3); 1743–44 (3).

33. Since the term "ballad opera" is notoriously imprecise we have not attempted a generic definition here but have retained instead the description of the play as it appeared originally in advertisements.

34. Both theatres produced the same play on the same night as or within a few days of the other at least once and as many as six times each season: 1735–36 (2); 1736–37 (6); 1737–38 (3); 1738–39 (2); 1739–40 (1); 1740–41 (4); 1741–42 (5); 1742–43 (1); 1743–44 (2); 1744–45 (1).

35. During the eight seasons in question both Smock Alley and Aungier Street theatres brought out thirty-six new mainpieces; Smock Alley staged thirty-six new afterpieces, Aungier Street twenty-nine.

36. It should be noted in regard to the completeness of the record of Dublin performances during these seasons that theatre managers and benefit recipients made a special effort to advertise plays which were new to Dublin as well as long-term revivals. It seems to us unlikely that many plays in these categories have escaped notice in the calendar.

37. The pantomimes referred to are: Edward Phillips's *The Royal Chace* (over thirty consecutive performances at Covent Garden); William Pritchard's *The Fall of Phaeton* (twenty-two at Drury Lane); and two anonymous pantomimes, *Harlequin Restored; or, Taste a la Mode* (over forty at Drury Lane) and *Harlequin Shipwrecked* (eleven at Goodman's Fields). The plays which successfully premiered in London this season include: George Lillo's tragedy *Fatal Curiosity;* (seven Haymarket performances); Henry Fielding's *Tumble Down Dick* (twenty-one at the Haymarket); Thomas Philips's *The Rival Captains* (eight at the Haymarket); Aaron Hill's tragedy *Alzira* (nine at Lincoln's Inn Fields); James Sterling's tragedy *The Parricide* (five at Goodman's Fields), Abraham Langford's farce *The Lover His Own Rival* (fourteen at Goodman's Fields); Elizabeth Cooper's *The Nobleman* (three at the Haymarket); and Robert Drury's *The Rival Milliners* (seven London performances).

An explanation for the curious fact that many extraordinarily successful London pantomimes were not performed in Dublin may lie in the nature of the genre itself, it being very difficult to transport and reproduce from memory or drawings any piece that has mimimal dialogue or other textual elements and which relys so heavily on large casts, and requires expensive (usually new) scenery, machinery, costumes and exotic specialist performers such as equilibrists and tumblers.

# The Theatrical Seasons, 1720–1745

## 1720–1721 Season

Theatre operating: Smock Alley.

*Smock Alley Company:*
The number of recorded casts for this season is so few that the precise make-up of the Smock Alley Company must remain a matter for conjecture. Clearly, Thomas Elrington, Thomas Griffith, Lewis Layfield, and Benjamin Husband were members.

The evidence of the cast lists from the preceding and succeeding seasons suggests that any or all of the following actors and actresses may have been with the company during the 1720–21 season; no evidence exists to indicate that they were performing elsewhere:

(1719–20) Daugherty, Dumott, Henry Giffard, Thomas Hallam (this "Mr. Hallam" who first joined the company ca. 1707 is mistakenly identified as "Adam Hallam" in Clark, 1955, 124 and *passim*), James Vanderbank, John Watson (since 1713), John Watson, Jr., Miss Wolfe, Mrs. Martin (since 1714), Miss Waters, Ralph Elrington, Mrs. Giffard.

Dancers: Mrs. Moreau, née Miss Schoolding (since 1713), and presumably, therefore, Mons. Anthony Moreau.

(1721–22) Francis Elrington, Frisby, Mrs. Giffard, Mrs. Lyddal, Nancy Lyddal, H. Norris, Jr., Smith, Mrs. Vanderbank.

*Repertory:*
Mainpieces: Recorded performances: 5.
Afterpieces: None recorded.
Premieres: *Wexford Wells.*
Entr'acte entertainments: None recorded.
Command performances: None recorded.
Benefits:

Pre-February: Author—1.
Post-February: Manager—1; charity—1.

## 1720

Exact performance date unknown      SA.      *King Richard II.*

*Cast:* Duke of York—Hewlet; Lord Salisbury—Frisby; Bishop of Carlisle—Husband; Bolingbroke—Giffard; Earl of Northumberland—Layfield; Lord Ross—Watson; Lord Willoughby—Dogherty; Exton—Vanderbank; Lieutenant of Tower—Hallam; Queen—[Mrs.] Giffard; Lady Piercy—[Mrs.] Lyddal.

*Miscellaneous:* The title page of a promptbook of *King Richard II* in the Folger Shakespeare Library reads: "The Tragedy of King Richard the II: As it is Acted at the Theatre in Lincoln's-Inn-Fields. Altered from Shakespeare By Mr. Theobald. London: Printed for G. Strahan at the Golden Ball . . . 1720."

The cast is listed as above in the prompter's hand. All of the actors could have been at Smock Alley this season. The part of Richard, played in London by Ryan, and that of Duke of Aumerle, played in London by Smith, are both followed by a stroke (——) in the promptbook. At Smock Alley these parts may well have been played by Thomas Elrington and Thomas Griffith.

On p. 58 the names of Hallam, Doctor, Trefusis, and Vanderbank are appended to the following stage direction: "Exton [i.e., Vanderbank] and the Guard break in; part of them hurry away the Queen; the King snatches a sword, kills two of them, and in the Scuffle is killed by Exton." Since Hallam was playing the Lieutenant of the Tower, it seems possible that Doctor and Trefusis were playing tertiary roles in this scene. At any rate Doctor's name also appears at the bottom of the list of *Dramatis Personae* next to "Scene—The Tower of London," which might suggest that he was playing one of the Tower Guards. Trefesis had acted at Smock Alley for many years in minor roles (see Clark 1955, *passim*)].

### NOVEMBER

5    Sat.    SA.    *The Jew of Venice.*
*Cast:* None recorded.
*Miscellaneous:* [William Shakespeare's *The Merchant of Venice* adapted by George Granville, Lord Lansdowne.]

7    Mon.    SA.    *Wexford Wells; or, Summer Assizes.*
*Cast:* Capt. Novite—Griffith; Innkeeper—L. Layfield.
*Benefit:* Author [Matthew Concanen.]

*Miscellaneous:* [See Matthew Concanen, *Poems upon Several Occasions* (Dublin, 1722), pp. 30–31, for a "Prologue to Wexford Wells, Spoken by Mr. Giffard." See *Carson's Dublin Intelligence,* 5 Nov. 1720, for "A Ballad Sung by Mr. Layfield, who Acted the Inn-Keeper."

Nicoll 1977–79 (2:315) cites a Dublin printing of *Wexford Wells* in 1721, but no Smock Alley performance. The play is not listed in *LS.* Exhaustive inquiry has failed to locate a copy of the supposed Dublin edition.]

## 1721

APRIL

1   Sat.   SA.   *Hamlet.*
*Cast:* None recorded.
*Benefit:* The Distressed Weavers of the City.
*Miscellaneous:* Prologue by Dr. Thomas Sheridan, spoken by T. Elrington; Epilogue by Dr. Jonathan Swift, spoken by Griffith. [See "A Prologue Spoke by Mr. Elrington at the Theatre-Royal on Saturday the First of April. In the Behalf of the Distressed Weavers" (Dublin, 1721), BL. 1890 e. 5. f. 67; "An Epilogue As it was spoke by Mr. Griffith on Saturday the First of April" (Dublin, 1721), BL. 1890 e. 5. f. 68.]
*Financial:* Benefit raised £73 [*Gentleman's Journal,* (London), 15 Apr. 1721.]

[Passion Week 3–8 April]

JUNE

26   Mon.   SA.   *The Provoked Wife.*
*Cast:* Constant—Husband; Griffith—Razor.
*Benefit:* Griffith.

## 1721–1722 Season

Theatre operating: Smock Alley.

*Smock Alley Company:*
F. Elrington, R. Elrington, T. Elrington, Frisby, H. Giffard, Mrs. Giffard, Mrs. Grace, Griffith, T. Hallam, Husband, Mrs. Knapp, L. Layfield, Mrs. Lyddal, Nancy Lyddal, Mrs. Martin, Henry Norris, Jr., Smith, Vanderbank, Mrs. Vanderbank, J. Watson, Jr.,

Dancers: Probably Mr. and Mrs. Moreau.

*Repertory:*
Mainpieces: Recorded performances: 6.
Afterpieces: None recorded.
Possible performances: The advertisements for *Amphitryon; or, The Two Socias* at SA 3 Feb. 1738 state: "Not acted here these 16 years." Those for *Mithradates, King of Pontus* SA 1 Mar. 1742 state: "Not acted these 20 years."
Premiere: *The Rival Generals.*
Entr'acte entertainment: Dancing advertised.
Command Performances: 1
Benefits: Actor—2.

## 1721

[Exact date unavailable]      SA.      *Fatal Extravagance.*

*Cast:* [In undated Dublin edition] Belmour—T. Elrington; Courtney—Giffard; Bargrave—Smith; Louisa—Mrs. Giffard.
*Miscellaneous:* By Aaron Hill [Nicoll 1977–79 (2:336) indicates that the title-page of the 1720 London edition declares the author to be Joseph Mitchell, but it was included in Hill's *Works* 1760. This performance may have been of the original one act version].

[Exact date unavailable.].      SA.      *Love for Love.*

*Cast:* [printed in 1722 Dublin edition] Sir Sampson Legend—Vanderbank; Valentine—Giffard; Scandal—Husband; Tattle—J. Watson, Sr.; Ben—Griffith; Foresight—Hallam; Jeremy—R. Elrington; Trapland—F. Elrington; Buckram—H. Norris, Jr.; Angelica—Mrs. Knapp; Mrs. Foresight—Mrs. Vanderbank; Mrs. Frail—Mrs. Lyddal; Miss Prue—Miss Lyddal; Nurse—Mrs. Martin; Jenny—Mrs. Grace.

### OCTOBER

16   Mon.   SA.   *The Rover; or, The Banished Cavaliers.*
*Cast:* Rover—T. Elrington; Ned Brand—Griffith; Belvil—Husband.
*Command Performance:* Duke and Duchess of Dorset.
*Dancing:* With several new entertainments of dance never performed before.

**1722**

JANUARY

20   Sat.   SA.   *Othello.*
*Cast:* Othello—T. Elrington.
*Miscellaneous:* [Stockwell 1938, 59, cites W. H. Grattan-Flood, "Early
Shakespeare Representations in Ireland," *R E. S.,* 2, (Jan. 1926), 93, who
believes that there were performances of *Othello* on 15 and 20 January. We
can find no evidence of the 15 January performance.]
*Benefit:* T. Elrington.

MARCH

[Exact date unavailable]     SA.     *The Rival Generals.*
*Cast:* [listed in 31 Mar. 1722 Dublin edition] Iagello—Smith; Guiscardo—
Husband; Perolto—Frisby; Spinoli—F. Elrington; Lorenzo—R. Elrington;
Astromont—T. Elrington; Honorio—Giffard; Leonalta—Mrs. Lyddal;
Eloisa—Mrs. Knapp; Sygismunda—Miss Lyddal; Eugenia—Mrs. Grace.
*Miscellaneous:* [Premiere. See Concanen's "To the Author of the Rival Gen-
erals" in *Miscellaneous Poems* for lines praising the author, James Sterling,
as a native Irish playwright.]

APRIL

2   Mon.   SA.   *Oedipus.*
*Cast:* None listed.
*Benefit:* Husband.

[Passion Week 19–24 April]

## 1722–1723 Season

Theatre operating: Smock Alley.

*Smock Alley Company:*
F. Elrington, R. Elrington, T. Elrington, Frisby, Giffard, Mrs. Giffard, Mrs.
Grace, Griffith, T. Hallam, Husband, Mrs. Knapp, L. Layfield, Mrs. Lyddal,
Miss Nancy Lyddal, Mrs. Martin, H. Norris, Jr., T. Philips, Rosco, Schoold-
ing, Vanderbank, Mrs. Vanderbank, J. Watson, Jr.

Dancers: Moreau and Mrs. Moreau.

Scene Designer: Johann Vanderhagen.

*Repertory:*
Mainpieces: Recorded performances: 39 of 33 different plays (excluding 2 unspecified plays).
Afterpieces: 2 for 2 performances. This is the first season in which an afterpiece is recorded: *The What D'ye Call It,* 1 Apr. 1723.
Possible Performances: The advertisement for the performance of *The Adventures of Half an Hour* at AS on 20 Mar. 1735 states that the farce has not been acted "these 12 Years." See also the performance at NBDS on 28 Feb. 1732. See *Miscellaneous* of 8 Oct. 1722 for a possible performance of a farce entitled *Punch Turned Schoolmaster.*
Premiere: *The Deceit.*
Entr'acte Entertainments: None recorded.
Command Performances: None recorded. Government Nights: 3.
Benefits:
Pre-February: Manager—1; Actor—4; Charity—1.
Post-February: Manager—1; Actor—3.

*Significant events of this season:*
In the autumn of 1722 Edward Hopkins, the Chief Secretary to the Lord Lieutenant of Ireland, the Duke of Grafton, was appointed Master of the Revels in Ireland "with an increase in the customary salary of £300 a year, which was apparently, to be obtained from the players" (Swift 1910, 306). We may deduce from Swift's poem entitled "Billet to the Company of Players," that in order to avoid paying the £300 annual license fee which Hopkins imposed, Thomas Elrington applied to the Lord Mayor of Dublin for a license which permitted the SA company to perform as strolling players thus circumventing the fee.
    The calendar is silent on this affair. Apparently a compromise was arrived at, for an anonymous "Epilogue *to* Mr. Hoppy's *Benefit-Night, at* S-A" (quoted in Stockwell 1938, 52, and incorrectly identified as Swift's) implies that Hopkins was granted an annual benefit night at Smock Alley with guaranteed profit of £100 in lieu of his license fee. No record exists of Hopkins receiving a benefit after this season. Perhaps it was at this time that Thomas Elrington purchased from Hopkins the post of Deputy Master of the Revels formerly held by Ashbury.

**1723**

[Exact date unavailable]     SA.     *The Deceit.*
*Cast:* [listed in 1723 Dublin edition] Sir Peter Purblind—H. Norris, Jr.; Sir

John Corpulent—Schoolding; Charles—R. Elrington; Hearty—J. Watson, Sr.; Stretchwell—Rosco; Saygrace—T. Philips; Lucinda—Miss Lyddal; Miss Dolly—Mrs. Grace; Abigail—Mrs. Martin.
*Miscellaneous:* [Premiere. Comedy by Henry Norris, Jr. No reference to this play in *LS;* Nicoll does not list Dublin performance].

OCTOBER

8    Mon.    SA.    *The Rival Queens; or, The Death of Alexander the Great.*
*Cast:* None listed.
*Miscellaneous:* The principal Characters new Dressed.

"The Theatre Royal in Dublin is now Repairing, and will be put into such secure Substantial Order, that the Ladies and Gentry, can't have any Apprehensions of Danger for the future, and will open on Monday October the 8th with the Play of Alexander the Great. The principal Characters new Dressed, the Stage Enlarged and Ornamented after the manner of the Theatres in London, with large lofty Scenes entirely new and Painted by Mr. Vanderhegan, lately arrived from London" (*Harding's Impartial News-letter,* 2 Oct. 1722). See section on scenery in introduction.

*Afterpiece:* [See Concanen's *Miscellaneous Poems* for the text of "A Prologue to the Farce of Punch Turned Schoolmaster, spoken by Mr. Griffith, written by Mr. Sheridan," which suggests that a piece of that title was performed at SA this evening. A letter from Swift to Charles Ford dated 15 Apr. 1721 may suggest that this play was also performed in Dublin around that date. The prologue states that the play included a mock–puppet show and a satirical comment on the poor houses at SA resulting from the recent opening of Stretch's Puppet Theatre. The prologue also verifies that the farce was performed prior to the tragedy].

20    Sat.    SA.    Unspecified "Play."
*Miscellaneous:* Government Night; Anniversary of King George II's Coronation.

25    Thur.    SA.    *The Spanish Fryar.*
*Cast:* [listed in 1723 Dublin edition] Torrismond—T. Elrington; Gomez— Griffith; Bertram—R. Elrington; Alphonso—Schoolding; Lorenzo—Giffard; Raymond—F. Elrington; Pedro—J. Watson, Jr.; Dominic—Vanderbank; Leonora—Mrs. Knapp; Teresa—Mrs. Grace; Elvira—Mrs. Vanderbank.

29   Mon.   SA.   Unspecified "Play."
*Miscellaneous:* Government night; Anniversary of Prince of Wales' Birth.

NOVEMBER

5   Mon.   SA.   *Tamerlane.*
*Cast:* Bajazet—T. Elrington.
*Miscellaneous:* Government night; Anniversary of King William's Birth.

8   Thur.   SA.   *The Provoked Wife.*
*Cast:* Razor—Griffith.

19   Mon.   SA.   *The Tender Husband; or, The Accomplished Fools.*

## 1723–1724 Season

Theatre Operating: Smock Alley.

*Smock Alley Company:*
F. Elrington; R. Elrington; T. Elrington; Giffard; Mrs. Giffard; Mrs. Grace; Griffith; Master Adam Hallam; Thomas Hallam; Husband; Mrs. Knapp; L. Layfield; Mrs. Lyddal; Lyon (or Lyons); Mrs. Martin; H. Norris, Jr.; T. Philips; Rosco; Vanderbank; Mrs. Vanderbank; J. Watson, Sr.; J. Watson, Jr.

Dancers: Moreau; Mrs. Moreau.

*Repertory:*
Mainpieces: Recorded performances: 26 (of 23 different pieces including one unspecified "play").
Afterpieces: None recorded.
Entr'acte entertainments: None recorded, but the dancer Moreau received a benefit so there was almost certainly dancing.
Command Performances: None recorded.
Benefits:
Pre-February—Actor: 3.
Post-February—Actor: 4.

**1723**

OCTOBER

21   Mon.   SA.   Unspecified "Play."

*Miscellaneous:* Government night: Anniversary of the Coronation of George I.

**NOVEMBER**

4    Mon.    SA.    *Tamerlane.*
*Cast:* Bajazet—T. Elrington.
*Miscellaneous:* Government night; Anniversary of birth of William III.

18    Mon.    SA.    *Henry IV, with the Humours of Sir John Falstaff.*
*Cast:* Hotspur—T. Elrington; Falstaff—Griffith.

21    Thur.    SA.    *The Busy Body.*
*Cast:* Marplot—Griffith.

25    Mon.    SA.    *Cato.*
*Cast:* Cato—T. Elrington.

28    Thur.    SA.    *The Busy Body.*
*Cast:* None listed.

**DECEMBER**

2    Mon.    SA.    *Oroonoko; or, The Royal Slave.*
*Cast:* Oroonoko—T. Elrington; Daniel—Griffith; Ben—Giffard.

5    Thur.    SA.    *The Mistake; or, The Wrangling Lovers.*
*Cast:* Don Carlos—Giffard.

9    Mon.    SA.    *Hamlet.*
*Cast:* Hamlet—T. Elrington; Gravedigger—Griffith.
*Benefit:* F. Elrington.

12    Thur.    SA.    *Love for Love.*
*Cast:* Ben—Griffith.

16    Mon.    SA.    *Jane Shore.*
*Cast:* Dumont—T. Elrington.

30    Mon.    SA.    *The Unhappy Favourite; or, The Earl of Essex.*
*Cast:* Essex—T. Elrington.

**1724**

JANUARY

[Exact date unavailable].     SA.     *A Wife and No Wife.*
*Cast:* [listed in 1724 Dublin edition] Justice Quibble—Vanderbank; Captain Gallant—R. Elrington; Modish—Watson; Commick—Hallam; Scribble—T. Philips; Boy—A. Hallam; Lady Quibble—Mrs. Moreau; Miss Flirt—Mrs. Grace; Pert—Mrs. Martin.
*Miscellaneous:* [By Charles Coffey. Premiere; Irish author. Farce. Nicoll 1977–79 (2:315), follows Baker's *Biographia Dramatica* (1812, 1:408) in listing Coffey's farce as never having been acted, but as having been printed at London in an unverified 1732 octavo edition. Ample evidence of its Smock Alley production, however, appears in a hitherto unrecorded Dublin edition, appended to the copy of Coffey's *Poems and Songs* (Dublin, 1724), in the Joly Collection, N.L.I. The play bears the following title page: "Wife and No Wife, a New Farce of One Act. As it was Perform'd by His Majesty's Servants at the Theatre in Dublin with great Applause. Dublin, 1724." The cast is listed as above. Not listed in *LS.*]

6     Mon.     SA.     *Aesop; or, The Politick Statesman.*
*Cast:* Aesop—Lyon.

9     Thur.     SA.     *The Orphan; or, The Unhappy Marriage.*
*Cast:* Chamont—T. Elrington.
*Benefit:* Vanderbank.

13     Mon.     SA.     *The Pilgrim.*
*Cast:* Pilgrim—T. Elrington.

16     Thur.     SA.     *Othello.*
*Cast:* Othello—T. Elrington; Roderigo—Griffith.
*Benefit:* Moreau.

20     Mon.     SA.     *The Beaux' Stratagem.*
*Cast:* Archer—T. Elrington; Scrub—Griffith.

23     Thur.     SA.     *The Distrest Mother.*
*Cast:* Orestes—T. Elrington.
*Benefit:* Mrs. Ashbury.

27     Mon.     SA.     *The Merry Wives of Windsor.*
*Cast:* Sir Hugh—T. Elrington.

[Passion Week 20 March–4 April]

MAY

13　Wed.　SA.　*The Conscious Lovers.* V
*Cast:* None listed.
*Miscellaneous:* [A "new" prologue, delivered by Husband (see BL broadside 839. m. 1–192) and a "new" epilogue, spoken by Mrs. Knapp, thought lost, are transcribed in W. J. Lawrence, Notebook 4:106–12.]

18　Mon.　SA.　*The Captives.*
*Cast:* Sophernes—T. Elrington.
*Benefit:* T. Elrington.

JUNE

10　Wed.　SA.　*King Lear and His Three Daughters.*
*Cast:* None listed.
*Miscellaneous:* [W. J. Lawrence, 4: 113 is the only source for this performance.]

11　Thurs.　SA.　*Venice Preserved.*
*Cast:* Belvidera—Mrs. Knapp.
*Benefit:* Mrs. Knapp.

29　Mon.　SA.　*Hamlet.*
*Cast:* Hamlet—T. Elrington; Gravedigger—Griffith.
*Benefit:* Watson.

JULY

6　Mon.　SA.　*Love Makes a Man; or, The Fop's Fortune.*
*Cast:* Don Carlos—T. Elrington; Don Cholerick—Griffith.
*Benefit:* Hallam.

## 1724–1725 Season

Theatre operating: Smock Alley.

*Smock Alley Company:*
Alcorn, Dash, Davis, F. Elrington, R. Elrington, T. Elrington, H. Giffard, Mrs. Giffard, Mrs. Grace, Griffith, A. Hallam, Husband, Mrs. Knapp, L.

Layfield, Mrs. Lyddal, Mrs. Martin, Moore, Moreau, Mrs. Moreau, H. Norris, Jr., Rosco, Spiller, Mrs. Spiller (from LIF.), Mrs. Sterling (formerly Miss Nancy Lyddal), Vanderbank, J. Watson, Jr.

*Repertory:*
Mainpieces: Recorded performances: 11 (of 7 different pieces excluding 2 unspecified plays).
Afterpieces: None recorded.
Possible performances: The advertisement for *Aesop* at AS on 7 June 1740 states: "Not acted these 15 years." This reference may, however, be to the recorded performance at SA on 6 June 1726.
Entr'acte Entertainments: None recorded.
Command Performances: 0.
Benefits: 3—Managers.

---

**1724**

[Exact date unavailable.]     SA.     *The Conscious Lovers.*

*Cast:* [listed in 1725 Dublin edition] Wisewod—Vanderbank; Loveless—Giffard; Sir Novelty—Watson; Elder Worthy—Rosco; Young Worthy—R. Elrington; Snap—Griffith; Sly—Moore; Amanda—Mrs. Knapp; Narcissa—Mrs. Sterling; Hillaria—Mrs. Moreau; Flareit—Mrs. Grace; Woman to Amanda and Maid to Flareit—Mrs. Martin.

[Exact date unavailable.]     SA.     *The Amorous Widow; or, The Wanton Wife.*

*Cast:* [listed in 1725 Dublin edition] Lovemore—T. Elrington; Barnaby Brittle—Griffith; Sir Peter Pride—L. Layfield; Cunningham—Giffard; Merryman—Vanderbank; Clodpole—F. Elrington; Jeremy—Dash; Jeffery—Alcorn; Lady Pride—Mrs. Martin; Lady Laycock—Mrs. Vanderbank; Mrs. Brittle—Mrs. Knapp; Philadelphia—Mrs. Sterling; Prudence—Mrs. Grace; Damaris—Mrs. Spiller.

[Exact date unavailable.]     SA.     *The Double Gallant; or, The Sick Lady's Cure.*

*Cast:* [listed in 1725 Dublin edition] Sir Soloman Sadlife—Vanderbank; Clerimont—Watson; Careless—R. Elrington; Atall—Giffard; Capt. Strut—L. Layfield; Sir Squabble Splithair—H. Norris, Jr.; Saunter—F. Elrington; Sir Harry Atall—Alcorn; Wilful—Moore; Supple—Rosco; Finder—Davis;

Lady Sadlife—Mrs. Moreau; Lady Dainty—Mrs. Knapp; Clarinda—Mrs. Spiller (lately arrived from London); Sylvia—Mrs. Sterling; Wishwell—Mrs. Martin; Situp—Mrs. Grace.

[Exact date unavailable.]    SA.    *She Would and She Would Not; or, The Kind Imposter.*

*Cast:* [listed in 1725 Dublin edition] Don Manuel—Vanderbank; Don Philip—Husband; Octavio—R. Elrington; Trappanti—Griffith; Soto—F. Elrington; Hypolita—Mrs. Knapp; Rosara—Mrs. Moreau; Flora—Mrs. Sterling; Viletta—Mrs. Martin.

[Exact date unavailable.]    SA.    *Tunbridge Walks; or, The Yeoman of Kent.*

*Cast:* [listed in 1725 Dublin edition] Reynard—Giffard; Woodcock—Vanderbank; Loveworth—Rosco; Squib—Moore; Maiden—J. Watson, Jr.; Belinda—Mrs. Sterling; Hillaria—Mrs. Spiller; Mrs. Goodfellow—Mrs. Martin; Penelope—Mrs. Grace.

# 1724

## NOVEMBER

30    Mon.    SA.    *All for Love.*
*Cast:* Antony—T. Elrington; Cleopatra—Mrs. Knapp; Octavia—Mrs. Spiller (from LIF).
*Benefit:* T. Elrington.

## DECEMBER

3    Thur.    SA.    *Love for Love.*
*Cast:* None listed.
*Benefit:* Griffith.

# 1725

## MARCH

1    Mon.    SA.    Unspecified "Play."
*Miscellaneous:* Government Night: Birthday of Caroline, Princess of Wales.

[Passion Week 22–27 March]

APRIL

22    Thur.    SA.    *Love for Love.*
*Cast:* Ben—Griffith.
*Miscellaneous:* Birthday Lord Carteret. [Occasional Prologue and Epilogue written by "C[harles] C[offey]" and spoken by T. Elrington and Griffith, respectively (BL 1890. e. 5. 98). See also T. C. D. Irish Pamphlets 1725–27 (A 7–4, fol. 110) for a satirical broadside referring to this as an "empty" prologue.]

MAY

28    Fri.    SA.    Unspecified "Play."
*Miscellaneous:* Government night: Birthday George I. With a Prologue spoken by Mr. Griffith on this occasion. [See BL 839. m. 23, 1–192 for text as well as another prologue "Written by J[oseph] T[refusis?], lately one of his Majesty's Servants," Dublin 1725.]

JUNE

24    Thur.    SA.    *The Twin Rivals.*
*Cast:* None listed.
*Miscellaneous:* Masons in attendance.
*Comment:* "Griffith was Secretary to the Grand Lodge, and greatly beloved by the brotherhood; his benefits were, in consequence, constantly bespoke by the grand master, who, attended by the brethren, always walked in procession to the theatre, and sat on the stage those nights. This circumstance ensured him a full house, from which, and his gold tickets, he reaped great emolument" (Hitchcock 1788–93, 1:57–58.)
    "After the Entertainment they all went to the Play, with their Aprons, etc. the private Brothers sat in the Pit, but the *Grand Master,* Deputy Grand Master, and Grand Wardens, in the Government's box, at the Conclusion of the Play, Mr. *Griffith,* the Player, who is a Brother, sung the Free Mason's Apprentice's Song, the Grand Master and the whole Brotherhood joyning in the Chorus" (*DWJ,* 26 June 1725). [June 24 was St. John's Day, a Festival Day of the Freemasons and Dublin tailors (Frederick Armitage, *A Short Masonic History* (London, 1911), 2:39). This performance seems to mark the inauguration of annual Masonic nights (the dates shifting from year to

year) at the Theatre Royal for Griffith's benefit which continued until the late 1730s.]
*Benefit:* Griffith.

## 1725-1726 Season

Theatre operating: Smock Alley.

*Smock Alley Company:*
Alcorn, Dash, Davis, F. Elrington, R. Elrington, T. Elrington, H. Giffard, Mrs. Giffard, Mrs. Grace, Griffith, A. Hallam, Husband, Mrs. Knapp, L. Layfield, Mrs. Lyddal, Mrs. Martin, Moore, H. Norris, Jr., Rosco, Simms, Mrs. Sterling, Vanderbank, Mrs. Vanderbank, J. Watson, Jr.

*Repertory:*
Mainpieces: Recorded performances: 11 (of 7 different pieces excluding 1 unspecified "play").
Afterpieces: None recorded.
Possible Performances: In Notebook 4, 125ff., W. J. Lawrence gives his reasons for suspecting that the Rev. James Sterling's tragedy *The Parricide* was first performed in Dublin ca. 1726. The notebook contains Lawrence's transcription of an undated manuscript epilogue to the play, spoken by Mrs. Sterling. The performance of *The Tempest* on 15 Sept. 1735 AS states that the play was "not acted here but once these 10 years."
Entr'acte entertainment: None recorded.
Command Performances: None recorded (two Government nights).
Benefits:
Pre-February—None recorded.
Post-February—Actor: 1, House servant—1, Other—1.

## 1725

[Exact date unavailable.]      SA.      *The Island Princess; or, The Generous Portuguese.*

*Cast:* [listed in 1727 Dublin edition] Armusia—T. Elrington; Ruidias—F. Elrington; Piniero—Rosco; King of Tidore—Giffard: Governor—Vanderbank; King of Bakam—Alcorn; Prince of Syana—J. Watson, Jr.; Townsman—Griffith; Townsman—L. Layfield; Townsman—Simms; Quisara—Mrs. Sterling; Panura—Mrs. Grace.

*Miscellaneous:* Performed before May 1726, when Griffith went to Drury Lane in London.

[Exact date unavailable.]     SA.     *The Northern Lass; or, The Nest of Fools.*

*Cast:* [listed in 1726 Dublin edition] Sir Philip Luckless—T. Elrington; Sir Paul Squelch—L. Layfield; Mr. Tridewell—Giffard; Mr. Bullfinch—Vanderbank; Mr. Widgin—J. Watson, Jr.; Mr. Nonsense—Griffith; Anvil—Rosco; Pate—F. Elrington; Beavis—Alcorn; Howd'ye—Hallam; Clerk—Dash; Vex'em—Simms; Fitchow—Mrs. Vanderbank; Mrs. Constance—Mrs. Sterling; Constance Holdup—Mrs. Grace.

*Miscellaneous:* Performed before May 1726, when Griffith went to Drury Lane in London.

[Exact date unavailable.]     SA.     *Anna Bullen; or, Virtue Betrayed.*

*Cast:* [listed in 1726 Dublin edition] King Henry—Vanderbank; Cardinal—F. Elrington; Northumberland—Rosco; Percy—Giffard; Rochford—R. Elrington; Anna Bullen—Mrs. Knapp; Lady Diana Talbot—Mrs. Sterling; Lady Elizabeth—Mrs. Vanderbank.

**1725**

OCTOBER

[Exact date unavailable.]     SA.     Concert.
*Cast:* Signora Stradiotti.
*Miscellaneous:* [This performance may have taken place in October or in September. The confusion arises from an item in the *St. James's Evening Post* of 2–4 November 1725 dated "Dublin Oct. 13" which reads as follows: "On the 26th Instant [*sic*] at our Theatre here was performed the first Consort of Musick by the famous Italian singer Stradiotti, lately arrived here. His Excellency Lord Carteret and his Lady, together with the Lord Chancellor, with a numerous Concourse of the Nobility and Gentry were present. . . ." September 26 fell on a Sunday, a day when no public entertainments were permitted.

    Whether it took place in September, October, or November, this concert predates the one of 8 December which Walsh and Boydell cite as the first given by Signora Stradiotti in Dublin.]

20     Wed.     SA.     Unspecified "Play."
*Miscellaneous:* Government Night: Anniversary of George I Coronation.

NOVEMBER

4    Thur.    SA.    *Tamerlane.*
*Miscellaneous:* Government Night: Birthday William III; Carteret present.

DECEMBER

8    Wed.    SA.    Concert of Handel Arias.
*Cast:* Sung by Signora Stradiotti.
*Miscellaneous:* [Walsh 1973, 23, cites the original libretto in T. C. D. "A Cantata composed by Philip Percival, Esq." Both Walsh and Boydell 1988, 42, observe that Sga. Stradiotti was "the first Italian *prima donna* to sing in Ireland." She was also the first to sing Handel's arias there. See concert performance of uncertain date above.]


**1726**

JANUARY

[Exact date unavailable].         SA.    *The Enchanter; or, Harlequin Merlin.*
*Cast:* None listed.
*Miscellaneous:* Music by Dr. Musgrave Heighington. [Boydell 1988, 42, notes that *FDJ,* 8 Feb. 1726 announces that this music has been printed and published by Neal.]

[Passion Week 4–9 April]

APRIL

21    Thur.    SA.    *King Henry IV, with the Humours of Sir John Falstaff.*
*Cast:* Hotspur—T. Elrington.
*Benefit:* Eastham (boxkeeper).

MAY

9    Mon.    SA.    *Theodosius; or, The Force of Love.*
*Cast:* None listed.
*Benefit:* Husband.

JUNE

6    Mon.    SA.    *Aesop; or, The Politick Statesman.*
*Cast:* None listed.

*Miscellaneous:* [Coffey may have acted in this play. See the performance of his *The Beggar's Wedding,* 24 Mar. 1729.]
*Benefit:* Charles Coffey.

## 1726–1727 Season

Theatre operating: Smock Alley.

*Smock Alley Company* (probable):
Alcorn, Dash, F. Elrington, R. Elrington, T. Elrington, H. Giffard, Mrs. Giffard, Griffith, A. Hallam, Husband, Mrs. Knapp, L. Layfield, Mrs. Lyddal, Mrs. Martin, H. Norris, Jr., Rosco, Simms, Mrs. Sterling, Vanderbank, Mrs. Vanderbank, J. Watson, Jr.

Dancers: Moreau and Mrs. Moreau.

*Repertory:*
Mainpieces: Recorded performances: 1 (18th-century tragedy).
Afterpieces: None recorded.
Possible performances: Advertisements for the performance of *The Rival Queans, with the Humours of Alexander the Great* SA 18 Feb. 1737 state that the piece was "Not acted in Dublin these 10 years."
Entr'acte Entertainments: None recorded.
Command Performances: None recorded (one Government night).
Benefits: None recorded.

## 1726

NOVEMBER

4     Fri.     SA.     *Tamerlane.*
*Cast:* None listed.
*Miscellaneous:* Government Night: Anniversary birth King William III.

## 1727–1728 Season

Theatre operating: Smock Alley.

*Smock Alley Company:*

Alcorn, Dash, F. Elrington, R. Elrington, T. Elrington, H. Giffard, Mrs. Giffard, Griffith, Hamilton, Mrs. Hamilton, Husband, L. Layfield, Mrs. Lyddal, Esther Lyddal, H. Norris, Jr., Reynolds, Mrs. Reynolds, Rosco, Sheridan, Simms, Mrs. Sterling, Vanderbank, Mrs. Vanderbank, J. Watson, Jr.

*Repertory:*
Mainpieces: Recorded performances: 12 (all of *The Beggar's Opera*). [*The Beggar's Opera* was certainly performed at SA more than 12 times this season. On 10 May 1728 Swift informed Alexander Pope that Gay's ballad opera had been performed twenty times (Swift 1963–65, 3:285). The popularity of the piece at benefits late in the season and the many performances of the work the following season suggest perhaps as many as thirty in its first season at Smock Alley.]
Afterpieces: None recorded.
Possible Performance: The advertisement for *the Double Gallant* of 5 Mar. 1733 at SA states that it has not been "acted here these 5 years."
Entr'acte entertainments: None recorded.
Command performances: None recorded.
Benefits: Manager—1; Actor—1.

---

**1728**

MARCH

[Exact date unavailable.]        SA.        *The Beggar's Opera.*
*Cast:* Polly—Mrs. Sterling; Macheath—L. Layfield.
*Miscellaneous:* [The precise date of this performance is not known, but Thursday, the 14th, seems a likely one for the first performance in Dublin. See *Comment* 16 March SA.]

16        Sat.        SA.        *The Beggar's Opera.*
*Cast:* None listed.
*Comment:* "Saturday night last [i.e. 16 Mar. 1728] the Beggar's Opera was a second time performed at our theatre with great applause; his Excellency the Lord Carteret being present, the Boxes were so crowded with Ladies, and the Pit and Stage with Gentlemen that it was remarked above half the people in the Gallery were Persons of Distinction in Disguise. That Place was also so crowded that great Numbers of our Citizens were forced to postpone the Pleasure of seeing the Performance Till Thursday next (*DI*, 19 Mar. 1728).
Swift wrote to John Gay that Dublin was "as full of it . . . as London

can be, continual[ly] acting and house Cramm'd and the Lord Lieut[enant] severall times there, laughing his heart out" (Swift 1963–65, 3:276).

21    Thur.    SA.    *The Beggar's Opera.*
*Cast:* None listed.
*Comment:* "[The Beggar's Opera was] so far the Topick of General Conversation that they who have not seen it, are hardly thought worth speaking to by their Acquaintance, and are only Admitted into Discourse on their Promise of going to see it the first Opportunity." Indeed, before the end of the month the attendance had reached such proportions "that boxes are bespoke for sixteen or eighteen nights in advance" (*DI*, 23 Mar. 1728).

"This Day will be published Namby Pamby's new Epilogue to the Beggar's Opera. Written by Mr. Gay, as it was spoken at the Theatre in this City" (*DI*, 19 Mar. 1728).

23    Sat.    SA.    *The Beggar's Opera.*
*Cast:* None listed.

30    Sat.    SA.    *The Beggar's Opera.*
*Cast:* None listed.

APRIL

1    Mon.    SA.    *The Beggar's Opera.*
*Cast:* None listed.

4    Thur.    SA.    *The Beggar's Opera.*
*Cast:* None listed.

6    Sat.    SA.    *The Beggar's Opera.*
*Cast:* None listed.

8    Mon.    SA.    *The Beggar's Opera.*
*Cast:* None listed.

11    Thur.    SA.    *The Beggar's Opera.* V.
*Cast:* None listed.
*Benefit:* Mrs. Sterling.
*Miscellaneous:* 10th performance.
    "Mrs. Sterling, who acted Polly Peachum's part in the Beggar's Opera, played it with so much applause, that the House called out that she might have a benefit night, and obliged the players to give it her, which she had on

Thursday, and received £105. 14s., and beside 30 odd pounds thrown to her on the Stage . . ." (*DG*, 9–13 Apr. 1728).

[On this day there appeared "An excellent new ballad inscribed to the Irish Polly Peachum on her Benefit of *The Beggar's Opera*. Given at the General Desire of the Nobility and Gentry of Dublin, April XI, MDCCXXVIII. By a Person of Honour." BL 839. m. 23–167.]

*Financial:* Receipts for this benefit were £105 14s., plus "thirty odd Pounds thrown to her on the Stage" (*DG*, 9–13 Apr. 1728).

13   Sat.   SA.   *The Beggar's Opera.*
*Cast:* Polly—Mrs. Sterling.
*Miscellaneous:* Eleventh time in this Kingdom.

MAY

[On 10 May 1728 Swift wrote to Alexander Pope reporting the 20th performance of *The Beggar's Opera* in Dublin (Swift 1963–65, 3:285).]

JUNE

[At the invitation of the Drogheda Corporation the SA company left for that city on 11 June to perform *The Beggar's Opera* a few nights. They intended to play it again in Dublin on 18 June for Griffith's benefit, but later decided to extend their stay in Drogheda and therefore could not return in time to act "with Due Decorum" on the 18th (*DI*, 11, 15, and 18 June 1728). The provincial performances involved some cast changes; the issue of the *DI* of 15 June 1738 observes: "Miss [Esther] Lyddel being rec[k]oned to do Polly Peachum, so well, as worthily to rival her Sister, Mrs. Sterling. . . ." Boydell 1988, 45, places these Drogheda performances the following summer.]

24   Mon.   SA.   *The Beggar's Opera.*
*Cast:* None listed.
*Benefit:* Griffith.

# 1728—1729 Season

Theatre operating: Smock Alley.

*Smock Alley Company:*
Alcorn, Dash, Mrs. Davis (or Davies), Delane, F. Elrington, Ralph Elrington, Richard Elrington, T. Elrington (from DL in April), H. Giffard, Mrs. Giffard, Griffith, Husband, L. Layfield, Lewis Layfield, Jr., Robert Layfield, Jack

Layfield, Mrs. Lester, Mrs. Lyddal, Esther Lyddal, Mrs. Mathews, Nelson, H. Norris, Jr., Mrs. Norris, Paget, Rosco, Mrs. Seale, Sheridan, Simms, Mrs. Sterling, Vanderbank, Mrs. Vanderbank, J. Watson, Jr.

Dancers: The Moreaus danced at LIF in London entire 1728–29 season after coming from Paris *LS,* pt. 2, vol. 2, 991.

House Servants: Eastham (boxkeeper), Morgan (officekeeper), Wright (Treasurer).

*Repertory:*
Mainpieces: Recorded performances: 26 (of 16 different pieces excluding 1 unspecified "Play").
[As the entry for 7 October 1728 suggests, there were certainly more performances of *The Beggar's Opera* than the six recorded. Hitchcock (I:42) erroniously places the 40th performance (since its premiere—the advertisement for the performance of 7 Oct. states that it is only the second of this season) on 28 Dec. instead of 16 Dec. 1728. The illnesses of both Griffith and Mrs. Sterling mentioned in *DI,* 31 Dec. 1728 and 18 Jan. 1729 delayed further presentation of the play for five weeks. At this time Swift wrote some reflections upon "this Dramatick Piece, so singular in the Subject, and the Manner, so much an Original." Swift vigorously defended "several worthy Clergymen in this City [who] went privately to see The Beggar's Opera represented," and he berated "the fleering Coxcombs in the Pit [who] amused themselves with making Discoveries and spreading the Names of those Gentlemen around the Audience" (*The Intelligencer,* (Dublin, 1728), no. III, pp. 3–7).]
Afterpieces: Total Performances: 4.
Premieres:
*Chuck; or, The School-Boy's Opera*
*The Beggar's Wedding*
Possible Performances: The advertisement for the performance of *The Indian Emperor* in *FDJ,* 1 Feb. 1732 states that the play has not been acted "these four years." There may also have been an unrecorded performance of *The District Mother,* see performance of 7 Apr. 1729. *DI,* 14 June 1729 indicates that "a new Entertainment called *Flora; or, Hob's Opera* is in rehearsal at the theatre and will be soon exhibited to the town. . . ." *FDJ,* 13–16 Sept. 1729 states that *Flora* has been published "As it is Acted . . . at the Theatre in Dublin."
Entr'acte entertainments: Singing and dancing.
Command Performances: None recorded (4 Government nights).
Benefits:
Pre-February: Manager—2, Actor—2.
Post-February: Manager—1, Actor—4, Author—1, House Servants—3.

*Significant events:*
Newspaper advertisements for the performance of 27 Jan. 1729 include the earliest known instances of two practices occasionally applied on special nights in Dublin theatres: 1. the "laying together" of the boxes and the pit, either whole or in part, at the higher box-seat charge; 2. the "railing in" of the front benches in the upper gallery to form a "box" quite separate from the area to the rear. This second device was continued only a few years. The notices (for Layfield's benefit) also specified, for the first time in Dublin, the various admission fees.

## 1728

[Exact date unavailable.]     SA.     *Rule a Wife and Have a Wife.*

*Cast:* [listed first in 1761 Dublin edition]: Duke of Medina—Rosco; Don Juan—R. Elrington; Periz—H. Giffard; Alonzo—J. Watson, Jr.; Sanchio—Paget; Leon—L. Layfield; Cacafogo—Vanderbank; Lorenzo—Sheridan; Margarita—Esther Lyddal; Estifania—Mrs. Sterling; Althea—Mrs. Lester; Clara—Mrs. Norris; Old Woman—H. Norris, Jr.; Maid—Alcorn.

### OCTOBER

7     Mon.     SA.     *The Beggar's Opera.*
*Cast:* None listed.
*Miscellaneous:* Second performance this season.

11     Fri.     SA.     *Love for Love.*
*Cast:* None listed.
*Miscellaneous:* Government Night: Anniversary of King George II's Coronation. Special occasional prologue spoke by Griffith.
*Command:* Lords Justice.

30     Wed.     SA.     Unspecified "Play."
*Miscellaneous:* Government Night: Anniversary of King George II's Birth.

### DECEMBER

2     Mon.     SA.     *The Beggar's Opera.*
*Cast:* None listed.
*Miscellaneous:* 38th performance [presumably since its Dublin premiere. Griffith spoke a prologue on English poetry in which Gay was eulogised.]
*Benefit:* Griffith.

5    Thur.    SA.    *The Beggar's Opera.*
*Cast:* None listed.

16    Mon.    SA.    *The Beggar's Opera.*
*Cast:* None listed.
*Miscellaneous:* 40th time [since its premiere.]
*Benefit:* Vanderbank.

19    Thur.    SA.    *The Provoked Husband; or, A Journey to London.*
*Cast:* None listed.

21    Sat.    SA.    *The Provoked Husband.*
*Cast:* None listed.
*Miscellaneous:* Second time.

**1729**

JANUARY

13    Mon.    SA.    *The Provoked Husband.*
*Cast:* None listed.
*Miscellaneous:* Third time.

20    Mon.    SA.    *The Beaux' Stratagem.*
*Cast:* Archer—Giffard; Gibbet—F. Elrington; Sullen—L. Layfield; Boni-
face—Vanderbank; Dorinda—Esther Lyddal; Lady Bountiful—Mrs. Vand-
erbank; Mrs. Sullen—Mrs. Sterling (her first appearance since her illness).
*Miscellaneous:* Government night: Anniversary of birth of Prince of Wales.
Boxes free to the Ladies. With a new occasional prologue spoken by F.
Elrington [published in *DI,* 21 Jan. 1729.]

23    Thur.    SA.    *The Beggar's Opera.*
*Cast:* None listed.

27    Mon.    SA.    *The Conscious Lovers.*
*Cast:* None listed.
*Miscellaneous:* Benefit at the desire of several persons of quality. The boxes
and pit will be laid together. Pit and boxes, a British Crown; middle gallery,
2s.; box in the upper gallery, 1s.
*Benefit:* Layfield.
                                        and
*Afterpiece: Chuck; or, The School-Boy's Opera.*
*Cast:* [listed in 1729 Dublin edition]: Tom Chuck—Master Robert Layfield;

Ned Sneak—Master Jack Layfield; Will Satchel—Nelson; Ezekiel Careful—
Norris; Dyonisius, the Schoolmaster—Paget; Miss Polly Sampler—Master
Richard Elrington; Suky Sly—Master Lewis Layfield.
*Miscellaneous:* [By Charles Coffey. The only known copy of this piece, a
small octavo of sixteen leaves, is in the Bodleian Library, Oxford. It bears
the title page: "Chuck: or, the School-Boy's Opera, Done on the Plan of the
Beggar's Opera in Verse, Heroick, Lyrick, Comick, and Tragick. The Songs
adapted to Italian Airs, Ballad Tunes, etc. With a Preface, containing some
Remarks on the Beggar's Opera. Dedicated to the Author of the Beggar's
Opera. By Mr. Cibber. Dublin: Printed, and Sold by James Hoey and George
Faulkner, at the Pamphlet Shop in Skinner-Row, opposite the Tholsel. 1729."
　*Chuck* was published in Dublin on 15 Feb. 1729 (*FDJ,* 15 Feb. 1729), but
Coffey concealed his authorship. In the preface he claimed, no doubt play-
fully, that he, rather than the author of the "fortunate" *Beggar's Opera,* was
"the first who thought of Burlesquing the Italian Opera." On the title page
he had attributed authorship to Colley Cibber, but the Dublin public knew
well that Gay had first offered his piece to Cibber, the Drury Lane manager,
and that Cibber had made the costly mistake of refusing to produce it.
　No performance listed in *LS;* Nicoll 1977–79, 2: 367, does not mention
an author or Dublin publication, but follows Baker 1812, 2:102, listing an
unverified 1736 London edition.]
*Music:* The piece contains seventeen original lyrics, sung "to the Tunes of
old English Ballads, Italian Airs, and Childish Ditties" (*FDJ,* 21 and 25 Jan.
1729).

FEBRUARY

27　Thur.　SA.　*The Constant Couple.*
*Cast:* None listed.
*Miscellaneous:* [Norris spoke an "entertaining Prologue while riding on an
Ass, to the great Diversion of the Audience." Published in *DI,* 1 Mar. 1729.]
*Benefit:* H. Norris, Jr.
and
*Afterpiece: The Cobler of Preston.*
*Cast:* None listed.

MARCH

1　Thur.　SA.　*The Recruiting Officer.*
*Cast:* None listed.
*Miscellaneous:* Government night: Anniversary of Queen Caroline's birth.
Lords Justice present. With a special prologue spoken by Griffith (published
in *DI,* 4 Mar. 1729).

3   Mon.   SA.   *King Lear and His Three Daughters.*
*Cast:* None listed.
*Benefit:* Mrs. Seale.
*Miscellaneous:* [Mrs. Seale joined the company in the current season and had been acquiring some notoriety as the protegé of James O'Hara, the second Lord Tyrawley. Consequently, a crowded house greeted her "notwithstanding the Mean Insinuations Publish'd . . . throughout This City . . . by some Malicious Persons, to hinder the Success of the Play." (*DI,* 4 Mar. 1729). She left Ireland for the Haymarket Theatre three weeks later. (*DI,* 25 Mar. 1729.)
   Norris spoke a new prologue in the character of a Nobody.]
*Singing and Dancing:* Singing and Dancing between the pieces. The song of "Mad Tom of Bedlam" to be sung by a Gentleman for his Diversion.

                                    and

*Afterpiece: Hob; or, The Country Wake.*
*Cast:* Hob—Griffith.

13   Thur.   SA.   *The Beggar's Opera.*
*Cast:* None listed.
*Benefit:* Eastham (boxkeeper).
*Miscellaneous:* Griffith spoke the prologue of Nobody.

24   Mon.   SA.   *The Beggar's Wedding.*
*Cast:* [listed in 1729 Dublin edition] Alderman Quorum—Vanderbank; Chaunter—F. Elrington; Hunter—L. Layfield; Dash—Nelson; Mump—Alcorn; Swab—Dash; Scrip—Norris; Cant—Paget; Griff—Sheridan; Gage—Watson; Phebe—Mrs. Sterling; Mrs. Chaunter—Mrs. Lyddal; Tippet—Mrs. Vanderbank.
*Miscellaneous:* [ballad opera, later revived as *Phoebe*] First time on any stage. Boxes one British Crown, Pit 3s. British, Middle Gallery, 2s., Box in Upper Gallery 1s. There was a thin house, the Town being empty.
   [A "Preface to the Reader," which appears only in the 1729 Dublin edition, indicates that Coffey submitted his manuscript to Griffith on 30 Oct. 1728, but Griffith elected not to undertake production while *The Beggar's Opera* was still drawing large houses. Finally, "at the General Desire of our Quality . . . with a Variety of Songs, Humourous Dances and other Decorations" (*DI,* 22 Mar. 1729) the play was announced at the higher admission prices customary on special nights.
   In his preface Coffey blamed the failure of the play in Dublin on drastic revisions of his script. The Smock Alley production wholly eliminated the parts of the six lusty female beggars who held singing bouts with "a hearty Bouze of Usquebagh" and also cut the closing wedding ceremony that gave title to the ballad opera. If, Coffey observes, this colorful climax to the play's design had not been omitted, the last scene "which seem'd to lagg

and pull so much [at Smock Alley], wou'd have concluded with infinitely more Life, Spirit, and Success" (Coffey 1724, ii–iii).

See also a satirical broadside on Coffey's lack of theatrical success entitled "Doctor Anthony's Advice to the Hibernian Aesop." BL 1890. e. 5, no. 106. The entry for Coffey in the DNB states: "Being deformed in person he acted Aesop at the Theatre in Dublin." See also Baker 1812, 1:93.]
*Singing and Dancing:* Includes six songs with Irish tunes, among them: "Ellen-a-Roon" and "The Highway to Dublin." See F. L. Harrison, "Music, Poetry and Polity in the Age of Swift," *Eighteenth-Century Ireland* 1 (1986); 37–63.

27    Thur.    SA.    *The Beggar's Wedding.*
*Cast:* None listed.
*Miscellaneous:* [This performance met with "great Applause but before a thin Audience, the Town at present being very Empty" (*DI*, 29 Mar. 1729).]

29    Sat    SA.    *The Beggar's Wedding.*    V.
*Cast:* None listed.
*Benefit:* Author [Charles Coffey].
*Miscellaneous:* [The benefit was advertised as being the author's "sole emolument".]
*Comment:* "I was most ungratefully us'd in bringing it on, in the worst Season of the whole Year; it was acted for my Benefit on Saturday the 29th of *March* last, when almost every Body was out of Town at the Circuits, when those few Gentlemen that remain'd, either went or were preparing to go to the Curragh, which happen'd the Wednesday following; and what was as unfortunate as the rest was, that the Day immediately preceded Passion Week, a time so solemn, that people were more anxious for the preservation of their Souls than the Recreation of their Minds, and notwithstanding all the Difficulties it still liv'd and came off with Appause, tho' before a very thin Audience" (Coffey 1724, iv).

[Passion Week 31 March–5 April]

APRIL

7    Mon.    SA.    *Oroonoko; or, The Royal Slave.*
*Cast:* Oroonoko—Delane (the Gentleman who played Orestes lately) [but no performance of *The Distrest Mother* is recorded this season. Presumably, that night would have been Delane's stage debut.]
*Benefit:* Morgan (officekeeper).

21    Mon.    SA.    *The Mourning Bride.*
*Cast:* None listed.
*Benefit:* Wright (treasurer).

MAY

[Exact date unavailable.]     SA.     *The Way of the World.*
*Cast:* None listed.
*Benefit:* Mrs. Sterling.
*Miscellaneous:* [Around May 1729, Mrs. Sterling had as her benefit play *The Way of the World.* "The New Epilogue Spoke and Sung by Polly Peachum at Her Benefit Play: The Way of the World. Printed for J. Carr, in Silver Court in Castle-Street, and Sold by the Stationers," (Dublin, n. d.) is in the T. C. D. Library, A.7.5.f.108.]

5     Thur.     SA.     *The Committee; or, The Faithful Irishman.*
*Cast:* Careless—Giffard; Teague—Griffith; Abel—F. Elrington; Ruth—Mrs. Sterling; Arabella—Esther Lyddal.
*Benefit:* Griffith.

JUNE

5     Thur.     SA.     *The Rover; or, The Banished Cavaliers.*
*Cast:* None listed.
*Benefit:* Vanderbank.

16     Mon.     SA.     *Tamerlane.*
*Cast:* None listed.
*Singing and Dancing:* Dancing by M. and Mme. Moreau. [The Moreaus arrived in Dublin from London on 12 June. Their stay must have been a brief one for *DI,* 2 Dec. 1729 states: "the famous French Dancing Master; who has been for some time past on his travels thru' England and France, is again come over to make his residence here. . . .".]
   Singing: Some celebrated Italian songs by Mrs. Davies "a famous singer, who came over with Mr. Elrington." [Boydell 1988, 45, believes that this Mrs. Davis "was probably a pupil of Pepusch," and not the Mrs. Davis who appeared in London in 1730 as Mrs. Clegg.]

## 1729–1730 Season

Theatre operating: Smock Alley.

*Smock Alley Company:*
Alcorn, Dash, Mrs. Davis, Delane, F. Elrington, R. Elrington, T. Elrington, Myrton Hamilton, Mrs. Hamilton, Husband, L. Layfield, Mrs. Lyddal, H.

Norris, Jr., Paget, George Sheridan, Simms, Mrs. Sterling, Vanderbank, Mrs. Vanderbank, Madame Violante, John Ward, Mrs. Ward, J. Watson, Jr. [The Giffards went to GF and T. Griffith to DL in the autumn].

Dancers: James Cummins, John Duval, Lalauze, Leigh, Moreau, Mrs. Moreau, W. Phillips, Pitt, Miss Violante.

House Servants: Eastham (boxkeeper, died sometime prior to his benefit taken by his widow on 2 Apr. 1730), P. Kelly (pit doorkeeper), LeRoux (boxkeeper), Morgan (officekeeper), Wright (treasurer).

*Repertory:*
Mainpieces: Recorded performances: 24 (of 19 different pieces excluding 2 unspecified plays and 4 unspecified "Entertainments").
Afterpieces: Total Performances: 6.
Entr'acte entertainments: Although the record of dancing is slight, the unspecified "Entertainments" presented by Madame Violante's company which had recently arrived from London may have included many dances.
Command Performances: None listed (3 Government Nights).
Benefits:
Pre-February: Manager—1.
Post-February: Actor—13, House servants—4.
[Mrs. Davis evidently received a benefit in late February or early March 1730 for a satirical "Prologue upon the Beaux, for Mrs. Davis's Benefit, at Smock-alley," aimed at Violante's company, appeared at about that time. In T. C. D. Broadside Collection and reprinted in Gilbert 1854–59, III:190.]

*Significant events:*
During November Dublin was hit with a grave epidemic, the worst since 1665, in which no fewer than 993 people died. "Most of the Gentlemen belonging to the Playhouse [were] severely afflicted with Colds and Coughs," and Lewis Layfield suffered from "a violent Fever." By early December, however, the company had fully recovered (*DI*, 6 Dec. 1729).

**1729**

[Exact date unavailable.]      SA.      *Philaster; or, Love Lies a Bleeding.*

*Cast:* [listed first in 1734 Dublin edition] King—F. Elrington; Philaster—Giffard; Pharamond—Griffith; Dion—Husband; Clerimont—Rosco; Thrasiline—J. Watson, Jr.; Old Captain—Vanderbank; Country Fellow—H.

Norris, Jr; Arethasa—Mrs. Sterling; Galatea—Mrs. Vanderbank; Megra—
Mrs. Moreau; Eutrasia—Mrs. Seale.

OCTOBER

30    Thur.    SA.    Unspecified "Play."
*Miscellaneous:* Government Night; Anniversary of George II Birthday.

NOVEMBER

10    Mon.    SA.    Unspecified "Play."
*Miscellaneous:* [*DI,* 15 Nov. 1739 reported that on this date "in the Theatre,
one Fl———r, a Gentleman who had more wit than Manners, was struck
off the Stage by the Grenadiers in Waiting, and put in the Guard, for turning
up his B———ch to the Audience, who hissed him for coming too forward
with his Hat on his Head, when the Lady Carteret was present".]

DECEMBER

6    Sat.    SA.    *The Necromancer; or, Harlequin Doctor Faustus.*
*Cast:* None listed.
*Miscellaneous:* With new Scenes, Shapes, and Machines.

13    Tues.    SA.    Unspecified Entertainments.
*Cast:* Entertainments by Madame Violante's Company.

30    Sat.    SA.    Unspecified Entertainments.
*Cast:* Madame Violante, Miss Violante, Lalauze, and W. Phillips.

**1730**

JANUARY

13    Tues.    SA.    Unspecified Entertainments.
*Cast:* Entertainments by Madame Violante's Company.

19    Mon.    SA.    *The Constant Couple.*
*Cast:* None listed.
*Miscellaneous:* Government Night: Anniversary of Frederick, Prince of
Wales' Birthday. Boxes free to the Ladies.
*Deferred:* Performance originally advertised for Sat. 17 Jan. 1730.

20   Tues.   SA.   Unspecified Entertainments.
*Cast:* Entertainments by Madame Violante's Company.
*Singing and Dancing:* Dancing: "The French Peasants."


FEBRUARY

12   Thur.   SA.   *Theodosius.*
*Cast:* None listed.
*Benefit:* Griffith's Family in his absence.
*Miscellaneous:* [See Mrs. Barber's *Poems on Several Occasions* for a "Prologue to Theodosius" which may have been spoken during this performance.]

and

*Afterpiece: The What D'Ye Call It.*
*Cast:* None listed.


23   Mon.   SA.   *Lady Jane Grey.*
*Cast:* None listed.
*Benefit:* Mrs. Sterling.
*Singing and Dancing:* [Mrs. Sterling spoke and sang a new opera epilogue as the Ghost of Lady Jane. The epilogue included three songs and was mildly satirical on the beaux. See BL 1890. 3. 5, 1–247.]


MARCH

2   Mon.   SA.   Unspecified "Play."
*Command:* Lord and Lady Carteret.
*Miscellaneous:* Government Night: Anniversary of Queen Caroline's Birth. The Ladies appeared dressed in Silks of the Manufacture of this Kingdom.


9   Mon.   SA.   *Cato.*
*Cast:* None listed.
*Command:* Lord and Lady Carteret.
*Benefit:* Moreau.
*Miscellaneous:* [W. J. Lawrence, Notebook 4:59, mentions the publication of a pamphlet, now lost, entitled "An Epistle to Mr. Thomas Elrington, occasioned by the Murder of the tragedy of Cato last Monday Night," Dublin, 1730, but he does not elaborate.]
*Singing and Dancing:* Unspecified dancing.

and

*Afterpiece: The What D'Ye Call It.*
*Cast:* None listed.

17    Mon.    SA.    *The Cheats of Harlequin; or, The Jealous Farmer Outwitted.*
*Cast:* None listed.
*Benefit:* Miss Violante.
*Miscellaneous:* Entertainments by Mme. Violante's Company.


19    Thur.    SA.    *Hamlet.*
*Cast:* Hamlet—T. Elrington; Gravedigger—L. Layfield.
*Benefit:* Mrs. Ward.


21    Sat.    SA.    *The Cheats of Harlequin.*
*Cast:* None listed.
*Benefit:* Madame Violante.
*Miscellaneous:* Entertainments by Mme. Violante's Company including Mme. and Miss Violante on the tight rope.
    Prices: Boxes 5/5, Pit 3/3, Middle Gallery 2/2, Box in Upper Gallery 1/1.
    [Mme. Violante, having received an invitation to perform in Cork, set out for that destination after this performance (*DI*, 24 Mar. 1730).]
*Singing and Dancing:* Comic dances by Lalauze.


[Passion Week 23–28 March]


APRIL


2    Thur.    SA.    *A Bold Stroke for a Wife.*
*Cast:* None listed.
*Benefit:* Widow Eastham and Le Roux (Box-keeper)
                              and
*Afterpiece: The Stage Coach.*
*Cast:* None listed.


9    Thur.    SA.    *The Beaux' Stratagem.*
*Cast:* Archer—T. Elrington.
*Benefit:* Norris.
*Miscellaneous:* Boxes 1 British Crown, Pit 3s.
*Singing and Dancing:* Dancing, "The Black Joke" performed in the dress of a man and a woman from the Fingal district of County Dublin by Pitt and one of his scholars.
                              and
*Afterpiece: The What D'Ye Call It.*
*Cast:* Timothy Peascod—Norris.

13    Mon.    SA.    *The Unhappy Favourite; or, The Earl of Essex.*
*Cast:* Essex—T. Elrington.
*Benefit:* Mrs. Lyddal.
*Deferred:* Deferred from 6 Apr. 1730.


16    Thur.    SA.    *Aurengzebe; or, The Great Mogul.*
*Cast:* Morat—T. Elrington; Aurengzebe—Delane.
*Benefit:* Alcorn.


20    Mon.    SA.    *King Richard III.*
*Cast:* Richard—F. Elrington.
*Benefit:* Mr. and Mrs. Hamilton.


23    Thur.    SA.    *The Provoked Husband; or, A Journey to London.*
*Cast:* None listed.
*Benefit:* Wright (treasurer).


27    Mon.    SA.    *The Mourning Bride.*
*Cast:* None listed.
*Benefit:* Mrs. Moreau.

and

*Afterpiece: Flora; or, Hob's Opera.*
*Cast:* [listed in 1730 Dublin edition] Sir Testy—Vanderbank; Friendly—Ward; Dick—Norris; Hob—Layfield; Old Hob—Paget; Flora—Mrs. Sterling; Betty—Mrs. Hamilton; Hob's Mother—Mrs. Lyddal.
*Miscellaneous:* [As Boydell observes, (1988, 46) the play was probably already being performed with success when the notice of its publication in September 1730 appeared also indicating that the piece was being acted "at the Theatre in Dublin." A fourth impression was advertised on 24 October 1729.]


30    Thur.    SA.    *The Merry Wives of Windsor.*
*Cast:* None listed.
*Benefit:* Morgan (officekeeper).

and

*Afterpiece: The School Boy; or, The Comical Rivals.*
*Cast:* None listed.


MAY


4    Mon.    SA.    *A Bold Stroke for a Wife.*
*Cast:* None listed.
*Benefit:* Sheridan and Widow Lestor.

7     Thur.     SA.     *The Amorous Widow; or, The Wanton Wife.*
*Cast:* None listed.
*Benefit:* P. Kelly (pit doorkeeper).

14     Thur.     SA.     *The Constant Couple.*
*Cast:* None listed.
*Benefit:* John Duval (lately from London).
*Singing and Dancing:* Dancing by M. and Mme. Moreau, John Duval, Leigh, and others.

and

*Afterpiece: Flora.*
*Cast:* None listed.

21     Thur.     SA.     *The Revenge.*
*Cast:* Alonzo—Delane; Zanga—R. Elrington; Leonora—Mrs. Sterling; Isabella—Mrs. Hamilton.
*Benefit:* Cummins and Dash.
*Miscellaneous:* First time here.

25     Mon.     SA.     *The Old Batchelour.*
*Cast:* None listed.


## 1730–1731 Season

---

Theatres operating: Smock Alley; "New Booth", Dame St.; Stretch's "Great Booth," Dame Street.

---

*Smock Alley Company:*
Alcorn, Dash, Delane, F. Elrington, Ralph Elrington; Richard Elrington; T. Elrington, Griffith, Hamilton, Mrs. Hamilton, Husband, L. Layfield, R. Layfield, Mrs. Lyddal, Neale, Mrs. Neale, Nichols, H. Norris, Jr., Sheridan, Simms, Mrs. Sterling, Vanderbank, Mrs. Vanderbank, J. Ward, Mrs. Ward, John Watson, Jr.

House Servants: Morgan (officekeeper).

*Repertory:*
Mainpieces: Recorded performances: 14 (including 2 unspecified plays).
Afterpieces: Recorded performances: 2
Possible performance: The advertisement for *The Tender Husband* at AS 15 Apr. 1736 says "not acted here these 5 years," and that for *She Would and She Would Not* at SA on 22 Dec. 1740 states: "Not acted these 10 years."

Entr'acte entertainments: Singing and Dancing advertised for two perfor-
mances.
Command performances: None recorded (5 Government nights).
Benefits: Manager—1, Actor—5, House Servants—1, Charity—1.

---

*"New Booth," Dame Street (Madame Violante's Company):*
Cummins, J. Duval, Master Lefavre, Lalauze, Moreau, Mrs. Moreau, Pitt,
Mme. Violante, Mlle. Violante.

House Servants: Mager (officekeeper).

*Repertory:*
Mainpieces: Recorded performances: 12 (including 5 unspecified entertain-
ments).
Afterpieces: The bulk of the plays performed were of entertainments which
would normally have been considered afterpieces.
Premieres:
*Jealous Husband Deceived; or, Harlequin Metamorphosed*
*The Burgomaster Tricked; or, The Intrigues of Harlequin and Columbine*
*The Birth of Harlequin; or, The Triumph of Love.*
Entr'acte entertainments: Several.
Command Performances: None recorded.
Benefits: Post-February: Manager—1, Actor—8, House Servant—1.

---

*Stretch's "Great Booth," Dame St. Company:*
"Young actors," including Mr. and Mrs. John Ward.

*Repertory:*
Mainpiece: Only one recorded performance of one Restoration comedy.
Benefit: Actor—1.
*Significant events:*
The first Dublin newspaper advertisement to list the complete cast of the
main piece, to specify the curtain time, and to advertise singing as a part of
the program would appear to be that for the performance of *King Richard
III* at SA on 22 Mar. 1731.

---

**1730**

OCTOBER

19    Mon.    SA.    *The Recruiting Officer.* V.
*Cast:* None listed.
*Miscellaneous:* Government Night: Anniversary George II's Coronation.

30　　Fri.　　SA.　　Unspecified "Play."
*Miscellaneous:* Government Night: Anniversary of George II's Birth.

NOVEMBER

4　　Wed.　　SA.　　Unspecified "Play" [probably *Tamerlane.*]
*Miscellaneous:* Government Night: Anniversary of King William III's Birth.

DECEMBER

[Exact date unavailable.]　　SA.　　*The Contrivances.*

*Cast:* [listed in 1731 Dublin edition] Argus—Vanderbank; Hearty—Husband; Rovewell—L. Layfield; Robin—Alcorn; 1st Mob—Dash; 2nd Mob—Hamilton; 3rd Mob—Norris; Woman Mob—Sheridan; Boy—R. Layfield; Arethusa—Mrs. Hamilton; Betty—Mrs. Vanderbank.

*Miscellaneous:* A Comi-farcical Opera. [Although no performance record survives, *FDJ*, 26–29 Dec. 1730, states that Henry Carey's *The Contrivances* "is now acting at the Theatre-Royal in Dublin with great *applause* and will speedily be published." This edition appeared in 1731.]

**1731**

JANUARY

20　　Wed.　　SA.　　*The Provoked Husband; or, A Journey to London.* V.
*Cast:* None listed.
*Miscellaneous:* Government Night: Anniversary of Frederick, Prince of Wales's Birth.

FEBRUARY

11　　Thur.　　SA.　　*The Way of the World.*
*Cast:* None listed.
*Benefit:* Mrs. Neale.

MARCH

1　　Mon.　　SA.　　*Love for Love.*
*Cast:* None listed.
*Miscellaneous:* Government Night: Anniversary of Queen Caroline's Birth.

8    Mon.    SA.    *Julius Caesar.*
*Cast:* None listed.
*Benefit:* Delane.

8    Mon.    NBDS.    *The Burgomaster Tricked; or, The Intrigues of Harlequin and Columbine.*
*Cast:* None listed.
   *Miscellaneous:* [Mme. Violante and Lalauze returned from their visit to Cork ca. 17 Nov. 1730 and began performing at NBDS ca. Jan. 1731.]
   To begin promptly at 6 o'clock. Admission: Pit, 2s. 6d.; Middle Gallery, 1s.; Upper Gallery, 6d. They will perform Mondays, Tuesdays, and Saturdays during the Lent Season.
*Singing and Dancing:* "The White Joke Dance" by the Old Woman with Pierrot in a Basket performed by Cummins.

15    Mon.    NBDS.    "Several New Entertainments."
*Cast:* None listed.
*Benefit:* Mrs. Moreau.

22    Mon.    SA.    *King Richard III.*
*Cast:* Richard—Ward; King Henry—T. Elrington; Prince Edward—Mrs. Hamilton; Duke of York—Richard Elrington; Buckingham—Ralph Elrington; Richmond—Delane; Stanley—Alcorn; Norfolk—Dash; Tressel—Simms; Lord Mayor—Vanderbank; Catesby—Neale; Ratcliff—Watson; Tyrrel—Norris; Blunt—Hamilton; Dighton—Sheridan; Forrest—Nichols; Lady Anne—Mrs. Sterling; Lady Elizabeth—Mrs. Ward; Duchess of York—Mrs. Lyddal. [*DWJ*, 20 Mar. 1731 casting differs: Prince Edward—"Mr. Hamilton", Simms—Oxford.]
*Benefit:* Mr. and Mrs. Ward.
*Miscellaneous:* At the particular Desire of several Ladies of Quality. Not acted this season. To begin exactly at 6 o'clock. A new lyrical epilogue spoken by Mrs. Sterling as "Lady Anne's Ghost."
                               and
*Afterpiece: The What D'Ye Call It.*
*Cast:* Timothy Peascod—L. Layfield; Sir Roger—Vanderbank; Kitty Carrott—Mrs. Ward.
*Singing and Dancing:* With the song beginning "'Twas When the Seas were Roaring, etc." sung by Vanderbank. [Boydell 1988, 48, indicates that Mrs. Vanderbank sang this song.]

23    Tues.    NBDS.    *The Jealous Husband Deceived; or, Harlequin Metamorphosed.*
*Cast:* None listed.
*Benefit:* Lalauze.
*Miscellaneous:* [Premiere.]

29   Mon.   SA.   *The Rival Queens; or, The Death of Alexander the Great.*
*Cast:* [listed in 1730 Dublin edition] Alexander—T. Elrington; Clytus—Delane; Lysimachus—Ralph Elrington; Cassander—Husband; Hephestion—Watson; Polypherchon—Vanderbank; Perdiccas—Ward; Philip—Dash; Thessalus—Sheridan; Meleager—Neale; Aristander—Simms; Eumenes—Hamilton; Sysigambis—Mrs. Vanderbank; Statira—Mrs. Sterling; Roxana—Mrs. Ward; Parisates—Mrs. Hamilton.
*Benefit:* Watson.
*Singing and Dancing:* Several unspecified entertainments of singing and dancing.


APRIL


3   Sat.   NBDS.   *The Burgomaster Tricked.*
*Cast:* None listed.
*Benefit:* Moreau.
*Singing and Dancing:* Dancing by Mme. Violante, Lalauze, M. and Mme. Moreau.


[Passion Week 12–17 April]


22   Thur.   SA.   *The Distrest Mother.*
*Cast:* None listed.
*Benefit:* Morgan (officekeeper).
*Miscellaneous:* Not Acted this Season.
and
*Afterpiece: The Stage Coach Opera.*
*Cast:* Squire Somebody—L. Layfield; Tom Jolt—Vanderbank.
*Miscellaneous:* Written originally in French by Monsieur Moliere, and translated into English by Mr. Motteaux and Mr. Farquhar, an opera in one act altered after the Manner of the Beggar's Opera.
   [Anonymous ballad-opera. W. J. Lawrence in "The Mystery of 'The Stage Coach'," *MLR* 27 (1932): 392–97, mistakes the SA performance of Farquhar's *The Stage Coach,* on 2 Apr. 1730, for this, the Dublin premiere of *The Stage Coach Opera,* and Nicoll 1977–79, 2:448, repeats the error. The operatic version, which Lawrence attributes to W. R. Chetwood on slight evidence, was published only in Ireland despite the wording on the title page: "The Stage Coach Opera: As it is Acted at the Theatre Royal in Drury-Lane. Written originally by Mr. Geo. Farquhar. Dublin . . . 1741." Joly Collection, NLI See also *LS* 3:59–217.]
*Singing and Dancing:* With gentle and humourous songs, properly adapted to old English, Scotch, and Irish Tunes.

23    Fri.    NBDS.    Unspecified "Play."
*Benefit:* Madame Violante.
*Miscellaneous:* Attended by one of the greatest Companys seen at Publick Divertions this Season.

MAY

5    Wed.    Stretch.    *The Double Dealer.*
*Cast:* None listed.
*Benefit:* Mr. and Mrs. Ward.
*Miscellaneous:* Never acted in this Kingdom. "At the Great Booth in Dame St." [Hitchcock's assertion to the contrary (1:55) this booth could hardly have been Madame Violante's "New Booth" since her own company was playing there regularly at this time. Almost certainly this "Great Booth" was the one in Dame St. owned by Mr. Stretch, the puppeteer.]
*Comment:* "We are informed that a great Number of Ladies and Gentlemen, have bespoke this Play, and that the Town in general appear ready and willing to encourage our young Comedians; who have of late separated Themselves from those of the Theatre-Royal, but upon what Account we cannot yet tell" (*FDJ*, 27 Apr.–1 May 1731).

10    Mon.    NBDS.    "Several new Entertainments."
*Cast:* None listed.
*Benefit:* Patt. Mager (officekeeper).

13    Thur.    SA.    *Hamlet.*
*Cast:* Hamlet—T. Elrington; Horatio—J. Elrington; Gravedigger—Griffith; Ophelia—Mrs. Sterling.
*Benefit:* Griffith.
and
*Afterpiece: The Stage Coach Opera.*
*Cast:* As 22 Apr. 1731.
*Miscellaneous:* Never performed here but once. It "went off with great applause" (*FDJ*, 17 May 1731).

17    Wed.    NBDS.    "Several New Entertainments."
*Cast:* None listed.
*Benefit:* Master Lefavre.

26    Wed.    NBDS.    Unspecified "Entertainments."
*Cast:* None listed.
*Benefit:* Cummins.
*Miscellaneous:* To begin exactly at 6 o'clock.

JUNE

7   Mon.   SA.   *Themistocles, the Lover of His Country.*
*Cast:* None listed.
*Miscellaneous:* For the entertainment of the Lords Justice.

14   Mon.   SA.   *The Beggar's Opera.*
*Cast:* None listed.
*Benefit:* Vanderbank.
*Miscellaneous:* The last Time the Company will perform this Season.

24   Thur.   SA.   *Cato.*
*Cast:* All male parts performed by Free Masons.
*Benefit:* Distressed Free Masons.
*Miscellaneous:* With Prologue and Epilogue suitable to the Occasion.
*Singing and Dancing:* Songs properly adapted to the Occasion.

28   Mon.   NBDS.   *The Burgomaster Tricked.*
*Cast:* None listed.
*Benefit:* John Duval.

JULY

15   Tues.   NBDS.   "Several New Entertainments."
*Cast:* None listed.
*Benefit:* Pitt (formerly of SA).
*Miscellaneous:* Prices: Pit 2/8, Middle Gallery 1/1, Upper Gallery 6d. English.

AUGUST

2   Mon.   NBDS.   *The Birth of Harlequin; or, The Triumph of Love.*
V.
*Cast:* None listed.
*Miscellaneous:* A new entertainment.

## 1731–1732 Season

Theatres Operating: Smock Alley; "New Booth," Dame St.

*Smock Alley Company:*
Alcorn, Barret (from GF), Dash, F. Elrington, J. Elrington, Nancy Elrington,

Ralph Elrington, T. Elrington, Griffith, Hamilton, Mrs. Hamilton, Husband, L. Layfield, R. Layfield, Mrs. Lyddal, Mrs. Matthews, Mrs. Moreau, Master Mott, Mrs. Neale, Reynolds, Mrs. Reynolds, Rosco, Mrs. Seale, Mrs. Shane, Simms, Sheridan, Mrs. Sterling, Vanderbank, Mrs. Vanderbank, J. Watson, Jr.

Dancers: W. Delamain.

House Servants: Wright (treasurer).

*Repertory:*
Mainpieces: Recorded performances: 33 (of 25 different pieces, including 5 unspecified plays).
Afterpieces: Recorded performances: 9.
Possible Performances: The advertisement for the performance of *Rule a Wife and Have a Wife* at SA on 7 Feb. 1734 states that the play was "not acted these three years."
   *The Ignoramus; or, The English Lawyer* was printed in Dublin in 1736 without mention of dates or place of performance but with the following cast: Husband, R. Elrington, Layfield, Rosco, F. Elrington, Simms, Watson, Vanderbank, Alcorn, Mrs. Moreau, Mrs. Sterling, Mrs. Matthews, and Mrs. Vanderbank. Since Mrs. Sterling retired in May 1732, and Alcorn died in May 1733, the date of performance was probably sometime in 1731.
Premieres:
*Love and Ambition*
*Johnny Bow-Wow*
Entr'acte entertainments: Singing—4; Dancing—5.
Command Performances: 5 (5 Government Nights).
Benefits:
Pre-February: Manager—1; Actor—1; Author—1 (perhaps 2).
Post-February: Manager—1; Actor—11; House Servant—1.

*"New Booth," Dame Street Company:*
Master Barnes, Miss Betty Barnes, Master Barrington, Master Beamsley, Miss Corbally, Master Fitzgerald, Miss Ruth Jenks, Master Lefavre, Miss Macay, Neale, Master Oates, Master Peters, Master Roan, Master Isaac Sparks, Madame Violante, Mlle. Violante, Master White, Master Woffington, Miss Woffington.

Dancers: Lalauze.

*Repertory:*
Mainpieces: Recorded performances: 6 (including 3 unspecified entertainments).

Afterpieces: Recorded performances: 1 farce.
Premiere: *The Cobler of Preston's Opera.*
Entr'acte entertainments: None recorded.
Command Performances: None recorded.
Benefits: Manager—1; Actor—2.
*Significant events:*
Advertisements for the performance of *Damon and Phillida* at SA on 16
Dec. 1731 contain the earliest Dublin reference to seating ladies on the stage
and to lighting the playhouse with wax tapers, two practices which were not
commonly advertised at special productions until after 1740, see *FDJ,* 11
Dec. 1731.

## 1731

[Exact date unavailable, but before May 1732.]     SA.     *The Jovial Crew.*

*Cast:* [listed in 1732 Dublin edition]: Oldrents—Dash; Hearty—Vanderbank;
Springlove—Ralph Elrington; Randal—Alcorn; Oliver—F. Elrington; Vin-
cent—Sheridan; Hillard—L. Layfield; Justice Clack—Griffith; Rachel—
Mrs. Sterling; Muriel—Mrs. Reynolds; Amy—Mrs. Neale.

### SEPTEMBER

21     Tues.     SA.     *The London Merchant; or, The History of George
Barnwell.*
*Cast:* [listed in the 1731 Dublin edition] Thorowgood—Vanderbank; Barn-
well—T. Elrington; George Barnwell—Ralph Elrington; Trueman—J. Elrin-
gton; Blunt—Alcorn; Maria—Mrs. Sterling; Millwood—Mrs. Seale; Lucy—
Mrs. Lyddal.
*Command:* Duke of Dorset.
*Miscellaneous:* At the particular Desire of several Persons of Quality. New
Prologue spoke by Elrington. [The prologue and an epilogue were subse-
quently printed, see T. C. D. broadside A-7-5 no. 230.]

23     Thur.     SA.     *Hamlet.*
*Cast:* None listed.

25     Sat.     SA.     *The London Merchant.*
*Cast:* None listed.

30     Sat.     SA.     *The Spanish Fryar; or, The Double Discovery.* V.
*Cast:* None listed.

*Comment:* In a letter dated 4 Oct. 1731 Mrs. Pendarvis (later Delany) says: "Well, after that [i.e. dinner] to the play we went, 'The Spanish Fryar' tolerably well acted. The house is small but neat and very well lighted, the gentlemen all sit in the pit" (Delany 1861, 1:294).

OCTOBER

11   Mon.   SA.   Unspecified "Play."
*Miscellaneous:* Government Night: Anniversary of George II's Coronation.

30   Sat.   SA.   Unspecified "Play."
*Miscellaneous:* Government Night: Anniversary of George II's birth.

NOVEMBER

4   Thur.   SA.   Unspecified "Play."
*Miscellaneous:* Government Night: Anniversary of birth of William III.

6   Sat.   NBDS.   Unspecified "Entertainments."
*Miscellaneous:* "Next Saturday [i.e. 6 Nov. 1731] we all go to see Madame Violante, and next week our ridottos will begin; masquerades are not talked of, but a scheme is laid for operas, which I hope will succeed." [The Crow St. Music Hall opened on 30 Nov. 1731 with a ridotto. See Delany 1861, 1:309.]

13   Sat.   NBDS.   Unspecified "Entertainments."
*Benefit:* Madame Violante.
*Comment:* Duke and Duchess of Dorset present with "the finest Company of Ladies and Gentlemen that was ever seen on the like Occasion, who were all exceedingly Diverted with her Entertainments" (*DI,* 18 Nov. 1731).

24   Wed.   NBDS.   Unspecified "Entertainments."
*Benefit:* Mons. Lalauze.

27   Sat.   SA.   *The Provoked Husband; or, A Journey to London.*
*Cast:* None listed.
*Command:* Duke of Dorset, Lord Chancellor, Lords Justice.

DECEMBER

[Exact date unavailable.]   NBDS.   *The Beggar's Opera.*
*Cast:* [Hitchcock (1:49) lists the cast] Macheath—Miss Betty Barnes, alias Mrs. Martin and Mrs. Workman; Peachum—Master Isaac Sparks; Lockit—Master Beamsley; Filch—Barrington ("celebrated for Irishmen and low

comedy"); Lucy—Miss Ruth Jenks ("who died some years afterwards"); Mrs. Peachum—Miss Mackay; Polly—Miss Woffington.

*Miscellaneous:* [The epilogue to *The Cobler of Preston's Opera* (see below, performance of February 1732) alludes to an earlier "Lilliputian" play at the New Booth and unmistakably identifies it as *The Beggar's Opera.* This production became so popular that by the end of the summer the ballad opera, presented in Madame Violante's "Irish Manner," had been "perform'd 96 times in Dublin with great Applause." W. J. Lawrence Notebook 4:91, says that 96 performances is probably an exaggeration and suggests that the 16 performances cited by J. Ried in *Notitia Dramatica* is probably nearer the number. Hitchcock's assertion (1:48) that Madame Violante brought out *The Beggar's Opera* "before it had been seen in Dublin" is clearly incorrect. He continues: "they drew crouded houses for a considerable length of time, and the Children of Shakespeare's and Johnson's [*sic*] day, were not more followed, or admired, then those tiny genuises." Madame Violante took this company to London in August and opened with *The Beggar's Opera* at the Haymarket Theatre on 4 Sept. for a run of at least three performances there and at Richmond Wells. See *LS*, 3:1:231–32.]

6  Mon.  SA.  *The Funeral; or, Grief A-la-Mode.*
*Cast:* None listed.
*Command:* Lord Kingston, Irish Grand Master.
*Benefit:* Griffith.
*Miscellaneous:* Mason's Night. [Griffith was Secretary to the Grand Lodge]. Boxes and pit laid together at one British crown, Gallery 2 British shillings, box in the upper gallery, 1s. 6d.

With a new occasional prologue spoke by Griffith dressed as a Mason and a new epilogue in the form of a dialogue between Griffith and Mrs. Sterling in the characters of a Mason and his wife.
*Singing and Dancing:* Masonic songs sung between the acts.
*Comment:* "On Monday last The Funeral or Grief A-la-Mode, was acted for the Benefit of Mr. Griffith, one of the Managers of our Theatre Royal and of the Ridotto, when the following Nobility and Gentry honoured him with their Presence, viz.; The Right Hon. the Lord Kingston, Grand Master of all Ireland, The Right Hon. the Lord Netervill, Deputy Grand Master, The Right Hon. the Lord Southwell, and Mr. Dillon Polard Hamson, Wardens. The Right Hon. the Lord Athenree, the Right Hon. the Lord Blaney who all sat in the King's box, several Members of the Honourable House of Commons in the Pit, all in their Gloves and white Leather Aprons, several Citizens of Worth and Representative wore the same in the galleries. The Ladies wore yellow ribbons and blue ribbons on their Breasts, being the proper Colours of that Ancient and Right Worshipful Society. In the Songs of Masonry all the Brothers stood up and joined in the Chorus, which made a fine Harmony. There was a crowded House and splendid Appearance upon

the Occasion: So that we may justly say, our City at present vies with any in Europe, for Polite Diversions and elegant Entertainments, which in a great Manner is owing to Mr. Griffith, who endeavoured all in his Power, to keep what little Money we have in this poor Country; and our Absentees may be assured of having Pleasure much Cheaper at home than Abroad. There was a Prologue and an Epilogue Spoken suitable to the Occasion" (*FDJ*, 7–11 Dec. 1731).

9     Thur.     SA.     *Love and Ambition*. V.
*Cast:* Matheady—F. Elrington; Samur—Ralph Elrington; Cosmez—L. Layfield; Haly—J. Elrington; Doran—Hamilton; Hamet—Alcorn; Reseck—T. Elrington; Odamus—Vanderbank; Abdallah—Dash; Caleb—Reynolds; Alzeyda—Nancy Elrington; Leiza—Mrs. Sterling.
*Miscellaneous:* [Premiere.] A "very witty Prologue" "written by a Friend" and spoke by Mr. R. Elrington and a "very humourous Epilogue" written by James Sterling and spoken by Mrs. Sterling. The prologue includes the following lines which suggest that rival theatres had been taking some custom away from SA:

> Long hath the Muse beheld with secret Rage,
> The Fair and Gay, desert her falling Stage;
> Blend with vile Crouds, and prostitute their Taste,
> At paultry Booths and Theatres debas'd;
> And gape, like Children, at distorted Shapes,
> Shrill wooden Heroes, Harlequins, and Apes,

*FDJ*, 18–21 Apr. 1730 states that *Love and Ambition* will be performed "next week," though for some reason it was deferred until this season.
*Comment:* "On Thursday the new Tragedy of Love and Ambition was acted at our Theatre Royal, before a very numerous Audience, and their Graces the Duke and Duchess of Dorset were both present. There never was a Play more universally applauded by loud Claps from the Gentry, who shewed their entire Satisfaction, and liking of the Performance. There was a very witty Prologue spoken by R. Elrington, and a very humourous Epilogue by Mrs. Sterling" (*FDJ*, 7–11 Dec. 1731).
"We hear that the Town next week is to be entertained by a new Play called Love and Ambition; and tho' the author be of this Country, 'tis generally talked that the Excellence of the Performance is like to prevail over the general Prejudice which the Nobility and Gentry of this Kingdom have for some years had to the Manufactures of their own Country" (*FDJ*, 23–27 Nov. 1731).
"Notwithstanding there was last Monday Night a Ridotto, a Latin Play acted by Dr. Sheridan's Scholars, and two or three Lodges of Free Masons, yet the new Tragedy of Love and Ambition was played to a vast Audience,

and met with the kindest Reception; and is again to be performed this Night for the Author's Benefit" (*FDJ*, 14–18 Dec. 1731).

11   Sat.   SA.   *Love and Ambition.*
*Cast:* None listed.
*Miscellaneous:* Second performance.

13   Mon.   SA.   *Love and Ambition.*   V.
*Cast:* None listed.
*Benefit:* The Author [James Darcy].
*Comment:* According to *FDJ*, 14 Dec. 1731, this and the performance of 11 Dec. drew "vast" audiences "who express'd their entire Satisfaction at the Diction of the Poetry."

16   Thur.   SA.   *Theodosius.*
*Cast:* None listed.
*Command:* Duke and Duchess of Dorset.
*Benefit:* L. Layfield.
*Miscellaneous:* For the better Convenience of the Ladies that shall sit on the Stage, the Whole's to be illuminated with Wax Candles.
   At the Desire of several Persons of Distinction, a new Epilogue on Luxury in Dress, will be spoken by Mrs. Sterling, designed for His Majesty's Birthday, but prevented by her Sickness.
*Singing and Dancing:* Entertainment includes "Peggy Grieves Me" after Mrs. Barbier's Manner, and first Part of the duet of the Chorus in the Opera of Porus, by Master Mott.
   [Mrs. Barbier, an English contralto, arrived in Dublin in early December 1731 and gave concerts at the newly opened concert hall in Crow St. Included in the program of her benefit concert on 4 Dec. was the "English" ballad "Peggy Grieves Me." Boydell believes Master Mott was a boy soprano (1988, 49).]

and

*Afterpiece: Damon and Phillida; or, Hymen's Triumph.* V.
*Cast:* Arcas—Ralph Elrington; Aegon—Hamilton; Corydon—Alcorn; Cimon—Reynolds; Mopsus—R. Layfield; Damon—L. Layfield; Phillida—Mrs. Reynolds.
*Miscellaneous:* Never performed here. [Walsh (1973, 43) followed by Boydell, cites the original libretto as proof that the first performance of this piece took place on 11 Jan. 1732, but clearly this performance predates it.]
   For the better convenience of the Ladies that shall sit on the Stage, the Whole's to be illuminated with Wax Candles.
*Singing and Dancing:* With dancing proper to same. [The singing of Layfield and Mrs. Reynolds was so popular that on the evenings of 16, 18, and 20 Dec. they had to repeat all their songs twice, see also 21 Dec. 1731.]

18   Sat.   SA.   *Love and Ambition.* V.
*Cast:* None listed.
*Benefit:* Darcy (second benefit).

and

*Afterpiece: Damon and Phillida.*
*Cast:* None listed.


20   Mon.   SA.   *Love and Ambition.* V.
*Cast:* None listed.
*Miscellaneous:* Fifth performance.

and

*Afterpiece: Damon and Phillida.* V.
*Cast:* None listed.


**1732**

JANUARY

17   Mon.   SA.   *Love and Ambition.* V.
*Cast:* None listed.

and

*Afterpiece: Damon and Phillida.* V.
*Cast:* None listed.
*Miscellaneous:* [Walsh 1973, 43, followed by Boydell cites the original libretto indicating a performance of this piece on 11 January. We can find no record of that performance.]


20   Thur.   SA.   Unspecified "Play."
*Miscellaneous:* Government night: Anniversary of Frederick, Prince of Wales's Birth.


24   Mon.   SA.   *The Devil to Pay; or, The Wives Metamorphosed.*
*Cast:* [Listed in 1732 Dublin edition] Loverule—Sheridan; Jobson—L. Layfield; Doctor—Dash; Butler—F. Elrington; Cook—Reynolds; Footman—Hamilton; Coachman—Alcorn; Lady Loverule—Mrs. Lyddal; Lucy—Mrs. Hamilton; Nell—Mrs. Reynolds; Lettice—Mrs. Seale.
*Miscellaneous:* [The original libretto lists a Mrs. Shane in the role of Lettice. Walsh and Boydell overlook this performance citing 24 Feb. 1732 as the date of the Dublin premiere.]
*Music:* Music arranged by Mr. Seedo. [Walsh 1973, 44, believes this composer to be Mr. Sidow or Sydow who worked in London at about this time.]

FEBRUARY

[Exact date unavailable]    NBDS.    *The Cobler of Preston's Opera.*
*Cast:* Sir Charles Burton—Master Oates; Capt. Jolly—Master Barnes; Lorenzo—Master Roan; Diego—Master Fitzgerald; Constable—Master White; Butler—Master Lefavre; Countryman—Master Woffington; Kit Sly—Master Peters; Betty—Miss Corberry; Joan—Mlle. Violante; Cicely Grundy—Miss Woffington.
*Miscellaneous:* SA had put this ballad opera into rehearsal in October 1731 with Lewis Layfield as Kit Sly. The rehearsal announcement for *The Cobler of Preston* "turn'd into an Opera" asserted that according to "the Best Judges" there had not "appear'd on any Stage so good a Performance since The Beggar's Opera," and that "our Town will be very agreeably entertain'd, if Wit and Humour can have any Influence." Furthermore, it stated that the "New Piece [was] Irish Manufacture, so 'tis hoped 'twill meet with the Reception suitable to its Desart" (*FDJ*, 26–30 Oct. 1731). Sometime in November or December, however, the SA management decided not to perform the piece.
The prologue refers to "our youthful Author." W. J. Lawrence (1922, 403) believes the author may have been William Dunkin (1709?–65), who took his B.A. at Trinity College, Dublin, in 1729 and M.A. in 1731. By reason of his clever occasional poems Swift thought him a "Man of Genius, and the best Poet we have. . . ." (Swift 1755–65, 5:96).
*FDJ*, 29 Feb.–4 Mar. 1732 announces the publication of this piece. The title page of the only printed edition reads: "The Cobler of Preston. An Opera, As it is Acted at the New Booth in Dublin, with great Applause. Dublin . . . 1732" (Joly Collection, N.L.I.). The head and running titles read "The Cobler of Preston's Opera".]

[Exact date unavailable.]    SA.    *The Indian Emperor.*
*Cast:* None listed.
*Benefit:* Vanderbank.
*Miscellaneous:* "Next week Mr. Vanderbank is to have the Indian Emperor for his benefit . . . which has not been acted these four years." [But this is the first recorded performance of his play during our period.]

14    Mon.    SA.    *Woman is a Riddle; or, The Way to Win a Widow.*
*Cast:* None listed.
*Benefit:* T. Elrington.
*Comment:* "Whereas it was inserted in Saturday's Newspapers, that the diverting Comedy called Woman is a Riddle, is to be acted at the Booth, for a Benefit; these are to inform the Town, the said Play being revived, is to be acted on Monday next . . . at the Theatre Royal, for the Entertainment

of the . . . Lord Chancellor . . . the Judges, and the Rest of the Hon. Society of King's Inns, for the Benefit of Mr. Elrington" (*FDJ*, 5–8 Feb. 1732).

17    Thur.    SA.    *The Island Princess; or, The Generous Portuguese.*
*Cast:* None listed.
*Benefit:* Ralph Elrington.

24    Thur.    SA.    *The Relapse; or, Virtue in Danger.*
*Cast:* None listed.
*Command:* Duke and Duchess of Dorset.
*Benefit:* Mrs. Lyddal.
*Miscellaneous:* Prices: Boxes 5/5, Pit 3/3, Middle Gallery 2/2, Upper Gallery 1/1.
*Singing and Dancing:* Singing—Master Mot. Dancing—Delamain.
and
*Afterpiece: The Devil to Pay; or, The Wives Metamorphosed.*
*Cast:* As 24 Jan. 1732.

28    Mon.    SA.    *Hamlet.*
*Cast:* None listed.
*Benefit:* Alcorn.
and
*Afterpiece: Damon and Phillida.*
*Cast:* None listed.

28    Mon.    NBDS.    *The Provoked Husband; or, A Journey to London.*
*Cast:* None listed.
*Benefit:* Neale.
*Miscellaneous:* At the particular desire of several Ladies of Quality.
and
*Afterpiece: The Adventures of Half an Hour.*
*Cast:* None listed.
*Miscellaneous:* Never played here.

MARCH

1    Wed.    SA.    Unspecified "Play."
*Miscellaneous:* Government Night: Anniversary of Queen Caroline's Birth.

6    Mon.    SA.    *The Way of the World.*
*Cast:* None listed.
*Benefit:* Mr. and Mrs. Hamilton.
*Miscellaneous:* A tragi-comi-pastoral-farcical opera.

*Singing and Dancing:* With several entertainments of singing and dancing by Master Mott and Delamain.

and

*Afterpiece: The Wedding.*
*Cast:* None listed.
*Miscellaneous:* Never acted here before.

APRIL

[Passion Week 3–8 April]

13    Thur.    SA.    *The Merry Wives of Windsor.*
*Cast:* None listed.
*Benefit:* Wright (treasurer).
*Singing and Dancing:* With several Entertainments of dancing.

and

*Afterpiece: The Judgment of Paris.*
*Cast:* None listed.
*Miscellaneous:* A pastoral ballad opera never performed here. [T. A. Arne's musical version of Congreve's masque was not written until 1740 (Boydell 1988, 51). This piece may be the anonymous *Judgment of Paris; or, The Triumphs of Beauty* a ballad opera which premiered 6 May 1731 at LIF and which was revived for 7 performances in 1733, then disappeared.]

24    Mon.    SA.    *Julius Caesar.*
*Cast:* Antony—Barret (lately arrived from the Theatre in Goodman's Fields).
*Benefit:* Husband.

MAY

4    Thur.    SA.    *Macbeth.*
*Cast:* Macbeth—T. Elrington; Duncan—Barret; Hecate—Griffith.
*Benefit:* Watson.

and

*Afterpiece: Damon and Phillida.*
*Cast:* None listed.

8    Mon.    SA.    *A Bold Stroke for a Wife.*
*Cast:* None listed.
*Benefit:* Mrs. Neale.

15    Mon.    SA.    *Love for Love.*
*Cast:* Valentine—F. Elrington.

*Command:* Lord Chancellor, the Chancellor of the Exchequer, the Judges, and the Society of the King's Inns.
*Benefit:* F. Elrington.
*Singing and Dancing:* With several entertainments of singing and dancing.

19     Fri.     SA.     *Johnny Bow-Wow; or, The Wicked Gravedigger.*
*Cast:* None listed.
*Benefit:* L. Layfield.
*Miscellaneous:* [This "farcical opera" is recorded in Reid's *Notitia Dramatica,* cited in Lawrence 1922, 403. It was evidently a topical piece about the lunatic necrophiliac called "Johnny Bow-Wow" who was sentenced to be transported in 1732.
     Not listed in either *LS* or Nicoll.]

22     Mon.     SA.     *The Beggar's Opera.*
*Cast:* None listed.
*Benefit:* Mrs. Sterling.
*Miscellaneous:* The last Time of Mrs. Sterling's performing on the Stage. Mrs. Sterling will speak a new Occasional Epilogue [printed in Sterling 1734.]
*Deferred:* "It is hoped that her play, being postponed from the 15th will be no disappointment to her Friends the Rt. Hon. the Judges, and the Hon. Society of the King's Inns" (*FDJ,* 29 Apr.–2 May 1732).
     [Mrs. Sterling (*née* Nancy Lyddal) was frequently ill throughout this period and frequently deferred performances. She evidently died within a few months of retiring. Her husband, James Sterling, remarried in 1734.]

JUNE

5     Mon.     SA.     *Love Makes a Man.*
*Cast:* Don Cholerick—Griffith; Don Carlos—T. Elrington.
*Command:* Lord Netterville, Deputy Grand Master.
*Benefit:* Griffith.
*Miscellaneous:* Masons' Night. With a new Epilogue to the Freemasons.

26     Mon.     SA.     *The Provoked Husband.*
*Cast:* Townly—T. Elrington; Lady Townly—Mrs. Neale.
*Benefit:* Vanderbank.
*Miscellaneous:* With several unspecified "Entertainments" never performed here before.
     [This was probably Thomas Elrington's last performance for in mid-July he contracted "a malignant fever" and died on 22 July. He was buried next to Joseph Ashbury in St. Michan's Church, Dublin (*FDJ,* 29 July 1732, and Hitchcock 1788–93, 1:63).]

and

*Afterpiece: Damon and Phillida.*
*Cast:* None listed.

## 1732–1733 Season

Theatres operating: Smock Alley; "New Booth", Dame St. (Violante's), moved to Rainsford St.; "Great Booth," George's Lane.

*Smock Alley Company:*
Alcorn (died in April), Mrs. Bellamy (*née* Seale), Miss Butcher (or Boucher), Dash, F. Elrington, J. Elrington, Ralph Elrington, Gough (or Goff), Griffith, Hamilton, Mrs. Hamilton, Husband (to RS in Feb.), L. Layfield, Master R. Layfield, Mrs. Lyddal, Mrs. Neale, Parker, Mrs. Parker, T. Philips, Reynolds, Mrs. Reynolds, Sheridan, Vanderbank, Mrs. Vanderbank, J. Watson, Jr., Mrs. Wrightson.

Dancers: Moreau, Mrs. Moreau.

House Servants: Morgan (officekeeper), Wright (Treasurer).

Scene Painter: Vanderhagen

Summer: Delane (from Goodman's Fields), L. Ryan (from Covent Garden).

*Repertory:*
Mainpieces: Recorded performances: 31 (of 26 different pieces, including 2 unspecified plays).
Afterpieces: Total of 16 afterpiece performances advertised.
Possible performances: The advertisement for *The Anatomist* at SA 30 Apr. 1739 states: "Not performed here these 6 years."
Premiere: *All Vows Kept.*
Entr'acte entertainments: Dancing advertised only once, but M. and Mrs. Moreau were with the company all season.
Command Performances: 2, (all by Lords Justice; 3 Government nights).
Benefits:
Pre-February: Manager—1; Actor—1; Charity—1.
Post-February: Actor—14; Charity—1; House Servants—2.

*"New Booth," Dame St. Company* (until Dec. 1732 when the Lord Mayor forbade performances and the company moved to *Rainsford St.*):

*Repertory:*
Mainpieces: Recorded performances: 3.
Entr'acte entertainments: None recorded.
Benefits:
Pre-February: Actor—1.
Post-February: Actor—1.

---

*Rainsford St. Company:*
Miss Barnes, Barret, John Barrington, Charles Bourne (or Byrne), Daniel,
L. Duval, J. Hinde, Husband, Miss Mackay, Moore, Ravenscroft, Mrs.
Ravenscroft, Roch, Mrs. Smith, Luke Sparks, Mrs. Talent.

*Repertory:*
Mainpieces: Recorded performances: 7 (including 1 unspecified play).
Afterpieces: Total of 2 afterpiece performances recorded.
Premiere: *The Fate of Ambition.*
Entr'acte entertainments: 2 dancing, 1 singing advertised.
Command Performances: None recorded.
Benefits: Post-February: Manager—1; Actor—3.

---

*"Great Booth," George's Lane, Company* (opened not later than May 1733):
James Cummins, James Walsh.

*Repertory:*
A triple bill consisting of a pantomime and two farces on 6 June 1733 is the
only one recorded for this theatre.
*Significant events:*
An epidemic of fever caused cancellations at the theatres during the spring
of 1733.

## 1732

### OCTOBER

5    Thur.    SA.    *The Island Princess; or, The Generous Portuguese.*
*Cast:* None listed.
*Comment:* "We hear that there are great Improvements made in the Theatre
Royal, and that the Managers have entertained several new Actors and Actresses; but that the Play or Opera of the Island Princess cannot be acted
until Thursday next, by Reason the new Scenes are not yet finished" (*FDJ,*
26–30 Sept. 1732).

30    Mon.    SA.    *Love Makes a Man.*
*Cast:* None listed.
*Command:* Lords Justice.
*Miscellaneous:* Government Night: Anniversary of King George II's Birth.

NOVEMBER

[Oct. or Nov., Exact date unavailable.]    NBDS.    *The Inconstant; or, The Way to Win Him.*
*Cast:* L. Sparks—Principal Character; Barrington—Principal Character; Miss Mackay—Principal Character.

[ca. Nov. 1732, Exact date unavailable.]    NBDS.    Unspecified Program.
*Benefit:* Miss Mackay.
*Miscellaneous:* [Chetwood 1749, 63, says the benefit took place and that "Several Ladies of the first Rank expous'd her Cause and brought upwards of forty Pounds to the Occasion".]

DECEMBER

[ca. Dec. 1732, Exact date unavailable.]    NBDS.    *Woman is a Riddle.*
*Cast:* None listed.
*Benefit:* The Company.
*Miscellaneous:* [The Lord Mayor forbade further performances by the unlicensed company at NBDS but allowed them a farewell benefit which attracted "a good house" to the Booth. Chetwood 1749, 63.]

4    Mon.    SA.    *The Rover; or, The Banished Cavaliers.*
*Cast:* None listed.
*Benefit:* Griffith.

15    Fri.    NBDS.    *Julius Caesar.*
*Cast:* Antony—T. Sheridan. Other parts by young gentlemen in Dr. Sheridan's School.

**1733**

JANUARY

1    Sat.    Dublin Castle    *The Distrest Mother.*
*Cast:* Freemason Players.
*Benefit:* Freemason Players.

*Comment:* "We hear that . . . Lord Kingsland ordered a Play and Entertainment, with Dances and Songs, for the Entertainment of the . . . Free-Masons, and for the Benefit of all the Free-Mason Players, to be acted on New Years Day next. . . ." (*FDJ,* 5–9 Dec. 1732).

[Hitchcock 1788–94, 1:75–76, notes that at this time, "Private playing was also much in fashion. In January 1732/33 the Distrest Mother was acting at the council chamber in the Castle of Dublin. Lord Viscount Mountjoy, Lord Viscount Kingsland, and other persons of quality of both sexes supported the different characters. The room was filled up in the most elegant stile. All the chambers and passages were illuminated with wax. There was a crowded audience of persons of the first rank in the kingdom, and the whole was conducted with the greatest regularity and decorum".]

20  Sat.  SA.  Unspecified "Play."
*Cast:* None listed.
*Miscellaneous:* Government Night: Anniversary of Frederick, Prince of Wales's Birth.

29  Mon.  SA.  *The Mourning Bride.*
*Cast:* None listed.
*Benefit:* Vanderbank.
                              and
*Afterpiece: Damon and Phillida; or, Hymen's Triumph.*
*Cast:* Not listed.

**FEBRUARY**

5  Mon.  SA.  *The Way of the World.*
*Cast:* None listed.
*Command:* Lord Chamberlain, the Chancellor of the Exchequer, Judges, Society of King's Inns.
*Benefit:* F. Elrington.
                              and
*Afterpiece: The Devil to Pay; or, The Wives Metamorphosed.*
*Cast:* Not listed.

5  Mon.  RS.  *Love for Love.*
*Cast:* Sir Sampson—Moore; Valentine—Husband; Tattle—Ravenscroft; Foresight—Bourne; Trapland—Daniel; Ben—L. Sparks; Jeremy—Roch; Angelica—Mrs. Ravenscroft; Mrs. Foresight—Mrs. Smith; Mrs. Frail—Miss Mackay; Miss Prue—Miss Barnes; Nurse—Mrs. Talent.
*Miscellaneous:* [Opening Night of the "New Theatre in Ransford Street"; the company was advertised as "the Earl of Meath's Comedians" (*DEP,*

1–3 Feb. 1733). Managed by Husband and Duval. With a Prologue on the Occasion.

*PO*, 13–17 Feb. 1733 states that this theatre was opened on 3 Feb. 1733, though all advertisements indicate that the first performance took place on 5 Feb. 1733.]

15   Thur.   SA.   *The Tender Husband; or, The Accomplished Fools.*
*Cast:* None listed.
*Benefit:* Mrs. Neale.

and

*Afterpiece: The Contrivances; or, More Ways than One.*
*Cast:* None listed.

19   Mon.   SA.   *King Lear and His Three Daughters.*
*Cast:* Lear—F. Elrington; Edgar—Ralph Elrington.
*Benefit:* Ralph Elrington.
*Miscellaneous:* At the Desire of several Persons of Quality.

19   Mon.   RS.   *The Fate of Ambition; or, The Treacherous Favourite.*
*Cast:* None listed.
*Benefit:* The Family of the recently-deceased Author [Abbot Forster].
*Miscellaneous:* [Premiere. No recorded London performance; not listed in Nicoll.]
*Comment:* "A bad performance everyway, but charity carried us hither. I wish people would be content with one's money, and not insist on one's presence—it is hard to sacrifice three hours to nonsense wilfully. Poor old Abbot! I believe he is no great loss to the world, nor the world to him" (Delany 1861, 1:401–2).

"This piece was played a few nights, the author, whose name I cannot learn, had a benefit, and it was then consigned to oblivion" (Hitchcock 1788–93, 1:80).

MARCH

1   Thur.   SA.   *The Recruiting Officer.*
*Cast:* Sylvia—Mrs. Bellamy.
*Miscellaneous:* [Government Night; Anniversary of Queen Caroline's Birth. With a new Prologue on the Occasion spoken by Griffith and an Epilogue spoken by Mrs. Bellamy in the character of Sylvia.

A poem in *FDJ*, 6–10 Mar. 1733 indicates that Mrs. Bellamy performed her part in both men's and women's dress, apparently with great success. See also *DEP*, 10 Mar. 1733. Evidently this is the first Dublin record of such a performance.]

1   Thur.   RS.   Unspecified "Play."
*Cast:* None listed.

5   Mon.   SA.   *The Double Gallant; or, The Sick Lady's Cure.*
*Cast:* None listed.
*Benefit:* Mrs. Bellamy.
*Miscellaneous:* Not acted here these five years.
and
*Afterpiece: Damon and Phillida.*
*Cast:* Not listed.

8   Mon.   SA.   *The Beggar's Opera.*
*Cast:* None listed.
*Benefit:* Miss Butcher.
*Miscellaneous:* Being the last Time of performing it.
and
*Afterpiece: The Necromancer; or, Harlequin Doctor Faustus.*
*Cast:* Harlequin—R. Elrington.

15   Thur.   SA.   *The Amorous Widow; or, The Wanton Wife.*
*Cast:* None listed.
*Benefit:* Mr. and Mrs. Reynolds.
and
*Afterpiece: The Devil to Pay.*
*Cast:* None listed.

[Passion Week 19–23 March]

[Spring 1733, exact date unavailable.]   SA.   *All Vows Kept.*
*Cast:* [listed in 1733 Dublin edition] Count Colloni—F. Elrington; Her-
cules—J. Elrington; Ursino—T. Philips; Vincentio—Watson; Trivoltio—R.
Elrington; Bumbardo—L. Layfield; Pedro—Vanderbank; Lopez—Griffith;
Ariomana—Mrs. Neale; Parthenia—Mrs. Bellamy; Lavinia—Mrs. Wright-
son; Nurse—Miss Butcher; Maid—Mrs. Parker.
*Miscellaneous:* [Premiere. Mrs. Bellamy spoke an Epilogue in Male Attire.]
   The title page of the first Dublin edition reads: "All Vows Kept. A Comedy.
As it is acted at the Theatre Royal in Smock Alley. Dublin . . . 1733." (in
Dix Collection, N. L. I). Neither the Dublin nor London edition, both dated
1733, gives evidence of authorship. Nicoll 1977–79, 2:319, names Captain
Downes as the playwright on the authority of Baker 1812, 2:19, who in turn
identifies the author as nephew and aide of the Rev. John Hoadley, Arch-
bishop of Dublin from 1730 to 1742. The appearance of Mrs. Parker in the
cast indicates performance before the end of the 1732–33 season, because
she joined the RS company in the autumn of 1733.]

29   Thur.   SA.   *Cephalus and Procris; or, Harlequin Grand Volgi.*
*Cast:* None listed.
*Miscellaneous:* [Pantomime. "The Scenes are finer Painted than any ever seen in this Kingdom, done by the famous Mr. Vanderhagen" (*FDJ*, 24–27 Mar. 1733).
   Mons. Roger (choreographer at DL during the 1729–30 season) had previously inserted *Harlequin Grand Volgi* as a comic interlude to *Cephalus and Procris* at DL 15 Sept. 1735. See *LS*, 3:1:88 and 511.]

APRIL

16   Mon.   SA.   *The Old Batchelour.*
*Cast:* None listed.
*Benefit:* Mrs. Lyddal.
*Singing and Dancing:* With several Entertainments of dancing by Mr. and Mrs. Moreau.

and

*Afterpiece: The What D'Ye Call It.*
*Cast:* None listed.

16   Mon.   RS.   *Hamlet.*
*Cast:* Hamlet—Moore.
*Benefit:* L. Duval.
*Singing and Dancing:* With Entertainments of dancing composed by M. Du Vall.

19   Thur.   SA.   *The Careless Husband.*
*Cast:* None listed.
*Benefit:* Mrs. Neale (2nd).
*Miscellaneous:* At the particular Desire of several Persons of Quality. By Reason of the Sickness which was lately so rife in this City, Mrs. Neale's Benefit not being sufficient to defray the necessary charge of the house, it was proposed by several Gentlemen and Ladies, that she should have another.

and

*Afterpiece: The What D'Ye Call It.*
*Cast:* None listed.

30   Mon.   SA.   *Love's Last Shift.*
*Cast:* None listed.
*Benefit:* Watson.

and

*Afterpiece: The Necromancer.*
*Cast:* None listed.

MAY

3   Thur.   SA.   *King Henry IV, with the Humours of Sir John Falstaff.*
*Cast:* None listed.
*Benefit:* Gough.
*Miscellaneous:* At the Desire of several Persons of Quality.

                              and

*Afterpiece: The Cheats of Scapin.*
*Cast:* Scapin—Gough.


3   Thur.   RS.   *The Beaux' Stratagem.*
*Cast:* None listed.
*Benefit:* Hinde.
*Miscellaneous:* With the original Epilogue spoken by Hinde.
*Singing and Dancing:* Several Entertainments of Singing and Dancing between the Acts.

                              and

*Afterpiece: The Contrivances.*
*Cast:* None listed.


5   Sat.   SA.   *The Beggar's Opera.*
*Cast:* None listed.
*Miscellaneous:* For the entertainment of the Lord Chancellor, the Judges, and the Society of King's Inn.

                              and

*Afterpiece: Cephalus and Procris; or, Harlequin Grand Volgi.*
*Cast:* Harlequin—R. Elrington.


7   Mon.   RS.   *The Beggar's Opera.*
*Cast:* None listed.
*Benefit:* Barret [Boydell 1988, 52, spells this "Barnett".]


8   Tues.   SA.   *The Funeral.*
*Cast:* None listed.
*Benefit:* Mr. and Mrs. Parker and Sheridan.

                              and

*Afterpiece: The Necromancer.*
*Cast:* None listed.


21   Mon.   SA.   *The Provoked Husband; or, A Journey to London.*
*Cast:* None listed.
*Benefit:* Widow of the late Mr. Alcorn.

*Miscellaneous:* [Boydell 1988, 53, cites RS as the venue of this performance but we can find no evidence that it took place anywhere but at SA.]

and

*Afterpiece: The Country Wedding; or, The Nuptials of Roger and Jean.*
*Cast:* None listed.
*Miscellaneous:* The comic part of *Acis and Galatea;* not acted these ten years.

[Boydell 1988, 53, indicates that this piece is *Acis, Galatea, and Polyphemus,* music by John Eccles, text by Motteaux.]

24    Thur.    SA.    *Woman is a Riddle.*
*Cast:* None listed.
*Benefit:* Morgan (office-keeper).

and

*Afterpiece: The Devil to Pay.*
*Cast:* None listed.
*Miscellaneous:* Desired.

28    Mon.    SA.    *Love Makes a Man.*
*Cast:* None listed.
*Benefit:* Wright (treasurer).

and

*Afterpiece: Damon and Phillida.*
*Cast:* None listed.

JUNE

6    Wed.    GBGL.    *Harlequin Triumphant; or, The Father Deceived.*
*Cast:* None listed.
*Benefit:* Walsh and Cummins (dancing masters).
*Miscellaneous:* A "grotesque Opera."

[John Weaver, pantomime choreographer and author of *A History of Mimes and Pantomimes* (London 1728), p. 58 writes: "By *Grotesque Dancing,* I mean only such Characters as are quite out of Nature, as Harlequin, Scaramouch, Pierrot, &c. tho' in the natural Sense of the Word, *Grotesque* among masters of our profession [i.e. dancing masters], takes in all *comic* Dancing whatever: But here I have confin'd this Name only to such Characters where, in lieu of regulated Gesture, you meet with distorted and ridiculous *Actions,* and Grin and Grimace take up entirely that Countenance where the *Passions* and *Affections* of the Mind should be expressed."]

and

*Afterpiece: The Tavern Bilkers.*
*Cast:* None listed.
*Miscellaneous:* "A new entertainment."

and

*Afterpiece: The Cheats of Scapin.*
*Cast:* None listed.
*Singing and Dancing:* With a variety of dancing and music, particularly several concertos on harp and "Jack Latin" on pipes by two of the best masters in this Kingdom.

7    Thur.    RS.    *The Way of the World.*
*Cast:* None listed.
*Benefit:* Mrs. Lyddal (from Smock Alley).
and

*Afterpiece: Damon and Phillida.*
*Cast:* Not listed.
*Miscellaneous:* At the Desire of several Persons of Quality.

18    Mon.    SA.    *The Mourning Bride.*
*Cast:* None listed.
*Benefit:* R. Elrington
*Miscellaneous:* The last Time of the Company performing this season.
and

*Afterpiece: The Necromancer.*
*Cast:* Harlequin—R. Elrington.

### Summer Season

25    Mon.    SA.    *Macbeth.* V.
*Cast:* Macbeth—Delane (from Goodman's Fields); Macduff—L. Ryan (from Covent Garden).
*Miscellaneous:* [This is the first record of a summer season in Ireland during this period.]
*Comment:* "They drew a very crouded House, and gave great satisfaction" (Hitchcock 1788–93, 1:82).

28    Thur.    SA.    *The Provoked Husband.*
*Cast:* Townly—Delane; Manly—Ryan.

JULY

2    Mon.    SA.    *King Henry IV, with the Humours of Sir John Falstaff.*
*Cast:* None listed.

5    Thur.    SA.    *Hamlet.*
*Cast:* None listed.

9    Mon.    SA.    *Othello.*
*Cast:* None listed.
*Benefit:* Delane.


12    Thur.    SA.    *The Constant Couple; or, A Trip to the Jubilee.*
*Casts:* None listed.
*Benefit:* Ryan.
*Miscellaneous:* "Being the last time of the Company performing this season the company being obliged to play at Cork the 20th of July" (*FDJ,* 26–30 July 1733). [This is the first record of a tour by a Dublin company since 1713.]


## 1733–1734 Season


Theatres operating: Smock Alley/Aungier St. (after March); Rainsford St.; "Great Booth," George's Lane.


*Smock Alley / AS Company:*
Addy, Mrs. Bellamy, Mrs. Butcher?, Miss Butcher, Butler, F. Elrington, J. Elrington, Ralph Elrington, Richard Elrington?, Gough, Griffith, Samuel Hinde, Miss Jones, L. Layfield, Meek, Mrs. Moreau, Mrs. Neale, Mrs. Orfeur (from London in May), Mrs. Page, Master Peters, T. Philips, Ranalow, Reed, Mrs. Reynolds, Seivers, Sheridan, Vanderbank, Mrs. Vanderbank, Warham, J. Watson, Jr., Mrs. Wrightson.

Dancers: Moreau? and Mrs. Moreau.

House Servants: Dryden (Treasurer), Mrs. Eastham (dresser), LeRoux (box-keeper), Morgan (pit officekeeper).


*Repertory:*
Mainpieces: Recorded performances: 23 (19 different pieces, including 2 unspecified plays).
Afterpieces: Total of 12 afterpiece performances advertised: SA 6; AS 6.
Premiere: *More Ways Than One to Gain a Wife.*
Entr'acte entertainments: Dancing advertised only once.
Command Performances: 3, (6 Government nights).
Benefits:
Pre-February: Manager—1, Actor—1.
Post-February: Manager—1, Actor—10, House Servants—3.

*Rainsford St. Company:*
Miss Barnes, Barrington, Bourne, L. Duval, J. Hinde, Husband, Johnston, Mrs. Lyddal, Mrs. Lyons (from London), Miss Mackay, Parker, Mrs. Parker, L. Sparks, Walsh.

*Repertory:*
Mainpieces: Recorded performances: 8.
Afterpieces: Recorded performances: 6
Entr'acte and other Entertainments: Singing and Dancing advertised 3 times.
Command Performances: 1.
Benefits:
Pre-February: Charity—1.
Post-February: Actor—6.

*"Great Booth," George's Lane Company:*
Connor (musician), Cummins (dancer), Walsh (dancer).

*Repertory:*
Mainpieces: Recorded performances: 5.
Afterpieces: Recorded performances: 5
Entr'acte entertainments: Singing and Dancing advertised for 4 nights.
Command Performances: 1.
Benefits: Actor—4.

## 1733

OCTOBER

4    Thur.    SA.    *Love for Love.*
*Cast:* None listed.
*Miscellaneous:* [Duke and Duchess of Dorset present; Parliament opened on this day. With a new prologue to their Graces upon their first coming to the play since their happy return to Ireland, spoken by Griffith.]

11    Thur.    SA.    Unspecified "Play."
*Miscellaneous:* Government Night: Anniversary of King George II's Coronation.

30    Tues.    SA.    *The Merry Wives of Windsor.* V.
*Cast:* None listed.
*Miscellaneous:* Government Night: Anniversary of King George II's Birth; Duke of Dorset and other persons of distinction present.

5   Mon.   SA.   *Tamerlane.* V.
*Cast:* None listed.
*Miscellaneous:* Government Night: Anniversary of King William III's Birth.
[*FDJ*, 3–6 Nov. 1733 indicates that the play is being performed in honour of the anniversary of the delivery from "the horrid Gunpowder Plot."
Occasional Prologue spoken by Griffith.]

12   Mon.   SA.   *Tamerlane.* V.
*Cast:* None listed.
*Miscellaneous:* [Government Night: *FDJ*, 10–13 Nov. 1733 explains that the play was performed for a second time this month because the Duke of Dorset had attended a banquet at the Boyne Club in honour of King William on 5 Nov. and "the lateness of the Dinner prevented their going to the Play of Tamerlane that Night".]

29   Thur.   SA.   *The Twin Rivals.*
*Cast:* None listed.
*Command:* Viscount Kingsland, Grand Master of the Free-Masons.
*Benefit:* Griffith.
*Miscellaneous:* With a prologue and epilogue proper for the occasion.
*Singing and Dancing:* With a Free Mason song between every act.
*Comment:* "The House was so full before the Society came, that Seats were erected around the Stage, whereon sat the Nobility and Gentlemen Free-Masons, who made a most beautiful and magnificent Appearance" (*FDJ*, 27 Nov.–1 Dec. 1733).

30   Fri.   GBGL.   *Woman's Revenge; or, A Match at Newgate.*
*Cast:* None listed.
*Benefit:* Connor and Cummins.
*Miscellaneous:* Requested by several Persons of Quality. The Booth is made very commodious and warm.
*Singing and Dancing:* With several entertainments of dance by Mr. Cummins and others. The whole to open with a full concert of trumpets, etc. Mr. Connor will perform several pieces on the German and small flutes.

DECEMBER

8   Sat.   RS.   *The Old Batchelour.*
*Cast:* None listed.
*Miscellaneous:* The Duke and Duchess of Dorset and the Earl of Meath present.

10   Mon.   RS.   *A Bold Stroke for a Wife.*
*Cast:* None listed.
*Benefit:* Annual Play to Benefit the Charity Children Educated in St. Catherine's Parish.
*Miscellaneous:* [Duke and Duchess of Dorset present.]

**1734**

JANUARY

21   Mon.   SA.   Unspecified "Play."
*Miscellaneous:* Government Night: anniversary of Frederick, Prince of Wales's Birth.

28   Mon.   SA.   *Love for Love.*
*Cast:* Valentine—R. Elrington; Ben—Griffith.
*Benefit:* Warham.
                    and
*Afterpiece: Damon and Phillida.*
*Cast:* Damon—L. Layfield; Phillida—Mrs. Reynolds.

FEBRUARY

1   Fri.   GBGL.   *Oroonoko; or, The Royal Slave.*
*Cast:* A Company of Young Gentlemen.
*Benefit:* A Young Gentleman.
*Singing and Dancing:* Singing and Dancing between the Acts.
                    and
*Afterpiece: Damon and Phillida.*
*Cast:* None listed.

7   Thur.   SA.   *Rule a Wife and Have a Wife.*
*Cast:* None listed.
*Benefit:* Ralph Elrington.
*Miscellaneous:* Not acted these three years.
                    and
*Afterpiece: The Necromancer.*
*Cast:* Harlequin—R. Elrington.

13   Wed.   RS.   *Woman is a Riddle.*
*Cast:* None listed.
*Benefit:* Miss Barnes.

and

*Afterpiece: The Mock Doctor.*
*Cast:* None listed.

13    Wed.    GBGL.    *The Distrest Mother.*
*Cast:* None listed.
*Benefit:* Walsh (dancing master).
*Miscellaneous:* At the Desire of several Persons of Quality. Anniversary of the Coronation of William III.
*Singing and Dancing:* Singing and Dancing between the acts

and

*Afterpiece: The Mock Doctor.*
*Cast:* None listed.

and

*Afterpiece: The Tavern Bilkers.*
*Cast:* None listed.

14    Thur.    SA.    *The Way of the World.*
*Cast:* None listed.
*Benefit:* Mrs. Bellamy.

18    Mon.    SA.    *King Lear and His Three Daughters.*
*Cast:* None listed.
*Command:* Duke and Duchess of Dorset.
*Benefit:* Miss (probably Mrs.) Butcher.
*Deferred:* Newspaper advertisements announce that this is for variously "Miss" and "Mrs." Butcher. It may be that a mother and daughter with that surname were working at SA at this time.

and

*Afterpiece: Flora.*
*Cast:* None listed.

18    Mon.    RS.    *The Conscious Lovers.*
*Cast:* None listed.
*Benefit:* Mrs. Lyddal.
*Miscellaneous:* At the Desire of several Ladies of Quality.

and

*Afterpiece: Tom Thumb the Great.*
*Cast:* None listed.
*Miscellaneous:* [Mrs. Laetitia Pilkington (1748–54, 3:155) relates the anecdote of Swift laughing only twice in his life, once was at the killing of the ghost in *Tom Thumb*. This must have been during a Dublin performance since Swift left England for good in 1727 and the play had its London premiere on 24 Apr. 1730.]

20    Wed.    RS.    *Sir Harry Wildair.*
*Cast:* None listed.
*Benefit:* Miss Mackay.

and

*Afterpiece: The Devil to Pay.*
*Cast:* None listed.

25    Mon.    SA.    *The Double Gallant.*
*Cast:* None listed.
*Benefit:* Phillips and Mrs. Reynolds.

and

*Afterpiece: The Devil to Pay.*
*Cast:* None listed.

25    Mon.    RS.    *King Henry IV, with the Humours of Falstaff.* V.
*Cast:* None listed.
*Command:* Duke and Duchess of Dorset.
*Benefit:* J. Hinde.
*Miscellaneous:* By the Rt. Hon. Earl of Meath's Comedians.
*Singing and Dancing:* Singing and Dancing between the Acts.

and

*Afterpiece: The Mock Lawyer.*
*Cast:* None listed.
*Miscellaneous:* Never yet performed here.

28    Thur.    SA.    *A Bold Stroke for a Wife.*
*Cast:* None listed.
*Command:* Duke and Duchess of Dorset.
*Benefit:* Gough and Miss Butcher. [See SA performance of 18 Feb.

and

*Afterpiece: The Cheats of Scapin.*
*Cast:* None listed.

MARCH

1    Fri.    SA.    *Tunbridge Walks; or, The Yeoman of Kent.*
*Cast:* None listed.
*Miscellaneous:* [The Duke and Duchess of Dorset present; Government night; Anniversary of Queen Caroline's birth. Occasional Prologue spoken by Griffith. Boxes free to the Ladies.

Last recorded performance in the original Smock Alley theatre. Mr. Sheridan was to have had his benefit on 4 Mar. at SA, but "Part of the House falling, prevented it. . . ." Patrons were asked to hold their ticket until a benefit could be arranged at the new theatre in AS (*FDJ,* 5–9 Mar. 1734).]

9    Sat.    AS.    *The Recruiting Officer.* V.
*Cast:* Plume—J. Elrington; Balance—L. Layfield; Brazen—R. Elrington; Worthy—Watson; Kite—Vanderbank; Bullock—F. Elrington; Recruit—Reed; Recruit—Butler; Sylvia—Mrs. Bellamy; Melinda—Mrs. Wrightson; Rose—Mrs. Moreau; Lucy—Mrs. Reynolds.
*Miscellaneous:* [Opening Performance at new AS theatre. Duke and Duchess of Dorset present. Occasional prologue spoken by Griffith.]
*Comment:* "Last Saturday, the 9th of March, the new Theatre-Royal in Angiers-street, was opened to a very numerous Audience. It is allowed by all Travellers to be, by much, the finest in Europe. It was honoured the first Night with the Presence of their Graces the Duke and Duchess of Dorset, attended by most of the Nobility and Gentry of the Kingdom, to see the Comedy of the Recruiting Officer; and a new Prologue, proper to the Occasion, was spoken by Mr. Griffith, one of the Managers; and received with universal Applause" (*FDJ*, 9–12 Mar. 1734).

APRIL

[Passion Week 8–13 April]

22    Mon.    AS.    *Hamlet.*
*Cast:* Ophelia—Mrs. Neale.
*Benefit:* Mrs. Neale.
*Miscellaneous:* Mrs. Neale "is in an unhappy State of Health" (*FDJ*, 16–20 Apr. 1734).

25    Thur.    AS.    *The Committee.*
*Cast:* None listed.
*Benefit:* Griffith.
                              and
*Afterpiece: The Tragedy of Chrononhotonthologos.* V.
*Cast:* [listed in 1735 Dublin edition] Chrononhotonthologos—Philips; Bombardinion—Layfield; Aldiborontiphoscophornio—Watson; Rigdum Funnidos—Gough; Captain of Guards—Butler; Doctor—Sheridan; Cook—Ranalow; King of Fiddlers—Seivers; King of the Antipodes—Addy; Dumb—Meek; Signor Scacciatinello—Hinde; Cupid—Master Peters; Fadladinida—Mrs. Reynolds; Tatlanthe—Mrs. Page; Lady at Court—Mrs. Bellamy; Lady at Court—Mrs. Butcher; Signora Sicarina—Miss Jones; Venus—Mrs. Vanderbank.

29    Mon.    AS.    *The Old Batchelour.*
*Cast:* None listed.
*Benefit:* Watson.
*Deferred:* Originally advertised for performance on 7 Mar. 1734.

and

*Afterpiece: Chrononhotonthologos.*
*Cast:* None listed.


MAY


16     Thur.     AS.     *Theodosius.*
*Cast:* Pulcheria—Mrs. Orfeur (from LIF).
*Benefit:* Philips and Mrs. Reynolds.
and
*Afterpiece: More Ways than One to Gain a Wife.*
*Cast:* None listed.
*Miscellaneous:* ["A diverting Ballad-Opera as perform'd in DL," but not listed in Nicoll or *LS.*]


20     Mon.     AS.     *The Miser.*
*Cast:* None listed.
*Benefit:* F. Elrington.
*Miscellaneous:* For the Entertainment of the Lord Chancellor, Chancellor of the Exchequer, the Judges, and Society of King's Inns.
and
*Afterpiece: The Necromancer.*
*Cast:* None listed.


21     Tues.     RS.     *The Recruiting Officer.*
*Cast:* None listed.
*Benefit:* Johnston.
*Miscellaneous:* At the particular Desire of several Persons of Quality.
*Singing and Dancing:* Several Songs and Dances between the acts.


24     Fri.     RS.     *The Fair Penitent.*
*Cast:* None listed.
*Benefit:* Mr. and Mrs. Parker.
*Miscellaneous:* To which will be added the new scene of the Lottery, as it is now drawing in London (*DEP,* 14–18 May 1734).
*Singing and Dancing:* Several Entertainments of Singing and Dancing, the former to be performed by a Gentlewoman just arrived from London [i.e. Mrs. Lyons].
and
*Afterpiece: The Lottery.*
*Cast:* Lovemore—Mrs. Lyons (from London).

30   Thur.   AS.   *The Twin Rivals.*
*Cast:* None listed.
*Benefit:* Morgan (pit officekeeper).
*Miscellaneous:* With several unspecified entertainments.

and

*Afterpiece: Chrononhotonthologos.*
*Cast:* None listed.


JUNE


6   Thur.   AS.   *Love's Last Shift.*
*Cast:* None listed.
*Benefit:* LeRoux (boxkeeper) and Mrs. Eastham (dresser).
*Singing and Dancing:* With several entertainments of dancing.

and

*Afterpiece: The Devil to Pay.*
*Cast:* None listed.


12   Wed.   GBGL.   *The Beaux' Stratagem.*
*Cast:* None listed.
*Command:* At the Particular Desire of Viscount Kingsland.
*Benefit:* Leigh and Walsh (dancing masters).
*Miscellaneous:* Pit and Boxes, British half crown, Middle gallery, 1s. 6d., Upper gallery, 1s.
[Since Viscount Kingsland was Grand Master of the Irish Freemasons, it seems likely that Leigh and Walsh were also Masons.]
*Singing and Dancing:* With a variety of music and dancing.
   *Comment:* "N. B. The Booth is in good Order for the Reception of the Quality, being well wainscotted and lined with woolen cloath, and will be finely illuminated after a new manner" (*FDJ*, 1–4 June 1734).

and

*Afterpiece: Flora.*
*Cast:* None listed.

and

*Afterpiece: The Tavern Bilkers.*
*Cast:* None listed.


13   Thur.   AS.   *The Miser.*
*Cast:* None listed.
*Benefit:* Dryden (Inspector [i.e. Treasurer] of the Theatre-Royal).
*Miscellaneous:* Dryden is "a near Relation of the celebrated John Dryden, Esq., Poet laureat" (*FDJ*, 4–8 June 1734).

18    Tues.    GBGL.    *The Orphan.*
*Cast:* None listed.
*Benefit:* Mrs. Lyons (from London).
*Miscellaneous:* [This program was originally advertised for performance at RS on 29 May 1734. Boydell 1988, 56, overlooks the apparent cancellation. *BD* contains no entry for any Mrs. Lyons.]

and

*Afterpiece: The Lottery.*
*Cast:* Lovemore—Mrs. Lyons.

## 1734–1735 Season

Theatres Operating: Aungier St.; Rainsford St. (The RS Company arrogated unto itself the title of "His Majesty's Company of Comedians" on the strength of Duval's appointment in January 1735 to the Deputy Mastership of the Revels. The company gave occasional performances at the "Great Booth," Georges Lane).

*Aungier St. Company:*
Boyton, Miss Broad, F. Elrington, Ralph Elrington, Griffith, S. Hinde, L. Layfield, R. Layfield; Miss Mackay, Peters, T. Philips, Vanderbank, Mrs. Vanderbank, J. Watson, Jr., Mrs. Wrightson.

Singers: Mrs. Davis (or Davies), Mrs. Raffa (one night only).

Dancers: W. Delamain, Moreau, Mrs. Moreau?, Pitt, Master Pitt (also at RS), Miss Woffington.

House Servants: Dryden (Treasurer); Le Roux (boxkeeper); Dickson (printer).

Summer: Delane (from GF), H. Giffard (from GF).

*Repertory:*
Mainpieces: Recorded Performances: 26 (of 21 different pieces, 2 unspecified plays and one concert).
Afterpieces: Recorded performances—11 of 8 different pieces.
Entr'acte entertainments: One full concert of instrumental music; 9 performances contained singing or dancing.
Command Performances: 4 (5 Government nights).
Benefits:
Pre-February: Actor—1.

Post-February: Manager—1; Actor—12; House Servants—3.

*Rainsford St. Company:*
J. Aicken, Miss Barnes, Barrington, Bourne, Dash, George Dogherty (found murdered on 13 Aug. 1735), L. Duval, Gough, J. Hinde (1 Dec. 35 to 18 Mar. 36), Husband, Mrs. Lyddal, Meeks, Nanfan, Mrs. Page, Master Pitt (from AS), I. Sparks, L. Sparks, Walsh, J. Ward, Mrs. Ward.

*Repertory:*
Mainpieces: Recorded Performances: 7 at RS, 3 at GBGL (of 9 different pieces).
Afterpieces: Recorded performances: 5.
Premieres: *Punch's Opera.*
Entr'acte entertainments: 6 performances advertise singing and dancing.
Command Performances: 1.
Benefits:
Pre-February: Actor—1; Charity—1.
Post-February: Manager—1; Actor—5.

**1734**

SEPTEMBER

9    Mon.    RS.    *A Bold Stroke for a Wife.*
*Cast:* None listed.
*Benefit:* Dash and Mrs. Page.
*Miscellaneous:* At the Desire of several Ladies of Quality.
*Singing and Dancing:* With several entertainments of singing and dancing between the acts.

and

*Afterpiece: Damon and Phillida.*
*Cast:* None listed.

OCTOBER

11    Fri.    AS.    *The Merry Wives of Windsor.*
*Cast:* None listed.
*Command:* Lords Justice.
*Miscellaneous:* Government Night: Anniversary of Coronation of King George II. Boxes free to Ladies. Occasional Prologue spoken by Griffith.

30   Wed.   AS.    Unspecified "Play."
*Cast:* None listed.
*Miscellaneous:* Government Night: Anniversary of the birth of George II.

NOVEMBER

4   Mon.   AS.    *Tamerlane.*
*Cast:* None listed.
*Miscellaneous:* Government Night: Anniversary of birth of William III; at the particular desire of the Boyne Society.

DECEMBER

11   Thur.   AS.    Concert of Vocal and Instrumental Music.
*Cast:* Vocal Parts—Mrs. Davis.
*Benefit:* Mrs. Davis.
*Miscellaneous:* Tickets one British Crown. [Venue moved from the Music Hall in Crow St.]
   [Boydell 1988, 55, believes that this Mrs. Davis was the wife of Mr. Davis the composer and harpsicord player and mother of Miss Davis the child prodigy harpsicord player and sister of John Clegg, the composer.]

14   Sat.   GBGL.    *The Tender Husband.*
*Cast:* None listed.
*Benefit:* A Distressed Officer with a Large Family.
*Miscellaneous:* By the particular Desire of several Persons of Quality.
*Singing and Dancing:* With several entertainments of dancing between the acts.
                              and
*Afterpiece: The Stage Coach.*
*Cast:* None listed.

16   Mon.   AS.    *King Henry VIII. V.*
*Cast:* King—L. Layfield; Wolsey—F. Elrington.
*Miscellaneous:* [Although no other recorded performance exists, this play was apparently performed another six or seven times by 7 Jan. 1735 (see *Comment* below).]
*Comment:* "The Play of King Henry VIIIth, which hath been so greatly admired, and hath met with so much Success in London for its fine Appearance, is now in Rehearsal at the Theatre-Royal in Aungier-street; and in order to encourage our Diversions, the Rt. Hon. William Conolly, Esq.; hath given 50 guineas to decorate it, which will make a most splendid Figure, there having been upwards of 300 l. already laid out for Dresses to the said Play" (*FDJ,* 10–14 Dec. 1734).

"For some Time past this Town hath been entertained in the most agreeable Manner, with the celebrated Play of Henry VIII, and the Coronation of Anna Bullen, at the Theatre-Royal in Aungier-street. It hath already been acted six or seven times to very numerous Audiences; and many People have gone away for want of Room. The Procession of the Coronation is the finest Sight that hath ever been seen in this Kingdom. It was to have been acted last Thursday night [i.e. 2 Jan. 1735]; but His Majesty King Henry VIII, Queen Catherine, and two other great Persons, were overturned in a Hackney Coach near Ringsend, which hindered the Town from being entertained that Night with the Presence of their Majesties. By the Fall His Majesty received a large deep Cut on his Forehead, his first Royal Consort had her two Arms and Sides bruised; one of the Attendants had his Nose broke; and the other got a very black Eye. P. S. We hear their Majesties are on the mending Hand, and will soon make their publick Appearance (*FDJ*, 4–7 Jan. 1735).

## 1735

JANUARY

20    Mon.    AS.    Unspecified "Play."
*Cast:* None listed.
*Miscellaneous:* Government Night: Anniversary of birth of Prince of Wales.

27    Mon.    AS.    *The Chances.*
*Cast:* None listed.
*Benefit:* R. Elrington.
*Miscellaneous:* Never acted here. By Beaumont and Fletcher, revised by the Duke of Buckingham. Several unspecified entertainments between the Acts.
                                  and
*Afterpiece: The Devil to Pay.*
*Cast:* None listed.

FEBRUARY

3    Mon.    AS.    *King Henry VIII.*
*Cast:* None listed.
*Command:* Judges.
*Benefit:* F. Elrington.
*Miscellaneous:* With the Procession of the Coronation of Anna Bullen and the Ceremony of the Champion. Prices: Boxes 5/5, Balconies 4/4, Pit 3/3, Gallery 2/2.

3    Mon.    RS.    *The Beggar's Opera.*
*Cast:* Macheath—Ward; Mrs. Peachum and Diana Trapes—Mrs. Lyddal.
*Benefit:* Mrs. Lyddal.
*Miscellaneous:* Boxes, 4s. 4d., Pit, British half-crown, Gallery, 1s. 6d.

and

*Afterpiece: The Stage Coach.*
*Cast:* None listed.

10    Mon.    AS.    *Macbeth.*
*Cast:* None listed.
*Benefit:* Vanderbank.
*Miscellaneous:* To which will be added the Ceremony of the coronation [in Henry VIII].
*Singing and Dancing:* With several entertainments of singing and dancing proper to the Play.

13    Thur.    AS.    *Othello.*
*Cast:* Othello—A Gentleman from London.

13    Thur.    RS.    *The Way of the World.*
*Cast:* None listed.
*Benefit:* L. Duval.
*Miscellaneous:* With a burlesque from the beggar's coronation in *The Royal Merchant* by His Majesty's Company of Comedians; With the whole procession of the Beggar's Coronation; By the particular Desire of several Persons of Quality; Boxes, 4s. 4d., Pit, 2s. 6d., Gallery, 1s. 6d.
*Singing and Dancing:* With several entertainments of dancing.

17    Mon.    AS.    *The Country Wife.*
*Cast:* None listed.
*Benefit:* Griffith.
*Miscellaneous:* Mason's Night. Not acted in this Kingdom these 20 years.
*Comment:* "The Most Ancient and Rt. Worshipful Society of Free Masons, being assembled, at the Grand Lodge, on Tuesday last [i.e. 4 Mar. 1735] and taking into consideration the great and publick Affront given them by Mr. Griffith, in chusing so vile and obscene a play for their entertainment, as that called the Country Wife; and likewise by omitting several Entertainments, mentioned in his printed Bills, viz. a grand piece of Musick, Dancing, and a Frost Scene, etc. And they highly resenting so flagrant and palpable an Indignity done them, did (among other things) resolve, that the said Gentleman ought never to have any Recommendation from the Grand Lodge; and hope the future Grand Officers will never encourage him" (*DEP*, 4–8 Mar. 1735).
    "The Resolution of the Grand Lodge of the Rt. Worshipful Society of Free

Masons, mentioned in this Paper of the 8th of last month, was not *printed* by Order of the Grand Lodge" (*DEP*, 5–8 Apr. 1735).

21    Fri.    AS.    *Acis and Galatea.*
*Cast:* Galatea—Mrs. Davis.
*Benefit:* Mrs. Davis.
*Miscellaneous:* The characters will be represented in proper dresses, with new Scenes of Gardens, Woods and Fountains, as in the Opera House of the Haymarket, where Mrs. Davis performed the part of Galatea. [Walsh 1973, 49, tells us that Mrs. Davis sang Eurilla, not Galatea, in the June 1732 Haymarket production. He also observes that the overture in *Ariadne* (see below) was probably its first Dublin performance.]
    The Pit and Boxes laid together at a British Crown, Gallery 2s. 6d. To begin at half past 6 o'clock.
*Singing and Dancing:* With an addition of new Pastoral Dances between the acts; the music for the dances composed by Mr. Davis.
    With an additional chorus of trumpets. A French horn and Kettle drum, and an additional song, which Mr. Handel composed for his own performance on the harpsicord alone, to be performed by Mr. Davis.
    The first Overture belongs to the Opera, the Overture of the second act of the Opera of Ariadne. The third Act, an Overture for a French Horn. The French Horn to be performed by the Lord Mountjoy's Gentleman.

MARCH

1    Sat.    AS.    *The Recruiting Officer.*
*Cast:* None listed.
*Miscellaneous:* Government Night; Anniversary of birth of Queen Caroline.
*Singing and Dancing:* An Ode set to Musick by Mr. Dubourg was sung by Mrs. Raffa.

6    Thur.    RS.    *The Unhappy Favourite; or, The Earl of Essex.*
*Cast:* Essex—Ward.
*Benefit:* Bourne (or Byrne).
*Miscellaneous:* By the particular Desire of several Persons of Quality.
*Singing and Dancing:* With several diverting entertainments between the acts; particular care shall be taken for a good stand of coaches; To begin at half past 6 o'clock.
                              and
*Afterpiece: The Stage Coach.*
*Cast:* Maccahone—Barrington.
*Singing and Dancing:* With the addition of a Teague song, as sung by him [Barrington] in *The Committee.*

8     Sat.     AS.     *Acis and Galatea.*
*Cast:* None listed.
*Miscellaneous:* Boxes, 5s. 5d., Balconies, 4s. 4d., Pit, 3s. 3d., Gallery, 2s. 2d.; To begin precisely at 7 o'clock.
*Comment:* "The last Time it was performed, it was not intended to be acted, but represented in characters sitting as in London; but now all the parts will be acted and performed without Book, Acis killed by Polypheme, and turned into Fountains and all the entrances and exits properly observed" (*DEP*, 1–4 Mar. 1735).

11     Tues.     RS.     *Punch's Opera; or, The Comical Humours of Acis and Galatea.*
*Cast:* None listed.
*Miscellaneous:* [Premiere. Not listed in Nicoll or *LS*].
*Comment:* "We hear the Players in Randsford-street, who were so successful in their Burlesque of the Coronation of Harry the Eighth, have prepared a humourous Entertainment in the nature of a Burlesque, on the Pastoral Opera of *Acis and Galatea.* . . ." (*FDJ*, 4–8 Mar. 1735).

13     Thur.     AS.     *Rule a Wife and Have a Wife.*
*Cast:* Copper Captain—R. Elrington.
*Benefit:* Mrs. Wrightson.

and

*Afterpiece: The Necromancer.*
*Cast:* Harlequin—W. Delamain.

17     Mon.     GBGL.     *A Bold Stroke for a Wife.*
*Cast:* Principal Characters: Sparks, Jr.; Bourne; Meeks; Gough.
*Benefit:* Walsh and Aicken.
*Miscellaneous:* Prices: Pit and Boxes one-half British guinea; First Gallery, 1s. 7½d.
*Singing and Dancing:* With Dancing between the Acts.
*Deferred:* Originally advertised for 12 Mar. 1735.

19     Wed.     GBGL.     *Punch's Opera.*
*Cast:* None listed.

20     Thur.     AS.     *Hamlet.*
*Cast:* Hamlet—R. Elrington.
*Benefit:* S. Hinde.
*Miscellaneous:* Tickets given out for *The Relapse* will be taken.
*Singing and Dancing:* With several entertainments of singing and dancing.

                              and

*Afterpiece: The Adventures of Half and Hour.*
*Cast:* None listed.
*Miscellaneous:* Not acted these 12 years [but see the performance at NBDS on 28 Feb. 1732].


24    Mon.    AS.    *The Silent Woman.*
*Cast:* Morose—Vanderbank.
*Benefit:* Philips.
*Singing and Dancing:* With several entertainments of singing and dancing between the acts.

                              and

*Afterpiece: Chrononhotonthologos.*
*Cast:* None listed.


APRIL


[Passion Week 31 March–5 April]


17    Thur.    AS.    *The Silent Woman.*
*Cast:* None listed.
*Benefit:* R. Layfield.
*Miscellaneous:* At the Desire of several Ladies of Quality.

                              and

*Afterpiece: Flora.*
*Cast:* None listed.
*Miscellaneous:* Being desired.


22    Tues.    AS.    *The Double Gallant; or, The Sick Lady's Cure.*
*Cast:* None listed.
*Miscellaneous:* With a new prologue "by an eminent Hand."

                              and

*Afterpiece: The Walking Statue; or, The Devil in the Wine Cellar.*
*Cast:* None listed.


23    Wed.    AS.    *The Merry Wives of Windsor.*
*Cast:* None listed.
*Benefit:* Christopher Dickson (printer).
*Miscellaneous:* By the particular Desire of several Persons of Quality, being St. George's Day.
*Singing and Dancing:* Dancing: "The Dusty Miller" by Mr. Pitt's son, a child of four years old, who performed once before at the Theatre in Rainsford Street.

and

*Afterpiece: The Necromancer.*
*Cast:* None listed.
*Miscellaneous:* With all its decorations.
*Singing and Dancing:* "The Dancing Devil" by Moreau.

30　Wed.　RS.　*The Siege of Damascus.*
*Cast:* None listed.
*Command:* Viscount Kingsland.
*Benefit:* Walsh.
*Miscellaneous:* Boxes, 3s., Pit, 2s., Gallery, 1s. [This was probably a night for the benefit of the Masons.]
*Singing and Dancing:* With a variety of dancing by the Highland Piper who dances at the Booth, and a Child of four years old [i.e. Master Pitt].

and

*Afterpiece: The Tavern Bilkers.*
*Cast:* None listed.

MAY

1　Thur.　AS.　*The Spanish Fryar.*
*Cast:* None listed.
*Benefit:* Miss Mackay.
*Miscellaneous:* At the particular Desire of several Persons of Quality.

and

*Afterpiece: The Adventures of Half an Hour.*
*Cast:* None listed.

5　Mon.　AS.　*The Way of the World.*
*Cast:* None listed.
*Command:* The Earl and Countess of Antrim.
*Benefit:* Watson.
*Singing and Dancing:* With several entertainments of dancing between the acts of Moreau, William Delamain, and Miss Woffington.

and

*Afterpiece: Tom Thumb.*
*Cast:* Tom Thumb—Miss Broad.
*Miscellaneous:* With the original epilogue in the character of Tom Thumb spoken by Miss Broad.

14　Wed.　RS.　*Othello.*
*Cast:* Othello—J. Hinde; Iago—Nanfan.
*Benefit:* Nanfan and J. Hinde.
*Miscellaneous:* With a Prologue and an Epilogue written by Dr. Swift [but

see performance of 1 Apr. 1721 SA], spoken in the year 1720 for the benefit of the Weavers, altered to their present circumstances.
*Singing and Dancing:* With several entertainments of singing and dancing.

JUNE

5    Thur.    AS.    *The Provoked Wife.*
*Cast:* None listed.
*Benefit:* S. Hinde.
*Miscellaneous:* By the particular Desire of several Persons of Quality.
*Singing and Dancing:* With several entertainments of singing and dancing.
                                      and
*Afterpiece: The Necromancer.*
*Cast:* None listed.

9    Mon.    AS.    *Love's Last Shift.*
*Cast:* None listed.
*Benefit:* Boyton.

                                      and
*Afterpiece: Damon and Phillida.*
*Cast:* None listed.

12   Thur.    AS.    *The Old Batchelour.*
*Cast:* None listed.
*Benefit:* Wm. Dryden (Treasurer) and Peter LeRoux (boxkeeper).
*Miscellaneous:* Last Time of Performing this Season.
*Singing and Dancing:* With a variety of singing and dancing.

                        *Summer Season*

30   Mon.    AS.    *Rule a Wife and Have a Wife.*
*Cast:* Copper Captain—Giffard (from GF); Leon—Delane (from GF).
*Benefit:* Giffard.
*Miscellaneous:* [*DEP,* 5 July 1735, reports that Giffard and Delane accompanied the AS company to the Carlow races "thereby to render the Diversions more agreeably pleasant to the Ladies."]

## 1735–1736 Season

Theatres operating: Aungier St.; Rainsford St. (moved to Smock Alley after 11 Dec. 1735).

*Aungier St. Company:*

Mrs. Bellamy, F. Elrington, Ralph Elrington, Green, Griffith, Hornby (from TR Bath), Mrs. Hornby (the Hornbys left Dublin in January), Loughlin, Miss Mackay, Miss Naylor, T. Philips, Reed, Mrs. Reynolds, Sheridan, Vanderbank, Mrs. Vanderbank, J. Watson, Jr., Miss Woffington (also dancer), Mrs. Wrightson.

Dancers: Connor, Cummins, W. Delamain, Samuel Hinde, Moreau, Naylor, Miss Vanderbank, Walsh.

Singer: Signora Maria Negri (one performance).

Musicians: J. Johnson; Call. MacCarty; Woder.

House Servants: Mrs. Eastham (boxkeeper); LeRoux (boxkeeper); Morgan (officekeeper).

*Repertory:*
Mainpieces: Recorded performances: 52 (of 35 different pieces, including ridottos, serenata, and concert).
Afterpieces: Recorded performances: 18 (of 13 different pieces).
Premieres:
*The Maid's Last Prayer.*
*The Medley.*
Entr'acte entertainments: Singing and/or dancing advertised on 6 evenings.
Command Performances: 14, (3 Government nights).
Benefits:
Pre-February: Manager—1, Actor—3.
Post-February: Actor—14, Author—1, House Servants—2.

---

*Rainsford St. / Smock Alley Company:*
Miss Barnes, Barrington, Beamsley, C. Bourne (also dancer), Miss Butcher (or Boucher), Cashell, Dash, L. Duval, W.(?) Hallam, J. Hinde, Husband, R. Layfield, Meeks (or Meek), Morgan (from CG), Redman, I. Sparks, L. Sparks, J. Ward, Mrs. Ward, Wetherilt.

Dancers: Cummins (from AS), Robert Delamain, John Morris, Pitt, Master Pitt.

House Servants: Dryden (Treasurer), Mrs. Bamford (dresser), Reilly (printer), Tyler.

*Repertory:*
Mainpieces: Recorded performances: RS—5, SA—43 = 48 (of 29 different pieces including one unspecified piece and one serenata).

Premiere: *Leonora.*

Afterpieces: Total recorded performances: 21 (of 11 different pieces, including one unspecified farce).

Premiere: *The Cooper Deceived.*

Entr'acte and other Entertainments: Five advertisements for singing and/or dancing.

Command Performances: 2 (1 Government night).

Benefits:

Pre-February: Charity—1.

Post-February: Manager—1; Actor—17; Actor—1; House Servants—4; Charity—5.

*Significant Events:*

The Rainsford St. Company moved to the new Smock Alley Theatre in December 1735.

---

**1735**

SEPTEMBER

8    Mon.    AS.    *Don John; or, The Libertine Destroyed.*

*Cast:* John—Ralph Elrington; Jacomo—Griffith.

*Miscellaneous:* Not acted here these 30 years. With proper Scenes, Machines, and Decorations, particularly all the Shepherd's Musick, set by the celebrated Mr. Purcell, performed by Hinde, Mrs. Reynolds, Miss Woffington, and others.

*Singing and Dancing:* Dancing by Moreau, Delamain, Cummins, and Miss Woffington.

15    Mon.    AS.    *The Tempest.*

*Cast:* None listed.

*Miscellaneous:* Not acted here but once these ten years. Common prices: boxes, 4s. 4d.; balconies, 3s. 3d.; pit, 2s. 6d.; gallery, 1s. 6d.

*Singing and Dancing:* With the original music, dances and decorations, particularly the song of "Dear pretty Youth, etc." by Miss Woffington, Singing Devils: Hinde, Naylor, and Mrs. Vanderbank; with a grand Fury dance by Moreau accompanied by Delamain, Cummins and Connor; A Sailor's Dance by Delamain; Pastoral Dance by Delamain and Miss Woffington.

*Deferred:* Originally advertised for 1 Sept.

29    Mon.    AS.    *The Albion Queens; or, The Death of Mary, Queen of Scotland.*

*Cast:* None listed.

OCTOBER

2    Thur.    AS.    *The Silent Woman.*
*Cast:* None listed.
*Command:* Duke and Duchess of Dorset.

9    Thur.    AS.    *The Miser.*
*Cast:* None listed.

10    Fri.    AS.    *The Beggar's Opera.*
*Cast:* Macheath—Mrs. Reynolds.
*Command:* Duke and Duchess of Dorset.

16    Thur.    AS.    *The Beggar's Opera.* V.
*Cast:* Macheath—Mrs. Reynolds.
*Command:* Duke and Duchess of Dorset.
*Miscellaneous:* Mrs. Reynolds performed in men's attire.
    [An Englishman, William Bulkley, was visiting Dublin at this time and stated that he attended this play and paid 18d. admission, "The Irish Channel and Dublin in 1735, Extracts from the Diary of William Bulkley," *The Journal of the Royal Society of Antiquaries of Ireland,* 5th series, 9 (1899): 58.]

20    Mon.    AS.    *Don John.*
*Cast:* None listed.

23    Thur.    AS.    *The Beggar's Opera.*
*Cast:* None listed.
*Command:* Duke and Duchess of Dorset.
*Miscellaneous:* [The only source for this performance is Boydell 1988, who cites *DEP,* 14–18 Oct. 1735.]

25    Sat.    AS.    Serenata.
*Miscellaneous:* [*DEP,* 8, 22, 25 Nov. 1735 announced that the managers had decided to "finish magnificently" the theatre's interior "for the accommodation of the nobility and gentry in a far more elegant manner than ever was in this Kingdon" and to present serenatas, oratorios, and ridottos each Saturday. See performance of 1 Nov. 1735 below.]

27    Mon.    AS.    *The Beggar's Opera.*
*Cast:* None listed.

30    Thur.    AS.    *The Provoked Husband.* V.
*Cast:* None listed.
*Command:* Duke and Duchess of Dorset.

*Miscellaneous:* Government Night: Anniversary of King George II Birth. [The Prologue for this performance is quoted in full in *DEP*, 8–11 Nov. 1735.]

NOVEMBER

1    Sat.    AS.    Serenata.
*Miscellaneous:* "As these Entertainments are conducted and managed by the Direction of Gentlemen, Lovers of Musick, which truly raises the Soul to a more than ordinary pitch, so it is expected that these Performances will be the most entertaining of any we ever had in this Kingdom; and in order to render the Expense as easy as possible we hear the Price is confined to that of a common Concert (*DEP*, 4–8 Nov. 1735).

3    Mon.    AS.    *The Beggar's Opera.*
*Cast:* None listed.

4    Tues.    AS.    *Tamerlane.* V.
*Cast:* None listed.
*Miscellaneous:* Government Night: Anniversary birth of William III. Performed to a very large audience.
   [William Bulkley attended this performance and paid "5s. English".]

6    Thur.    AS.    *King Henry VIII.*
*Cast:* None listed.

13    Thur.    AS.    *King Henry IV, with the Humours of Falstaff.*
*Cast:* None listed.

13    Thur.    RS.    *The Royal Merchant; or, The Beggar's Bush.*
*Cast:* [listed in 1736 Dublin edition] Woolfort—Cashell; Gerrard—Ward; Hubert—Morris; Florez—L. Sparks; Hemskirk—Husband; Vandunk—Morgan (from CG); Higgen—W. Hallam; Prig—Barrington; Snapp—Bourne; Ferrit-—Beamsley; Ginks—Meek; Boor—R. Layfield; Jaculine—Miss Barnes; Bertha—Miss Butcher.
*Miscellaneous:* [According to William Bulkley this comedy was played in its entirety. He paid the admission price of "2s. 10d. Irish".]

17    Mon.    AS.    *Tunbridge Walks; or, The Yeoman of Kent.*
*Cast:* None listed.

17    Mon.    RS.    *The Royal Merchant.*
*Cast:* None listed.

20    Thur.    AS.    *King Henry VIII.*
*Cast:* None listed.
*Miscellaneous:* With the Procession of the Coronation of Anna Bullen.

24    Mon.    AS.    *The Rehearsal.*
*Cast:* None listed.

27    Thur.    AS.    *The Pilgrim.*
*Cast:* None listed.

28    Fri.    RS.    *The Way of the World.*
*Cast:* None listed.
*Benefit:* The Charity Children in St. Catherine's Parish.

and

*Afterpiece: The Mock Doctor.*
*Cast:* None listed.

DECEMBER

1    Mon.    AS.    *Theodosius; or, The Force of Love.*
*Cast:* None listed.

1    Mon.    RS.    *The Royal Merchant*
*Cast:* None listed.
*Miscellaneous:* [The Rainsford St. Company acted at the new Smock Alley
Theatre after this date.]

4    Thur.    AS.    *Julius Caesar.*
*Cast:* None listed.

8    Mon.    AS.    *The Prophetess; or, The History of Dioclesian.*
*Cast:* None listed.
*Music:* [Walsh 1973, 55, states that this piece was a 1690 adaptation by
Thomas Betterton of Fletcher and Massinger's *The Prophetess* and that the
music was "almost certainly" by Henry Purcell.]

11    Thur.    AS.    *The Merry Wives of Windsor.*
*Cast:* None listed.

and

*Afterpiece: Flora.*
*Cast:* None listed.

11    Thur.    SA.    *Love Makes a Man.*
*Cast:* Don Carlos—Ward; Don Lewis—Wetherilt; Don Antonio—Dash; Don

Charino—Bourne; Don Duart—Cashell; Clody—Sparks; Sandro—Barrington; Governor—Redman; Louisa—Mrs. Ward; Elvira—Miss Butcher (or Boucher according to Hitchcock, 1:94); Angelina—Miss Barnes.

[Chetwood reverses the roles of Cashel and Wetherilt and adds that Miss Barnes has married and is "now" Mrs. Martin.]

*Miscellaneous:* [Opening of new Smock Alley Theatre.]

13     Sat.     AS.     *Aminta.*
*Cast:* None listed.
*Command:* Duke and Duchess of Dorset.
*Benefit:* Signora Maria Negri.
*Miscellaneous:* A Pastoral Opera. No silver tickets will be taken at the door.

[Nicoll 1977–79, 2:224, states that "In 1726 P. B. Du Bois issued a rather lame prose rendering of Tasso as "L'Aminta, Di Torquato Tasso, Favola Boscherecchia Tasso'a Aminta, A Pastoral Comedy, In Italian and English." *LS* lists a pastoral with this title by John Dancer performed in 1659.

Walsh 1973, 54, says: "It is tempting to suggest that this could have been the first performance of an Italian opera in Dublin but one must temper wishful thinking with manifest facts. The facts are that the likelihood of the performance having been sung entirely in Italian is improbable. With the exception of Negri the name of no other singer taking part has come down to us; had other Italians been engaged, their names would probably have been mentioned in the advertisements. . . . Extensive research has failed to identify the composer".]

15     Mon.     AS.     *The Pilgrim.*
*Cast:* None listed.
*Command:* Duke and Duchess of Dorset.
*Benefit:* Mrs. Reynolds.

                              and

*Afterpiece: Damon and Phillida.*
*Cast:* None listed.

15     Mon.     SA.     *King Henry IV, with the Humours of Falstaff.* V.
*Cast:* None listed.
*Miscellaneous:* [William Bulkley attended this performance and paid "2s. 3d. Irish." He states [incorrectly] that "this was the first play that ever was acted at the new Play-house in Smock Alley".]

17     Wed.     AS.     Ridotto.

18     Thur.    SA.     *The Twin Rivals.*
*Cast:* None listed.

22    Mon.    SA.    *The Recruiting Officer.* V.
*Cast:* None listed.
*Miscellaneous:* [William Bulkley attended this performance.]

29    Mon.    SA.    *The Royal Merchant.*
*Cast:* None listed.

**1736**

JANUARY

5    Mon.    AS.    *Hamlet.*
*Cast:* None listed.

15    Thur.    AS.    *Rule a Wife and Have a Wife.* V.
*Cast:* Estifania—Mrs Hornby.
*Benefit:* Mrs. Hornby.
and
*Afterpiece: The Honest Yorkshireman.* V.
*Cast:* [listed in 1736 Dublin edition] Gaylove—S. Hinde; Muckworm—
Hornby; Sapscull—Philips; Slango—Naylor; Blunder—Reed; Arabella—
Miss Woffington; Combbrush—Mrs. Reynolds.
*Miscellaneous:* "To be repeated on Thursday [i.e. 22 Jan. 1736] . . . taken
from a surreptitious copy, 'tis expected that the Author's genuine copy will
be still more entertaining" (*DEP*, 13–17 Jan. 1736).
     "'Tis reported, that Mr. Hornby the Proprietor of the Theatre-Royal in
Bath, will set out with all convenient speed for that place with his Family,
and a Company of Actors collected from our Theatres, to entertain the
Public in the approaching Seasons, and at the Hot-Well. Their place of
Rendevos [*sic*] will be Drogheda, and 'tis thought they will return to Dublin
next Winter" (*DEP*, 24–27 Jan. 1736).
*Singing and Dancing:* Overture composed by Dr. Pepusch, songs by Mr.
Carey.

15    Thur.    SA.    *The Man of Taste; or, The Guardian.*
*Cast:* None listed.

20    Tues.    SA.    *Love for Love.* V.
*Cast:* None listed.
*Command:* Duke and Duchess of Dorset.
*Miscellaneous:* Government Night: Anniversary birth of Frederick, Prince
of Wales.

20     Tues.     AS.     Unspecified "Play."
*Command:* Duke and Duchess of Dorset.

22     Thur.     AS.     *The Constant Couple.*
*Cast:* None listed.

                              and
*Afterpiece: The Honest Yorkshireman.*
*Cast:* None listed.

26     Mon.     AS.     *The Tempest.*
*Cast:* None listed.

29     Thur.     AS.     *The Merry Wives of Windsor.*
*Cast:* None listed.
*Benefit:* Griffith.
*Deferred:* Deferred from 15, then 22 Dec. 1735.

                              and
*Afterpiece: The Honest Yorkshireman.*
*Cast:* None listed.
*Miscellaneous:* At the particular Desire of several Persons of Quality.

FEBRUARY

4     Wed.     SA.     *Leonora; or, The Fatal Lover.*
*Cast:* None listed.
*Miscellaneous:* [Premiere.]

                              and
*Afterpiece: The Spaniard Deceived, or, Harlequin Worm Doctor.*
*Cast:* None listed.
*Miscellaneous:* [Premiere. "The best of its Kind ever yet exhibited" (*WO,* 3
Feb. 1736).

    Nicoll lists no play with this main title. He cites an anonymous pantomime
entitled *The Chymical Counterfeits; or, Harlequin Worm Doctor,* premiere
at GF 1734; *LS* lists no piece with this maintitle but also lists *Chymical
Counterfeits,* premiere 9 Dec. 1734 at GF.]
*Comment:* "A pantomime called Harlequin Spaniard was exhibited several
nights, and brought tolerable houses at SA theatre" (Hitchcock 1788–93,
1:98).

5     Thur.     AS.     *The Silent Woman.*
*Cast:* None listed.
*Command:* Duke and Duchess of Dorset.
*Benefit:* Mrs. Ashbury.
*Miscellaneous:* No person admitted behind the scenes under box prices.

and

*Afterpiece: Damon and Phillida.*
*Cast:* None listed.


9    Mon.    AS.    *Hamlet.*
*Cast:* None listed.
*Benefit:* The Author of the Farce [Prelleur].
*Singing and Dancing:* With several entertainments of singing and dancing, particularly "Old English Roast Beef, etc." as sung at Covent Garden, words and music by Leveridge, sung by Hinde; "Dusty Miller" dance by Moreau. With a new Prologue to the Town.

and

*Afterpiece: The Medley.*
*Cast:* Lovewin—Hinde; Sylvia—Mrs. Reynolds; Betty—Miss Woffington.
*Miscellaneous:* [Premiere. "A new ballad-farce of one act." By Prelleur. Nicoll lists only 1765 and 1778 works by this title; *LS* cites a dance and an overture of this title performed in 1734 and 1735.]
*Singing and Dancing:* With a new comic Medley Overture composed by Mr. Prelure [Prelleur], songs of farce set by Mr. Gladwin; the last Mr. Purcell's three part musical catch beginning, "Sum up all the Delights, etc." is to be sung by three voices in the Farce. At the end of the Farce dancing by W. Delamain and Miss Woffington.
[W. J. Lawrence states that neither Prelleur nor Gladwin was in Ireland at this time (Lawrence 1922, 404).]


9    Mon.    SA.    *Leonora.*
*Cast:* None listed.

and

*Afterpiece: The Spaniard Deceived.*
*Cast:* None listed.


11    Wed.    SA.    *Leonora.*
*Cast:* None listed.
*Benefit:* The Author of the Play [Anonymous].


12    Thur.    AS.    *The Funeral; or, Grief a-la-Mode.*
*Cast:* None listed.
*Command:* Duke and Duchess of Dorset.
*Benefit:* Ralph Elrington.
*Miscellaneous: Alexander the Great; or, The Rival Queens* was originally advertised for this night, but it was altered at the particular Desire of several Persons of Quality.

and

*Afterpiece:* A new Grotesque Entertainment never acted here. [Perhaps *The Spaniard Deceived*, See 3 April 1736.]


16    Mon.    SA.    *The Twin Rivals.*
*Cast:* None listed.
*Benefit:* Barrington.

and

*Afterpiece: Penelope.*
*Cast:* None listed.
*Miscellaneous:* [Ballad Opera by John Mottley assisted by T. Cooke.]


20    Fri.    SA.    *King Richard III.*
*Cast:* None listed.
*Benefit:* Mr. and Mrs. Ward.

and

*Afterpiece: The Stage Coach.*
*Cast:* None listed.


23    Mon.    AS.    Ridotto.
*Comment:* "The Appearance of Ladies and Gentlemen at the Riddotto . . . was so grand the like has not been seen here before, the streets were so thronged with coaches and chairs, that several Ladies were forced to wait above two hours before they could get up to the Play-House door" (*DEP,* 21–24 Feb. 1736).


23    Mon.    SA.    *King Lear and his Three Daughters.*
*Cast:* None listed.
*Benefit:* Cashell.

and

*Afterpiece: Flora.*
*Cast:* None listed.


26    Thur.    AS.    *The Conscious Lovers.*
*Cast:* Sealand—F. Elrington.
*Command:* Duke and Duchess of Dorset.
*Benefit:* Moreau.
*Miscellaneous:* Prices: Boxes, balconies and stage 5/5, Pit 3/3, Gallery 2/2.
*Singing and Dancing:* With several entertainments of singing and dancing between the acts.

and

*Afterpiece: The Devil to Pay.*
*Cast:* None listed.

27    Fri.    SA.    *The Double Dealer.*
*Cast:* None listed.
*Benefit:* Dryden (treasurer).
                              and
*Afterpiece: The Cooper Deceived.*
*Cast:* None listed.
*Miscellaneous:* [Premiere. Anonymous Pantomime? Nicoll 1977-79, 2:369, lists an anonymous pantomime entitled *The Cooper Deceived; or, Harlequin Executed* performed at GF in May 1748; *LS* lists only an anonymous pantomime called *The Cooper Outwitted; or, Harlequin Happy,* performed at DL from Apr. 1742.]

MARCH

2    Tues.    SA.    *Love for Love.*
*Cast:* None listed.
*Miscellaneous:* Government Night; Anniversary of birth of Queen Caroline. Boxes opened for the Ladies. With an occasional prologue.
*Deferred:* The play intended to be acted last night [1 Mar.] at the Theatre Royal in Smock Alley is put off till this Night, the Musick being obliged to attend at the Castle.
                              and
*Afterpiece: The Spaniard Deceived.*
*Cast:* None listed.

3    Wed.    AS.    Concert of Vocal and Instrumental Music.
*Benefit:* Woder.
*Miscellaneous:* [Francis Woder was listed as a State Musician in 1717 (Boydell 1988, 293).]

4    Thur.    AS.    *The Squire of Alsatia.*
*Cast:* None listed.
*Benefit:* Vanderbank.
*Miscellaneous:* Never acted here before. At the particular Desire of several Persons of Quality.

6    Sat.    SA.    *Love Makes a Man.*
*Cast:* None listed.
*Benefit:* Master Pitt.
*Singing and Dancing:* With several entertainments of singing and dancing between the acts.
                              and
*Afterpiece: Damon and Phillida.*
*Cast:* None listed.

8    Mon.    SA.    *The Gamester.*
*Cast:* None listed.
*Benefit:* Tyler.


15    Mon.    SA.    *The Miser.*
*Cast:* None listed.
*Benefit:* L. Duval.

and

*Afterpiece: The Spaniard Deceived.*
*Cast:* None listed.
*Miscellaneous:* A new Pantomime Entertainment lately performed with vast Applause.
*Singing and Dancing:* Concluding with a Riddotto al Fresco.


16    Tues.    RS.    *Othello.*
*Cast:* Othello—J. Hinde; Iago—I. Sparks.
*Benefit:* A Gentleman in Distress.
*Miscellaneous:* For the Entertainment of the Gentlemen Subscribers and the Gentlemen and Ladies of the Earl of Meath's Liberty. N. B. There will be a Guard procured to keep all quiet. Prices: Boxes British half-crown; Pit three British six-pences; Middle Gallery 1s.; Upper Gallery 6d.
   [Evidently the RS theatre was temporarily reopened for this performance.]

and

*Afterpiece: The Devil to Pay.*
*Cast:* None listed.


17    Wed.    SA.    *The Committee; or, The Faithful Irishman.* V.
*Cast:* Teague—Barrington.
*Benefit:* Sick and Decayed Freemasons.
*Miscellaneous:* [The prologue, spoken by Ward, and the epilogue, spoken by Mrs. Ward, as well as several songs sung at this performance are in the Halliday Collection of pamphlets No. 5, vol. 127, in the Royal Irish Academy and reprinted in Lepper and Crossle 1925, 474–82.]
*Singing and Dancing:* A song at the end of every act with the Grand Chorus and other Choruses, to be sung by the Masons; with dancing.
*Comment:* "St. Patrick's Day the Committee was performed to a larger assembly of Masons than had been known for many years. It was performed to the perfect satisfaction of the spectators, particularly the part of Teague, by Mr. Barrington" (*DEP,* 2–6 Mar. 1736).

and

*Afterpiece: The Cobler of Preston.*
*Cast:* None listed.

18   Thur.    AS.    *The Relapse.*
*Cast:* None listed.
*Command:* Duke and Duchess of Dorset.
*Benefit:* Mrs. Bellamy.
                              and
*Afterpiece: The Maid's Last Prayer.*
*Cast:* None listed.
*Miscellaneous:* "A new Ballad Opera never performed here."

20   Sat.    SA.    *Venice Preserved.*
*Cast:* None listed.
*Benefit:* Husband.

22   Mon.    SA.    *The Provoked Husband.*
*Cast:* None listed.
*Benefit:* L. Sparks.

24   Wed.    SA.    *Love Makes a Man.*
*Cast:* None listed.
*Benefit:* The Blue Coat Hospital in Queen St., to be applied to rebuilding
the same.
*Deferred:* Deferred from 11 Mar. 1736, tickets for *Oroonoko* intended to
have been performed will be taken.
                              and
*Afterpiece: The Mock Doctor.*
*Cast:* None listed.

25   Thur.    AS.    *The Fair Quaker of Deal; or, The Humours of the
Navy.*
*Cast:* None listed.
*Command:* Duke and Duchess of Dorset.
*Benefit:* Watson.
*Miscellaneous:* Not acted here these 50 years. Being particularly desired.
                              and
*Afterpiece: The Contrivances.*
*Cast:* None listed.
*Miscellaneous:* Altered from *The Honest Yorkshireman* at the particular
desire of several Ladies and Gentlemen of Quality.

27   Sat.    SA.    *Othello.*
*Cast:* None listed.
*Benefit:* Morris.
*Singing and Dancing:* With several entertainments of dancing between the
acts. At the particular desire of several Ladies of Quality.

29   Mon.   AS.   *The Mourning Bride.*
*Cast:* Osmyn—Ralph Elrington.
*Command:* Duke and Duchess of Dorset.
*Benefit:* W. Delamain.

and

*Afterpiece: The Mock Doctor.*
*Cast:* None listed.

31   Wed.   SA.   *King Richard III.*
*Cast:* None listed.
*Benefit:* Reilly (printer to the Theatre).
*Miscellaneous:* At the particular Desire of several Ladies of Quality.
*Singing and Dancing:* With several entertainments of singing and dancing.

and

*Afterpiece: Flora.*
*Cast:* None listed.

APRIL

1   Thur.   AS.   *The Fatal Marriage; or, The Innocent Adultery.*
*Cast:* None listed.
*Command:* Duke and Duchess of Dorset.
*Benefit:* Philips.

and

*Afterpiece: The Wrangling Lovers.*
*Cast:* None listed.
*Miscellaneous:* "By John Vanbrught." [This may be William Lyon's adaptation which Nicoll lists only in a 1745 Edinburgh edition.]

3   Sat.   AS.   *The Distrest Mother.*
*Cast:* None listed.
*Benefit:* Mrs. Jane Marmion.
*Miscellaneous:* At the particular Desire of several Ladies of Quality. Prices: Boxes 5/5; Lattice 4/4, Pit 3/3, Gallery 2/2.
*Singing and Dancing:* Dancing by Delamain and Miss Woffington.

and

*Afterpiece: Chrononhotonthologos.*
*Cast:* None listed.

3   Sat.   SA.   *The Beaux' Stratagem.*
*Cast:* None listed.
*Benefit:* John Johnson (musician).
*Singing and Dancing:* Dancing: End Act I a Pierrot by Morris; Act II Scotch Hornpipe by Pitts; Act III Wooden Shoe by Morris; Act IV Dance to the

Key of the Cel[?] by Master Pitt; Act V dance by Robert Delamain; End of Afterpiece a new Country Dance. Music to Play and Entertainment composed by John Johnson.

and

*Afterpiece: The Spaniard Deceived.*
*Cast:* None listed.
*Miscellaneous:* A new pantomime entertainment in grotesque characters.

5    Mon.    AS.    *Love's Last Shift.*
*Cast:* None listed.
*Command:* Duke and Duchess of Dorset:
*Benefit:* Miss Mackay.

and

*Afterpiece: The Necromancer.*
*Cast:* None listed.
*Miscellaneous:* Being desired.

5    Mon.    SA.    *Woman's a Riddle.*
*Cast:* None listed.
*Benefit:* Cummins and Morgan.
*Miscellaneous:* At the particular Desire of several Persons of Quality. Epilogue with Morgan riding on an ass.

and

*Afterpiece: The Stage Coach.*
*Cast:* Squire Somebody—Wetherilt; Macchone—Barrington.
*Singing and Dancing:* Several entertainments. At the particular desire of several Persons of Quality Barrington will sing "Teague's Travels" and one beginning "Arrah, my Judy"; Dancing by Morris, Pitt, and others.

7    Wed.    SA.    *King Henry IV, with the Humours of Falstaff.*
*Cast:* None listed.

8    Thur.    AS.    *Sir Courtly Nice; or, It Cannot Be.*
*Cast:* Sir Courtly—Watson.
*Command:* Duke and Duchess of Dorset.

and

*Afterpiece: Tom Thumb.*
*Cast:* Tom Thumb—"Little" Miss Naylor ("Mr. Naylor's 4 year old Daughter").
*Miscellaneous:* Miss Naylor dressed in a "Beautiful Roman Shape, with a Train borne by a Gentleman."

14    Wed.    SA.    *The Tender Husband.*
*Cast:* None listed.
*Benefit:* Wetherilt.

15    Thur.    AS.    *The Tender Husband.*
*Cast:* None listed.
*Command:* Duke and Duchess of Dorset.
*Benefit:* Mrs. Wrightson and Loughlin.
*Miscellaneous:* Not acted here [i.e. at AS] these 5 years; There will be particular Care taken in the Performance of the Entertainment.
and
*Afterpiece: The Necromancer.*
*Cast:* None listed.
*Miscellaneous:* Being desired. With three additional scenes never performed here.

15    Thur.    SA.    *Theodosius.*
*Cast:* None listed.
*Benefit:* Redman.

17    Sat.    SA.    *The Beggar's Opera.*
*Cast:* Macheath—R. Layfield.
*Benefit:* Layfield.

[Passion Week 19–24 April]

28    Wed.    SA.    *The Squire of Alsatia.*
*Cast:* None listed.
*Command:* Duke and Duchess of Dorset.

29    Thur.    AS.    *Pasquin.*
*Cast:* None listed.
*Benefit:* Philips.
*Miscellaneous:* A dramatic satire on the Times Being a Rehearsal of two Plays, viz. a Comedy called The Election; and a Tragedy called the Life and Death of Common Sense.
[For this night *DEP*, 17–20 Apr. 1736, advertises *Woman is a Riddle* and *Chrononhotonthologos,* benefit Sheridan and Connor, commanded by the Duke and Duchess of Dorset. Since Philips already had a benefit on 1 Apr., it is possible that this entry (from *FDJ*) is in error. However, the *DEP*, 24–27 Apr. 1736, advertises both of these pieces for this night.]

MAY

1    Sat.    SA.    *Pasquin.*
*Cast:* None listed.
*Miscellaneous:* First time performed here [i.e. at SA]. "Dramatic Satire on

the Times, Being the Rehearsal of two Plays: viz. a Comedy called the Election and a Tragedy called the Life and Death of Common Sense."

3    Mon.    SA.    *Pasquin.*
*Cast:* None listed.

5    Wed.    SA.    *Pasquin.*
*Cast:* None listed.

13    Thur.    AS.    *The Silent Woman.*
*Cast:* None listed.
*Command:* Duke and Duchess of Dorset.
*Benefit:* Morgan (pit officekeeper) and Green.
*Singing and Dancing:* Dancing by Moreau, W. Delamain, and Miss Woffington.

and

*Afterpiece: Tom Thumb.*
*Cast:* Tom Thumb—"Little" Miss Naylor; Train-bearer—A Gentleman.
*Miscellaneous:* Miss Naylor will wear a new dress after the Roman Manner.

17    Mon.    SA.    *Oroonoko.*
*Cast:* None listed.
*Benefit:* Miss Butcher.

and

*Afterpiece: The Devil to Pay.*
*Cast:* None listed.

18    Tues.    AS.    *Pasquin.*
*Cast:* None listed.
*Benefit:* Call. MacCarty (musician) and Walsh.
*Miscellaneous:* For the entertainment of the Gentlemen of the Charitable Society held at the Bull's Head in Fishamble St. Acted here but once. At the particular Desire of several Ladies of Quality; last time of performing it this season.

20    Thur.    AS.    *A Bold Stroke for a Wife.*
*Cast:* None listed.
*Command:* The Duke and Duchess of Dorset.
*Benefit:* LeRoux and Mrs. Eastham (boxkeepers).

24    Mon.    SA.    *Pasquin.*
*Cast:* None listed.
*Benefit:* L. Duval.
*Miscellaneous:* At the particular Desire of several Persons of Quality.

26    Wed.    SA.    *Macbeth.*
*Cast:* None listed.
*Benefit:* Mr. and Mrs. Ward.
*Miscellaneous:* With entertainments.

JUNE

2    Wed.    SA.    *The Squire of Alsatia.*
*Cast:* None listed.
*Benefit:* Morgan and Mrs. Bamford (dresser).
                              and
*Afterpiece: The Mock Lawyer.*
*Cast:* None listed.
*Miscellaneous:* Ballad Opera.

16    Wed.    SA.    *The Provoked Husband.* V.
*Cast:* None listed.
*Benefit:* A great Number of Poor Prisoners in the Four Courts Marshalsea.
*Comment:* " . . . a very small audience, occasioned by the thinness of the
Town, and proper persons to disperse tickets for those poor Creatures"
(*DEP,* 15–19 June 1736). [See performance of 25 June 1736 for a second
benefit.]
                              and
*Afterpiece: The Mock Lawyer.*
*Cast:* None listed.

21    Mon.    SA.    *Pasquin.*
*Cast:* None listed.
*Benefit:* Bourne (Byrne).
*Miscellaneous:* "The House was as cool as in March and therefore Persons
can sit in it with the Greatest Ease and Pleasure" (*DEP,* 15–19 June 1736).
*Singing and Dancing:* With entertainments of dancing, particularly "Two
Pierrots" and "Wooden Shoe Dance." "Two Punches" by Pitt and Byrne; a
Dance to "Jack Lattin" by Byrne.
                              and
*Afterpiece: The Mock Lawyer.*
*Cast:* None listed.

25    Fri.    SA.    *The Miser.*
*Cast:* None listed.
*Benefit:* Second Benefit for Prisoners in Four Courts Marshalsea.
*Miscellaneous:* The House being very small for the first benefit on 16 June
Duval has applied for a second such benefit. Last time of acting this Season.

With a new Prologue on the occasion by a member of the Charitable Musical
Society of the Bull's Head Club.
*Singing and Dancing:* With Singing and Dancing.

and

*Afterpiece:* Unspecified "Farce."

30    Wed.    SA.    *The Committee.*
*Cast:* None listed.
*Benefit:* Dryden (Treasurer).
*Miscellaneous:* The House is rendered so cool, that Persons can sit in it
with the greatest Ease and Pleasure.
*Singing and Dancing:* Dancing: "Wooden Shoe," "Pierrot in the Basket,"
and "Jack Lattin" by Pitt and Miss Barnes.

and

*Afterpiece: The Spaniard Deceived.*
*Cast:* None listed.

[The SA company may have acted until early July. *PO,* 3–6 July contains
the notice: "On Saturday Evening last [3 July], a Girl, Daughter of Mr.
Hartford, in SA, fell from the Gallery of the Play-house in said Street into
the Pitt and fractured her Scull, and died soon after."

Clark 1965, 2, says that the AS company went to Cork in July to open
a summer Theatre-Royal. They performed at Clonmell, Cork, and Carlow.
Hitchcock 1788–93, 1:97, reports that the SA company made a trip during
this summer to Belfast and Derry.]

## 1736–1737 Season

Theatres operating: Aungier St. (Theatre Royal with performances
advertised as acted by "His Majesty's Company of Comedians"); Smock
Alley (advertised as acting "By Permission of the Lord Mayor").

*Aungier St. Company:*
Miss Butcher (from SA?), Butler, Dash, J. Delamain, F. Elrington, J. Elring-
ton, Ralph Elrington (until 7 Jan.), Griffith, Jenkins (from GF), Miss Mackay,
Redman, Reed, Seivers, Sheridan, Vanderbank, Mrs. Vanderbank, Walsh, J.
Ward (from SA), Mrs. Ward, J. Watson, Jr., Mrs. Williamson (from London),
Miss Woffington.

Dancers: W. Delamain, Moreau.

Musicians: Blackwood, Lee.

House Servants: LeRoux (boxkeeper), John Morgan (pit officekeeper).


*Repertory:*
Mainpieces: Recorded performances: 37 (of 31 different pieces, excluding 3 ridottos).
Afterpieces: Total recorded performances: 18 (of 13 pieces, including unspecified farces: 2.
Premieres:
*Harlequin Turned Physician.*
*The Brave Irishman.*
Entr'acte entertainments: 10 performances advertise dancing, 1 singing.
Command Performances: 4 (6 Government nights).
Benefits:
Pre-February: Manager—1; Actor—1; House Servant—1; Charity—1.
Post-February: Manager—1; Actor—12; Charity—1.

*Smock Alley Company:*
Barrington, Beamsley, Mrs. Bullock, L. Duval, Ralph Elrington (From AS, after 7 Jan.), Fitzpatrick, Healy, Mrs. S. Hinde, Husband, Master Husband, Miller (from Edinburgh), C. Morgan, Mrs. Orfeur, T. Philips, Mrs. Ravenscroft, Mrs. Reynolds (from CG in March, formerly of AS), L. Sparks, Wetherilt, Mrs. Wetherilt.


Dancers: Miss Barnes, Dumont, S. Hinde (from AS), J. Morris, Pitt, Master Pitt.


House Servants: Dryden (Treasurer), Fox (pit doorkeeper), Lamb (pit officekeeper), Nimmo (prompter), Stockdill (carpenter).


Summer: Roger Bridgewater (from CG), Dennis Delane (from CG), Adam Hallam (from CG).


*Repertory:*
Mainpieces: Recorded performances: 55 (of 36 different pieces including one unspecified pantomime).
Afterpieces: Recorded Performances: 20 (of 13 different pieces).
Premieres: *The Comic Rivals.*
Entr'acte entertainments: 12.
Command Performances: 1, Masons.
Benefits:

Pre-February: Manager—2; Actor—1; Charity—3.
Post-February: Manager—2; Actor—12; House Servants—3; Charity—1.

## 1736

OCTOBER

11　Mon.　AS.　*The Recruiting Officer.*
*Cast:* Plume—J. Elrington; Kite—Vanderbank; Scale—R. Elrington; Brazen—Watson; Bullock—F. Elrington; Peniman—Griffith; Appletree—Reed; Worthy—Butler; Balance—Sheridan; Melinda—Mrs. Williamson (from London, her first appearance here); Sylvia—Miss Mackay; Rose—Miss Woffington; Lucy—Mrs. Vanderbank.
*Command:* Lords Justice.
*Miscellaneous:* Government Night: Anniversary of Coronation of George II; Balconies, 3s. 3d.; Pit, British half-crown; Gallery, 1s. 6d. British; To begin at 6 o'clock. With a new Occasional Prologue spoken by Griffith.
*Singing and Dancing:* Dancing by Moreau, William Delamain, and Miss Woffington.

18　Mon.　AS.　*The Provoked Husband.*
*Cast:* Lady Townly—Mrs. Williamson (her second appearance on this stage).
*Singing and Dancing:* Dancing by Moreau and W. Delamain.

25　Mon.　AS.　*The Spanish Fryar.*
*Cast:* Torrismond—J. Elrington; Leonora—Mrs. Williamson.
*Miscellaneous:* By particular Desire of several Persons of Quality.
*Singing and Dancing:* Dancing, particularly two Harlequins and a Columbine by Moreau, Delamain, and Miss Woffington.

28　Thur.　SA.　*King Henry IV, with the Humours of Falstaff.*
*Cast:* None listed.
*Benefit:* The Almshouse now Erecting in St. Werburgh's Parish, for the Reception of Reduced Housekeepers (Poor Widows of St. Werbergh's Parish).
*Financial:* Over £120 collected (*FDJ*, 26–30 Oct. 1736).

30　Sat.　AS.　*Tunbridge Walks; or, The Yeoman of Kent.*
*Cast:* None listed.
*Miscellaneous:* Government Night: Anniversary of birth of George II; "The Speaker of the House of Commons sat the Play out in the King's Box" (*DDA*, 1 Nov. 1736). Occasional Prologue spoke by J. Elrington.

NOVEMBER

1   Mon.   AS.   *Oroonoko.*
*Cast:* Oroonoko—Ward (from SA).

1   Mon.   SA.   *The Twin Rivals.*
*Cast:* Teague—Barrington.
*Singing and Dancing:* Dancing by Morris and others.

4   Thur.   AS.   *Tamerlane.*
*Cast:* None listed.
*Miscellaneous:* Government Night: Anniversary of birth of William III. "The usual Prologue" spoken by Elrington.
*Singing and Dancing:* Dancing by W. Delamain and Miss Woffington to the tune of "Lillibalero."

5   Fri.   SA.   *Tamerlane.*
*Cast:* None listed.
*Miscellaneous:* "For the Entertainment of the Lord Mayor and Aldermen of the City of Dublin. The Lord Mayor and Aldermen sat in the centre box reserved for the Mayor who appeared bearing his rod of office and wearing his Formalities. A group of Worshipful Citizens in their Gowns sat in adjoining boxes" (*DDA,* 6 Nov. 1736).
*Singing and Dancing:* Several Entertainments of Dancing.

8   Mon.   AS.   *The Beggar's Opera.*
*Cast:* Macheath—Jenkins (from GF).

8   Mon.   SA.   *Pasquin.*
*Cast:* None listed.

11   Thur.   AS.   *The Constant Couple.*
*Cast:* Wildair—Jenkins (lately from London).
*Singing and Dancing:* Several Entertainments of Dancing.

11   Thur.   SA.   *The Merry Wives of Windsor.*
*Cast:* Falstaff—Morgan.
                              and
*Afterpiece: The Stage Coach.*
*Cast:* Maccahone—Barrington.

15   Mon.   AS.   Ridotto.
*Deferred:* Deferred from 4 Nov. so the town can fill.

15    Mon.    SA.    *A Bold Stroke for a Wife.*
*Cast:* None listed.
*Singing and Dancing:* Several Entertainments of Dancing.
and

*Afterpiece: The Mock Lawyer.*
*Cast:* None listed.


18    Thur.    SA.    *Rule a Wife and Have a Wife.*
*Cast:* Estifania—Mrs. Bullock (from CG).
*Singing and Dancing:* Several Entertainments of Dancing, particularly "The Wooden Shoe" by Morris.
and

*Afterpiece: The Stage Coach.*
*Cast:* Maccahone—Barrington.


19    Fri.    AS.    *The Merry Wives of Windsor.* V.
*Cast:* None listed.
*Command:* Lords Justice.
*Miscellaneous:* Government Night: Anniversary of birth of Princess of Wales. With a new prologue on the Occasion, written by a young gentleman of our Society, and quoted in full in *DDA*, 21 Jan. 1736.
*Singing and Dancing:* Entertainments of Dancing.


22    Mon.    AS.    *Love Makes a Man.*
*Cast:* None listed.
*Command:* Viscount Tyrone, Grand Master of All Ireland.
*Benefit:* Griffith.
*Miscellaneous:* Masons' Night. With a Prologue to be spoke by a Free Mason; Epilogue by a Mason's Wife.
    [The Masons resumed their patronage of Griffith with this benefit despite the hurt feelings resulting from the *Country Wife* debacle of 1735. This was perhaps because Griffith was deeply in debt, as is clear from his letter of 8 Feb. 1736 to Swift pleading for financial assistance. See Swift 1963–65, 4:458–59.]
*Singing and Dancing:* Songs of Masonry between the Acts; Dancing by Moreau and Delamain.
and

*Afterpiece: Damon and Phillida.*
*Cast:* None listed.


22    Mon.    SA.    *The Provoked Husband.*
*Cast:* Lady Townly—Mrs. Bullock.
*Singing and Dancing:* Several Entertainments of Dancing.

25   Thur.   AS.   *Macbeth.*
*Cast:* Banquo—F. Elrington.
*Singing and Dancing:* Several Entertainments of Dancing.

25   Thur.   SA.   *The Old Batchelour.*
*Cast:* Laetitia—Mrs. Bullock.

29   Mon.   AS.   Ridotto.

**DECEMBER**

1   Wed.   SA.   *The City Wives' Confederacy.*
*Cast:* Clarissa—Mrs. Bullock.
*Miscellaneous:* Not acted these 8 years.

2   Thur.   AS.   *King Henry VIII.*
*Cast:* King—Vanderbank; Wolsey—F. Elrington.
*Benefit:* Vanderbank.
*Miscellaneous:* At the Desire of several Persons of Quality.

3   Fri.   SA.   *The Beaux' Stratagem.*
*Cast:* Sullen—Mrs. Bullock.
*Benefit:* The Charitable Infirmary of the King's Inn.
*Singing and Dancing:* Several Entertainments of Dancing by W. Delamain
and Miss Woffington.
*Financial:* "Yesterday se'enight the Money received at the Theatre in Smoak
Alley, for the Benefit of the Charitable Infirmary, amounted to 140 l" (*FDJ,*
11 Dec. 1736).

9   Thur.   AS.   *The Miser.*
*Cast:* Lovegold—F. Elrington.
*Benefit:* F. Elrington.
*Miscellaneous:* By particular Desire of several Persons of Quality. Altered
from Plautus by Moliere.
and

*Afterpiece: The Lover's Opera.*
*Cast:* None listed.
*Miscellaneous:* An Operatical Farce. Never acted in this Kingdom, as acted
over 30 nights at the Theatre Royal in London; Boxes 5s. 5d., Balconies 4s.
4d., Pit 3s. 3d., Gallery 2s. 2d.; To begin at 6 o'clock. At the Desire of several
Persons of Quality.

13   Mon.   AS.   *The City Wives' Confederacy.* V.
*Cast:* None listed.
*Benefit:* L. Duval.

16 Thur. AS. *Hamlet.*
*Cast:* None listed.
*Benefit:* J. Delamain.
*Miscellaneous:* Last time of acting before Christmas and no play at the other house this night.
*Singing and Dancing:* Several Entertainments of Dancing.


17 Fri. SA. *The Twin Rivals.*
*Cast:* None listed.
*Singing and Dancing:* Several Entertainments of Dancing.


20 Mon. AS. *The Old Batchelour.*
*Cast:* None listed.
*Benefit:* LeRoux (boxkeeper).
*Miscellaneous:* By the Charity of the Ladies.
*Singing and Dancing:* Several Entertainments of Dancing, particularly the last new Dance composed by M. Moreau, performed by him, William Delamain, and Miss Woffington.
and
*Afterpiece: Chrononhotonthologos.*
*Cast:* None listed.


22 Wed. SA. *The Provoked Husband.*
*Cast:* Lady Townly—Mrs. Bullock.
*Benefit:* The Prisoners in the Several Marshalseas.
*Miscellaneous:* By Order of the Charitable Musical Society. [See Whyte 1742 for a prologue that it states was designed to be spoken at this performance.]


**1737**

JANUARY

3 Mon. AS. *The Beggar's Opera.*
*Cast:* None listed.


3 Mon. SA. *The Committee.*
*Cast:* Teague—Barrington; Ruth—Mrs. Bullock.


7 Fri. SA. *Venice Preserved.*
*Cast:* Jaffier—R. Elrington; Belvidera—Mrs. Bullock.

10    Mon.    AS.    *Jane Shore.*
*Cast:* None listed.
*Miscellaneous:* Several unspecified "Entertainments."
and
*Afterpiece: The Rival Theatres; or, A Playhouse to be Lett.* [Probably *The Stage Mutineers; or, A Playhouse to be Lett.*]
*Cast:* [listed in 24 Jan. 1737 Dublin edition] First Manager—Ward; Second Manager—Reed; Pistol—Butler; Crambo—Watson; Truncheon—J. Elrington; Comic—Jenkins; Wardrobe Keeper—Dash; Prompter—Seivers; Coupee—Sheridan; Madame Haughty—Mrs. Williamson; Mrs. Squeamish—Miss Mackay; Miss Crotchet—Miss Woffington; Miss Lovemode—Miss Butcher.
*Miscellaneous:* A tragi-comi-farcical ballad opera. By "A Gentleman late of Trinity College, Cambridge, 1733" [i.e. Edward Phillips.]

10    Mon.    SA.    *The City Wives' Confederacy.*
*Cast:* None listed.
*Miscellaneous:* By particular Desire of several Ladies of Quality.

14    Fri.    SA.    *The City Wives' Confederacy.*
*Cast:* None listed.
and
*Afterpiece: The Mock Doctor.*
*Cast:* None listed.

17    Mon.    AS.    *Woman is a Riddle.*
*Cast:* None listed.
and
*Afterpiece: The Rival Theatres.*
*Cast:* None listed.
*Miscellaneous:* Third Night.

17    Mon.    SA.    *Rule a Wife and Have a Wife.*
*Cast:* Estafania—Mrs. Bullock.

20    Thur.    AS.    *Love for Love.* V.
*Cast:* None listed.
*Command:* Lords Justice.
*Miscellaneous:* Government Night: Anniversary of birth Frederick, Prince of Wales. With a new Occasional Prologue spoke by J. Elrington and written by a young Gentleman of our Society [of the King's Inns?]. Quoted in full in *DDA*, 21 Jan. 1736.

20    Thur.    SA.    Unspecified "Pantomime."

21     Fri.     SA.     *King Henry IV, Pt. 2, with the Humours of Sir John Falstaff, Justice Swallow, and Antient Pistol.*
*Cast:* None listed.

24     Mon.     AS.     *The Beaux' Stratagem.*
*Cast:* None listed.
                              and
*Afterpiece:* Unspecified "Pantomime."

26     Wed.     SA.     *The Provoked Husband.*
*Cast:* None listed.
*Command:* Lord Mayor, Aldermen, Sheriffs, and Common Council of the City of Dublin.
*Benefit:* L. Duval.
*Miscellaneous:* At the Request and for the entertainment of the Rt. Hon. Lord Mayor, Aldermen, Sheriffs, and Common Council of the City of Dublin.

27     Thur.     AS.     *The Way of the World.*
*Cast:* None listed.
*Benefit:* Moreau.

28     Fri.     SA.     *The Careless Husband.*
*Cast:* Lady Betty Modish—Mrs. Bullock.
*Benefit:* Mrs. Bullock.

FEBRUARY

1     Tues.     SA.     *Pasquin.* V.
*Cast:* None listed.
*Benefit:* Philips
*Miscellaneous:* A crowded Audience was present. With several unspecified "Entertainments."
                              and
*Afterpiece: The Devil to Pay.*
*Cast:* None listed.

2     Wed.     SA.     *The Committee.*
*Cast:* None listed.
*Benefit:* Barrington.
*Deferred:* Deferred from 31 Jan. 1737 "not knowing the said Day was appointed by Act of Parliament for the fast of the Martyrdom of King Charles, which falls on Sunday the 30th" (*DNL,* 25–29 Jan. 1737).

and

*Afterpiece: The Mock Lawyer.*
*Cast:* None listed.


3    Thur.    AS.      *The History and Fall of Caius Marius.*
*Cast:* None listed.
*Benefit:* J. Elrington.

and

*Afterpiece: Harlequin Turned Physician.*
*Cast:* Drunken Man—Reed; French Peasant—Moreau; Wife—Miss Woffington.
*Miscellaneous* [Premiere. Not listed in Nicoll or *LS.*]


4    Fri.    SA.      *The Conscious Lovers.* V.
*Cast:* None listed.
*Benefit:* Husband.
*Miscellaneous:* "Last Night [i.e. 4 Feb.] there was the fullest house at SA that has been this Season. . . ." (*DDA*, 5 Feb. 1737).
*Singing and Dancing:* Several Entertainments of Dancing.

and

*Afterpiece: Tom Thumb.*
*Cast:* Tom Thumb—Master Husband.


7    Mon.    SA.      *Love for Love.*
*Cast:* Angelica—Mrs. Bullock.
*Command:* Lord Viscount Tyrone, Grand Master of Ireland.
*Benefit:* Poor and Distressed Freemasons.
*Miscellaneous:* With a Prologue and Epilogue proper for the Occasion.
*Singing and Dancing:* With a Mason Song and a dance between every Act.

and

*Afterpiece: The Mock Lawyer.*
*Cast:* None listed.


8    Tues.    AS.      *The Miser.*
*Cast:* None listed.
*Benefit:* Widow Ashbury.

and

*Afterpiece:* Unspecified "Pantomime."


9    Wed.    SA.      *The Constant Couple.*
*Cast:* Sir Harry—R. Elrington.
*Benefit:* R. Elrington.
*Miscellaneous:* By particular Desire of several Persons of Quality.

and

*Afterpiece: The Mock Lawyer.*
*Cast:* None listed.

10    Thur.    AS.    *King Richard III.*
*Cast:* Gloster—Ward; King Henry—J. Elrington; Richmond—F. Elrington; Lord Mayor—Vanderbank.
*Benefit:* Mr. and Mrs. Ward.
*Miscellaneous:* A new Prologue on the Occasion. With several unspecified "Entertainments."
*Singing and Dancing:* Dance by W. Delamain and Miss Woffington in the character of a Free Mason and his Wife.

and

*Afterpiece: The Freemason's Opera.* [Probably W. R. Chetwood's *The Generous Freemason.*]
*Cast:* None listed.
*Miscellaneous:* Ballad Opera. As it was acted 76 Times in London; inscribed to that ancient and honourable Society. In which will be performed the whole ceremony of making a Free Mason. [*LS* lists only 10 performances of *The Generous Freemason* between 20 Aug. 1730 and its last recorded performance on 22 Aug. 1741.]

11    Fri.    SA.    *King Richard III.*
*Cast:* Gloster—Sparks (first time in character).
*Benefit:* L. Sparks.

and

*Afterpiece: The Cobler of Preston.*
*Cast:* None listed.

12    Sat.    AS.    *Hamlet.*
*Cast:* Hamlet—Ward; Ophelia—Miss Woffington.
*Benefit:* Mercer's Charitable Hospital in Stephens's St.
*Miscellaneous:* Hitchcock, 1:103, states that this is Miss Woffington's first appearance in a speaking character on that stage.
    Being the last Night of Term. The whole Receipts of the House this Night, is to be applied to the Charity, free of all Expenses.
*Singing and Dancing:* Several Entertainments of Dancing by W. Delamain.

14    Mon.    AS.    *The Orphan.*
*Cast:* None listed.
*Benefit:* Miss Woffington.

16    Wed.    SA.    *Love's Last Shift.*
*Cast:* None listed.
*Benefit:* Mr. and Mrs. Wetherilt.

and

*Afterpiece: The What D'Ye Call It.*
*Cast:* Timothy Peascod—Wetherilt.


17   Thur.   AS.   *The Funeral.*
*Cast:* None listed.
*Benefit:* Mrs. Williamson.
*Miscellaneous:* Not performed this Season. Several unspecified "Entertainments."
*Comment:* "N. B. Meeting with ungenerous usage from a partner [i.e. John Morgan, pit officekeeper, who was originally advertised to share this benefit] who has declined the Agreement, and put the whole expense of the house on myself; on which consideration, and being a stranger in the Kingdom, I hope the Town will favor me with their Company at Common Prices [signed Mrs. Williamson]" (*DDA,* 14 Feb. 1737).

and

*Afterpiece: The Devil to Pay.*
*Cast:* None listed.


18   Fri.   SA.   *Love Makes a Man.*
*Cast:* None listed.
*Benefit:* C. Morgan and Mrs. Ravenscoft.

and

*Afterpiece: The Rival Queans, with the Humours of Alexander the Great.*
*Cast:* Alexander—Morgan.
*Miscellaneous:* Not acted in Dublin these 10 years.


19   Sat.   AS.   *The Drummer.*
*Cast:* None listed.
*Benefit:* William Delamain.
*Miscellaneous:* Never Acted here.
*Singing and Dancing:* Dancing, particularly Act 1, Comic Dance by Moreau; Act 2, A New Dance to "The Berwick Jockey" by Miss Woffington; Act 3, A Scotch Jig to the Drought by Delamain; Act 4, Minuet and Louver by W. Delamain and Miss Woffington; Act 5, A Serious Dance by Delamain.

and

*Afterpiece: The Rival Theatres.*
*Cast:* None listed.


21   Mon.   AS.   *The Gamester.*
*Cast:* None listed.
*Benefit:* Reed.

and

*Afterpiece: The Honest Irishman; or, The Cockold in Conceit* [i.e. *The Brave Irishman*].
*Cast:* None listed.
*Miscellaneous:* [Premiere.] Written by a Gentleman of Trinity College, Dublin [i.e. Thomas Sheridan]. Particular care is taken that the Farce shall be played perfect.

21     Mon.     SA.     *The Careless Husband.*
*Cast:* None listed.
*Benefit:* Lamb (pit officekeeper) and Fox (pit doorkeeper).

24     Thur.     AS.     Ridotto.
*Deferred:* Deferred from 21 Jan. and again from 18 Feb. so that the Town can fill.

24     Thur.     SA.     *King Henry IV, Part 2.*
*Cast:* None listed.
*Benefit:* Master Pitt.
*Miscellaneous:* The last revived Play. At the particular Desire of several Ladies of Quality. With a new epilogue spoken by Master Pitt.

28     Mon.     SA.     *The Squire of Alsatia.*
*Cast:* None listed.
*Benefit:* Morris.

MARCH

1     Tues.     AS.     *The Beaux' Stratagem.*
*Cast:* None listed.
*Miscellaneous:* Government Night: Anniversary of birth of Queen Caroline.

7     Mon.     AS.     *The Squire of Alsatia.*
*Cast:* None listed.
*Benefit:* Miss Mackay.
*Singing and Dancing:* Several Entertainments of Dancing.
                                        and
*Afterpiece: Damon and Phillida.*
*Cast:* None listed.

7     Mon.     SA.     *The Royal Merchant.*
*Cast:* None listed.
*Benefit:* Dryden (Treasurer).
*Miscellaneous:* With the whole Procession of the Coronation of King Clause.

14    Mon.    SA.    *The Double Gallant.*
*Benefit:* Mrs. Orfeur and Miss Barnes.
*Cast:* Sick Lady—Mrs. Bullock.
*Singing and Dancing:* Several Entertainments of Dancing.

and

*Afterpiece: The What D'Ye Call It.*
*Cast:* None listed.

21    Mon.    SA.    *The Beggar's Opera.*
*Cast:* Macheath—Mrs. Reynolds (from CG); Lucy—Mrs. Samuel Hinde (her first appearance on any stage).
*Comment:* "The Beggar's Opera was got up for the purpose of introducing Mrs. Reynolds, the famous in the character of Macheath" (Hitchcock 1788–93, 1:98).

24    Thur.    AS.    *The Fair Quaker of Deal.*
*Cast:* None listed.
*Benefit:* Walsh and Butler.
*Singing and Dancing:* The Play will open with the Trumpet Overture of *Atalanthe* performed by the best hands. A variety of Dancing between the Acts. With an occasional epilogue in the character of Teague spoken by Mr. Reed.

and

*Afterpiece: The Cheats of Scapin.*
*Cast:* None listed.

24    Thur.    SA.    *Oroonoko.*
*Cast:* None listed.
*Singing and Dancing:* With entertainments of dancing, particularly "The Dutch Skipper and His Frow" by Hinde and Miss Barnes; "The Song of new Mad Tom" by Hinde, being the first time of his appearing on this stage.
*Comment:* "Mr. Hinde was the original in the song of Mad Tom in this kingdom, which he repeatedly sung on the stage with great applause" (Hitchcock, 1:98).

APRIL

2    Sat.    SA.    *The Orphan.*
*Cast:* None listed.
*Singing and Dancing:* With several entertainments of singing and dancing.

/          and

*Afterpiece: The King and the Miller of Mansfield.*
*Cast:* None listed.
*Miscellaneous:* A new dramatic tale.

[Passion Week 4–9 April]

11    Mon.    SA.    *King Charles I.*
*Cast:* None listed.
*Miscellaneous:* The Characters will be entirely new dressed, suitable to them
times. As it is now acting at the Theatre Royal in London. Written in imita-
tion of Shakespeare's style. [See Hitchcock, 1:98 for an amusing anecdote
about the writing of this play.]

25    Mon.    SA.    *The Beggar's Opera.*
*Cast:* None listed.
*Singing and Dancing:* Dancing by Hinde and Pitt.

29    Fri.    SA.    *Hamlet.*
*Cast:* None listed.
*Benefit:* Nimmo (Prompter).
*Singing and Dancing:* Entertainments of Dancing.
                                    and
*Afterpiece: The Devil to Pay.*
*Cast:* None listed.

MAY

2    Mon.    SA.    *The Hussar; or, Harlequin Restored.*
*Cast:* Harlequin—R. Elrington; Pierrot—J. Morris.
*Miscellaneous:* A new Pantomime with all the Scenes, Machines, and Decorations proper to the Entertainment.
    An advance notice in *FDJ* of 18 Apr. 1737 states: "Mr. Duval hath for some
time been practicing and getting up . . . *The Hussar.* . . . as no Expense has
been spared in the Scenes, Machines, Dresses, Sinkings, Flyings, and other
Decorations of the Entertainment, it therefore is not doubted but it will give
entire Satisfaction to the Town, nothing equal to it having ever been performed in this Kingdom before."

4    Wed.    SA.    *The Pilgrim.*
*Cast:* Pilgrim—Miller (from Edinburgh).
*Benefit:* L. Duval.
*Singing and Dancing:* With several Entertainments of Dancing
                                    and
*Afterpiece:* Unspecified "Farce."

5    Thur.    AS.    *The Inconstant.*
*Cast:* Young Mirabell—Bridges; Oriana—Miss Woffington.
*Benefit:* Blackwood (musician).
*Singing and Dancing:* With Dancing between the Acts.

                              and

*Afterpiece: The Devil to Pay.*
*Cast:* Jobson—Layfield.


9    Mon.    SA.    *The Beggar's Opera.*
*Cast:* None listed.
*Benefit:* Fitzpatrick and Healy.

                              and

*Afterpiece: The Mock Lawyer.*
*Cast:* None listed.


16    Mon.    AS.    *The Double Dealer.*
*Cast:* None listed.
*Benefit:* Watson.
*Miscellaneous:* At the particular Desire of several Persons of Quality.
*Singing and Dancing:* Dancing by Moreau, W. Delamain, and Miss Woffington.


16    Mon.    SA.    *A Bold Stroke for a Wife.*
*Cast:* None listed.
*Benefit:* Stockdill (Carpenter of the Playhouse).

                              and

*Afterpiece: The Comic Rivals; or, Columbine Coquette.*
*Cast:* None listed.
*Miscellaneous:* A new pantomime Interlude in Grotesque Characters never performed before. [Not listed in Nicoll or *LS*.]


17    Tues.    SA.    *Pasquin.*
*Cast:* None listed.
*Singing and Dancing:* Dancing: "The Squeeking Punch and Monkey" by Barrington; "The Dancing Punch" by Dumont, lately of Paris.

                              and

*Afterpiece: The Hussar.*
*Cast:* As 2 May 1737.
*Miscellaneous:* As it was acted at Mr. Duval's benefit with Applause.


20    Fri.    SA.    *The City Wives' Confederacy.*
*Cast:* None listed.
*Benefit:* Mrs. Reynolds.

                              and

*Afterpiece: Columbine Courtezan.*
*Cast:* None listed.
*Miscellaneous:* A comic, operatical, pantomime entertainment, never performed here. At the particular Desire of several Ladies of Quality.

23    Mon.    AS.    *The Merry Wives of Windsor.*
*Cast:* Falstaff—Vanderbank.
*Benefit:* Moreau.

and

*Afterpiece: The Hussar.*
*Cast:* None listed.

24    Tues.    AS.    *The Jew of Venice.*
*Cast:* None listed.
*Benefit:* Griffith, T. Elrington, Vanderbank.
*Miscellaneous:* For the Entertainment of the Lord Chancellor, Chancellor of the Exchequer, the Rt. Hon. and Hon. Judges, and the Rest of the Hon. Society of King's Inns.

and

*Afterpiece: The Virgin Unmasked.*
*Cast:* None listed.
*Miscellaneous:* Never acted here but once [but this is the first recorded performance].

JUNE

6    Mon.    AS.    *The Way of the World.*
*Cast:* None listed.
*Benefit:* Lee (musician).
*Singing and Dancing:* Several Entertainments of Dancing.

and

*Afterpiece: The Hussar.*
*Cast:* None listed.

*Summer Season*

A news item in *FDJ* of 4 June 1737 announces that *The Conscious Lovers,* intended as a benefit for some Gentlemen in Distress at SA, is put off "the Actors being at the Races in Mullingar." It states further that Duval, the manager, is now on his way from CG with Delane, Bridgewater, and Adam Hallam. They will perform "next Term" at SA. A news item from Athlone in the London *Daily Gazette* of June 1737 also refers to the journey to Dublin of these actors and adds Henry Giffard to the list. It states that the AS Company "intends to be at the Races at Clonmell to entertain . . . and at their Return from Cork design to entertain at Carlow, during the time of the Races."

    *PO,* 2–6 Aug. 1737, announces that the High Sheriff of Carlow "has given leave to Mr. Duval, for his Company to perform in the County Court-House during the Races there; and that Mr. Duval will give a Benefit-Night towards building the Church of Chade."

In September Duval responded to a claim by the AS company that only they would be permitted to play in Carlow: "I think proper to acquaint you, that my Company played here [in Carlow] in the Race Week on Tuesday and Saturday; and tho' it was usual for other Players to dismiss for want of Company on Saturdays, yet we played the Beggar's Opera on that Night, to the most crowded audience that ever was known here. . . . We likewise played the Monday following, and as to the Merit of the Companies, I humbly submit it to the Judgment of the Audiences. . . ." (PO, 3–6 Sept. 1737).

20   Mon.   SA.   *The Provoked Husband.*
*Cast:* Townly—A. Hallam (from CG); Manly—Bridgewater (from CG).

23   Thur.   SA.   *Othello.*
*Cast:* Othello—Delane (from CG); Iago—Hallam.

24   Fri.   SA.   *The Orphan.*
*Cast:* Principal Characters—Hallam; Bridgewater; Delane.

27   Mon.   SA.   *Julius Caesar.*
*Cast:* Brutus—Delane; Cassius—Bridgewater; Antony—Hallam.
*Miscellaneous:* "This Company intends in a short time to set out for Waterford . . . the English Gentlemen intend to accompany Mr. Duval there" (*DNL*, 21–25 June 1737).

30   Thur.   SA.   *Volpone.*
*Cast:* Volpone—Delane; Mosca—Hallam; Corbaccio—Bridgewater.
*Miscellaneous:* Never performed here.

JULY

12   Tues.   SA.   *Volpone.*
*Cast:* None listed.
*Benefit:* L. Duval.
*Miscellaneous:* By particular Desire of several Ladies of Quality. [This benefit may have been deferred. See SA 14 July 1737.]
*Singing and Dancing:* With a great Variety of Dancing.

14   Thur.   SA.   *The Spanish Fryar.*
*Cast:* Torrismond—Delane; Fryar—Bridgewater; Lorenzo—Hallam.
*Benefit:* Duval.
*Miscellaneous:* FDJ, 9–12 July 1737 and *DNL* of same date indicate that this performance is for Duval's benefit.

and

*Afterpiece: The Hussar.*
*Cast:* None listed.
*Miscellaneous:* Being particularly desired.

## 1737–1738 Season

Theatres operating: Aungier Street (Theatre Royal); Smock Alley (return to calling themselves "The Rt. Hon. The Lord Mayor's Company of Comedians").

*Aungier Street Company:*
Edward Bate, Bridges, Mrs. Bridges, Butler, Carmichael, F. Elrington, J. Elrington, Richard Elrington, Giles (from DL), Griffith, T. Jones, L. Layfield, R. Layfield, Redman, Reed, Vanderbank, Vaughn (from DL), J. Ward, Mrs. Ward, J. Watson, Jr., Miss Woffington (also dancer), Mrs. Woodward (from Edinburgh), Mrs. Wrightson.

Dancers: W. Delamain, Moreau, Pitt, Master Pitt.

Musicians: W. Connor.

House Servants: John Morgan (pit officekeeper).

*Repertory:*
Mainpieces: Recorded Performances: 29 (of 26 different pieces, including unspecified plays but excluding ridottos and ball).
Afterpieces: Recorded Performances: 16 (of 9 different pieces).
Premieres: *Polite Conversation.* (a)
Entr'acte Entertainments: Singing and/or Dancing advertised 8 times.
Command performances: 16 (4 Government nights).
Benefits:
Pre-February: Manager—1.
Post-February: Manager—1, Actor—11, House Servant—1, Charity—1.

*Smock Alley Company:*
Barrington, Mrs. Barry, Beamsley, Bourne, Mrs. Bullock, Cashell, L. Duval, Ralph Elrington, Este, Fitzpatrick, S. Hinde, Mrs. S. Hinde, Husband, Kennedy, Lamphrey, Mrs. Martin, Mrs. Mitchell, Morgan, Mrs. Morgan, Charles Morgan, Mrs. Orfeur, T. Philips, Prest, Mrs. Ravenscroft, Mrs. Reynolds, L. Sparks, Stepney, Mrs. Stepney, Walsh, Wetherilt, Mrs. Wetherilt, Worsdale.

Dancers: Miss Bullock, Cummins, Dumont, Mrs. Dumont, J. Morris.

Musicians: Connor, Fitzgerald, Lee, Mainwaring.

House Servants: Mrs. Bamford (dresser), Dryden (treasurer), Fox (pit door-keeper), Goff (upholsterer and former boxkeeper), Lamb (pit officekeeper), LeRoux (boxkeeper), Tudor (scene painter).

Summer: Henry Giffard, James Quin.

*Repertory:*
Mainpieces: Recorded Performances: 70 (of 44 different pieces).
Afterpieces: Recorded Performances: 49 (of 15 different pieces).
Premieres:
*The Sharper.*
*Three Humps.*
*No Death Like Marriage.* (a)
*The Jealous Farmer Deceived.* (a)
Entr'acte entertainments: Many evenings of singing and/or dancing.
Command Performances: 7.
Benefits:
Pre-February: Manager—1, Author—2.
Post-February: Manager—3, Actor—28; House Servants: 4, Charity—6.
*Significant events:* Theatres closed from 1 December 1737 until 7 January 1738 due to official mourning for the death of Queen Caroline.

---

**1737**

SEPTEMBER

15   Thur.   AS.   *Love for Love.*
*Cast:* None listed.
*Command:* Duke and Duchess of Devonshire.
*Miscellaneous:* There was a splendid Appearance of Nobility and Gentry. With a new Prologue spoken by Griffith in honour of the Duke and Duchess of Devonshire. [Miss Woffington's last recorded performance in Ireland for two years.]
*Singing and Dancing:* Dancing by Moreau, Delamain, Miss Woffington, Pitt, and Master Pitt.

22   Thur.   AS.   *The Spanish Fryar.*
*Cast:* None listed.
*Command:* Duke and Duchess of Devonshire.

22    Thur.    SA.    *The Man's Bewitched; or, The Devil to Do About Her.*
*Cast:* None listed.
*Miscellaneous:* "Mr. Duval being informed of the Inconveniences that the Audiences lay under by beginning too late, is determined for the Future to have the Curtain drawn up exactly at half an hour after 6 o'clock and never to dismiss" (*FDJ,* 13–17 Sept 1737).

29    Thur.    AS.    *The Country Lasses; or, The Custom of the Manor.*
*Cast:* None listed.
*Command:* Duke and Duchess of Devonshire.
*Miscellaneous:* Not acted these 20 years. Curtain rises at precisely half past six o'clock. The Company is resolved never to dismiss the Audience.
*Singing and Dancing:* Several entertainments of Dancing between the Acts.

**OCTOBER**

3    Mon.    SA.    *The Country Lasses.*
*Cast:* None listed.
*Miscellaneous:* The Lord Mayor's Company of Comedians; With all Decorations proper thereto, as it was performed with great applause at the Theatre Royal in London.
*Singing and Dancing:* With a Grand Rural Dance.

6    Thur.    AS.    *The Fair Penitent.*
*Cast:* None listed.
*Command:* Duke and Duchess of Devonshire.
*Miscellaneous:* With entertainments

10    Mon.    SA.    *The City Wives' Confederacy.*
*Cast:* None listed.
*Command:* Earl of Anglesey for the entertainment of the Duke and Duchess of Devonshire.
*Singing and Dancing:* With Dances, especially the Grand Rural Dance, as performed at the Theatre Royal, London, with dresses therein entirely new.

11    Tues.    AS.    *Tunbridge Walks; or, The Yeoman of Kent.*
*Cast:* None listed.
*Command:* Duke and Duchess of Devonshire.
*Miscellaneous:* Government Night; Anniversary of Coronation of George II. With a new Prologue for the Day.
and
*Afterpiece: The Hussar.*

*Cast:* Harlequin—Vaughn (lately arrived from DL, his first appearance in Ireland).
*Miscellaneous:* [*The Hussar* was performed before *Tunbridge Walks* with several alterations and additions of new scenes and machines.]

20    Thur.    AS.    *King Henry VIII.*
*Cast:* None listed.
*Command:* Duke and Duchess of Devonshire.

27    Thur.    AS.    *Love Makes a Man.*
*Cast:* None listed.
*Command:* Duke and Duchess of Devonshire.

31    Mon.    AS.    *The Tender Husband.*
*Cast:* None listed.
*Command:* Duke and Duchess of Devonshire.
*Miscellaneous:* Government Night; Anniversary of birth of George II; followed by a ball.

and

*Afterpiece: The Hussar.*
*Cast:* None listed.

NOVEMBER

3    Thur.    SA.    *The Pilgrim.*
*Cast:* None listed.
*Singing and Dancing:* Concluding with the last Grand new Rural Dance.

and

*Afterpiece: The Hussar.*
*Cast:* Harlequin—R. Elrington; Pierrot—Morris.

4    Fri.    AS.    Unspecified "Play"
*Miscellaneous:* Government Night; Anniversary of birth of William III.

7    Mon.    SA.    *Othello.*
*Cast:* None listed.

and

*Afterpiece: The Hussar.*
*Cast:* None listed.

10    Thur.    SA.    *Love and a Bottle.*
*Cast:* None listed.

and

*Afterpiece: The Hussar.*
*Cast:* None Listed.


14    Mon.    SA.    *The Squire of Alsatia.* V.
*Cast:* Sir William Belfond—Morgan; Sir Edward Belfond—T. Philips; Belfond, Sr.—Wetherilt; Belfond, Jr.—L. Sparks; Truman—Este; Cheatly—Beamsley; Shamwell—Cashell; Hackum—Barrington; Scrapeall—Bourne; Attorney—Husband; Lolpoop—C. Morgan; Termagant—J. Morris; Mrs. Termagant—Mrs. Reynolds; Teresa—Mrs. Ravenscroft; Isabella—Mrs. Morgan; Lucia—Mrs. Martin; Betty—Mrs. Hinde; Margaret—Mrs. Stepney.
*Command:* The Earl of Angelsey for the entertainment of the Duke and Duchess of Devonshire.
*Miscellaneous:* The Duke and Duchess of Devonshire were present; The crowded audience expressed great satisfaction with the new scenes and machines.

and

*Afterpiece: The Hussar.* V.
*Cast:* Harlequin—R. Elrington; Pierrot—Morris.


17    Thur.    SA.    *The Provoked Husband.*
*Cast:* None listed.
*Singing and Dancing:* Several entertainments of Dancing by Dumont, Morris, Mrs. Martin, and others.

and

*Afterpiece: The Hussar.*
*Cast:* None listed.


19    Sat.    AS.    Unspecified "Play."
*Miscellaneous:* Government Night; Anniversary birth of Princess of Wales.


21    Mon.    SA.    *Hamlet.*
*Cast:* None listed.
*Singing and Dancing:* Several entertainments of Dancing.

24    Thur.    AS.    *The Beggar's Opera.*
*Cast:* None listed.
*Command:* Duke and Duchess of Devonshire.
*Singing and Dancing:* With Entertainments of Dancing.

24    Thur.    SA.    *The Beggar's Opera.*
*Cast:* Macheath—Mrs. Reynolds.
*Miscellaneous:* At the Desire of several Persons of Quality.

and

*Afterpiece: The Hussar.*
*Cast:* None listed.

28    Mon.    SA.    *Man's Bewitched; or, The Devil to Do About Her.*
*Cast:* None listed.

and

*Afterpiece: The Hussar.*
*Cast:* None listed.

28    Mon.    AS.    Ridotto.
*Command:* Duke and Duchess of Devonshire.
*Miscellaneous:* The Theatre is fitted for this purpose; the Managers propose to give two Ridottos for a Moydore, paid at the time of subscribing.

30    Wed.    AS.    Ridotto.
*Command:* Duke and Duchess of Devonshire.
*Miscellaneous:* Undertaken by the Management of said Theatre.

30    Wed.    SA.    *The Way of the World.*
*Cast:* None listed.
*Miscellaneous:* By particular desire.

and

*Afterpiece: The Hussar.*
*Cast:* None listed.

[After this performance the theatres were closed because of the death of Queen Caroline, at the order of the Duke of Devonshire who declared official mourning until January 1738 much to the detriment, no doubt, of Mr. Pellish, "lately arrived from London," who was to play the King in *King Henry IV, Pt. 1* at SA 1 Dec. 1737 for his own benefit.]

**1738**

JANUARY

7    Sat.    SA.    *The Beggar's Opera.*
*Cast:* Macheath—Cashell.
*Miscellaneous:* Last time of performing it this season.
*Singing and Dancing:* Several entertainments of Dancing.

and

*Afterpiece: The Hussar.*
*Cast:* Harlequin—R. Elrington; Pierrot—Morris.

11    Wed.    SA.    *Love Makes a Man.*
*Cast:* None listed.
*Singing and Dancing:* Several entertainments of Dancing.

12    Thur.    AS.    *The Relapse; or, Virtue in Danger.*
*Cast:* Foppington—Giles (from DL).
*Command:* Duke and Duchess of Devonshire.
*Miscellaneous:* With several Entertainments.

16    Mon.    SA.    *The Busy Body.*
*Cast:* None listed.

                              and

*Afterpiece: A Cure for a Scold.*
*Cast:* [listed in 1738 Dublin edition] Manly—Este; Heartwell—Cashell; Sir
William—Philips; Gainlove—Morris; Margaret—Mrs. Reynolds; Flora—
Mrs. Martin.
*Miscellaneous:* [By James Worsdale. A ballad farce adaptation of *The Tam-
ing of the Shrew.*]

18    Wed.    SA.    *The City Wives' Confederacy.*
*Cast:* None listed.
*Benefit:* The Author [of the Farce (Worsdale)].
*Miscellaneous:* By the particular Desire of several Persons of Quality.

                              and

*Afterpiece: A Cure for a Scold.*
*Cast:* None listed.
*Comment:* ". . . Worsdale had The Cure for a Scold, altered from Shakespeare's Taming of a Shrew, into a ballad opera by Mr. Pilkington played
for his own benefit; I wrote a flaming Prologue to it, in honour of my fair
Countrywomen, and Worsdale insisted on my going to see it, assuring me
he would have a lettice [lattice] secured entirely for me, or any friends I
should please to bring, and would himself take care of placing me, and also
guarding me safe out, for really I was very much afraid of receiving some
insult.
     On these promises I ventured to go; when behold! the lettice was full;
but that was no matter, the Ladies, though my intimate friends, quickly
decamped, and Mrs. Dubourg, the Fidler's wife, declared she had like to
faint at the sight of the *odious creature!* The Rev. Mr. Gr——n also took to
his heels, so I had indeed the whole lettice for me and my Company, which
were two young Misses, daughters of my landlady" (L. Pilkington 1748–54,
2:301–2).

19    Thur.    AS.    *Macbeth.*
*Cast:* None listed.
*Command:* Duke and Duchess of Devonshire.

*Miscellaneous:* Not performed these two years; With all songs, flyings, sinkings, machines, and decorations proper to the play.
*Deferred:* Deferred from 28 Nov. 1737.

and

*Afterpiece: The Necromancer.*
*Cast:* Harlequin—Vaughn (from Drury Lane).

20    Fri.    SA.    *The Sharper.*
*Cast:* None listed. [But see cast for performance of 25 Jan. 1738 SA.]
*Miscellaneous:* [Premiere.] By Dr. Michael Clancy.

"The new Comedy which is now in rehearsal at the Theatre in Smock-Alley, was in different newspapers called The Charters, the Chartres, and Charters; now as none of these names were designed by the Author, the Public is hereby advertised that the name of that Play is *The Sharper.*" (*FDJ,* 20–24 Dec. 1737).

[Michael Clancy was born in Co. Clare in 1704 and attended Trinity College, Dublin, from 1721 to 1725. Later he apparently obtained his medical degree at Rheins. He came back to Dublin to practice medicine but in 1737 "had the misfortune of losing his sight by a cold, which rendered him incapable of exercising his profession." He turned to writing plays. A friend of Clancy's, seeking encouragement for the author, gave a copy of *The Sharper* to Swift for his comment. On Christmas Day, 1737, Swift wrote Clancy: "I have read it carefully, and with much Pleasure, on Account both of the Characters, and the Moral . . . I send you a small Present, in such Gold as will not give you Trouble to change [£5]; for I much pity your loss of Sight. . . ." Shortly afterwards Clancy gratefully acknowledged the gift: "I sent him a parcel of tickets, he kept but one, which he said he had paid for, and afterwards sent me two four pound pieces or more" (*The Memoirs of Michael Clancy, M.D.,* (Dublin, 1750), p. 52 and passim; Swift 1963–65, 4:81–82).]

23    Mon.    AS.    *Macbeth.*
*Cast:* None listed.
*Miscellaneous:* With original music, songs, sinkings, flyings proper to the play.

and

*Afterpiece: The Necromancer.*
*Cast:* None listed.

23    Mon.    SA.    *The Sharper.*
*Cast:* None listed.
*Miscellaneous:* Never performed but once.
*Singing and Dancing:* With entertainments of Dancing.

25   Wed.   SA.   *The Sharper.*
*Cast:* [listed in playbill of 25 Jan. 1738] Francisco—L. Sparks; Squire Fasten—R. Elrington; Puzzle Suit—Wetherilt; Trueman—Philips; Melefont—Este; Sawny—Cashell; Darey—Bourne; Angelica—Mrs. Reynolds; Lurewell—Mrs. Orfeur; Susanna Darey—Mrs. Ravenscroft. *Also,* in unspecified parts—Barrington, Beamsley, Fitzpatrick, S. Hinde, Morgan, C. Morgan, Stepney, Mrs. Barry, Mrs. S. Hinde, Mrs. Martin, Mrs. Stepney, Mrs. Morgan, Mrs. Wetherilt.
*Benefit:* The Author [Dr. Michael Clancy].
*Miscellaneous:* Never performed but twice. Prices: Boxes, Stage, Lattices, and Pit one British Crown, Gallery 2/2. No odd Money will be taken. Begins exactly at half past six o'clock. A Prologue spoken by Este and a new epilogue in the character of Susannah Dairy by Mrs. Ravenscroft.
[The cast is taken from the oldest surviving Irish playbill in the Grangerized copy of Augustin Daly's *Peg Woffington* at the Widener Library, Harvard University (reproduced in Stockwell 1938, 333). The Dramatis Personae to this piece printed in Clancy's *Memoirs* casts Byrne as Darey and Mrs. Pasqualino as Susanna Darey.]
*Deferred:* Deferred from 9 Jan. 1738.
*Comment:* "The last Time this Comedy was acted [perhaps this performance], there was the greatest Appearance of Nobility and Gentry that ever was seen at any Play in this Kingdom" (*FDJ,* 18–22 Apr. 1738).
"Whereas several evil-minded Persons at the Author's benefit on Wednesday the 25th Inst. did in a riotous and tumultuous Manner, assault many of the Servants belonging to the Theatre in Smock-alley, broke down the Gallery door and most of the Lamps and Windows thereof, together with two of the publick Lights, and notwithstanding a Detachment from the Main Guard came, and made diligent Search for such Rioters, none of them were found out. . . . Mr. Lewis Duvall, Master of said Theatre, offers a reward of 3 pounds for each offender convicted of the crime" (*FDJ,* 24–28 Jan. 1738).

26   Thur.   AS.   *Wit Without Money.*
*Cast:* [listed in 1738 Dublin edition] Valentine—Bridges; Master Lovegood—Redman; Francisco—Watson; Fountain—R. Layfield; Bellamour—Richard Elrington; Hairbrain—Carmichael; Lance—Reed; Shorthose—Griffith; Roger—Vaughn; Ralph—Ward; Humphrey—Butler; Lady Hartwell—Mrs. Ward; Isabella—Mrs. Bridges; Lucy—Mrs. Woodward (from Edinburgh).
*Command:* Duke and Duchess of Devonshire.
*Benefit:* Griffith.
*Miscellaneous:* Never acted in this Kingdom [but see Clark 1955, 33, for a probable 1638 or 1639 production]. Revised from Beaumont and Fletcher, with alterations.
*Singing and Dancing:* With entertainments of dancing between the acts by Moreau, Delamain, Pitt, and Master Pitt.

and

*Afterpiece: The Dragon of Wantley.*
*Cast:* More of More Hall—Giles (lately from London).
*Miscellaneous:* A new burlesque operatical farce never performed in this Kingdom. By Henry Carey, music by Lampe.

28    Sat.    SA.    *The Man's Bewitched.*
*Cast:* None listed.
*Singing and Dancing:* With entertainments of Dancing by Dumont and others.

and

*Afterpiece: Harlequin Triumphant; or, The Jealous Farmer Deceived.* [Title usually reversed].
*Cast:* None listed.
*Miscellaneous:* Never acted but once. [Anonymous pantomime. There is no record of an earlier performance.]

FEBRUARY

1    Wed.    SA.    *Pasquin.*
*Cast:* None listed.
*Miscellaneous:* At the particular Desire of several Ladies of Quality.

and

*Afterpiece: A Cure for a Scold.*
*Cast:* Principal Character—Worsdale.
*Miscellaneous:* Never acted but once.

3    Fri.    SA.    *Amphitryon; or, The Two Sosias.*
*Cast:* None listed.
*Benefit:* Barrington.
*Miscellaneous:* Not acted here these 16 years.

and

*Afterpiece: The Stage Coach.*
*Cast:* None listed.
*Miscellaneous:* Not acted here this season.

4    Sat.    SA.    *The Squire of Alsatia.* V.
*Cast:* None listed.
*Miscellaneous:* [Boydell 1988, 63, indicates that this benefit was sponsored by the Charitable Musical Society. In the course of the evening "the famous Mr. Murphy will perform on the Irish Harp" (*DNL,* 17–21 Dec. 1737).]
*Benefit:* Distressed Prisoners in the Several Marshalseas.
*Singing and Dancing:* With several Entertainments of Dancing.
*Financial:* "There was £128 in the House" (*DNL,* 4–7 Feb. 1738).

and

*Afterpiece: The Mock Doctor.*
*Cast:* None listed.


8     Wed.     SA.     *Timon of Athens; or, The Man Hater.*
*Cast:* None listed.
*Command:* Duke and Duchess of Devonshire.
*Benefit:* L. Duval.

and

*Afterpiece: A Cure for a Scold.*
*Cast:* None listed.


9     Thur.     AS.     *Sir Courtly Nice; or, It Cannot Be.*
*Cast:* None listed.
*Command:* Duke and Duchess of Devonshire.
*Benefit:* F. Elrington.
*Miscellaneous:* For the entertainment of the Lord Chancellor and Chancellor of the Exchequer, the Rt. Hon. and Hon. Judges, and the rest of the Society of King's Inns.

and

*Afterpiece: The Necromancer.*
*Cast:* None listed.


10     Fri.     SA.     *Love for Love.*
*Cast:* Miss Prue—Miss Bullock. All other parts to the best advantage.
*Benefit:* Miss Bullock (Mrs. Bullock's Daughter).
*Miscellaneous:* By particular desire. With a new prologue spoke by Miss Bullock. Prices: Boxes 5/5, Lattices 4/4, Pit 3/3, Gallery 2/2. To begin exactly at 6. 30 p.m.
   [Playbill quoted in Hitchcock 1788–93, 1:109–10].
*Singing and Dancing:* With Entertainments of Dancing between the Acts, viz. Act I the song of "Mad Tom" by Hinde; Act II "The Sailor's Dance" by Dumont and Mrs. Martin; Act III A new Dialogue to be sung between Este and Mrs. Reynolds; Act IV "Scotch Dance" by Morris and Mrs. Martin; Act V A new pantomime dance called "Pigmalion and the Ivory Statue" Statue of Ivory Maid by Miss Bullock.


13     Mon.     SA.     *The Double Gallant.*
*Cast:* None listed.
*Benefit:* Ralph Elrington.

and

*Afterpiece: The Hussar.*
*Cast:* None listed.

14    Tues.    SA.    *The Twin Rivals.*
*Cast:* None listed.
*Command:* Viscount Tyrone, Grand Master of Ireland.
*Benefit:* Sick and Decayed Masons.
*Miscellaneous:* With a Prologue and Epilogue suitable to the occasion.
*Singing and Dancing:* With Mason's Songs and Dances between the acts.
*Deferred:* Deferred from 27 Jan. 1738.
                              and
*Afterpiece: A Cure for a Scold.*
*Cast:* None listed.


16    Thur.    AS.    *King Lear and His Three Daughters.*
*Cast:* Lear—F. Elrington.
*Command:* Duke and Duchess of Devonshire.
*Benefit:* Vanderbank.


16    Thur.    SA.    *King Henry IV, with the Humours of Falstaff.*
*Cast:* None listed.
*Benefit:* Morris.
                              and
*Afterpiece: The Hussar.*
*Cast:* None listed.


18    Sat.    AS.    Ridotto.


18    Sat.    SA.    *The Constant Couple.*
*Cast:* None listed.
*Benefit:* Philips.
*Singing and Dancing:* With entertainments of Dancing.
                              and
*Afterpiece: A Cure for a Scold.*
*Cast:* None listed.


20    Mon.    AS.    Ridotto.
*Command:* Duke and Duchess of Devonshire.


22    Wed.    SA.    *Macbeth.*
*Cast:* None listed.
*Benefit:* Husband.
*Miscellaneous:* At the Desire of several Ladies of Quality. With music and decorations suitable to the play.
*Singing and Dancing:* With music and dancing.

and

*Afterpiece: The Hussar.*
*Cast:* None listed.


23    Thur.    AS.    *The Constant Couple; or, A Trip to the Jubilee.*
*Cast:* None listed.
*Command:* Duke and Duchess of Devonshire.
*Benefit:* Moreau.
*Miscellaneous:* At the particular Desire of several Persons of Quality.

and

*Afterpiece: The Dragon of Wantley.*
*Cast:* None listed.


24    Fri.    SA.    *Volpone.*
*Cast:* Volpone—L. Sparks.
*Benefit:* L. Sparks.
*Singing and Dancing:* With several Entertainments of Dancing.

and

*Afterpiece: The Hussar.*
*Cast:* None listed.


27    Mon.    AS.    *Wit Without Money.*
*Cast:* None listed.
*Command:* Duke and Duchess of Devonshire.
*Benefit:* The Charitable Infirmary on the Inn's Quay.
*Miscellaneous:* Never acted in this Kingdom but once; There will be a sufficient number of convenient seats erected on the Stage for the conveniency of the Ladies; The House will be illuminated with wax-lights.
*Deferred:* Deferred from 11 Feb. 1738.
*Comment:* The gala evening seems to have been spoiled by "great Flashes of Lightning, that put the Gentlemen in the Upper Gallery in such a Fright, that they cry'd out 'Fire,' and so terrified the Ladies that they were running they knew not where, but upon some Persons crying it was no such thing, and that the House was very safe, all was pretty quiet again; nevertheless a great many Ladies who were next the Door went away at that time, the Play being almost over" (*DEP*, 28 Feb. 1738).

and

*Afterpiece: The Dragon of Wantley.*
*Cast:* None listed.

MARCH

1    Wed.    SA.    *Pasquin.*
*Cast:* None listed.
*Benefit:* Lamb (pit officekeeper) and Fox (pit doorkeeper).
*Singing and Dancing:* With several Entertainments of Dancing.

and

*Afterpiece: The Hussar.*
*Cast:* None listed.

2    Thur.    AS.    *Jane Shore.*
*Cast:* None listed.
*Command:* Duke and Duchess of Devonshire.
*Benefit:* J. Elrington.

4    Sat.    SA.    *The Committee.*
*Cast:* None listed.
*Benefit:* Mr. and Mrs. Wetherilt.
*Singing and Dancing:* With several Entertainments of Dancing.

and

*Afterpiece: The Hussar.*
*Cast:* None listed.

6    Mon.    SA.    *The Beggar's Opera.*
*Cast:* Macheath—Mrs. Stepney; Locket—Mrs. Wetherilt; Peachum—Mrs.
Reynolds; Polly—Este; Lucy—Barrington; Mrs. Peachum—Cashell.
*Command:* Duke and Duchess of Devonshire.
*Benefit:* Dryden (Treasurer).
*Miscellaneous:* All the characters reversed. As it was performed at London
with great applause. The play will begin at precisely half past 6 o'clock,
there being a Ridotto that night. [This year, in addition to the hall on Crow
Street, another large auditorium used for both music and dancing called
Geminiani's Room opened. The hall was named after the Italian musician
Francisco Geminiani who gave concerts at the "Great Room" (*DNL*, 11 Feb.
1738)].
*Singing and Dancing:* With several Entertainments of Dancing.

and

*Afterpiece: The King and the Miller of Mansfield.*
*Cast:* None listed.

9    Thur.    SA.    *The Pilgrim.*
*Cast:* None listed.
*Command:* Duke and Duchess of Devonshire.
*Benefit:* Mr. and Mrs. Morgan.

and
*Afterpiece: The King and the Miller of Mansfield.*
*Cast:* None listed.


11    Sat.    SA.    *The Miser.*
*Cast:* None listed.
*Benefit:* Mrs. Reynolds.
*Singing and Dancing:* With several Entertainments of Dancing.
                                    and
*Afterpiece: A Cure for a Scold.*
*Cast:* None listed.


16    Thur.    AS.    *Measure for Measure.*
*Cast:* None listed.
*Command:* Duke and Duchess of Devonshire.
*Benefit:* Ward.
*Miscellaneous:* Never acted in this Kingdom.
*Singing and Dancing:* With several Entertainments of Dancing.
                                    and
*Afterpiece: Sir John Cockle at Court.*
*Cast:* None listed.
*Miscellaneous:* A Sequel to *The King and the Miller of Mansfield.*


16    Thur.    SA.    *King John.*
*Cast:* None listed.
*Benefit:* Mrs. Orfeur and Mrs. Ravenscroft.
*Singing and Dancing:* With several Entertainments of Dancing.
                                    and
*Afterpiece: Damon and Phillida.*
*Cast:* None listed.


18    Sat.    SA.    *Man's Bewitched.*
*Cast:* None listed.
*Benefit:* Thomas Kirby, a Prisoner in the Four Courts Marshalsea, Confined for the past 7 Years.
*Miscellaneous:* Pit and Boxes laid together at an English crown and the gallery 2s. 2d.
    [According to the *DNL* of 17 Mar. 1738, Kirby owed over £150. His "Liberty will be of Service to the Public, he being able to improve the Linen manufacture, in Printing and Dying as beautiful Colours and patterns as any now done in England. . . ."]
*Financial:* "The Neat Produce of the House was £66 15s." Kirby received a second benefit on 17 May, see below.

and
*Afterpiece: The King and the Miller of Mansfield.*
*Cast:* None listed.


20    Mon.    AS.    "Le Grand Ball by the Managers of the Theatre."
*Miscellaneous:* ". . . the house will be fitted up and illuminated in the same manner as at a ridotto; the tea tables will be in the 'beauffets,' which will be elegantly furnished with 'chocolate,' jellys, fruit, etc., but no wine or supper. Tickets at a British crown. . . . Doors open at 8 and the ball begins at 10" (*FDJ*, 17 Mar. 1738).


20    Mon.    SA.    *Julius Caesar.*
*Cast:* None listed.
*Command:* Duke and Duchess of Devonshire.
*Benefit:* Este.
*Singing and Dancing:* With several Entertainments of Dancing.
and
*Afterpiece: A Cure for a Scold.*
*Cast:* None listed.


23    Thur.    AS.    *Oedipus, King of Thebes.*
*Cast:* None listed.
*Command:* Duke and Duchess of Devonshire
*Benefit:* Bridges.
*Miscellaneous:* Not acted here these 20 years; founded on the Greek of Sophocles by the late Mr. Dryden and Mr. Lee; With all the Prodigies, Musick, and other Decorations proper to the Play.
    [The Duke and Duchess of Devonshire left Ireland for England on 26 Mar. 1738.]
*Singing and Dancing:* Music, see *Miscellaneous* above; With dancing between the acts by Moreau, Delamain, Pitt, and Master Pitt.
and
*Afterpieces: Sir John Cockle at Court.*
*Cast:* None listed.
*Miscellaneous:* As acting at the Theatre Royal in London.


23    Thur.    SA.    *The Way of the World.*
*Cast:* None listed.
*Benefit:* Mrs. Martin and Mrs. Barry.
*Singing and Dancing:* With several Entertainments of Dancing.
and
*Afterpiece: A Cure for a Scold.*
*Cast:* None listed.

[Passion Week 27 March–1 April]

APRIL

6　Thur.　SA.　*The Unhappy Favourite; or, The Earl of Essex.*
*Cast:* None listed.
*Miscellaneous:* Being particularly desired.
*Singing and Dancing:* With several Entertainments of Dancing.
and

*Afterpiece: The Devil to Pay.*
*Cast:* None listed.


14　Fri.　AS.　*The Merry Wives of Windsor.*
*Cast:* None listed.
*Benefit:* Reed and T. Jones.
and

*Afterpiece: The Cheats of Scapin.*
*Cast:* None listed.


14　Fri.　SA.　*Love Makes a Man.*
*Cast:* None listed.
*Benefit:* Cummins (dancer) and Leroux (boxkeeper).
and

*Afterpiece: The Stage Coach.*
*Cast:* None listed.


15　Sat.　SA.　*The Double Dealer.*
*Cast:* None listed.
*Benefit:* Mr. and Mrs. Stepney.
*Singing and Dancing:* With several Entertainments of Dancing.
and

*Afterpiece: Flora.*
*Cast:* None listed.


21　Fri.　SA.　*The Beaux' Stratagem.*
*Cast:* None listed.
*Benefit:* Lee (musician) and Mrs. Mitchell.
*Singing and Dancing:* With several Entertainments of Dancing.
and

*Afterpiece: The Mock Doctor.*
*Cast:* None listed.

24    Mon.    AS.    *The Silent Woman.*
*Cast:* None listed.
*Benefit:* Watson.
*Miscellaneous:* At the particular Desire of several Ladies of Quality.
                              and
*Afterpiece: The Necromancer.*
*Cast:* None listed.

25    Tues.    SA.    *Rule a Wife and Have a Wife.*
*Cast:* None listed.
*Benefit:* Kennedy and Mrs. Bamford (dresser).
*Miscellaneous:* Not acted this season.
*Singing and Dancing:* With several Entertainments of Dancing.
                              and
*Afterpiece: The Devil to Pay.*
*Cast:* None listed.

26    Wed.    SA.    *The Country Lasses.*
*Cast:* None listed.
*Command:* Lord and Lady Kingsland.
*Benefit:* Prest and Walsh.
*Singing and Dancing:* With a great Variety of Dancing.
                              and
*Afterpiece: The Mock Lawyer.*
*Cast:* None listed.

27    Thur.    AS.    *Lucius Junius Brutus, Father of His Country.*
*Cast:* None listed.
*Benefit:* Mrs. Ward and William Connor (musician).
*Miscellaneous:* Not acted these 20 years.
*Singing and Dancing:* With several Entertainments of Dancing.
                              and
*Afterpiece: Polite Conversation.*
*Cast:* None listed.
*Miscellaneous:* [Premiere. Made into 3 acts.
    The manuscript of Swift's realistic dialogues ridiculing the mechanical wit and coarseness of the fashionable small talk of the day circulated about Dublin privately. According to the *DNB*, Swift presented it to Mrs. Mary Barber (1690?–1757), a poetess and friend. Poor and in ill-health, she begged Swift to give her the work which was still in manuscript although largely written thirty years earlier. In the hope that its sale would relieve her poverty, he may have given her the piece in 1737 (*DNB*, 1:1068). Swift certainly gave a ms. of *Polite Conversation* to Lord Orrery who took it to London in July 1737 to be published for Mrs. Barber's benefit (Swift 1963–65, 6:39). Both

theatre companies had access to the manuscript after Mrs. Barber sold it to George Faulkner, who had it printed in 1738 [see Swift, *A Proposal for Correcting the English Tongue. . . . [etc.]*, ed. Herbert Davis and Louis Landa (Oxford: Basil Blackwell, 1957), pp. xxviii–xxxiv.]

27    Thur.    SA.     *The Sharper.*
*Cast:* None listed.
*Benefit:* Author [Michael Clancy].
*Miscellaneous:* With a new Prologue on the Occasion. At the particular Request of several Persons of Quality and Distinction. See also *Miscellaneous* for 25 Jan. 1738 SA.
*Comment:* "It [*The Sharper*] was five times acted at SA, and on the Author's Night, before the greatest Number of Nobility and Gentry, that ever was seen at one Meeting in this Kingdom" (Clancy 1750, 2:53).
*Deferred:* Deferred from 17 Apr. on Account of the Indisposition of a Principal Actor.

and

*Afterpiece: The Stage Coach.*
*Cast:* None listed.

28    Fri.    SA.     *Bonduca; or, The British Heroine.*
*Cast:* None listed.
*Benefit:* Mrs. Bullock.
*Miscellaneous:* Never acted in this Kingdom; Represents the Conquest of Britain by the Romans as now performed at the Theatre Royal in London. [But *LS* lists the most recent London revival at DL on 9 June 1731.]
*Singing and Dancing:* With several Entertainments of Dancing. [Contains the very popular song "Britons Strike Home."]

and

*Afterpiece: The Stage Coach.*
*Cast:* None listed.

**MAY**

1    Mon.    SA.     *The Provoked Husband.*
*Cast:* None listed.
*Benefit:* The Workhouse in St. Werburgh's Parish.
*Singing and Dancing:* With several Entertainments of Dancing.

and

*Afterpiece: The Mock Doctor.*
*Cast:* None listed.

3    Wed.    SA.     *The Old Batchelour.*
*Cast:* None listed.
*Benefit:* Lamphrey and S. Hinde.

and

*Afterpiece: No Death Like Marriage.*
*Cast:* None listed.
*Miscellaneous:* [Premiere. A new comic Opera, "By a Lady" (*FDJ*, 15 Apr. 1738). Not listed in either Nicoll or *LS*.]

4    Thur.    AS.    *The Indian Emperor; or, The Conquest of Mexico by the Spaniards.*
*Cast:* None listed.
*Command:* Viscount Tyrone for the entertainment of the Free Masons.
*Benefit:* Griffith.
*Singing and Dancing:* With several Entertainments of Singing and Dancing.

and

*Afterpiece: Damon and Phillida.*
*Cast:* None listed.

5    Fri.    SA.    *The Recruiting Officer.*
*Cast:* Plume—Cashell; Brazen—L. Sparks; Kite—Barrington.
*Benefit:* Cashell.

and

*Afterpiece: The Honest Yorkshireman.*
*Cast:* None listed.

6    Sat.    AS.    *Measure for Measure.*
*Cast:* None listed.
*Benefit:* Giles and Christopher Dickson (printer).
*Miscellaneous:* Never acted but once in this Kingdom; At the Desire of several Persons of Quality.
*Singing and Dancing:* Several Entertainments of Dancing.

and

*Afterpiece: Flora.*
*Cast:* Hob—L. Layfield.

8    Mon.    SA.    *Volpone.*
*Cast:* None listed.
*Benefit:* L. Duval.
*Singing and Dancing:* With Entertainments of Dancing by Mr. and Mrs. Dumont and Mr. Morris.

and

*Afterpiece: Polite Conversation.*
*Cast:* Miss Notable—Miss Bullock; Neverout—Wetherilt; Lord Sparkish—Este; Col. Atwit—Cashell; Lady Smart—Mrs. Ravenscroft; Lady Answerwell—Mrs. Wetherilt.

9    Tues.    AS.    *The Rival Queens; or, The Death of Alexander the Great.*
*Miscellaneous:* At the Desire of Several Persons of Quality.
*Cast:* None listed.
*Benefit:* Mrs. Bridges.

and

*Afterpiece: The What D'Ye Call It.*
*Cast:* None listed.

10    Wed.    SA.    *The Distrest Mother.*
*Cast:* None listed.
*Benefit:* Beamsley and Healy.
*Singing and Dancing:* With several Entertainments of Dancing.

and

*Afterpiece: The Anatomist; or, The Sham Doctor.*
*Cast:* None listed.

11    Thur.    AS.    *The Tempest.*
*Cast:* None listed.
*Benefit:* Mrs. Wrightson, Redman, and Bate.
*Singing and Dancing:* With several Entertainments of Dancing between the Acts.

and

*Afterpiece: The What D'Ye Call It.*
*Cast:* None listed.

12    Fri.    SA.    *The Double Dealer.*
*Cast:* [Listed on playbill of 12 May 1738] Maskwell—Este; Mellefont—Barrington; Brisk—Sparks; Touchwood—Philips; Sir Paul—Bourne; Froth—Wetherilt; Careless—Cashell; Lady Froth—Mrs. Bullock; Lady Touchwood—Mrs. Wetherilt; Lady Pliant—Mrs. Morgan; Cynthia—Mrs. Barry.
*Benefit:* Tudor (scene painter).
*Miscellaneous:* This is the second-oldest surviving Dublin playbill.

and

*Afterpiece: A Cure for a Scold.*
*Cast:* None listed.

15    Mon.    SA.    *The Three Humps.*
*Cast:* Donough O'Thoreen—Barrington.
*Miscellaneous:* In 3 Acts. [Premiere. Not listed in Nicoll or *LS.*]
*Singing and Dancing:* With several Entertainments of Dancing.

16    Tues.    SA.    *The Committee.*
*Cast:* None listed.
*Benefit:* Goff (upholsterer and former boxkeeper).

and

*Afterpiece: A Cure for a Scold.*
*Cast:* None listed.


17    Wed.    SA.    *The Way of the World.*
*Cast:* None listed.
*Benefit:* Thomas Kirby (second benefit).
*Miscellaneous:* See also 18 Mar. and 16 Nov.
*Financial:* The profit from the two performances was £95, so this performance netted £28 5s.

and

*Afterpiece: The Cobler of Preston.*
*Cast:* None listed.


19    Fri.    SA.    *The Twin Rivals.*
*Cast:* None listed.
*Benefit:* Fitzgerald and Mainwaring (musicians).
*Singing and Dancing:* With several Entertainments of Dancing.

and

*Afterpiece: A Cure for a Scold.*
*Cast:* None listed.


22    Mon.    SA.    *Love and a Bottle.*
*Cast:* None listed.
*Benefit:* Stepney and Mrs. Reynolds.
*Singing and Dancing:* With several Entertainments of Dancing.

and

*Afterpiece: Damon and Phillida.*
*Cast:* None listed.


*Summer Season*


JUNE


19    Mon.    SA.    *King Richard III.*
*Cast:* Gloster—Quin (from DL).


22    Thur.    SA.    *Othello.*
*Cast:* Othello—Quin.


26    Mon.    SA.    *Julius Caesar.* V.
*Cast:* Brutus—Quin.
*Benefit:* Quin.

*Miscellaneous:* The Town is so pleased with his performance, that despite the warm weather every Night he Acts there is a full House.
*Financial:* £126 in the House.

JULY

3    Mon.    SA.    *Cato.*
*Cast:* Cato—Quin.

13    Thur.    SA.    *The Merry Wives of Windsor.*
*Cast:* Falstaff—Quin.

17    Mon.    SA.    *The Spanish Fryar.*
*Cast:* Fryar—Quin.
*Benefit:* L. Duval.
*Miscellaneous:* Being positively the last time of his performing in this Kingdom [but see below].

24    Mon.    SA.    *The Careless Husband.*
*Cast:* Sir Charles—Giffard (from London).

27    Thur.    SA.    *The Constant Couple.*
*Cast:* Sir Harry—Giffard.

31    Mon.    SA.    *The Provoked Wife.*
*Cast:* Heartfree—Giffard; Sir John—Quin (being the last time of his performing in this kingdom).
*Benefit:* Giffard.

AUGUST

3    Thur.    SA.    *Cato.*
*Benefit:* Charitable Infirmary on the Inn's Quay.
*Cast:* Cato—Quin; Juba—Giffard.
*Miscellaneous:* Performed to the best House of the Season.

7    Mon.    SA.    *Hamlet.*
*Cast:* Hamlet—Giffard.

[Clark 1965, 7, says SA company toured Carlow and Drogheda from August to late October. *FDJ,* 5–9 Sept. 1738 states: "Mr. Duvall's Company of Comedians . . . will begin to perform there [Drogheda] on Monday next . . . and will continue to act there on Mondays, Wednesdays and Fridays till after the Races at Bellewstown."

It is possible that the AS company travelled to Waterford at some time after their last recorded performance on 5 May but prior to 5 Aug. 1738 since an advertisement in *FDJ,* 1–5 Aug. 1738 offers a reward for some traces and other tackle borrowed but not returned by the actor Vanderbank who was travelling thence.]

## 1738–1739 Season

Theatres Operating: Aungier Street (Theatre Royal); Smock Alley.

*Aungier St. Company:*
Bridges, F. Elrington, J. Elrington; Griffith, L. Layfield, Loughlin, Mrs. Moreau, Morgan, Vanderbank, Mrs. Vanderbank, J. Ward, J. Watson, Jr., Mrs. Wrightson.

Dancers: Master Cormack, R. Layfield, Moreau, Miss Moreau, Pitt, Master Pitt.

Musicians: McCarty.

*Repertory:*
Mainpieces: Recorded performances: 21 (of 20 different pieces, including 4 ridottos).
Afterpieces: Recorded Performances: 15 (of 13 different pieces, including unspecified farces).
Premieres:
*Turnus.*
*The Female Officer.* (a)
Entr'acte entertainments: 3 advertisements for dancing.
Command Performances: 3 (3 Government Nights).
Benefits:
Pre-February: Manager—1, Actor—7, Charity—2.
Post-February: Manager—1, Actor—5, Author—1, Charity—1.

*Smock Alley Company:*
Barrington, Mrs. Barry, Mrs. Bayley, Beamsley, Bourne, Mrs. Bullock (died Mar. 1739), Miss Harriet Bullock, Bushell, J. Duval, L. Duval, Ralph Elrington, Este, H. Eyre, J. Hamilton, Husband, Kennedy, Mrs. Martin, Mrs. Orfeur, Pellish (from London), T. Philips, Mrs. Reynolds, L. Sparks, Wetherilt.

Dancers: Cummins, W. Delamain, Dumont, J. Morris.

Musicians: W. Connor, W. Mainwaring, Thumoth, Woder.

House Servants: Dryden (treasurer), Fox (pit doorkeeper), Gibson (box-keeper), Healy (stage officekeeper), Lamb (pit officekeeper), Neil (box-keeper) [sic], Nimmo (prompter), Tudor (scene painter), Tyler (gallery officekeeper).

Summer: Delane (from CG), Milward (from DL), Woodward (from DL).

*Repertory:*
Mainpieces: Recorded performances: 73 (of 41 different pieces, including one treble bill with two mainpieces).
Afterpieces: Recorded Performances: 52 (of 23 different pieces, including unspecified farces).
Premieres:
*The Treacherous Husband.*
*Whittington and His Cat.* (a)
Entr'acte entertainments: Many performances of dancing or music; several ads for unspecified entertainments.
Command Performances: None listed.
Benefits:
Pre-February: Manager—2, Actor—1, Author—2, Charity—3.
Post-February: Manager—3, Actor—17, House Servants—11, Charity—7.

---

## 1738

OCTOBER

11    Wed.    AS.    *The Drummer; or, The Haunted House.*
*Cast:* None listed.
*Command:* Lords Justice.
*Miscellaneous:* Government Night: Anniversary of coronation of George II. Boxes free to the Ladies. A new Occasional Prologue spoke by Mr. Griffith.
*Singing and Dancing:* With entertainments of Dancing.

30    Mon.    AS.    *The Tender Husband.*
*Cast:* None listed.
*Command:* Lords Justice.
*Miscellaneous:* Government Night: Anniversary of birth of George II. The Lords Justice attended. With a new Prologue spoke by Mr. Griffith.
*Singing and Dancing:* Entertainments of Dancing between the Acts.
*Comment:* The Ladies made a very fine Appearance.

NOVEMBER

4     Sat.     AS.     *Tamerlane.*
*Cast:* None listed.
*Miscellaneous:* For the entertainment of the Hanover Club. Government Night; Anniversary of birth of William III. Boxes open to Ladies as on the Coronation and Birthday. Usual Prologue to the Day.

6     Mon.     SA.     *The Busy Body.*
*Cast:* None listed.
*Miscellaneous:* Whereas Complaints have been made of the Plays being done too late they will begin at 6 o'clock. [Duval's Company was performing in Drogheda until at least 28 Oct., when there was a benefit performance of *The Double Dealer* for the company ("last time of performing") advertised for that date.]

and

*Afterpiece: The Hussar.*
*Cast:* None listed.

9     Thur.     SA.     *The Beggar's Opera.*
*Cast:* Macheath—Mrs. Reynolds.
*Miscellaneous:* Mrs. Reynolds in male attire.
*Deferred:* Deferred from 2 Nov. 1738.

13     Mon.     AS.     *Hamlet.*
*Cast:* None listed.
*Benefit:* Almshouse in St. Warberg's Parish.

and

*Afterpiece: The Mock Lawyer.*
*Cast:* None listed.

13     Mon.     AS.     Ridotto.

16     Thur.     SA.     *The City Wives' Confederacy.*
*Cast:* None listed.
*Benefit:* Thomas Kirby (third benefit).
*Miscellaneous:* [The takings from the previous two benefits [i.e. 18 Mar. and 17 May 1738] at the end of the previous season (£95) being insufficient to enlarge him several Ladies and Gentlemen have requested a third benefit. *DNL,* 16–19 Dec. 1738 states that Kirby was discharged on 18 Dec. 1738, a sum of £110 (the Amount of the clear Produce of three Plays acted for his benefit) having been paid to his creditors. He later established himself in the linen printing business in Dublin.]
*Singing and Dancing:* With several entertainments of singing and dancing.

and

*Afterpiece: The Mock Lawyer.*
*Cast:* None listed.

20    Mon.    AS.    Ridotto
*Miscellaneous:* Second ridotto. Undertaken by the Managers of the Theatre.

22    Wed.    AS.    *The Committee.*
*Cast:* Teague—Griffith.
*Benefit:* Griffith.
*Miscellaneous:* The last time of his performing in that character. Epilogue delivered by Griffith riding on an Ass that never appeared on any stage.
    [It is possible that Griffith was considering retirement at this time. As much is suggested in *FDJ,* 18–21 Nov. 1738 which contains the following "Verses occasioned by a late Playbill, wherein a new Ass is promised to come on Stage":

> What prompts————[Griffith] thus to warn the Age,
> That soon he means to abdicate the Stage.
> Or is it Spleen? Or Conscious that thy Vein,
> Exhausted, can no longer Entertain?
> Whatever be the Cause, we must confess,
> His generous Care to make our Loss the less;
> For at the taking of his last Adieu,
> He gives us, in his Stead, an Ass that's New].

*Singing and Dancing:* With several Entertainments of Dancing between the Acts by Moreau, Pitt, Master Pitt, and others.
*Deferred:* Deferred from 20 Nov. 1738 at the Desire of several Persons of Quality.

and

*Afterpiece: The Wrangling Lovers.*
*Cast:* None listed.

23    Thur.    SA.    *The Constant Couple.*
*Cast:* None listed.
*Benefit:* L. Duval.

and

*Afterpiece: The Jealous Farmer Deceived; or, Harlequin Triumphant.*
*Cast:* None listed.
*Miscellaneous:* [Anonymous pantomime. Both *LS* and Nicoll list only a piece by Joseph Yarrow called *The Jealous Farmer Deceived; or, Harlequin a Statue* performed in Mar. 1739.]
*Singing and Dancing:* The whole to conclude with a Grand Entertainment of Dancing by Mrs. Bullock, it being the first time of her Appearance on stage in Dancing.

28    Tues.    SA.    *The Treacherous Husband.*
*Cast:* None listed.
*Miscellaneous:* [Premiere. Tragedy by Samuel Davey. Not listed in *LS;* Nicoll lists only a 1737 Dublin 8vo. edition. A prologue intended to be spoken at this performance is quoted in full in *FDJ,* 2–5 Dec. 1738.]
  As the Company intend to begin exactly at 6 o'clock, it will be done in time for those who are disposed to go to the Riddotto.

29    Wed.    AS.    *The Recruiting Officer.*
*Cast:* None listed.
*Benefit:* The Charitable Infirmary on the Inn's Quay.
*Miscellaneous:* At the desire of the Ladies Governesses, it is agreed that no places are to be kept. Prices: Boxes, pit, stage and lattices advanced to 5s. 5d., gallery 2s. 8½d.
*Financial:* £172 collected according to *DEP* and *FDJ,* 28 Nov.–2 Dec. 1738.

DECEMBER

4    Mon.    AS.    *Ignoramus; or, The English Lawyer.*
*Cast:* None listed.
*Benefit:* F. Elrington.
*Miscellaneous:* For the Entertainment of the Lord Chancellor, Chancellor of the Exchequer, Rt. Hon. and Hon. Judges, and the Rest of the Hon. Society of King's Inns.
*Singing and Dancing:* Entertainments of Dancing.
                                  and
*Afterpiece:* Unspecified "Farce."

5    Tues.    SA.    *The Committee.*
*Cast:* None listed.
*Singing and Dancing:* With several Entertainments of Dancing.
                                  and
*Afterpiece: The Jealous Farmer Deceived.*
*Cast:* None listed.

8    Fri.    SA.    *The Treacherous Husband.*
*Cast:* None listed.
*Benefit:* The Author [Samuel Davey.] Third night [since premiere?].
*Singing and Dancing:* With several Entertainments of Dancing.
                                  and
*Afterpiece:* Unspecified "Farce."

11    Mon.    SA.    *Volpone.*
*Cast:* None listed.
*Singing and Dancing:* With several Entertainments of Dancing.

and

*Afterpiece: The Jealous Farmer Deceived.*
*Cast:* None listed.

12   Tues.   AS.   *The Indian Emperor.*
*Cast:* None listed.
*Benefit:* Vanderbank.
*Miscellaneous:* The characters to be entirely new dressed in rich Feather Dresses after the Manner of the Indians, and the Spaniards dressed in new Spanish dresses.
*Singing and Dancing:* With several entertainments of Dancing.

and

*Afterpiece: Scaramouche Turned Old Woman.*
*Cast:* None listed.
*Miscellaneous:* [Premiere. Anonymous pantomime. Not listed in Nicoll or *LS.*]

14   Thur.   AS.   *The Miser.*
*Cast:* Lovegold—F. Elrington; Lappet—Mrs. Moreau (her first time performing it in Ireland).
*Benefit:* Moreau.
*Singing and Dancing:* With several entertainments of dancing by Moreau, Mrs. Moreau, Miss Moreau, Pitt, and Master Pitt.

and

*Afterpiece:* Unspecified "Farce."

14   Thur.   SA.   *The Treacherous Husband.*
*Cast:* None listed.
*Benefit:* The Author [Samuel Davey].
*Miscellaneous:* [This may have been the sixth night since its premiere.]

and

*Afterpiece: Whittington and His Cat.*
*Cast:* None listed.
*Miscellaneous:* [Hitchcock 1788–93, 1:104, mistakenly places this performance in 1739. Ballad-opera by Samuel Davey. Not listed in *LS;* Nicoll lists only a possible 1739 Dublin performance.]

18   Mon.   AS.   *Love Makes a Man.*
*Cast:* None listed.
*Benefit:* The Poor Distressed Prisoners in Various Marshalseas.

and

*Afterpiece: The What D'Ye Call It.*
*Cast:* None listed.

19    Tues.    SA.    *The Alchemist.*
*Cast:* None listed.
*Singing and Dancing:* With several Entertainments of Dancing.
and

*Afterpiece: The Jealous Farmer Deceived.*
*Cast:* None listed.


20    Wed.    AS.    Ridotto.
*Miscellaneous:* By Subscription. Tickets: Gentlemen, one-half gn.; Ladies,
1 British Crown.


**1739**


JANUARY


3    Wed.    SA.    *Cato.*
*Cast:* Cato—Pellish (from London).


4    Thur.    AS.    *The Silent Woman.*
*Cast:* None listed.
*Benefit:* Loughlin.
and

*Afterpiece: The Cobler of Preston.*
*Cast:* None listed.


11    Thur.    SA.    *The Beaux' Stratagem.*
*Cast:* None listed.
and

*Afterpiece: The Harlot's Progress* [*; or, The Ridotto Al'Fresco*].
*Cast:* Harlequin—Morris.
*Miscellaneous:* With new scenes painted by Mr. [Joseph] Tutor from the
celebrated drawings of Hogarth; the stage to be finely illuminated and
adorned with Statues, Festoons, etc.
    [We hear that there is now in rehearsal . . . a new pantomime entertain-
ment called *The Harlot's Progress; or, The Birth of Harlequin* [*sic*] . . ."
(*DNL,* of early Dec. 1738 quoted by W. J. Lawrence, Notebook 7:70).
    *Singing and Dancing:* Concluding with a Grand Masquerade dance; Mr.
Barrington (it being particularly desired) in the Bridewell Scene will sing
the Humourous Song called "Chau Raw."
*Comment:* "Whereas the Machinery of the Entertainment . . . was in the
Performance sometimes obstructed by the crouding of Gentlemen on the
Stage (notwithstanding the raising the Price to half a Guinea) it's then hoped

no Gentleman will take it ill their being refused Admittance behind the Scenes the Nights of performing said Entertainment" (*DDP*, 13 Jan. 1739).

15    Mon.    AS.    Ridotto.

15    Mon.    SA.    *The Old Batchelour.*
*Cast:* None listed.
and
*Afterpiece: The Harlot's Progress.*
*Cast:* Harlequin—Morris.

18    Thur.    SA.    *The Woman's Revenge; or, A Match at Newgate.*
*Cast:* None listed.
and
*Afterpiece: The Harlot's Progress.*
*Cast:* Harlequin—Morris.

22    Mon.    AS.    *All for Love.*
*Cast:* None listed.
*Benefit:* Widow Elrington.
and
*Afterpiece: The Cobler of Preston.*
*Cast:* None listed.

22    Mon.    SA.    *The Constant Couple.*
*Cast:* Sir Harry Wildair—R. Elrington.
*Benefit:* Henry Ussher (Being Nine Years and upwards confined in the Four Courts Marshalsea).
*Miscellaneous:* At the Desire of several Persons of Distinction; "N. B. This Gentleman's Grandfather was the Founder of Trinity College" (*DDP*, 18 Jan. 1739); Boxes and stage, 5s. 5d.; Lattices 4s. 4d.; Pit, 3s. 3d.
and
*Afterpiece: The Mock Doctor.*
*Cast:* None listed.

24    Wed.    AS.    *King Henry VIII.*
*Cast:* King—Ward (first time in character).
*Benefit:* Ward.
*Miscellaneous:* At the Desire of several Persons of Quality.
and
*Afterpiece: Margery; or, A Worse Plague Than the Dragon.*
*Cast:* None listed.

*Miscellaneous:* Never performed in this Kingdom; as altered from the Italian of Sig. Carini.
*Singing and Dancing:* With all the Music; with Entertainments of Dancing.

25     Thur.     SA.     *Volpone.*     V.
*Cast:* None listed.
*Benefit:* L. Duval.
*Comment:* "Last Night Volpone was played for the Benefit of Mr. Duval, at his Theatre in SA, to a very full and splendid Audience: The Performance of it gave universal Satisfaction, as most of his Plays do, he having introduced a certain Regularity of Management, which certainly must conduct all Theatrical Affairs to much more Advantage than they can be where no such Thing is used" (*DDP*, 26 Jan. 1739).

and

*Afterpiece: The Harlot's Progress.*
*Cast:* Harlequin—Morris.
*Miscellaneous:* "Whereas by the crowding of Gentlemen on the Stage the first Night of performing this Entertainment the same was greatly obstructed, but by keeping the Stage clear the last Night the same (with several Amendments and Alterations) gave entire Satisfaction to the Audience. . . . High Prices. No Person to be admitted behind the Scenes and no odd Money to be taken" (*DDP*, 19 Jan. 1739).

27     Sat.     AS.     *Julius Caesar.*
*Cast:* Antony—J. Elrington.
*Benefit:* J. Elrington.
*Miscellaneous:* At the Particular Desire of Several Persons of Distinction.
*Singing and Dancing:* With several Entertainments of Dancing.

and

*Afterpiece: The Walking Statue.*
*Cast:* None listed.

31     Wed.     SA.     *Love for Love.*
*Cast:* None listed.
*Benefit:* Husband.

and

*Afterpiece:* Unspecified "Farce."

FEBRUARY

1     Thur.     AS.     *The Emperor of the Moon.*
*Cast:* Harlequin—Morgan; Scaramouche—R. Layfield.
*Benefit:* Bridges.
*Miscellaneous:* At the Desire of several Persons of Quality; All the Scenes,

Machines and other Decorations (with a grand Machine representing the Zodiack and Moon World) being entirely new.

and

*Afterpiece: The Adventures of Half an Hour.*
*Cast:* None listed.

2    Fri.    SA.    *Woman's Revenge.*
*Cast:* None listed.

and

*Afterpiece: The Harlot's Progress.*
*Cast:* Harlequin—Morris.

6    Tues.    AS.    *The Tender Husband.*
*Cast:* None listed.
*Benefit:* Christopher Dickson (printer) and MacCarty (musician).

8    Thur.    SA.    *Macbeth.*
*Cast:* None listed.
*Benefit:* Ralph Elrington.

and

*Afterpiece: The Hussar.*
*Cast:* Harlequin—R. Elrington.

9    Fri.    AS.    *The Careless Husband.*
*Cast:* None listed.
*Benefit:* Sick and Distressed Freemasons.

15    Thur.    SA.    *The Squire of Alsatia.*
*Cast:* None listed.
*Benefit:* Wetherilt and Woder.

and

*Afterpiece: The Mock Lawyer.*
*Cast:* None listed.

16    Fri.    AS.    *The Fair Penitent.*
*Cast:* None listed.
*Benefit:* Mrs. Wrightson.

and

*Afterpiece:* Unspecified "Farce."

17    Sat.    SA.    *The Tender Husband.*
*Cast:* Clerimont—H. Eyre (first appearance on this stage).
*Benefit:* Philips.
*Miscellaneous:* Being particularly Desired; Eyre is a Gentleman who had

his Education in our University; Not performed here these three years. With a new Prologue to the Town on the Occasion spoke by Sparks.

and

*Afterpiece: The Hussar.*
*Cast:* Harlequin—Dumont.

21    Wed.    SA.    *The Twin Rivals.*
*Cast:* None listed.
*Benefit:* Valentine Kavan (a Sufferer from a late fire in Church St.)

22    Thur.    AS.    *Theodosius.*
*Cast:* None listed.
*Command:* Viscount Mountjoy, Grand Master of Ireland.
*Benefit:* Griffith.
*Miscellaneous:* Mason's Night. With a new Prologue and Epilogue suitable to the Occasion.
*Singing and Dancing:* With several Entertainments of Dancing.

and

*Afterpiece: The Rival Queans, with the Humours of Alexander the Great.*
*Cast:* Alexander the Great—Mr. Griffith "the Little".

26    Mon.    SA.    *The Fatal Extravagance.*
*Cast:* Louisa—Mrs. Bayley (first stage appearance); Bellmour—R. Elrington.
*Benefit:* Dryden (treasurer).

and

*Afterpiece: Woman's Revenge.*
*Cast:* None listed.

and

*Afterpiece: The Harlot's Progress.*
*Cast:* Harlequin—Morris.
*Miscellaneous:* With all the Decorations proper to it, concluded with a Ridotto al fresco, representing the Prospect of Vauxhall Gardens as they were fitted up for the Entertainment of the Nobility and Gentry of England.

MARCH

1    Thur.    SA.    *Woman is a Riddle.*
*Cast:* None listed.
*Benefit:* Dumont and Mrs. Martin.
*Singing and Dancing:* With several Entertainments of Dancing.

and

*Afterpiece: A Cure for a Scold.*
*Cast:* None listed.

3    Sat.    SA.    *Volpone.*
*Cast:* None listed.
*Benefit:* A Distressed Gentlewoman.
and
*Afterpiece: The Jealous Farmer Deceived.*
*Cast:* None listed.

5    Mon.    SA.    *Oroonoko.*
*Cast:* None listed.
*Benefit:* Gibson (boxkeeper).
*Miscellaneous:* At the particular Desire of several Persons of Quality.
*Singing and Dancing:* With several Entertainments of Dancing, particularly
"The Wooden Shoes" by Morris, being desired.
and
*Afterpiece: The Devil to Pay.*
*Cast:* None listed.

6    Tues.    SA.    *The Busy Body.*
*Cast:* None listed.
*Benefit:* Andrew Francis Cheney, a Prisoner in the Four Courts Marshalsea.
*Comment:* Cheney "is confined for fees and Chamber-rent, which he could
not raise to discharge, before he delivered up his Effects, upon his taking
the Benefit of the Insolvent Debtors Act" (*DG*, 20–24 Feb. 1739).
and
*Afterpiece: The King and the Miller of Mansfield.*
*Cast:* None listed.

8    Thur.    SA.    *Love's Last Shift.*
*Cast:* None listed.
*Benefit:* Este.
*Singing and Dancing:* With several Entertainments, particularly, a Concerto
on the Trumpet and a solo on the German Flute by Mr. Burk Thumoth.
and
*Afterpiece: The Harlot's Progress.*
*Cast:* Harlequin—Morris.

12    Mon.    SA.    *The Recruiting Officer.*
*Cast:* Rose—Miss Bullock (first stage appearance).
*Benefit:* W. Delamain.
and
*Afterpiece: The Jealous Farmer Deceived.*
*Cast:* None listed.

13    Tues.    SA.    "A Latin Play."
*Cast:* Rev. Mr. Ford's Scholars.

*Comment:* ". . . a Latin Play was performed with great Applause, by the Reverend Mr. Ford's Scholars, before a numerous and Learned Audience" (*DDP,* 15 Mar. 1739).

14    Wed.    SA.     *Hamlet.*
*Cast:* None listed.
*Benefit:* John Gregory (jeweller).

15    Thur.    SA.     *The Constant Couple.*
*Cast:* None listed.
*Benefit:* W. Mainwaring and W. Connor (musicians).
and

*Afterpiece: The Stage Coach.*
*Cast:* None listed.

19    Mon.    SA.     *The Provoked Husband.*
*Cast:* None listed.
*Benefit:* Mrs. Orfeur.
*Singing and Dancing:* With several Entertainments of Dancing.
and

*Afterpiece:* Unspecified "Farce."

20    Tues.    SA.     *Love and a Bottle.*
*Cast:* None listed.
*Benefit:* Mrs. Barry.
*Singing and Dancing:* With several Entertainments of Dancing.
and

*Afterpiece: Flora.*
*Cast:* None listed.

21    Wed.    SA.     *The Twin Rivals.*
*Cast:* Teague—Morris (first time in character).
*Benefit:* Lamb (pit officekeeper) and J. Duval.
*Singing and Dancing:* With several Entertainments of Dancing.
and

*Afterpiece:* Unspecified "Farce."

22    Thur.    AS.     *The Relapse.*
*Cast:* None listed.
*Benefit:* Watson.
*Miscellaneous:* At the Desire of several Persons of Quality.
and

*Afterpiece: Flora.*
*Cast:* None listed.

26   Mon.      AS.      *The Pilgrim.*
*Cast:* None listed.
*Benefit:* Mrs. Vanderbank.
*Miscellaneous:* [After this performance the AS company travelled to Cork for the spring Assizes (Clark 1965, 3).]
*Singing and Dancing:* Dancing, "Camargo" by Mrs. Moreau, "The Wooden Shoe" by Master Cormack, "The Huntsman and Hounds" by R. Layfield, "The Highlander and His Mistress" by Moreau, "Four Pierrots" by Pitt, Layfield, Master Pitt and Master Cormack.
                        and
*Afterpiece: The Devil to Pay.*
*Cast:* None listed.
                        and
*Afterpiece: Flora.*
*Cast:* None listed.

26   Mon.      SA.      *The City Wives' Confederacy.*
*Cast:* None listed.
*Benefit:* Cummins (dancer) and Bourne.
*Singing and Dancing:* A solo by Burk Thumoth, being particularly desired.
                        and
*Afterpiece: The Hussar.*
*Cast:* None listed.

29   Thur.     SA.      *The Unhappy Favourite; or, The Earl of Essex.*
*Cast:* None listed.
*Benefit:* Nimmo (prompter).

APRIL

9    Mon.      SA.      *The Spanish Fryar.*
*Cast:* None listed.
*Miscellaneous:* At the particular Desire of several Persons of Quality.
*Singing and Dancing:* With a variety of dancing.
                        and
*Afterpiece: The Jealous Farmer Deceived.*
*Cast:* None listed.

12   Thur.     SA.      *The Orphan.*
*Cast:* Page—Miss Bullock.
*Miscellaneous:* Being the last time of performing until after the Easter holidays.
*Singing and Dancing:* With several Entertainments of Dancing.

and
*Afterpiece: Chrononhotonthologos.*
*Cast:* None listed.

[Passion Week 16–21 April]

26    Thur.    SA.    *Venice Preserved.*
*Cast:* None listed.
*Benefit:* Husband.
*Miscellaneous:* Masons' Night.
                                            and
*Afterpiece:* Unspecified "Farce."

28    Sat.    SA.    *Othello.*
*Cast:* None listed.
*Benefit:* Mrs. Martin and Fox (pit doorkeeper).
                                            and
*Afterpiece:* Unspecified "Farce."

30    Mon.    SA.    *The Beggar's Opera.*
*Cast:* None listed.
*Benefit:* Philips and Gibson (boxkeeper).
*Deferred:* Deferred from 27 Apr. 1739.
                                            and
*Afterpiece: The Anatomist; or, The Sham Doctor.*
*Cast:* None listed.
*Miscellaneous:* Not performed here these 6 years.

MAY

2    Wed.    SA.    *Mustapha.*
*Cast:* None listed.
*Benefit:* L. Duval.
*Miscellaneous:* With several unspecified "Entertainments."

8    Tues.    AS.    Ridotto.

9    Wed.    SA.    *King Henry IV, with the Humours of Falstaff.*
*Cast:* None listed.
*Benefit:* A Gentlewoman in Distress.
                                            and
*Afterpiece: The Hussar.*
*Cast:* None listed.

10   Thur.   SA.   *The Committee.*
*Cast:* Teague—Morris (first time).
*Benefit:* Hamilton and Neil (boxkeeper).
*Miscellaneous:* "We hear that Mrs. Hamilton, who was on this Stage some Years ago and Sister to Mrs. Sterling, comes over from the TRDL to perform next season at the TRSA, Mr. Duval having agreed with Mr. Hamilton, who is now here . . ." (*DDP*, 1 May 1739).
*Singing and Dancing:* With several Entertainments of Dancing; with select pieces of music performed by Thumoth.
and

*Afterpiece: The Mock Doctor.*
*Cast:* None listed.


14   Mon.   SA.   *All for Love.*
*Cast:* None listed.
*Benefit:* Pellish.
and

*Afterpiece: A Cure for a Scold.*
*Cast:* None listed.


17   Thur.   SA.   *Love and a Bottle.*
*Cast:* None listed.
*Benefit:* Healy (stage officekeeper).
and

*Afterpiece: The What D'Ye Call It.*
*Cast:* None listed.


21   Thur.   AS.   *Turnus.*
*Cast:* None listed.
*Benefit:* The Author [Descaizeauz?].
*Miscellaneous:* [Premiere. Tragedy. Not listed in Nicoll or *LS*. The *BNL*, 3 Mar. 1772, reports: "Yesterday died much lamented by the curious in the phenomena of nature, the noted Chevalier Descaizeauz who resided for thirty years in a garret within the rules of a Fleet. He has left by his will, his tragedy of Turnus between the managers of our theatres and the King of France".]


21   Thur.   SA.   *Love for Love.*
*Cast:* None listed.
*Benefit:* Tyler (gallery officekeeper) and Bushell.
and

*Afterpiece:* Unspecified "Farce."

23    Wed.    SA.    *Oroonoko.*
*Cast:* None listed.
*Benefit:* Nimmo (prompter) and Kennedy.

and

*Afterpiece: The Anatomist.*
*Cast:* None listed.


JUNE


8    Fri.    SA.    *The City Wives' Confederacy.*
*Cast:* None listed.
*Benefit:* Richard Holliday, a Prisoner in the Four Courts Marshalsea for near 4 years.

and

*Afterpiece: The Honest Yorkshireman.*
*Cast:* None listed.


*Summer Season*


15    Fri.    SA.    *Hamlet.*
*Cast:* Hamlet—Milward (from DL).


18    Mon.    SA.    *Oroonoko.*
*Cast:* Oroonoko—Milward.


25    Mon.    SA.    *Othello.*
*Cast:* Othello—Delane (from CG).
*Benefit:* The Almshouse for "Widows of Decayed House-Keepers in St. Werburgh's Parish."
*Financial:* £145 in the House, *RNL,* 26 June 1739.


27    Wed.    SA.    *Tamerlane.*
*Cast:* Tamerlane—Delane; Bajazet—Milward.


29    Fri.    SA.    *The Orphan.*
*Cast:* Castalio—Milward; Chamont—Delane.
*Singing and Dancing:* With several Entertainments of Dancing.

and

*Afterpiece: The Hussar.*
*Cast:* Harlequin—Woodward (Lun, Jr. from LIF).

JULY

2   Mon.   SA.   *Julius Caesar.*
*Cast:* Brutus—Delane; Cassius—Milward.
*Benefit:* Milward.
*Miscellaneous:* Unspecified "Entertainments".

4   Wed.   SA.   *Volpone.*
*Cast:* Volpone—Delane; Voltore—Milward.

6   Fri.   SA.   *King Lear and His Three Daughters.*
*Cast:* Lear—Delane; Edgar—Milward.
*Singing and Dancing:* With several Entertainments of Dancing.

9   Mon.   SA.   *Macbeth.*   V.
*Cast:* Macbeth—Delane; Macduff—Milward.
*Benefit:* Delane.
*Comment:* ". . . had it not been for the Warmth of the Wheather [*sic*], he would have had a much greater Number of Auditors: However, many Persons of Quality and Distinction who had Tickets, did not attend, but gave him very handsome Presents, which amount to a considerable Sum" (*FDJ*, 10–14 July 1739).
*Financial:* Receipt for benefit £95.

12   Thur.   SA.   *The Distrest Mother.*
*Cast:* Pyrrhus—Delane; Orestes—Milward.
*Benefit:* J. Duval.
*Singing and Dancing:* With several Entertainments of Dancing.

14   Sat.   SA.   *The Conscious Lovers.*
*Cast:* Bevil, Jr.—Delane; Sealand—Milward.
*Benefit:* The Charitable Infirmary on the Inn's Quay.
*Miscellaneous:* Delane's last time of performing this season.

16   Mon.   SA.   *Love's Last Shift.*
*Cast:* Loveless—Milward; Sir Novelty—Woodward (his first appearance in Ireland).

and

*Afterpiece: Harlequin's Vagaries; or, Pierrot in Distress.* V.
*Cast:* Harlequin—Lun, Jr. [Woodward].
*Miscellaneous:* First time in this Kingdom.
*Singing and Dancing:* With entirely new music, scenes, machines and decorations; also a clever device designed by Woodward altering the stage "so that the Side Scenes from the Upper Part to the Lower, may move together

which will be of infinite use to the Plays, particularly to the Historical Ones of Shakespere" (*DNL*, 21 July 1739).

19    Thur.    SA.    *King Henry IV, with the Humours of Falstaff.*
*Cast:* Hotspur—Milward.
*Benefit:* Milward.

20    Fri.    SA.    *All for Love.*
*Cast:* Ventidius—Milward.
                              and
*Afterpiece:*    *Harlequin's Vagaries.*
*Cast:* Harlequin—Woodward.

23    Mon.    SA.    *Love Makes a Man.*
*Cast:* Charles—Milward; Clodio—Woodward.
*Benefit:* Woodward.
                              and
*Afterpiece: Harlequin's Vagaries.*
*Cast:* Harlequin—Woodward.

26    Thur.    SA.    *The Unhappy Favourite; or, The Earl of Essex.*
*Cast:* Essex—Milward.
                              and
*Afterpiece: Harlequin's Vagaries.*
*Cast:* Harlequin—Woodward.

30    Mon.    SA.    *Hamlet.*
*Cast: Hamlet*—Milward.
*Miscellaneous:* At the desire of several Ladies of Quality. Positively Milward's last time of performing.
                              and
*Afterpiece: Harlequin's Vagaries.*
*Cast:* Harlequin—Woodward.
*Miscellaneous:* Last time of performing it this season.

AUGUST

2    Thur.    SA.    *All for Love.*
*Cast:* Antony—Milward.
*Comment:* "Monday Evening, being the last Night Mr. Milward intended to Play this Season, after the Entertainment went on the Stage to return Thanks to the Publick, for the Favours conferred on him since his Arrival, and to take his Leave for this Year; which done, the Audience with one Voice called for Alexander, and Mr. Milward to shew his Willingness to oblige, enquired of the Actors, if the Play could be performed, and being answered in the

Negative, told the Audience, as he could not oblige them with that Play, he was ready to perform the Part of Mark Antony, in All for Love, or the World well Lost, which the Audience immediately agreed to . . . as it was the Request of the Audience, and the last Time of his Performance; 'tis not to be doubted, but the House will be as full as it was at Hamlet" (*DDP*, 1 Aug. 1739).

and

*Afterpiece: Harlequin's Vagaries.*
*Cast:* Harlequin—Woodward.
*Miscellaneous:* Last time of performing it this season.

6    Mon.    SA.    *The Rival Queens; or, The Death of Alexander the Great.*
*Cast:* Alexander—Milward (the last time of his performing this season).

and

*Afterpiece: Harlequin's Vagaries.*
*Cast:* Harlequin—Woodward.

9    Thur.    SA.    *The Squire of Alsatia.*
*Cast:* None listed.
*Benefit:* Thumoth (musician).
*Deferred:* Deferred from 6 Aug. 1739 by request so as not to conflict with Milward's farewell performance.

and

*Afterpiece: Harlequin's Vagaries.*
*Cast:* Harlequin—Woodward.

13    Mon.    SA.    *The Beggar's Opera.*
*Cast:* Macheath—Mrs. Reynolds.
*Benefit:* L. Duval.
*Miscellaneous:* Positively the last time of performing this season; Mrs. Reynolds performed in male attire.

and

*Afterpiece: Harlequin's Vagaries.*
*Cast:* Harlequin—Woodward.

## 1739–1740 Season

Theatres operating: Aungier Street (the Theatre Royal, with performances advertised as "By Command of The Duke and Duchess of Devonshire."); Smock Alley (acted "By Authority of the Rt. Hon. Luke Gardiner, Esq.," i.e. the Master of the Revels).

*Aungier Street Company:*

Mrs. Bayley, Bridges, F. Elrington, J. Elrington, Griffith, Lawler, L. Layfield, R. Layfield, Loughlin, Mrs. Lyddal, Vanderbank, J. Ward, Mrs. Ward, J. Watson, Jr., Miss Woffington, Wrightson, Mrs. Wrightson.

Dancers: Master Pitt, Walsh.

Musicians: Heron, Francis Woder, Callaghan MacCarty (or Carty).

*Repertory:*
Mainpieces: Recorded performances: 33 (of 27 different pieces, including 2 unspecified plays but excluding concert and ridottos).
Afterpieces: Recorded Performances: 19 (of 12 different pieces including unspecified farces).
Premieres:
*Tamar.*
*A Cure for Jealousy.* (a)
Entr'acte entertainments: Most performances include singing and/or dancing.
Command Performances: 11 (3 Government nights).
Benefits:
Pre-February: Manager—1; Actor—3.
Post-February: Manager—1; Actor—18; Author—2; House Servant—1.

---

*Smock Alley Company:*
Barrington, Mrs. Barry, Beamsley, Bourne, Miss Dalton, Doland, J. Duval, L. Duval, Dyer, Ralph Elrington, Este, Furnival, Mrs. Furnival, Miss Furnival, Giles, Gregory, Kennedy, Mrs. Orfeur, T. Philips, Mrs. Reynolds, I. Sparks, L. Sparks, Wetherilt, Mrs. Wetherilt, Worsdale.

Dancers: Miss Bullock, Cummins, W. Delamain, Dumont, Mrs. Dumont, Mrs. Martin, Moreau (from AS), J. Morris, Miss Elizabeth Thomson.

Musicians: Heron, Gunan, Burke Thumoth, Woder.

House Servants: Mrs. Bamford (dresser), Dryden (Treasurer), Gibson (boxkeeper), Lamb (pit officekeeper), Nimmo (prompter), James Reilly (stage doorkeeper), Tyler (gallery officekeeper).

Summer: Delane (from Covent Garden), H. Giffard (from Drury Lane), Oates (from Covent Garden), Stoppelaer (from Covent Garden).

*Repertory:*
Mainpieces: Recorded performances: 77 (of 47 different pieces, excluding concert).

Afterpieces: Recorded Performances: 62 (of 27 different pieces, including unspecified farces).
Premieres:
*The Faithful Shepherd.*
*The Miser Matched.*
*The Assembly.* (a)
*Matrimony Displayed.* (a)
*The Preceptor.* (a)
Entr'acte entertainments: Most performances advertise singing and/or dancing; trained marmaset.
Command Performances: 5.
Benefits:
Pre-February: Manager—1; Charity—2.
Post-February: Manager—1; Actor—16; Author—2; House Servants—4; Charity—11.
[Two of the "Charity" performances may have been to pay off debts to local merchants, i.e. Fitzgerald and Steward.]
*Significant events:*
In late December a spell of very cold weather gripped the country, lasting for over two months. There were violent storms, the River Liffey froze and many people died of exposure. *FDJ* of 13 Jan. 1740 reported: "We hear that the Proprietors of the Lamps of the City of Dublin have never been lay'd under greater Hardship in Lighting the Publick Lamps than at the Present Time . . . it being with the utmost Difficulty that Men can be procured to Light them, the Weather being so Exquisitely Cold, so that the Oyle, notwithstanding the Light, Freezeth in the Lamps." The bad weather adversely affected the theatrical revenues, many performances being postponed or cancelled.

---

**1739**

OCTOBER

11    Thur.    AS.    *Tunbridge Walks.*
*Cast:* None listed.
*Miscellaneous:* Government Night: Anniversary of Coronation of George II.

30    Tues.    AS.    Unspecified "Play."
*Miscellaneous:* Government Night: Anniversary of birth of George II.

NOVEMBER

1   Thur.   SA.   *Love's Last Shift.*
*Cast:* None listed.
*Miscellaneous:* First Time of the Company's playing this Season. Mr. Duval
is determined to begin positively at half an hour after Six each Night he
Plays.
*Singing and Dancing:* With a Variety of Dancing, particularly a dance by
Moreau being the first time of his Appearance on this [i.e. new SA] Stage.
                                    and
*Afterpiece: The Honest Yorkshireman.*
*Cast:* None listed.


5   Mon.   AS.   Unspecified "Play."
*Miscellaneous:* Government Night; Anniversary of birth of William III.


5   Mon.   SA.   *Tamerlane.*
*Cast:* None listed.
*Singing and Dancing:* Several entertainments of dancing between the Acts,
particularly a comic Dance by Moreau, being his second Time on this stage.


8   Thur.   AS.   Ridotto.   V.
*Miscellaneous:* Duke and Dutchess of Devonshire present.


8   Thur.   SA.   *The Twin Rivals.*
*Cast:* None listed.
*Miscellaneous:* The Scenes, Musick, Dances and other Decorations entirely
new.
*Singing and Dancing:* Entirely new Dances by Moreau, Dumont, Delamain,
Madam Dumont, Mrs. Martin, and Miss Thompson.
                                    and
*Afterpiece: Harlequin's Vagaries; or, Pierrot in Distress.*
*Cast:* None listed.


12   Mon.   SA.   *Love for Love.*
*Cast:* None listed.
*Command:* Earl of Anglesey.
*Miscellaneous:* For the entertainment of the Duke and Duchess of Devon-
shire.
                                    and
*Afterpieces: Harlequin's Vagaries.*
*Cast:* None listed.

15    Thur.    AS.    [*The Life and Death of*] *Sir Walter Raleigh.*
*Cast:* None listed.
*Command:* Duke and Duchess of Devonshire.
*Miscellaneous:* A new Prologue on the Occasion.
*Singing and Dancing:* With entertainments of dancing.

15    Thur.    SA.    *Sir Walter Raleigh.*
*Cast:* None listed.
*Miscellaneous:* New Prologue.
*Singing and Dancing:* With entertainments of dancing.
and

*Afterpiece: Harlequin's Vagaries.*
*Cast:* None listed.

19    Mon.    SA.    *Sir Walter Raleigh.*
*Cast:* None listed.
and

*Afterpiece: Harlequin's Vagaries.*
*Cast:* None listed.

21    Wed.    SA.    *Love's Last Shift.*
*Cast:* None listed.
*Miscellaneous:* By Authority of Rt. Hon. Luke Gardiner, Esq.
and

*Afterpiece: Harlequin's Vagaries.*
*Cast:* None listed.
*Miscellaneous:* With an additional Scene, in which will be introduced a wonderful Creature [probably a trained marmoset] lately arrived from Mexico, who performs several very surprizing Things.

22    Thur.    AS.    Ridotto.
*Miscellaneous:* The lattices are shut up.

26    Mon.    SA.    *Love Makes a Man.*
*Cast:* None listed.
and

*Afterpiece: The Preceptor; or, The Loves of Abelard and Heloise.*
*Cast:* None listed.
*Miscellaneous:* [Premiere. Ballad Opera in one act by William Hammond.] Seats erected on the stage for the accommodation of the Ladies; Boxes, pit, stage and lattices 1 English crown, gallery, 2 British Shillings, with the boxes laid open to the pit.
     [Nicoll lists only this performance; not listed in *LS.*]
*Comment:* "The Preceptor will be speedily published . . . N.B. This Piece

was not intended for the Press; but the Author, apprehending himself injured by a Misrepresentation of it, thinks himself obliged to Print it in his own Vindication" (*DNL,* 26–29 Dec. 1739).

29    Thur.    SA.    *The Provoked Husband.*
*Cast:* None listed.

and

*Afterpiece: The Preceptor.*
*Cast:* None listed.

DECEMBER

1    Sat.    SA.    Concert of "Alexander's Feast" [Dryden's "Ode to St. Cecilia's Day.]
*Miscellaneous:* [See Boydell 1988, 65.]

3    Mon.    SA.    *Hamlet.*
*Cast:* None listed.
*Miscellaneous:* By authority of Rt. Hon. Luke Gardiner.

and

*Afterpiece: Harlequin's Vagaries.*
*Cast:* None listed.
*Miscellaneous:* With several new and surprizing Things to be performed by the She Mexican Mermot.

6    Thur.    AS.    *The Relapse; or, Virtue in Danger.*    V.
*Cast:* None listed.
*Command:* Duke and Duchess of Devonshire.
*Benefit:* Griffith.
*Singing and Dancing:* Dancing between the Acts.
*Miscellaneous:* Mason's Night. With a new Prologue and Epilogue.
*Deferred:* Deferred from 29 Nov. 1739 by the command of Viscount Mountjoy, Grand Master of all Ireland.
*Comment:* "The Grand Master, Deputy Grand Master, and the Noblemen who had been Grand Masters, sat at the Upper end of the Stage, the Gentlemen ranged on Benches on each Side with Aprons and Gloves, they all joined in the chorus of Mason Songs, sung between the Acts, which greatly delighted the Audience" (*PO,* 8–11 Dec. 1739).

6    Thur.    SA.    *King Richard III.*
*Cast:* None listed.

and

*Afterpiece: Harlequin's Vagaries.*
*Cast:* None listed.

*Miscellaneous:* In which the Mexican Mermot performs several New and surprizing Things, being the last Time of its performing in this Kingdom.

13    Sat.    AS.    *The Way of the World.*
*Cast:* None listed.
*Benefit:* Woder and Heron (musicians).

and

*Afterpiece: The Hussar.*
*Cast:* None listed.

15    Sat.    AS.    *The Beggar's Opera.*
*Cast:* Polly—Miss Woffington.
*Command:* Duke and Duchess of Devonshire.
*Benefit:* F. Elrington.
*Miscellaneous:* For the Entertainment of the Judges.

17    Mon.    AS.    *The Beggar's Opera.*
*Cast:* None listed.
*Miscellaneous:* At the particular Desire of several Ladies of Quality. [*DDP*, 3 Jan. 1740 contains a adulatory poem inserted at the request of "S. R." entitled "On Miss Woffington's playing the Part of Polly" which perhaps suggests that Miss W. performed that part this night.]

17    Mon.    SA.    *King Henry IV, with the Humours of Falstaff.*
*Cast:* "All Parts as Usual."
*Benefit:* The Distressed Prisoners in the Several Marshalseas of this City.
*Miscellaneous:* By Appointment of the Charitable Musical Society at the Bull's Head. By authority of Luke Gardiner, Esq. Stage illuminated with wax. Prices: Boxes, Pit, Stage, Lattices, 1 British Crown, Gallery 2s. 3d. [Playbill in TCD Library OLS 194.2.3 no. 58.]
*Singing and Dancing:* With several Entertainments of Dancing.
*Comment:* The Charitable Musical Society has released 142 from Prison in 1737 and 141 in 1738 (*PO,* 1–4 Dec. 1739).

and

*Afterpiece: The What D'Ye Call It.*
*Cast:* None listed.

19    Wed.    AS.    Ridotto.

20    Thur.    SA.    *The Constant Couple.*    V.
*Cast:* Lady Lurewell—Mrs. Furnival (just arrived from Drury Lane).
*Singing and Dancing:* Several entertainments of dancing between the Acts by Moreau, Dumont, Morris, Delamain, and Miss Bullock.
*Benefit:* L. Duval.

and

*Afterpiece: The Lottery.*    V.
*Cast:* [listed in 1740 Dublin edition] Stocks—Barrington; Jack Stocks—
Witherilt; First Buyer—Bourne; Second Buyer—I. Sparks; Lovemore—
Este; Whisk—Beamsley; Chloe—Mrs. Reynolds; Mrs. Stocks—Mrs. Or-
feur; Jenny—Mrs. Martin; Lady—Mrs. Barry.
*Miscellaneous:* With the original Epilogue spoken by Mrs. Reynolds, in the
Character of Lady Lace. With a new Grand Additional Scene, which exactly
represents the Manner of Drawing the State Lotteries at Guild-Hall in Lon-
don. [The Dublin version is based on the fourth London edition with the
addition of this new scene according to W. J. Lawrence, Notebook 7:100.]
*Singing and Dancing:* Songs intirely new, and set to Musick by Mr. Seedo
[i.e., Sydow].


22    Sat.    SA.    *The Beaux' Stratagem.*
*Cast:* Mrs. Sullen—Mrs. Furnival.
                              and
*Afterpiece: The Lottery.*
*Cast:* None listed.


24    Mon.    SA.    *The Distrest Mother.*
*Cast:* Hermione—Mrs. Furnival.
                              and
*Afterpiece: The Lottery.*
*Cast:* None listed.


31    Mon.    AS.    *The Busy Body.*
*Cast:* None listed.
*Miscellaneous:* [This performance may have been cancelled.]


31    Mon.    SA.    *The Distrest Mother.*
*Cast:* Hermione—Mrs. Furnival.
                              and
*Afterpiece: The Lottery.*
*Cast:* None listed.


**1740**


JANUARY


3    Thur.    SA.    *The Old Batchelour.*
*Cast:* Laetitia—Mrs. Furnival.

and

*Afterpiece: Harlequin's Vagaries.*
*Cast:* None listed.


7   Mon.   SA.   *The Miser Matched; or, A Trip to Brussels.*
*Cast:* None listed.
*Miscellaneous:* Comedy written by Mr. Skiddy. [Premiere. No record in Nicoll or *LS*.]
*Singing and Dancing:* With entertainments of dancing.


21   Mon.   AS.   Ridotto.
*Command:* Duke and Duchess of Devonshire.


21   Mon.   SA.   *The Provoked Wife.*   V.
*Cast:* Lady Fanciful—Mrs. Furnival.
*Miscellaneous:* "Whereas the Nobility and Gentry in Consideration of the great Charge Mr. Duval has been at in getting up Plays, Entertainments, etc. have subscribed for six plays to be acted at the Theatre Royal in Smock Alley, the first to be the Provoked Wife on Thursday [i.e. 17 January, but deferred to this date]" (*FDJ*, 12–15 Jan. 1740).

Mr. Duval has erected in the Pit (which he designs to continue during the frost) a fire Engine, in which is kept a large Fire burning the whole time of Performance, which warmed the House, so as to give great Satisfaction to the Audience.
*Singing and Dancing:* Several entertainments of dancing between the Acts.

and

*Afterpiece: The Honest Yorkshireman.*
*Cast:* None listed.


24   Thur.   SA.   *The Orphan.*   V.
*Cast:* Monimia—Mrs. Furnival.
*Miscellaneous:* Second Subscription Night [*DNL* says Third]. "Several Stoves were placed in such a manner as rendered the house very warm, so that the Fires in the Gallery were put out before the play was half over" (*DNL*, 22–26 Jan. 1740).

[Boydell 1988, 66, places this performance on 26 January ].
*Singing and Dancing:* With entertainments of dancing, particularly a new Grand Entertainment of Dancing between four Highlanders and their Mistresses, by Moreau, Dumont, Morris, Delamain, Madam Dumont, Mrs. Martin, Miss Bullock, and Miss Thomson.

and

*Afterpiece: The Lottery.* V.
*Cast:* None listed.

26    Sat.    AS.    *The Fair Quaker of Deal.*
*Cast:* Fair Quaker—Miss Woffington.
*Benefit:* Mrs. Wrightson.

and

*Afterpiece: The Devil to Pay.*
*Cast:* Nell—Miss Woffington.

28    Mon.    SA.    *The Funeral.*
*Cast:* None listed.
*Miscellaneous:* Never acted here.
*Singing and Dancing:* Several entertainments of dancing between the Acts, particularly the new dance between four Highlanders.

and

*Afterpiece: Briton's Strike Home! or, The Sailor's Rehearsal.*
*Cast:* None listed.
*Miscellaneous:* Never acted in this Kingdom. Third Subscription Night. "Being the Rehearsal of a Farce on board the Spanish Prize the St. Joseph, and supposed to be performed by the English Sailors that guarded that Prize, while they lay at Spithead, and was actually taken from the Bravery, Spirit, and Humour of those gallant Fellows, when on their Duty there" (*DNL*, 19–22 Jan. 1740).

31    Thur.    SA.    *The Faithful Shepherd.*
*Cast:* None listed.
*Benefit:* Dr. Sheridan's Family.
*Miscellaneous:* Never performed here.
*Comment:* "Now in Rehearsal . . . a new Pastoral Tragedy, called the Faithful Shepherd translated from the Pastor Fido of the celebrated Guarini, by the late Reverend Dr. Thomas Sheridan, and now fitted for the stage by his Son" (*FDJ*, 8–12 Jan. 1740).

FEBRUARY

2    Tues.    AS.    Concert of Vocal and Instrumental Music.
*Benefit:* Richard Davis.
*Singing and Dancing:* Thumoth—Trumpet Concerto accompanied by Kettle Drum; Sig. and Signa. Palma—Concerto and Solo on German Flute and Overture for *Esther* on two German Flutes, and "The Early Horn."

7    Thur.    SA.    *Hamlet.*
*Cast:* None listed.
*Benefit:* Ralph Elrington.
*Singing and Dancing:* Several Entertainments.

8    Fri.    AS.    Ridotto.
*Benefit:* Widow Elrington.

9    Sat.    SA.    *Love's Last Shift.*
*Cast:* Amanda—Mrs. Furnival.
*Benefit:* Mrs. Furnival.
*Miscellaneous:* With a new Epilogue on the Occasion spoken by Mrs. Furnival. [Both Mrs. Furnival and the dancer Walsh advertised benefits for this night (see below, 18 Feb. 1740 SA). Walsh sought to force Mrs. Furnival to change her night by abusing her, but she remained firm, gained the sympathy of the Town, and Walsh had to change his own night.]
*Singing and Dancing:* With several entertainments of singing and dancing, at the End of the third Act will be sung, a new Ballad, made by Mr. Worsdale. The Printed Song to be given gratis at the Theatre.
*Deferred:* Deferred from 2 Feb. 1740, see 18 Feb. 1740 AS.
and

*Afterpiece: A Cure for a Scold.*
*Cast:* None listed.

11    Mon.    SA.    *Jane Shore.*
*Cast:* Jane Shore—Mrs. Furnival.
*Miscellaneous:* Fourth Subscription Night.
*Singing and Dancing:* With entertainments of dancing.
and

*Afterpiece: Harlequin's Vagaries.*
*Cast:* None listed.

13    Wed.    AS.    *Sir Courtly Nice; or, It Cannot Be.*
*Cast:* Sir Courtly—Bridges.
*Benefit:* Bridges.
and

*Afterpiece: The Virgin Unmasked; or, An Old Man Taught Wisdom.*
*Cast:* Lucy—Miss Woffington.
*Miscellaneous:* Never acted here.

18    Mon.    AS.    *The Way of the World.*
*Cast:* Sir Wilful Witwoud—Vanderbank; Petulant—F. Elrington; Millamant—Miss Woffington.
*Command:* Duke and Duchess of Devonshire.
*Benefit:* Walsh (dancer).
*Singing and Dancing:* With several entertainments of singing and dancing between the Acts.
*Comment:* "The above Play was not fixed to the 9th Instant to oppose Mrs. Furnival's Interest, on the contrary she is the Aggressor and knew that I

was confined to the said Day two Days before she put off her Play from Saturday the 2d or printed Bill or Ticket for the 9th" (*DDP*, 4 Feb. 1740). *Deferred:* Deferred from 9 Feb. 1740. This date retained by Boydell 1988, 66.

and

*Afterpiece: The Devil to Pay.*
*Cast:* Jobson—L. Layfield; Nell—Miss Woffington.

18    Mon.    SA.    *The Spanish Fryar.*
*Cast:* None listed.
*Benefit:* Barrington.
*Singing and Dancing:* With entertainments of dancing.

and

*Afterpiece:* Unspecified "Farce."

19    Tues.    AS.    *Tamar, Prince of Nubia.*
*Cast:* None listed.
*Miscellaneous:* A "new Tragedy by Michael Clancey, M. D. written on the late Revolution in China, and the Conquest of that Empire by the Tartars. . . . The Mortals and Customs produced in this Story, are collected from Duhald's History of China, and from Observations on the Memoirs and Relations of Pallafaux, Bishop of Osma" (*PO*, 22–26 Dec. 1739). [Nicoll lists only this performance; not listed in *LS*.]
*Deferred:* Deferred from 28 Jan. 1740 due to "the excessively cold weather."

21    Thur.    AS.    *All for Love.*
*Cast:* None listed.
*Command:* Duke and Duchess of Devonshire.
*Benefit:* The Author of the Farce [Matthew Gardiner].
*Deferred: DNL*, 26–29 Dec. 1739 indicates that at the Desire of several Persons of Quality *The Sharpers* was first deferred to 25 Jan. 1740 at SA but was switched to AS "Mr. Duval's House being engaged each night of the term." It was again deferred to this date because of bad weather.

and

*Afterpiece: The Sharpers; or, The Female Matchmaker.*
*Cast:* [listed in 1740 Dublin edition] Sir John Friendly—Morris; Trueman—Beamsley; Freelove—Gemea; Feignlove—Este; Wellfort—Giles; Lady Friendly—Mrs. Wetherilt; Loveit—Mrs. Martin; Wheedle—Mrs. Reynolds.
*Miscellaneous:* Ballad opera of one act in two scenes by Matthew Gardiner. A new Prologue "by a Friend" to be spoken before the farce by Miss Woffington. An epilogue by William Este and spoken by an actress [transcribed by W. J. Lawrence, Notebook 7:82.]

21   Thur.   SA.   *The Double Dealer.*
*Cast:* Maskwell—L. Sparks; Lady Froth—Mrs. Furnival.
*Benefit:* T. Philips.

and

*Afterpiece: The Hussar.*
*Cast:* Harlequin—Delamain (first time in character); Pierrot—Morris.
*Miscellaneous:* The Machinery will be entirely new painted, new Garlands and Arches of Flowers for the Dance; in which will be introduced the little Mexican Mermot, being the last Time of its Appearance in this Kingdom.
*Singing and Dancing:* Concluded with the Grand Rural Dance, composed by Dumont.

and

*Afterpiece: The Raree Show; or, The Fox Trapped.*
*Cast:* None listed.
*Miscellaneous:* [Ballad Opera by Joseph Paterson. Nicoll lists a 1739 York edition and 1740 Chester edition; not listed in *LS*.]

23   Sat.   SA.   Concert of Music.
*Benefit:* Burk Thumoth.
*Miscellaneous:* Mr. Thumoth [spelled variously Thumoth/Tumond/Tumont] will perform several Grand Concerts on the Trumpet and Solos on the German Flute.
*Deferred:* Mr. Thumoth begs Pardon for putting off his Concert [originally advertised for 6 Feb., then 15 Feb.], but he was disappointed in the other House.

25   Mon.   AS.   *King Lear and His Three Daughters.*
*Cast:* None listed.
*Benefit:* Callaghan MacCarty and Mrs. Ward.
*Singing and Dancing:* With entertainments of singing and dancing between the acts.

and

*Afterpiece: The Virgin Unmasked.*
*Cast:* Lucy—Miss Woffington.
*Miscellaneous:* Afterpiece at the particular Desire of several Persons of Quality.

25   Mon.   SA.   *The Royal Merchant.*
*Cast:* None listed.
*Benefit:* Mr. and Mrs. Wetherilt.
*Miscellaneous:* With the whole Procession of the Coronation of King Clause.

and

*Afterpiece: Harlequin's Vagaries.*
*Cast:* None listed.

27   Wed.   AS.   *The Double Gallant; or, The Sick Lady's Cure.*
*Cast:* None listed.
*Command:* Duke and Duchess of Devonshire.
*Benefit:* Watson.

MARCH

1   Sat.   AS.   *The Conscious Lovers.*
*Cast:* Phillis—Miss Woffington.
*Benefit:* Miss Woffington.

and

*Afterpiece: The Female Officer; or, The Lady's Voyage to Gibraltar.*
*Cast:* Female Officer—Miss Woffington.
*Miscellaneous:* [Premiere. Farce by Henry Brooke, adaptation of Shadwell's *The Humours of the Army.* Nicoll cites Brooke's *Works,* 1778, but no performance; not listed in *LS.*]

3   Mon.   SA.   *The Committee.*
*Cast:* None listed.
*Command:* Duke and Duchess of Devonshire.
*Benefit:* Cummins (dancer).

and

*Afterpiece: The Hussar.*
*Cast:* None listed.

4   Tues.   SA.   *The City Wives' Confederacy.*
*Cast:* None listed.
*Benefit:* Mr. and Mrs. Dumont.

and

*Afterpiece: The Hussar.*
*Cast:* Harlequin—W. Delamain; Hussar—Philips; Petit Maitre—Dumont; His Man—I. Sparks; Pierrot—Morris; Columbine—Mrs. Martin.

8   Sat.   SA.   *The Tempest.*
*Cast:* Hippolita—Mrs. Furnival.
*Benefit:* Dryden (treasurer).
*Miscellaneous:* As the Whole will be attended with a great Expence, and the Performance to be very exact, it is hoped that no Gentlemen will take it ill if they are refused Admittance behind the Scenes.
*Singing and Dancing:* With the Songs, Dances, and Decorations proper to it and the original music.

and

*Afterpiece: The Harlot's Progress.*
*Cast:* None listed.

*Singing and Dancing:* At the end of which will be a grand Masquerade Dance, and also the delightful Prospect of Vauxhall Gardens.


12     Wed.     AS.     *Hamlet.*
*Cast:* Queen—Mrs. Lyddal.
*Command:* Duke and Duchess of Devonshire.
*Benefit:* J. Elrington and Mrs. Lyddal.
*Comment: FDJ,* 8–11 Mar. 1740 recommends Mrs. Lyddal to the public because of her "uncommon worth" and suggests that she is very old and ill with the following lines of verse:

> On Life's last Stage, alas! she soon must tread,
> The fatal Sisters hover round her Head.
> Then seize the Moment, plead her Cause ye Fair,
> Be Virtue, Merit, suppliant Age your Care.

[Mrs. Lyddal was long on the Dublin stage. Clark finds her in Dublin as early as the 1716–17 season (Clark 1955, 162). She was evidently the mother of three actress daughters: Mary (Molly or Anna Marcella, later Mrs. Henry Giffard), Esther (later Mrs. Bland, then Mrs. John Hamilton, then Mrs. Sweeney) and Nancy (later Mrs. James Sterling) who were also acting in Dublin during this period.]

and

*Afterpiece: The Female Officer.*
*Cast:* None listed.


13     Thur.     AS.     *The Provoked Husband.*
*Cast:* None listed.
*Benefit:* A Gentleman in Distress.

and

*Afterpiece: The Virgin Unmasked.*
*Cast:* None listed.


13     Thur.     SA.     *The Fair Penitent.*
*Cast:* None listed.
*Benefit:* Este.
*Miscellaneous:* At the Desire of several Persons of Quality.

and

*Afterpiece: A Cure for Jealousy.*
*Cast:* None listed.
*Miscellaneous:* Written by Mr. Este. Never performed. [Ballad Farce by William Este. Not listed in *LS;* Nicoll lists only this performance].

15    Sat.    AS.    *The Pilgrim.*
*Cast:* None listed.
*Command:* Duke and Duchess of Devonshire.
*Benefit:* Mrs. Bayley.
*Singing and Dancing:* With entertainments of dancing.
and
*Afterpiece: The Female Officer.*
*Cast:* None listed.

15    Sat.    SA.    *The Mourning Bride.*
*Cast:* Almeria—Mrs. Furnival.
*Command:* Duke and Duchess of Devonshire.
*Miscellaneous:* Fifth Subscription Play. Never performed here [i.e. at AS, but see performance of 29 Mar. 1736].
and
*Afterpiece: The Devil to Pay.*
*Cast:* None listed.

19    Wed.    SA.    *Rule a Wife and Have a Wife.*
*Cast:* None listed.
*Benefit:* Sick and Distrest Freemasons.
*Miscellaneous:* With a new Prologue and Epilogue.
*Singing and Dancing:* With several Songs suitable to the Occasion.

20    Thur.    SA.    *Love for Love.*
*Cast:* Valentine—R. Elrington; Angelica—Mrs. Furnival; Miss Prue—Miss Bullock.
*Benefit:* W. Delamain.
and
*Afterpiece: The Honest Yorkshireman.*
*Cast:* None listed.

22    Sat.    AS.    *The Country Lasses.*
*Cast:* None listed.
*Command:* Duke and Duchess of Devonshire.
*Benefit:* Master Pitt (dancer).
*Singing and Dancing:* Several entertainments of dancing between the Acts.
and
*Afterpiece: The Female Officer.*
*Cast:* Female Officer—Miss Woffington.

24    Mon.    AS.    "Mr. Delamayne's Beau Monde."
*Command:* Duke and Duchess of Devonshire.
*Miscellaneous:* [Perhaps a ridotto.]

27    Thur.    SA.    *King Richard III.*
*Cast:* Queen Elizabeth—Mrs. Furnival.
*Benefit:* Moreau.
*Singing and Dancing:* With the following Entertainments of Dancing between the Acts: Act 1, "The Grecian Sailor" by Delamain; Act 2, a Dance to the Tune of "Camargo" by Miss Moreau; Act 3, A Punch's Dance by Dumont; Act 4, "The Highlander and his Mistress" by Moreau and Mrs. Moreau; Act 5, a Dance to the Tune of "The Drought" by Miss Moreau.

and

*Afterpiece: Harlequin's Vagaries.*
*Cast:* None listed.

29    Sat.    SA.    *The Constant Couple.*
*Cast:* None listed.
*Benefit:* Mrs. Furnival.
*Miscellaneous:* At the request and for the entertainment of several noble Lords and Hon. Members of Parliament.
*Singing and Dancing:* With several entertainments of singing and dancing.

and

*Afterpiece: Harlequin's Vagaries.*
*Cast:* None listed.

APRIL

[Passion Week 21 March–5 April]

7    Mon.    SA.    *The Double Dealer.*
*Cast:* None listed.
*Benefit:* A Distressed Family.
*Miscellaneous:* Unspecified "Entertainments."

and

*Afterpiece:* Unspecified "Farce."

9    Wed.    SA.    *The Recruiting Officer.*
*Cast:* Silvia—Mrs. Furnival.
*Miscellaneous:* Sixth Subscription Night.
*Singing and Dancing:* With a Variety of Dancing.

and

*Afterpiece: Tom Thumb.*
*Cast:* None listed.

11    Fri.    SA.    *Venice Preserved.*
*Cast:* None listed.
*Benefit:* A Distressed Family.
*Miscellaneous:* Several unspecified Entertainments.

and

*Afterpiece: The Honest Yorkshireman.*
*Cast:* None listed.


14    Mon.    SA.    *The Beggar's Opera.*
*Cast:* None listed.
*Benefit:* James Reilly (stage doorkeeper).
*Singing and Dancing:* With several Dances.

and

*Afterpiece: The Stage Coach.*
*Cast:* None listed.


15    Tues.    AS.    *King Henry VIII.*
*Cast:* None listed.
*Benefit:* R. Layfield.

and

*Afterpiece: Flora.*
*Cast:* None listed.


16    Wed.    SA.    *The Conscious Lovers.*
*Cast:* None listed.
*Command:* Viscount Mountjoy.
*Benefit:* Richard Holliday, son of Mr. John Holiday, of Bride's Street, Mercer.
*Singing and Dancing:* Diverting Entertainments and Dancing between the Acts.


17    Thur.    SA.    *Theodosius.*
*Cast:* None listed.
*Benefit:* Gibson (boxkeeper).
*Miscellaneous:* Not acted these three years; A Part of the Pit is taken in in a Manner entirely new, which makes it equally commodious as the Boxes, and will prevent the Ladies being crouded by the other Part of the Pit. Mr. Gibson begs that the Ladies will send Directions by their Servants how many Places they will have.

and

*Afterpiece: The Devil to Pay.*
*Cast:* Nell—a young Gentlewoman (her first appearance on any stage).


18    Fri.    SA.    *The Orphan.*
*Cast:* None listed.
*Benefit:* Author of the Farce [Worsdale].

and

*Afterpiece: The Assembly.*
*Cast:* Lady Scandal—Worsdale.
*Miscellaneous:* [Premiere. Farce? by James Worsdale. Nicoll attributes the plays to Pitcairne and lists only this performance; not listed in *LS*. Worsdale played Lady Scandal at the particular desire of several Ladies of Quality.]

19    Sat.    AS.    *The Way of the World.*
*Cast:* None listed.
*Benefit:* A Distressed Family.

21    Mon.    SA.    *The Beaux' Stratagem.*
*Cast:* None listed.
*Benefit:* Whitnall, Wilkes, and B. Mainwaring [musicians].
*Miscellaneous:* With a new Prologue and Epilogue written by Mr. Wilkes.

and

*Afterpiece: The Honest Yorkshireman.*
*Cast:* None listed.

23    Wed.    SA.    *The Miser.*
*Cast:* None listed.
*Benefit:* Mrs. Martin and Mrs. Bamford.
*Singing and Dancing:* With a variety of dances.
*Deferred:* The play and the day was altered by the Desire of several Persons of Quality and all the Tickets given out for the Miser will be received that Day [i.e. the play was first deferred to 7 and then 10 Apr. and the program changed to *The Man's Bewitched* and *The Lover's Opera,* but the play was deferred again to this date and the program restored at the particular desire of several persons of quality].

and

*Afterpiece: The Lover's Opera.*
*Cast:* None listed.
*Miscellaneous:* Ballad opera by William Rufus Chetwood.

24    Thur.    SA.    *Love and a Bottle.*
*Cast:* None listed.
*Benefit:* The Author of the Farce.

and

*Afterpiece: Matrimony Displayed; or, A Cure for Love.*
*Cast:* None listed.
*Miscellaneous:* Never performed. [Anonymous Farce. Nicoll lists only this performance; not listed in *LS*.]

25     Fri.     AS.     *The Constant Couple.*
*Cast:* Sir Harry—Miss Woffington (first time in character).
*Benefit:* Ward.
*Miscellaneous:* Miss Woffington as Sir Harry at the Desire of several Persons of Quality; To begin exactly at 7 o'clock. [Miss Woffington's performance elicited an adulatory poem in *FDJ,* 17 May 1740.]
*Singing and Dancing:* "The Life of a Beau" sung by Miss Woffington in character at the Desire of several Persons of Quality.
*Comment:* "The dreadful severe winter in 1739–40, for a long time put a stop to all public diversions. The poverty and distresses of the lower classes of people at that time can scarcely be described. The theatre felt this general calamity in its full force, and for near three months was entirely closed. In the April following, just after the opening, Miss Woffington, now high in estimation, by desire of several persons of quality, appeared for the first time in the character of Sir Harry Wildair, and charmed the town to an uncommon degree" (Hitchcock 1788–93, 1:106–7). [Hitchcock is clearly incorrect in his assertion that the theatres closed during this period, although some performances were certainly affected.]
                                                    and
*Afterpiece: The Emperor of the Moon.*
*Cast:* None listed.
*Miscellaneous:* With all the Scenes, Machines, Flyings and other Decorations (with a grand Machine representing the Zodiack and Moon World) entirely new.

26     Sat.     AS.     *The Beggar's Opera.*
*Cast:* None listed.
*Benefit:* Loughlin.
*Deferred:* Deferred from 26 Mar. 1740.

26     Sat.     SA.     *Hamlet.*
*Cast:* None listed.
*Benefit:* John Steward (former wine merchant in Abbey St.)
*Miscellaneous:* At the Desire of several Persons of Quality. [Boydell 1988, 67, places this performance on 27 Apr.]
*Singing and Dancing:* With entertainments of dancing.
                                                    and
*Afterpiece: Flora.*
*Cast:* None listed.

28     Mon.     SA.     *Rule a Wife and Have a Wife.*
*Cast:* None listed.
*Benefit:* Dom. Gunan (musician) and Miss Dalton.
*Singing and Dancing:* With entertainments of dancing.

and

*Afterpiece: The Stage Coach.*
*Cast:* None listed.

29    Tues.    AS.    *The Miser.*
*Cast:* Lovegold—F. Elrington; Lappet—Miss Woffington.
*Benefit:* Vanderbank.
*Miscellaneous:* Not Acted here these two Years.
*Singing and Dancing:* With several entertainments of singing and dancing.

and

*Afterpiece:* Unspecified "Farce."

MAY

1    Thur.    AS.    *The Recruiting Officer.*
*Cast:* Silvia—Miss Woffington.
*Benefit:* Mr. and Mrs. Wrightson.

and

*Afterpiece:* Unspecified "Farce."

2    Fri.    SA.    *Jane Shore.*
*Cast:* None listed.
*Benefit:* Nimmo (prompter), Dyer, and Kennedy.

and

*Afterpiece: The Mock Lawyer.*
*Cast:* Mock Lawyer—I. Sparks; Justice Lovelaw—Morris; Valentine—Giles; Dash—Dyer; Laetitia—Miss Barry.
*Singing and Dancing:* With all the songs.

3    Sat.    AS.    *Rule a Wife and Have a Wife.*
*Cast:* Estifania—Miss Woffington.
*Benefit:* Dr. Michael Clancy.
*Miscellaneous:* By subscription of the Nobility and Gentry.

and

*Afterpiece: The Female Officer.*
*Cast:* Female Officer—Miss Woffington.

3    Sat.    SA.    *The Twin Rivals.*
*Cast:* None listed.
*Benefit:* Miss Bullock.
*Singing and Dancing:* With entertainments of dancing.

and

*Afterpiece: Damon and Phillida.*
*Cast:* None listed.

5    Mon.    SA.    *The Plain Dealer.*
*Cast:* Plain Dealer—L. Sparks.
*Benefit:* L. Duval.
*Miscellaneous:* As revised by the Duke of Buckingham; Sparks will perform
"being recovered from his late Indisposition."
*Singing and Dancing:* With entertainments of dancing; "Mr. Worsdale's Ob-
ligations to several Ladies of Quality and Fashion, oblige him to entertain
them with the Song of the Medley at the above [Duval's] Benefit" (*FDJ*, 29
Apr.–3 May 1740).

and

*Afterpiece: Harlequin's Vagaries.*
*Cast:* None listed.


7    Wed.    SA.    *The Royal Merchant.*
*Cast:* None listed.
*Benefit:* Lambe (pit officekeeper) and Tyler.

and

*Afterpiece:* Unspecified "Farce."


8    Thur.    SA.    *The Albion Queens; or, The Death of Mary, Queen
of Scotland.*
*Cast:* Queen—Mrs. Furnival.
*Benefit:* Doland and Miss Thomson.
*Miscellaneous:* Gentlemen and Ladies may depend that every thing will be
performed in the Manner expressed; and that particular Care will be taken
to have the Play done with great Decorum, the Stage being to be hung in
Mourning during that celebrated dying Scene of Queen Mary, and every
other Embellishment proper to the Play; and as this will occasion some
extraordinary Expence, no Money under the full Price will be taken in any
Part of the House, till after the Play.
   At the end of the *DDP*, 6 May 1740 advertisement for this performance
we find this notice of fraud in connection with benefit tickets:

> Whereas a Person about a Week ago went to a Noble Lord near Bolton Street
> and with a forg'd Letter in the name of Miss Thomson fraudulently obtain'd a Sum
> of Money for Tickets, which Miss Thomson had give the Day before to the same
> Noble Lord. If anyone will discover the said Person so that he may be convicted
> . . . they shall receive a Guinea reward by me. [signed] Elizabeth Thomson.

*Singing and Dancing:* Dancing: Act 1, A Shepherdess by Miss Thomson;
Act 2, a Peasant Dance by Mons. and Mlle. Dumont; Act 3, A new Dance
between a Boatswain and his Mistress by Pitt and Miss Thomson; Act 4,
"The Dusty Miller" by Moreau; Act 5, A Dance between a Pierrot and a
Pierrottess by Morris and Miss Thomson.

and

*Afterpiece: The Lottery.*
*Cast:* Jack Stocks—Wetherilt.


12    Mon.    AS.    *The Beggar's Opera.*
*Cast:* Macheath—R. Layfield; Polly—Miss Woffington.
*Benefit:* Christopher Dickson (printer).

and

*Afterpiece: The Female Officer.*
*Cast:* Female Officer—Miss Woffington; Knockmedown—R. Layfield.


12    Mon.    SA.    *The Way of the World.*
*Cast:* None listed.
*Benefit:* Gregory.
*Singing and Dancing:* With entertainments of singing and dancing.

and

*Afterpiece: Damon and Phillida.*
*Cast:* None listed.


14    Wed.    SA.    *The Committee.*
*Cast:* None listed.
*Benefit:* A Family in Distress.
*Deferred:* This benefit may have been deferred, see 24 May 1740 SA.

and

*Afterpiece:* Unspecified "Farce."


16    Fri.    SA.    *The Distrest Mother.*
*Cast:* None listed.
*Benefit:* A Large Family in great Distress.
*Miscellaneous:* The whole to Conclude with a new diverting Entertainment representing a Bull Beating, as it is performed in Madrid before the Court of Spain.
*Singing and Dancing:* With Dancing between the Acts.

and

*Afterpiece: The What D'Ye Call It.*
*Cast:* None listed.


19    Mon.    SA.    *The Mourning Bride.*
*Cast:* None listed.
*Benefit:* For the Support of several Poor Prisoners in The Four Courts Marshalseas at a Pennyworth of Bread a Day.
*Singing and Dancing:* With entertainments of dancing between the Acts.

and
*Afterpiece: The What D'Ye Call It.*
*Cast:* Brisk—Mrs. Furnival.


20    Tues.    SA.    *The Provoked Husband.*
*Cast:* None listed.
*Benefit:* Phillip Fitzgerald (merchant of Charleville).
*Miscellaneous:* Benefit for Fitzgerald because "all his worldly Substance [was] consumed in Ashes."
*Singing and Dancing:* With Dancing
and
*Afterpiece: The Lottery.*
*Cast:* None listed.


22    Thur.    AS    *The Merry Wives of Windsor.*
*Cast:* None listed.
*Benefit:* Griffith.
*Miscellaneous:* Not acted this season; Masons' night.
*Singing and Dancing:* Several entertainments of dancing between the Acts.
*Deferred:* Deferred from 13 May 1740.
and
*Afterpiece: Robin Hood and Little John.*
*Cast:* None listed.
*Miscellaneous:* A Humourous Droll, never performed here.


22    Thur.    SA.    *The Relapse; or, Virtue in Danger.*
*Cast:* None listed.
*Benefit:* J. Duval and the Author of *The Sharpers* [Matthew Gardiner].
and
*Afterpiece: The Sharpers.*
*Cast:* None listed.


24    Sat.    SA.    *Love for Love.*
*Cast:* None listed.
*Benefit:* Mrs. McDonnell and her Distressed Family.
*Miscellaneous:* Tickets delivered out for *The Committee* will be taken, see 14 May 1740 SA.
and
*Afterpiece: The Stage Coach.*
*Cast:* None listed.

26    Mon.    SA.    *The Busy Body.*
*Cast:* Marplot—Wetherilt.
*Benefit:* Gibson (boxkeeper).
*Miscellaneous:* By Desire.
*Singing and Dancing:* With entertainments of dancing.

and

*Afterpiece: The Cheats of Scapin.*
*Cast:* None listed.

29    Thur.    AS.    *The Beaux' Stratagem.*
*Cast:* None listed.
*Benefit:* Lawler [*FDJ*, 20–24 May 1740 spells the name Lawless].

and

*Afterpiece:* Unspecified "Farce."

JUNE

2    Mon.    SA.    *Tamerlane.*
*Cast:* Moneses—Furnival (from London, his first appearance on this stage).
*Singing and Dancing:* With dancing between the Acts.
*Deferred:* Deferred from 29 May.

and

*Afterpiece: The Virgin Unmasked.*
*Cast:* Lucy—Miss Furnival (her first appearance on any stage).

5    Thur.    SA.    *The Beaux' Stratagem.*
*Cast:* Archer—Furnival.
*Miscellaneous:* Being particularly desired.
*Singing and Dancing:* With entertainments of dancing.

and

*Afterpiece: The Virgin Unmasked.*
*Cast:* Lucy—Miss Furnival (in which she appeared with great Applause, this being the second Time of her Performance).

7    Sat.    AS.    *Aesop; or, The Politick Statesman.*
*Cast:* Aesop—Ward; Unspecified Part—Frank Elrington, Vanderbank, Jo. Elrington, Bridges.
*Benefit:* J. Elrington and Bridges.
*Miscellaneous:* Not acted these 15 years.
*Singing and Dancing:* Several entertainments of dancing between the Acts.
*Deferred:* Deferred from 5 June because of bread riots (see *Significant Events* p. 279).

and

*Afterpiece: The Female Officer.*
*Cast:* Female Officer—Miss Woffington.

12     Thur.     SA.     *Oedipus.*
*Cast:* None listed.
*Miscellaneous:* Never acted here before.
*Singing and Dancing:* With entertainments and dancing.

and

*Afterpiece: The Virgin Unmasked.*
*Cast:* Lucy—Miss Furnival.

### Summer Season

16     Mon.     SA.     *Oroonoko.*
*Cast:* Oroonoko—Delane (just arrived from Covent Garden).

19     Thur.     SA.     *Cato.*
*Cast:* Cato—Delane.

23     Mon.     SA.     *Julius Caesar.*
*Cast:* Brutus—Delane.

26     Thur.     SA.     *The Rival Queens.*
*Cast:* Alexander—Delane.

30     Mon.     SA.     *Othello.*
*Cast:* Othello—Delane.
*Benefit:* Delane.
*Miscellaneous:* Last time but one of his performing this season.

JULY

3     Thur.     SA.     *Macbeth.*
*Cast:* Macbeth—Delane.

5     Sat.     SA.     *Love for Love.*
*Cast:* None listed.
*Command:* Earl of Anglesey, Grand Master.
*Benefit:* A Distressed Mason.

8     Tues.     SA.     *The Beaux' Stratagem.*
*Cast:* Archer—Oates (from Covent Garden).
*Benefit:* Oates.

*Miscellaneous:* Oates, "the son of a late worthy citizen of Dublin, has not been in this Kingdom these 25 years."

and

*Afterpiece: The Lottery.*
*Cast:* None listed.


14    Thur.    SA.    *The Beggar's Opera.*
*Cast:* Macheath—Stoppelaer (from Covent Garden).

and

*Afterpiece: The Devil to Pay.*
*Cast:* Loverule—Stoppelaer.
*Singing and Dancing:* In which he will introduce "The Early Horn," accompanied by French Horns.


24    Thur.    SA.    *The Provoked Husband.*
*Cast:* None listed.

and

*Afterpiece: The Harlot's Progress.*
*Cast:* Beau Mordecai—Stoppelaer.
*Miscellaneous:* [Stoppelaer played the original Beau Mordecai at the premiere performance of this piece at DL on 31 Mar. 1733.]


28    Mon.    SA.    *King Henry IV, with the Humours of Falstaff.*
*Cast:* Falstaff—Giffard (from Drury Lane).
*Miscellaneous:* Giffard never appeared on this stage in this character.


AUGUST


20    Wed.    SA.    *Oedipus.*
*Cast:* Oedipus—Delane.
*Benefit:* Mrs. Wetherilt.
*Miscellaneous:* Last time of his performing this season.
*Deferred:* Deferred from 18 Aug. 1740.


[Duval's company performed in the Drogheda Assembly Room on 25 and 27 Aug. On 17 Sept. they left that town for the Carlow races after which they returned to Drogheda, giving a "play" there on 12 Oct. on the occasion of the anniversary of the Coronation of George II (*FDJ*, 19–23 Aug. and 13–16 Sept. 1740; *DNL*, 11–14 Oct. 1740).]

## 1740—1741 Season

Theatres operating: Aungier St.; Smock Alley.

*Aungier Street Company:*
Bardin (from England), Barrington (from Smock Alley), Bridges, Mrs. Bridges, Mrs. Elmy (from England), J. Elrington, Griffith, James, L. Layfield, Mrs. Martin (from Smock Alley), Mrs. Mitchell, Mrs. Pasquilino (from Smock Alley), Mrs. Reynolds (from Smock Alley), Vanderbank, J. Ward, Mrs. Ward, J. Watson, Jr., Worsdale, Wrightson, Mrs. Wrightson.

Dancers: Baudouin, Cantarino (rope dancer from Paris), Cormack, Dumont (from SA), Mrs. Dumont (from SA), Fromont (from Drury Lane), Pitt, Master Pitt, Miss Thomson.

Musicians: Delahoyde, McCarty, Walsh.

House Servants: Joseph Tudor (scene painter).

Summer: Mlle. Chateauneuf (dancer from Drury Lane), Mrs. Clive (singer from Drury Lane), Giles (dancer from Smock Alley), Lalauze (dancer from Drury Lane), Lewis Layfield, Jr. (dancer), Mrs. Martin (dancer from Smock Alley), Oates (from Covent Garden), Quin (from Drury Lane), L. Ryan (from Covent Garden).

*Repertory:*
Mainpieces: Recorded performances: 57 (of 42 different pieces, including 3 unspecified plays).
Afterpieces: Recorded Performances: 31 (of 16 different pieces). 2 evenings of triple bills.
Premieres:
*The Intriguers.* (a)
*The Judgment of Paris; or, The Nuptials of Harlequin.* (a)
*Vernon Triumphant.* (a)
*The Ridiculous Bridegroom.* (a)
*L'Arlequin Mariner.* (a)
Entr'acte entertainments: Dancing advertised for several performances.
Command Performances: 2 (1 Government Night).
Benefits:

Pre-February: Manager—1; Charity—1.
Post-February: Manager—1; Actor—21.

*Smock Alley Company:*
Bardin (18 Dec.–20 Jan.), Barrington (until 4 Apr.), Mrs. Barry, Beamsley, Mrs. Carmichael (formerly Miss Furnival), Doland, L. Duval, Mrs. Elmy (18 Dec.–20 Apr.), F. Elrington, Ralph Elrington, Este, Mrs. Furnival, Gregory, Husband, Kennedy, L. Layfield (from Aungier Street 16 Apr.–   ), Mrs. Martin (to AS), Meek, Morgan, Mrs. Morgan, Charles Morgan, Miss Orfeur, Mrs. Pasquilino (until 7 Mar.), T. Philips, Mrs. Reynolds (until 15 Apr.), I. Sparks, Vaughn (from GF), Wetherilt, Mrs. Wetherilt.

Dancers: Cummins (died in Apr.), W. Delamain, Giles, Moreau, Mrs. Moreau, Miss Moreau, J. Morris, W. Phillips, Mrs. W. Phillips.

Musicians: Bartel Mainwaring, Master Woder.

House Servants: Mrs. Bamford (dresser), Dryden (treasurer), Fox (pit door-keeper), Gibson (boxkeeper), Lamb, Tudor (scene painter, also at AS), Tyler.

*Repertory:*
Mainpieces: Recorded performances: 60 (of 41 different pieces).
Afterpieces: Recorded performances: 51 (of 24 different pieces).
Entr'acte entertainments: Dancing advertised for most performances. Some rope dancing and other equilbres.
Command Performances: 1.
Benefits:
Pre-February: Manager—2; Actor—1; Charity—3.
Post-February: Manager—2; Actor—26; House Servant—5; Charity—3.
*Significant events:*
During the autumn of 1740 the conditions among the poor became steadily worse. Grain became scarce and the price rose precipitously. In November and December, living conditions became even more difficult when the weather became very cold with rain and snow. There was a sudden thaw, and on 23 December the Liffey overflowed causing "the greatest flood ever known" (*DG*, 27 Dec. 1740).

The cool spring and summer reduced the potato and grain harvests even further and resulted in severe famine. In Irish tradition 1741 is remembered as *bliadhain an air* (the year of the slaughter) when between 200,000 and 400,000 souls perished from starvation and epidemic (See *NHI*, p. 34).

---

**1740**

OCTOBER

11   Sat.   AS.   *The Beaux' Stratagem.*
*Cast:* Archer—Bardin; Mrs. Sullen—Mrs. Elmy.
*Miscellaneous:* Bardin and Mrs. Elmy from the Theatre Royal, Drury Lane, their first time appearing in this Kingdom.

30   Thur.   AS.   Unspecified "Play."
*Command:* Lords Justice.
*Miscellaneous:* Government Night; Anniversary of birth of George II.

NOVEMBER

1   Sat.   AS.   Unspecified "Play."
*Miscellaneous:* At the particular Desire of several Persons of Quality. In Honour of Admiral Vernon's Birthday.

4   Tues.   AS.   Unspecified "Play" [probably *Tamerlane*].
*Miscellaneous:* Government Night; Anniversary of birth of William III.

10   Mon.   SA.   *The Funeral.*
*Cast:* None listed.
*Miscellaneous:* [The SA company had performed in Drogheda on 11 Oct. and again on 31 Oct. for Duval's benefit according to Clark 1965, 2.]
*Singing and Dancing:* Several Entertainments of Dancing by Moreau, Morris, and Delamain.
                                        and
*Afterpiece: The Virgin Unmasked.*
*Cast:* None listed.

12   Wed.   AS.   *The Rehearsal.*
*Cast:* Bayes—Bardin.
*Deferred:* Deferred from 10 Nov. because of the "extraordinary Machinery and Decoration."

14   Fri.   SA.   *The City Wives' Confederacy.*
*Cast:* None listed.

and
*Afterpiece: Harlequin's Vagaries.*
*Cast:* None listed.

15    Sat.    AS.    *The Rehearsal.*
*Cast:* None listed.

17    Mon.    AS.    *The Rehearsal.*
*Cast:* None listed.
*Miscellaneous:* Third Night. At the desire of several persons of quality.

17    Mon.    SA.    *King Henry IV, with the Humours of Falstaff.*
*Cast:* Falstaff—Vaughn (from Goodman's Fields).

24    Mon.    SA.    *The Rehearsal.*
*Cast:* Bayes—Wetherilt.
*Miscellaneous:* Never performed here before. "Mr. Bardin, alias Bays, who lately appeared in that Character at the TRAS thinks it necessary to inform the Town, that for several very good reasons he has declined any further performance in that Theatre" (*DNL,* 18–22 Nov. 1740).
*Singing and Dancing:* Concludes with a Grand Dance called "The Country Wedding."
*Deferred:* Deferred from 20 Nov., "as the same will require a great deal of Trouble and expence. Mr. Duval is determined to have it performed in the strongest and most exact Manner his Company is capable of" (*DEP,* 1, 15, 18 Nov. 1740).

27    Thur.    SA.    *The Rehearsal.*
*Cast:* Bayes—Wetherilt.
*Miscellaneous:* Second Night.
    "NB. Whereas Complaints have been made, that Numbers of Persons nightly Shift from Box to Box, and into the Pit, so to the Stage, which appears on Enquiry, that it is to avoid paying; for the further Prevention thereof, an Office is kept for the Boxes, where all Gentlemen are requested to take Tickets before they go in" (*FDJ,* 22–25 Nov. 1740). [W. J. Lawrence, Notebook 8:31, believes that this shows that the post-Restoration practice of collecting the price of admission in the boxes after the audience had assembled (the collector being the boxkeeper) was in vogue up to this time.]

DECEMBER

1    Mon.    SA.    *The Rehearsal.*
*Cast:* None listed.

3     Wed.     SA.     *The Rehearsal.*
*Cast:* None listed.
*Miscellaneous:* Fourth Night. Last time of performing it this season.

                                    and

*Afterpiece: Harlequin's Vagaries.*
*Cast:* None listed.


4     Thur.     AS.     *Love for Love.*
*Cast:* None listed.
*Benefit:* The Charitable Infirmary on Inn's Quay.
*Miscellaneous:* Stage illuminated with wax.
*Singing and Dancing:* Dancing by Dumont, Fromont, Baudouin, Pitt, Master Pitt, Cormick, Mrs. Dumont, Miss Thomson.


4     Thur.     SA.     *The Way of the World.*
*Cast:* None listed.
*Benefit:* For the Enlargement of Poor Distressed Pensioners in the Marshalsea.
*Deferred:* From 1 Dec. Boydell 1988, 68, retains earlier date. This benefit may have been deferred further; see below 15 Dec. which cites the same program for the same charity.

                                    and

*Afterpiece: The Mock Lawyer.*
*Cast:* None listed.


8     Mon.     AS.     *Hamlet.*
*Cast:* None listed.
*Benefit:* Griffith.
*Miscellaneous:* At the Request of several ladies of quality.

                                    and

*Afterpiece:* Sequel to *The Rehearsal.*
*Cast:* None listed.


8     Mon.     SA.     *Greenwich Park; or, The Merry Citizens.*
*Cast:* None listed.
*Miscellaneous:* Never Acted in this Kingdom.

                                    and

*Afterpiece: The Virgin Unmasked.*
*Cast:* None listed.


11     Thur.     AS.     *Jane Shore.*
*Cast:* None listed.

and

*Afterpiece: The Judgment of Paris; or, The Nuptials of Harlequin.*
*Cast:* None listed.
*Miscellaneous:* Never done here; as it was originally performed at the Opera in Paris. The Judgment of Paris is composed by M. Baudouin, consisting of several Interludes both serious and comic. The Recitative, Airs, Musick, Dances, Sinkings, Flyings, Machines, and other Decorations are entirely new. Scenes painted by Mr. Joseph Tudor. The Whole new dressed. To conclude with the Nuptials of Harlequin and Colombine in the magnificent Temple of Hymen.
    [Although there are several pieces with the same maintitle, neither *LS* nor Nicoll lists a pantomime with this subtitle.]

15    Mon.    SA.    *The Way of the World.*    V.
*Cast:* "All Parts as Usual."
*Benefit:* For the Release of Poor Prisoners in the several Marshalseas.
*Miscellaneous:* [Item in *FDJ*, 16–20 Dec. 1740 quotes from the Prologue and indicates that there was a "crouded audience".]
*Financial:* £207 in the House.

and

*Afterpiece: The Virgin Unmasked.*
*Cast:* None listed.

18    Thur.    AS.    *The Careless Husband.*
*Cast:* Foppington—Bardin (from AS); Lady Betty—Mrs. Elmy (from AS).
*Miscellaneous:* Bardin and Mrs. Elmy the first time of their appearing on this stage. Desire of Several Ladies of Quality.
*Deferred:* Deferred from 12 Dec. 1739.

29    Mon.    AS.    *The Successful Straingers.*
*Cast:* None listed.

and

*Afterpiece: The Judgment of Paris.*
*Cast:* None listed.

29    Mon.    SA.    *The Mourning Bride.*
*Cast:* None listed.

and

*Afterpiece: The Intriguing Chambermaid.*
*Cast:* Lettice—Mrs. W. Phillips.
*Singing and Dancing:* After the farce a variety of dancing, particularly "The English Maggot" by Phillips, in which he introduces his Horn Pipe and the pantomime miller's dance, "Double Jealousy."

**1741**

2    Fri.    SA.    *Love for Love.*
*Cast:* None listed.
*Singing and Dancing:* Dancing by Phillips.
                              and
*Afterpiece: The Intriguing Chambermaid.*
*Cast:* None listed.

8    Thur.    SA.    *The Rehearsal.*
*Cast:* None listed.
*Miscellaneous:* Being desired.
*Singing and Dancing:* Dancing, "The Drunken Peasant" by Phillips.
                              and
*Afterpiece: The Virgin Unmasked.*
*Cast:* None listed.

12    Mon.    SA.    *The Committee.*
*Cast:* None listed.
*Singing and Dancing:* With several Entertainments of Dancing, particularly
the "English Maggot" by Phillips, with the last new "Miller's Dance" by
Phillips, Mrs. Moreau, etc.
                              and
*Afterpiece: The Intriguing Chambermaid.*
*Cast:* None listed.

19    Mon.    SA.    *Pasquin.*
*Cast:* None listed.
*Miscellaneous:* At the particular Desire of several Persons of Quality. To
begin precisely at 6 o'clock on account of the Assembly. [See also 16 Feb.
1741 SA.]
*Singing and Dancing:* Several entertainments of dancing.

20    Tues.    AS.    *The Rehearsal.*
*Cast:* Bayes—Bardin.
*Miscellaneous:* With some improvements of the scenery and decorations;
N. B. Two thorough bred Horses, with fine Furniture, will make their appearance in the Grand Battle, and all the others are new-bitted and perfectly
ridden. Admission prices lowered to: Boxes, 4s. 4d.; Lattices, 3s. 3d.; Pit,
2s. 8½d.; Gallery, 1s. 7½d. in order to entertain the Publick in the most cheap
(tho' elegant) Manner.
    [Sometime prior to this performance the control of affairs at AS passed

from the hands of the actor-managers (Griffith, F. Elrington, L. Layfield, Moreau, and Wetherilt). The public was promised that the new management "are Persons who are qualified to discern the Method to please . . . and [will] furnish the Auditors with the best Plays by the best Authors, as well as procure the best Performers in all Characters. . . . The Gentlemen, the Proprietors of the Theatre-Royal in Aungier-Street, have disposed matters under so happy a Regulation and Oeconomy, that the many Enormities, which hitherto disgusted the Audience, will, for the Future, be avoided, and no Care, Labour, or Expense, will be spared to render the Theatre the Seat of Rational Pleasure . . ." (*DNL*, 17–20 Jan. 1741). Discussed above in introduction.]

21    Wed.    SA.    *The Twin Rivals.*
*Cast:* None listed.
*Benefit:* The Poor Distressed Families [Housekeepers] in several Parishes.
*Miscellaneous:* By Appointment of the Charitable Musical Society at the Bear on College Green.
*Miscellaneous:* [Prologue written by Rev. Pilkington quoted in full in *DNL*, 20–24 Jan. 1741.]
*Financial:* £168 8s. in the House.

22    Thur.    AS.    *Love Makes a Man.*    V.
*Cast:* None listed.

24    Sat.    SA.    *The Careless Husband.*
*Cast:* None listed.
*Benefit:* L. Duval.
*Singing and Dancing:* Several entertainments of dancing.
*Deferred:* Duval's benefit first deferred from 18 Dec. 1739 at the Desire of several Persons of Quality then from 22 Dec. by particular desire.
and
*Afterpiece: The Intriguing Chambermaid.*
*Cast:* None listed.

27    Tues.    AS.    *Love Makes a Man.*
*Cast:* None listed.
*Singing and Dancing:* With Entertainments of Dancing.
and
*Afterpiece: The Judgment of Paris.*
*Cast:* None listed.

27    Tues.    SA.    *The Unhappy Favourite; or, The Earl of Essex.*
*Cast:* None listed.

and

*Afterpiece: Harlequin Metamorphosed; or, Columbine Courtezan.*
*Cast:* Harlequin—W. Phillips; Columbine—Mrs. W. Phillips; Pierrot—
Morris.
*Miscellaneous:* Pantomime. Composed by William Phillips. As this Enter-
tainment will be very Expensive, it is hoped it will meet with due Encourage-
ment. The Painting by Mr. Joseph Tutor. All the Scenes and Dresses are
entirely new, and done to imitate the Original, as it was performed with great
Applause in London.

[This may be an adaptation of an anonymous pantomime entitled *Cupid
and Psyche; or, Columbine Courtezan* performed at DL on 4 Feb. 1734 and
played 20 times with Phillips as Harlequin during the 1738–39 season under
the subtitle.]

29　　Thur.　　SA.　　*The Fair Penitent.*
*Cast:* None listed.
*Benefit:* Mrs. Furnival.
*Miscellaneous:* At the particular Desire of several Persons of Quality.

and

*Afterpiece: The Devil to Pay.*
*Cast:* None listed.

31　　Sat.　　AS.　　*A Bold Stroke for a Wife.*
*Cast:* None listed.

and

*Afterpiece: The Author's Farce; or, The Pleasures of the Town.*
*Cast:* None listed.
*Miscellaneous:* Into which will be introduced an operatical puppet show
never acted before; in which will be shewn the whole Court of Dulness, with
Abundance of Singing and Dancing and several other Entertainments. Also
the Comical and diverting Humours of Somebody and Nobody; Punch and
his wife Joan to be performed by living Figures some of them six foot high;
the whole to conclude with the Siege and taking of Porto Bello by Six Ships.
The Puppets in the show are to be all alive and merry, and to be performed
by figures as large and big as living persons. It was performed 50 nights
successively in London, to entire Satisfaction.
*Singing and Dancing:* See *Miscellaneous.*

31　　Sat.　　SA.　　*The Author's Farce.*
*Cast:* None listed.
*Miscellaneous:* In which will be introduced an operatical puppet show,
called the Pleasures of the Town. The puppets in the Show are to be alive
and merry, and to be performed by Figures as large and big as living Persons.

Care will be taken here to have the same performed with the Greatest Exactness, and no Expence will be spared to rendering it pleasing and agreeable.

## 1741-1742 Season

Theatres operating: Aungier Street; Smock Alley.

*Aungier St. Company:*
Bardin, Barrington, Mrs. Bayley, Bridges, Butler@, Mrs. Cibber, Mrs. Davis, Dyer@, Mrs. Elmy@, F. Elrington, J. Elrington, Richard Elrington@, Giles, Griffith, Harvey@, L. Layfield, L. Layfield Jr.@, R. Layfield@, Lee, Mrs Martin, Mrs. Pasquilino, Pellish, Price@, Quin, Mrs. Reynolds@, I. Sparks@, L. Sparks, Cornelius Swan, Vanderbank, J. Watson, Jr., Wetherilt, Mrs. Wetherilt (on 22 June only), Worsdale [@ = named only in playbill for a cancelled production of *Samson Agonistes*. See *Miscellaneous* AS 15 March 1742 for details.]

Dancers: Mlle. Chateauneuf, Moreau, Mrs. Moreau, Oates (at SA also), Oates, Jr. (at SA also), Master Pitt (also at SA?)

Musicians: Callaghan McCarty.

House Servants: Thomson (prompter).

Summer: Mrs. Arne, Delane.

*Repertory*
Mainpieces: Recorded performances: 80 (of 41 different pieces, including 2 unspecified plays but excluding 2 concerts).
Afterpieces: Recorded Performances: 17 (of 8 different pieces).
Premieres:
*The Betrayer of His Country.*
*Nature.*
Entr'acte entertainments: Music, singing or dancing advertised for many performances.
Command Performances: 14 (1 Government night).
Benefits:
Pre-February: Actor—6.
Post-February: Actor—24; Author—1; House Servant—1; Charity—3.

*Smock Alley Company:*
Beamsley, Mrs. Chetwood, Dolland, L. Duval, Ralph Elrington, Este, Furni-

val, Mrs. Furnival, Gregory, Husband, Kennedy, Lamb, Mrs. Mackay, Meek, Mrs. Mitchell, C. Morgan, John Morris, P. Morris, Jr. (or is this same as P. Morris?, *BD* throws no light on this), T. Philips, Mrs. Sampson, I. Sparks, Thompson, Wetherilt, Mrs. Wetherilt (at AS in June), T. Wright (from DL, until 27 Feb.).

Dancers: Miss Bullock, Mlle. Chateauneuf (on 29 Jan. only), Cormack, W. Delamain, McNeil, Moreau (29 Jan. only), Patrick Morris, Oates (from CG, also at AS), Oates, Jr. (at AS also), Master Pitt.

Musicians: John Blackwood, Charles, Francis Dowdal, George Fitzgerald, Dominick Gunan, William Heron, Thomas Johnson, Kountze, Bartle Mainwaring, William Mainwaring, Winch, Francis Woder.

House Servants: Mrs. Bamford (dresser); William Rufus Chetwood ("manager," i.e. prompter); Dryden (treasurer); Thomas Ludlow (machinist); O'Neil (boxkeeper); Compton Roe (?); Tyler.

Summer: Signora Barbarini (dancer, from CG); Henry Delamain (dancer, from DL); Garrick (from GF); H. Giffard (from GF); Mrs. Moreau (dancer, summer only); Miss Moreau (dancer, summer only); Thomas Walker (from GF); Mrs. Woffington (from DL).

*Repertory:*
Mainpieces: Recorded performances: 82 (of 40 different pieces). Afterpieces: Recorded Performances: 55 (of 17 different pieces including unspecified farces).
Premieres: *Parthian Hero.*
Entr'acte entertainments: Music, singing, or dancing advertised for most performances.
Command Performances: 2.
Benefits:
Pre-February: Actor—3; House Servant—3; Charity—3.
Post-February: Actor—31; Author—1; House Servant—2; Charity—5.

---

**1741**

OCTOBER

12   Mon.   AS.     *The Recruiting Officer.*
*Cast:* Balance—Quin.
*Command:* Duke and Duchess of Devonshire.

*Miscellaneous:* Government Night: Anniversary of coronation of George II.
With a new occasional Prologue.
*Singing and Dancing:* Dancing by Mlle. Chateauneuf.

14    Wed.    SA.    *As You Like It.*
*Cast:* Rosalind—Mrs. Furnival.
*Miscellaneous:* Opening Night of season. First time in Ireland. With entirely
new Decorations.

"On Wednesday next Mr. Duvall opens the theatre of SA, with Shakespeare's Comedy called As You Like it, with entire new Decorations. This
Comedy was performed upwards of 40 Times at DL last Season. The Character of Rosalind is drawn in so inimitable a manner by that great Author, that
it is judged to exceed most of the Womens Characters in his Comedies"
(*FDJ*, 6–10 Oct. 1741).

"We hear that on Monday next [i.e. 14 Sept. 1741] Mr. Duval's Company
of Comedians sets out from Belfast for the Races of Catherlough, and that
he intends to open the Theatre in Dublin on the first Monday in October,
and hopes to entertain the Town in a very agreeable Manner, they being now
preparing several Plays (never performed here) under the Direction of Mr.
Chetwood from the TR DL" (*DNL*, 8–12 Sept. 1741).

"We are assured Mr. Duvall (in order to entertain the Town in the most
agreeable manner) has engaged a Machinist from the Theatre-royal in Drury-
lane, and is fitting up his House in Smock-alley, in an entire new manner,
after the Model of those in London, and is now getting up several new
Plays, Farces and Pantomime Entertainments, under the Direction of Mr.
Chetwood. He proposes to open, as soon as the Theatre can be got ready,
with the Tragedy of King Lear and his Three Daughters; the Part of King
Lear to be performed by Mr. Wright, from the Theatre-royal in Drury-lane"
(*FDJ*, 29 Sept.–3 Oct. 1741).

Hitchcock (1:116) says, "By his [Chetwood's] direction a machinist from
one of the London theatres was engaged, who first worked the wings by
means of a barrel underneath, which moved them together at the same time
with the scenes. This was publicly boasted of as a master-piece of mechanism; at present it is well understood and constantly practised."

*DG*, 21–24 Dec. 1742 indicates that "Tom Ludlow, Machinist to the Theatre in Smock-Alley, lately arriv'd from England, has found out an Infallible
Method of Curing Smoaky Chimnies. . . ."

[Chetwood had first appeared in Dublin as assistant manager to Ashbury
in 1714 (Clark 1955, 153). He returned to London and was prompter at Drury
Lane theatre. He became deeply in debt early in 1741 and was imprisoned.
Rescued from jail with the help of a Covent Garden benefit, he travelled to
Dublin where, as "director," he seems not to have been too successful since
by 15 Feb. Thomas Philips had taken over the duties of that office (see

performance of 15 Feb. 1742 SA). For Chetwood's own account see his *History* (Chetwood 1749), 73).]
*Singing and Dancing:* Dancing between the acts by Oates, Jr. from TR CG.

15    Thur.    AS.    *As You Like It.*
*Cast:* Jaques—Quin.
*Command:* Duke and Duchess of Devonshire.
*Miscellaneous:* Never acted in this Kingdom [in *FDJ* ad of 6–10 Oct. 1741. The claim changes to "never acted here" in *FDJ,* 10–13 Oct. 1741].

"We hear that there is in Rehearsal at the Theatre-royal in AS, that celebrated Play of Shakespeare, called, As You Like It, which will be acted in a few Days after they open" (*FDJ,* 29 Sept.–3 Oct. 1741).
*Singing and Dancing:* With the Original Songs, new Cloathes, and all other Decorations proper to the Play. Dancing by Moreau and Mlle. Chateauneuf.

19    Mon.    AS.    *As You Like It.*
*Cast:* Jaques—Quin.
*Miscellaneous:* Second Night. With the original songs, new clothes, and all decorations proper to the play. The Duke and Duchess of Devonshire present.
*Singing and Dancing:* Dancing by Mlle. Chateauneuf.

19    Mon.    SA.    *As You Like It.*
*Cast:* Rosalind—Mrs. Furnival.
*Miscellaneous:* With new Scenes, Clothes and Decorations.
*Singing and Dancing:* Dancing by Oates, Sr. and Oates, Jr.

22    Thur.    AS.    *Timon of Athens.*
*Cast:* Apemantus—Quin.
*Singing and Dancing:* Dancing by Mlle. Chateauneuf.

22    Thur.    SA.    *King Lear and His Three Daughters.*
*Cast:* Lear—T. Wright (from DL).
*Singing and Dancing:* Between the acts a concerto on French horn by Mr. Winch, who has performed several years in Mr. Handel's operas and oratorios.
and
*Afterpiece: Harlequin's Vagaries; or, Pierrot in Distress.*
*Cast:* Harlequin—Oates, Jr.; Columbine—Mrs. Chetwood; Pierrot—J. Morris.
*Miscellaneous:* With several Additions and Alterations, as performed at the TRDL.

"We hear Mr. Duval is getting up a new Pantomime Entertainment, which will be performed there in a few Days, the Character of Harlequin to be performed by Mr. Oats, Junior" (*FDJ*, 13–17 Oct. 1741).

26    Mon.    AS.    *King Richard III.*
*Cast:* Richard—Quin.
*Singing and Dancing:* Dancing by Mlle. Chateauneuf.

26    Mon.    SA.    *The City Wives' Confederacy.*
*Cast:* Clarissa—Mrs. Furnival; Flippanta—Mrs. Chetwood.
                              and
*Afterpiece: Harlequin's Vagaries.*
*Cast:* As 22 Oct. 1741.

29    Thur.    SA.    *The Fair Penitent.*
*Cast:* Sciolto—Wright; Calista—Mrs. Furnival.
*Miscellaneous:* Wright's second time of performing in this kingdom.
*Singing and Dancing:* With Dancing.
                              and
*Afterpiece: Harlequin's Vagaries.*
*Cast:* None listed.

30    Fri.    AS.    Unspecified "Play."
*Miscellaneous:* Government Night; Anniversary of birth of George II.

NOVEMBER

2    Mon.    AS.    *Cato.*
*Cast:* Cato—Quin.
*Benefit:* Quin.
*Singing and Dancing:* With several Entertainments of Dancing Mlle. Chateauneuf, Mr. and Mrs. Moreau.

2    Mon.    SA.    *The Rehearsal.*
*Cast:* Bayes—Wetherilt
*Miscellaneous:* The Players, Horsemen, Foot Soldiers, Heralds, Bishops, Cardinals, Mayor, Judges, and Serjeants at Arms, to be performed with the utmost care and Exactness, with Mr. Bays's Grand Battle, Dances, etc. as it was done at the TR CG.
                              and
*Afterpiece: Harlequin's Vagaries.*
*Cast:* None listed.

4    Wed.    AS.    Unspecified "Play" [probably *Tamerlane*].
*Miscellaneous:* Government Night; Anniversary of birth of William III.

5    Thur.    SA.    *The Mourning Bride.*
*Cast:* Almeria—Mrs. Furnival.

and

*Afterpiece: Harlequin's Vagaries.*
*Cast:* None listed.


9    Mon.    AS.    *The Provoked Wife.*
*Cast:* Sir John—Quin.
*Singing and Dancing:* Dancing by Mlle. Chateauneuf, M. and Mrs. Moreau.


9    Mon.    SA.    *The Twin Rivals.*
*Cast:* None listed.

and

*Afterpiece: Harlequin's Vagaries.*
*Cast:* None listed.


12    Thur.    AS.    *Venice Preserved.*
*Cast:* Pierre—Quin.
*Singing and Dancing:* Dancing by Mlle. Chateauneuf and Moreau.


12    Thur.    SA.    *The Merchant of Venice.*    V.
*Cast:* Shylock—Wright; Portia—Mrs. Furnival; Launcelot—Wetherilt.
*Miscellaneous:* As it was originally written by Shakespeare and performed thirty Nights last season at the TR DL. [*LS* lists 21 performances of *The Merchant* during the 1740–41 season.]

and

*Afterpiece: The Strollers.* V.
*Cast:* None listed.
*Miscellaneous:* Never acted in this Kingdom. [A farce by Captain John Durant Breval. Nicoll 1977–79, 2:300, says: "This play is taken from *The Play is the Plot* [by Breval, 1718]; as Breval was alive in 1723, the alteration may be ascribed to him. A ballad opera of the same title appeared at CG in May 1734. This was no doubt the earlier farce embellished with songs." *LS* indicates that this work was revived several times after 1723, particularly in 1739 at CG (2) and 12 May 1741 at DL.]


16    Mon.    AS.    *Macbeth.*
*Cast:* Macbeth—Quin.
*Singing and Dancing:* With several Entertainments of Dancing by Mlle. Chateauneuf and M. and Mrs. Moreau.


16    Mon.    SA.    *The Merchant of Venice.*
*Cast:* None listed.

*Miscellaneous:* As they were performed on Thursday last to the entire satisfaction of the Audience.

and

*Afterpiece: The Strollers.*
*Cast:* None listed.

19     Thur.     AS.     *As You Like It.*
*Cast:* Jaques—Quin.
*Command:* Duke and Duchess of Devonshire.
*Singing and Dancing:* Moreau and Mlle. Chateauneuf.

19     Thur.     SA.     *King Lear and His Three Daughters.*
*Cast:* Lear—Wright.
*Miscellaneous:* By the particular Desire of several Persons of Quality.

and

*Afterpiece: The Virgin Unmasked.*
*Cast:* Lucy—Mrs. Chetwood.

23     Mon.     AS.     *King Richard III.*
*Cast:* Gloster—Quin.

26     Thur.     AS.     *Cato.*
*Cast:* Cato—Quin.

26     Thur.     SA.     *The Lancashire Witches.*
*Cast:* Teague O'Dively—J. Morris.
*Miscellaneous:* Never acted in this Kingdom; by Thomas Shadwell, Poet Laureate, with Music composed by Mr. Barret. "With all the Music, Songs, Sinkings, Flyings, and Decorations suitable thereto. There is prepared two new Flyings for the witches to fly with; and also the Wings and Scenes on the stage made to move in a moment, by an engine obtained at a great Expense; the stage entirely new painted and illuminated in a beautiful Manner; and 'tis hoped that said Comedy by the grand Alteration of the Stage, will be done in the same Taste and Manner that it was done in London, where it was done with great Applause" (*FDJ*, and *DNL*, 10–14 Nov. 1741).
[*FDJ*, calls the piece *Teague O'Dively; or, The Lancashire Witches.*]
*Deferred:* Deferred from 23 Nov. 1741: "The Machinery for this Play cannot possibly be finished till Thursday next, and the Company (being unwilling to exhibit an imperfect Performance to the Town) are obliged to defer it till then. . . ." (*DNL*, 21–24 Nov. 1741).
[During the play Charles Morgan was to fly on the back of a witch but "Thro' the ignorance of the workers in the machinery, the fly broke, and they fell together, but thro' Providence neither of them were hurt" (Chetwood 1749, 139).]

30    Mon.    AS.    *King Henry IV, with the Humours of Falstaff.*
*Cast:* Falstaff—Quin.

30    Mon.    SA.    *The Mourning Bride.*
*Cast:* Almeria—Mrs. Furnival; King—Wright; Osmyn—R. Elrington.
*Benefit:* Mrs. Furnival.
*Singing and Dancing:* With Dancing.
                              and
*Afterpiece: Harlequin's Vagaries.*
*Cast:* None listed.

DECEMBER

3    Thur.    AS.    *Sequil to King Henry IV, with the Humours of Sir
John Falstaff and Justice Shallow* [*King Henry IV, Pt. 2*].
*Cast:* Falstaff—Quin.
*Singing and Dancing:* Dancing by Mlle. Chateauneuf and Moreau.

3    Thur.    SA.    *The Lancashire Witches.*
*Cast:* None listed.
*Miscellaneous:* Never acted but once. Particular Care is taken, that the
Flyings and machinery may be performed without the least Danger [see
*Miscellaneous* for 26 Nov. 1741.]

7    Mon.    AS.    *The Provoked Wife.*
*Cast:* Sir John Brute—Quin.
*Benefit:* Mlle. Chateauneuf.
*Miscellaneous:* At the particular Desire of several Ladies of Quality. Stage,
Boxes, and Lattices laid together at one British Crown.
*Singing and Dancing:* With several entertainments of Dancing.

7    Mon.    SA.    *Pamela.*
*Cast:* Pamela—Mrs. Furnival.
*Miscellaneous:* This Comedy has been performed 18 Nights successively in
London, and still continues to be acted there with universal Applause (*DNL*,
1–5 Dec. 1741).
    [By James Dance or Henry Giffard. The question of authorship is obscure
according to Nicoll 1977–79, 2:435.]
    Although *FDJ*, 2–6 June indicates that the play is in rehearsal and will be
performed on Thursday, 18 June 1741, a letter to George Faulkner in *FDJ*,
22–26 Dec. 1741 makes it clear that that performance did not take place:

    Sir. I saw in your Paper some days ago the Comedy Pamela advertised to be
    played at Smock Alley, which was accordingly done. You may remember, last

spring I showed you the manuscript of one written on the same subject by me which was read and approved of by the Gentlemen the Proprietors of the Theatre Royal in Aungier-Street, and by them ordered into Rehearsal and you advertised it to be played. The arrival of Mr. Quin, Mrs. Clive, and Mr. Ryan, put it off 'til the Winter. Now, Sir, I write this to clear myself of the imputation of having sent my copy to London after having agreed with, and been well treated by the Proprietors of the Theatre Royal. The Comedy at Smock Alley is not that written by me, therefore I do not hold myself anyway accountable for its Faults, if it has any, neither would I assume any of its Merits. In publishing this in your Paper, you will oblige, Sir, Your Friend and humble Servant H. Eyre. Thurs. Dec. 24, 1741. P.S. I had almost forgotten to tell you that my comedy Pamela is to be acted some nights in February, for my sole and entire benefit, by the favour of the Proprietors of the Theatre Royal in Aungier-Street.

10     Thur.     AS.     *The Merry Wives of Windsor.*
*Cast:* Falstaff—Quin.

10     Thur.     SA.     *Pamela.*
*Cast:* None listed.
*Benefit:* Chetwood ("Director of the Theatre in Smock Alley").
*Miscellaneous:* At the Request of Several Persons of Distinction; Second Night; Chetwood described as "an utter Stranger to this Country."
*Singing and Dancing:* With entertainments of dancing between the acts.

and

*Afterpiece: Nancy; or, The Parting Lovers.*
*Cast:* None listed.

and

*Afterpiece: Harlequin's Vagaries.*
*Cast:* None listed.

12     Sat.     AS.     *The Conscious Lovers.*
*Cast:* Indiana—Mrs. Cibber (her first appearance in Ireland); Bevil, Jr.—Quin.
*Miscellaneous:* [According to *PO*, 5 Dec. 1741 Mrs. Cibber arrived in Dublin on 3 Dec.].
*Comment:* "After the first few nights they played to empty benches. On one occasion when he [Sheridan] went to Aungier Street the two played to a beggarly £8. Mrs. Cibber had been guaranteed a certainty, and one of the subscribers to the house who was a guarantor had to made good the deficientcy [*sic*] out of his own pocket. Quin, when he saw how things were going, refused each night to let the curtain go up till he had been paid. Very often his nightly stipend exceeded the whole takings" (Sheridan 1771, 8.).

14    Mon.    SA.    *The Provoked Husband.*
*Cast:* None listed.
*Benefit:* The Prisoners in the various Marshalseas.
*Singing and Dancing:* With several Entertainments of Dancing.
*Miscellaneous:* At the application of the Charitable Musical Society.
*Financial:* £190 collected (*DG*, 15–19 Dec. 1741).


17    Thur.    AS.    *Venice Preserved.*
*Cast:* Pierre—Quin; Belvidera—Mrs. Cibber (her second performance in this kingdom).
*Command:* Duke and Duchess of Devonshire.
*Singing and Dancing:* Dancing by Oates, Jr., his first time dancing on this stage.


17    Thur.    SA.    *The Merchant of Venice.*
*Cast:* None listed.
*Benefit:* L. Duval.
*Miscellaneous:* By the particular Desire of several Persons of Quality. With several Entertainments.
                              and
*Afterpiece: The Blind Beggar of Bethnal Green.*
*Cast:* None listed.


18    Fri.    AS.    Concert of Vocal and Instrumental Music.
*Benefit:* Miss Davis.
*Miscellaneous:* By Subscription. Single Tickets a British Crown; Gallery a British half-crown.
*Singing and Dancing:* "The Echo" song from *Comus* with other favourite songs from that masque; two new English songs never performed here before.
*Deferred:* Deferred from 5 Dec. due to the illness of Miss Davis.


19    Sat.    AS.    Concert of Vocal and Instrumental Music.
*Benefit:* Signior Dionysius Barbatielli.
*Miscellaneous:* With a Ball. Theatre finished after the Ridotto Manner. Tickets a British Crown; gallery a half-crown.


21    Mon.    AS.    *The Orphan.*
*Cast:* Chamont—Quin; Monimia—Mrs. Cibber.


22    Tues.    SA.    *Venice Preserved.*
*Cast:* Belvidera—Mrs. Furnival.

and

*Afterpiece: The Lying Valet.*
*Cast:* Sharp—Wetherilt.
*Miscellaneous:* A new farce as it is presently performing in London.

31    Thur.    AS.    *Love's Last Shift.*
*Cast:* Amanda—Mrs. Cibber.
*Singing and Dancing:* Dancing by Mlle. Chateauneuf, Moreau, and Oates.

31    Thur.    SA.    *The Lancashire Witches.*
*Cast:* None listed.

and

*Afterpiece: The Lying Valet.*
*Cast:* None listed.


## 1742

### JANUARY

7    Thur.    AS.    *Comus.*
*Cast:* Comus—Quin; Lady—Mrs. Cibber; Euphrosyne and Sabrina—Mlle.
Chateauneuf (her first appearance as an actress).
*Miscellaneous:* With the original Music and all the Decorations proper to
the Mask. [Boydell 1988, 76, puts Mrs. Cibber in the role of Euphrosyne.]

9    Sat.    SA.    *Jane Shore.*
*Cast:* None listed.
*Deferred:* From 7 Jan.

and

*Afterpiece: The Rival Sorcerers; or, Harlequin Victorious.*
*Cast:* Harlequin—R. Elrington (who has not appeared in this character in
four years); Columbine—Mrs. Chetwood.
*Miscellaneous:* [Premiere. Pantomime by Ludlow, the machinist.] In which
will be introduced the surprizing Serpent in the same manner as it was
performed in the celebrated entertainment of Orpheus and Euridice at
TRCG; With new habits, scenes, flyings, sinkings, Inchantments, with other
Decorations never performed before. [Not listed in Nicoll or *LS* under either
title, but see below 29 Jan. 1742 SA where it is indicated that this piece is
by Ludlow, the machinist.]

11    Mon.    AS.    *Comus.*
*Cast:* As 7 Jan. 1742

14    Thur.    SA.    *The Busy Body.*
*Cast:* None listed.

and

*Afterpiece: The Rival Sorcerers.*
*Cast:* As 7 Jan. 1742.


15    Fri.    SA.    *The Fair Penitent.*
*Cast:* None listed.
*Benefit:* Widow Cummins.
*Deferred:* Deferred from 7 Jan. 1742 at the particular Request of several
Ladies of Quality.

and

*Afterpiece: The Rival Sorcerers.*
*Cast:* None listed.


16    Sat.    AS.    *Julius Caesar.*
*Cast:* Brutus—Quin.


18    Mon.    AS.    *Old Batchelour.*
*Cast:* Heartwell—Quin; Laetitia—Mrs. Cibber.


18    Mon.    SA.    *The Constant Couple.*
*Cast:* None listed.
*Benefit:* Dryden (Treasurer).
*Singing and Dancing:* With Songs, etc.

and

*Afterpiece: The Lancashire Witches.*
*Cast:* Teague O'Divelly—J. Morris.


[*PO*, 20–24 Jan. 1741 reports that on Wednesday, 20 Jan. "One Parsons, a
Taylor, was killed in a Fray at the Play-house in AS, for which three Fellows
were committed to Newgate."]


21    Thur.    AS.    *Measure for Measure.*
*Cast:* Duke—Quin; Isabella—Mrs. Cibber.
*Singing and Dancing:* Dancing by Mlle. Chateauneuf, Moreau, and Oates.


22    Fri.    AS.    *Love's Last Shift.*
*Cast:* None listed.
*Command:* Lord Tullamore, Grand Master.
*Benefit:* Sick and Distressed Freemasons.
*Miscellaneous:* [See also 5 Feb. 1742, below.]

22     Fri.     SA.     *Love for Love.*
*Cast:* None listed.
*Benefit:* Master Pitt.
*Singing and Dancing:* With several Entertainments of Dancing.
and

*Afterpiece: Harlequin's Vagaries.*
*Cast:* None listed.


23     Sat.     AS.     *Measure for Measure.*
*Cast:* None listed.


25     Mon.     AS.     *The Plain Dealer.*
*Cast:* Manly—Quin.
*Miscellaneous:* Never performed here.
*Singing and Dancing:* Dancing by Mlle. Chateauneuf, Moreau, and Oates.


25     Mon.     SA.     *The Beaux' Stratagem.*
*Cast:* None listed.
*Benefit:* Poor Distressed Families.
*Miscellaneous:* By appointment for the Charitable Musical Society at the
Bear on College Green. House illuminated with wax.
*Singing and Dancing:* With several entertainments of dance.
and

*Afterpiece: The Lying Valet.*
*Cast:* None listed.


28     Thur.     AS.     *The Spanish Fryar.*
*Cast:* Fryar—Quin; Queen—Mrs. Cibber.
*Benefit:* Quin.
*Singing and Dancing:* Dancing by Mlle. Chateauneuf, Moreau, and Oates.


28     Thur.     SA.     *Jane Shore.*
*Cast:* None listed.
and

*Afterpiece: The Rival Sorcerers.*
*Cast:* None listed.


29     Fri.     SA.     *King Richard III.*
*Cast:* Gloster—Thompson (who never appeared on this stage in this
Kingdom).
*Benefit:* Thomas Ludlow (Machinist and Composer of the Entertainment.)
*Miscellaneous:* [There is no entry for Ludlow in *BD*, *LS*, or Nicoll.]

*Singing and Dancing:* Dancing by Mlle. Chateauneuf, Oates, Sr., and Moreau [their only performance at SA this season].
*Deferred:* Originally advertised for 21 Jan. 1742 then for 23 Jan.

and

*Afterpiece: The Rival Sorcerers.*
*Cast:* None listed.
*Miscellaneous:* ". . . composed by Ludlow" (*DNL*, 26 Jan. 1742).


FEBRUARY


1    Mon.    AS.    *The Fair Penitent.*
*Cast:* Horatio—Quin (last time of his performing in this kingdom); Calista—Mrs. Cibber.
*Benefit:* Mrs. Cibber.
*Miscellaneous:* At the Desire of Persons of Quality.
*Singing and Dancing:* Dancing by Mlle. Chateauneuf, Moreau, and Oates.


4    Thur.    AS.    *The Old Batchelour.*
*Cast:* Laetitia—Mrs. Cibber.
*Command:* Duke and Duchess of Devonshire.
*Benefit:* F. Elrington.
*Miscellaneous:* For the Entertainment of the Lords Justice, Lord Chancellor, etc.


4    Thur.    SA.    *King Henry IV, with the Humours of Falstaff.*
*Cast:* Falstaff—J. Morris (first time in character).
*Benefit:* J. Morris.
*Miscellaneous:* At the particular Desire of several persons of quality.
*Singing and Dancing:* With several Entertainments of Dancing.

and

*Afterpiece: The Rival Sorcerers.*
*Cast:* None listed.


5    Fri.    AS.    *Love's Last Shift.*
*Cast:* None listed.
*Command:* Lord Tullamore, Grand Master.
*Benefit:* Distressed Freemasons.
*Deferred:* This performance may have been deferred from 22 Jan.


6    Sat.    SA.    *Jane Shore.*
*Cast:* Jane Shore—Mrs. Furnival.
*Miscellaneous:* By particular desire.

and

*Afterpiece: The Rival Sorcerers.*
*Cast:* None listed.

8    Mon.    AS.    *The Betrayer of His Country*    V.
*Cast:* None listed.
*Miscellaneous:* [Premiere.] By the Author of *Gustavus Vasa* [i.e. Henry Brooke]. Boxes, 5s. 5d.; Pit 3s. 3d.; Gallery, 2s. 2d.
    [Hitchcock 1788–94, 1:117, confuses this play with *The Patriot* (3 Dec. 1744 SA) and mistakenly states that in Feb. 1741 "'Gustavus Vasa; or the Deliverer of his Country' was got up with much care and attention at AS, and was performed several nights with great success."
    This play was revised as *The Earl of Westmoreland* and performed in Dublin on 13 and 23 May 1745 at SA. In 1754 it was again retitled *Injured Honour* and acted, according to Nicoll, although there is no record of a performance of a play with that title either in London or Dublin.]

8    Mon.    SA.    *Oroonoko.*
*Cast:* Oroonoko—R. Elrington; Imoinda—Mrs. Furnival.
*Benefit:* Ralph Elrington.
*Singing and Dancing:* With several Entertainments of Dancing.
                                    and
*Afterpiece: The Rival Sorcerers.*
*Cast:* None listed.

9    Tues.    AS.    *The Conscious Lovers.*
*Cast:* Bevil, Jr.—Quin; Indiana—Mrs. Cibber.
*Benefit:* The Charitable Infirmary.

11    Thur.    SA.    *The Humorous Lieutenant.*
*Cast:* Lieutenant—Wetherilt.
*Benefit:* Wetherilt.
*Miscellaneous:* Never Performed here.
*Singing and Dancing:* With several Entertainments of Dancing.
                                    and
*Afterpiece:* Unspecified "Farce."

13    Sat.    SA.    *King Lear and His Three Daughters.*
*Cast:* Lear—Wright; Cordelia—Mrs. Furnival.
*Benefit:* Wright.
*Miscellaneous:* Neither the Play or Entertainment will be performed again till next Season.
                                    and

*Afterpiece: Thomas Koulikan, the Persian Hero [; or, The Distressed Princess]*.
*Cast:* None listed.
*Miscellaneous:* Interspersed with Harlequin's Descent from the Sun and his Adventures upon Earth, with new scenes and machines.

[Anonymous farce. *LS* lists one performance at a Booth at Bartholemew Fair 22 Aug. 1741; Nicoll 1977–79, 2: 385, gives subtitle and cites BF booths Turbott and Yeates for Aug. 1741. On p. 452 Nicoll cites a piece: "The Persian Hero; or the Noble Englishman. With the comical humours of Toby and Dorcas Guzzle of Preston seems to be the same as Thamas Kouli Kan, the Persian Hero. . . . It also appeared as The King of Persia or the Noble Englishman. With the comical humours of Sir Andrew Ague-cheek at the Siege of Babylon, BF, Lee and Woodward, 1741. Probably the same as The Noble Englishman (1722). . . .".].

15   Mon.   SA.   *The Tempest; or, The Enchanted Island.*
*Cast:* None listed.
*Benefit:* T. Philips.
*Miscellaneous:* (Never performed in this Kingdom before). With the original Music, Flyings, Sinkings, Risings, Thunder, Lightening, Rain, Showers of Fire, all executed in the same Manner as at the Theatre Royal Drury Lane.

[There were six prior performances of a play with this title in Dublin—presumably performances of the Davanent-Dryden operatic version, which this also seems to be. *The Tempest* was revived after several years at DL during the 1739–40 season.]

"As Mr. Philips has been at an extraordinary expence with Carpenters, Painters, etc. in order to have both the Play and Entertainment performed in the most regular Manner, he humbly hopes no Gentleman will take it ill, that they are refused Admittance under full Price the whole Performance, this being the only Night either the Play or Entertainment will be acted till next Winter" (*FDJ*, 9–13 Feb. 1742).

and

*Afterpiece: The Hussar.*
*Cast:* None listed.
*Miscellaneous:* By particular command; not performed this season. All scenes, Machines, and decorations entirely new.

16   Tues.   AS.   *The Betrayer of His Country.*
*Cast:* None listed.
*Miscellaneous:* With entirely new dresses and machines. New prologue and epilogue; epilogue spoken by Mrs. Cibber.

18     Thur.     AS.     *The Fair Penitent.*
*Cast:* Calista—Mrs. Cibber.
*Command:* Duke and Duchess of Devonshire.
*Benefit:* Griffith.
*Singing and Dancing:* Dancing by Mlle. Chateauneuf and others.
and
*Afterpiece: The Necromancer.*
*Cast:* Harlequin—Oates.
*Singing and Dancing:* With all the songs and dances belonging to the entertainment.


18     Thur.     SA.     *The Distrest Mother.*
*Cast:* Orestes—R. Elrington; Andromache—Mrs. Furnival.
*Miscellaneous:* [*DNL* says Mrs. Furnival plays the role of Hermione.]
*Benefit:* Este.
*Singing and Dancing:* With several Entertainments of Dancing.
and
*Afterpiece: The Rival Sorcerers.*
*Cast:* None listed.


19     Fri.     AS.     *Venice Preserved.*
*Cast:* Belvidera—Mrs. Cibber.
*Benefit:* Barrington.
*Miscellaneous:* By the particular Desire of several Persons of Quality.
*Singing and Dancing:* With several Entertainments of Dancing. At the end of the Play Mr. Barrington will sing his Roratorio.
and
*Afterpiece:* Unspecified "Farce."


22     Mon.     AS.     *The Spanish Fryar.*
*Cast:* Queen—Mrs. Cibber.
*Benefit:* Vanderbank.
*Singing and Dancing:* Dancing between the Acts by Mlle. Chateauneuf and others.


22     Mon.     SA.     *Macbeth.*
*Cast:* Lady Macbeth—Mrs. Furnival (first time in character).
*Benefit:* [Mr.] Furnival.
*Miscellaneous:* At the particular Desire of several Ladies of Quality.
*Singing and Dancing:* Dancing between the Acts.
and
*Afterpiece:* Unspecified "Farce."

25    Thur.    AS.    [*Epicoene; or,*] *The Silent Woman.*
*Cast:* None listed.
*Command:* Duke and Duchess of Devonshire.
*Benefit:* I. Sparks.
*Miscellaneous:* Not acted these four years.
*Singing and Dancing:* With several Entertainments of Dancing.
*Deferred:* From 11 Feb.

and

*Afterpiece: The Necromancer.*
*Cast:* None listed.


25    Thur.    SA.    *The Conscious Lovers.*
*Cast:* Indiana—Mrs. Furnival.
*Benefit:* William Delamain.
*Miscellaneous:* For the better Accommodation of the Ladies four new Boxes
will be formed in an elegant Manner on the Stage, and three rows of the Pit
will be let into boxes. The Boxes will be illuminated with wax-lights.
    [Boydell 1988, 78, indicates that Delamain shared this benefit with Mrs.
Furnival. This seems unlikely in light of the fact that Mrs. Furnival was a
principal performer and had never previously shared a benefit with anyone.]
*Singing and Dancing:* With several Entertainments of Dancing between the
Acts.

and

*Afterpiece: The Lying Valet.*
*Cast:* Sharp—Wetherilt.


26    Fri.    AS.    *Comus.*
*Cast:* None listed.
*Command:* Lords Justice.
*Benefit:* L. Layfield.


27    Sat.    AS.    *The Orphan.*
*Cast:* Monimia—Mrs. Cibber.
*Benefit:* Mrs. Pasquilino.
*Miscellaneous:* Play to begin at 6 o'clock and to end at half past 8 o'clock
to oblige the Ladies. [See *Miscellaneous* SA 27 Feb.]
*Singing and Dancing:* Singing by Mlle. Chateauneuf, particularly "The
Cuckoo."


27    Sat.    SA.    *The Merchant of Venice.*
*Cast:* Shylock—Wright; Portia—Mrs. Furnival.
*Benefit:* Winch (musician).
*Miscellaneous:* To begin at exactly 6 o'clock so Ladies and Gentlemen may
go to the Assemblies.

*Singing and Dancing:* With several favourite concertos on the French horn by Winch.

and

*Afterpiece: The Lying Valet.*
*Cast:* None listed.

MARCH

1    Mon.    AS.    *The Way of the World.*
*Cast:* None listed.
*Benefit:* Moreau.
*Singing and Dancing:* Dancing by Mlle. Chateauneuf.

and

*Afterpiece: The Necromancer.*
*Cast:* None listed.

1    Mon.    SA.    *Mithridates, King of Pontus.*
*Cast:* None listed.
*Benefit:* Husband.
*Miscellaneous:* Not acted these 20 years.
*Singing and Dancing:* With several Entertainments of Dancing.

and

*Afterpiece: The Rival Sorcerers.*
*Cast:* None listed.

4    Thur.    AS.    *The Betrayer of His Country.*
*Cast:* None listed.
*Benefit:* The Author [Henry Brooke].
*Miscellaneous:* Third time. Several improvements in dress and machinery. New prologue and epilogue; epilogue spoke by Mrs. Cibber.
*Singing and Dancing:* Second scene opened with vocal music by Mrs. Cibber and others.
*Deferred:* Deferred from 25 Feb. 1742.

4    Thur.    SA.    *The Constant Couple.*
*Cast:* Sir Harry—M. de Rheiner.
*Benefit:* M. De Rheiner (A Distressed Foreign Gentleman).
*Singing and Dancing:* With several new English and Italian Songs to be sung by him.
*Deferred:* Deferred from 2 Mar. 1742. See *Comment* below.
*Comment:* "The unhappy Situation this Gentleman labours under is pretty well known to the Publick; and as he has no other means to extricate himself from his present Distress; it is humbly hoped that the Ladies and Gentlemen will favour him with their Presence, since he would not have attempted to

appear on the Stage (which he never did before) were it not to endeavour to entertain the Audience to the best of his Abilities.

M. De Rheiner has been obliged to put off his Day, which was to have been Tuesday next, on account of all the best Musick's being engaged to Mr. Handel's concert and as he was obliged to give a considerable Praemium to obtain another Day, besides other extraordinary Expences, he humbly hopes that no Person will desire Admittance for less than full Prices during the whole Performance" (*DNL*, 23–27 Feb. 1742).

8     Mon.     AS.     *The Committee.*
*Cast:* None listed.
*Benefit:* J. Elrington and Callaghan MacCarty (musician).
*Singing and Dancing:* Mrs. Cibber being sick, Mlle. Chateauneuf will sing "The Cuckoo."

8     Mon.     SA.     *The Busy Body.*
*Cast:* Marplot—Wetherilt.
*Benefit:* Mrs. Wetherilt and Gregory.
                    and
*Afterpiece: The Hussar.*
*Cast:* None listed.

9     Tues.     SA.     *The Provoked Husband.*
*Cast:* Townly—R. Elrington; Lady Townly—Mrs. Furnival.
*Benefit:* A Certain Gentleman in Distress.
                    and
*Afterpiece: The Lying Valet.*
*Cast:* None listed.

11     Thur.     SA.     *The Distrest Mother.*
*Cast:* None listed.
*Benefit:* L. Duval.
*Miscellaneous:* At the particular Desire of several Ladies of Quality; Four new Boxes formed in an elegant fashion on the stage with the three Rows in the Pit let into Boxes. With a variety of entertainments.

12     Fri.     AS.     *Love's Last Shift.*
*Cast:* Amanda—Mrs. Cibber.
*Benefit:* Bridges.
*Miscellaneous:* [*The Siege of Damascus*, Eudocia—Mrs. Cibber was originally advertised for this night, then *Measure for Measure*, Isabella—Mrs. Cibber.] Roaratorio at the end of the Play.
*Singing and Dancing:* Dancing by Mlle. Chateauneuf and others.
*Deferred:* Deferred from 11 Mar. 1742.

and
*Afterpiece: The Judgment of Paris, with the Nuptials of Harlequin and Columbine.*
*Cast:* Columbine—Mlle. Chateauneuf (her first appearance in Character); Harlequin Paris—Oates.
*Miscellaneous:* As Mlle. Chateauneuf honours this Entertainment with her Performance, the Town may be assured it will be got up in the most exact and careful Manner.


15　Mon.　AS.　*Nature.*
*Cast:* None listed.
*Miscellaneous:* [Premiere. Comedy by Mr. Dixon. Not listed in Nicoll or *LS*.]
　　"The Company finding it impossible to get up the Tragedy of *Sampson* [*sic*] *Agonistes*, [in] the Time propos'd, as it requires the most extraordinary Application in Study, as well as in Musical Parts, both Vocal and Instrumental, have prevail'd on the Author, to a longer day. . . . To make him Satisfaction adequate to his friendly Intention of serving the Company, they have with the greatest Pleasure accepted of *Nature*, a new Comedy since finish'd by him for that purpose, and look'd upon by some of the politest Judges to be as innocently diverting and entertaining as any on the Stage. The story being true in the chief Circumstances and the Ground-work laid by those Great Masters Shakespeare and Fletcher tho' so nicely apply'd in the greatest Adaptation, as to make it appear an Original peculiarly design'd to have due Honour aid to the *Fair Sex*, to whom there is the greatest Reason to hope that it will give more real Satisfaction than anything that has appear'd for many years. Tickets delivered for *Samson Agonistes* will be taken the first night, and every other, during its Performance" (*Dublin Mercury*, 6 Mar. 1742).
　　[*Samson Agonistes*, with all proper decorations, "originally by the Sublime Milton" with music by Handel was initially advertised for 25 Jan., then 8 Mar. and finally this date. According to John O'Keeffe (1826, 1:18–21) Mr. Dixon, a painter and linen copperplate printer, adapted Milton's tragedy. Baker writes: "I remember to have seen in the possession a gentleman in Dublin (one Mr. Dixon) an alteration of this poem [*Samson Agonistes*], said by himself to be his own, so as to render it fit for the stage: and the same gentleman also shewed me a bill for the intended performance" (Baker 1812, 2:240). The playbill is now in the possession of Mrs. William S. Clark.]


15　Mon.　SA.　*The Country Wife.*
*Cast:* Mrs. Pinchwife—Mrs. Chetwood; Horner—R. Elrington; Sparkish—Wetherilt; Pinchwife—J. Morris; Lady Fidget—Mrs. Furnival.
*Benefit:* Mrs. Chetwood and Woder (musician).

*Miscellaneous:* This Comedy is performed as it was revised by the late Sir Richard Steele, for the Theatre Royal in DL; To begin exactly at 6 o'clock.

and

*Afterpiece: The Rival Sorcerers.*
*Cast:* Columbine—Mrs. Chetwood; Pierrot—J. Morris.
*Miscellaneous:* Last time of performing it this season.

16    Tues.    SA.    *The Parthian Hero; or, Beauty in Distress.*
*Cast:* None listed.
*Benefit:* Matt. Gardiner, the Author.
*Miscellaneous:* With a "new" prologue by a Gentleman very well known in the polite world. [First recorded performance of this tragedy by Matthew Gardiner.]
*Singing and Dancing:* Hornpipe solo by Master Pitt; "Scotch Dance" by McNeil; "A Peasant" by P. Morris; and dance by Miss Bullock and Delamain.
*Deferred:* Deferred from 28 Jan. then 6 Mar. because of the shortness of time, and hurry of the Benefit, rendering it impossible to get it sufficiently perfect for the entertainment of the audience.

18    Thur.    AS.    *The Twin Rivals.*
*Cast:* None listed.
*Benefit:* Mlle. Chateauneuf.
*Miscellaneous:* By the particular Desire of several Persons of Quality. [*Siege of Damascus* originally advertised.]
*Singing and Dancing:* Singing and Dancing between the Acts: 1. A Spanish Escapade by Moreau 2. "Blow, blow, thou Winter Wind," by Mlle. Chateauneuf, and, by particular desire, with a serious dance. 3. "La Paisant Dequise" a new dance by Mlle. Chateauneuf and Mr. Oates. 4. "The Lass of St. Osyth" sung by Mlle. Chateauneuf. 5. A new comic dance by Mlle. Chateauneuf and Mr. Oates.

and

*Afterpiece: Damon and Phillida.*
*Cast:* None listed.

18    Thur.    SA.    *The Royal Merchant.*
*Cast:* None listed.
*Benefit:* Beamsley and a Reduced Gentleman.
*Miscellaneous:* With the whole Procession of the Coronation of King Clause; in which will be introduced the ceremony of the Champion as done at Beggar's Bush.

and

*Afterpiece: The Rival Sorcerers.*
*Cast:* A Lilliputian Company.

22    Mon.    AS.    *Love for Love.*
*Cast:* None listed.
*Singing and Dancing:* Dancing by Mlle. Chateauneuf, Moreau, and Oates.
and
*Afterpiece: The Judgment of Paris.*
*Cast:* Columbine—Mlle. Chateauneuf.

22    Mon.    SA.    *The Double Dealer.*
*Cast:* None listed.
*Benefit:* Dolland and a Distressed Family.
*Singing and Dancing:* With several Entertainments of Dancing.
and
*Afterpiece: The Rival Sorcerers.*
*Cast:* None listed.

23    Tues.    AS.    *The Distrest Mother.*
*Cast:* Andromache—Mrs. Cibber; Hermione—Mrs. Furnival.
*Benefit:* Bardin.
*Deferred:* Deferred from 15 Feb. 1742.

23    Tues.    SA.    *Mithridates, King of Pontus.*
*Cast:* Semandra—Mrs. Furnival.
*Benefit:* O'Neil (boxkeeper).
*Miscellaneous:* The Publick may be assured, that Mrs. Furnival will perform
the Character of Semandra in the above Play, notwithstanding what has been
reported to the contrary. With several unspecified "Entertainments."
and
*Afterpiece: The Stage Coach.*
*Cast:* Maccahone—J. Morris.

25    Thur.    AS.    *The Relapse.*
*Cast:* None listed.
*Benefit:* Mrs. Martin.
*Singing and Dancing:* Singing and Dancing by Mlle. Chateauneuf and others.
Barrington will sing his Roaratorio.
and
*Afterpiece: The Stage Coach.*
*Cast:* Maccahone—Barrington.

25    Thur.    SA.    *The Relapse.*
*Cast:* Berinthia—Mrs. Furnival; Foppington—Oates.
*Benefit:* Oates.
*Miscellaneous:* Not performed here this season; At the particular Desire of
several Persons of Quality.

*Singing and Dancing:* With several entertainments of singing and dancing at the end of every act. By particular desire, at the end of the Play will be introduced a humourous Ballad written by Sir John Suckling upon himself, setting forth his Expedition, valourous Exploits, and merry Adventures, against the Scots, in the Reign of King Charles I.

and

*Afterpiece: The Lying Valet.*
*Cast:* None listed.


26    Fri.    SA.    *The Mourning Bride.*
*Cast:* None listed.
*Benefit:* For the Maintenance of the Poor Prisoners in the Marshalseas, at one Pennyworth of Bread a Day to each of them, distributed under the Direction of the Rev. Dean Maturin.

and

*Afterpiece: The Lying Valet.*
*Cast:* None listed.


29    Mon.    SA.    *King Henry IV, with the Humours of Falstaff.*
*Cast:* Falstaff—J. Morris.
*Benefit:* P. Morris, Jr. (dancer) [Patrick and J. Morris, Jr. were evidently brothers.]
*Miscellaneous:* Changed from *The Merry Wives of Windsor* at the particular Desire of several Persons of Quality.

and

*Afterpiece: The Hussar.*
*Cast:* Harlequin—P. Morris; Columbine—Mrs. Chetwood; Pierrot—J. Morris (last time of his performing that character this season).


30    Tues.    AS.    *The Pilgrim.*
*Cast:* None listed.
*Benefit:* Widow Shewell and her Helpless Orphans.
*Miscellaneous:* By the Benevolence of a Noble Peer, and the Gentlemen Proprietors of the TR.
*Comment:* "The World is so well acquainted with the late Mr. Shewell's Misfortunes, and the necessitous Circumstances in which his poor Family were left, that 'tis hoped the Public will . . . raise them from the deplorable Condition they at present Labour under" (*Dublin Mercury,* 13 and 20 Mar. 1742). [Two weeks later Mrs. Shewell died leaving the family in an even more desperate condition (*DNL,* 20 Apr. 1742). A short, sentimental poem addressed to the unfortunate Mrs. Shewell appears in *FDJ,* 16–20 Mar. 1742.]
*Singing and Dancing:* Dancing by Mlle. Chateauneuf, Moreau, and others.

and

*Afterpiece: Damon and Phillida.*
*Cast:* None listed.

APRIL

1    Thur.    AS.    *Love Makes a Man.*
*Cast:* None listed.
*Benefit:* Giles and Lee.
*Miscellaneous:* At the Desire of Persons of Quality.
*Singing and Dancing:* Dancing by Mlle. Chateauneuf, Moreau, and Oates.
and
*Afterpiece: The Judgment of Paris.*
*Cast:* None listed.
*Miscellaneous:* Carefully revised and altered.

1    Thur.    SA.    *The Fair Penitent.*
*Cast:* None listed.
*Benefit:* Mrs. Mackay.

3    Sat.    AS.    *Hamlet.*
*Cast:* None listed.
*Benefit:* Mrs. Sampson and Kountze (drummer).
*Singing and Dancing:* With several Entertainments of Dancing.
and
*Afterpiece: The Lying Valet.*
*Cast:* None listed.

5    Mon.    AS.    *The Double Gallant.*
*Cast:* Lady Dainty—Mrs. Cibber (her first time of performing since her late Indisposition).
*Singing and Dancing:* Dancing by Mlle. Chateauneuf, Moreau, and Oates.
and
*Afterpiece: The Judgment of Paris.*
*Cast:* Columbine—Mlle. Chateauneuf.

5    Mon.    SA.    *The Careless Husband.*
*Cast:* Foppington—Wetherilt; Lady Betty—Mrs. Furnival.
*Benefit:* Mrs. Furnival.
*Miscellaneous:* With several unspecified "Entertainments".
and
*Afterpiece: The Virgin Unmasked.*
*Cast:* Lucy—Mrs. Chetwood.

8    Thur.    AS.    *The Siege of Damascus.*
*Cast:* Eudocia—Mrs. Cibber.
*Singing and Dancing:* Dancing by Mlle. Chateauneuf, Moreau, and Oates.


[Passion Week 12–17 April]

[The first rehearsal of Handel's *Messiah* was scheduled for 8 Apr. at the Fishamble St. Music Hall but was deferred until the 9th (Boydell 1988, 80). The first performance took place at noon on 13 Apr.]

22    Thur.    SA.    *The Busy Body.*
*Cast:* Marplot—Wetherilt; Miranda—Mrs. Furnival.
*Benefit:* Tyler and Meek.

and

*Afterpiece: The Rival Sorcerers.*
*Cast:* None listed.

26    Mon.    AS.    *The Siege of Damascus.*
*Cast:* Eudocia—Mrs. Cibber.
*Command:* Lords Justice.
*Singing and Dancing:* Dancing by Mlle. Chateauneuf, Moreau, and Oates.

29    Thur.    AS.    *The Orphan.*
*Cast:* Monimia—Mrs. Cibber; Chamont—Pellish (his first appearance on this stage).
*Singing and Dancing:* Dancing by Mlle. Chateauneuf, Moreau, and Oates.

29    Thur.    SA.    *Jane Shore.*
*Cast:* Jane Shore—Mrs. Furnival.
*Benefit:* Dominick Gunan.

MAY

3    Mon.    AS.    *The Man of Mode.*
*Cast:* Sir Foppling—Bardin; Loveit—Mrs. Cibber.
*Miscellaneous:* Never Performed Here.
*Singing and Dancing:* Dancing by Mlle. Chateauneuf, Moreau, and Oates.

4    Tues.    AS.    *Comus.*
*Cast:* Lady—Mrs. Cibber.

6    Thur.    AS.    *Comus.*
*Cast:* Lady—Mrs. Cibber.
*Miscellaneous:* By the particular Desire of several Persons of Quality.

*Singing and Dancing:* Mrs. Cibber will sing in character "Sweet Echo"; Dancing by Mlle. Chateauneuf, Moreau, and Oates.

11    Tues.    SA.    *The Recruiting Officer.*
*Cast:* None listed.
*Benefit:* Mrs. Mitchell.
*Singing and Dancing:* With Dancing.
                                      and
*Afterpiece: The Mock Doctor.*
*Cast:* None listed.

12    Wed.    SA.    *The Careless Husband.*
*Cast:* None listed.
*Benefit:* A Gentleman in Distress in the Four Courts Marshalsea.
                                      and
*Afterpiece: The Virgin Unmasked.*
*Cast:* None listed.

13    Thur.    AS.    *The Man of Mode.*
*Cast:* As 3 May 1742.
*Benefit:* Bardin.
*Singing and Dancing:* Dancing by Mlle. Chateauneuf, Moreau, and Oates.

13    Thur.    SA.    *Love for Love.*
*Cast:* None listed.
*Benefit:* Lamb, Kennedy, and Compton Roe.
                                      and
*Afterpiece: The Mock Doctor.*
*Cast:* None listed.

15    Sat.    AS.    *Othello.*
*Cast:* Othello—Swan; Desdemona—Mrs. Cibber (her first time in that character).
*Benefit:* Worsdale.
*Miscellaneous:* Othello will be attempted by a Gentleman [i.e. Swan], whose friendship for Mr. Worsdale has engaged him in the undertaking.

17    Mon.    AS.    *The Beggar's Opera.*
*Cast:* Polly—Mrs. Cibber (her first appearance in that character).
*Miscellaneous:* [Mary Nash in her biography of Mrs. Cibber (Nash 1977, 166) reveals that Mrs. Cibber had long wanted to try the part of Polly but had been unable to because in London the part belonged exclusively to her rival, Mrs. Clive.]
*Singing and Dancing:* Dancing by Mlle. Chateauneuf, Moreau, and Oates.

*Comment:* "After the departure of Mr. Quinn for London . . . so great was her [Mrs. Cibber's] character, that she continued to draw houses, especially in Polly in The Beggar's Opera, which was often repeated, and allowed by the first judges to be superior to any that ever played it" (Hitchcock 1788–94, 1:117).
*Deferred:* From 10 May.

18    Tues.    AS.    *The Provoked Wife.*
*Cast:* Sir John—L. Sparks.
*Benefit:* Watson.
*Miscellaneous:* At the Desire of several Ladies of Quality.
*Singing and Dancing:* With Dancing. Barrington (being desired) will sing his celebrated Roratorio.
*Deferred:* Deferred from 17 May "on Extraordinary Occasion."
and
*Afterpiece: The Stage Coach.*
*Cast:* Maccahone—Barrington.

19    Wed.    SA.    *The Squire of Alsatia.*
*Cast:* Squire—Wetherilt; Teresa—Mrs. Furnival.
*Benefit:* William and Barty. Mainwaring (musicians).
*Miscellaneous:* At the request of the Charitable Musical Society on College Green; Not acted this season.
*Singing and Dancing:* Mr. Mainwaring will play his own Medley Overture and Mr. Charles, with his second, will perform the "Water Music," being the first time of his appearing on the stage, in which he will be accompanied on the kettle drum by Mr. Kounty [i.e. Kountze]; With Entertainments of Dancing between every act.
*Deferred:* Deferred from 17 May 1742.
and
*Afterpiece: The Anatomist; or, The Sham Doctor.*
*Cast:* Crispin—Wetherilt (his first time in character).

20    Thur.    AS.    *The Beggar's Opera.*    V.
*Cast:* Polly—Mrs. Cibber (her second performance in character).
*Singing and Dancing:* Dancing by Mlle. Chateauneuf, Moreau, and Oates.

21    Fri.    AS.    *The Double Gallant.*
*Cast:* Atall—Bardin; Lady Dainty—Mrs. Elmy; Lady Sadlife—Mrs. Pasquilino.
*Benefit:* Oates.
*Miscellaneous:* By the particular Desire of several Persons of Quality.
*Singing and Dancing:* Between the Acts: Act 1, Violin Concerto by Mr. Oates; Act 2, "The Peasant Disguised" by Mlle. Chateauneuf and Oates;

Act 3, "The Dusty Miller" by Moreau; Act 4, "Grand Peasant Dance" by
Mlle. Chateauneuf and Oates; Barrington will perform his "Roaratorio."
and
*Afterpiece: The Judgment of Paris.*
*Cast:* Columbine—Mlle. Chateauneuf; Harlequin—Oates.

24    Mon.    AS.    *The Beggar's Opera.*
*Cast:* Polly—Mrs. Cibber (third performance).
*Miscellaneous:* By the particular Desire of several Persons of Quality.
*Singing and Dancing:* Dancing by Mlle. Chateauneuf, Moreau, and Oates.

27    Thur.    AS.    *The Beggar's Opera.*
*Cast:* Polly—Mrs. Cibber (fourth time).
*Singing and Dancing:* Dancing by Mlle. Chateauneuf, Moreau, and Oates.

27    Thur.    SA.    *Love for Love.*
*Cast:* None listed.
*Benefit:* McNeil (dancer) and Mrs. Bamford (dresser).
*Singing and Dancing:* With several Entertainments of Dancing between the
Acts.
and
*Afterpiece: The Virgin Unmasked.*
*Cast:* None listed.

31    Mon.    AS.    *Venice Preserved.*
*Cast:* Belvidera—Mrs. Cibber.
*Benefit:* Mrs. Cibber.
*Singing and Dancing:* Dancing by Mlle. Chateauneuf, Moreau, and Oates.
and
*Afterpiece: The Devil to Pay.*
*Cast:* None listed.

**JUNE**

1    Tues.    SA.    *The Careless Husband.*
*Cast:* Lady Betty—Mrs. Furnival; Foppington—Wetherilt.
*Miscellaneous:* At the particular Desire of several Ladies of Quality; The
last time of the Company's performing until after their return from the Carlow Races.
and
*Afterpiece:* Unspecified "Farce."

4   Fri.   AS.   *The Distrest Mother.*
*Cast:* Andromache—Mrs. Cibber (her first time in character).
*Benefit:* Mrs. Pasquilino.
*Singing and Dancing:* Dancing by Mlle. Chateauneuf, Moreau, and Oates.
*Deferred:* Deferred from 24 May.

11   Fri.   AS.   *Oroonoko.*
*Cast:* Oroonoko—Swan; Imoinda—Mrs. Cibber.

*Summer Season*

16   Wed.   SA.   *The Constant Couple.*
*Cast:* Sir Harry—Mrs. Woffington (from DL.)
*Miscellaneous:* "We hear that Mr. Delane, Mr. Garrick, and Miss Woffington are hourly expected from England to play Smock Alley Theatre, and that they open with the Constant Couple, or a Trip to the Jubilee; and next Richard, the part of Sir Harry Wildair by Miss Woffington, the part of Richard by Mr. Garrick" (*DNL,* 8–12 June 1742). [Garrick and Miss Woffington arrived in Dublin from Chester on 14 June, Delane arrived from Holyhead on 15 June (*DNL,* 12–15 June 1742). Hitchcock, 1:118, places this performance on 15 June.]

18   Fri.   SA.   *King Richard III.*
*Cast:* Gloster—Garrick (from GF, his first appearance in this Kingdom); King Henry—Giffard (from GF); Lady Anne—Mrs. Woffington; Queen Elizabeth—Mrs. Furnival.

21   Mon.   AS.   *Oroonoko.*
*Cast:* Oroonoko—Delane (from DL).

21   Mon.   SA.   *The Orphan.*
*Cast:* Chamont—Garrick (his second appearance on this stage); Monimia—Mrs. Furnival.

22   Tues.   AS.   *King Richard III.*
*Cast:* Gloster—Delane.
*Benefit:* Mrs. Wetherilt.
*Singing and Dancing:* Dancing by Mlle. Chateauneuf, Moreau, and Oates.

24   Thur.   AS.   *The Beggar's Opera.*
*Cast:* Polly—Mrs. Cibber.
*Benefit:* Thomson (prompter).
*Miscellaneous:* Last time but one of the Company's performing this season.
*Singing and Dancing:* Dancing by Mlle. Chateauneuf and Moreau.

24    Thur.    SA.    *King Lear and His Three Daughters.*
*Cast:* Lear—Garrick; Edgar—Giffard; Cordelia—Mrs. Woffington.
*Benefit:* Garrick.
*Comment:* During this performance, while Garrick as Lear lay with his head in Cordelia's [Mrs. Woffington] lap, "a Gentleman threw himself down on the other side of the fair Princess, and without the least regard to her rank, began to treat her with the utmost indecency. Resentment followed on her part and abuse on his. Mr. Garrick was silent, but could not help casting an eye of indignation at so brutal a scene, which was considered so daring an insult by the gentlemen, that two or more of his comrades searched for him after the play was over, vowing dreadful imprecations that they would put him to death" (Sheridan 1758, 15.)
    A short, unremarkable poem entitled "Verses to Garrick" is found in *DNL,* 26–29 June 1742.

                                        and

*Afterpiece: The Lying Valet.*
*Cast:* Sharp—Garrick.
*Miscellaneous:* By particular desire.


26    Sat.    SA.    *The Busy Body.*
*Cast:* None listed.
*Singing and Dancing:* Dancing by Signora Barbarini (her first appearance in this Kingdom), End of Act 2, "The Italian Peasants" by Signa. Barbarina and Henry Delamain, from the Opera in Paris and others; End of Play "The Rural Assembly" by Signa. Barbarina, Henry Delamain and others.


28    Mon.    SA.    *The Orphan.*
*Cast:* Chamont—Garrick.
*Singing and Dancing:* Dancing by Signora Barbarina.
*Comment:* "Yesterday Evening their Excellencies the Lords Justice were at the Theatre in Smock Alley to see Mr. Garrick and Mrs. Barbarina perform" (*FDJ,* 26–29 June 1742).


29    Tues.    AS.    *Othello.*
*Cast:* Othello—Delane; Desdemona—Mrs. Cibber (being particularly desired).
*Command:* Lords Justice.


30    Wed.    SA.    *Love Makes a Man.*
*Cast:* Clodio—Garrick; Carlos—Giffard; Angelina—Mrs. Woffington.
*Singing and Dancing:* Dancing by Signa. Barbarina and Henry Delamain and others.

JULY

3    Sat.    SA.    *The Rehearsal.*
*Cast:* Bayes—Garrick.
*Singing and Dancing:* Dancing by Signa. Barbarina.
*Comment:* "Last Saturday Night the Comedy called the Rehearsal was acted
. . . to a very brilliant and polite Audience; and though Mr. Garrick has
given a general Satisfaction in his several Performances, yet in the Character
of Bayes he shewed so particular an Excellence, as no one before who has
attempted that Part here, could ever yet arrive at" (*DNL,* 3–6 July 1742).

5    Mon.    SA.    *The Careless Husband.*
*Cast:* Foppington—Garrick; Sir Charles—Giffard; Lady Betty—Mrs. Wof-
fington.
*Benefit:* Signora Barbarini (dancer).
*Singing and Dancing:* With several new Entertainments of Dancing by
Signa. Barbarini.

6    Tues.    AS.    *The Distrest Mother.*
*Cast:* Pyrrhus—Delane; Andromache—Mrs. Cibber (her last performance
his season).
*Command:* Lords Justice.
*Miscellaneous:* With the original epilogue spoken by Mrs. Cibber.
*Singing and Dancing:* Dancing by Mlle. Chateauneuf.
*Comment:* "After a few unsuccessful attempts, Aungier Street Theatre
closed with Mrs. Cibber's Andromache . . ." (Hitchcock, 1:119).

8    Thur.    SA.    *King Richard III.*
*Cast:* Gloster—Garrick; King Henry—Giffard; Lady Anne—Mrs. Wof-
fington.
*Benefit:* Mrs. Woffington.
*Miscellaneous:* At the particular Desire of several Ladies of Quality; the last
time of his performing the character this season.
*Singing and Dancing:* Dancing by Signora Barbarini and H. Delamain.
                                 and
*Afterpiece: The Virgin Unmasked.*
*Cast:* Lucy—Mrs. Woffington.

12    Mon.    SA.    *Venice Preserved.*
*Cast:* Pierre—Garrick; Jaffier—R. Elrington; Belvidera—Mrs. Furnival.
*Miscellaneous:* [Hitchcock, 1:119, states that Giffard played Jaffier.]
    A letter signed by the proprietors of SA and published in the *FDJ,* 13 July
1742, indicates that the Lord Mayor had engaged a box for this performance
but, through some mistake of the boxkeeper, there was none available when

he arrived. The proprietors apologized profusely and vowed to "always take care for the future his Lordship shall never be so ill-used again."]
*Singing and Dancing:* Dancing by Signora Barbarini and H. Delamain.
and

*Afterpiece: The Virgin Unmasked.*
*Cast:* Lucy—Mrs. Cibber.

15   Thur.   SA.   *The Rehearsal.*
*Cast:* Bayes—Garrick (the last time of his performing the character this season).
*Singing and Dancing:* With new Entertainments of Dancing by Signora Barbarini and H. Delamain.

22   Thur.   SA.   *The Beaux' Stratagem.*
*Cast:* Archer—R. Elrington; Scrub—Wetherilt; Mrs. Sullen—Mrs. Woffington.
*Benefit:* H. Delamain.
*Singing and Dancing:* Dancing by Signora Barbarini and H. Delamain (lately arrived from the Opera in Paris).

23   Fri.   SA.   *The Rehearsal.*
*Cast:* Bayes—Garrick.
*Command:* Lords Justice.
*Singing and Dancing:* Dancing, particularly a new Grand Ballet by Signora Barbarini and H. Delamain.

26   Mon.   SA.   *The Old Batchelour.*
*Cast:* Fondlewife—Garrick; Laetitia—Mrs. Woffington.
and

*Afterpiece: The School-Boy.*
*Cast:* Master Johnny—Garrick.

29   Thur.   SA.   *King Lear and His Three Daughters.*
*Cast:* Lear—Garrick; Edgar—R. Elrington; Cordelia—Mrs. Woffington.
*Miscellaneous:* At the particular Desire of several Persons of Quality.
*Singing and Dancing:* Dancing by Signora Barbarini and H. Delamain.

AUGUST

2   Mon.   SA.   *The Constant Couple.*
*Cast:* Sir Harry—Mrs. Woffington.
*Miscellaneous:* By the particular Desire of several Persons of Quality; the last time Garrick or Mrs. Woffington will perform those characters this season.

*Singing and Dancing:* Dancing, Act 2, a Louvre and Minuet by Signora Barbarini and H. Delamain; end of play, a new Scots Dance by Signa. Barbarina, etc.

and

*Afterpiece: The Lying Valet.*
*Cast:* Sharp—Garrick.

5    Thur.    SA.    *The Rehearsal.*
*Cast:* Bayes—Garrick.
*Miscellaneous:* Positively the last time of his appearing in that character this season.
*Singing and Dancing:* Dancing by Signa. Barbarina.

9    Mon.    SA.    *Oroonoko.*
*Cast:* Oroonoko—Walker (from GF).
*Benefit:* H. Delamain (second).
*Miscellaneous:* By the particular Desire of several Persons of Quality.
*Singing and Dancing:* Dancing between every Act by Signora Barbarini and H. Delamain.

12    Thur.    SA.    *Hamlet.*
*Cast:* Hamlet—Garrick (first time in character); Queen—Mrs. Furnival; Ophelia—Mrs. Woffington.
*Command:* Lords Justice.
*Benefit:* Garrick (second).
*Miscellaneous:* By particular desire.
    "Mr. Garrick thinks it proper to acquaint the Town, that he did not take the Fair Penitent (as it was given out) for his Benefit; that play being disapproved of by several Gentlemen and Ladies. . . ."; Last performances by Garrick, Mrs. Woffington and Signora Barbarini [but see below 19 Aug.]
*Singing and Dancing:* Dancing by Signora Barbarini and H. Delamain; particularly a new Musset by Signa. Barbarina and a new Grand Ballet by Signa. Barbarina, Henry Delamain, and others.
[The dances advertised for this evening and subsequent nights may not have been performed. The following letter, probably by Thomas Philips, the SA manager, appeared in *FDJ,* 14 Aug. 1742:

> Whereas an Advertisement was yesterday published and handed about the Coffee Houses, containing a Sort of an Excuse from the Music, for their Non-attendance at the Play house in Smock Alley, on Thurs. the 10th of this Instant August, at the Play of Hamlet, for Mr. Garrett's Benefit: Now being apprehensive that the said Advertisement is calculated to injure the Company of said Theatre in the Opinion of the Town, They therefore think themselves obliged to inform the Public that upon Examination of the Play House Accompt Books, they find that since the Management of the Company has been committed to the Care of the

Persons, now concerned, there is not one Night's Sallery due to the Musick, altho' they insist in their Advertisement that there were 4 Nights; And they further beg Leave to say, that being disappointed of Music on the above Night, they sent to the Band, desiring them to attend as usual, and that whatever appeared to be justly due to them, should the following Day be paid; and tho' two Acts of the Play were then over, the Person who applied to them on the Company's Behalf, offered to pay them down the Money for that Night's Performance, that the Lords Justices who were then in the House might not be disappointed of the Dances mentioned in the Bills: and tho' several of the said Band actually belonged to the Castle and State Music, yet they peremptorily refused to come, as did also Mr. John Blackwood who is an annual Servant to the Company, and had in his Custody the Copies of the Dances, etc. And they further take leave to observe that the said Band carried their ill Behaviour so far as to enter into a Combination to intimidate several other performers from supplying their Places, by threatening, that whoever should play in the Music Rooms of said Theatre, should never be engaged, or concerned in any Band or Concert of Music with them [word illegible] which is humbly submitted to the Consideration of the Public."

Later that week in *DNL,* 17 Aug. 1742, Woder responded that he had applied to Philips: "for arrears of four nights' salary (exclusive of four months' arrears) and told him if they were not by Thursday following paid, or secured to pay in six months the entire amount due them, they would no longer attend the House, to which Phillips replied he would get other Music to attend, which reply [was] reported to the Band . . . so Woder and his Band considered themselves Discharged from that night and every other. [signed] Will. Heron, Fra. Woder, Bart. Manwaring, Tho. Johnson, Geo. Fitzgerald, John Blackwood, Fran. Dowdal, and Will Manwaring."]

19   Thur.   SA.   *The Recruiting Officer.*
*Cast:* Capt. Plume—Garrick; Sylvia—Mrs. Woffington.
*Miscellaneous:* [*PO,* 21–24 Aug. 1742 states that Garrick, Mrs. Cibber, and the other English players returned to England on 23 Aug.]

## 1742–1743 Season

Theatres operating: Aungier St.; Smock Alley.

*Aungier St. Company:*
Mrs. Arne, Baildon (from London), Bardin, Barrington, Bourne, Boyton, Bridges, Miss Davies (singer from CG), Dyer, Mrs. Elmy (until 18 Apr.), F. Elrington, J. Elrington, Mrs. Furnival, Griffith, R. Layfield, Mrs. Pasquilino, Pellish, Master John Carteret Pilkington, Reynolds, I. Sparks, L. Sparks, Swan, Mrs. Sybilla, Thomas Walker, Walsh, J. Watson, Jr.

Dancers: Moreau.

Musicians: Alcock, Anderus, T. A. Arne (conductor), Charles, Jeronimo, John Neale, Master Neale, Short.

Summer: Mlle. Chateauneuf (dancer from England), Havard (from DL), Muilment (dancer from DL), Picq (dancer from CG).

*Repertory:*
Mainpieces: Recorded performances: 64 (of 36 different pieces).
Afterpieces: Recorded performances: 25 performances of 16 different pieces.
Entr'acte entertainments: Singing and/or dancing advertised for many performances after January.
Command Performances: 6 (No Government Nights advertised).
Benefits:
Pre-February: Actor—1.
Post-February: Actor—28; Manager—1; Charity—2.

---

*Smock Alley Company:*
Baker, Mrs. Bayley, Beamsley, Miss Bullock, T. Cibber (from LIF in May), L. Duval, Mrs. Elmy (from AS 18 Apr.), Ralph Elrington, William Este (died 24 Jan. 1743), H. Giffard (from LIF in May), Mrs. Giffard (in May), Husband, Lee, Mrs. Lyon, Mrs. Mitchell, Morgan, J. Morris, Mrs. J. Morris, Oates, Miss Orfeur, T. Philips, Mrs. Reynolds, Richard Sheridan, T. Sheridan, Mrs. Elizabeth Storer (from England), Walker, Wetherilt (died 5 June), Mrs. Wetherilt, Worsdale, Wright.

Tumblers and equilbrists: Dominique, Madame Dominique, Madame German, Guitar, Jonno, "Russian Boy."

Dancers: W. Delamain, P. Morris, Jr., Master Pitt.

Musicians: Cormick, Pockrich (glasses).

House servants: Dryden (treasurer), Neil (boxkeeper), Tyler.

*Repertory:*
Mainpieces: Recorded performances: 74 (of 42 different pieces).
Afterpieces: Recorded performances: 45 performances of 25 different pieces including unspecified farces.
Premieres:
*Harlequin Triumphant.* (a)
*The Rival Beaux.* (a)
Entr'acte entertainments: Equilibres and tumbling earlier in season; singing and/or dancing advertised for most performances from beginning of season.

Command Performances: (No Government Nights advertised).
Benefits:
Pre-February: Actor—5; Charity—4.
Post-February: Actor—23; House Servants—3; Charity—1.

---

**1742**

OCTOBER

11    Mon.    AS.    *The Tender Husband.*
*Cast:* None listed.
*Miscellaneous:* Government Night; Anniversary of Coronation of George II.

30    Sat.    AS.    *The Recruiting Officer.*
*Cast:* None listed.
*Miscellaneous:* Government Night; Anniversary of birth of George II.

NOVEMBER

1    Mon.    SA.    Rope Dancing, Tumbling, Vaulting, Equilibres, and Ground Dancing, etc.
*Cast:* A Company of celebrated Germans, Dutch, Italians, and French.
*Miscellaneous:* "This Company having met with Success in most Courts in Europe, they hope to have the Honour of pleasing in this Kingdom, whose Reputation for encouraging People of Merit, and Elegancy of Taste, is the only Motive of their coming here; and tho' their Stay here can be only to perform at most Ten or Twelve Nights, being all engaged to be at Paris in December, they will perform something New and Surprising every Night, to endeavour to merit the Approbation of so judicious an Assembly" (*DNL*, 26–30 Oct. 1742).

4    Thur.    AS.    *Tamerlane.*
*Cast:* Tamerlane—Swan; Bajezet—Walker (his first appearance on this stage).
*Command:* Lords Justice.
*Miscellaneous:* [Government Night?]; For the entertainment of the Hanover Club; Tamerlane played by the Gentleman who played Othello for Mr. Worsdale's Benefit [i.e. Swan]. With the usual prologue spoken by Sparks.

8    Mon.    AS.    *Cato.*
*Cast:* Cato—Pellish.

8    Mon.    SA.    Rope Dancing, Tumbling, Vaulting, Equilibres, and Ground Dancing, etc.
*Cast:* As 1 Nov. 1742 SA.
*Miscellaneous:* Madam German will dance the Slack Rope, and perform on the Vaulting Rope, never attempted by any Woman in this Kingdom before. The famous Monsr. Dominique and the celebrated Monsr. Guitar, will perform the surprising Tumble over a Man on Horseback, never done here before. The Pierrot to the Rope, and Clown to the Tumbling, to be performed by Jonno.

11    Thur.    SA.    Rope Dancing, Tumbling, Vaulting, Equilibres, and Ground Dancing etc.
*Cast:* As 1 Nov. 1742 SA.

13    Sat.    SA.    Rope Dancing, Tumbling, etc.
*Cast:* As 1 Nov. 1742 SA.

15    Mon.    SA.    Rope Dancing, Tumbling, etc.
*Cast:* As 1 Nov. 1742 SA.
*Miscellaneous:* This Company will perform several Exercises never before done in this Kingdom.

18    Thur.    AS.    *Othello.*
*Cast:* Othello—Swan.
*Miscellaneous:* First Subscription Night. The Manager of AS proposes a subscription series of Shakespeare plays, one a week for eight weeks. Principal characters in each play new dressed. Each Subscriber to take eight box tickets for £1 12s. being 4s. 4d. each; each fourth play to be a new one. Places saved for subscribers up to 6 o'clock; prices raised for non-subscribers.
    [*FDJ,* 1–4 Jan. 1743 contains a prologue, smacking strongly of sour grapes, spoke by Swan on this occasion. Swan suggests that the exotic performances of Dominique and his troupe are hurting AS receipts. The opening lines are worth reproducing here insofar as they help to give us a more vivid conception of the contents of the SA programs of "entertainments."

> Oppressed by foreign Arts, the drooping Stage,
> In Shakespear's Name demands your honest Rage.
> Whilst Anticks vault o'r Sense and Nature's Laws,
> Invade the Muses Seat and gather rude applause
> From Boys who stare away their slender Wits,
> And teeming Dames diverted into Fits.
> With guarded step high poised upon the Rope,
> The Dancer traverses the tottering Slope;
> Wanton extends her half-dressed Limbs in Air
> And kindles Blushes in each modest Fair.

Lo! next succeeds the Tumblers plastick Train
Perversely raising awkward Mirth from Pain;
Degraded in the Serpent's tortuous Coil,
See one climb downwards win ingeneous Toil.
  The next as wide from Nature shows his Skill,
He swallows upwards his preposterous Meal,
Inverts high Heaven's intent in forming Man,
Prone to the Earth his Head, sublime his Feet profane,
Distorted Nature shocks the aching Sight,
And horrid Wonders dreadfully delight.
The vaultring Tribe, to close the Monstrous Scene,
With all their skill prepare the nice Machine;
O'er Tyres of Men, thro' Tubs the gaping Crowd,
Sees Leap Frog spring by mighty force of—Wood.

A good-natured reply to Swan's priggish prologue written by Jonno and published in French ("for want of Knowledge in the English Tongue") appeared in the next issue of *FDJ*, a translation of which was provided the following week.]

and

*Afterpiece: The Mock Lawyer.*
*Cast:* None listed.

18     Thur.     SA.     Rope Dancing, Tumbling, etc.
*Cast:* As 1 Nov. 1742 SA.

22     Mon.     AS.     *The Distrest Mother.*
*Cast:* Hermione—Mrs. Furnival.

22     Mon.     SA.     *The Old Batchelour.*
*Cast:* Belinda—Mrs. Storer (from CG).
*Miscellaneous:* "On Sunday last [i.e. 14 Nov. 1742] arrived from Liverpool, the SA Company of Comedians, and on Monday next intend to entertain the Town with Shakespear's Tempest . . . the Part of Dorinda to be performed by Mrs. Storer from the Theatre-Royal, Covent Garden, in which she will introduce several Songs proper to the Character" (*DNL,* 13–16 Nov. 1742).
*Singing and Dancing:* Mrs. Storer will sing several songs proper to the character.

and

*Afterpiece: The Contrivances.*
*Cast:* Lovewell—Baker (his first appearance in this Kingdom); Arethusa—Mrs. Storer.
*Singing and Dancing:* Mrs. Storer will sing all the songs proper to the character.

23     Tues.     SA.     Rope Dancing, Tumbling, etc.

*Cast:* As 1 Nov. 1742     SA.

*Miscellaneous:* Particularly, M. Guitar will dance on the Rope with two Boys first, and afterwards two Men tied to his Feet. M. Dominique will perform the Running Board, with several new Tumbles off it, never seen before; he fires off two Pistols when he makes the great Somerset. He also performs (being desired) the Equiliber of the Table. The Russian Boy will perform a new surprizing Equiliber of the Chairs, supported by four small Spindles a Foot and a half high, never seen here before.

25     Thur.     AS.     *The Merry Wives of Windsor.*
*Cast:* Mrs. Page—Mrs. Furnival.
*Miscellaneous:* Second Subscription Night.

"Whereas there have been great complaints made by the Ladies that the Boxes in the Aungier Street Playhouse were excessive cold, the Manager of said Theatre thinks proper to advertize, that apprehending the same proceeded from Holes cut in the Door by Servants waiting in the Passage, and want of Curtains over the door, he has made all the Boxes quite close, and gotten Curtains to every Door, and given orders that no Servants shall wait in said Passage, which he hopes will answer, and if not [he] will execute any Method [he] shall be advized [of] for warming the House, or otherwise for the Convenience and Satisfaction of the Audience, [and] he has likewise got a new Set of Lamps to burn Tallow at the Front of the Stage, the Oyle being offensive, and has mended all the Seats round the House" (*FDJ,* 23 Nov. 1742).

27     Sat.     SA.     Rope Dancing, Tumbling, etc.
*Cast:* As 1 Nov. 1742 SA.
*Miscellaneous:* Particularly, Madam German performs the surprising Jump over the Ribbon on the Rope, and dances with Fetters on her Feet. M. Guitar and M. Dominique perform the surprising Tumble over the Double Fountain, never performed here. M. Dominique will perform several Tumbles and Equilibers with the Chair, and also performs the Great Somersets backwards and forwards off the Plank 18 Foot high.

29     Mon.     AS.     *King Henry IV, with the Humours of Falstaff.*
*Cast:* None listed.
*Miscellaneous:* Third Subscription Night.
                              and
*Afterpiece: Damon and Phillida.*
*Cast:* Phillida—Miss Davies (from CG); Damon—Reynolds.

29     Mon.     SA.     *The Beggar's Opera.*
*Cast:* Macheath—Mrs. Reynolds; Polly—Mrs. Storer.

**DECEMBER**

2  Thur.  SA.  *The Beggar's Opera.*
*Cast:* None listed.

and

*Afterpiece: The Contrivances.*
*Cast:* None listed.

4  Sat.  SA.  Rope Dancing, Tumbling, etc.
*Cast:* As 1 Nov. 1742 SA.
*Miscellaneous:* Particularly, Madam German performs on the Rope with Rowlers on her Feet. Guitar tumbles over 12 Men with 24 Swords. And Dominique performs the surprising Equiliber of the Hoop, in which he will stand on his Head, and is drawn up 40 Foot high, then fires a Pistol, and is let down in the same Posture.

6  Mon.  AS.  *Twelfth Night.*  V.
*Cast:* None listed.
*Miscellaneous:* Fourth Subscription Night. Never acted in this Kingdom before; with new habits proper to the play.

7  Tues.  SA.  Rope Dancing, Tumbling, etc.
*Cast:* As 1 Nov. 1742 SA.
*Miscellaneous:* By Permission of the Rt. Hon. Luke Gardiner. With entertainments, Particularly, Madam German performs on the Rope with Stilts, never done here but once and will also perform on the Slack Rope. The Russian Boy performs some new Equilibres. Dominique performs the surprising Equilibes of the Circle never attempted by any but himself, in which he will stand on his Head, and is drawn up 40 feet high, then fires two Pistols, and is let down in the same Posture. He also tumbles through the Hogshead, with a fire in the middle and a lighted torch in each hand. Guitar and Dominique perform the surprising Tumble of the Double Fountain. [Playbill quoted in Hitchcock 1788–94, 1:122.]

9  Thur.  AS.  *Twelfth Night.*
*Cast:* None listed.
*Miscellaneous:* Acted but once in this Kingdom; with habits proper to the play.

9  Thur.  SA.  *The Tempest.*  V.
*Cast:* Dorinda and Amphitrite—Mrs. Storer.
*Comment:* "We hear the Smock Alley Company leave Liverpool the first fair Wind, and intend to open the Theatre here, with the Tempest; or, The Enchanted Island, the Part of Dorinda with the Song of "Dear Pretty Youth,"

and several other songs proper for the Character, to be performed by Mrs. Sterer [Storer] from the Theatre-Royal in Covent Garden, London" (*DG*, 9–13 Nov. 1742).

". . . (having procured the original Music for the Tempest) in order to have the same done in the most regular Manner they do not perform there on Monday next [i.e. 6 Dec.], being obliged to make great Alterations to the Stage" (*DG*, 30 Nov.–4 Dec. 1742).

"We hear they are making great Preparations at the Theatre in Smock-Alley for reviving of the Tempest on Thursday next, with the Songs, Dances, Sinkings, Flyings, Machinery, and all other Decorations, as performed at the Theatres in London. The Music was composed by the late famous Mr. Henry Purcel, and taken from the best Manuscript, being sent over by Mr. Garrick on this Occasion. The Scenes, Machines, Dresses, and other Decorations, are entirely new" (*DG*, 4–7 Dec. 1742). [Walsh 1973, 75, doubts that Purcell's music was used in this production.]

10    Fri.    SA.    Rope Dancing, Tumbling, etc.
*Cast:* None listed.

13    Mon.    AS.    *Julius Caesar.*
*Cast:* None listed.
*Miscellaneous:* Fifth Subscription Night.

13    Mon.    SA.    *The Tempest.*
*Cast:* As 9 Dec. 1742.

14    Tues.    SA.    *The Beggar's Opera.*
*Cast:* Macheath—J. Morris; Polly—Mrs. Storer.
*Benefit:* A Child that has the Money of the House Owing.
*Miscellaneous:* At the particular Desire of several Persons of Quality. [*Double Dealer* and *Mock Doctor* originally advertised but changed at the particular desire of several Ladies of Quality.]
*Singing and Dancing:* With several Entertainments of Dancing.
and
*Afterpiece: The Mock Doctor.*
*Cast:* None listed.

16    Thur.    AS.    *Twelfth Night.*
*Cast:* None listed.
*Miscellaneous:* With new habits proper to the play.

16    Thur.    SA.    *The Wonder, A Woman Keeps a Secret.*
*Cast:* None listed.
*Benefit:* Mrs. Storer.

*Miscellaneous:* Never acted here. [An Epilogue, spoken by Walker on Mrs. Storer's benefit night, is quoted in full in *DNL,* 18–21 Dec. 1742.]
*Singing and Dancing:* Several Entertainments of Singing and Dancing between the Acts. Singing by Mrs. Storer.

and

*Afterpiece: The Virgin Unmasked.*
*Cast:* Lucy—Mrs. Storer.

20     Mon.     SA.     *Hamlet.*
*Cast:* None listed.

and

*Afterpiece: The Queen of Spain; or, Farinelli in Madrid.*
*Cast:* Farinelli—Mrs. Storer.
*Miscellaneous:* A Tragical, Comical, Operatical, Farcical, Pantomimical and Political Burlesque Scene between the King and Queen of Spain, Farinelli, and English Sailors, on the Posture of Affairs as they stood in the Beginning of Admiral Vernon's Expedition to America.
    Being the first time of her appearing in boy's cloathes in this Kingdom.

21     Tues.     SA.     *The Grand Sultan; or, Harlequin Captive.*
*Cast:* Grand Sultan—Dominique; Harlequin—Jonno; Pierrot—Guitar; Sultaness—Madame German; Columbine—Madame Dominique (from Paris; her first appearance in Ireland).
*Miscellaneous:* [Premiere of anonymous pantomime, though probably by Dominique.] With performances on the rope and new tumbling.
*Singing and Dancing:* With a Tambourine dance.

22     Wed.     SA.     *The Beggar's Opera.*
*Cast:* Macheath—Walker (who performed it originally at the theatres in London); Polly—Mrs. Storer.
*Benefit:* Walker.
*Miscellaneous:* Walker performed the character over 300 times in London, oftner than any character was ever played by one person.
    Mr. Walker having received an Epilogue (which he gratefully acknowledges) from an unknown Hand designs to make the intended Use of it.

and

*Afterpiece: Hob; or, The Country Wake.*
*Cast:* None listed.

27     Mon.     SA.     *The Grand Sultan.*
*Cast:* As 21 Dec. 1742.
*Miscellaneous:* It is hoped no Gentleman will take it amiss being refused Admittance behind the Scenes, the Stage being so crowded the last Night,

the Performers could not possibly go through with the Entertainment as they intended, with several new Additions.

30    Thur.    SA.    *The Grand Sultan.*
*Cast:* Pierrot—J. Morris; Sultan—Mons. Dominique; Harlequin—Jonno; Colombine—Madame Dominique.
*Miscellaneous:* Also rope dancing and tumbling. [*The Double Dealer* and *The Dragon of Wantley* originally advertised for this night.]


**1743**


JANUARY


1    Sat.    AS.    *Othello.*
*Cast:* None listed.


3    Mon.    AS.    *The Royal Merchant.*
*Cast:* King Clause—F. Elrington (his first appearance since his late indisposition).
*Miscellaneous:* Seventh Subscription Night.
*Deferred: As You Like It* originally advertised but deferred by desire of the Subscribers.
                               and
*Afterpiece: Damon and Phillida.*
*Cast:* Phillida—Miss Davies.


3    Mon.    SA.    *The Double Dealer.*
*Cast:* None listed.
                               and
*Afterpiece: The Dragon of Wantley.*
*Cast:* Margery—Mrs. Storer.
*Singing and Dancing:* With all the Songs, Recitativo, original Musick composed by Mr. Lampe, and with Decorations as perfect as at Covent Garden.
*Comment:* "The Dragon of Wantley . . . met with extraordinary Applause in London, having been acted at CG upwards of 40 Nights successively. This Piece is reckoned equal in its Ridicule to the Beggar's Opera, but greatly exceeding it in the Musick, which is in as grand a Taste as that of the Italian Operas, the Burlesque being confined to the Poverty of Expression, ill Choice and Inconsistency of the Fable, and ridiculous Incidents generally running through those darling Amusements" (*DNL,* 28 Dec. 1742–1 Jan. 1743).

4     Tues.     SA.     *The Grand Sultan.*
*Cast:* As 30 Dec. 1742.
*Miscellaneous:* The stage being kept clear the last Night of Performance, the Entertainment was done to the Satisfaction of the whole Assembly.

6     Thur.     SA.     *Hamlet.*
*Cast:* None listed.
*Miscellaneous:* All characters entirely new dressed.
and

*Afterpiece: The Dragon of Wantley.*
*Cast:* None listed.
*Singing and Dancing:* With the original music, composed by Mr. Lampe, songs, recitativo, and all decorations as performed in London.

10     Mon.     AS.     *Comus.*     V.
*Cast:* Comus—Swan; First Spirit—L. Sparks; Second Spirit—Watson; Elder Brother—Bardin; Younger Brother—J. Elrington; Lady—Mrs. Elmy; Pastoral Nymph and Sabrina—Mrs. Arne; Chief Bachannal—Baildon (from London); Second Pastoral Nymph—Mrs. Sybilla; Euphrosyne—Miss Davies. [Hitchcock, 1:127, ascribes this role to Mrs. Baildon.]
*Miscellaneous:* With new Habits, Scenes, Machines, Risings, Sinkings, Flyings and other Decorations. Original prologue spoke by Swan, epilogue by Mrs. Furnival. Pit and boxes laid together at 5s. 5d., Lattices 5s. 5d., Gallery, 2s. 8½d. because of the great expence of the Production.
*Singing and Dancing:* Mr. Arne will accompany the performance on the harpsicord; the Orchestra will be doubled and there will be a row in the pit for the music; Mrs. Arne will sing "Sweet Echo" accompanied by Mr. Neal from England, who performed it originally; Mrs. Sybilla is a Scholar of Mr. Arne's; all choruses performed in parts as originally in England and never done here before.

10     Mon.     SA.     *The Spanish Fryar.*
*Cast:* None listed.
*Singing and Dancing:* Singing between the acts by Mrs. Storer.
and

*Afterpiece: The Hussar; or, Harlequin Restored.*
*Cast:* None listed.

11     Tues.     SA.     *Harlequin Triumphant in His Amours.*
*Cast:* Harlequin—Jonno; Petit Maitre—Guitar; Pierrot—Dominique; Scaramouche—P. Morris, Jr.; Columbine—Madame Dominique.
*Benefit:* Jonno (tumbler).
*Miscellaneous:* [Anonymous pantomime probably by Dominique.] In which will be introduced the scene of the Skeleton, in the French Manner; Being

the last Time of performing in this Kingdom. Guitar will tumble over 15 men's heads with four boys on his shoulders; Dominique will tumble the Double Fountain.

*Singing and Dancing:* With several Entertainments of Dancing, by Jonno, Cormick, and others.


13    Thur.    AS.    *Comus.*    V.
*Cast:* As 10 Jan. 1743.


13    Thur.    SA.    *The Tempest.*
*Cast:* Dorinda and Amphitrite—Mrs. Storer.

and

*Afterpiece: The Hussar.*
*Cast:* None listed.


15    Sat.    SA.    Rope Dancing, Tumbling, etc.
*Cast:* Guitar, etc.
*Benefit:* Guitar.
*Miscellaneous:* Guitar will go through the whole Exercise of Tumbling, never seen here before; he will tumble over 15 men's Heads with five Boys on his Shoulders; he will also perform the tumble of the Arch, never done here before. He will likewise perform on the Rope with two Men tied to his Feet.


17    Mon.    AS.    *Comus.*
*Cast:* As 10 Jan. 1743.
*Miscellaneous:* It is hoped it will not be taken ill, that none can be admitted behind the Scenes; Mr. Swan advertised the Publick, that whereas the Town are desirous to see the Masque of Comus at the usual Prices, notwithstanding it is really performed at a much greater Expence than any Theatrical Entertainment exhibited in this Kingdom; yet not being entirely new (tho' all the Musical Parts were never performed here) it will be performed on Monday next at 5s. 5d. Boxes and Lattices; Pit 3s. 3d., Gallery 2s. 2d.


17    Mon.    SA.    *The Tempest.*
*Cast:* Dorinda and Amphitrite—Mrs. Storer.
*Miscellaneous:* Several Entertainments between the Acts.
*Singing and Dancing:* In which will be introduced a new Political Ballad on the Behaviour of the French General in Bohemia and the United Fleets of France and Spain at Toulon, written and sung by Mr. Worsdale in the character of a Sailor.

and

*Afterpiece: The Hussar.*
*Cast:* None listed.

18    Tues.    SA.    *Harlequin Triumphant in His Amours.*
*Cast:* None listed.
*Benefit:* Dominique, Madame German, and the Russian Boy (tumblers).
*Miscellaneous:* By Particular Desire; with new scenes, particularly Harlequin enfant trouve; Being positively the last time of performing in this Kingdom.
    Madame German will perform stiff rope and sword dances never seen here; two boys will perform on the rope; A great Variety of new Tumbling by Dominique, particularly his tumbling through a Hogshead with 24 Swords pointed at each End; Jonno will perform The Pierrot on the Rope.
*Singing and Dancing:* With entertainments of comic dancing by Mr. Cormick, etc., particularly a dance between Harlequin and Harlequinetta by Dominique and Madame German.

20    Thur.    AS.    *The Provoked Husband.*    V.
*Cast:* None listed.
*Command:* Lords Justice.
*Miscellaneous:* With a new prologue for the day written by Mr. Griffith, author of the state prologues, spoken by Mr. Bardin.
*Comment:* The Lords Justice were present this evening and there was a splendid appearance of Ladies (*DG,* 18–22 Jan. 1743).

20    Thur.    SA.    *The Tempest.*
*Cast:* Dorinda and Amphitrite—Mrs. Storer.
                                    and
*Afterpiece: The Hussar.*
*Cast:* None listed.
*Singing and Dancing:* In which will be introduced the new Political Ballad on the Behaviour of the French Generals in Bohemia, and the United Fleets of France and Spain at Toulon, written and sung by Mr. Worsdale in the Character of a Sailor.

24    Mon.    AS.    *Comus.*
*Cast:* As 10 Jan. 1743 AS.
*Miscellaneous:* The last time of performing it this season.
*Comment:* "It having been insinuated that the Masque of Comus is performed on Monday Night with intent to oppose the intended Charity of Vicar's Street Society, Mr. Swan advertises the publick, that he is willing to defer the same till Tuesday, if said Society will defer their Club, and provide him a sufficient band of music, otherwise he hopes the Town will excuse him, there being no other day this Season on which the same can possibly be performed, the principal person's being engaged to play at their Club every Tuesday" (*FDJ,* 18–22 Jan. 1743).

24    Mon.    SA.    *The Recruiting Officer.*
*Cast:* None listed.
*Benefit:* Fund for Reception of Sick and Wounded Poor taken into Dr. Stevens's Hospital.
*Miscellaneous:* By appointment of the Charitable Musical Society in Vicar's St.
*Singing and Dancing:* With several Entertainments of Dancing.
*Deferred:* From 15 Jan.

and

*Afterpiece:* Unspecified "Farce."


26    Wed.    SA.    *The Committee.*
*Cast:* Teague—J. Morris.
*Benefit:* Tomasin Jones and her Distrest Parents.
*Singing and Dancing:* With several Entertainments of Dancing.
*Deferred:* Deferred from 25 Jan. 1743 at the particular desire of several Ladies of Quality.

and

*Afterpiece: The Devil to Pay.*
*Cast:* None listed.


27    Thur.    AS.    *Twelfth Night.*
*Cast:* None listed.
*Benefit:* L. Sparks.
*Singing and Dancing:* Entertainments of Singing and Dancing.

and

*Afterpiece: The Vintner Tricked [; or, A Match at Newgate].*
*Cast:* None listed.
*Miscellaneous:* Never acted here. [Anonymous farce. Although Clark 1965, 337, attributes authorship to Henry Ward, the authorship of this farce remains unclear. It is perhaps an adaptation of Aphra Behn's *The [Woman's] Revenge; or, A Match at Newgate.* The advertisement for 28 Feb. 1743 AS indicates the full title of the afterpiece as above. *LS* lists Bullock's play, *A Match in Newgate; or, The Vintner Tricked,* as well as two farces with this title: one, anon. 9 Apr. 1746 DL; the other by Henry Ward, HAY 7 June 1769 with performances for several seasons thereafter. Nicoll (1977–79, 2:363) lists two pieces with this main title, the one by Henry Ward, (but premiering DL Apr. 1746); and a farce by Joseph Yarrow entitled *Trick upon Trick; or, The Vintner Outwitted,* York 1742 (2:364); he does not list Bullock's comedy by this title but cites Aphra Behn's.]

28    Fri.    SA.    *Rule a Wife and Have a Wife.*
*Cast:* None listed.
*Benefit:* A Distressed Family.
*Singing and Dancing:* With several Entertainments of Dancing.
*Deferred:* Deferred from 20 Jan. 1743 due to the birthday of Prince of Wales.

and

*Afterpiece: A Cure for a Scold.*
*Cast:* None listed.


29    Sat.    SA.    *King Richard III.* V.
*Cast:* Gloster—a Gentleman [i.e. Thomas Sheridan] (his first appearance on any stage).
*Miscellaneous:* "As not only the Players but the Audience in general, have frequently complained of the ill Effects of a crowded Stage, it is to be hoped that no Gentleman will take it ill that he is refused admittance behind the Scenes on that Night, under the above-mentioned Price [half-guinea], but more particularly on this Occasion; it is to be hoped his Complaisance will be greater, when he considers that the Confusion which a Person must necessarily be under on his first appearance, will be greatly heightened by having a Number of People about him, and his Perplexity on his Exits and Entrances, (things with which he is but little acquainted) must be greatly increased by having a Crowd to bustle thro'" (*FDJ,* 22–25 Jan. 1743).
*Singing and Dancing:* With several Entertainments of Singing and Dancing between the acts.
*Comment:* "Saturday Night last the celebrated Play of Richard III was exhibited at the Theatre in Smock Alley, to a most polite and crowded Audience, who expressed the highest Satisfaction and Approbation of the Performance. It was in particular allowed, by all the judicious, that the Gentleman who played King Richard, in most Parts of that Character vastly excelled whatever had at any Time been seen [in] the Kingdom before" (*DG,* 25 Jan.–1 Feb. 1743).


FEBRUARY


1    Tues.    SA.    *The Busy Body.*
*Cast:* None listed.
*Benefit:* John Neale (hautboy from London).
*Singing and Dancing:* Between the Acts Neale will perform solos and concertos on the Hautboy and a piece on the German flute; Mr. Charles and his Second, a French Horn Concerto; Mrs. Storer, a Song; Master Neale, a 10 year-old, will perform a Violin Concerto and "Elin-a-Roon" with all Variations.

                                    and
*Afterpiece: The Lying Valet.*
*Cast:* Sharp—Wetherilt.


2    Wed.    AS.    *The Mourning Bride.*
*Cast:* None listed.
*Benefit:* Bridges.
*Singing and Dancing:* With Entertainments.
                                    and
*Afterpiece: Damon and Phillida.*
*Cast:* None listed.


3    Thur.    AS.    *Comus.*
*Cast:* Comus—Swan; Principal Bacchanal—Baildon (from London); Second
Pastoral Nymph–Mrs. Sybilla (a Scholar of Mr. Arne's); Pastoral Nymph
and Sabrina—Mrs. Arne.
*Benefit:* Bardin.
*Miscellaneous:* Brought forward from 10 Feb.
*Singing and Dancing:* "Sweet Echo"—Mrs. Arne, accompanied by Mr.
Neale from England, who performed it originally; with all the Choruses in
Parts as originally in England, and never performed here before; the whole
conducted by Mr. Arne, who accompanies the Performance on the Harp-
sicord.


3    Thur.    SA.    *Mithridates.* V.
*Cast:* Mithridates—Sheridan.
*Miscellaneous:* Never performed here before. By Racine. [Translator
anonymous.]
     "As several People have imagined on Account of the Name, that this play
is the same, or much of a piece with Lee's Mithradates: This is to assure
the Public, that this is exactly taken from Racine. Those who understand
French may easily see that neither the Story, the Plot, the Circumstances,
or the Characters, have the least Affinity with the other" (*FDJ*, 18–22 Jan.
1743). [Nicoll lists only the versions by Lee and Kimble 1802; *LS* lists an
anonymous 1722 translation of Racine's play.]


4    Fri.    SA.    *Volpone.*
*Cast:* None listed.
*Benefit:* J. Morris.
                                    and
*Afterpiece: The Brave Irishman; or, Captain O'Blunder.*
*Cast:* O'Blunder—J. Morris.
*Miscellaneous:* A new farce. [By Thomas Sheridan. *DNL*, 22–25 Jan. 1743
gives the title: *Captain O'Blunder; or, The Brave Irishman*].

7    Mon.    AS.    *The Scornful Lady.*
*Cast:* The Scornful Lady—Mrs. Furnival.
*Command:* Lords Justice.
*Benefit:* Mrs. Furnival.
*Miscellaneous:* Never acted in this Kingdom; At the particular Desire of several Ladies of Quality.

and

*Afterpiece: Flora.*
*Cast:* None listed.

7    Mon.    SA.    *Othello.*
*Cast:* Othello—R. Elrington.
*Benefit:* Ralph Elrington.

and

*Afterpiece: The Dragon of Wantley.*
*Cast:* None listed.

9    Wed.    AS.    *The Miser.*
*Cast:* Lovegold—F. Elrington.
*Benefit:* F. Elrington.
*Miscellaneous:* For the Entertainment of the Lords Justice.

10    Thur.    AS.    *Love and Glory.*
*Cast:* None listed.
*Benefit:* Mrs. Arne.
*Miscellaneous:* Words by Thomas Philips; music by T. A. Arne. A Grand Sonata by Mr. Arne in Honour of the Nuptials of the Prince and Princess of Wales; Pit, Boxes and Lattices laid together at 5s. 5d.; upper Gallery 1s. 6d.

and

*Afterpiece: Miss Lucy in Town.*
*Cast:* None listed.
*Miscellaneous:* A new farce.
*Singing and Dancing:* All the Songs composed by Arne. As performed at TR DL.

11    Fri.    SA.    *The Squire of Alsatia.*
*Cast:* None listed.
*Benefit:* Wetherilt.
*Miscellaneous:* With several Entertainments between the Acts.
*Deferred:* Deferred from 10 Feb. 1743.

and

*Afterpiece: The Rival Beaux; or, Vanity Reclaimed.*
*Cast:* None listed.

*Miscellaneous:* Includes a humourous scene (taken from life) between an eminent painter and a celebrated actress.

[Premiere of anonymous farce. Not listed in Nicoll or *LS. Lying Valet* originally advertised.]

12    Sat.    AS.    *Love for Love.*

*Cast:* Valentine—Swan (his first appearance in character); Angelica—Mrs. Furnival.

*Benefit:* Charles (French Horn musician).

*Miscellaneous:* No Servant to be admitted into the Upper Gallery without a Ticket from Mr. Charles. Five tickets to each subscriber at one guinea for a box, 12 British shillings for the pit, and 8 British shillings for the gallery; charge to non-subscribers: Boxes, 5s. 5d.; Pit, 3s. 3d.; Gallery, 2s. 2d.

*Singing and Dancing:* With a grand [subscription] concert of vocal and instrumental music; before the play the Overture in *Artaxerxes* with French Horns, Kettle Drums, Trumpets, composed by Sig. Vinci; End Act 1, a favourite hunting song called "The Early Horn" by Mr. Baildon (being the first time of his singing in that Character in this Kingdom) accompanied with the French Horn by Mr. Charles; End Act 2, French Horn Solo by Charles to show the perfection of the instrument; End Act 3, a favourite song by Miss Davis, composed by Mr. Arne; End Act 4, clarinet concerto by Charles; End of Play, grand concert, overture in *Saul* with the Dead march, I. A song by Mr Baildon; II. The Water Music, III. The March in *Scipio,* IV. Grand Chorus in *Atalanta,* composed by Mr. Handel.

and

*Afterpiece: The Vintner Tricked.*

*Cast:* Visard—Sparks.

*Miscellaneous:* [*FDJ,* 8–12 Feb. 1743 cites title as *A Match at Newgate; or, The Vintner Tricked.*]

14    Mon.    AS.    *Comus.*

*Cast:* None listed.

*Command:* Lords Justice.

*Benefit:* Swan.

*Miscellaneous:* [*Love for Love* originally advertised, Valentine—Swan.]

*Deferred:* Deferred from 8 Feb. 1743.

14    Mon.    SA.    *The Island Princess; or, The Generous Portuguese.*

*Cast:* Armusia—R. Elrington; Quisara—Mrs. Storer.

*Benefit:* T. Philips.

*Miscellaneous:* First performance in this Kingdom [but see performances of 5 Oct. 1732 and earlier]. With all the original music, songs, dances, and other Decorations.

*Singing and Dancing:* Music procured from DL. Several songs in character by Mrs. Storer. Entertainments between the Acts, viz. Act 1, The Dialogue beginning "Since Times are so Bad" by Morris and Mrs. Reynolds; in Act 2, an Entertainment between Vulcan and Venus by Worsdale and Mrs. Bailey; Act 3, "Lovely Charmer" by Mrs. Storer, "The Rake and the Widow" by Morris and Worsdale; Act 4, "Stay John e'er You Leave Me" by Worsdale and Mrs. Reynolds, "The Enthusiastic Song" by Baker.

With the original prologue sung by Mrs. Reynolds.

*Comment:* "Sir: As the Opera of the Island Princess is to be performed on Monday next at the TRSA, I had the Curiosity to hear a Practice of it, and I own it gave me a good deal of Satisfaction to hear so much of the great Purcell's Productions performed in so agreeable a Manner; for, in Justice to the Performers, I must say, they have truly entered into the Humour of the Comick Songs, the Serious ones, with the Epilogue, will be performed to great Satisfaction by Mrs. Storer" (*DNL,* 5–8 Feb. 1743).

and

*Afterpiece: Hymen.*
*Cast:* Hymen—Worsdale; Married Couple—Mrs. Lyon and Mrs. Reynolds; Followers of Hymen—Delamain, Lee, Baker, Oates, Morgan, Miss Bullock, Mrs. Wetherilt, and Mrs. Bayley.
*Miscellaneous:* With the original epilogue sung by Mrs. Storer.

17    Thur.    SA.    *The Amorous Widow; or, The Wanton Wife.*
*Cast:* None listed.
*Benefit:* Dryden (treasurer).
*Miscellaneous:* Never acted here.
*Singing and Dancing:* With a great variety of singing and dancing.

and

*Afterpiece: The Dragon of Wantley.*
*Cast:* None listed.

18    Fri.    AS.    *Amphitryon; or, The Two Sosias.*
*Cast:* None listed.
*Benefit:* Barrington.

and

*Afterpiece: The Vintner Tricked.*
*Cast:* None listed.
*Miscellaneous:* [Title given as *The Match in Newgate.*]
With the Roaratorio.

21    Mon.    SA.    *King Richard III.*
*Cast:* Gloster—Sheridan.
*Benefit:* Thomas Sheridan.
*Miscellaneous:* "N. B. Whereas several unruly Persons, disguised like Servants, endeavoured to break down the Partition between the Gallery for the

Footmen and the Pay Gallery, the last Play Night [i.e. this night]: At the particular Desire of several Gentlemen and Ladies then present, the Managers have ordered that no one be admitted but such as have tickets given them by the Box keeper; and do hereby promise a Reward of two Guineas to any Person or Persons who shall discover any one of the said Offenders, so that they may be convicted according to Law" (*DNL*, 22–26 Feb. 1743).

22    Tues.    AS.    *Love Makes a Man.*
*Cast:* None listed.
*Benefit:* The Dublin Society.
*Miscellaneous:* By Appointment to the Bull's Head Society, profits to go to the Dublin Society for the Improvement of Husbandry and other useful Arts; the Lord Mayor and Aldermen to be present.
                                    and
*Afterpiece:* Unspecified "Farce."

23    Wed.    AS.    *Jane Shore.*
*Cast:* None listed.
*Benefit:* Moreau.
*Singing and Dancing:* Several entertainments of singing and dancing.
                                    and
*Afterpiece:* Unspecified "Farce."

24    Thur.    AS.    *The Country Wife.*
*Cast:* None listed.
*Benefit:* Mrs. Elmy.
*Singing and Dancing:* Several entertainments of singing and dancing.
                                    and
*Afterpiece: The What D'Ye Call It.*
*Cast:* None listed.

26    Sat.    AS.    *The Distrest Mother.*
*Cast:* Pyrrhus—L. Sparks; Orestes—J. Elrington; Andromache—Mrs. Pasquilino; Hermione—Mrs. Furnival.
*Benefit:* Griffith.
*Singing and Dancing:* Dancing by Moreau; Songs by Miss Davis, particularly "Brow of the Hill" being desired; end of Play, Barrington will give his Roaratorio after the Italian Manner; all Songs adapted to the Occasion.
*Deferred:* From 21 Feb. because of Griffith's "tedious Indisposition."
                                    and
*Afterpiece: Flora.*
*Cast:* Hob—R. Layfield; Flora—Miss Davis.

28    Mon.    AS.    *As You Like It.*
*Cast:* None listed.
*Benefit:* Mrs. Pasquilino.
*Miscellaneous:* Several unspecified entertainments.
and

*Afterpiece: A Match in Newgate; or, The Vintner Tricked.*
*Cast:* None listed.

**MARCH**

3    Thur.    AS.    *The Scornful Lady.*
*Cast:* None listed.
*Benefit:* R. Layfield.
*Singing and Dancing:* With Entertainments.
and

*Afterpiece:* Unspecified "Farce."

3    Thur.    SA.    *Hamlet.* V.
*Cast:* Hamlet—Sheridan.
*Singing and Dancing:* Several entertainments of singing and dancing.
*Deferred:* Deferred from 24 Feb., then 28 Feb. when it was advertised that Sheridan had recovered from "his late Indisposition."

7    Mon.    AS.    *Cato.*
*Cast:* Cato—Swan.
*Deferred:* From 3 Mar., then 5 Mar. "because the extraordinary Hands of Musick were engaged at the Assembly."
and

*Afterpiece: Miss Lucy in Town.*
*Cast:* None listed.
*Singing and Dancing:* With vocal parts by Baildon, Mrs. Sybilla, and Miss Davis.

7    Mon.    SA.    *The Twin Rivals.*
*Cast:* None listed.
*Benefit:* Neil (boxkeeper) and Mrs. Wetherilt.
*Singing and Dancing:* Several entertainments of singing and dancing.
and

*Afterpiece:* Unspecified "Farce."

10    Thur.    SA.    *King Henry IV, with the Humours of Falstaff.*
*Cast:* Falstaff—J. Morris; Hotspur—R. Elrington; King Henry—Husband; Prince of Wales—Wright.
*Benefit:* W. Delamain.
*Miscellaneous:* At the Desire of several Ladies of Quality.

*Singing and Dancing:* Entertainments: Before play, a Grand Concert of Music, Charles will perform on the French Horn; after Act 1, song "The Brow of the Hill" by Mrs. Storer; Act 2, Dance by Delamain; Act 3, French Horn Solo, Charles; Act 4, a new Song, by Worsdale; Act 5, Dance by Delamain.

and

*Afterpiece:* Unspecified "Farce."


11    Fri.    AS.    *Tamerlane.*
*Cast:* Bajazet—A Gentleman from England.


14    Mon.    SA.    *The Merchant of Venice.*
*Cast:* Shylock—Wright; Launcelot—Wetherilt; Portia—Mrs. Wetherilt.
*Benefit:* Beamsley.
*Singing and Dancing:* With Entertainments of Singing and Dancing.

and

*Afterpiece: The Dragon of Wantley.*
*Cast:* None listed.


17    Thur.    SA.    *Julius Caesar.* V.
*Cast:* Brutus—T. Sheridan.
*Miscellaneous:* At the particular Desire of several Persons of Quality; All the principal Characters to be entirely new Dressed.
*Singing and Dancing:* Singing by Mrs. Storer; Entertainments of Dancing.


21    Mon.    SA.    *A Bold Stroke for a Wife.*
*Cast:* None listed.
*Benefit:* Gregory, Guitar, and Morgan.
*Miscellaneous:* At the Desire of several Ladies of Quality; last time of Guitar's performing in this Kingdom; Not acted here these four years.
*Singing and Dancing:* After Act 1, a Peasant dance by Mr. Guitar; Act 2, a dance by Delamain; Act 4, a song by Mrs. Storer.

After the play a variety of tumbling by Mr. Guitar, particularly, he will vault over the largest Horse that can be procured with a Man on him, and three Men before his Head. He will likewise perform the great and surprising Tumble (never performed in this Kingdom) of the Arch. He will also tumble over a Ribon ten Feet from the Ground, he being the only Man that ever performed it. And several other entertainments of Tumbling, never performed in this Kingdom before, particularly, he vaults over a Giant 8 Foot 3 inches high.

and

*Afterpiece: The Stage Coach*
*Cast:* Maccahone—J. Morris.

24   Thur.   AS.    *The Fatal Marriage; or, The Innocent Adultery.*
*Cast:* None listed.
*Benefit:* I. Sparks and Dyer.
*Miscellaneous:* Several unspecified entertainments.

and

*Afterpiece: The Vintner Tricked.*
*Cast:* None listed.

24   Thur.   SA.    *The Beaux' Stratagem.*
*Cast:* None listed.
*Benefit:* Oates.
*Miscellaneous:* The last time of the Company's performing until after the Easter holidays.
*Singing and Dancing:* With Dancing by Delamain and others.
*Deferred:* Deferred from 23 Mar. 1743.

and

*Afterpiece: The Country Wedding; or, The Nuptials of Roger and Jean.*
*Cast:* None listed.
*Miscellaneous:* The Comic part from *Acis and Galatea.* [See 21 May 1733 SA].

25   Fri.   SA.    *Hamlet.*
*Cast:* Hamlet—T. Sheridan.
*Miscellaneous:* At the Desire of several Ladies of Quality.
*Singing and Dancing:* Several entertainments of singing and dancing.

[Passion Week 28 March–2 April]

APRIL

4   Mon.   SA.    *Julius Caesar.*
*Cast:* Brutus—Sheridan.
*Miscellaneous:* At the Desire of several Ladies of Quality; All Characters new dressed.

7   Thur.   SA.    *King Richard III.*
*Cast:* Gloster—Sheridan.
*Miscellaneous:* At the particular Desire of several Persons of Quality.

11   Mon.   AS.    *The Fair Penitent.*
*Cast:* Calista—Mrs. Furnival.
*Benefit:* Mrs. Furnival.
*Miscellaneous:* Several unspecified entertainments.

12    Tues.    SA.    *Love Makes a Man.*
*Cast:* Don Carlos—Sheridan.
*Benefit:* J. Morris.
*Miscellaneous:* Morris's second benefit; Mr. Sheridan's first time appearing in comedy.
*Singing and Dancing:* With Dancing.

and

*Afterpiece: The Brave Irishman; or, Captain O'Blunder.*
*Cast:* O'Blunder—J. Morris.


14    Thur.    SA.    *Othello.*
*Cast:* Othello—Sheridan.


18    Mon.    SA.    *The Provoked Husband.*
*Cast:* Townly—Sheridan; Lady Townly—Mrs. Elmy (from AS).


21    Thur.    AS.    *Comus.*
*Cast:* None listed.
*Deferred:* From 19 Apr.

and

*Afterpiece: Miss Lucy in Town.*
*Cast:* None listed.


21    Thur.    SA.    *Othello.*
*Cast:* Othello—Sheridan.
*Benefit:* Sheridan.


25    Mon.    AS.    *Comus.*
*Cast:* Lady—Mrs. Furnival; Pastoral Nymph and Sabrina—Mrs. Arne.
*Miscellaneous:* Last time of performing it this season.
*Singing and Dancing:* "Sweet Echo" by Mrs. Arne. Conducted by Arne, who will accompany on the harpsicord.

and

*Afterpiece: Miss Lucy in Town.*
*Cast:* None listed.


25    Mon.    SA.    *The Way of the World.*
*Cast:* None listed.
*Benefit:* Husband.
*Miscellaneous:* Several unspecified entertainments.

and

*Afterpiece:* Unspecified "Farce."

26   Tues.   AS.   *Love's Last Shift.*
*Cast:* Amanda—Mrs. Furnival.
*Benefit:* Walsh and Miss Davies.
*Singing and Dancing:* With a Grand Concert of Music in which Mr. Alcock, Jeronimo, Anderus, and Short, all lately come here, will perform on their different instruments, which variety will render this entertainment most agreeable; with singing.

and

*Afterpiece: The Virgin Unmasked.*
*Cast:* Lucy—Miss Davies.

27   Wed.   AS.   *Venice Preserved.*
*Cast:* None listed.
*Benefit:* Bourne and Boyton.
*Miscellaneous:* "Mr. Bourne being indisposed by being Lame, hopes his Friends will excuse his not waiting on them according to Custom, and will favour him with their Company at his Play" (*DNL,* 16–19 Apr. 1743).

and

*Afterpiece: The Vintner Tricked.*
*Cast:* None listed.

28   Thur.   SA.   *The Recruiting Officer.*
*Cast:* None listed.
*Command:* Lord Mayor.
*Benefit:* A Distressed Family.
*Singing and Dancing:* With Entertainments of Singing and Dancing.

and

*Afterpiece:* Unspecified "Farce."

29   Fri.   SA.   *Julius Caesar.*
*Cast:* Brutus—Sheridan; Cassius—Richard Sheridan (his first appearance on any stage).
*Miscellaneous:* [Richard was Thomas' elder brother by three years. He did not take to the stage as a profession. About 1765 he was, according to John O'Keeffe, "a snug, cosy friendly little man with a nice post in the Custom House and lived in Moor St."]
*Singing and Dancing:* With Dancing.
*Financial:* In his "Proper Reply" T. Cibber says that he was told that the house brought in about £50 this night.

30   Sat.   AS.   *King Richard III.*
*Cast:* Gloster—Genous.
*Benefit:* Genous.
*Deferred:* Deferred from 29 Apr. 1743: "I thought it proper to give this

publick Notice to those Gentlemen and Ladies who design to favour me with their Company at my Play, on Friday next, in Aungier-Street, that I designed to appear in the Character of Richard III, before ever I heard that Mr. Sheridan had any such Design; which I can prove by several Gentlemen, Witnesses; but being informed, some Time after, that Mr. Sheridan designed to play that Character for his own Benefit: Out of good nature to him I declined appearing in that Character till this Term, and therefore fixed on Friday next for my Benefit, being informed by Mr. Philips, some Time ago, who belongs to Smock-Alley Theatre, that Mr. Sheridan positively would not play that Week, there being three Benefit Plays in said Theatre. And whereas I am now informed that the Play of Julius Caesar is given out for Smock-Alley for the same Night of my Play; I humbly make this Request to my Friends, that they will not decline serving me, (tho' opposed the same Night at the other House) as I have just Reason to believe it is done with a Design to hurt me in my Play, but rather look upon the Opposition, as a Piece of the greatest ill Nature, and hope that my Friends will look on it in its true Light, and shew it so to others; which then will undoubtedly turn out rather to the Advantage than otherwise. . . . [signed] John Genous April 23, 1743" (*DNL*, 19–23 Apr. 1743).

MAY

2    Mon.    AS.    *Julius Caesar.*
*Cast:* Brutus—Pellish; Cassius—Walker (by particular desire); Portia—Mrs. Pasquilino.
*Benefit:* Pellish.
*Miscellaneous:* At the particular Desire of several Persons of Quality.
                                        and
*Afterpiece: The Mock Doctor.*
*Cast:* Mock Doctor—I. Sparks.

2    Mon.    SA.    *Hamlet.*
*Cast:* Hamlet—T. Sheridan.

3    Tues.    SA.    *The Old Batchelour.*
*Cast:* None listed.
*Benefit:* Richard Pockrich.
*Miscellaneous:* First time the Glasses were ever introduced in Concert; he will perform one of Vivaldi's Season's called Spring; "The Early Horn," sung by Baildon; "Hark ye Little Warbling Choirs" sung by Mrs. Storer; "Ellin A Roon"; "Jack Latten"; "The Black Joke"; with additional variations, some of which cannot be executed on any instrument but the Glass; the principal parts in all the above musick to be played on Glasses.
*Commentary:* "As this Kingdom of late has greatly encouraged all Inven-

tions, and Improvement in Arts and Sciences, it is to be hoped this Invention, in the Science of Music, will meet with Encouragement.

Some perhaps who have seen a Sketch of it in its Infancy, or upon accidental Glasses, may be apt to conclude, they have seen all that can be done upon them, but they can scarcely have an idea of the Perfection the Inventor has brought them to.

This being the first Time that Glasses were ever introduced in Concert, it is hoped that Curiosity will induce the Town to see what has so much surprized all those who have heard them, even at the greatest Disadvantage.

All Gentleman that love a cheerful Glass, will undoubtedly be zealous in the Affair" (*FDJ*, 26–30 Apr. 1743).

7    Sat.    AS.    *Rosamond.*
*Cast:* King Henry—Baildon; Sir Trusty—R. Layfield; Page—Master J. C. Pilkington (his first appearance on any stage); Rosamond—Mrs. Sybilla; Grideline—Miss Davies; Queen Eleanor—Mrs. Arne.
*Benefit:* Arne.
*Miscellaneous:* [Opera by T. A. Arne (music), text by Addison. First recorded Dublin performance (Walsh 1973, 326).] To prevent mistakes Ladies are desired to take their places in Time, and on the Day of Performance to send their Servants to keep Places before five o'clock.
and

*Afterpiece: Tragedy of Tragedies; or, The Life and Death of Tom Thumb the Great.*
*Cast:* Tom—Master Pilkington; King—Baildon; Lord Grizzle—R. Layfield; Queen Dollalolla—Miss Davies; Princess Huncamunca—Mrs. Sybilla; all the other Characters by a select Company of burlesque Opera Singers.
*Miscellaneous:* [Arne's opera version of Fielding's burlesque opera; first recorded Dublin performance (Walsh 1973, 326). Later retitled *Opera of Operas; or, Tom Thumb the Great.*]

9    Mon.    AS.    *The Beaux' Stratagem.*
*Cast:* None listed.
*Benefit:* L. Duval (from SA).
*Singing and Dancing:* With Dancing.
*Commentary:* "I humbly presume to give this public notice to the Nobility, Gentry, and others, that I am under the greatest Obligations to the Proprietors of Aungier Street Theatre for giving me the 9th of May for my Benefit; Mr. Thomas Philips and his Company of Comedians, as he impudently terms them, having disappointed me of it, tho' often applied to this Winter, unless I would take it upon their own ill-natured and oppressive terms; neither would they suffer Mr. Sheridan, who is under their Influence, as he alleges, to play for me, and therefore refused me that Service: But indeed I need not at this Day, wonder at their dealing so cruelly by me, being so inured to

their base and ungrateful Treatment, who under the shew of the sincerest Friendship, confirmed by the most sacred and solemn vows, have undone me and my family, and possessed themselves of my property in the Theatre in Smock-alley, broke all their Contracts to me, and now employ the Profits of the said Theatre to my further Ruin; although they are, upon a fair Account, even in the first of their own fraudulent Agreement 387 l. 9s. 11d. or thereabouts in my Debt, as I hope to make appear in a court of Equity, from whence alone I can expect Relief; and further to distress me and my Family, have also cut off all subsistance from me, so that I and my Family would have wanted, only for the good nature of my Subscribers of Smock-alley. And I do assure the Publick, that any Opposition that I ever gave to the just Demands of my Subscribers, and which they are fully sensible of, was owing to the wicked, false, and designing Misrepresentations of Contrivances of said Philips. And as my Endeavors were ever to entertain the Town in the best Manner, I humbly beg their Protection and Favour at this Time, being in a most distressed fit of the Gout, and unable to wait upon them in Person, which shall ever be acknowledged by their most distressed and afflicted, but most obedient and obliged humble servant. Lewis Duval" (*DNL*, 23–26 Apr. 1743 and *FDJ*, 26–30 Apr. 1743).

"I thought it impossible that any Thing Mr. Duval should say, could have induced me to address the Publick, but the impudent and scandalous Falshoods he has set forth in the Dublin News-Letter of the 26th Inst. have obliged me to inform the Town of the true state of the Case:

In April 1741, Mr. Duval had brought his Affairs into so great Distress, that he had not credit for the incidental Charge of a Night's Playing; in these circumstances he called the Company together, and told them, that unless they would stand by him, and take the Management into their Hands, he and his Family were utterly undone; his Wife joined in this Application, both drowned in Tears. This had such an Effect, that the present Lessees immediately joined into an Article with him, which is calculated much more for his Interest than theirs, though he would now deny the same (could there be a possibility of gaining Belief), and in the whole Proceedings of his Quarrel with the Proprietors (which shall be re-printed if Occasion requires) he acknowledges his Obligations to his Company, though he is now doing every Thing in his power to ruin them.

As to the State of his Account, it is hardly worth answering, the Assertion is so bare-faced a Piece of Impudence and Ignorance; for the Lessees have had the House but two Years and a few Days, so that had he never received a Shilling, his Demand could have been but 200 l. But in looking over his Accounts, I find, he has been paid, in the two Years in Cash, and for his Use, 579 l. 7s. 9d. As to his Benefit, Mr. Wetherilt applied to him, as soon as we came from England, to take it (according to his Agreement) in Michaelmas Term; but his Answer was, that he would stay till after Christmas. When we fixed out Days, we sent to him, and he would return no positive

Answer; so that we set apart Thursday the 24th of February, which we settled for him, though another Person's Day. At this time he fixed his whole Scheme of destroying the Company; which proving of no Effect, about the 4th Instant he sent to have Monday the 2d of May, which, tho' fixed for the Widow of Mr. Este, (that we might have no Dispute) was settled for him, and Mrs. Este obliged to defer hers (tho' her Tickets were Printing) to Monday the 9th of May. He then sent Word, unless Mr. Sheridan played for him he would not take the Day; I replied, that Mr. Sheridan was under no contract with us, but to play when he pleased and that the Company could not compel him to act, but that he should have any Play he pleased, acted in the best manner the Company could perform it. As to his Salary not being paid constantly, besides the above reason that the Company have already paid much more than was due to him, there is an additional one, viz. One of the Company, at his Request, lately became Bail for him for a large sum of Money, which he has not thought proper to pay, but has suffered Process to issue against the Bail, which is therefore obliged to pay the Debt, Mr. Duval thinking it more prudent to keep out of the Way than to surrender himself in Discharge of his Bail. Upon the whole, if any Gentlman will give himself the Trouble to see it, I will make every Circumstance above recited appear plain matter of Fact, so hope the wicked Assertions of Mr. Duval will have no Effect to the Prejudice of the Company. . . . [signed] Thomas Philips April 29, 1743.

The above-named 24th of February was my Benefit Day, but at the Instance of the Company I declined it for Mr. Duval. [signed] James Worsdale.

The 2d of May was fixed for me by the Company, but on Mr. Duval's Message, Mr. Wetherilt and Mr. Philips came to me, and begged me to take Monday the 9th, that if possible they might have no Dispute with him. [signed] Frances Este" (*DNL*, 26–30 Apr. 1743).

and

*Afterpiece:* Unspecified "Farce."

<br>

9     Mon.     SA.     *The Provoked Husband.*
*Cast:* Townly—T. Sheridan.
*Benefit:* Widow Este.
*Miscellaneous:* At the particular Desire of several Persons of Quality. *Volpone* originally advertised.
*Singing and Dancing:* Singing by Worsdale and Mrs. Storer.
*Financial:* T. Cibber in his "Proper Reply" says this performance brought in only about £20.

and

*Afterpiece: The Lying Valet.*
*Cast:* Sharp—Wetherilt.

11    Wed.    AS.    *The Conscious Lovers.* V.
*Cast:* None listed.
*Benefit:* Hospital for Incurables.
*Miscellaneous:* By Appointment to the Charitable Music Society of Crow St.; a "most crowded Audience" is reported to have attended.

and

*Afterpiece: The Stage Coach.*
*Cast:* None listed.


12    Thur.    AS.    *Love for Love.*
*Cast:* None listed.

and

*Afterpiece: The Tragedy of Tragedies.* [*Opera of Operas.*]
*Cast:* As 7 May 1743.


12    Thur.    SA.    *The Careless Husband.* V.
*Cast:* Foppington—T. Cibber (from LIF; his first appearance in this Kingdom); Sir Charles—H. Giffard (from LIF); Lady Betty—Mrs. Giffard (from LIF; her first appearance on this stage).
*Miscellaneous:* [*DNL* reports that T. Cibber arrived in Dublin on 27 Apr. 1743.]


13    Fri.    AS.    *The Royal Merchant.*
*Cast:* None listed.
*Benefit:* Watson.
*Singing and Dancing:* With Singing and Dancing.

and

*Afterpiece:* Unspecified "Farce."


16    Mon.    SA.    *The Relapse.*
*Cast:* Foppington—Cibber; Loveless—Giffard; Berintha—Mrs. Giffard.

and

*Afterpiece: The Mock Doctor.*
*Cast:* Mock Doctor—Cibber.
*Miscellaneous:* By particular desire.


17    Tues.    AS.    *The Merchant of Venice.*
*Cast:* None listed.
*Benefit:* Tyler.
*Singing and Dancing:* Singing by Mrs. Storer; Dancing.
*Deferred:* Deferred from 10 May due to Mr. Elrington's Illness.

and

*Afterpiece: The Contrivances.*
*Cast:* None listed.

18    Wed.    SA.    *The Busy Body.*
*Cast:* None listed.
*Benefit:* Mrs. Mitchell and Master Pitt.
*Singing and Dancing:* With Singing and Dancing.
and
*Afterpiece: The Honest Yorkshireman.*
*Cast:* None listed.

19    Thur.    SA.    *The Old Batchelour.*
*Cast:* Fondlewife—Cibber; Belmour—Giffard; Laetitia—Mrs. Giffard.
*Miscellaneous:* With a Humourous Epilogue to be spoke by No-body.
*Singing and Dancing:* After the Play there will be a Cantata sung by Mrs. Storer.
and
*Afterpiece: The School-Boy.*
*Cast:* Johnny—Cibber.

25    Wed.    AS.    *The Siege of Damascus.*
*Cast:* Eudocia—Mrs. Furnival.
*Benefit:* Swan.
*Singing and Dancing:* With Several Entertainments.
*Deferred:* Deferred from 20 May because the band was engaged at the last performance of the season of the Musical Society in Fishamble St.

30    Mon.    SA.    *The Non-Juror.*
*Cast:* Dr. Wolf—Cibber; Heartly—Giffard; Maria—Mrs. Giffard.
*Miscellaneous:* Not acted here these 25 years; no play next week on account of the holidays. With a Prologue spoke by No-body.

JUNE

2    Thur.    SA.    *The Man of Mode.*
*Cast:* Sir Fopling—Cibber; Dorimant—Giffard; Loveit—Mrs. Giffard.
*Miscellaneous:* Never acted here.

3    Fri.    AS.    *The Distrest Mother.*
*Cast:* Orestes—Walker.
*Benefit:* Walker.
*Miscellaneous:* Several unspecified entertainments.
and
*Afterpiece: The Walking Statue; or, The Devil in the Wine Cellar.*
*Cast:* None listed.

6    Mon.    SA.    *The Orphan.*

*Cast:* Monimia—Mrs. Giffard; Polydore—Cibber (his first time in Character); Chamont—Wright; Castilio—Giffard; Acasto—Beamsley; Ernesto—Oates; Serina—Mrs. Bayley; Page—Miss Orfeur.
*Benefit:* Mrs. Giffard.
*Miscellaneous:* At the Desire of several Ladies of Quality. [Wetherilt was billed to play the Chaplain this date but he died on 5 June 1743.]
*Singing and Dancing:* Singing and Dancing: Act 1, Scotch Dance by Delamain; Act 2, a Song by Mrs. Storer, beginning "Ye Verdant Plains"; Act 3, Peasant Dance by P. Morris; Act 4, Song by Mrs. Storer, beginning "Love Sounds the Alarm"; End of Play, The Basket Dance by P. Morris.

and

*Afterpiece: The Mock Doctor.*
*Cast:* Mock Doctor—Cibber.

11    Sat.    AS.    *Rosamond.*
*Cast:* As 7 May 1743.
*Benefit:* Baildon and Mrs. Sybilla.
*Miscellaneous:* Being the last time of Mrs. Arne exhibiting any Performance this Season; Master Pilkington's third appearance on any stage; To prevent Mistakes, Ladies are desired to take their Places in time, and on the Day of Performance to send their Servants to keep places before five o'clock. N. B. To induce the Town to personate their Benefit, Mr. Baildon and Mrs. Sybilla, have prevailed on Mr. Arne, (notwithstanding the great Expence attending the Performance) to exhibit at the usual Benefit Prices, viz. Boxes, Stage and Lattices, 5s. 5d., Pit, 3s. 3d., First Gallery, 2s. 2d.
*Deferred:* Deferred from 27 May "Mrs. Arne being taken violently Ill, and forbidden by her physician to attempt performing at the Hazard of her Life."

and

*Afterpiece: The Tragedy of Tragedies. [Opera of Operas.]*
*Cast:* As 8 May 1743.

11    Sat.    SA.    *The Rehearsal.*
*Cast:* Bayes—Cibber; Johnson—Giffard; Smith—Wright.
*Miscellaneous:* As it was performed at the Theatre Royal Covent Garden for 40 nights. With all Songs, Dances, Machines, and all other Decorations proper to the Play, concluding with the Representation of a Grand Battle by Mr. Bay's new-raised Troops; At the particular Desire of several Persons of Quality; Anniversary of the Coronation of George II.

By particular desire a Prologue spoke by No-body. [This prologue was spoken by T. Cibber and printed at the end of *Cibber and Sheridan; or, A Dublin Miscellany.*]
*Deferred:* "Whereas the Play of the Rehearsal was postponed from Thursday [i.e. 9 June] to Friday on Account of the Indisposition of one of the Principal Performers, the Managers of Smock Alley Theatre, not reflecting that it was

the 10th of June, they shew that it was meerly Accidental, and without any Design to give Offence; think proper to inform the Public that the Performance is deferred till this present Saturday, it being the Anniversary of His Majesty's happy Accession to the Throne" (*DG,* 7–11 June 1743).

13    Mon.    SA.    *The Conscious Lovers.*
*Cast:* Tom—Cibber; Bevil, Jr.—Giffard; Indiana—Mrs. Giffard.
*Miscellaneous:* At the particular Desire of several Ladies of Quality.
*Singing and Dancing:* With Songs and Dancing, particularly: End Act 1, Scot's Dance by Delamain; in Act 2, a Song by Mrs. Storer; End Act 3, Peasant Dance by Morris; End Act 4, A Cantata by Mrs. Storer; End farce, a Basket Dance by Morris, after which will be spoke an Epilogue (wrote by the celebrated comedian Jo. Haynes, of facetious Memory) spoke by Mr. Cibber riding on an Ass.
With a new Prologue addressed to the Ladies and Gentlemen of this Kingdom by Mr. Cibber; and Epilogue.
                              and
*Afterpiece: The Jovial Crew.*
*Cast:* Master Oliver and Justice Clack—Cibber.

16    Thur.    AS.    *The Miser.*
*Cast:* None listed.
*Miscellaneous:* No after-money will be taken the whole performance.
*Singing and Dancing:* Dancing by Mullement, Picq and Mlle. Chateauneuf, just arrived from England.

18    Sat.    AS.    *A Bold Stroke for a Wife.*
*Cast:* None listed.
*Miscellaneous:* No after-money will be taken.
*Singing and Dancing:* Dancing by Moreau, Picq, and Mlle. Chateauneuf, lately arrived from England; viz. Act 2, a Grand Serious Dance by Picq and Mlle. Chateauneuf; Act 3, a Pastoral Dance by Moreau and others; Act 4, a Tambourine by Mlle. Chateauneuf; Act 5, a Grand Ballet, "Le Rendezvous Gallant" by Moreau, Picq, and Mlle. Chateauneuf.

20    Mon.    AS.    *Othello.*
*Cast:* None listed.

20    Mon.    SA.    *The Constant Couple.*
*Cast:* Sir Harry—Giffard; Clincher, Jr.—R. Sheridan; Beau Clincher—Cibber; Standard—Wright; Angelica—Mrs. Bayley; Lady Lurewell—Mrs. Giffard.
*Benefit:* Giffard.

*Miscellaneous:* At the Desire of several Ladies of Quality. [*DG*, and *FDJ*, for 7-11 June 1743 advertise Mrs. Elmy in the part of Angelica.]

With a new Prologue to be spoke by Mr. Rich. Sheridan on his appearing in Comedy.

*Singing and Dancing:* With Singing and Dancing.

and

*Afterpiece:* Unspecified "Farce."

22    Wed.    SA.    *A Bold Stroke for a Wife.*
*Cast:* None listed.
*Benefit:* Lee.

and

*Afterpiece: The Devil to Pay.*
*Cast:* None listed.

23    Thur.    AS.    *King Henry IV, with the Humours of Falstaff.*
*Cast:* None listed.
*Singing and Dancing:* Dancing by Moreau, Picq, and Mlle. Chateauneuf.

23    Thur.    SA.    *King Lear and His Three Daughters.*
*Cast:* Lear—T. Sheridan (his first time in Character); Edgar—Giffard; Gentleman Usher—Cibber; Cordelia—Mrs. Giffard.
*Deferred:* Deferred from 16 June because of an Indisposition on the part of T. Sheridan.

27    Mon.    SA.    *The Fair Penitent.*
*Cast:* Horatio—T. Sheridan; Altamont—Giffard; Lothario—Cibber (his first time in Character); Calista—Mrs. Giffard.
*Singing and Dancing:* With Singing by Mrs. Storer and Dancing between the Acts.

28    Tues.    AS.    *Love's Last Shift.*
*Cast:* None listed.
*Benefit:* Mrs. Barker and her Children.
*Deferred:* Deferred from 21 June 1743 "on account of the Indisposition of Mrs. Furnival."
*Financial:* In his "Proper Reply" T. Cibber says that this house was less than £20 and was "the very worst audience they have known a long while."

and

*Afterpiece: The Stage Coach.*
*Cast:* None listed.

30    Thur.    AS.    *The Beaux' Stratagem.*
*Cast:* None listed.

*Singing and Dancing:* Dancing by Moreau, Picq, and Mlle. Chateauneuf, viz. Act. 2, new dance by Moreau and Mlle. Chateauneuf; Act 3, new comic danced called "The Jealous Peasants" by Moreau, Picq, and Mlle. Chateauneuf; Act 5, a Grand Ballet "La Rendezvous Gallant" by Moreau, Picq, and Mlle. Chateauneuf and others.

30    Thur.    SA.    *King Richard III.*
*Cast:* Gloster—T. Sheridan; King Henry—Giffard; Richmond—Cibber; Queen Elizabeth—Mrs. Giffard.
*Miscellaneous:* Being the last time of performing that play this season.
*Financial:* In his "Proper Reply" T. Cibber, addressing T. Sheridan, says that this performance brought in less than £30 "and caused about £15 worth of tickets to be given away to puff for you."

JULY

4    Mon.    AS.    *Love for Love.*
*Cast:* Valentine—Swan; Angelica—Mrs. Furnival.
*Benefit:* Mlle. Chateauneuf.
*Miscellaneous:* At the particular Desire of several Persons of Quality.
*Singing and Dancing:* With Dancing.

5    Tues.    SA.    *The Fair Penitent.*
*Cast:* As 27 June 1743.
*Benefit:* Father, Mother, and Widow of the late Mr. Wetherilt.
*Singing and Dancing:* Several entertainments of singing and dancing.
                            and
*Afterpiece: The Contrivances.*
*Cast:* Robin—Cibber; Arethusa—Mrs. Storer.

7    Thur.    SA.    *Cato.*
*Cast:* Cato—T. Sheridan (first time in character; last time but one of his performing this season); Juba—Giffard; Marcia—Mrs. Giffard; Syphax—Cibber.
                            and
*Afterpiece: The Brave Irishman.*
*Cast:* O'Blunder—J. Morris.

9    Sat.    AS.    *Twelfth Night.*
*Cast:* Viola—Mrs. Furnival; Sebastian—Swan; Malvolio—I. Sparks.
*Benefit:* Picq.
*Singing and Dancing:* Dancing, particularly, Act 1, a Pastoral Dance by Picq and others; Act 2, "Badinage Provencal" by Picq and Mlle. Chateauneuf and others; Act 3, Comic Pantomime Dance, Picq, Moreau and Mlle. Cha-

teauneuf; Act 4, Italian Sailor Dance by Moreau; End, The Louvre and Minuet by Picq and Mlle. Chateauneuf.
*Deferred:* Put off to this date at the Desire of several Ladies of Quality.

11　Mon.　AS.　*Lady Jane Grey.*
*Cast:* Lady Jane—Mrs. Furnival.
*Benefit:* Muilment (dancer from DL).
*Miscellaneous:* Last time of the company's acting in Town this season.
*Singing and Dancing:* With a variety of new dancing by Moreau, Picq, and Mlle. Chateauneuf.

12　Tues.　SA.　*The Rehearsal.*
*Cast:* Bayes—Cibber; Johnson—Giffard.
*Command:* Lords Justice.
*Miscellaneous:* In his "Proper Reply" T. Cibber says that the audience was dismissed because of poor attendance "tho' at the time the Audience were sent away, every one allows, there was a better Prospect of an Audience, than there was at the same hour, to the Play of *Cato.*"
*Singing and Dancing:* With Singing and Dancing between the Acts.
and
*Afterpiece: The Brave Irishman.*
*Cast:* O'Blunder—J. Morris.

14　Thur.　SA.　*Cato.*
*Cast:* As 7 July 1743, but without Sheridan (see below).
*Miscellaneous:* [Upon arriving at the theatre to play Cato, Sheridan learned that no one had been paid in several weeks. The members of the band refused to play, and the actors were dejected. He also learned that Thomas Philips had absconded, taking with him some of the costumes. When Sheridan dressed for his part, he discovered that the cape which he had worn before "to give him more dignity and gravity" had been taken by Philips. Although he was offered a new robe made for Husband to wear as Julius Caesar, Sheridan refused it and became incensed at Cibber's comment: "Damn me if I care what you do, the Play shall not stand for you." Infuriated, Sheridan rushed onto the stage to dismiss the audience, only to find that he had lost his voice. Cibber followed, proposing to read the part of Cato as well as acting his own. When the audience agreed to the substitution, Sheridan removed his costume and angrily left the theatre, asserting that he was through with acting.

A paper war ensued. Sheridan defended his action, and when Cibber castigated Sheridan the town began taking sides. The Trinity College students supported Sheridan and wrote to *FDJ,* accordingly:

Trinity College, Dublin July 17, 1743 . . . upon a strict and impartial Enquiry into the Reasons of Mr. Sheridan's not appearing Thursday last [i.e. 14 July] in the Character of Cato, we find them so strong and satisfactory, that our Resolution, we hope, will be favourably looked on, of seeing him righted, and the Insolence of others properly chastised, who either thro' Envy or malice, would remove the strongest Inducement we have for frequenting the Play-House. . . . (*FDJ*, 16–19 July 1743)

Alarmed at their vehemence, Sheridan went to the college and solicited a promise not to disturb Cibber's performance of *Othello* on 21 July. The pledge, however, was broken and a riot occurred at the theatre that night. John Pilkington explains why:

After we made this Promise Cibber's letter came out in which we [students] were attacked by the manner in which he treated our Advertisement, such insolence from a person of his Character, tho' it deserved the highest Punishment, yet, should we not have carried Matters so far [the riot], had we not heard, and the events justified it, that Mr. Cibber had a Party of Ruffians and other desperate Fellows to oppose us. Notwithstanding all the Series of Provocations, we are willing to suffer him to play his own benefit or any other Characters that are fit for him, provided he behaves himself well, Mr. Sheridan having earnestly entreated us that we might. As there were Distinction and Merit then present who might have taken Exception to our Behaviour that night, we publickly declaim any Design of offending them which we should have done at that Time, could we have been heard. (J. Pilkington 1760, 168)

The affair fizzled out later in the summer though readers in Dublin and London were amused by two published collections of Sheridan-Cibber letters relevant to the dispute. (See Sheldon 1967, 40–47, for a detailed account of the *Cato* affair).

and

*Afterpiece: The Brave Irishman.*
*Cast:* None listed.

18   Mon.   SA.   *The Careless Husband.*
*Cast:* Foppington—Cibber; Sir Charles—Giffard; Lady Betty—Mrs. Giffard.
*Singing and Dancing:* Singing by Mrs. Storer.

and

*Afterpiece: The Brave Irishman.*
*Cast:* None listed.

19   Tues.   AS.   *The Distrest Mother.*
*Cast:* Pyrrhus—Pellish; Orestes—Walker; Andromache—Mrs. Pasquilino; Hermione—Mrs. Furnival; Cleone—A Debutante (never appeared on any stage).
*Command:* Lords Justice.
*Benefit:* Walker.
*Miscellaneous:* With the original Prologue and Epilogue.
*Singing and Dancing:* With Singing and Dancing.

*Deferred:* Deferred from 5 July so as not to interfere with the Widow Wetherilt's benefit.

and

*Afterpiece: The Walking Statue.*
*Cast:* None listed.


21    Thur.    SA.    *Othello.*
*Cast:* Othello—Cibber; Cassio—Giffard; Iago—Wright; Roderigo—J. Morris; Desdemona—Mrs. Giffard.
*Miscellaneous:* [This performance was disrupted by a riot. See above 14 July 1743 SA.]


25    Mon.    SA.    *Macbeth.*
*Cast:* None listed.
*Deferred:* Deferred from 14 July at the desire of several persons of quality.


28    Thur.    AS.    *Cato.*
*Cast:* Cato—T. Sheridan (his first appearance on this stage and his last time of performing this season).
*Command:* Lords Justice.
*Miscellaneous:* No person to be admitted to the upper Gallery but such as have liveries and have received tickets from the Boxkeeper.
*Singing and Dancing:* Several entertainments of dancing by Mullement.
*Commentary:* ". . . at the particular desire of a very considerable number of ladies and gentlemen, Mr. Sheridan played the part of Cato a few nights afterwards [after the riots] at AS theatre to a very splendid audience, and received every tribute of applause which his late unfair treatment, and masterly performance of the character merited. The night following the theatre closed" (Hitchcock 1788–94, 1:134–35).


AUGUST


1    Mon.    SA.    *King Henry IV, Part 2.*
*Cast:* Pistol—Cibber.
*Benefit:* T. Cibber (second).
*Miscellaneous:* With the Humours of Sir John Falstaff, Justice Swallow, and Ancient Pistol (by desire); Last time of the Company's acting this season.

A new Prologue by Cibber on the Occasion of the Glorious Success of British Arms under His Majesty in Germany; An Epilogue spoke by Nobody.
*Singing and Dancing:* With Entertainments of Singing and Dancing.
*Deferred:* Deferred from 28 July.

and

*Afterpiece: The Lottery.*
*Cast:* Jack Stocks—Cibber; Chloe—Mrs. Storer.
*Singing and Dancing:* Intermixed with songs.

[Broadbent 1908, 18–19, states that the SA company were so successful in Liverpool in the previous summer "that they were induced to come here the following year." No other record of their activities in Liverpool has survived.]

## 1743–1744 Season

Theatres Operating: Aungier St.; Smock Alley. [At the beginning of this season the companies of the two theatres united, though after three weeks a group of those not chosen for the united company or disaffected with the parts they were given to play reopened the SA theatre in competition with AS. This enterprise was unsuccessful, and after 2 Feb. 1744 the two companies again merged using both theatres for performances.]

*United Company:*
Bardin, Barrington, Spranger Barry, Mrs. Bayley, Beamsley, Miss Bullock, Miss C. Douglas, Miss M. Douglas, Dyer, Mrs. Elmy, F. Elrington, J. Elrington, R. Elrington (after 6 Feb.), Mrs. Furnival, Griffith (died 23 Jan. 1744), Hall, Harvey, Husband, R. Layfield, Mrs. R. Layfield, C. Morgan, Miss Rogers, Mrs. Sampson, I. Sparks, L. Sparks, Vanderbank, Mrs. Vanderbank, Walker, J. Watson, Jr., Mrs. White, Worsdale, Wright.

Singers: Mrs. Arne, Miss Davies, Thomas Lowe (from DL), Mrs. Pasquilino.

Dancers: Mlle. Chateauneuf, W. Delamain, Dumont, Moreau,

Musicians: Arne.

House Servants: Neale (boxkeeper); Layfield (perhaps L. or R.) may have acted as Treasurer (see 22 Dec. 1743 AS).

*Repertory:*
Mainpieces: Recorded performances: 90 (of 38 different pieces). [It is perhaps worth noting the *DC,* 30 June 1744 reference to the "50th" performance of *The Beggar's Opera* when only 12 are recorded this season.]
Afterpieces: Total: 54 performances of 19 different pieces including unspecified farce.

Premieres: *Love and Loyalty.*
Entr'acte entertainments: Most programs include entertainments of singing and dancing.
Command Performances: 10 including one Government night.
Benefits:
Pre-February: Actor—6.
Post-February: Actor—12; Charity—1; Author—1; Houseservant—1.

---

*Smock Alley Company* (3 Nov. 1743 to 2 Feb. 1744):
Dale, Ralph Elrington, Jenkins, L. Layfield, Mason, J. Morris, Mynitt, Mrs. Mynitt, Mrs. W. Phillips, T. Sheridan (to CG after 16 Jan.).

Singers: Mrs. Storer.

Dancers: P. Morris, W. Phillips, Mlle. Roland (from LIF).

House Servants: Darby (boxkeeper), Dryden (treasurer).

Repertory:
Mainpieces: Recorded performances: 14 (11 different pieces).
Afterpieces: Recorded Performances: 9 performances of 5 different afterpieces.
Premieres:
*The Death of Abel.*
*The Prude.*
Entr'acte entertainments: Many programs of singing and dancing.
Command Performances: None.
Benefits:
Pre-February: Actor—5; Houseservant—1.
Post-February: Actor—5; Manager—1; Charity—2; Author—1; House-servant—1.

---

## 1743

OCTOBER

11    Tues.    AS.    *The Conscious Lovers.*
*Cast:* Bevil, Jr.—J. Elrington; Sealand—F. Elrington; Myrtle—L. Sparks; Tom—Bardin; Sir John—Husband; Humphrey—Beamsley; Cimberton—Morgan; Daniel—Dyer; Phillis—Mrs. Furnival; Indiana—Mrs. Pasquilino;

Mrs. Sealand—Mrs. Sampson; Lucinda—Mrs. Bayley; Isabella—Mrs. White.
*Command:* Duke and Duchess of Devonshire.
*Miscellaneous:* The Gentlemen Proprietors of the two Playhouses, being convinced one Theatre sufficient, have now settled. Government Night: Anniversary of Coronation of George II. With a new Prologue for the day spoke by Mr. Wright from SA.
*Singing and Dancing:* Dancing by M. Dumont, lately arrived from Paris.


13    Thur.    AS.    *Othello.*
*Cast:* Othello—Walker.


17    Mon.    AS.    *The Constant Couple.*
*Cast:* Sir Harry—Hall (a Gentleman who never appeared on any Stage before); Lady Lurewell—Mrs. Furnival.
*Miscellaneous:* By His Majesty's United Company of Comedians.
*Singing and Dancing:* Dancing by Moreau, Dumont, and Mlle. Chateauneuf.


20    Thur.    AS.    *Venice Preserved.*
*Cast:* Jaffier—Wright; Pierre—L. Sparks; Belvidera—Mrs. Furnival.
*Singing and Dancing:* Dancing by Moreau, Delamain, and Mlle. Chateauneuf, particularly an Italian dance after the Manner of Faussana by Delamain and Mlle. Chateauneuf.


24    Mon.    AS.    *The Old Batchelour.*
*Cast:* Heartwell—Husband; Fondlewife—F. Elrington; Laetitia—Mrs. Furnival; Belinda—Mrs. Elmy.


27    Thur.    AS.    *The Constant Couple.*
*Cast:* As 17 Oct. 1743.
*Miscellaneous:* At the particular Desire of several Persons of Quality; Hall's second time of appearing on any stage.
*Singing and Dancing:* As 20 Oct.


31    Mon.    AS.    *Love's Last Shift.*
*Cast:* Sir William—Vanderbank; Loveless—J. Elrington; Sir Novelty—Bardin; Flareit—Mrs. Elmy; Amanda—Mrs. Furnival.
*Command:* Duke and Duchess of Devonshire.
*Miscellaneous:* Government Night; Anniversary of birth of George II; Boxes open for the Ladies. A new Prologue for the Day.
*Singing and Dancing:* Dancing by Moreau, Dumont, and Mlle. Chateauneuf.

NOVEMBER

3    Thur.    AS.    *The Mourning Bride.*
*Cast:* None listed.
*Command:* Duke and Duchess of Devonshire.
*Singing and Dancing:* Dancing by Moreau, Delamain, and Mlle. Chateauneuf.


3    Thur.    SA.    *King Richard III.*
*Cast:* Gloster—T. Sheridan; King Henry—R. Elrington; Queen Elizabeth—Mrs. Mynitt (her first appearance here); The other parts by Persons who never appeared on this Stage.
*Miscellaneous:* The Managers of the Theatre in SA intend to perform Plays as usual there this Season; and will open on Thursday the 3d of November. They are determined always to begin precisely at 6 o'clock; By Permission of the Lord Mayor.

[The reopening of SA produced a barrage of letters in the newspapers asserting that Elrington had acquired the theatre and its properties in an underhanded manner. Hitchcock states: "The new company of rejected actors thinking themselves aggrieved, had the address, by fraudulent means, I believe, to obtain the old lease of Smock Alley from Duval, the principal proprietor, and took possession, determined, desperate as their situation was, to form an opposition" (1:137). Sheldon (1967) believes that "Sheridan would not knowingly have adhered to anything dishonest, that records show that the financial affairs of the two theatres were in a great snarl at this time; there may have been no fraud, just confusion and a long-standing want of funds. Furthermore, certain matters of ownership were under litigation and therefore unsettled at the moment" (p. 48 and p. 71n. Sheldon does not cite the source of the financial "records" she refers to here).

Another letter (possibly written by Duval) which appeared in *FDJ*, 1 Nov. 1743 throws additional light on the controversy.

> Mr. Faulkner, I cannot help taking Notice of a Paragraph in your Journal of Saturday last (Octr. 29th 1743) wherein 'tis said that the Managers of Smock-alley Play-house propose opening their House on Thursday next with Richard the Third, the Part of Richard by Mr. Sheridan, King Henry by Mr. Elrington, and the Rest of the Parts by Persons who never appeared on that Stage; and that as they always spared no Expence to entertain the Town, they hoped the Favour of the Publick etc.
>
> The Modesty of this Advertisement is of a Piece with all their other Actions; I must therefore beg Leave to lay before the Publick the Steps that were taken by these new Managers to bring their Affairs to bear—1st as there is a Decree in the High Court of Chancery for 800£ and Costs, which is to be paid to the Proprietors of the House the 8th instant, this is to be shuffled off by a Bill of Reversal, advised by a new Manager, tho' without any Hopes of succeeding even in his own chimerical Brain—2nd—The Cloaths and Scenes were publickly sold for Rent due to the Ground Landlord near a Year ago, and those Managers had the Favour

granted to them by the Persons (whose Property they were then and are now) to act and play with them without Fee or Reward; and tho' by a Trick these Managers have got them again in their Possession, yet their Modesty does not dare to say they have the least Shadow of Right in them.—3rd—They owe their Players about £500, and rather than to offer Payment of one Shilling to them, have either run away, absconded, or denied their Debts; so 'tis no Wonder they sent for a strolling Company from the North to perform with them.—4th They obtained a Lease from a weak Man, under Oppression, by Fraud; and though they have not complied even with any one Condition of such Lease, yet their Modesty is still the same to keep him out of his Right, and oblige him to throw himself on the Protection of a noble Lord, and the Charity of the Publick.—And now let the Publick judge whether these Managers deserve their Favour, or their Resentment; for, surely,—
—To act in a House they have no Right to;
—To act with Cloaths and Scenes that don't belong to them;
—To act with Strollers, without paying their Players;
—To act by a Lease neither good in itself, nor having paid the Conditions of it,—are sufficient Reasons to conclude the whole Attempt is an Affront to common Sense and common Justice, and ought to bring that just Indignation on the Heads of these Managers, which becomes an honest, just and brave People; for Robbing by Tricks of Law is always esteemed the worst Kind of Thievery.

I must further observe, the Person, who is to act the Part of King Richard [Sheridan], if I am rightly informed, has made it his Business to attend the Houses of all Persons of Quality and Distinction (he could have Access to) and implore them to countenance him and his Undertaking, exciting their Compassion towards him, as an Act of Generosity and Charity to him, as an injured Person:—now I must assure all Persons of Quality etc. (and I can prove it true) that this Player, when he attended the Gentlemen of Aungier-street, was received by them with such Terms of Civility and Profit, as no Man but himself could refuse: the Terms they offered would amount to near six Pounds a week, and, as he pretended a delicate Constitution, they submitted to his playing but once a Week for it:—surely, no Man can be an Object of Charity, or compassion, that has refused such a Sum (a Sum never yet given to any Player in this Kingdom, except to Quin and others, who came here (like Birds of Prey) to carry away what they could, and which the Gentlemen, since their Union are determined never to countenance again) and a Sum the Gentlemen thought four Times too much for his Merit;—but this Player did not only refuse six Pounds a week, but insisted to have equal Profit with the Gentlemen, who have expended very large Sums in their Undertaking, and are at the Charge of Maintaining not only their own Company, but, out of a Desire to oblige the Town, have engaged all Smock-alley Players that ever applied to them.

As to the Person who is to play King Henry [R. Elrington], the Gentlemen upon Application did engage him at the same Salary and Benefit as usual; so neither the one nor the other are Objects of Charity, and consequently are not forced to do any ill Act of Subsistence. Now what the Fate of the poor Strollers from the North will be, no one knows, for, as these two Kings are to divide the Profits, which I suppose is all the Money they can finger (as they did last Winter) it would have been more human in these Managers to have engaged a Set of Players out of Punch's Theatre, who would have been content with the Honour of acting with these Heroes, and never mutiny for Want of Subsistence.]

7    Mon.    AS.    *The Miser.*
*Cast:* None listed.
*Miscellaneous:* No after-money will be taken in any part of the House.

*Singing and Dancing:* Dancing by Moreau, Delamain, and Mlle. Chateauneuf.

and

*Afterpiece: The Devil to Pay.*
*Cast:* Loverule—Lowe (from DL, his first appearance in this Kingdom).
*Miscellaneous:* Walsh 1973, 70, and Boydell 1988, 95, cite the performance of *The Beggar's Opera* at AS on 8 Dec. as Lowe's first Dublin appearance.
*Singing and Dancing:* In which character will be introduced the song "The Early Horn" with several entertainments of singing, particularly after Act 3 the favourite song in *Alexander's Feast* called "The Happy Pair" sung by Lowe.

10    Thur.    AS.    *The Fair Penitent.*
*Cast:* None listed.
*Singing and Dancing:* Dancing by Moreau, Delamain, and Mlle. Chateauneuf.

and

*Afterpiece: The Devil to Pay.*
*Cast:* Loverule—Lowe (his second appearance in this Kingdom).

12    Sat.    AS.    *The Beaux' Stratagem.*
*Cast:* Aimwell—J. Elrington; Mrs. Sullen—Mrs. Furnival.
*Singing and Dancing:* Dancing by Moreau, Delamain, and Mlle. Chateauneuf.

and

*Afterpiece: The Devil to Pay.*
*Cast:* Loverule—Lowe (third appearance).
*Singing and Dancing:* "The Early Horn" and other entertainments of singing by Lowe, particularly, a favourite Ballad, called "Stella and Flavia."

14    Mon.    AS.    *The Twin Rivals.*
*Cast:* None listed.

14    Mon.    SA.    *Cato.*
*Cast:* Cato—T. Sheridan; Syphax—R. Elrington.
*Singing and Dancing:* Singing by Mrs. Storer, Dancing by Madam Roland (her second appearance on the Irish Stage).

17    Thur.    AS.    *Comus.*
*Cast:* Comus—Wright; Pastoral Nymph and Sabrina—Mrs. Arne; Bachannal and Attendant Spirit—Lowe.
*Miscellaneous:* At the particular desire of several Persons of Quality. A Row of the Pit taken into the Orchestra.
*Singing and Dancing:* Mrs. Arne will sing "Sweet Echo."; With all the

Choruses in Parts as originally in England; with an extraordinary Band of Music provided for the Occasion. The whole conducted by Mr. Arne, who accompanies the Performance on the Harpsicord; Dancing by Moreau, Delamain, and Mlle. Chateauneuf.

17   Thur.   SA.   *Julius Caesar.*
*Cast:* Brutus—Sheridan; Cassius—R. Elrington.
*Benefit:* T. Sheridan.
*Singing and Dancing:* Dancing by Madam Roland; Singing by Mrs. Storer.
                                  and
*Afterpiece: The Brave Irishman.*
*Cast:* O'Blunder—J. Morris.

19   Sat.   AS.   *Comus.*
*Cast:* Comus—Wright; Pastoral Nymph and Sabrina—Mrs. Arne; Bachannal and Attendant Spirit—Lowe; Euphrosyne—Miss Davis.
*Command:* Duke and Duchess of Devonshire.
*Miscellaneous:* New Prologue spoken by Hall.
*Singing and Dancing:* "The Wanton God" sung by Mlle. Chateauneuf; Dancing by Moreau, Delamain, and Mlle. Chateauneuf.

24   Thur.   AS.   *Comus.*
*Cast:* As 17 Nov. 1743.
*Command:* Duke and Duchess of Devonshire.

26   Sat.   AS.   *Hamlet.*
*Cast:* Hamlet—Hall; Queen—Mrs. Furnival; Ghost—Gentleman.
*Benefit:* Hall.
*Miscellaneous:* With a new Prologue spoken by Mr. Wright.
*Singing and Dancing:* Singing and Dancing: Singing and Dancing between the Acts.

28   Mon.   AS.   *The Beggar's Opera.*
*Cast:* Macheath—Lowe; Peachum—L. Sparks; Lockit—Beamsley; Filch—Dyer; Polly—Mlle. Chateauneuf; Lucy—Mrs. Bayley; Mrs. Peachum—Miss Davies.
*Miscellaneous:* Being prepared with the utmost Propriety; At the particular Desire of several Persons of Quality. Front Row of Pit taken into the Orchestra.
*Deferred:* Deferred from 24 Nov. 1743.

28   Mon.   SA.   *Cato.*
*Cast:* As 14 Nov.
*Benefit:* William Dryden (treasurer).

*Singing and Dancing:* With a variety of Singing and Dancing by Mrs. Storer and Mme. Roland, etc.

and

*Afterpiece:* Unspecified "Farce."

**DECEMBER**

1 Thur. AS. *The Beggar's Opera.*
*Cast:* Macheath—Lowe; Lucy—Mrs. Bayly; Polly—Mlle. Chateauneuf.
*Singing and Dancing:* With Entertainments of Dancing.

1 Thur. SA. *King Richard III.*
*Cast:* Richard—T. Sheridan; King Henry—R. Elrington; Catesby—J. Morris.
*Benefit:* J. Morris.
*Singing and Dancing:* Dancing by Morris, Mme. Roland, and Others.

and

*Afterpiece: The Brave Irishman.*
*Cast:* O'Blunder—J. Morris.

5 Mon. AS. *The Beggar's Opera.*
*Cast:* As 1 Dec. 1743.

8 Thur. AS. *The Beggar's Opera.*
*Cast:* As 1 Dec. 1743, but Lucy—Miss Davies.
*Command:* Duke and Duchess of Devonshire.
*Miscellaneous:* Part of the Pit will be taken into the Orchestra, there being an extraordinary Band of Music provided on this Occasion, conducted by Mr. Arne who will accompany on the Harpsicord.
*Singing and Dancing:* With Dancing.

8 Thur. SA. *Macbeth.*
*Cast:* Macbeth—T. Sheridan (his first time in Character); Hecate—J. Morris; Macduff—R. Elrington.
*Singing and Dancing:* Vocal parts by Mrs. Storer and the best Voices that can be procured; with the original Dances, Music, and Decorations, particularly a Scaramouche Dance by Phillips, never performed by him but at the Opera in Paris, and at the End of the Play the "Drunken Peasant."

and

*Afterpiece: The Devil to Pay.*
*Cast:* Nell—Mrs. W. Phillips (her first appearance this season).

12 Mon. AS. *The Beggar's Opera.*

*Cast:* Macheath—Lowe; Filch—Dyer; Lucy—Miss Davies; Mrs. Peachum—Mrs. Vanderbank; Polly—Mlle. Chateauneuf.
*Command:* Duke and Duchess of Devonshire.
*Miscellaneous:* Fifth Night; A Row of the Pit will be taken into the Orchestra.

15    Thur.    AS.    *The Beggar's Opera.*
*Cast:* As 12 Dec. 1743.
*Benefit:* Mlle. Chateauneuf.
*Miscellaneous:* Sixth Night.

15    Thur.    SA.    *Julius Caesar.*
*Cast:* Brutus—Sheridan; Cassius—R. Elrington.
*Benefit:* W. Phillips.
*Singing and Dancing:* With several new Entertainments of Singing and Dancing.
                                  and
*Afterpiece: The Hussar; or, Harlequin Restored.*
*Cast:* Harlequin—W. Phillips; Pierrot—P. Morris; Columbine—Mrs. W. Phillips.
*Miscellaneous:* With several Alterations and Additions.

17    Sat.    AS.    *Comus.*
*Cast:* Bacchanal and Attendant Spirit—Lowe; Euphrosyne—Mlle. Chateauneuf; Pastoral Nymph and Sabrina—Mrs. Arne.
*Benefit:* Lowe.
*Singing and Dancing:* With Dancing; Singing, "Sweet Echo" by Mrs. Arne.
                                  and
*Afterpiece: The Devil to Pay.*
*Cast:* Loverule—Lowe; Nell—Mlle. Chateauneuf (her first time in that character).
*Singing and Dancing:* Singing, "Early Horn" by Lowe.

19    Mon.    AS.    *The Beggar's Opera.*
*Cast:* As 12 Dec. 1743.
*Miscellaneous:* Seventh Night.
*Singing and Dancing:* With Dancing.

19    Mon.    SA.    *The Beggar's Opera.*
*Cast:* Macheath—Mrs. Storer; Lucy—Mrs. W. Phillips; Polly—Mlle. Roland.
*Singing and Dancing:* A Scaramouch Dance by Phillips and Others.

22    Thur.    AS.    *Comus.*

*Cast:* Comus—Wright; Pastoral Nymph and Sabrina—Mrs. Arne; Bacchanal and Attendant Spirit—Lowe; Euphrosyne—Miss Davies.
*Miscellaneous:* By particular Desire of the Proprietors Sig. Pasqualino will perform thro' the Opera; Row of Pit laid into Boxes; Last Time of Acting till after the holidays.

"Whoever have any lawful Demands on the TRAS, are desired to bring them to Mr. Layfield, at his House in Marlbro Bowling-Green" (*DNL*, 17–20 Dec. 1743).

22    Thur.    SA.    *Venice Preserved.*
*Cast:* Pierre—T. Sheridan (his first time in Character).
*Benefit:* T. Sheridan.
*Singing and Dancing:* Singing by Mrs. Storer; Dancing by Mlle. Roland and Phillips.

and

*Afterpiece: The Brave Irishman.*
*Cast:* None listed.

JANUARY

2    Mon.    AS.    *Amphitryon; or, The Two Sosias.*
*Cast:* Jupiter—Wright; Sosia—Barrington.
*Singing and Dancing:* With Several Entertainments of Singing and Dancing between the Acts, viz. End Act 1, "Vitumnus and Pomona," a Cantata, by Lowe; Dance by M. Dumont; In Act 3, a Song, "If Love be a Fault," by Lowe in Character; End Act 3, Dance by Moreau; In Act 4, a new Italian Dance by Dumont and Mlle. Chateauneuf; End Act 4, "Vo'Solcado" a masterly song of Sig. Farinelli's, by Mrs. Arne; End of Play, Tambourine by Mlle. Chateauneuf.

and

*Afterpiece: Miss Lucy in Town.*
*Cast:* Cantileno—Lowe; Mrs. Haycock—Mrs. R. Layfield; Miss Lucy—Miss Davies.
*Miscellaneous:* A Sequel to *The Virgin Unmasked.* Cantileno is a burlesque upon the Italian Singers. [Several newspapers cast "Mr." R. Layfield in the role of Mrs. Haycock.]
*Singing and Dancing:* Music by Dr. Arne.

2    Mon.    SA.    *The Committee.*
*Cast:* Teague—J. Morris.

and

*Afterpiece: The Honest Yorkshireman.*
*Cast:* None listed.

*Singing and Dancing:* Singing by Mrs. Storer, particularly "The Life of a Beau"; Dancing by Phillips and Mlle. Roland.

5   Thur.    AS.    *The Beggar's Opera.*
*Cast:* Macheath—Lowe; Peachum—L. Sparks; Lockit—Beamsley; Filch—Dyer; Polly—Mlle. Chateauneuf; Lucy—Miss Davies; Mrs. Peachum—Mrs. Vanderbank.
*Miscellaneous:* At the particular Desire of several Ladies of Quality; Eighth Night.
*Singing and Dancing:* With several Entertainments of Dancing.

9   Mon.    AS.    *The Beaux' Stratagem.*
*Cast:* Archer—Hall; Dorinda—Miss Campbellina Douglas (her first appearance on any stage).
                              and
*Afterpiece: The Dragon of Wantley.*
*Cast:* Moore of Moore Hall—Lowe; Margery—Mrs. Arne (her first appearance in any comic character); Mauxalinda—Mlle. Chateauneuf; Gubbins—Worsdale; Dragon—R. Layfield.
*Singing and Dancing:* With all the Choruses; Conducted by Arne who will accompany on the Harpsicord.

12   Thur.    AS.    *The Winter's Tale.*
*Cast:* Leontes—Wright; Paulina—Mrs. Furnival.
*Miscellaneous:* Never Acted in this Kingdom.
*Singing and Dancing:* Entertainments of Dancing by Moreau, Delamain, and Mlle. Chateauneuf.
                              and
*Afterpiece: The Dragon of Wantley.*
*Cast:* Cast as 9 Jan. 1744.

16   Mon.    AS.    *The Winter's Tale.*
*Cast:* None listed.
*Miscellaneous:* Never acted in this Kingdom but once.
*Singing and Dancing:* With Dancing.
                              and
*Afterpiece: The Dragon of Wantley.*
*Cast:* Cast as 9 Jan. 1744.

16   Mon.    SA.    *Hamlet.*
*Cast:* Hamlet—T. Sheridan; Ghost—R. Elrington; Queen—Mrs. Mynitt; Ophelia—Mrs. W. Phillips.
*Benefit:* Mrs. Phillips, Madam Roland, and P. Morris.
*Miscellaneous:* Sheridan's last performance this season.

*Singing and Dancing:* With Singing and Dancing, Act 1, "Elin a Roon" by Mrs. Storer; Act 2, "Quaker's Sermon" on Violin by Phillips; Act 3, the new Scaramouche Dance by Phillips, etc.; Act 4, the "Drunken Peasant" by Phillips.

and

*Afterpiece: The Hussar.*
*Cast:* Harlequin—W. Phillips; Pierrot—P. Morris; Columbine—Mrs. W. Phillips.
*Miscellaneous:* With several adaptations and additions by Phillips.

19    Thur.    AS.    *The Fatal Extravagance.*
*Cast:* None listed.
*Miscellaneous:* Never acted in this Kingdom before.

and

*Afterpiece: The Dragon of Wantley.*
*Cast:* As 9 Jan. 1744.

20    Fri.    AS.    *The Constant Couple.*
*Cast:* None listed.
*Miscellaneous:* Government Night; Anniversary of birth of Prince of Wales.

23    Mon.    AS.    *The Beggar's Opera.*
*Cast:* As 5 Jan. 1744.
*Command:* Duke and Duchess of Devonshire.
*Benefit:* Wright.
*Singing and Dancing:* With Singing and Dancing.
*Comment:* "Theatre Royal, Jan. 20, 1743-4. To prevent the ill Consequences of any Disappointment to the Nobility and Gentry, or raising Displeasure in the Town, on having my name inserted, without my Leave in Mr. Wright's Play-bill, on a Night I neither intended to play, or was obliged by my Articles in any Manner to perform. . . ."

Whereas Mr. Wright in his Play-bill of the Beggar's Opera advertised to be acted on 23 Jan. "presumed without the Permission or Approbation of the Proprietors, and contrary to any Agreement made with them by me for such Purpose, to insert my Name as a performer in the Part of Miss Polly . . . I hereby give notice, that I shall not then, on any Account appear or Perform. Marye Chateauneuf."

The "next day" Wright answered that he indeed did have the Proprietors' permission "this will easily appear, as I no more could or dared, get my Bills printed without the Proprietors consent, or put a command at the top of them, unless it was given me, then Mrs. Chateauneuf refuses to perform her Part, now it is commanded. T. Wright."

In the same issue another advertisement signed "Marye Chateauneuf" appears in which she repeats her first notice and adds that she refuses to perform "the Night of his Benefit, or Benefit Night of any other Player, during my stay in this Kingdom."

Then follows: "In answer to Mr. [*sic*] Chateauneuf's repeated Notice, I say, that I don't doubt his having Malice and Ill-nature enough to hinder his Daughter's performing in any Actor's Benefit; but I do certainly know, that he dares not refuse to let Mrs. Chateauneuf play for the Entertainment, and by the express Command of the Government, and therefore do positively assert she must play. T. Wright" (*FDJ*, 18–21 Jan. 1744).

26    Thur.    AS.    *Love for Love.*
*Cast:* Valentine—Lowe; Ben—I. Sparks; Angelica—Mrs. Furnival.
*Benefit:* Widow of Thomas Griffith.
*Miscellaneous:* At the particular Desire of several Ladies of Quality; This benefit was originally advertised for Griffith himself, but he died on 23 Jan. 1744 after a "long and severe Indisposition."
and

*Afterpiece: The Devil to Pay.*
*Cast:* Loverule—Lowe.
*Singing and Dancing:* With "Early Horn" by Lowe in Character.

28    Sat.    AS.    *King Henry IV, Part 2.*
*Cast:* Prince of Wales—Arne (his first attempt of this Kind).
*Benefit:* Mrs. Arne.
*Command:* Duke and Duchess of Devonshire.
*Singing and Dancing:* Singing by Lowe and Mrs. Arne; Dancing by Dumont and Mlle. Chateauneuf.
and

*Afterpiece: The Dragon of Wantley.*
*Cast:* None listed.

31    Tues.    AS.    *As You Like It.*
*Cast:* None listed.
*Benefit:* Barrington.
*Miscellaneous:* With the Roaratorio.
*Singing and Dancing:* Singing by Lowe; Dancing by Mlle. Chateauneuf.
and

*Afterpiece: The Stage Coach.*
*Cast:* None listed.

**FEBRUARY**

1    Wed.    AS.    *Comus.*
*Cast:* Lady—Mrs. Elmy.
*Benefit:* Mrs. Elmy.

*Singing and Dancing:* Vocals by Lowe, Mrs. Arne, Mlle. Chateauneuf, Miss Davies, etc.

and

*Afterpiece: Nancy; or, The Parting Lovers.*
*Cast:* Trueblue—Lowe; Nancy—Mlle. Chateauneuf.
*Miscellaneous:* Interlude. Never acted here [i.e. at AS].


2    Thur.    AS.    *Amphitryon.*
*Cast:* Jupiter—Wright; Sosia—Barrington; Phaedra—Mrs. Furnival.
*Singing and Dancing:* With several Entertainments of Singing and Dancing between the Acts.


2    Thur.    SA.    *Love Makes a Man.*
*Cast:* Clodio—Hall.
*Benefit:* Mynitt, Mason, L. Layfield, Dale, and Jenkins.
*Miscellaneous:* By Permission of the Lord Mayor and by the particular favour and Indulgence of the Rt. Hon. and Hon. Renters and Proprietors of Both Theatres being the last Time of the Company's Playing in Town; Prices: Stage and Boxes 5s. 5d., Lattices 4s. 4d., Pit 2s. 8½d., Gallery 1s. 7½d., Upper Gallery 1s. 1d.
*Deferred:* Originally advertised for 1 Feb. 1744.

and

*Afterpiece: The Mock Doctor.*
*Cast:* None listed.


4    Sat.    SA.    *The Beggar's Opera.*
*Cast:* Macheath—Lowe; Lucy—Mrs. Bayly; Polly—Mlle. Chateauneuf.
*Singing and Dancing:* With Dancing, viz. End Act 1, a Clown by Mr. Phillips; End Act 3, a hornpipe by Phillips and others, the whole conducted by Arne who will accompany on the harpsicord.


6    Mon.    AS.    *The Merchant of Venice.*
*Cast:* Bassanio—R. Elrington (from SA); Antonio—J. Elrington; Prince of Morocco—Beamsley; Tubal—I. Sparks; Launcelot—Barrington; Gobbo—Morgan; Salarino—Watson; Salanio—Dyer; Duke—Vanderbank; Gratiano—L. Sparks; Lorenzo—Lowe; Shylock—Wright; Portia—Mrs. Furnival; Nerissa—Miss Bullock; Jessica—Miss Douglas.
*Benefit:* Mrs. Furnival.
*Miscellaneous:* As written by Shakespeare. At the particular Desire of several Ladies of Quality. First performance by the united company.
*Singing and Dancing:* Lowe will sing songs proper to the character. Dancing by Moreau, Delamain, and Mlle. Chateauneuf. [Hitchcock 1788-94, 1:144-45 quotes the playbill which says dancing by Dumont, Mlle. Chateauneuf and Morris.]

and

*Afterpiece: The Virgin Unmasked.*
*Cast:* Lucy—Mlle. Chateauneuf (her first time in character); Quaver—Lowe.

9    Thur.    AS.    *Jane Shore.*
*Cast:* Jane Shore—Mrs. Pasquilino; Gloster—I. Sparks; Alicia—Mrs. Furnival.
*Benefit:* I. Sparks.
*Miscellaneous:* At the particular Desire of several Ladies of Quality.
*Singing and Dancing:* Dancing by Dumont and Mlle. Chateauneuf.

and

*Afterpiece: The Dragon of Wantley.*
*Cast:* Moore—Lowe; Margery—Mrs. Arne (her first appearance in any comic character); Mauxalinda—Mlle. Chateauneuf; Gubbins—Worsdale; Dragon—Layfield.

11    Sat.    AS.    *The Fatal Marriage; or, The Innocent Adultery.*
*Cast:* None listed.
*Command:* Judges.
*Benefit:* F. Elrington.
*Deferred:* Deferred from 2 Feb. 1744.

13    Mon.    AS.    *The Spanish Fryar.*
*Cast:* None listed.
*Command:* Lord Southwell, Grand Master.
*Benefit:* Sick and Distressed Free and Accepted Masons.

and

*Afterpiece: Damon and Phillida.*
*Cast:* Unspecified Parts: Lowe, Mrs. Arne, Mlle. Chateauneuf.

15    Wed.    SA.    *Othello.*
*Cast:* Othello—Barry (his first appearance on any stage); Iago—Wright; Duke—Vanderbank; Brabantio—Beamsley; Roderigo—Morgan; Cassio—J. Elrington; Lodovico—Bardin; Montano—Watson; Desdemona—Mrs. Bayley; Emilia—Mrs. Furnival.
*Benefit:* Spranger Barry.
*Miscellaneous:* Boxes, 5s. 5d.; Pit, 3s. 3d.; Gallery, 2s. 2d.
    The playbill, quoted in Hitchcock, adds: "By order of the proprietors, Tickets given out for this play at the TRAS will be taken the same night at the TRSA."
    [W. J. Lawrence notes that "as Barry was not a member of the United Company, he virtually hired the theatre by making himself responsible— perhaps paying in advance—the charges of the house. This was a lucky arrangement for him as he scooped in all the profits. After his success the

Proprietors feared to be pestered to death by other aspirants and thought proper to issue a warning advertisement by way of deterrent" (Lawrence, 11:19–20). *FDJ*, 17 Feb. 1744, published this warning: "No other person who is not a member of the United Company [note that this implies that SA is under the control of the united company by this date] to be allowed to benefit under the full sum of £50 sterling, to be paid into the hands of the Treasurer eight days before the fixed time of Performance. By order of the Board of Proprietors."]

*Singing and Dancing:* Singing and dancing between the acts by Lowe and Mlle. Chateauneuf.

16     Thur.     AS.     *Venice Preserved.*
*Cast:* Pierre—Sparks; Jaffier—Wright; Belvidera—Mrs. Pasquilino.
*Benefit:* Mrs. Pasquilino.
*Singing and Dancing:* With Entertainments of Singing and Dancing.

and

*Afterpiece: The Dragon of Wantley.*
*Cast:* Moore—Lowe; Margery—Mrs. Arne; Mauxalinda—Mlle. Chateauneuf.

18     Sat.     SA.     *The Death of Abel.*
*Cast:* Principal Characters: Lowe, Mrs. Arne, Mlle. Chateauneuf.
*Miscellaneous:* [Premiere.] By Subscription. The Stage will be disposed in the same Manner as at Mr. Handel's Oratorios in London. Prices: Pit, Boxes, Lattices one half guinea; First gallery 2s. 8½ d.; Upper Gallery 2s. 2d.; Ladies are requested to sit in the Pit, as well as Boxes, as is the Custom in the Operas and Oratorios in London; for which purpose the Pit Seats will be made thoroughly clean.

"Mrs. Arne proposes to exhibit at the TRAS four Performances disposed in the Manner of the Oratorios in London, viz. two performances of The Distresses and Conquests of King Alfred composed by the Command of H.R.H. the Prince of Wales and performed at his Palace at Cliefdon and two performances of a new Oratorio called *The Death of Abel*. Both composed by Mr. Arne, the Principal Characters to be performed by Mr. Lowe an Mrs. Arne" (*FDJ*, 24–28 Jan. 1744).

20     Mon.     SA.     *Twelfth Night.*
*Cast:* None listed.
*Benefit:* L. Duval.
*Miscellaneous:* The above Play is the first Benefit Mr. Duval has presumed to trouble the Town with since the Union of the Theatres; to which he contributed all that lay in his Power, by delivering up all his Interest to the Gentlemen Proprietors.

and

*Afterpiece: The Dragon of Wantley.*
*Cast:* Principal Characters: Lowe and Mlle. Chateauneuf.

22    Wed.    SA.    *The Miser.*    V.
*Cast:* Lovegold—F. Elrington.
*Benefit:* Hospital for Incurables.
*Miscellaneous:* By Appointment of the Charitable Society in Crow St.
"Whereas in the last printed playbills giving Notice that no places were to be kept in any part of the House has been inconvenient to many persons of Quality; it is now ordered that places may be taken in any part of the House by ladies who are pleased to send to the Boxkeeper, who shall attend at the playhouse on Wednesday at 3 o'clock for that purpose. The Stage will be built and enclosed . . . in order to keep the Ladies warm. The house to be illuminated with wax lights" (*FDJ*, 31 Jan. 1744).
[See *FDJ*, 3 Mar. 1744 for some lines addressed to F. Elrington regarding his performance as Lovegold.]
*Singing and Dancing:* With Entertainments of Singing and Dancing.
*Financial:* "Last Wednesday, at the play of the Miser (for the benefit of the Hospital of Incurables) there was the most numerous polite Audience that ever appeared at a Play in this Kingdom, the Profits whereof amounted to more than two hundred Pounds. . . ." (*FDJ*, 25–28 Feb. 1744).
and
*Afterpiece: The Dragon of Wantley.*
*Cast:* None listed.

25    Sat.    SA.    *The Death of Abel.*
*Cast:* As 18 Feb. 1744.
*Miscellaneous:* Second Night.

28    Tues.    AS.    *The Way of the World.*
*Cast:* Petulant—F. Elrington; Marwood—Mrs. Furnival.
*Benefit:* R. Layfield.
*Singing and Dancing:* Dancing, viz. End Act 1, Scots Dance by Phillips; Act 2, Tambourine Dance by Mlle. Chateauneuf; Act 3 a Punch by M. Dumont; Act 4, Pierrot in the Basket by Morris; Act 5, The Drunken Peasant by Phillips.
and
*Afterpiece: The Dragon of Wantley.*
*Cast:* None listed.

29    Wed.    AS.    *The Disappointment; or, The Robbers Reclaimed.*
*Cast:* Principal Character—Lowe; Principal Character—Mlle. Chateauneuf.
*Benefit:* The Author [John Randal].
*Miscellaneous:* [Premiere.] With an occasional Prologue and Epilogue.

"It is hoped, that the Town in General and University in Particular; who were ever remarkable in supporting Pieces of this Nature will be so kind as to favour the Author with their Company on the Night of the Performance" (*PO*, 28 Feb. 1744).

[Nicoll 1977–79, 2:351 lists "*The Disappointment . . .* altered from a Farce after the Manner of the Beggar's Opera by John Randal, 1732." *LS* lists an anonymous play of the same title, performed once at YB in 1734, and *The Disappointment; or, The Mother in Fashion* by T. Southerne, which had only two performances pre-1700. Gagey suggests H. Carey as the author.]
*Singing and Dancing:* As it is of the Opera Kind the principle Characters will be performed by Lowe and Madam. Chateauneuf; in which will be introduced a Song, proper to those times called "Britons Strike Home, etc."

MARCH

1    Thur.    AS.    *The Rehearsal.*
*Cast:* Bayes—Bardin.
*Benefit:* Bardin.
*Singing and Dancing:* Vocals by Lowe, Worsdale, and others.

2    Fri.    SA.    *Othello.*
*Cast:* Othello—Barry (his second Appearance on any Stage).
*Benefit:* S. Barry (second).
*Deferred:* Deferred from 21 Feb. 1744 due to Barry's sudden Indisposition.

6    Tues.    AS.    *The Merchant of Venice.*
*Cast:* None listed.
*Benefit:* Neil (boxkeeper).
*Miscellaneous:* At the particular Desire of several Ladies of Quality.
                    and
*Afterpiece: The Devil to Pay.*
*Cast:* Loverule—Lowe; Nell—Mlle. Chateauneuf.
*Singing and Dancing:* Singing: "The Early Horn" by Lowe.

7    Wed.    AS.    *Twelfth Night.*
*Cast:* None listed.
*Benefit:* Dumont.
*Miscellaneous:* At the particular Desire of several Ladies of Quality.
*Singing and Dancing:* Songs in Character by Lowe; with several Entertainments of Singing and Dancing.

9    Fri.    SA.    *Venice Preserved.*
*Cast:* Pierre—Barry (his first Appearance in that Character).

10    Sat.    SA.    *The Judgment of Paris.*
*Cast:* None listed.
*Miscellaneous:* Third Subscription Night. Prices: Pit, Boxes, Lattices 10/6, 1st Gallery 2/8½, Upper Gallery 2/2.
*Singing and Dancing:* With all the Choruses as performed at the TRDL.
[*The Judgment of Paris* "Written by Congreve and New Set by Mr Arne" (*LS*, pt. 3:2:974) was performed at DL on 12 and 19 March and 17 April 1742.]

and

*Afterpiece: Alfred.*
*Cast:* None listed.
*Miscellaneous:* "a new Serenata . . . never performed but at his [the Prince of Wales'] Palace at Cliefden, which concludes with ["Rule, Britannia"]. . . . The reason of not performing this Saturday is that the Musick Writers could not possibly get the Musick finished" (*FDJ,* 28 Feb.–3 Mar. 1744).

[Boydell 1988, 98, quotes in full an advertisement for the 30 May 1743 performance of these pieces given at Mr. Neale's Great Room in Fishamble St. At that performance the principal parts were sung by Lowe, Colgan, and Mrs. Arne. The advertisement concludes: "This performance will be done to great Advantage on account of the Organ, and the Assistance of Mr. Colgan, several Gentlemen in the Chorusses, who could not perform in the Theatre."

This was, as Boydell indicates, the first public performance of Thomas Arne's version of the masque *Alfred* written by James Thomson and David Mallet for performance at the birthday celebration for Frederick, Prince of Wales's eldest daughter, Princess Augusta, at Cliveden House on 1 August 1740. Arne's masque, variously entitled *The Distresses of Alfred the Great, King of England, With his Conquest of the Danes, Alfred the Great,* and *The Distresses and Conquest of King Alfred,* was a drastic revision of the Thomson/Mallet masque that retains little of the original dialogue and adds nine new songs (some of which may have been composed by Charles Burney). For an extended discussion of the masques of *Alfred* see John C. Greene, *The Plays of James Thomson: A Critical Edition,* vol. 2 (New York: Garland, 1987), pp. 301–13.]


12    Mon.    AS.    *The Conscious Lovers.*
*Cast:* Sir John—Husband; Indiana—Mrs. Pasquilino; Phillis—Mrs. Furnival.
*Benefit:* Watson.
*Miscellaneous:* At the particular Desire of several Ladies of Quality.
*Singing and Dancing:* With Entertainments of Singing and Dancing.

and

*Afterpiece: Damon and Phillida.*
*Cast:* Damon—Lowe; Phillida—Mlle. Chateauneuf.

13    Tues.    AS.    *The Mourning Bride.*
*Cast:* None listed.
*Benefit:* William Delamain.
*Singing and Dancing:* Dancing, viz. End Act 1, A serious Dance by Moreau; Act 2, a favourite song by Lowe; Act 3, Tambourine Dance by Mlle. Chateauneuf.; Act 4, Pierrot in the Basket by Morris; Act 5, The Drunken Peasant by Phillips.

and

*Afterpiece: The Devil to Pay.*
*Cast:* As 6 Mar. 1744.
*Singing and Dancing:* "The Early Horn" by Lowe.


14    Wed.    AS.    *Love for Love.*
*Cast:* None listed.
*Benefit:* Misses Mary and Cambellina Douglas Daughters of the late Rt. Rev. George, Lord Mornington.
*Miscellaneous:* At the particular Desire of several Ladies of Quality.
*Singing and Dancing:* With Entertainments of Singing and Dancing.


15    Thur.    AS.    *The Beggar's Opera.*
*Cast:* Macheath—Lowe; Polly—Mlle. Chateauneuf.
*Benefit:* Mlle. Chateauneuf.
*Miscellaneous:* At the particular Desire of several Ladies of Quality.
*Singing and Dancing:* With entertainments of singing and dancing between the Acts.

and

*Afterpiece: The Virgin Unmasked.*
*Cast:* Quaver—Lowe; Lucy—Mlle. Chateauneuf; (the other parts as usual).


17    Sat.    SA.    *The Judgment of Paris.*
*Cast:* None listed.
*Miscellaneous:* The Last Subscription Night.

and

*Afterpiece: Alfred.*
*Cast:* None listed.


[Passion Week 19–24 March]


29    Thur.    AS.    *Comus.*
*Cast:* Comus—Wright; Pastoral Nymph and Sabrina—Mrs. Arne; Bacchanal and Attendant Spirit—Lowe; Euphrosyne—Miss Davies.
*Miscellaneous:* At the particular Desire of several Ladies of Quality; the last Time of performing it this Season.

*Singing and Dancing:* Dancing by Dumont and Mlle. Chateauneuf; "Sweet Echo" by Mrs. Arne; with all the Choruses.

APRIL

2    Mon.    SA.    *The Merchant of Venice.*
*Cast:* Shylock—Wright; Bassanio—R. Elrington; Antonio—J. Elrington; Gratiano—L. Sparks; Lorenzo—Lowe; Portia—Mrs. Furnival.
*Miscellaneous:* At the particular Desire of several Ladies of Quality.
*Singing and Dancing:* Lowe sings songs proper to Character.
                    and
*Afterpiece: Rosamond.*
*Cast:* King Henry—Lowe; Sir Trusty—R. Layfield; Grideline—Miss Davies; Queen—Mrs. Arne; Rosamond—Mlle. Chateauneuf.
*Miscellaneous:* [Premiere. *DG,* 3–7 Apr. 1744 contains an epilogue spoken this night.]

5    Thur.    SA.    *The Way of the World.*
*Cast:* None listed.
                    and
*Afterpiece: Rosamond.*
*Cast:* As 2 Apr. 1744.

9    Mon.    SA.    *The Prude; or, Win Her and Wear Her.*
*Cast:* The Prude—Mrs. Furnival; Teague—Barrington; Sappira—Mrs. Pasquilino.
*Miscellaneous:* Written by a retired University Gentleman. With an Epilogue by Mrs. Furnival.
    [Nicoll lists two much later plays called *The Prude,* none with subtitle; *LS* lists none.]
                    and
*Afterpiece: Rosamond.*
*Cast:* Grideline—Miss Davies; King Henry—Lowe; Sir Trusty—Layfield; Rosamond—Mlle. Chateauneuf; Page—Young Person who never appeared on any Stage; Queen Eleanor—Mrs. Arne.

10    Tues.    SA.    *The Prude.*
*Cast:* None listed.
*Miscellaneous:* Second Night; Written by a Gentleman late of the University. Prologue spoken by Sparks, an Epilogue spoken by Mrs. Furnival.
                    and
*Afterpiece: Rosamond.*
*Cast:* As 9 Apr. 1744.
*Miscellaneous:* Written by Mr. Addison, Music by Arne.

12    Thur.    SA.    *The Prude.*
*Cast:* None listed.
*Benefit:* The Author.

and

*Afterpiece: Rosamond.*
*Cast:* None listed.


13    Fri.    AS.    *The Recruiting Officer.*
*Cast:* None listed.
*Benefit:* Worsdale.
*Miscellaneous:* At the particular Desire of several Ladies of Quality.

and

*Afterpiece: The Dragon of Wantley.*
*Cast:* None listed.


14    Sat.    SA.    *The Beggar's Opera.*
*Cast:* Macheath—Lowe; Lucy—Mrs. Bayley; Polly—Mlle. Chateauneuf.
*Singing and Dancing:* With Dancing.

and

*Afterpiece: The Virgin Unmasked.*
*Cast:* Quaver—Lowe; Lucy—Mlle. Chateauneuf.


16    Mon.    AS.    *Woman is a Riddle.*
*Cast:* None listed.
*Benefit:* Morris.
*Singing and Dancing:* With entertainments of singing and dancing.

and

*Afterpiece:* Unspecified "Farce."


18    Wed.    AS.    *The Provoked Husband.*
*Cast:* None listed.
*Benefit:* J. Elrington.

and

*Afterpiece: The Devil to Pay.*
*Cast:* None listed.


19    Thur.    SA.    *As You Like It.*
*Cast:* Amiens—Lowe; Jacques—Wright; Touchstone—Barrington; Rosalind—Mrs. Furnival.
*Singing and Dancing:* "Blow, blow ye Winter Wind" and "Under the Greenwood Tree" sung by Lowe.

and

*Afterpiece: Rosamond.*

*Cast:* King Henry—Lowe; Rosamund—Mlle. Chateauneuf; Queen Elenor—
Mrs. Arne.

23     Mon.     SA.     *Woman is a Riddle.*
*Cast:* None listed.
*Miscellaneous:* At the particular Desire of several Ladies of Quality.

                              and

*Afterpiece: Margery; or, A Worse Plague than the Dragon.*
*Cast:* None listed.
*Miscellaneous:* Never performed in this Kingdom [but see AS 24 Jan. 1739].

26     Thur.    SA.     *Theodosius; or, The Force of Love.*
*Cast:* Varanes—Barry (his first time in Character).
*Benefit:* Barry.
*Singing and Dancing:* "As the original Songs and Choruses of the Play were
never performed in this Kingdom, for want of Musick and Performances
equal to such an undertaking Mr. Arne has been prevailed upon to set the
same to new music" (*FDJ,* 17–21 Apr. 1744). [W. H. Grattan Flood remarks:
"We know that Arne never had any scruples about replacing Purcell's music
by his own, and it is not likely that much persuasion was necessary to make
him rewrite the *Theodosius* music" (Flood 1906a, 224).]

30     Mon.     SA.     *The Beggar's Opera.*
*Cast:* None listed.

                              and

*Afterpiece: The Hussar.*
*Cast:* Harlequin—W. Phillips.

MAY

2      Wed.     AS.     *King Henry IV, with the Humours of Falstaff.*
*Cast:* None listed.
*Benefit:* Beamsley and I. Sparks.

                              and

*Afterpiece: The Vintner Tricked.*
*Cast:* None listed.

3      Thur.    SA.     *Othello.*
*Cast:* Othello—Barry; Iago—Wright; Desdemona—Mrs. Pasquilino; Emilia—Mrs. Furnival.

                              and

*Afterpiece: The Hussar.*
*Cast:* Harlequin—W. Phillips; Conjurer—R. Layfield.

7   Mon.   SA.   *The Recruiting Officer.*
*Cast:* Plume—Wright; Kite—L. Layfield; Silvia—Mrs. Furnival; Melinda—Mrs. Pasquilino; Brazen—I. Sparks.

10   Thur.   SA.   *Theodosius.*
*Cast:* Theodosius—J. Elrington; Leontine—F. Elrington; Varanes—Barrington; Marcian—L. Sparks; Pulcheria—Mrs. Pasquilino; Athenais—Mrs. Furnival.
*Miscellaneous:* At the particular Desire of several Ladies of Quality.
and
*Afterpiece: The Vintner Tricked.*
*Cast:* None listed.

17   Thur.   AS.   *The Miser.*
*Cast:* Lovegold—F. Elrington; Lappet—Mrs. Furnival.
and
*Afterpiece: The Hussar.*
*Cast:* Harlequin—W. Phillips.

21   Mon.   AS.   *Jane Shore.*
*Cast:* Jane Shore—Mrs. Pasquilino; Gloster—I. Sparks; Alicia—Mrs. Furnival.
and
*Afterpiece: The Hussar.*
*Cast:* None listed.

23   Wed.   SA.   *Woman is a Riddle.*
*Cast:*   Vainwit—Sparks;   Vulture—Morris;   Courtwell—R. Elrington; Manly—J. Elrington; Aspin—Harrington; Butler—I. Sparks; Miranda—Mrs. Pasquilino; Clarinda—Mrs. Bayley; Necessary—Miss Bullock; Betty—Mrs. Phillips.
*Benefit:* P. Morris and Mlle. Roland.
*Miscellaneous:* At the particular Desire of several Ladies of Quality.
*Singing and Dancing:* With entertainments of singing and dancing, viz. Act I "The Dutch Skipper" by Phillips; end Act IV a dance called "La Marie" and the Louvre and Minuet by Moreau and Mlle. Roland.
and
*Afterpiece: The Devil to Pay.*
*Cast:* Loverule—J. Morris; Nell—Mlle. Roland (her first time in character).

24   Thur.   AS.   *Love and Loyalty; or, Publick Justice.* V.
*Cast:* King of Arragon—Wright; Ramirez—L. Sparks; Sebastian—Walker; Rinaldo—Beamsley; Alonzo—R. Elrington; Provost—Watson; Captain—

Morgan; Victoria—Mrs. Furnival; Bellamante—Miss Rogers (her first appearance on any stage).
*Miscellaneous:* By Mr. Thomas Walker, a tragedy. [Premiere. Nicoll 1977–79, 2:363 says this is an Irish revival of Walker's play *The Fate of Villainy;* see also Chetwood 1749, 247.]
*Comment:* "Mr. Walker's new Tragedy received prodigious Applause on Thursday night and will be acted again on Monday next. All the Actors performed admirably, and the whole was conducted with decent Propriety. The Publication of this piece is expected and much desired" (*FDJ,* 22–26 May 1744).

25    Fri.    SA.    *The Recruiting Officer.*
*Cast:* None listed.
*Benefit:* Dryden (treasurer).
*Miscellaneous:* For the Entertainment of the Officers and Gentlemen of the several Regiments of Horse and foot Militia of the City of Dublin.
*Deferred:* Deferred from 7 Apr.

28    Mon.    AS.    *Love and Loyalty.*
*Cast:* None listed.
*Miscellaneous:* [A benefit for the author, Thomas Walker, was advertised for 1 June 1744 with an Overture, select Pieces of Musick adapted to the subject of each Act, particularly the Dead March in *Saul* by Handel, and singing by Mrs. Storer, particularly "Consider Fond Shepherd." However, Chetwood tells us that Walker "not being able to pay in half the common expences, the Doors were order'd to be kept shut; but I remember, few people came to ask the reason. However, I fear this Disappointment hasten'd his death, for he survived it but three days" (Chetwood 1749, 247).]

JUNE

7    Thur.    SA.    *Macbeth.*
*Cast:* Macbeth—Barry (his first time in character); Hecate—L. Layfield; Lady Macbeth—Mrs. Furnival.

JULY

2    Mon.    AS.    *The Beggar's Opera.*
*Cast:* Macheath—Lowe; Polly—Mlle. Chateauneuf; Lucy—Mrs. Bayley; Peachum—Bardin; Lockit—Vanderbank; Mrs. Peachum—Mrs. Vanderbank; Diana Trapes—Mr. [*sic*] Layfield; Mrs. Slamerkin—Mrs. Elmy.
*Command:* Lords Justice.
*Miscellaneous:* "Fiftieth" Performance [presumably since its AS premiere]. Positively the last time of the Company's performing in Town this Season.

14    Sat.    SA.    *The Conscious Lovers.*
*Cast:* Bevil Jr.—Delane (the last time of his performing this season); Seland—Milward.
*Benefit:* The Charitable Infirmary on Inns Quay.

## 1744–1745 Season

Theatres operating: United Company at SA and AS (spectacular productions only as AS); Capel St.

*United Company:*
Bardin, Barrington, S. Barry, Beamsley, L. Duval, Michael Dyer, Mrs. Dyer (formerly Miss Harriot Bullock, m. 26 Dec.), F. Elrington, J. Elrington, Ralph Elrington, Richard Elrington, Foote (from DL., to CAP in Jan. 1745), Mrs. Furnival, Husband, L. Layfield, L. Layfield, Jr., R. Layfield, Mrs. Mitchell, C. Morgan (died in May), Oates, Parsons, Mrs. Pasquilino (left stage in Nov.), Quin (from CG in Aug.), T. Sheridan, I. Sparks, L. Sparks, Vanderbank, J. Watson, Jr.

Singers: Miss Carleton, Miss Davies, Mrs. Storer.

Dancers: Moreau, Mrs. Moreau?, Master Pitt.

Musicians: Alcock, Oates.

House Servants: Dryden (Treasurer), Neil (boxkeeper).

*Repertory:*
Mainpieces: Recorded Performances: 60 (of 33 different pieces).
Afterpieces: Recorded performances: 26 performances of 15 different pieces including unspecified farces.
Premieres: *The Patriot.*
Entr'acte entertainments: Many performances of singing and dancing/advertised at SA, one at AS.
Command Performances: 4 (no Government Nights advertised).
Benefits: (SA)
Pre-February: Actor—4; Author—1.
Post-February: Actor—21; Author—2; Charity—3; House Servant—1.
Benefits: (AS)
Post-February: Actor—1; Charity—1.

*Capel Street Company* (advertised as acting "By Permission of the Rt. Hon. Lord Mayor of the City of Dublin"):
Bourne, Brouden, Mrs. Brouden, Bunbury, Corry, Foote (from SA in Jan.), Hall, Kirkpatrick, Miss Lewis, Marshall (from England), Mitchell, Morgan, J. Morris, O'Brien, W. Phillips, Mrs. W. Phillips, Rivers, Townsend, Wright.

Dancers: Cormick, Walsh.

Musicians: Fitzgerald, Walsh.

House Servants: Boynton (wardrobe keeper), Mrs. Kathrens (pit office-keeper).

*Repertory:*
Mainpieces: Recorded performances: 32 (of 20 different pieces).
Afterpieces: Recorded performances: 21 performances of 10 different pieces.
Premieres:
*The Oculist.* (a)
*The Prize.* (a)
Entr'acte entertainments: One performance of singing and dancing advertised.
Command Performances: None.
Benefits:
Post-February: Actor—11.

---

## 1744

### SEPTEMBER

27    Thur.    SA.      *The Recruiting Officer.*
*Cast:* None listed.
*Benefit:* Mrs. Mitchell.
*Miscellaneous:* Boxes, 4s. 4d.; Lattices, 3s. 3d.; Pit, 2s. 6d. British; Gallery, 1s. 7½d.
*Singing and Dancing:* With entertainments of singing and dancing.

### OCTOBER

11    Thur.    SA.      *The Constant Couple.*
*Cast:* None listed.

*Miscellaneous:* Government Night; Anniversary of coronation of George II. Boxes open to the Ladies.

[After this performance the United Company travelled to Kilkenny where they intended "speedily to entertain the city with their best plays" (*FDJ*, 16 Oct. 1744).]

25　　Thur.　　AS.　　*The Rehearsal.*
*Cast:* Bayes—Foote (from DL).
*Miscellaneous:* With a Grand Battle by new rais'd Horse and Foot.

30　　Tues.　　SA.　　*Twelfth Night.*
*Cast:* None listed.
*Command:* Lords Justice.
*Miscellaneous:* [Government Night; Anniversary of birth of King George II.]

"Several Gentlemen and Ladies of distinction have applied to the Proprietors of the Theatre that ladies might be admitted into the Pit at the same price as the Gentlemen are, which is the custom in every Town in Ireland but Dublin, the said proprietors being willing to encourage theatrical performances have given orders for the future, Ladies will be admitted into the Pit accordingly" (*FDJ*, 27–30 Oct. 1744). [There is no evidence that the ladies used the privilege for many years except at a few benefits when, as in the past, the front rows of the pit were railed off for them. O'Keeffe states that as late as 1770 no women sat in the main portion of the pit at any Dublin theatre (O'Keeffe 1826, 1:287).]

NOVEMBER

5　　Mon.　　SA.　　*Venice Preserved.*
*Cast:* Pierre—Barry.
*Singing and Dancing:* Dancing by Moreau.

8　　Thur.　　SA.　　*Venice Preserved.*
*Cast:* Pierre—Barry.

and

*Afterpiece: Damon and Phillida.*
*Cast:* Damon—Dyer; Phillida—Mrs. Storer.

12　　Mon.　　SA.　　*Macbeth.*
*Cast:* Macbeth—Barry.
*Miscellaneous:* [An adulatory letter in praise of Barry as Macbeth appeared in *FDJ*, 21 Nov. 1744.]

15   Thur.   SA.   *The Relapse.*
*Cast:* Foppington—Foote.
*Benefit:* Foote.
*Miscellaneous:* Ladies admitted to the Pit at the same Price as Gentlemen.


26   Mon.   SA.   *King Lear and His Three Daughters.*
*Cast:* Lear—Barry (his first time in that character).
*Benefit:* Barry.


**DECEMBER**


3   Mon.   SA.   *The Patriot.* V.
*Cast:* Gustavus Vasa—Barry; Principal Character—Foote.
*Miscellaneous:* [A revision of Henry Brooke's *Gustavus Vasa,* which had been banned by the Lord Chamberlain in London on 10 Mar. 1739. This play is remarkable for affording both Barry and Foote their first original parts.]
*Comment:* [See Delany 1861, 2:336–37, for the observation: "I don't find it greatly approved of, but they say it is miserably acted. He will not print it till it has made its appearance on the English stage."]


6   Thur.   SA.   *The Patriot.*
*Cast:* As 3 Dec. 1744.


10   Mon.   SA.   *The Patriot.* V.
*Cast:* As 3 Dec. 1744.
*Benefit:* The Author [Henry Brooke].
*Comment:* "Last Monday night at the TRSA The Patriot was played for the third time . . . upon giving another play for Thursday, The Patriot was loudly called for. . . ." There is no other record that *The Patriot* was performed again.


11   Tues.   SA.   *Tunbridge Walks; or, The Yeoman of Kent.*
*Cast:* None listed.
*Benefit:* Mrs. Storer.
                                    and
*Afterpiece: The Contrivances.*
*Cast:* None listed.


22   Sat.   SA.   *The Royal Merchant.*
*Cast:* Florez—L. Sparks; Clause—F. Elrington; Jaculine—Mrs. Storer; Bertha—Miss Bullock.

*Miscellaneous:* Prices: Stage 5/5, Boxes and Lattices 4/4, Pit 2/8½, Gallery 1/7½.

*Singing and Dancing:* Singing by Mrs. Storer, dancing by Moreau.

## 1745

### JANUARY

14   Mon.   SA.   *Othello.*

*Cast:* Othello—Barry.

*Deferred:* Deferred from 10 Jan. because of "bad weather" but see a performance of that date.

15   Thur.   CAP.   *The Merchant of Venice.*

*Cast:* Duke—Rivers; Prince of Morocco—Brouden; Antonio—Townsend; Bassanio—Marshall; Grantiano—Hall; Lorenzo—Corry; Shylock—Wright (his first appearance this season); Tubal—Bourne; Launcelot—Morgan; Portia—Mrs. Brouden; Nerissa—Mrs. W. Phillips; Jessica—Miss Lewis.

*Miscellaneous:* Opening Performance of the New Theatre in Capel Street; By Permission of the Rt. Hon. Lord Mayor of Dublin. Prices: Boxes, 4s. 4d.; Lattices, 3s. 3d.; Pit, 2s. 2d.; first gallery, 1s. 1d.; second gallery 6½d.; To begin precisely at half past six o'clock; no odd Money taken until after Act 3; Doors will open at five o'clock, where Servants will be allowed to keep Places." "Mr. Phillips, to remove any Reflections or injurious Aspersions, calculated to Prejudice him in the Prosecution of this Affair, will take care to obtain the Judgment and Certificate of the best Master Builders, as to its Warmth, Strength, and Security. . . . the Doors will be open at 5 o'clock when servants will be allowed to keep Places. Gentlemen who are pleased to subscribe to Mr. Phillips Theatre are desired to send in their Money by Wednesday next for no subscriptions will be received after— Those Gentlemen to have their names engraved on their respective Ticket: otherwise they will not be admitted" (*FDJ*, 12–15 Jan. 1745).

[Stretch's Puppets reopened on 16 Jan. and performed Tuesdays, Wednesdays, Fridays, and Saturdays at 6 o'clock.]

21   Mon.   CAP.   *The Merchant of Venice.*

*Cast:* None listed.

                              and

*Afterpiece: The Mock Doctor.*

*Cast:* None listed.

22　Tues.　CAP.　*Hamlet.*
*Cast:* Hamlet—Marshall.

28　Mon.　CAP.　*The Constant Couple.*
*Cast:* Sir Harry—Foote (from SA); Standard—Marshall.

29　Tues.　CAP.　*The Constant Couple.*
*Cast:* None listed.

FEBRUARY

1　Fri.　SA.　*King Richard III.*
*Cast:* Gloster—Sheridan.
*Benefit:* Sheridan.
*Singing and Dancing:* Singing by Mrs. Storer, Dancing by Moreau.
and
*Afterpiece: The Honest Yorkshireman.*
*Cast:* Arabella—Mrs. Storer.

4　Mon.　CAP.　*The Constant Couple.*
*Cast:* None listed.

6　Wed.　SA.　*The Conscious Lovers.*
*Cast:* Bevil, Jr.—Barry.
*Benefit:* Parsons.
*Miscellaneous:* With Entertainments.
and
*Afterpiece: Damon and Phillida.*
*Cast:* None listed.

7　Thur.　SA.　*The Spanish Fryar.*
*Cast:* Torrismond—Elrington.
*Benefit:* Ralph Elrington.
and
*Afterpiece: The Devil to Pay.*
*Cast:* None listed.

8　Fri.　SA.　*The Royal Merchant.*
*Cast:* None listed.
*Benefit:* Barrington.
*Singing and Dancing:* With singing and dancing between the acts, particularly the "Roaratorio."
and
*Afterpiece:* Unspecified "Farce."

8    Fri.    CAP.    *The Drummer.*
*Cast:* Tinsel—Foote (first time).

and

*Afterpiece: The Virgin Unmasked.*
*Cast:* None listed.


9    Sat.    CAP.    *Venice Preserved.*
*Cast:* Pierre—Foote.
*Benefit:* Foote.

and

*Afterpiece:* [*The Debauchee; or,*] *The Credulous Cuckold.*
*Cast:* Fondlewife—Foote.
*Miscellaneous:* [Anonymous adaptation of a comedy by Aphra Behn.]


11    Mon.    SA.    *The Twin Rivals.*
*Cast:* Young Woudbe—L. Sparks; Teague—Barrington; Aurelia—Mrs. Furnival.
*Command:* Lords Justice.
*Benefit:* L. Sparks.
*Singing and Dancing:* With Singing by Mrs. Storer and Dancing by Moreau; Barrington will sing his "Roaratorio."

and

*Afterpiece:* Unspecified "Farce."


11    Tues.    CAP.    *Hamlet.*
*Cast:* Hamlet—Bunbury (his first appearance on any stage).


12    Tues.    CAP.    *Venice Preserved.*
*Cast:* Pierre—Foote.

and

*Afterpiece: The Credulous Cockold.*
*Cast:* None listed.


13    Wed.    SA.    *Macbeth.*
*Cast:* Macbeth—Barry; Lady Macbeth—Mrs. Furnival.
*Command:* Judges.
*Benefit:* F. Elrington.
*Miscellaneous:* "N. B. It being apprehended that the usual appearance of Ladies usual at Dr. Taylor's Lecture ['to Prove the Seat of Vision with the Anatomical and Optic Experiments'], might prejudice Mr. Elrington in his Benefit, the Doctor has been pleased to defer his lecture . . ." (*FDJ,* 9–12 Feb. 1745).
*Singing and Dancing:* Singing by Mrs. Storer, Dancing by Moreau and Master Pitt.

and
*Afterpiece: The Honest Yorkshireman.*
*Cast:* None listed.


14    Thur.    CAP.    *Othello.*
*Cast:* Othello—Bunbury.


15    Fri.    SA.    *The Miser.*
*Cast:* Lovegold—F. Elrington; Lappet—Mrs. Furnival.
*Benefit:* Dryden (treasurer).
*Singing and Dancing:* With singing and dancing.
                              and
*Afterpiece: The Honest Yorkshireman.*
*Cast:* None listed.


16    Sat.    CAP.    *Hamlet.*
*Cast:* Hamlet—Bunbury.
*Benefit:* Bunbury.
                              and
*Afterpiece: The Mock Doctor.*
*Cast:* Mock Doctor—Bunbury.


18    Mon.    SA.    *Theodosius.*
*Cast:* Varanes—Barry.
*Benefit:* Barry.
*Singing and Dancing:* Singing by Mrs. Storer, Dancing by Moreau.
                              and
*Afterpiece: The Honest Yorkshireman.*
*Cast:* None listed.


18    Mon.    CAP.    *The Constant Couple.*
*Cast:* Sir Harry—Foote.
*Comment:* An anonymous letter dated 20 Feb. 1745 now in the British Library and quoted in the entry for Samuel Foote in *BD* says: "The attention of the Publick has been lately taken up by the two rival theatres, the old one in Smock-Alley and a new one, under the direction of Mr. Foote in Capel-Street; but the last is in the greatest esteem at present, Mr. Foote having played Wildair, Bayes, and Pierre five times each, to as crowded Audiences as ever were known." We have record this season of Foote appearing in only four performances of *The Constant Couple,* one of *The Rehearsal,* and two of *Venice Preserved* prior to the date of this letter.
                              and
*Afterpiece: The Credulous Cuckold.*
*Cast:* None listed.

20    Wed.    SA.    *Twelfth Night.*
*Cast:* None listed.
*Benefit:* The Hospital of Incurables.
*Miscellaneous:* By Appointment of the Charitable Musical Society. Theatre illuminated with wax; The stage commodiously built for the ladies as the pit must be kept entirely for the Gentlemen; Prices: Boxes, stage, lattices and pit, 5s. 5d.; Gallery 2s. 8½d.
*Singing and Dancing:* Singing by Mrs. Storer; the Crow Street Band will entertain between the acts.
*Comment:* "Last Wednesday Night there was the greatest Appearance at the Play for the Benefit of the Hospital for the Incurables, that ever was seen" (*FDJ*, 19–23 Feb. 1745).
*Financial:* The accounts of the Charitable Musical Society presented in *FDJ*, 29 Jan.–2 Feb. 1745 indicate that the proceeds from the benefit play for Hospital for Incurables in 1743–44 season was £196 11s. 11d.

and

*Afterpiece: The Vintner Tricked.*
*Cast:* None listed.


21    Thur.    SA.    *The Squire of Alsatia.*
*Cast:* None listed.
*Benefit:* Neil (boxkeeper) and Morgan.

and

*Afterpiece:* Unspecified "Farce."


25    Mon.    SA.    *Julius Caesar.*
*Cast:* None listed.
*Benefit:* Husband.
*Miscellaneous:* With several Entertainments.

and

*Afterpiece:* Unspecified "Farce."
*Cast:* None listed.


25    Mon.    CAP.    *The Relapse.*
*Cast:* Foppington—Foote.

and

*Afterpiece: The Stage Coach.*
*Cast:* None listed.


28    Thur.    SA.    *The Patriot.*
*Cast:* None listed.
*Benefit:* Author [Henry Brooke, second].
*Miscellaneous:* Fourth performance this season. [The advertisement clearly

states that Brooke's benefit will take place on this, the fourth night of the play being performed.]
*Deferred:* Deferred from 26 Feb. "on account of some additional Scenes, and the new Casting of some of the Parts."

MARCH

4    Mon.    SA.    *Venice Preserved.*
*Cast:* Pierre—Barry; Belvidera—Mrs. Furnival.
*Command:* Lords Justice.
*Benefit:* Mrs. Furnival.
*Singing and Dancing:* With entertainments of singing and dancing.
and
*Afterpiece:* Unspecified "Farce."

4    Mon.    CAP.    *Sir Courtly Nice.*
*Cast:* Sir Courtly—Foote.
*Benefit:* Foote (second).
and
*Afterpiece: The Credulous Cuckold.*
*Cast:* None listed.

5    Tues.    SA.    *The Merry Wives of Windsor.*
*Cast:* Falstaff—Vanderbank; Sir Hugh—Barrington.
*Benefit:* Oates and Alcock (Musicians).
*Singing and Dancing:* Some favourite pieces on the bassoon will be performed by Alcock, viz. "Eleen O'Roon" and "Come Listen to my Ditty" with some new Graces set by Mr. Dubourg and a Concerto set on purpose for the Basson by Mr. Boyce; with several entertainments of singing and dancing by Mrs. Storer and Moreau.
and
*Afterpiece: The Devil to Pay.*
*Cast:* Jobson—Barrington; Nell—Mrs. Storer.

5    Tues.    CAP.    *The Beaux' Stratagem.*
*Cast:* None listed.
and
*Afterpiece: Harlequin Imprisoned; or, The Spaniard Outwitted.*
*Cast:* Harlequin—W. Phillips; Columbine—Mrs. W. Phillips.
*Miscellaneous:* [Premiere.]

11    Mon.    CAP.    *The Merchant of Venice.*
*Cast:* None listed.

and

*Afterpiece: Harlequin Imprisoned.*
*Cast:* Second Dwarf—Famous Little Irishman.

13    Wed.    CAP.    *The Constant Couple.*
*Cast:* None listed.

and

*Afterpiece: Harlequin Imprisoned.*
*Cast:* None listed.

14    Thur.    SA.    *The Pilgrim.*
*Cast:* None listed.
*Command:* Lords Justice.
*Benefit:* Vanderbank.

and

*Afterpiece: The Devil to Pay.*
*Cast:* None listed.
*Miscellaneous:* Being desired.

18    Mon.    SA.    *The Tempest.*
*Cast:* None listed.
*Benefit:* Beamsley and I. Sparks.

and

*Afterpiece: The Mock Doctor.*
*Cast:* Mock Doctor—I. Sparks.

18    Mon.    CAP.    *Man's Bewitched; or, the Devil to Do about Her.*
*Cast:* None listed.

and

*Afterpiece: Harlequin Imprisoned.*
*Cast:* Dwarfs—Three Lilliputians.

19    Tues.    CAP.    *King Lear and His Three Daughters.*
*Cast:* Lear—Wright; Cordelia—Mrs. Phillips.
*Benefit:* Mrs. W. Phillips.

21    Thur.    AS.    *The Twin Rivals.*
*Cast:* Young Wouldbe—L. Sparks; Teague—Barrington; Aurelia—Mrs. Furnival.

and

*Afterpiece: The Necromancer.*
*Cast:* Harlequin—Gentleman from DL (his first appearance in Ireland); Faustus's Man—Morgan; Miller—Moreau; Miller's Man—I. Sparks; Miller's Wife—Mrs. Moreau; Hero—Dyer; Leander—Mrs. Storer; Helen—Mrs.

Charleton; Dancing Devil—Moreau; Two Spirits—Miss Charleton and Miss Davies; Grand Spirit and Charos—R. Layfield.

*Miscellaneous:* "N. B. As it is intended that the above Entertainment shall be exhibited with the utmost elegance and Propriety, it cannot possibly be performed in Smock Alley, for want of Room to work the necessary Scenery, Machinery, etc. and as the reviving it in Aungier-Street has been attended with a very great expense, it is therefore humbly hoped Gentlemen will not take it ill, that, to prevent the Passages being stopt up, and the Performers obstructed, no persons whatsoever will be admitted behind the Scenes, nor any odd Money taken in any part of the House, during the whole Performance" (*FDJ,* 16–19 Mar. 1745).

21    Thur.    CAP.    *Love Makes a Man.*
*Cast:* Don Cholerick—Wright (his first time in that character).
*Benefit:* Wright.

and

*Afterpiece: The Brave Irishman.*
*Cast:* None listed.

22    Fri.    CAP.    *The Funeral.*
*Cast:* None listed.
*Benefit:* Boynton (wardrobe keeper).
*Miscellaneous:* At the particular Desire of several Ladies of Quality.
*Singing and Dancing:* Singing and Dancing between the Acts by Miss Carlton and Moreau.

and

*Afterpiece: The Mock Doctor.*
*Cast:* None listed.

25    Mon.    SA.    *Julius Caesar.*
*Cast:* Antony—Barry.
*Benefit:* L. Duval.

and

*Afterpiece: Flora; or, Hob in the Well.*
*Cast:* None listed.

25    Mon.    CAP.    *King Richard III.*
*Cast:* Gloster—Wright.
*Benefit:* Mrs. Kathrens (pit officekeeper).

26    Tues.    SA.    *The Distrest Mother.*
*Cast:* Orestes—Barry (his first time in that character).
*Command:* Lords Justice.
*Benefit:* Bardin.

*Miscellaneous:* Prices: Boxes, stage, and lattices 5/5, Pit 3/3, upper gallery 1/1. After the play the little Woman who has of late so much excited the Curiosity of the Publick, will appear and entertain the Audience with a facetious Epilogue on the Occasion.

*Singing and Dancing:* With all the singing and musick as originally performed in London. Singing and Dancing by Mrs. Storer and Moreau.

*Deferred:* Deferred from 11 Mar. because of Barry's Indisposition. Barry was "suddenly taken ill" about 7 Mar. (*FDJ*, 5–9 Mar. 1745.)

and

*Afterpiece: Flora.*
*Cast:* Hob—Bardin.


26     Tues.     CAP.     *Love and a Bottle.*
*Cast:* None listed.
*Benefit:* Hall.

and

*Afterpiece: The Lying Valet.*
*Cast:* Sharp—Hall.


28     Thur.     SA.     *The Committee.*
*Cast:* None listed.
*Benefit:* Mrs. Mitchell.

and

*Afterpiece: The Devil to Pay.*
*Cast:* None listed.


APRIL


1     Mon.     SA.     *Othello.*
*Cast:* Othello—Barry.
*Benefit:* L. Layfield.

and

*Afterpiece: The Picture; or, The Cuckold in Conceit.*
*Cast:* None listed.


1     Mon.     CAP.     *Love Makes a Man.*
*Cast:* Don Cholerick—Wright; Clodio—Hall.

and

*Afterpiece: Harlequin Imprisoned.*
*Cast:* Dwarfs—Lilliputians; A Famous Giantess [probably a facetious reference to "the Famous Little Irishwoman" of earlier performances.]


4     Thur.     AS.     *The Distrest Mother.*
*Cast:* Orestes—Barry.

and

*Afterpiece: The Necromancer.*
*Cast:* Harlequin—L. Layfield, Jr.

[Passion Week 8–13 April]

15    Mon.    AS.    *The Fair Quaker of Deal; or, The Humours of the Navy.*
*Cast:* None listed.

and

*Afterpiece: The Necromancer.*
*Cast:* Harlequin—Layfield, Jr. (by desire).
*Miscellaneous:* [AS theatre was used only 3 times this season before *The Necromancer* was staged, after which it was used 6 times.]

15    Mon.    CAP.    *Love and a Bottle.*
*Cast:* None listed.

and

*Afterpiece: The Walking Statue.*
*Cast:* None listed.

19    Fri.    AS.    *King Henry V; or, The Conquest of France by the English.*
*Cast:* King—Barry.
*Miscellaneous:* Never acted in this Kingdom. With the memorable Battle of Agincourt.
*Comment:* "A Noble piece excellently performed, almost in a wilderness. The major part of the audience were about half a score of Ladies in the Boxes, whose good taste were I a poet, should be celebrated in verse" (*DC,* 27 Apr. 1745).

22    Mon.    SA.    *Venice Preserved.*
*Cast:* None listed.
*Benefit:* Prisoners in the Four Courts Marshalsea.

25    Thur.    SA.    *The Distrest Mother.* V.
*Cast:* Orestes—Barry; Pyrrhus—L. Sparks.
*Benefit:* New Lying-In Hospital in George's Lane.
*Miscellaneous:* For the satisfaction of the Ladies the House will be illuminated with Wax tapers. Prices: Boxes, Pit, Stage, 5/5, Gallery 2/8½. An occasional Prologue (written by Rev. William Dunkin D.D.) spoken by Bardin and quoted in *FDJ,* 27–30 Apr. 1745.
*Financial:* The Benefit amounted to about £150 and some charitable persons have subscribed £15 a year (*FDJ,* 23–27 Apr. 1745).

29    Mon.    SA.    *King Henry IV, with the Humours of Falstaff.*
*Cast:* Hotspur—Barry (his first time in character); King—F. Elrington;
Prince of Wales—Richard Elrington; Falstaff—Vanderbank.
*Benefit:* Mrs. Storer.
*Miscellaneous:* Not acted this season.
*Singing and Dancing:* With Entertainments of Singing, in Act 4 "Sheen
Shees Agu Surfeiam," a favourite Irish Song by Mrs. Storer; Dancing.
[Boydell has observed (1988, 103) that the precise title of this song is unclear.
For discussion see Nicolas Carolan, "Gaelic Song," in *Popular Music in
18th-Century Dublin* (Dublin, 1985).]
                                   and
*Afterpiece: The School-Boy.*
*Cast:* Master Johnny—Mrs. Storer.

MAY

2    Thur.    AS.    *King Henry V.*
*Cast:* King—Barry.
*Miscellaneous:* With new Scenes, Habits, and Decorations.

6    Mon.    AS.    *Hamlet.*
*Cast:* None listed.
*Benefit:* Joseph Elrington.
*Singing and Dancing:* With entertainments of singing and dancing.
                                   and
*Afterpiece:* Unspecified "Farce."

6    Mon.    CAP.    *The Revenge.*
*Cast:* None listed.
                                   and
*Afterpiece: The Oculist; or, Harlequin Fumigated.*
*Cast:* None listed.
*Miscellaneous:* [Premiere. Anonymous pantomime. Nicoll 1977-79, 2:380,
lists an anonymous farce by this title; not listed in *LS*.]

7    Tues.    CAP.    *The Double Dealer.*
*Cast:* None listed.
*Benefit:* Walsh and Fitzgerald (musicians).
                                   and
*Afterpiece:* Unspecified "Pantomime."

9    Thur.    AS.    *Comus.*
*Cast:* Vocal parts by Layfield, Dyer, Mrs. Storer, Miss Davis, and others.

*Miscellaneous:* With Habits, Scenes, Machines, Flyings, Sinkings, Risings, etc., proper to the Opera.

9    Thur.    CAP.    *King Richard III.*
*Cast:* Gloster—Wright; King—Gentleman.
*Benefit:* J. Morris.

13    Mon.    SA.    *The Earl of Westmoreland.*
*Cast:* Westmoreland—Barry.
*Miscellaneous: The Betrayer of his Country* revised. As great care has been taken and much expended in the Painting of the new Scenes no Gentlemen will be permitted on the Stage that the performance may not be interrupted the first night. Prices: Boxes and lattices 5/5, Pit 3/3, Gallery 2/2, Upper Gallery 1/1.
  Prologue spoke by Bardin, Epilogue spoke by Mrs. Furnival.
[This play was advertised again for 16 May but the house was dismissed because of poor attendance (*FDJ,* 21 May 1745).]
*Singing and Dancing:* A Song to be printed and dispensed gratis on the Night of Performance set to Music by Dubourg and performed by Mrs. Storer in the character of a Nun.

14    Tues.    CAP.    *Julius Caesar.*
*Cast:* Brutus—Gentleman from London; Antony—O'Brien (his first stage appearance).
*Benefit:* O'Brien.

and

*Afterpiece: The Brave Irishman.*
*Cast:* None listed.

23    Thur.    SA.    *The Earl of Westmoreland.*
*Cast:* None listed.
*Benefit:* Author [Henry Brooke].
*Miscellaneous:* [Brooke apologised to the audience who had been turned away from the cancelled performance on 16 May, assuring them "that he was not apprized of the Disappointment til One Hour before the opening of the House" (*FDJ,* 21 May 1745).]

27    Mon.    SA.    *Othello.*
*Cast:* Othello—Sheridan (lately arrived from TRDL); Iago—L. Sparks; Cassio—J. Elrington; Brabantio—Bardin; Roderigo—Dyer; Desdemona—Mrs. Dyer; Emilia—Mrs. Furnival.
*Miscellaneous:* [Harriet Bullock married Michael Dyer on 26 Dec. 1744 (*FDJ,* 29 Dec. 1744).]

30　Thur.　SA.　*Macbeth.*
*Cast:* Macbeth—Barry; Lady Macbeth—Mrs. Furnival.
*Benefit:* Watson.
*Miscellaneous:* At the particular Desire of several Ladies of Quality. Prices: Boxes 5/5, lattices 4/4, pit 3/3, gallery 2/2, upper gallery 1/1.
*Singing and Dancing:* With entertainments of singing and dancing by Mrs. Storer and Moreau; With the Songs, Dances, Flyings, Sinkings proper to the Play.

and

*Afterpiece: The Vintner Tricked; or, The White Fox Chase.*
*Cast:* None listed.


31　Fri.　SA.　*Hamlet.*
*Cast:* Hamlet—Sheridan; Queen—Mrs. Furnival.


JUNE


6　Thur.　SA.　*Julius Caesar.*
*Cast:* Brutus—Sheridan; Antony—Barry.


11　Tues.　AS.　*King Henry V.*
*Cast:* King—Barry.
*Miscellaneous:* With New Habits, Scenes, and Decorations proper to the Play. Anniversary of His Majesty's Accession to the Throne. With the original Prologue and Chorus after the Manner of the Ancients, to be performed by Mr. Sparks.


13　Thur.　SA.　*King Richard III.* V.
*Cast:* Gloster—Sheridan.
*Benefit:* Sheridan.
*Miscellaneous:* Performed to the greatest applause ever heard. Sheridan is to perform but four times more this season. The play to begin precisely at half past 6 o'clock.


17　Mon.　SA.　*Cato.*
*Cast:* Cato—Sheridan; Sempronius—L. Sparks; Lucius—Beamsley; Juba—J. Elrington; Syphax—F. Elrington; Portius—Bardin; Marcus—Dyer; Decius—Watson; Lucia—Mrs. Dyer; Marcia—Mrs. Furnival.


20　Thur.　CAP.　*Jane Shore.*
*Cast:* Hastings—O'Brien.
*Benefit:* Kirkpatrick and O'Brien.

and

*Afterpiece: The Mock Doctor.*
*Cast:* None listed.

24    Mon.    SA.    *Othello.*
*Cast:* Othello—Barry.

JULY

3    Wed.    CAP.    *The Orphan.*
*Cast:* None listed.
*Benefit:* Morgan.

and

*Afterpiece: The Prize; or, Harlequin's Artifice.*
*Cast:* None listed.
*Miscellaneous:* [Anonymous pantomime. Not listed in *LS* or Nicoll.]

11    Thur.    SA.    *Hamlet.*
*Cast:* Hamlet—Sheridan.
*Miscellaneous:* [Sheridan is reported being "so well recovered from his Indisposition" that he can perform this night; At the particular Desire of several Persons of Quality. *Macbeth* was originally advertised to be performed.]

15    Mon.    SA.    *King Richard III.*
*Cast:* Gloster—Sheridan.
*Miscellaneous:* At the particular Desire of several Persons of Quality.

25    Thur.    SA.    *The Revenge.*
*Cast:* Zanga—Sheridan (his first time in that character); Leonora—Mrs. Furnival.
*Miscellaneous:* Never acted there before.
*Singing and Dancing:* Singing by Mrs. Storer.

AUGUST

1    Thur.    AS.    *Cato.*
*Cast:* Cato—Quin (from CG).
*Benefit:* Lying-In Hospital in George's Lane.
*Miscellaneous:* Requested by the Gentlemen Trustees of the Hospital. It is requested that the Ladies lay aside their Hoops for the Night. Prices for boxes, pit, stage, and lattices 5s. 5d.
*Financial:* The money received at this play amounted to above £130, exclusive of the charges of the house, which was between £30 and £40" (*FDJ,* 30 July–3 Aug. 1745).

5    Mon.    SA.    *Macbeth.*
*Cast:* Macbeth—Sheridan.
*Benefit:* Sheridan.
*Miscellaneous:* "As it is the last Time Mr. Sheridan can perform here this season, several persons of distinction who formerly bespoke the play of Macbeth, when the acting of it was prevented by his sudden Indisposition do now insist upon its being played instead of The Revenge [which was advertised for Sheridan's benefit on 30 July 1745].

and

*Afterpiece: Damon and Phillida.*
*Cast:* Damon—Dwyer; Phillida—Mrs. Storer.

# Selected Bibliography/Works Cited

## Manuscripts

Burney Collection. BL.

Dix Collection. NLI.

Epilogues. BL.

Great Britain. Public Record Office, London

    MS Domestic Entry Book.

    MS. Domestic Signet Office Papers.

    MS. Patent Rolls, Charles II.

    MS. State Papers, Ireland.

Ireland. Office of the Registry of Deeds, Dublin

    MS. Transcripts of Deeds, 1708—1760.

    Survey of Dublin Streets Leading to the Castle, Dublin, 1751.

    Public Record Office, Dublin. Transcribed by W. J. Lawrence in "Notebooks" cited below prior to the 1922 fire which destroyed the following manuscripts:

    MS. British Departmental Papers.

    MS. Chancery Patent Rolls.

    MS. Irish Parliamentary Papers.

    MS. Signet Office Docket Books.

    MS. Treasury Ledgers.

Kemble, John Philip. "Manuscript Diary Record of the Theatre Royal from the *Dublin Journal,* 1730–51." Shaw Collection, Widener Library, Harvard University.

Lawrence, William J. "Notebooks for a History of the Irish Stage." University of Cincinnati Library.

Mason, William Monck. "Collection for a History of the City of Dublin." Egerton MS. 1773, BL.

————. "Collection for a History of the Irish Stage." Egerton MS. 1763, BL.

Orrery Papers. "Letter from Counsellor Tighe to Lord Orrery." Vol. 6. Dublin, 26 Jan. 1743.

Prologues, BL.

Smock Alley Theatre, Dublin, Epilogues and Prologues. MS. English 674 F, Widener Library; Trinity College, Dublin, Library A. 7. 5. f. 108; Folger Shakespeare Library.

Ware, Robert. "The History and Antiquities of Dublin Collected from Authentic

Records and MSS. Collection of Sir James Ware" and MS. De Rebus Eblanae 74, 75, Gilbert Collection, Pearce St. Library, Dublin.

## Maps

*An Exact Survey of the City and Suburbs of Dublin.* John Rocque (BL).
Flintscroft Property Rental Volume of Maps. Muniment Room, City Hall, Dublin.
*A Map of the City and Suburbs of Dublin, 1738.* Charles Brooking (BL).
*Map of Dublin, 1756.* John Rocque. Muniment Room, City Hall, Dublin.
*Map of Dublin, c. 1800.* Longford. NLI.

## Newspapers

*Carson's Dublin Intelligence* [DI]:1720–32 (BL; GIL; NLI; RIA).
*Daily Gazeteer,* London [*LDG*]:1738–40 (BL).
*Dublin Courant* [*DC*]:1744–45; 1746–52 (NLI).
*Dalton's Dublin Impartial Newsletter* [*DDIN*]:1734 (RIA; TCD).
*Dublin Daily Advertiser* [*DDA*]:1736–38 (BL: COL: NLI; RIA).
*Dublin Daily Post* [*DDP*]:1730–37 (COL; RIA; NLI).
*Dublin Evening Post* [*DEP*]:1732–41 (DM; NLI; RIA).
*Dublin Gazette* [*DG*]:1720–44 (BL; RIA).
*Dublin Mercury* [*DM*]:1722–24 (GIL; BL); 1725 (BL); 1742 (COL).
*Dublin Weekly Journal* [*DWJ*]:1725–31 (COL); 1734–37 (RIA).
*Esdall's Newsletter* [*ENL*]:1744 (BL; COL; NLI).
*Exshaw's Gentleman's And London Magazine.*
*Faulkner's Dublin Journal* [*FDJ*]:1726 (BL); 1727 (GIL); 1729–37 (RIA); 1736–42 (BL); 1737–38 (Linen Hall, Belfast); 1741–49 (Marsh's); 1744–46 (TCD).
*Harding's Impartial News-Letter* [*HIN*]:1722 (BL; COL; GIL).
*Hoey's Dublin Journal* [*HDJ*]:1730–36 (GIL; BL).
*Hume's Dublin Courant* [*HDC*]:1720–26 (BL; COL).
*The Intelligencer* (Dublin, 1728).
*Pue's Occurrences* [*PO*]:1726–45 (BL; COL; GIL; TCD).
*Reilly's Dublin Courant* [*DC*]:1744–45 (BL; NLI; TCD).
*Reilly's Dublin News-Letter* [*RNL*]:1737, 1739 (Lough Fea); 1739–41 (NLI; RIA).
*St. James's Evening Post* [*SJEP*]:1723–24 (BL); 1726 (GIL); 1732–35 (Marsh's).
*Weekly Oracle* [*WO*]:1735–37 (BL).

## Printed Works

Adair, Rev. Patrick. 1866. *A True Narrative of the Rise and Progress of the Presbyterian Church in Ireland.* Belfast: C. Aitchison.
Armitage, Frederick. 1909–11. *A Short Masonic History.* 2 vols. London: H. Weare.
Baker, David Erskine. 1764. *The Companion to the Playhouse: or, an Historical Account of all the Dramatic Writers. . . .* 2 vols. London: Becket et al.

————. 1812. *Biographia Dramatica; or, A Companion to the Playhouse,* 3 vols. London: Longman.

Barber, Mary. 1734. *Poems on Several Occasions.* London: C. Rivington.

Barrington, Sir Jonah. 1827–32. *Personal Sketches of His Own Times.* 3 vols. London: Colburn and Bentley.

Bellamy, George Anne. 1785. *An Apology for the Life of George Anne Bellamy.* 6 vols. 3rd ed. London: privately published.

Boaden, James. 1827. *Memoirs of Mrs. Siddons.* 2 vols. London: H. Colburn.

————. 1831. *Life of Mrs. Jordan.* 2 vols. London: Edward Bull.

Boydell, Brian. 1988. *A Dublin Musical Calendar, 1700–1760.* Dublin: Irish Academic Press.

Broadbent, R. J. 1908. *Annals of the Liverpool Stage.* Liverpool: E. Howell.

Brooke, Henry. 1792. *Poetical Works.* Edited by Charlotte Brooke. 4 vols. 3rd ed. Dublin: privately published for the editor.

Bulkley, William. 1899. "The Irish Channel and Dublin in 1735, Extracts from the Diary of William Bulkley, of Bryndda, near Almwich, Angelsy, a Grand Jurror of That County." *Journal of the Royal Society of Antiquaries of Ireland* 5th series, 9 (1899): 56–81.

*The Buskin and Sock; Being Controversial Letters Between Mr. Thomas Sheridan, Tragedian, and Mr. Theophilus Cibber, Comedian.* Dublin, 1743; rpt. London, 1743.

*Calendar of Ancient Records of Dublin.* Edited by Sir John T. Gilbert. 17 vols. Dublin, 1889–1922.

Carolan, Nicholas. 1985. "Gaelic Song." In *Popular Music in Eighteenth-Century Dublin.* Dublin.

Chetwood, William Rufus. 1749. *A General History of the Stage.* London: W. Owen.

————. N.d. "The Dramatic Congress. A Short State of the Stage under the Present Management." BL and Bodliean.

*Cibber and Sheridan; or, The Dublin Miscellany. Containing All the Advertisements, Letters, Addresses, Replys, Apologys, Verses, etc., etc., etc. Lately publish'd on Account of the Theatric Squabble. . . .* 8 vols. Dublin, 1743.

Clancy, Michael. 1750. *The Memoirs of Michael Clancy, M.D.* 2 vols. Dublin: S. Powell.

Clark, William Smith. 1955. *The Early Irish Stage: The Beginnings to 1720.* Oxford: Oxford University Press.

————. 1965. *The Irish Stage in the County Towns, 1720–1800.* Oxford: Oxford University Press.

Coffey, Charles. 1724. *Poems and Songs.* Dublin.

*Comical Pilgrim; or, Travels of a Cynick Philosopher, thro' the most Wicked Parts of the World, Namely, England, Wales, Scotland, Ireland, and Holland. . . . Being a General Satyr on the Vices and Follies of the Age.* 2nd ed. London, 1722.

Concanen, Matthew. 1722. *Poems upon Several Occasions.* Dublin: E. Dobson.

————. 1724. *Miscellaneous Poems . . . by Several Hands.* London: J. Peele.

Cooke, William. 1804. *Memoirs of Charles Macklin.* London.

Craig, Maurice. 1952. *Dublin: 1660–1860.* Dublin: Allen Figgis, 1952; rpt. 1980.

Crookshank, Anne, and The Knight of Glin. 1978. *The Painters of Ireland c. 1660–1920.* London: Barrie and Jenkins.

Daly, Augustin. 1888. *Woffington. A Tribute to the Actress and Women.* Philadelphia: privately published.

Delany, Mrs. Mary. 1861. *The Autobiography and Correspondence of Mary Granville, Mrs. Delany.* 3 vols. 1st series, edited by Lady Llanover. London: R. Bentley.

*A Description of the City of Dublin in Ireland, . . . By a Citizen of London, who liv'd Twenty Years in Ireland.* London, 1732.

Dibden, James C. 1888. *The Annals of the Edinburgh Stage.* Edinburgh: R. Bentley.

*Dictionary of National Biography.* 63 vols. Edited by Leslie Stephen and Sidney Lee.

*Doctor Anthony's Advice to the Hibernian Aesop; or, An Epistle to the Author of the B[eggar']s W[eddin]g.* Dublin, 1729.

*Dramatic Miscellanies.* 3 vols. Dublin, 1784.

Dunkin, William. 1769–70. *Select Poetical Works.* 2 vols. Dublin: W. G. Jones.

Dunton, John. 1699. *The London Scuffle.* London: privately published.

Fitz-Simon, Christopher. 1983. *The Irish Theatre.* London: Thames and Hudson.

Flood, W. H. Grattan. 1906a. "Dublin City Music (1560–1780)." *Journal of the Royal Society of Antiquaries of Ireland.* Part 3, no. 32 (September 1906).

———. *History of Irish Music.* 1906b. 2nd ed. Dublin: Brown and Nolan.

———. 1926. "Thomas Sheridan's *The Brave Irishman.*" *Review of English Studies.* July 1926.

*Four Letters, Originally written in French, Relating to the Kingdom of Ireland.* Dublin, 1739.

G. N. S. 1814. "Anecdotes of Vander Hagen." *The Monthly Museum; or, Dublin Literary Repertory.* (May 1814): 473.

Gagey, Edmond M. 1937. *Ballad Opera.* New York: Columbia University Press.

Garrick, David. 1831–32. *The Private Correspondence of David Garrick.* 2 vols. Edited by James Boaden. London: Colburn and Bentley.

———. 1963. *The Letters of David Garrick.* Edited by David M. Little and George M. Kahrl, with associate editor Phoebe DeK. Wilson. 3 vols. Cambridge: Harvard University Press.

Genest, John. 1832. *Some Account of the English Stage, From the Restoration in 1660 to 1830.* 10 vols. Bath: T. Rodd.

*Gentleman's Journal.* London, 1721.

Gilbert, Sir John T. 1854–59. *A History of the City of Dublin.* 3 vols. Dublin: McGlushan.

Gilliland, Thomas. 1808. *The Dramatic Mirror: Containing the History of the Stage from the Earliest Period to the Present Time.* 2 vols. London: Chappele.

*Green Room Gossip; or, Gravity Gallinit.* London, 1809.

Halliday Pamphlets, RIA.

Harrison, F. L. 1986. "Music, Poetry and Polity in the Age of Swift." *Eighteenth-Century Ireland.* I (1986): 37–63.

Haslewood, Joseph. 1795. *The Secret History of the Green Room.* 2 vols. London: J. Owen.

———. N.d. Smith Collection of Theatrical Clippings. BL.

Highfill, Philip H. *et al.* 1973–92. *A Biographical Dictionary of Actors, Actresses, Musicians, Dancers, Managers, and Other Stage Personnel in London, 1660–1800.* 16 vols. Carbondale: Southern Illinois University Press.

Hitchcock, Robert. 1788–94. *An Historical View of the Irish Stage.* 2 vols. Dublin: Marchbank.

Hogan, Charles B. 1952–57. *Shakespeare in the Theatre, 1701–1800.* 2 vols. Oxford: Clarendon Press.

Hughes, Samuel C. 1889. *The Church of St. John the Evangelist.* Dublin: Hodges and Figgis.

———. 1904. *The Pre-Victorian Drama in Dublin.* Dublin: Hodges and Figgis.

Hume, Robert D., ed. 1980. *The London Theatre World, 1660–1800.* Carbondale and Edwardsville: Southern Illinois University Press.

———. 1983. *The Rakish Stage: Studies in English Drama, 1660–1800.* Carbondale and Edwardsville: Southern Illinois University Press.

———. 1988. *Henry Fielding and the London Theatre 1728–1737.* Oxford: Clarendon Press.

Irish Pamphlets, 1725–27. TCD.

Joly Collection. NLI.

Kavanagh, Peter. 1946. *The Irish Theatre.* Tralee: Kerryman.

Langhans, Edward. 1981. *Restoration Promptbooks.* Carbondale and Edwardsville: Southern Illinois University Press.

Lawrence, William J. 1913. *"Beggar's Opera* in Dublin." *Irish Times,* 15 Aug. 1913.

———. 1922. "Early Irish Ballad Opera and Comic Opera." *Musical Quarterly* (July 1922): 400.

———. 1932. "The Mystery of *The Stage Coach." MLR* 27 (1932): 393–97.

Lenihan, Maurice. 1866. *Limerick: Its History and Antiquities.* Dublin: Hodges and Smith.

Lepper, J. H., and Philip Crossle. 1925. *History of the Grand Lodge of Free and Accepted Masons of Ireland.* 2 vols. Dublin: published for the Lodge of Research.

Lewes, Charles Lee. 1805. *Memoirs.* 4 vols. London: R. Phillips.

[Lloyd, Edmund.] 1732. *A Description of the City of Dublin.* Dublin, n.p.

*The London Stage, 1660–1800.* Edited by William Van Lennep, et al. 5 parts in 11 vols. Edwardsville and Carbondale: Southern Illinois University Press, 1960–68.

Lovejoy, J. 1890. "Diary of a Tour in 1732 through Parts of England, Wales, Ireland, and Scotland." Roxburghe Club.

Luckombe, Phillip. 1783. *A Tour through Ireland in 1779.* 2nd ed. London: Lowndes.

Mac Gregor, John J. 1821. *A New Picture of Dublin.* Dublin: published for Johnson and Deas.

Madden, Dr. Samuel. 1738. "Reflections and Resolutions Proper for the Gentlemen of Ireland." Dublin.

Maddockes, Charles and James Belcher. 1723. *Account of Secret Service Money.* 6 vols. Dublin.

Maxwell, Constantia. 1936. *Dublin Under the Georges.* London: Harrap.

*Memoirs of the Celebrated Mrs. Woffington.* N.p., n.d.

Milhous, Judith, and Robert Hume. 1990. "John Rich's Covent Garden Account Books for 1735–36." *Theatre Survey* 31 (November 1990): 200–241.

Molloy, J. Fitzgerald. 1897. *The Romance of the Irish Stage.* 2 vols. London: Downey.

Moody, T. W., and W. E. Vaughan. 1986. *A New History of Ireland.* Vol. 4. Oxford: Clarendon Press.

Murphy, Arthur. 1801. *Life of Garrick.* 2 vols. London.

Nash, Mary. 1977. *The Provok'd Wife*. London: Hutchinson.

Nicoll, Allardyce. 1977–79. *A History of English Drama, 1660–1900*. Vols. 1–3. 4th ed. Cambridge: Cambridge University Press.

O'Keeffe, John. 1826. *Recollections of the Life of John O'Keeffe, Written by Himself.* 2 vols. London: Colburn.

O'Neill, James. J. 1920. "A Bibliographical Account of Irish Theatrical Literature." *Bibliographical Society of Ireland.* 1 (1920): 60–88.

Packenham, Christine P., Countess of Longford. 1936. *A Biography of Dublin*. London: Methuen.

Pasquali, N. 1750. *Twelve English Songs*. London.

Pasquin, Anthony [Williams, John]. 1796. *An Authentic History of the Professors of Painting . . . in Ireland*. Dublin.

Philips, Katherine. 1705. *Letters from Orinda to Poliarchus*. London: Lintot.

Pilkington, John Carteret. 1760. *The Real Story of John Carteret Pilkington*. London.

Pilkington, Laetitia. 1748–54. *Memoirs of Mrs. Laetitia Pilkington, Written by Herself.* 3 vols. London: Griffiths.

*Present State of the Stage in Great Britain and Ireland. And the Theatrical Characters of the Principal Performers, In both Kingdoms, Impartially Considered.* London, 1793.

*A Prologue to Julius Caesar, As it was Acted at Madam Violante's Booth, December the 15th, 1732, by some of the young Gentlemen in Dr. Sheridan's School.* Broadside. Folger.

"Punch and Judy," *Irish Independent*, 29 Aug. 1905.

[Roach, John]. 1814. *Authentic Memoirs of the Green Room*. London: Roach.

Rosenfeld, Sybil and Edward Croft-Murray. 1965–66. "A Checklist of Scene Painters Working in Great Britain and Ireland in the 18th century (2)." *Theatre Notebook* 19 (1965–66): 49–64.

Shadwell, Charles. 1720. *The Works of Charles Shadwell*. 2 vols. Dublin: Risk, et al.

Shakespeare, William. *King Richard II*. Promptbook. Folger.

Shaw Collection. Widener Library, Harvard University.

Sheldon, Esther K. 1967. *Thomas Sheridan of Smock-Alley*. Princeton: Princeton University Press.

"The Sheridan Family," *The Ancestor*. April 1904.

Sheridan, Thomas. 1747. *A Full Vindication of the Conduct of the Manager of the Theatre-Royal, Written by Himself.* Dublin.

———. 1758. *An Humble Appeal to the Publick, Together with some Considerations on the Present critical and dangerous State of the Stage of Ireland . . .* Dublin.

———. 1771. *An Appeal to the Public: containing an account of the rise, progress, and establishment of the first regular Theatre in Dublin: with the causes of its decline and ruin . . .* Dublin.

———. 1772. *Mr. Sheridan's Speech addressed to a Number of Gentlemen Assembled with a View of considering the best Means to establish one good Theatre in this city*. Dublin.

Schneider, Ben Ross Jr. 1979. *Index to the London Stage, 1660–1800*. Carbondale and Edwardsville: Southern Illinois University Press.

*Some Observations on the Present State of Ireland, particularly with Relation to the Woolen Manufacture*. Dublin, 1731.

Sterling, James. 1734. *Poetical Works*. Dublin.

Stockwell, La Tourette. 1938. *Dublin Theatres and Theatre Customs, 1737–1820*. Kingsport, Tenn.

Strickland, W. G. 1913. *A Dictionary of Irish Artists*. 2 vols. Dublin: Maunsel.

Swift, Jonathan. 1727–28. *A Short View of the State of Ireland*. Dublin.

———. 1728. *Gulliveriana*. London.

———. 1755–65. *Works of Jonathan Swift*. Edited by Deane Swift. 16 vols. London: Bathurst.

———. 1910. *Poems of Jonathan Swift*. Edited by William E. Browning 2 vols. London.

———. 1939–68. *The Prose Works of Jonathan Swift*. Edited by Herbert Davis *et al.* 14 vols. Oxford: Blackwell.

———. 1958. *The Poems of Jonathan Swift*. Edited by Harold Williams. 2nd ed. 3 vols. Oxford: Clarendon Press.

———. 1963–65. *The Correspondence of Jonathan Swift*. 5 vols. Edited by Harold Williams. Oxford: Clarendon Press.

*Theatrical Biography; or, Memoirs of the Principal Performers of the Three Theatre Royals*. 2 vols. London, 1772.

*The Thespian Dictionary; or, Dramatic Biography of the Eighteenth Century*. London, 1802.

Townsend, Horatio. 1852. *An Account of the Visit of Handel to Dublin*. Dublin: McGlashan.

———. 1860. *History of Mercer's Hospital in Dublin*. Dublin: Herbert.

*The Tricks of the Town laid open, or a Companion for Country Gentlemen*. Dublin.

Victor, Benjamin. 1761–71. *The History of the Theatres in London and Dublin from 1730 to the Present Time*. 2 vols. London: T. Davies.

———. 1776. *Original Letters, Dramatic Pieces, and Poems*. 3 vols. London: Becket.

Walsh, Thomas J. 1973. *Opera in Dublin 1705–1797: The Social Scene*. Dublin: Allen Figgis.

Weaver, John. 1728. *A History of Mimes and Pantomimes*. London: Roberts.

Whyte, Laurence. 1740. *Poems on Various Subjects*. Dublin: S. Powell.

———. 1742. *Poems*. 2nd ed. Dublin: S. Powell.

Whyte, Samuel. 1772. *The Shamrock; or, Hibernian Cresses*. Dublin: Marshbank.

———. 1792. *Poems*. 2nd ed. Dublin: R. Marchbank.

———. 1800. *Miscellaneous Nova*. Dublin: Marshbank.

Wilkinson, Tate. 1790. *Memoirs of His Own Life*. 4 vols. York: Wilson, Spence, Mawman.

# Dublin Stage Personnel Index (1720–1745)

Key: * = Summer season only; UC = United Company

Addy (SA 33–34).
Aicken, James (GBGL 34–35).
Alcock [musician] (AS 42–43) (UC 44–45).
Alcorn (SA 24–25, 25–26, 26–27?, 27–28?, 28–29, 29–30, 30–31, 31–32, 32–33, died April 1733).
Anderus [musician] (AS 42–43).
Arne, Susannah Marie. *See* Cibber, Mrs. Theophilus
Arne, Thomas Augustine [musician] (AS 42–43) (UC 43–44).
Arne, Mrs. Thomas Augustine (AS 41–42, 42–43) (UC 43–44).
Ayre. *See* Eyre, H.
Baildon, [Joseph?] (from London, AS 42–43).
Baker (SA 42–43).
Bamford, Mrs. Anne [dresser] (RS/SA 35–36) (SA 37–38, 39–40, 40–41, 41–42).
Barbarini, Signora. *See* Campanini, Barbarina
Bardin, Peter (from England, AS and SA 40–41) (AS 41–42, 42–43) (UC 43–44, 44–45).
Barnes, Master (NBDS 31–32).
Barnes, Miss and Mrs. *See* Martin Mrs. Christopher
Barret (from GF, SA 31–32) (RS 32–33).
Barrington, John (RS 32–33, 33–34, 34–35, RS/SA 35–36) (SA 36–37, 37–38, 38–39, 39–40, 40–41, to AS in Apr.) (AS 41–42, 42–43) (UC 43–44, 44–45).
Barry, Spranger (UC 43–44, 44–45).
Barry, Mrs. (SA 37–38, 38–39, 39–40, 40–41).
Bate, Edward [printer to the theatre?] (AS 37–38).

Baudouin [dancer] (AS 40–41).
Bayley [or Bailey or Baily], Mrs. (SA 38–39) (AS 39–40, 41–42?) (SA 42–43) (UC 43–44).
Beamsley, John (RS/SA 35–36) (SA 36–37?, 37–38, 38–39, 39–40, 40–41, 41–42, 42–43) (UC 43–44, 44–45).
Bellamy, Mrs. [*née* Miss Seale, *see also*] (SA 28–29, 31–32, 32–33, 33–34) (AS 35–36).
Blackwood, John [musician] (AS 36–37) (SA 41–42).
Bourne [or Byrne], Charles (RS 32–33, 33–34) (GBGL 34–35) (RS/SA 35–36) (SA 37–38, 38–39, 39–40, 42–43) (CAP 44–45).
Boynton [wardrobe-keeper] (CAP 44–45).
Boyton (AS 34–35, 42–43).
Bridges, [William?] (AS 37–38, 38–39, 39–40, 40–41, 41–42, 42–43).
Bridges, Mrs. [William?] (AS 37–38, 40–41).
Bridgewater, Roger (from CG, SA 36–37*).
Broad, Miss (AS 34–35).
Brouden [or Broudin], Mrs. (CAP 44–45).
Bullock, Mrs. Christopher [*née* Jane Rogers] (SA 36–37, 37–38, 38–39, died Mar. 1739).
Bullock, Miss Harriet [*see also* Dyer, Mrs. Michael] (SA 37–38, 38–39, 39–40, 41–42?, 42–43) (UC 43–44).
Bunbury (CAP 44–45).
Burke [musician] (SA 39–40?).
Bushell (SA 38–39).
Butcher, Miss [*see also* Ward, Mrs. John] (SA 32–33, 33–34) (RS/SA 35–36) (AS 36–37).

Eastham [boxkeeper, died before 2 Apr. 1730] (SA 29–30).

Eastham, Mrs. [dresser] (SA 33–34) (AS 35–36).

Elmy, Mrs. Mary [William?] [née Morse or Moss] (from England, AS and SA 40–41) (AS 41–42) (SA 42–43) (UC 43–44).

Erlington, Francis (SA 20–21?, 21–22, 22–23, 23–24, 24–25, 25–26, 26–27, 27–28?, 28–29, 29–30, 30–31, 31–32, 32–33, 33–34) (AS 34–35, 35–36, 36–37, 37–38, 38–39, 39–40) (SA 40–41) (AS 41–42, 42–43) (UC 43–44, 44–45).

Elrington, Joseph (SA 31–32, 32–33, 33–34) (AS 36–37, 37–38, 38–39, 39–40, 40–41, 41–42, 42–43) (UC 43–44, 44–45).

Erlington, Nancy [see also Mrs. Wrightson] (SA 31–32).

Elrington, Ralph (SA 20–21?, 21–22, 22–23, 23–24, 24–25, 25–26, 26–27?, 27–28?, 28–29, 29–30?, 30–31, 31–32, 32–33, 33–34) (AS 34–35, 35–36, 36–37) (AS and SA after Jan. 36–37) (SA 37–38, 38–39, 39–40, 40–41, 41–42, 42–43) (UC and SA 43–44, 44–45).

Elrington, Richard (SA 28–29, 30–31) (AS 37–38, 41–42) (UC 44–45).

Elrington, Thomas (SA 20–21, 21–22, 22–23, 23–24, 24–25, 25–26, 26–27?, 27–28?, from DL in Apr., 28–29, 29–30, 30–31, 31–32).

Este, William (SA 37–38, 38–39, 39–40, 40–41, 41–42, died Jan. 1743).

Eyre [perhaps Ayre], H. (SA 38–39).

Fitzgerald, Master (NBDS 31–32).

Fitzgerald, George [musician] (SA 37–38, 41–42) (CAP 44–45).

Fitzpatrick (SA 36–37, 37–38).

Foote, Samuel (from DL, UC and CAP 44–45).

Fox [pit doorkeeper] (SA 36–37, 37–38, 38–39, 40–41).

Frisby, [Richard?] (SA 20–21?, 21–22, 22–23).

Fromont, J. Baptiste L. [dancer] (from DL, AS 40–41).

Furnival, Thomas (SA 39–40, 41–42).

Furnival, Elizabeth "Fanny" [Mrs. Thomas] (SA 39–40, 40–41, 41–42) (AS 42–43) (UC 43–44, 44–45).

Furnival, Miss. See Carmichael.

Garrick, David (from GF, SA 41–42*).

German [or Garman], Mme. [tumbler and equilibrist] (SA 42–43).

Gibson [boxkeeper] (SA 38–39, 39–40, 40–41).

Giffard, Henry (SA 20–21?, 21–22, 22–23, 23–24, 24–25, 25–26, 26–27?, 27–28?, 28–29) (AS from GF 34–35*) (SA 37–38*, from DL 39–40*, 41–42*, from LIF, 42–43).

Giles (from DL, AS 37–38) (SA 39–40, and AS 40–41*) (AS 41–42).

Goff [same as Gough?] [upholsterer and former boxkeeper] (SA 37–38).

Gough (SA 32–33, 33–34) (GBGL 34–35).

Mrs. Grace (SA 20–21?, 21–22, 22–23, 23–24, 24–25).

Green (AS 35–36).

Gregory (SA 39–40, 40–41, 41–42).

Griffith, Thomas (SA 20–21, 21–22, 22–23, 23–24, 24–25, 25–26, 26–27?, 27–28?, 28–29, 30–31, 31–32, 32–33, 33–34) (AS 34–35, 35–36, 36–37, 37–38, 38–39, 39–40, 40–41, 41–42, 42–43) (UC 43–44, died Jan. 1744).

Guitar, Mons. [tumbler and equilibrist] (SA 42–43).

Gunan, Dominic [musician] (SA 39–40, 41–42).

Hall (UC 43–44) (CAP 44–45).

Hallam, Adam [earlier Master] (SA 23–24, 24–25, 25–26, 26–27?, from CG, 36–37*).

Hallam, Thomas (SA 20–21?, 21–22, 22–23, 23–24).

Hallam, [William?] (RS/SA 35–36).

Hamilton, John (SA 38–39).

Hamilton, Myrton (SA 27–28, 29–30, 30–31, 31–32, 32–33).

Hamilton, Mrs. Sarah Myrton [née Lyddal] (SA 27–28, 29–30, 30–31, 31–32, 32–33).

Harvey (AS 41–42) (UC 43–44?).

Havard, William (from DL, AS 42–43*).

Healy [stage officekeeper] (SA 36–37, 38–39).

Heron, William [musician] (AS 39–40) (SA 41–42)

Hinde, James (RS 32–33, 33–34, 34–35, RS/SA 35–36).

McCarty [or M'Carty or McCarthy], Callaghan [musician] (AS 35–36, 38–39, 39–40, 40–41, 41–42).

McNeil, Gordon [dancer] (SA 41–42).

Meeks (AS 33–34) (GBGL 34–35) (RS/SA 35–36) (SA 40–41, 41–42).

Miller (from Edinburgh, SA 36–37).

Milward, William (from DL, SA 38–39*).

Mitchell (CAP 44–45).

Mitchell, Mrs. [née Mackay] (SA 37–38) (AS 40–41) (SA 41–42, 42–43) (UC 44–45).

Moore (SA 24–25, 25–26) (same person? RS, 32–33).

Moreau, Anthony [dancer] (SA 20–21?, 21–22, 22–23, 23–24?, 24–25, 29–30) (NBDS 30–31) (SA 32–33) (AS 34–35, 35–36, 36–37, 37–38, 38–39) (SA 39–40, 40–41) (AS and SA 41–42?) (AS 42–43) (UC 43–44, 44–45).

Moreau, Mrs. Anthony [née Schoolding] [dancer] (SA 20–21?, 21–22, 22–23, 23–24, 24–25, 28–29, 29–30) (NBDS 30–31) (SA 32–33, 33–34) (AS 38–39) (SA 40–41) (AS 41–42) (SA 41–42*?) (UC 44–45).

Moreau, Miss [dancer] (AS 38–39) (SA 40–41?, 41–42*?).

Morgan (SA 37–38) (AS 38–39?) (SA 40–41, 42–43) (CAP 44–45).

Morgan, Mrs. (SA 37–38, 40–41).

Morgan, Charles (from CG, RS/SA 35–36) (SA 36–37, 37–38, 40–41, 41–42?) (UC 43–44, 44–45, died May 1745).

Morgan, John [pit officekeeper] (SA 29–30, 30–31, 32–33, 33–34) (AS 35–36, 36–37, 37–38).

Morris, John [dancer] (RS/SA 35–36) (SA 36–37, 37–38, 38–39, 39–40, 40–41, 41–42, 42–43) (SA 43–44) (CAP 44–45).

Morris, Mrs. John (SA 42–43?).

Morris, Patrick [dancer] (SA 41–42, 43–44).

Morris, Patrick Jr. (SA 41–42, 42–43).

Mot [or Mott], Master [singer] (SA 31–32.

Muilment [or Mullement] [dancer] (from DL, AS 42–43*).

Mynitt, William (SA 43–44).

Mynitt, Mrs. William (SA 43–44).

Nanfan (RS 34–35).

Naylor (AS 35–36).

Naylor, Miss (AS 35–36).

Neal [or O'Neil] [boxkeeper] (SA 38–39, 41–42, 42–43) (UC 43–44, 44–45).

Neale, [Charles?] (SA 30–31) (NBDS 31–32).

Neale, Mrs. [Charles?] (SA 30–31, 31–32, 32–33, 33–34).

Neale, John [musician] (AS 42–43).

Neale, Master [musician] (AS 42–43).

Negri, Miss Maria (AS 35–36).

Nelson (SA 28–29).

Nichols [or Nicholls] (SA 30–31).

Nimmo [prompter] (SA 36–37, 38–39, 39–40).

Norris, Henry Jr. ["Jubilee Dickey Jr."] (SA 20–21?, 21–22, 22–23, 23–24?, 24–25, 25–26, 26–27?, 27–28?, 28–29, 29–30, 30–31, died 1731).

Norris, Mrs. (SA 28–29).

Oates, James [known first as "Master"] (NBDS 31–32) (from CG, SA 39–40) (AS 40–41*, and SA 41–42) (SA 42–43) (UC 44–45).

Oates, James Jr. (SA and AS 41–42).

Oates [musician?] (UC 44–45).

O'Brien, Francis (CAP 44–45).

Orfeur, Mrs. Elizabeth (from London, SA 33–34, 36–37, 37–38, 38–39, 39–40, 40–41).

Orfeur, Miss (SA 42–43).

Page, Mrs. (SA 33–34) (RS 34–35).

Paget, William (SA 28–29, 29–30).

Parker (SA 32–33) (RS 33–34).

Parker, Mrs. (SA 32–33) (RS 33–34).

Parsons (UC 44–45).

Pasquilino, Mrs. [see also Mrs. Ravenscroft] (SA and AS? 40–41) (AS 41–42, 42–43) (UC 43–44, 44–45, retired in Nov.).

Pellish (from London, SA 38–39) (AS 41–42, 42–43).

Peters, Master (NBDS 31–32) (SA 33–34) (AS 34–35?).

Philips [or Phillips], Thomas (SA 22–23, 23–24, 32–33, 33–34) (AS 34–35, 35–36) (SA 36–37, 37–38, 38–39, 39–40, 40–41, 41–42, 42–43).

Phillips, William "Harlequin" [dancer] (SA 29–30, 40–41, 43–44) (CAP 44–45).

Phillips, Mrs. William (SA 40–41, 43–44) (CAP 44–45).

Picq, Charles [dancer] (from CG, AS 42–43*).

Pilkington, Master John Carteret (AS 42–43).

Pitt, George (SA 29–30) (NBDS 30–31) (AS 34–35?) (RS/SA 35–36) (SA 36–37?) (AS 37–38, 38–39, 40–41).

Pitt, Master [dancer] (AS and RS 34–35) (RS/SA 35–36) (SA 36–37) (AS 37–38, 38–39, 39–40, 40–41) (SA 41–42?) (SA 42–43) (UC 44–45).

Pockrich, Richard [musician: musical glasses] (SA 42–43).

Prest (SA 37–38).

Price (AS 41–42).

Quin, James (SA 37–38*) (From DL, AS 40–41*, and SA 41–42) (from CG, UC 44–45*).

Raffa, Mrs. (AS 34–35).

Ranalow (SA 33–34).

Ravenscroft (RS 32–33).

Ravenscroft, Mrs. [see also Mrs. Pasqualino] (RS 32–33) (SA 36–37, 37–38).

Redman, Samuel (RS/SA 35–36) (AS 36–37?, 37–38).

Reed (SA 33–34) (AS 35–36, 36–37, 37–38).

Reilly, James [stage doorkeeper] (SA 39–40).

Reilly [or Rielly] [printer] (RS/SA 35–36).

Reynolds, Richard (SA 28–29?, 31–32, 32–33) (AS 42–43).

Reynolds, Mrs. Richard (SA 28–29?, 31–32, 32–33, 33–34) (AS 35–36) (from CG, SA 36–37, 37–38, 38–39, 39–40) (AS 40–41) (AS 41–42) (SA 42–43).

Rivers (CAP 44–45).

Roan, Master (NBDS 31–32).

Roch (RS 32–33).

Roe, Compton [musician?] (SA 41–42).

Rogers, Miss Elizabeth ["Lilliputian Polly"] (UC 43–44).

Roland, Mlle. Catherine [dancer] (from LIF, SA 43–44).

Rosco, James (SA 22–23, 23–24?, 24–25, 25–26, 26–27?, 27–28?, 28–29).

"Russian Posture Boy" [posture maker and equilibrist] (SA 42–43).

Ryan, Lacy (from CG, SA 32–33*) (from CG, AS 40–41*).

Sampson, Mrs. (SA 41–42) (UC 43–44).

Schoolding (SA 22–23).

Seale, Mrs. See Mrs. Bellamy

Seivers (SA 33–34) (AS 36–37).

Sheridan, George (SA 27–28?, 28–29, 29–30, 30–31, 31–32, 32–33, 33–34) (AS 35–36, 36–37).

Sheridan, Richard (SA 42–43).

Sheridan, Thomas (SA 42–43, 43–44) (UC 44–45).

Short [musician] (AS 42–43).

Simms (SA 25–26, 26–27?, 27–28?, 28–29?, 29–30?, 30–31).

Smith (SA 20–21?, 21–22).

Smith, Mrs. (RS 32–33).

Sparks, Isaac (RS 34–35, RS/SA 35–36) (SA 39–40, 40–41) (AS 41–42, 42–43) (UC 43–44, 44–45).

Sparks, Luke (RS 32–33, 33–34) (GBGL 34–35) (RS/SA 35–36) (SA 36–37, 37–38, 38–39, 39–40) (AS 41–42, 42–43) (UC 43–44, 44–45).

Spiller, Mrs. James (From LIF, SA 24–25).

Stepney (SA 37–38).

Stepney, Mrs. (SA 37–38).

Sterling, Mrs. Nancy. [neé Lyddal] (SA 24–25, 25–26, 26–27?, 27–28, 28–29, 29–30, 30–31, 31–32).

Stockdill [carpenter] (SA 36–37).

Stoppelaer, Charles (from CG, SA 39–40).

Storer, Elizabeth [Mrs. Charles] [singer] (from London, SA 42–43, 43–44) (UC 44–45).

Swan, George Cornelius (AS 41–42, 42–43).

Sybilla, Mrs. [stage name Sybilla Gronaman] [singer] (AS 42–43).

Talent, Mrs. (RS 32–33).

Thompson (SA 41–42).

Thomson [prompter] (AS 41–42).

Thomson [or Thompson], Miss Elizabeth [dancer] (SA 39–40, 40–41).

Thumoth, Burk [musician] (SA 38–39, 39–40?).

Townsend (CAP 44–45).

Trefusis, Joseph (SA 20–21?).

Tudor, Joseph [scene-painter] (SA 37–38, 38–39) (AS 40–41).

Tyler [gallery officekeeper] (RS/SA 35–36) (SA 38–39, 39–40, 40–41, 41–42, 42–43).

Vanderbank, James (SA 20–21?, 21–22, 22–23, 23–24, 24–25, 25–26, 26–27?, 27–28?, 28–29, 29–30, 30–31, 31–32, 32–33, 33–34) (AS 34–35, 35–36, 36–37, 37–38, 38–39, 39–40, 40–41, 41–42) (UC 43–44, 44–45).

Vanderbank, Mrs. James (SA 20–21?, 21–22, 22–23, 23–24?, 25–26, 26–27?, 27–28?, 28–29, 29–30?, 30–31?, 31–32?, 32–33, 33–34) (AS 34–35?, 35–36, 36–37, 38–39) (UC 43–44).

Vanderbank, Miss (AS 35–36).

Vanderhagen, Johann [scene-painter] (SA 22–23, 32–33).

Vaughn, [Henry?] (from DL, AS 37–38) (from GF, SA 40–41).

Violante, Sgna. or Mme. (SA 29–30) (NBDS 30–31, 31–32) (GBGL 32–33).

Violante, Miss or Mlle. (SA 29–30) (NBDS 30–31?, 31–32) (GBGL 32–33).

Walker, Thomas (from GF, SA 41–42*) (SA and AS 42–43) (UC 43–44).

Walsh [musician] (CAP 44–45).

Walsh, James [dancer] (GBGL 32–33) (RS and GBGL 33–34) (GBGL 34–35) (AS 35–36, 36–37) (SA 37–38) (AS 39–40, 40–41, 42–43).

Ward, John (SA 29–30) (SA and GBDS 30–31) (RS 34–35, RS/SA 35–36) (AS 36–37, 37–38, 38–39, 39–40, 40–41).

Ward, Mrs. John [neé Sarah Butcher] (SA 29–30) (SA and GBDS 30–31) (RS 34–35?, RS/SA 35–36) (AS 36–37, 37–38, 39–40, 40–41).

Warham (SA 33–34).

Waters, Miss (SA 20–21?).

Watson, John Sr. (SA 20–21?, 23–24).

Watson, John Jr. (SA 20–21?, 21–22, 22–23, 23–24, 24–25, 25–26, 26–27?, 27–28?, 28–29, 29–30?, 30–31, 31–32, 32–33, 33–34) (AS 34–35, 35–36, 36–37, 37–38, 38–39, 39–40, 40–41, 41–42, 42–43) (UC 43–44, 44–45).

Wetherilt, Robert (RS/SA 35–36) (SA 36–37, 37–38, 38–39, 39–40, 40–41) (AS 41–42) (SA 41–42, 42–43, died June).

Wetherilt, Mrs. Robert (SA 36–37, 37–38, 39–40, 40–41) (AS 41–42) (SA 41–42, 42–43).

White, Mrs. (UC 43–44).

White, Master (NBDS 31–32).

Whitnall [musician] (SA 39–40?).

Wilks [musician] (SA 39–40?).

Williamson, Mrs. (AS 36–37).

Winch [musician] (SA 41–42).

Woder, Francis [musician] (AS 35–36) (SA 38–39) (AS 39–40) (SA 41–42).

Woder, Master [musician] (SA 40–41).

Woffington, [John?] Master (NBDS 31–32).

Woffington, Margaret "Peg" [Miss, later Mrs.] (NBDS 31–32) (AS 34–35, 35–36, 36–37, 37–38, 39–40) (from DL, SA 41–42).

Wolfe, Miss (SA 20–21?).

Woodward, Henry (from DL, SA 38–39).

Woodward, Mrs. [not Mrs. Henry Woodward] (from Edinburgh, AS 37–38).

Worsdale, James (SA 37–38, 39–40) (AS 40–41, 41–42) (SA 42–43) (UC 43–44).

Wright [treasurer] (SA 28–29, 29–30, 31–32, 32–33).

Wright, Thomas (from DL, SA 41–42, 42–43) (UC 43–44) (CAP 44–45?).

Wrightson (AS 39–40, 40–41).

Wrightson, Mrs. Nancy [neé Elrington, see also] (SA 32–33, 33–34) (AS 34–35, 35–36, 37–38, 38–39, 39–40, 40–41).

# Author-Play Index

See Mainpiece and Afterpiece indexes for play type, venues, and performance dates. @ indicates afterpiece.

@*Scaramouche Turned Old Woman* (P) 1738

@*Sequel to the Rehearsal* (Burl.) 1741

@*Spaniard Deceived, The; Or, Harlequin Worm Doctor* (P) 1736

@*Stage Coach Opera, The* (BO) 1730

@*Thomas Koulikan, The Persian Hero; Or, The Distressed Princess* (P) 1741

*Three Humps, The* (C) 1738

@*Vernon Triumphant; Or, The British Sailors* (F) 1741

@*Vintner Tricked, The; Or, A Match at Newgate* (F) 1743

ARNE, THOMAS A.
*Death of Abel, The* (Oratorio) 1744
@*Judgment of Paris, The* (BO) after Congreve 1740
*Love and Glory* (Masque) Thomas Philips music Arne 1734
*Opera of Operas, The; Or; Tom Thumb the Great* (See Mrs. Eliza Haywood)
*Rosamond* (Opera) adaptation of Addison/Clayton 1733

BAKER, THOMAS
*Tunbridge Walks; Or, The Yeoman of Kent* (C) 1714

BANKS, JOHN
*Albion Queens, The; Or, The Death of Mary, Queen of Scotland* (T) 1704
*Anna Bullen; Or, Virtue Betrayed* (T) 1682
*Unhappy Favourite, The; Or, The Earl of Essex* (T) 1681

BEAUMONT, FRANCIS AND FLETCHER, JOHN
*Philaster; Or, Love Lies a Bleeding* (C) adapted by Settle 1695
*Scornful Lady, The* (C)
*Wit Without Money* (C)

BEHN, APHRA
@*Credulous Cockhold, The [The Debauchee; Or,]* (F) 1677
*Emperor of the Moon, The* (F) 1687

*Rover, The; Or, The Banished Cavaliers* (C) 1677

BETTERTON, THOMAS
*Amorous Widow, The; Or, The Wanton Wife* (C) 1670

BREVAL, CAPT. JOHN
@*Strollers, The* (F) 1723

BROME, SIR RICHARD
*Jovial Crew, The* (BO) adaptation by Roome, Concanen, and Yonge 1732
*Northern Lass, The; Or The Nest of Fools* (C) 1662

BROOKE, HENRY
*Earl of Westmoreland, The; Or, The Betrayer of his Country* (T) 1742
@*Female Officer, The; Or, The Lady's Voyage to Gibraltar* (F) 1740
*Patriot, The* (T) revision of *Gustavus Vasa* 1744

BULLOCK, CHRISTOPHER
@*Adventures of Half an Hour, The* (F) 1716
@*Cobler of Preston, The* (F) 1716
*Woman is a Riddle; Or, The Way to Win a Widow* (C) 1717
*Woman's Revenge, The; Or, A Match at Newgate* (C) 1715

CAREY, HENRY
@*Chrononhotonthologos* (Burl.) 1734
@*Contrivances, The; Or, More Ways Than One* (BO) 1715
@*Dragon of Wantley, The* (Burl.) music by Lampe 1737
@*Honest Yorkshireman, The* (BO) 1735
@*Margery; Or, A Worse Plague Than the Dragon* (Burl.) 1738
@*Nancy; Or, The Parting Lovers* (Int.) 1739

CENTLIVRE, SUSANNAH
*Bold Stroke for a Wife, A* (C) 1709
*Busy Body, The* (C) 1709
*Gamester, The* (C) 1705
*Man's Bewitched, The; Or, The Devil to Do About Her* (C) 1709

*Nuptials of Roger and Jean* (Operetta) 1733

ESTE, WILLIAM
@*Cure for Jealousy, A* (F) 1740

ETHEREGE, GEORGE
*Man of Mode, The* (C) 1676

FARQUHAR, GEORGE
[*Beaux'*] *Stratagem, The* (C) 1707
*Constant Couple, The* (C) 1699
*Inconstant, The; Or, The Way to Win Him* (C) 1702
*Love and a Bottle* (C) 1699
*Recruiting Officer, The* (C) 1706
*Sir Harry Wildair* (C) 1701
@*Stage Coach, The* (F) 1704
*Twin Rivals, The* (C) 1703

FENTON, ELIJAH
*Mariamne* (T) 1723

FIELDING, HENRY
@*Author's Farce, The; Or, The Pleasures of the Town* (F) 1730
@*Intriguing Chambermaid, The* (F) 1734
@*Lottery, The* (BO) 1732
*Miser, The* (C) 1733
@*Miss Lucy in Town* (F) music by Arne 1742
@*Mock Doctor, The* (BO) 1732
*Pasquin* (Dr. Satire) 1736
@*Tragedy of Tragedies; Or, Tom Thumb the Great* (Burl.) 1730
@*Virgin Unmasked, The; Or, An Old Man Taught Wisdom* (BO) 1735

FLETCHER, JOHN
*Humorous Lieutenant, The* (C)
*Pilgrim, The* (C) adapted by Vanbrugh 1700
*Prophetess, The; Or The History of Dioclesian* with Massinger
*Royal Merchant, The; Or, The Beggar's Bush* (C) with Massinger
*Rule a Wife and Have a Wife* (C)

FORSTER, ABBOT
*Fate of Ambition, The; Or, The Treacherous Favourite* (T) 1733

GARDINER, MATTHEW
*Parthian Hero, The; Or Beauty in Distress* (T) 1741
@*Sharpers, The; Or, The Female Matchmaker* (BO) 1740

GARRICK, DAVID
@*Lying Valet, The* (F) 1741

GAY, JOHN
*Acis and Galatea* (Pastoral Opera) music by Handel 1731
*Beggar's Opera, The* (BO) 1728
*Captives, The* (T) 1724
@*What D'ye Call It, The* (F) 1715

HAMMOND, WILLIAM
@*Preceptor, The; Or, The Loves of Abelard and Heloise* (BO) 1739

HANDEL, GEORGE FREDERIC
*Acis and Galatea* (Pastoral Opera) with Gay 1731

HAVARD, WILLIAM
*King Charles I* (T) 1737

HAWKER, ESSEX
@*Wedding, The* (BO) 1729

HAYWOOD, ELIZABETH MRS.,
HATCHETT, WILLIAM
@*Opera of Operas, The; Or, Tom Thumb the Great* (Burl. opera) musical adaptation of Fielding's *Tragedy of Tragedies* 1733

HEIGHINGTON, M. DR.
@*Enchanter, The; Or, Harlequin Merlin* (P) 1725

HILL, AARON
*Fatal Extravagance* (T) 1721
@*Walking Statue, The; Or, The Devil in the Wine Cellar* (F) 1710

HIPPISLEY, JOHN
@*Flora; Or, Hob's Opera* [*Flora; Or, Hob in the Well*] (BO) 1729

HOWARD, ROBERT SIR
*Committee, The; Or, The Faithful Irishman* (C) 1662

RAVENSCROFT, EDWARD
  @Anatomist, The; Or, The Sham
    Doctor (F) 1696

RICH, JOHN
  @Necromancer; Or, Harlequin Doc-
    tor Faustus (P) 1723

ROGER, MONS.
  @Cephalus and Procris; Or, Harle-
    quin Grand Volgi (Masque) 1730

ROWE, NICHOLAS
  Fair Penitent, The (T) 1703
  Jane Shore (T) 1714
  Lady Jane Grey (T) 1715
  Tamerlane (T) 1701

RYAN, LACY
  Cobler of Preston's Opera, The (BO)
    1728

SEWELL, GEORGE
  Sir Walter Raleigh [The Life and
    Death of] (T) 1719

SHADWELL, CHARLES
  Fair Quaker of Deal, The (C) 1710

SHADWELL, THOMAS
  Don John; Or, The Libertine De-
    stroyed (Droll) 1675
  Lancashire Witches, The (C) 1681
  Squire of Alsatia, The (C) 1688

SHAKESPEARE, WILLIAM
  As You Like It
  Hamlet, Prince of Denmark
  Jew of Venice, The (C) adapted by
    George Granville (See also Mer-
    chant of Venice)
  Julius Caesar
  King Henry IV [Pt. 1] with the Hu-
    mours of Sir John Falstaff
  King Henry IV, Pt. 2
  King Henry V
  King Henry VIII
  King John
  King Lear and His Three Daughters
    adapted by Tate
  King Richard II
  King Richard III

Macbeth
Measure for Measure
Merchant of Venice, The. See also
  Jew of Venice, The
Merry Wives of Windsor, The
Othello
Tempest, The; Or, The Enchanted Is-
  land (Opera) adapted by Davanent
  (1667) then T. Shadwell (1674)
Timon of Athens; Or, The Man Hater
Twelfth Night
Winter's Tale, The

SHERIDAN, THOMAS
  @Brave Irishman, The; Or, Captain
    O'Blunder (F) 1737
  Faithful Shepherd, The (F) 1736

SKIDDY, MR.
  Miser Matched, The; Or, A Trip to
    Brussels (C) 1740

SOUTHERNE, THOMAS
  Fatal Marriage, The; Or, The Inno-
    cent Adultery (C) 1694
  Oroonoko; Or, The Royal Slave (T)
    1695

STEELE, RICHARD SIR
  Conscious Lovers, The (C) 1722
  Funeral, The; Or, Grief A-la-mode
    (C) 1701
  Tender Husband, The; Or, The Ac-
    complished Fools (C) 1705

STERLING, JAMES
  Rival Generals, The (T) 1722

TATE, NAHUM
  See SHAKESPEARE King Lear and
    His Three Daughters

THOMSON, JAMES AND MALLET, DAVID
  @Alfred (Masque) 1740

VANBRUGH, JOHN SIR
  Aesop; Or, The Politick Statesman
    (C) 1696–97
  City Wives' Confederacy, The (C)
    1705
  Mistake, The; Or, The Wrangling
    Lovers (C) 1706
  Provoked Wife, The (R) 1697

*Relapse, The; Or Virtue in Danger*
   (C) 1696
@*Wrangling Lovers, The* (F) adaptation of *The Mistake* 1735

VILLIERS, GEORGE, EARL OF
BUCKINGHAM
   *Chances, The* (C) 1682
   *Rehearsal, The* (Burl.) 1671

WALKER, THOMAS
   *Love and Loyalty; Or, Publick Justice*
      (T) 1744

WEAVER, JOHN

@*Tavern Bilkers, The* (F) 1702

WORSDALE, JAMES
   @*Assembly, The* (F) 1740
   @*Cure for a Scold, A* (BO) 1735
   @*Queen of Spain, The; Or, Farinelli
      in Madrid* (Mus. Ent.) 1741

WYCHERLEY, WILLIAM
   *Country Wife, The* (C) 1675
   *Plain Dealer, The* (C) 1676

YOUNG, EDWARD
   *Revenge, The* (T) 1721

# Index of Main- and Afterpieces

## Mainpiece Index

Asterisk indicates benefit performance.

Total Performances

*Acis and Galatea* (Pastoral Opera) Gay music Handel 1731     2
1734–35: AS FEB. 21*, MAR. 8

*Aesop; or, The Politick Statesman* (C) Vanbrugh 1696–97     5
1723–24: SA JAN. 6
1725–26: SA JUNE 6*
1739–40: AS JUNE 7*
1740–41: AS JULY 18, 20

*Albion Queens, The; Or, The Death of Mary, Queen of Scotland* (T)
  Banks 1704     3
1735–36: AS SEPT. 29
1739–40: SA MAY 8*
1740–41: SA APR. 20*

*Alchemist, The* (C) Jonson     1
1738–39: SA DEC. 19

*All for Love* (T) Dryden 1677     7
1724–25: SA NOV. 30*
1738–39: AS JAN. 22*
        SA MAY 14*, JULY 20, AUG. 2*
1739–40: AS FEB. 21*
1740–41: SA MAR. 10*

*All Vows Kept* (C) Capt. Downes 1733     1
1732–33: SA Spring, EXACT DATE UNKNOWN

*Aminta* (Pastoral) John Dancer? 1660 alteration by P. Dubois 1726     1
1735–36: AS DEC. 13*

*Amorous Widow, The; Or, The Wanton Wife* (C) T. Betterton 1670     5
1722–23: SA 22 NOV.
1724–25: SA EXACT DATE UNKNOWN
1729–30: SA MAY 7*
1732–33: SA MAR. 15*

424

1736–37: AS NOV. 8, JAN. 3
         SA MAR. 21, APR. 25, MAY 9*
1737–38: SA NOV. 24, JAN. 7, MAR. 6*
         AS NOV. 24
1738–39: SA NOV. 9, APR. 30*, AUG. 13*
1739–40: AS DEC. 15*, 17, MAR. 26*, APR. 26*, MAY 12*
         SA APR. 14*, JULY 14
1740–41: AS MAR. 7*
1741–42: AS MAY 17, 20, 24, 27, JUNE 24*
         SA AUG. 21
1742–43: SA NOV. 29, DEC. 2, 14*, 22*
1743–44: SA DEC. 19, FEB. 4, APR. 14, 30
         AS NOV. 28, DEC. 1, 5, 8, 12, 15*, 19, JAN. 5, 23*, MAR. 15*,
         JULY 2

*Beggar's Wedding, The* (BO) Charles Coffey 1729                          3
1728–29: SA MAR, 24, 27, 29*

*Betrayer of his Country, The.* See *Earl of Westmoreland, The*

*Bold Stroke for a Wife, A* (C) S. Centlivre 1709                        16
1729–30: SA APR. 2*, MAY 4*
1731–32: SA MAY 8*
1733–34: RS DEC. 10*
         SA FEB. 28*
1734–35: RS SEPT. 9*
         GBGL MAR. 17*
1735–36: AS MAY 20*
1736–37: SA NOV. 15, MAY 16*
1740–41: AS JAN. 31, JUNE 8
         SA FEB. 5*
1742–43: SA MAR. 21*, JUNE 22*
         AS JUNE 18

*Bonduca; Or, The British Heroine* (O) George Powell 1696                1
1737–38: SA APR. 28*

*Busy Body, The* (C) S. Centlivre 1709                                  13
1723–24: SA NOV. 21, 28
1737–38: SA JAN. 16
1738–39: SA NOV. 6, MAR. 6*
1739–40: AS DEC. 31 (CANCELLED?)
         SA MAY 26*
1740–41: SA JAN. 14, MAR. 8*, APR. 22*, JUNE 26
1742–43: SA FEB. 1*, MAY 18*

*Captives, The* (T) Gay 1724                                             1
1723–24: SA MAY 18*

*Careless Husband, The* (C) C. Cibber 1704                              14
1722–23: SA DEC. 6
1732–33: SA APR. 19*

1744–45: SA MAR. 28*

*Comus* (Masque) Milton, adapted by J. Dalton 1712                    24
1740–41: AS AUG. 6, 10, 12
1741–42: AS JAN. 7, 11, FEB. 26*, MAY 4, 6
1742–43: AS JAN. 10, 13, 17, 24, FEB. 3*, 14*, APR. 21, 25
1743–44: AS NOV. 17, 19, 24, DEC. 17*, 22, FEB. 1*, MAR. 29
1744–45: AS MAY 9

*Conscious Lovers, The* (C) Steele 1722                    25
1722–23: SA JAN. 10, 17, 24, 28, MAR. 7
1723–24: SA MAY 13
1724–25: SA EXACT DATE UNKNOWN
1728–29: SA JAN. 27*
1733–34: RS FEB. 18*
1735–36: AS FEB. 26*
1736–37: SA FEB. 4*
1738–39: SA JULY 14*
1739–40: AS MAR. 1*
         SA APR. 16*
1740–41: SA APR. 8*, MAY 20*
1741–42: AS DEC. 12, FEB. 9*
         SA FEB. 25*
1742–43: AS MAY 11*
         SA JUNE 13*
1743–44: AS OCT. 11, MAR. 12*, JULY 14*
1744–45: SA FEB. 6*

*Constant Couple, The* (C) Farquhar 1699,                    32
1728–29: SA FEB. 27*
1729–30: SA JAN. 19, MAY 14*
1732–33: SA JULY 12*
1735–36: AS JAN. 22
1736–37: AS NOV. 11
         SA FEB. 9*
1737–38: SA FEB. 18*, 23*, JULY 27
1738–39: SA NOV. 23*, JAN. 22*, MAR. 15*
1739–40: SA DEC. 20, MAR. 29*
         AS APR. 25*
1740–41: AS MAR. 21*
         SA APR. 22*
1741–42: SA JAN. 18*, MAR. 4*, JUNE 16, AUG. 2
1742–43: SA JUNE 20*
1743–44: AS OCT. 17, 27, JAN. 20
1744–45: SA OCT. 11
         CAP JAN. 28, 29, FEB. 4, 18, MAR. 13

*Country Lasses, The; Or, The Custom of the Manor* (C) C. Johnson 1715    4
1737–38: AS SEPT. 29
         SA OCT. 3, APR. 26*
1739–40: AS MAR. 22*

*Country Wife, The* (C) Wycherley 1675                    4

1739–40: AS FEB. 27*
1740–41: AS APR. 16
1741–42: AS APR. 5, MAY 21*

*Drummer, The; Or, The Haunted House* (C) Addison 1716                    3
1736–37: AS FEB. 19*
1738–39: AS OCT. 11
1744–45: CAP FEB. 8

*Earl of Westmoreland, The; Or, The Betrayer of his Country* (T) Brooke
  1742                                                                    5
1741–42: AS FEB. 8, 16, MAR. 4*
1744–45: SA MAY 13, 23*

*Emperor of the Moon, The* (F) A. Behn 1687                               2
1738–39: AS FEB. 1*
1739–40: AS APR. 25* (AS AFTERPIECE)

*Epicoene; Or, The Silent Woman.* See *The Silent Woman*

*Fair Quaker of Deal, The* (C) C. Shadwell 1710                          4
1735–36: AS MAR. 25*
1736–37: AS MAR. 24*
1739–40: AS JAN. 26*
1744–45: AS APR. 15

*Fair Penitent, The* (T) N. Rowe 1703                                    16
1733–34: RS MAY 24*
1737–38: AS OCT. 6
1738–39: AS FEB. 16*
1739–40: SA MAR. 13*
1740–41: SA JAN. 29*, MAY 14*, JUNE 19*
1741–42: SA OCT. 29, JAN. 15*, APR. 1*
         AS FEB. 1*, 18*
1742–43: AS APR. 11*
         SA JUNE 27, JULY 5*
1743–44: AS NOV. 10

*Faithful Shepherd, The* (F) T. Sheridan 1736                            1
1739–40: SA JAN. 31*

*Fatal Extravagance* (T) A. Hill 1721                                    4
1721–22: SA EXACT DATE UNKNOWN
1738–39: SA FEB. 26*
1740–41: AS FEB. 21*
1743–44: AS JAN. 19

*Fatal Marriage, The; Or, The Innocent Adultery* (C) Southerne 1694      5
1722–23: SA DEC. 17*
1735–36: AS APR. 1*
1740–41: SA FEB. 19*
1742–43: AS MAR. 24*

1741–42: SA FEB. 11*

*Ignoramus, The; Or, The English Lawyer* (C) Anon. 1716                              1
1738–39: AS DEC. 4*

*Inconstant, The; Or, The Way to Win Him* (C) Farquhar 1702                          2
1732–33: NBDS OCT. OR NOV. EXACT DATE UNKNOWN
1736–37: AS MAY 5*

*Indian Emperor, The* (T) Dryden 1667                                                3
1731–32: FEB. EXACT DATE UNKNOWN
1737–38: AS MAY 4*, DEC. 12*

*Island Princess, The; Or, Generous Portuguese* (O) P. Motteux 1699                  4
1725–26: SA EXACT DATE UNKNOWN
1731–32: SA FEB. 17*
1732–33: SA OCT. 5
1742–43: SA FEB. 14*

*Jane Shore* (T) Rowe 1714                                                          16
1723–24: SA DEC. 16
1736–37: AS JAN. 10
1737–38: AS MAR. 2*
1739–40: SA FEB. 11, MAY 2*
1740–41: SA APR. 9*, JUNE 8*
          AS DEC. 11
1741–42: SA JAN. 9, 28, FEB. 6, APR. 29*
1742–43: AS FEB. 23*
1743–44: AS FEB. 9*, MAY 21
1744–45: CAP JUNE 20*

*Jew of Venice, The* (C) George Granville (See also *Merchant of Venice*)            2
1720–21: SA 5 NOV.
1736–37: AS MAY 24*

*Johnny Bow-wow; Or, The Wicked Gravedigger* (BO) Anon. 1732                          1
1731–32: SA MAY 19*

*Jovial Crew, The* (BO) Brome                                                        2
1731–32: SA EXACT DATE UNKNOWN
1742–43: SA JUNE 13* (AS AFTERPIECE)

*Julius Caesar* Shakespeare                                                         23
1722–23: SA JAN. 21*
1730–31: SA MAR. 8*
1731–32: SA APR. 24*
          NBDS DEC. 15
1735–36: AS DEC. 4
1736–37: SA JUNE 27
1737–38: SA MAR. 20*, JUNE 26*
1738–39: AS JAN. 27*
          SA JULY 2*

*King Lear and his Three Daughters* Tate after Shakespeare          18
1723–24: SA JUNE 10
1728–29: SA MAR. 3*
1732–33: SA FEB. 19*
1733–34: SA FEB. 18*
1735–36: SA FEB. 23*
1737–38: AS FEB. 16*
1738–39: SA JULY 6
1739–40: AS FEB. 25*
1740–41: AS FEB 17*, AUG. 17*
1741–42: SA OCT. 22, NOV. 19, FEB. 13*, JUNE 24*, 29
1742–43: SA JUNE 23
1744–45: SA NOV. 26*
          CAP MAR. 19*


*King Richard II* Shakespeare          1
1720–21: SA EXACT DATE UNKNOWN

*King Richard III* Shakespeare          28
1729–30: SA APR. 20*
1730–31: SA MAR. 22*
1735–36: SA FEB. 20*, MAR. 31
1736–37: AS FEB. 10*
          SA FEB. 11*
1737–38: SA JUNE 19
1739–40: SA DEC. 6, MAR. 27*
1740–41: AS APR. 29*
1741–42: SA JAN. 29*, JUNE 18, JULY 8*
          AS OCT. 26, NOV. 23, JUNE 22*
1742–43: SA JAN. 29, FEB. 21*, APR. 7, JUNE 30
          AS APR. 30*
1743–44: SA NOV. 3, DEC. 1*
1744–45: SA FEB. 1*, JUNE 13*, JULY 15
          CAP MAR. 25*, MAY 9*


*Lady Jane Grey* (T) Rowe 1715          2
1729–30: SA FEB. 23*
1742–43: AS JULY 11*


*Lancashire Witches, The* (C) T. Shadwell 1681          4
1741–42: SA NOV. 26, DEC. 3, 31, JAN. 18* (AS AFTERPIECE)


*Leonora; Or, The Fatal Lover* (T) Anon. 1736          3
1735–36: SA FEB. 4, 9, 11*


*London Merchant, The* (T) Lillo 1731          3
1731–32: SA SEPT. 21, 25
1740–41: SA APR. 27*


*Love and a Bottle* (C) Farquhar 1699          8
1737–38: SA NOV. 10, MAY 22*
1738–39: SA MAR. 20*, MAY 17*

1739–40: SA APR. 24*
1740–41: SA APR. 30*
1744–45: CAP MAR. 26*, APR. 15

*Love and Ambition* (T) J. Darcy 1731      6
1731–32: SA DEC. 9, 11, 13*, 18, 20, JAN. 17

*Love and Glory* (Masque) Thomas Philips, music T. A. Arne 1734      1
1742–43: AS FEB. 10*

*Love and Loyalty; Or, Publick Justice* (T) T. Walker 1744      2
1743–44: AS MAY 24, 28

*Love for Love* (C) Congreve 1695      34
1721–22: SA EXACT DATE UNKNOWN
1723–24: SA DEC. 12
1724–25: SA DEC. 3*, APR. 22
1728–29: SA OCT. 11
1730–31: SA MAR. 1
1731–32: SA MAY 15*
1732–33: RS FEB. 5
1733–34: SA OCT. 4, JAN. 28*
1735–36: AS JAN. 20
        SA MAR. 2*
1736–37: AS JAN. 20
        SA FEB. 7*
1737–38: SA FEB. 10*
        AS SEPT. 15
1738–39: SA JAN. 31*, MAY 21*
1739–40: SA NOV. 12, MAR. 20*, MAY 24*, JULY 5*
1740–41: SA JAN. 2
        AS DEC. 4*, JUNE 3*
1741–42: AS MAR. 22
        SA JAN. 22*, MAY 13*, 27
1742–43: AS FEB. 12*, MAY 12, JULY 4*
1743–44: AS JAN. 26*, MAR. 14*

*Love Makes a Man* (C) C. Cibber 1700      27
1722–23: SA FEB. 14*
1723–24: SA JULY 6*
1731–32: SA JUNE 5*
1732–33: SA OCT. 30, MAY 28*
1735–36: SA DEC. 11, MAR. 6*, 24*
1736–37: SA FEB. 18*
        AS NOV. 22*
1737–38: SA JAN. 11, APR. 14*
        AS OCT. 27
1738–39: SA JULY 23*
        AS DEC. 18*
1739–40: SA NOV. 26
1740–41: AS JAN. 22, 27
        SA MAR. 16*, APR. 14*

1741–42:  AS APR. 1*
          SA JUNE 30
1742–43:  AS FEB. 22*
          SA APR. 12*
1743–44:  SA FEB. 2*
1744–45:  CAP MAR. 21*, APR. 1


*Love's Last Shift* (C) C. Cibber 1696                                        19
1722–23:  SA JAN. 7
1732–33:  SA APR. 30*
1733–34:  AS JUNE 6*
1734–35:  AS JUNE 9*
1735–36:  AS APR. 5*
1736–37:  SA FEB. 16*
1738–39:  SA MAR. 8*, JULY 16
1739–40:  SA NOV. 1, 21, FEB. 9*
1740–41:  AS SEPT. 3*
1741–42:  SA DEC. 31, JAN. 22*, FEB. 5*, MAR. 12*
1742–43:  AS APR. 26*, JUNE 28*
1743–44:  AS OCT. 31


*Lucius Junius Brutus, Father of his Country* (T) Lee 1680                     1
1737–38:  AS APR. 27*


*Macbeth* Shakespeare                                                         21
1722–23:  SA DEC. 3*
1731–32:  SA MAY 4*
1732–33:  SA JUNE 25
1734–35:  AS FEB. 10*
1735–36:  SA MAY 26*
1736–37:  AS NOV. 25
1737–38:  AS JAN. 19, 23
          SA FEB. 22*
1738–39:  SA FEB. 8*, JULY 9*
1739–40:  SA JULY 3
1741–42:  AS NOV. 16
          SA FEB. 22*
1742–43:  SA JULY 25
1743–44:  SA DEC. 8, JUNE 7
1744–45:  SA NOV. 12, FEB. 13*, MAY 30*, AUG. 5*


*Man of Mode, The* (C) Etherege 1676                                          3
1741–42:  AS MAY 3, 13*
1742–43:  SA JUNE 2


*Man of Taste, The; Or, The Guardian* (C) J. Miller 1735                       1
1735–36:  SA JAN. 15


*Man's Bewitched, The; Or, The Devil to Do About Her* (C) S. Centlivre
    1709                                                                       6
1737–38:  SA SEPT. 22, NOV. 28, JAN. 28, MAR. 18*
1740–41:  SA FEB. 24*

*Mistake, The; Or, The Wrangling Lovers* (C) Vanbrugh 1706 (See also
   *Wrangling Lovers, The* afterpiece)        2
1722–23: SA APR. 18
1723–24: SA DEC. 5


*Mithradates, King of Pontus* (T) Lee 1678       2
1741–42: SA MAR. 1*, 23*


*Mithradates* (T) Anon. trans. of Racine 1742?       1
1742–43: SA FEB. 3


*Mourning Bride, The* (T) Congreve 1697       16
1722–23: SA APR. 1*
1728–29: SA APR. 21*
1729–30: SA APR. 27*
1732–33: SA JAN. 29*, JUNE 18*
1735–36: AS MAR. 29*
1739–40: SA MAR. 15, MAY 19*
1740–41: SA DEC. 29, FEB. 26*
1741–42: SA NOV. 5, 30*, MAR. 26*
1742–43: AS FEB. 2*
1743–44: AS NOV. 3, MAR. 13*


*Mustapha* (T) D. Mallet 1739       1
1738–39: SA MAY 2*


*Nature* (C) Dixon 1742       1
1741–42: AS MAR. 15


*Non-juror, The* (C) C. Cibber 1718       1
1742–43: SA MAY 30


*Northern Lass, The; Or The Nest of Fools* (C) Brome 1662       1
1725–26: SA EXACT DATE UNKNOWN


*Oedipus, King of Thebes* (T) Dryden and Lee 1678       5
1721–22: SA APR. 2*
1722–23: SA APR. 6
1737–38: AS MAR. 23*
1739–40: SA JUNE 12, AUG. 20*


*Old Batchelour, The* (C) Congreve 1693       17
1729–30: SA MAY 25
1732–33: SA APR. 16*
1733–34: AS APR. 29*
      RS DEC. 8
1734–35: AS JUNE 12*
1736–37: SA NOV. 25
      AS DEC. 20*
1737–38: SA MAY 3*
1738–39: SA JAN. 15
1739–40: SA JAN. 3

1741–42: AS JAN. 18, FEB. 4*
         SA JULY 26
1742–43: SA NOV. 22, MAY 3*, 19
1743–44: AS OCT. 24

*Oroonoko; Or, The Royal Slave* (T) Southerne 1695                    16
1722–23: SA JAN. 31*
1723–24: SA DEC. 2
1728–29: SA APR. 7*
1733–34: GBGL FEB. 1
1735–36: SA MAY 17*
1736–37: SA MAR. 24
         AS NOV. 1
1738–39: SA MAR. 5*, MAY 23*, JUNE 18
1739–40: SA JUNE 16
1740–41: SA MAY 1*
1741–42: SA FEB. 8*, AUG. 9*
         AS JUNE 11, 21

*Orphan, The; Or, The Unhappy Marriage* (T) Otway 1680                17
1723–24: SA JAN. 9*
1733–34: GBGL JUNE 18*
1736–37: AS FEB. 14*,
         SA APR. 2, JUNE 24
1738–39: SA APR. 12, JUNE 29
1739–40: SA JAN. 24, APR. 18*
1740–41: AS FEB. 3
1741–42: AS DEC. 21, FEB. 27*, APR. 29
         SA JUNE 21, 28
1742–43: SA JUNE 6*
1744–45: CAP JULY 3*

*Othello* Shakespeare                                                34
1721–22: SA JAN. 20*
1722–23: SA DEC. 10*
1723–24: SA JAN. 16*
1732–33: SA JULY 9
1734–35: AS FEB. 13
         RS MAY 14*
1735–36: RS MAR. 16*
         SA MAR. 27*
1736–37: SA JUNE 23
1737–38: SA NOV. 7, JUNE 22
1738–39: SA APR. 28*, JUNE 25*
1739–40: SA JUNE 30
1740–41: SA MAY 21*
         AS JUNE 22*
1741–42: AS MAY 15*, JUNE 29
1742–43: AS NOV. 18, JAN. 1, JUNE 20
         SA FEB. 7*, APR. 14, 21*, JULY 21
1743–44: SA FEB. 15*, MAR. 2*, MAY 3
         AS OCT. 13
1744–45: SA JAN. 14, APR. 1*, MAY 27, JUNE 24

CAP FEB. 14

*Pamela* (C) Dance? 1742                                                                2
1741–42:  SA DEC. 7, 10*

*Parthian Hero, The; Or Beauty in Distress* (T) M. Gardiner 1741          1
1741–42:  SA MAR. 16*

*Pasquin* (Dr. Satire) Fielding 1736                                                   14
1735–36:  AS APR. 29*, MAY 18*
          SA MAY 1, 3, 5, 24*, JUNE 21*
1736–37:  SA NOV. 8, FEB. 1*, MAY 17
1737–38:  SA FEB. 1, MAR. 1*
1740–41:  SA JAN. 19, FEB. 16

*Patriot, The* (T) H. Brooke 1744 rev. of *Gustavus Vasa*                    4
1744–45:  SA DEC. 3, 6, 10*, FEB. 28*

*Philaster; Or, Love Lies a Bleeding* (C) Settle after Beaumont and
     Fletcher 1695                                                                         1
1728–29:  SA EXACT DATE UNKNOWN

*Pilgrim, The* (C) Vanbrugh after Fletcher 1700                                11
1723–24:  SA JAN. 13
1735–36:  AS NOV. 27, DEC. 15*
1736–37:  SA MAY 4*
1737–38:  SA NOV. 3, MAR. 9*
1738–39:  AS MAR. 26*
1739–40:  AS MAR. 15*
1740–41:  AS APR. 15*
1741–42:  AS MAR. 30*
1744–45:  SA MAR. 14*

*Plain Dealer, The* (C) Wycherley 1676                                           2
1739–40:  SA MAY 5*
1741–42:  AS JAN. 25

*Prophetess, The; Or The History of Dioclesian* Fletcher and Massinger    1
1735–36:  AS DEC. 8

*Provoked Husband, The; Or, A Journey to London* (C) C. Cibber 1728       32
1728–29:  SA DEC. 19, 21, JAN. 13
1729–30:  SA APR. 23*
1730–31:  SA JAN. 20.
1731–32:  NBDS FEB. 28*
          SA NOV. 27, JUNE 26*
1732–33:  SA MAY 21*, JUNE 28
1735–36:  AS OCT. 30
          SA MAR. 22*, JUNE 16*
1736–37:  SA NOV. 22, DEC. 22*, JAN. 26*, JUNE 20
          AS OCT. 18
1737–38:  SA NOV. 17, MAY 1*

1738–39: SA MAR. 19*
1739–40: AS MAR. 13*
       SA NOV. 29, MAY 20*, JULY 24
1740–41: AS JUNE 25*
1741–42: SA DEC. 14*, MAR. 9*
1742–43: AS JAN. 20
       SA APR. 18, MAY 9*
1743–44: AS APR. 18*

*Provoked Wife, The* (R) Vanbrugh 1697                8
1720–21: SA JUNE 26*
1722–23: SA NOV. 8
1734–35: AS JUNE 5*
1737–38: SA JULY 31*
1739–40: SA JAN. 21
1741–42: AS NOV. 9, DEC. 7*, MAY 18*

*Prude, The; Or, Win Her And Wear Her* (C) Anon. 1744      3
1743–44: SA APR. 9, 10, 12*

*Punch's Opera; Or, The Comical Humours of Acis and Galatea* (Burl)
   Anon. 1735                                                2
1734–35: RS MAR. 11
       GBGL MAR. 19

*Recruiting Officer, The* (C) Farquhar 1706          25
1722–23: SA DEC. 13
1728–29: SA MAR. 1
1730–31: SA OCT. 19
1732–33: SA MAR. 1
1733–34: AS MAR. 9
       RS MAY 21*
1734–35: AS MAR. 1
1735–36: SA DEC. 22
1736–37: AS OCT. 11
1737–38: SA MAY 5*
1738–39: SA MAR. 12*
       AS NOV. 29*
1739–40: SA APR. 9
       AS MAY 1*
1740–41: SA MAY 8*
1741–42: SA MAY 11*, AUG. 19
       AS OCT. 12
1742–43: SA JAN. 24*, APR. 28*
       AS OCT. 30
1743–44: AS APR. 13*
       SA MAY 7, 25*
1744–45: SA SEPT. 27*

*Rehearsal, The* (Burl) Buckingham 1671           22
1735–36: AS NOV. 24
1740–41: AS NOV. 12, 15, 17, JAN. 20, APR. 2*

SA NOV. 24, 27, DEC. 1, 3, JAN. 8, FEB. 9*, JUNE 16*
1741–42: SA NOV. 2, JULY 3, 15, 23, AUG. 5
1742–43: SA JUNE 11, JULY 12
1743–44: AS MAR. 1*
1744–45: AS OCT. 25


*Relapse, The; Or, Virtue in Danger* (C) Vanbrugh 1696                    12
1731–32: SA FEB. 24*
1735–36: AS MAR. 18*
1737–38: AS JAN. 12
1738–39: AS MAR. 22*
1739–40: SA MAY 22*
          AS DEC. 6*
1740–41: SA MAR. 7*
1741–42: AS MAR. 25*
          SA MAR. 25*
1742–43: SA MAY 16
1744–45: SA NOV. 15*
          CAP FEB. 25


*Revenge, The* (T) E. Young 1721                    3
1729–30: SA MAY 21*
1744–45: CAP MAY 6
          SA JULY 25


*Rival Generals, The* (T) J. Sterling 1722                    2
1721–22: SA MAR. EXACT DATE UNKNOWN
1722–23: SA APR. 29*


*Rival Queens, The; Or, The Death of Alexander the Great* (T) Lee 1677                    5
1722–23: SA OCT. 8
1730–31: SA MAR. 29*
1737–38: AS MAY 9*
1738–39: SA AUG. 6
1739–40: SA JUNE 26


*Rosamond* (Opera) Addison and T. A. Arne 1733                    8
1742–43: AS MAY 7*, JUNE 11*
1743–44: SA APR. 2, 5, 9, 10, 12, 19 (ALL AS AFTERPIECE)


*Rover, The; Or, The Banished Cavaliers* (C) Behn 1677                    3
1721–22: SA OCT. 16
1728–29: SA JUNE 5*
1732–33: SA DEC. 4*


*Royal Merchant, The; Or, The Beggar's Bush* (C) Fletcher and Massinger                    13
1735–36: RS NOV. 13, 17, DEC. 1
          SA DEC. 29
1736–37: SA MAR. 7*
1739–40: SA FEB. 25*, MAY 7*
1740–41: AS MAY 11*
1741–42: SA MAR. 18*

1731–32: SA SEPT. 30
1734–35: AS MAY 1*
1736–37: AS OCT. 25
          SA JULY 14*
1737–38: SA JULY 17*
          AS SEPT. 22
1738–39: SA APR. 9
1739–40: SA FEB. 18*
1741–42: AS JAN. 28*, FEB. 22*
1742–43: SA JAN. 10
1743–44: AS FEB. 13*
1744–45: SA FEB. 7*

*Squire of Alsatia, The* (C) T. Shadwell 1688                                    14
1735–36: AS MAR. 4*
          SA APR. 28*, JUNE 2*
1736–37: SA FEB. 28*
          AS MAR. 7*
1737–38: SA NOV. 14, FEB. 4*
1738–39: SA FEB. 15*, AUG. 9*
1740–41: SA MAR. 5*, JUNE 4*
1741–42: SA MAY 19*
1742–43: SA FEB. 11*
1744–45: SA FEB. 21*

*Stratagem, The.* See *Beaux' Stratagem, The*

*Successful Straingers, The* (T) William Mountfort 1689                            1
1740–41: AS DEC. 29

*Tamar, Prince of Nubia* (T) M. Clancy (1739)                                     1
1739–40: AS FEB. 19

*Tamerlane* (T) Rowe 1701                                                        19
1722–23: SA NOV. 5, MAY 9
1723–24: SA NOV. 4
1725–26: SA NOV. 4
1726–27: SA NOV. 4
1728–29: SA JUNE 16
1733–34: SA NOV. 5, 12
1734–35: AS NOV. 4
1735–36: AS NOV. 4
1736–37: AS NOV. 4
          SA NOV. 5
1738–39: AS NOV. 4
          SA JUNE 27
1739–40: SA NOV. 5, JUNE 2
1740–41: AS JULY 1
1742–43: AS NOV. 4, MAR. 11

*Tempest, The; Or, The Enchanted Island* (Opera) Davanent and Dryden
    (1667) then Shadwell (1674) after Shakespeare                               12

1735–36: AS SEPT. 15, JAN. 26
1737–38: AS MAY 11*
1739–40: SA MAR. 8*
1740–41: SA MAR. 12*
1741–42: SA FEB. 15*
1742–43: SA DEC. 9, 13, JAN. 13, 17, 20
1744–45: SA MAR. 18*

*Tender Husband, The; Or, The Accomplished Fools* (C) Steele 1705          11
1722–23: SA NOV. 19*
1732–33: SA FEB. 15*
1734–35: GBGL DEC. 14*
1735–36: SA APR. 14*
         AS APR. 15*
1737–38: AS OCT. 31
1738–39: AS OCT. 30, FEB. 6*
         SA FEB. 17*
1740–41: AS MAY 13*
1742–43: AS OCT. 11

*Themistocles, The Lover of his Country* (T) Dr. Samuel Madden 1729          1
1730–31: SA JUNE 7

*Theodosius; Or, The Force of Love* (T) Lee 1680          13
1722–23: SA NOV. 26
1725–26: SA MAY 9*
1729–30: SA FEB. 12*
1731–32: SA DEC. 16*
1733–34: AS MAY 16*
1735–36: AS DEC. 1
         SA APR. 15*
1738–39: AS FEB. 22*
1739–40: SA APR. 17*
1740–41: SA FEB. 2*
1743–44: SA APR. 26*, MAY 10
1744–45: SA FEB. 18*

*Three Humps, The* (C?) Anon. 1738:          1
1737–38: SA MAY 15

*Timon of Athens; Or, The Man Hater* Shakespeare          2
1737–38: SA FEB. 8*
1741–42: AS OCT. 22

*Treacherous Husband, The* (T) Samuel Davey 1737          3
1738–39: SA NOV. 28, DEC. 8*, 14*

*Tunbridge Walks; Or, The Yeoman of Kent* (C) T. Baker 1714          8
1722–23: SA DEC. 20
1724–25: SA EXACT DATE UNKNOWN
1733–34: SA MAR. 1
1735–36: AS NOV. 17

1736–37: AS OCT. 30
1737–38: AS OCT. 11
1739–40: AS OCT. 11
1744–45: SA DEC. 11*

*Turnus* (T) Chev. Descaizeauz? 1738                                    1
1738–39: AS MAY 21*

*Twelfth Night* Shakespeare                                            9
1742–43: AS DEC. 6, 9, 16, JAN. 27*, JULY 9*
1743–44: SA FEB. 20*
        AS MAR. 7*
1744–45: SA OCT. 30, FEB. 20*

*Twin Rivals, The* (C) Farquhar 1703                                  22
1724–25: SA JUNE 24*
1733–34: SA NOV. 29*
        AS MAY 30*
1735–36: SA DEC. 18, FEB. 16*
1736–37: SA NOV. 1, DEC. 17
1737–38: SA FEB. 14*, MAY 19*
1738–39: SA FEB. 21*, MAR. 21*
1739–40: SA NOV. 8, MAY 3*
1740–41: SA JAN. 21*, APR. 16*
        AS MAY 7
1741–42: AS MAR. 18*
        SA NOV. 9
1742–43: SA MAR. 7*
1743–44: SA NOV. 14
1744–45: SA FEB. 11*
        AS MAR. 21

*Unhappy Favourite, The; Or, The Earl of Essex* (T) J. Banks 1681      8
1722–23: SA DEC. 31
1723–24: SA DEC. 30
1729–30: SA APR. 13*
1734–35: RS MAR. 6*
1737–38: SA APR. 6
1738–39: SA MAR. 29*, JULY 26
1740–41: SA JAN. 27

Unspecified Entertainments or Program                                 9
1729–30: SA DEC. 13, 30, JAN. 13, 20
1730–31: NBDS MAR. 15*, MAY 10*, MAY 17*, MAY 26*, JULY 15*
1731–32: NBDS NOV. 6, NOV. 13*, NOV. 24*
1732–33: NBDS EXACT DATE UNKNOWN

Unspecified Play                                                      35
1722–23: SA OCT. 20, 29
1723–24: SA OCT. 21
1724–25: SA MAR. 1, MAY 28
1725–26: SA OCT. 20

1728–29: SA OCT. 30
1729–30: SA OCT. 30, NOV. 10, MAR. 2
1730–31: NBDS APR. 23
         SA OCT. 30, NOV. 4
1731–32: SA OCT. 11, 30, NOV. 4, JAN. 20, MAR. 1
1732–33: SA JAN. 20
         RS MAR. 1
1733–34: SA OCT. 11, JAN. 21
1734–35: AS OCT. 30, JAN. 20
1735–36: SA JAN. 20
1737–38: AS OCT. 31, NOV. 4, 19
1739–40: AS OCT. 30, NOV. 5
1740–41: AS OCT. 30, NOV. 1, 4
1741–42: AS OCT. 30, NOV. 4


*Venice Preserved; Or, A Plot Discovered* (T) Otway 1682                25
1722–23: SA FEB. 7*
1723–24: SA JUNE 11*
1735–36: SA MAR. 20*
1736–37: SA JAN. 7
1738–39: SA APR. 26*
1739–40: SA APR. 11*
1740–41: SA MAY 6*
1741–42: AS NOV. 12, DEC. 17, FEB. 19*, MAY 31*
         SA DEC. 22,* JULY 12
1742–43: AS APR. 27*
1743–44: AS OCT. 20, FEB. 16*, NOV. 5
         SA DEC. 22*, MAR. 9
1744–45: CAP FEB. 9*, 12
         SA NOV. 5, 8, MAR. 4*, APR. 22*


*Volpone* (C) Jonson                                                   10
1736–37: SA JUNE 30, JULY 12*
1737–38: SA FEB. 24*, MAY 8*
1738–39: SA DEC. 11, JAN. 25*, MAR. 3*, JULY 4
1740–41: AS JULY 13
1742–43: SA FEB. 4*


*Way of the World, The* (C) Congreve 1700                              25
1728–29: SA MAY* EXACT DATE UNKNOWN
1730–31: SA FEB. 11*
1731–32: SA MAR. 6*
1732–33: SA FEB. 5*, JUNE 7*
1733–34: SA FEB. 14*
1734–35: RS FEB. 13*
         AS MAY 5*
1735–36: RS NOV. 28*
1736–37: AS JAN. 27*, JUNE 6*
1737–38: SA NOV. 30, MAR. 23*, MAY 17*
1739–40: AS DEC. 13*, FEB. 18*, APR. 19*
         SA MAY 12*
1740–41: SA JUNE 1*, DEC. 4*, 15*
1741–42: AS MAR. 1*

1742–43: SA APR. 25*
1743–44: AS FEB. 28*
          SA APR. 5

*Wexford Wells; Or, The Summer Assizes* (C) Concanen 1721                    1
1720–21: SA NOV. 7*

*Wife and No Wife, A* (C) Coffey 1724                                         1
1723–24: SA EXACT DATE UNKNOWN

*Wife's Relief, The; Or, The Husband's Cure* (C) C. Johnson 1711             1
1740–41: AS FEB. 24*

*Winter's Tale, The* Shakespeare                                             2
1743–44: AS JAN. 12, 16

*Wit Without Money* (C) Beaumont and Fletcher                                2
1737–38: AS JAN. 26*, FEB. 27*

*Woman is a Riddle; Or, The Way to Win a Widow* (C) Bullock 1717            12
1722–23: SA NOV. 28, DEC. 5
1731–32: SA FEB. 14*
1732–33: SA MAY 24*
          NBDS* ca. NOV. EXACT DATE UNKNOWN
1733–34: RS FEB. 13*
1735–36: SA APR. 5*
1736–37: AS JAN. 17
1738–39: SA MAR. 1*
1743–44: AS APR. 16*
          SA APR. 23; MAY 23*

*Woman's Revenge, The; Or, A Match at Newgate* (C) Bullock 1715              5
1733–34: GBGL NOV. 30*
1738–39: SA JAN. 18, FEB. 2, 26 (AS AFTERPIECE)
1740–41: SA FEB. 7*

*Wonder, The, A Woman Keeps a Secret* (C) Centlivre 1714                     1
1742–43: SA DEC. 16*

# Afterpiece Index

*Adventures of Half an Hour, The* (F) Bullock 1716                           4
1731–32: NBDS FEB. 28*
1734–35: AS MAR. 20*, MAY 1*
1738–39: AS FEB. 1*

*Alfred* (Masque) Thomson and Mallet 1740                                    2
1743–44: SA MAR. 10, 17

*Anatomist, The; Or, The Sham Doctor* (F) Ravenscroft 1696                   8
1737–38: SA MAY 10*

1734–35: AS MAR. 24*
1735–36: AS APR. 3*
1736–37: AS DEC. 20*
1738–39: SA APR. 12
1740–41: SA FEB. 19*

*Chuck; Or, The School-Boy's Opera* (BO) Anon. 1736                     1
1728–29: SA JAN. 27*

*Cobler of Preston, The* (F) Bullock 1716                               6
1728–29: SA FEB. 27*
1735–36: SA MAR. 17*
1736–37: SA FEB. 11*
1737–38: SA MAY 17*
1738–39: AS JAN. 4*, 22*

*Columbine Courtezan* (P) Anon. 1737?                                   1
1736–37: SA MAY 20*

*Comic Rivals, The; Or, Columbine Coquette* (P) Anon. 1737?            1
1736–37: SA MAY 16*

*Contrivances, The; Or, More Ways Than One* (BO) H. Carey 1715        11
1730–31: SA DEC. EXACT DATE UNKNOWN
1732–33: SA FEB. 15*
        RS MAY 3*
1735–36: AS MAR. 25*
1740–41: SA FEB. 12*, APR. 9*
1742–43: SA NOV. 22, DEC. 2, MAY 17*, JULY 5*
1744–45: SA DEC. 11*

*Cooper Deceived, The* (P) Anon. 1736?                                 1
1735–36: SA FEB. 27*

*Country Wedding, The; Or, The Nuptials of Roger and Jean* (Operetta)
  Eccles and Motteaux                                                  2
1732–33: SA MAY 21*
1742–43: SA MAR. 24*

*Credulous Cockhold, The* [*The Debauchee; Or,*] (F) Behn 1677         4
1744–45: CAP FEB. 9*, 12, 18, MAR. 4*

*Cure for Jealousy, A* (F?) William Este 1740?                         1
1739–40: AS MAR. 13*

*Cure for a Scold, A* (BO) Worsdale 1735                              17
1737–38: SA, JAN. 16, 18, FEB. 1, 8*, 14*, 18*, MAR. 11*, 20*, 23*,
        MAY 12*, 16*, 19*
1738–39: SA MAR. 1*, MAY 14*
1739–40: SA FEB. 9*
1740–41: AS APR. 25*
1742–43: SA JAN. 28*

*Damon and Phillida; Or, Hymen's Triumph* (O) C. Cibber 1729    35
1731–32: SA DEC. 16*, 18*, 20, FEB. 28*, MAY 4, JUNE 26*
1732–33: SA JAN. 29*, MAR. 5*, MAY 28*, JUNE 7*
1733–34: SA JAN. 28*
        GBGL FEB. 1*
        RS SEPT. 9*
1734–35: AS JUNE 9*
1735–36: AS DEC. 15*, FEB. 5*
        SA MAR. 6*
1736–37: AS NOV. 22*, MAR. 7*
1737–38: SA MAR. 16*, MAY 22*
        AS MAY 4*
1739–40: SA MAY 3*, 12*
1741–42: AS MAR. 18*, 30*
1742–43: AS NOV. 29, JAN. 3, FEB. 2*
1743–44: AS FEB. 13*, MAR. 12*
1744–45: SA NOV. 8, FEB. 6*, AUG. 5


*Devil to Pay, The; Or, The Wives Metamorphosed* (BO) C. Coffey 1731    49
1731–32: SA JAN 24*, FEB 24*
1732–33: SA FEB. 5*, MAR. 15*, MAY 24*
1733–34: RS FEB. 20*
        SA FEB. 25*
        AS JUNE 6*
1734–35: AS JAN. 27*
1735–36: AS FEB. 26*
        RS MAR. 16*
        SA MAY 17*
1736–37: SA FEB. 1*, APR. 29*
        AS FEB 17*, MAY 5*
1737–38: SA APR. 6, 25*
1738–39: SA MAR. 5*
        AS MAR. 26*
1739–40: AS JAN. 26*, FEB. 18*
        SA MAR. 15, APR. 17*, JULY 14
1740–41: SA JAN. 29*, FEB. 24*
        AS FEB. 17*, JUNE 22*, 29*, JULY 1, 23
1741–42: AS MAY 31*
1742–43: SA JAN. 26*, JUNE 22*
1743–44: AS NOV. 7, 10, 12, DEC. 17*, JAN. 26*, MAR. 6*, 13*, APR.
        18*
        SA DEC. 8, MAY 23*
1744–45: SA FEB. 7*, MAR. 5*, 14*, 28*


*Dragon of Wantley, The* (Burl) H. Carey and Lampe 1737    19
1737–38: AS JAN. 26*, FEB. 23*, 27*
1742–43: SA JAN. 3, 6, FEB. 7*, 17*, MAR. 14*
1743–44: AS JAN. 9, 12, 16, 19, 28*, FEB. 9*, 16*, 28*, APR. 13*
        SA FEB. 20*, 22*


*Enchanter, The; Or, Harlequin Merlin* (P) Dr. H. Heighington 1725?    1
1725–26: SA JAN. EXACT DATE UNKNOWN

*Female Officer, The; Or, The Lady's Voyage to Gibraltar* (F) H. Brooke, 1740  
1739–40: AS MAR. 1*, 12*, 15*, 22* MAY 3*, 12*, JUNE 7*  7

*Flora; Or, Hob's Opera* [*Flora; Or, Hob in the Well*] (BO) Hippisley 1729  20  
1729–30: SA APR. 27*, MAY 14*  
1733–34: SA FEB. 18*  
        NBGL JUNE 12*  
1734–35: AS APR. 17*  
1735–36: AS DEC. 11  
        SA FEB. 23, MAR. 31*  
1737–38: SA APR. 15*  
        AS MAY 6*  
1738–39: SA MAR. 20*  
        AS MAR. 22*, 26*  
1739–40: AS APR. 15*, 26*  
1740–41: SA JUNE 4*  
1742–43: AS FEB. 7*, 26*  
1744–45: SA MAR. 25*, 26*  

*Freemason's Opera, The* [*The Generous Freemason*] (BO) Chetwood, 1730?  1  
1736–37: AS FEB. 10*  

*Grand Sultan, The; Or, Harlequin Captive* (P) Anon. 1742?  4  
1742–43: SA DEC. 21, 27, 30, JAN. 4 (ALL AS A MAINPIECE)  

*Harlequin Imprisoned; Or, The Spaniard Outwitted* (P) Anon. 1745?  5  
1744–45: CAP MAR. 5, 11, 13, 18, APR. 1  

*Harlequin Metamorphosed; Or, Columbine Courtezan* (P) Anon. 1740?  6  
1740–41: SA JAN. 27, FEB. 7*, 14, MAR. 2, 7*, JUNE 8*  

*Harlequin Triumphant in His Amours* (P) Anon. 1742?  2  
1742–43: SA JAN. 11*, 18* (BOTH AS MAINPIECE)  

*Harlequin Triumphant; Or, The Father Deceived* (P) Anon. 1733?  1  
1732–33: NBGL JUNE 6* (AS A MAINPIECE)  

*Harlequin Turned Physician* (P) Anon. 1737?  1  
1736–37: AS FEB. 3*  

*Harlequin's Vagaries; Or, Pierrot in Distress* (P) Anon. 1739?  33  
1738–39: SA JULY 16, 20, 23*, 26, 30, AUG. 2, 6, 9*, 13*  
1739–40: SA NOV. 8, 12, 15, 19, 21, DEC. 3, 6 JAN. 3, FEB. 11, 25*,  
        MAR. 27*, 29*, MAY 5*  
1740–41: SA NOV. 14, DEC. 3  
1741–42: SA OCT. 22, 26, 29, NOV. 2, 5, 9, 30*, DEC. 10*, JAN. 22*  

*Harlot's Progress, The; Or, The Ridotto Al' Fresco* (P) T. Cibber 1733  9  
1738–39: SA JAN. 11, 15, 18, 25*, FEB. 2, 26*, MAR. 8*  
1739–40: SA MAR. 8*, JULY 24

*Hob; Or, The Country Wake* (Int.) C. Cibber 1715
2
1728–29: SA MAR. 3*
1742–43: SA DEC. 22*


*Honest Irishman, The.* See *Brave Irishman, The*


*Honest Yorkshireman, The* (BO) H. Carey 1735
18
1735–36: AS JAN. 15*, 22, 29*
1737–38: SA MAY 5*
1738–39: SA JUNE 8*
1739–40: SA NOV. 1, JAN. 21, MAR. 20*, APR. 11*, 21*
1740–41: SA FEB. 2*, MAY 14*
1742–43: SA MAY 18*
1743–44: SA JAN. 2
1744–45: SA FEB. 1*, 13*, 15*, 18*


*Hussar, The; Or, Harlequin Restored* (P) Anon. 1737?
48
1736–37: SA MAY 2 (AS MAINPIECE), 17, JULY 14*
          AS MAY 23*, JUNE 6*
1737–38: SA NOV. 3, 7, 10, 14, 17, 24, 28, 30, JAN. 7, FEB. 13*, 16*,
          22*, 24*, MAR. 1*, 4*
          AS OCT. 11, 31
1738–39: SA NOV. 6, FEB. 8*, 17*, MAR. 26*, MAY 9*, JUNE 29
1739–40: SA FEB. 21*, MAR. 3*, 4*
          AS DEC. 13*
1740–41: SA FEB. 26*, MAR. 10*, JUNE 16*
1741–42: SA FEB. 15*, MAR. 8*, 29*
1742–43: SA JAN. 10, 13, 17, 20
1743–44: SA DEC. 15*, JAN. 16*, APR. 30, MAY 3
          AS MAY 17, 21


*Hymen* (Operetta?) Anon. 1743?
1
1742–43: SA FEB. 14*


*Intriguers, The* (F?) Anon. 1741?
1
1740–41: AS MAY 7*


*Intriguing Chambermaid, The* (F) Fielding 1734
5
1740–41: SA DEC. 29, JAN. 2, 12, 24*, MAR. 5*


*Jealous Farmer Deceived, The; Or, Harlequin Triumphant* (P) Anon.
  1738?
8
1737–38: SA JAN. 28
1738–39: SA NOV. 23*, DEC. 5, 11, 19, MAR. 3*, 12*, APR. 9


*Jealous Husband Deceived, The; Or, Harlequin Metamorphosed* (P)
  Anon. 1731?
1
1730–31: NBDS MAR. 23* (AS MAINPIECE).


*Judgment of Paris, The* (Masque) Congreve 1701
1
1731–32: SA APR. 13*

*Judgment of Paris, The* (BO) Arne after Congreve 1740                    2
1743–44: SA MAR. 10, 17

*Judgment of Paris, The; Or, The Nuptials of Harlequin* (P) Anon. 1741?    10
1740–41: AS DEC. 11, 29, JAN. 27, FEB. 24*
          SA FEB. 9*
1741–42: AS MAR. 12*, 22, APR. 1*, 5, MAY 21*

*King and the Miller of Mansfield, The* (Dr. Satire) Dodsley 1737          6
1736–37: SA APR. 2
1737–38: SA MAR. 6*, 9*, 18*
1738–39: SA MAR. 6*
1740–41: AS MAR. 7*

*Lottery, The* (BO) Fielding, 1732                                        11
1733–34: RS MAY 24*
          NBGL JUNE 18*
1739–40: SA DEC. 20*, 22, 24, 31, JAN. 24, MAY 8*, 20*, JULY 8*
1742–43: SA AUG. 1*

*Lover's Opera, The* (BO) Chetwood, 1728–29                                2
1736–37: AS DEC. 9*
1739–40: SA APR. 23*

*Lying Valet, The* (F) Garrick, 1741                                      14
1741–42: SA DEC. 22, 31, JAN. 25*, FEB. 25*, 27*, MAR. 9*, 25*, 26*,
          JUNE 24*, AUG. 2
          AS APR. 3*
1742–43: SA FEB. 1*, MAY 9*
1744–45: CAP MAR. 26*

*Mad Captain, The* (BO?) Anon. 1741?                                       1
1740–41: SA FEB. 5*

*Maid's Last Prayer, The* (F?) Anon. 1736?                                 1
1735–36: AS MAR. 18*

*Margery; Or, A Worse Plague Than the Dragon* (Burl.) Carey 1738           2
1738–39: AS JAN. 24*
1743–44: SA APR. 23

*Matrimony Displayed; Or, A Cure for Love* (F) Anon. 1740?                 1
1739–40: SA APR. 24*

*Medley, The* (Ballad-farce) Prelleur and Gladwin 1736                     1
1735–36: AS FEB. 9*

*Miss Lucy in Town* (F) Fielding and Arne 1742                             5
1742–43: AS FEB. 10*, MAR. 7, APR. 21, 25
1743–44: AS JAN. 2

*Mock Doctor, The* (BO) Fielding 1732                                     23

1742–43: AS MAY 7*, JUNE 11*

*Penelope* (BO) Mottley and Cooke 1728                                                1
1735–36: SA FEB. 16

*Picture, The; Or, The Cockold in Conceit* (F) James Miller 1745                      1
1744–45: SA APR. 1*

*Polite Conversation* (Satire) J. Miller after Swift 1737                             2
1737–38: AS APR. 27*
         SA MAY 8*

*Preceptor, The; Or, The Loves of Abelard and Heloise* (BO) Wm.
   Hammond 1739                                                                       2
1739–40: SA NOV. 26, 29

*Prize, The; Or, Harlequin's Artifice* (P) Anon. 1745?                                1
1744–45: CAP JULY 3*

*Queen of Spain, The; Or, Farinelli in Madrid* (Mus. Ent.) Worsdale 1741             4
1740–41: AS APR. 16, 21*, MAY 13*
1742–43: SA DEC. 20

*Raree Show, The; Or, The Fox Trapped* (BO) Joseph Paterson 1739                      1
1739–40: SA FEB. 21

*Ridiculous Bridegroom, The* (BO?) Anon. 1741?                                        1
1740–41: AS FEB. 21*

*Rival Beaux, The; Or, Vanity Reclaimed* (F?) Anon. 1743?                             1
1742–43: SA FEB. 11*

*Rival Queans, The, With the Humours of Alexander the Great* (F) C.
   Cibber 1710                                                                        2
1736–37: SA FEB. 18*
1738–39: AS FEB. 22*

*Rival Sorcerers, The; Or, Harlequin Victorious* (P) T. Ludlow 1741?                 14
1741–42: SA JAN. 9, 14, 15*, 28, 29*, FEB. 4*, 6, 8*, 18*, MAR. 1*,
         15*, 18*, 22*, APR. 22*

*Rival Theatres, The; Or, A Playhouse to be Let* (*The Stage Mutineers*)
   (Burl.) E. Phillips 1733                                                           3
1736–37: AS JAN. 10, 17, FEB. 19*

*Robin Hood and Little John* (BO) Anon. 1730.                                         1
1739–40: AS MAY 22*

*Scaramouche Turned Old Woman* (P?) Anon. 1738?                                       1
1738–39: AS DEC. 12*

*Schoolboy, The* (F) C. Cibber 1703                                                   5

1741–42: SA FEB. 13*

*Tragedy of Tragedies; Or, Tom Thumb the Great* (Burl) Fielding 1730        9
[SEE ALSO *Opera of Operas*]
1733–34: RS FEB. 18*
1734–35: AS MAY 5*
1735–36: AS APR. 8*, MAY 13*
1736–37: SA FEB. 4*
1739–40: SA APR. 9
1742–43: AS MAY 7* (As *Opera of Operas*), 12, JUNE 11*

Unspecified Farce        52
1735–36: SA JUNE 25*
1736–37: SA MAY 4*
1738–39: AS DEC. 4*, 8, 14*, FEB. 16*
        SA DEC. 8*, JAN. 31*, MAR. 19*, 21*, APR. 26*, 28*, MAY
        21*
1739–40: SA FEB. 18*, APR. 7*, MAY 7*, 14*
        AS APR. 29*, MAY 1*, 29*
1740–41: SA APR. 14*, 20*, 27*, MAY 8*, 20*, 21*, JUNE 19*
        AS MAY 8*, 11*
1741–42: SA FEB. 11*, 22*, JUNE 1
        AS FEB. 19*
1742–43: SA JAN. 24*, MAR. 7*, 10*, APR. 25*, 28*, JUNE 20
        AS FEB. 22*, 23*, MAR. 3*, MAY 9*, 13*
1743–44: SA NOV. 28*
        AS APR. 16*
1744–45: SA FEB. 8*, 11*, 21*, 25*, MAR. 4*
        AS MAY 6*

Unspecified Pantomime        5
1735–36: AS FEB. 12*
1736–37: SA JAN. 20
        AS JAN. 24, FEB. 8*
1744–45: CAP MAY 7*

*Vernon Triumphant; Or, The British Sailors* (F?) Anon. 1741?        1
1740–41: AS APR. 29*

*Vintner Tricked, The; or, A Match at Newgate* (F) Anon.        10
1742–43: AS JAN. 27*, FEB. 12*, 18*, 28*, MAR. 24*, APR. 27*
1743–44: AS MAY 2*
        SA MAY 10
1744–45: SA FEB. 20*, MAY 30* (W/SUBTITLE *The White Fox Chase*).

*Virgin Unmasked, The; Or, An Old Man Taught Wisdom* (BO) Fielding
    1735        28
1736–37: AS MAY 24*
1739–40: AS FEB. 13*, 25*, MAR. 13*
        SA JUNE 2, 5, 12
1740–41: SA NOV. 10, DEC. 8, 15*, JAN. 8, MAR. 3*
        AS JUNE 25*, JULY 18, 20, AUG. 3

# General Index

This index includes items discussed in the text of the introduction and those items in the calendar that are not incorporated into the Dublin Stage Personnel index (p. 403), the Author-Play index (p. 410), and the Index of Main- and Afterpieces (p. 424). No effort is made here to index all references to the individual Dublin playhouses or to all benefit and command performances, for which see calendar entries for individual seasons.